THE COLLECTED
SHORT STORIES OF
LOUIS L'AMOUR

Bantam Books by Louis L'Amour

ASK YOUR BOOKSELLER FOR THE BOOKS YOU HAVE MISSED.

NOVELS

Bendigo Shafter
Borden Chantry
Brionne
The Broken Gun
The Burning Hills
The Californios
Callaghen
Catlow
Chancy
The Cherokee Trail
Comstock Lode
Conagher
Crossfire Trail
Dark Canyon
Down the Long Hills
The Empty Land
Fair Blows the Wind
Fallon
The Ferguson Rifle
The First Fast Draw
Flint
Guns of the Timberlands
Hanging Woman Creek
The Haunted Mesa
Heller with a Gun
The High Graders
High Lonesome
Hondo
How the West Was Won
The Iron Marshal
The Key-Lock Man
Kid Rodelo
Kilkenny
Killoe
Kilrone
Kiowa Trail
Last of the Breed
Last Stand at Papago Wells
The Lonesome Gods
The Man Called Noon
The Man from the Broken Hills
The Man from Skibbereen
Matagorda
Milo Talon
The Mountain Valley War
North to the Rails
Over on the Dry Side

Passin' Through
The Proving Trail
The Quick and the Dead
Radigan
Reilly's Luck
The Rider of Lost Creek
Rivers West
The Shadow Riders
Shalako
Showdown at Yellow Butte
Silver Canyon
Son of a Wanted Man
Taggart
The Tall Stranger
To Tame a Land
Tucker
Under the Sweetwater Rim
Utah Blaine
The Walking Drum
Westward the Tide
Where the Long Grass Blows

SHORT STORY
COLLECTIONS

Beyond the Great Snow
   Mountains
Bowdrie
Bowdrie's Law
Buckskin Run
The Collected Short Stories of
   Louis L'Amour (vols. 1–4)
Dutchman's Flat
End of the Drive
From the Listening Hills
The Hills of Homicide
Law of the Desert Born
Long Ride Home
Lonigan
May There Be a Road
Monument Rock
Night over the Solomons
Off the Mangrove Coast
The Outlaws of Mesquite
The Rider of the Ruby Hills
Riding for the Brand
The Strong Shall Live
The Trail to Crazy Man
Valley of the Sun

War Party
West from Singapore
West of Dodge
With These Hands
Yondering

SACKETT TITLES

Sackett's Land
To the Far Blue
   Mountains
The Warrior's Path
Jubal Sackett
Ride the River
The Daybreakers
Sackett
Lando
Mojave Crossing
Mustang Man
The Lonely Men
Galloway
Treasure Mountain
Lonely on the Mountain
Ride the Dark Trail
The Sackett Brand
The Sky-Liners

THE HOPALONG
CASSIDY NOVELS

The Riders of the High
   Rock
The Rustlers of West Fork
The Trail to Seven Pines
Trouble Shooter

NONFICTION

Education of a Wandering
   Man
Frontier
THE SACKETT
   COMPANION: A
   Personal Guide to the
   Sackett Novels
A TRAIL OF MEMORIES:
   The Quotations of Louis
   L'Amour, compiled by
   Angelique L'Amour

POETRY

Smoke from This Altar

THE
COLLECTED
SHORT STORIES
OF
LOUIS L'AMOUR

THE ADVENTURE STORIES:

Volume Four

Louis L'Amour

BANTAM BOOKS

THE COLLECTED SHORT STORIES OF LOUIS L'AMOUR
The Adventure Stories: Volume Four
A Bantam Book / November 2006

Published by Bantam Dell
A Division of Random House, Inc.
New York, New York

Book design by Glen Edelstein

Bantam Books is a registered trademark of Random House, Inc., and the colophon is a trademark of Random House, Inc.

ISBN-13: 978-0-553-80494-2
ISBN-10: 0-553-80494-4

Printed in the United States of America
Published simultaneously in Canada

www.bantamdell.com

10 9 8 7 6 5 4 3 2 1
BVG

CONTENTS

THE COLLECTED SHORT STORIES OF LOUIS L'AMOUR

Beyond the Great Snow Mountains

When the burial was complete, she rode with her son into the hills.

The Go-log tribesmen, sharing her sorrow for their lost leader, stood aside and allowed her to go. Lok-sha had been a great man and too young to die.

Only in the eyes of Norba and his followers did she detect the triumph born of realization that nothing now stood between him and tribal control. Nothing but a slender woman, alien to their land, and Kulan, her fourteen-year-old son.

There was no time to worry now, nor was there time for grief. If ever they were to escape, it must be at once, for it was unlikely such opportunity would again offer itself.

It had been fifteen years since the plane in which she was leaving China crashed in the mountains near Tosun Nor, killing all on board but herself. Now, as if decreed by fate, another had come, and this one landed intact.

Shambe had brought the news as Lok-sha lay dying, for long ago the far-ranging hunter had promised if ever another plane landed, he would first bring the news to her.

If the fierce Go-log tribesmen learned of the landing, they would kill the survivors and destroy the plane. To enter the land of the Go-log was to die.

It was a far land of high, grass plateaus, snowcapped mountains, and rushing streams. There among the peaks were born three of the greatest rivers of Asia—the Yellow, the Yangtze, and the Mekong—and there the Go-log lived as they had lived since the time of Genghis Khan.

Splendid horsemen and savage fighters, they lived upon their herds of yaks, fat-tailed sheep, horses, and the plunder reaped from caravans bound from China to Tibet.

Anna Doone, born on a ranch in Montana, had taken readily to the hard, nomadic life of the Go-log. She had come to China to join her father, a medical missionary, and her uncle, a noted anthropologist. Both were killed in Kansu by the renegade army that had once belonged to General Ma. Anna, with two friends, attempted an escape in an old plane.

Riding now toward this other aircraft, she recalled the morning when, standing beside her wrecked plane, she had first watched the Go-log approach. She was familiar with their reputation for killing interlopers, but she had a Winchester with a telescopic sight and a .45-caliber Colt revolver.

Despite her fear, she felt a burst of admiration for their superb horsemanship as they raced over the plain. Seeing the rifle ready in her hands, they drew up sharply, and her eyes for the first time looked upon Lok-sha.

Only a little older than her own twenty-one years, he was a tall man with a lean horseman's build, and he laughed with pure enjoyment when she lifted the rifle. She was to remember that laugh for a long time, for the Go-log were normally a somber people.

Lok-sha had the commanding presence of the born leader of men, and she realized at once that if she were to survive, it would be because he wished it.

He spoke sharply in his own tongue, and she replied in the dialect of Kansu, which fortunately he understood.

"It is a fine weapon," he said about the rifle.

"I do not wish to use it against the Go-log. I come as a friend."

"The Go-log have no friends."

A small herd of Tibetan antelope appeared on the crest of a low ridge some three hundred yards away, looking curiously toward the crashed plane.

She had used a rifle since she was a child, killing her first deer when only eleven. Indicating the antelope, she took careful aim and squeezed off her shot. The antelope bounded away, but one went to its knees, then rolled over on its side.

The Go-log shouted with amazement, for accurate shooting with their old rifles was impossible at that range. Two of the riders charged off to recover the game, and she looked into the eyes of the tall rider.

"I have another such rifle, and if we are friends, it is yours."

"I could kill you and take them both."

She returned his look. *"They,"* she said, indicating the others, "might take it from me. You would not, for you are a man of honor, and I would kill you even as they killed me."

She had no doubt of her position, and her chance of ever leaving this place was remote. Whatever was done, she must do herself.

He gestured toward the wreck. "Get what you wish, and come with us."

Her shooting had impressed them, and now her riding did also, for these were men who lived by riding and shooting. Lok-sha, a *jyabo* or king of the Go-log people, did not kill her. Escape being impossible, she married him in a Buddhist ceremony, and then to satisfy some Puritan strain within her, she persuaded Tsan-Po, the lama, to read over them in Kansu dialect the Christian ceremony.

Fortunately, the plane had not burned, and from it she brought ammunition for the rifles, field glasses, clothing, medicines, and her father's instrument case. Best of all, she brought the books that had belonged to her father and uncle.

Having often assisted her father, she understood the emergency treatment of wounds and rough surgery. This knowledge became a valuable asset and solidified her position in the community.

As soon as Anna's son was born, she realized the time would come when, if they were not rescued, he would become *jyabo,* so she began a careful record of migration dates, grass conditions, and rainfall. If it was in her power, she was going to give him the knowledge to be the best leader possible.

Lok-sha was sharply interested in all she knew about the Chinese to the east, and he possessed the imagination to translate the lessons of history into the practical business of command and statecraft. The end had come when his horse, caught on a severe, rocky slope, had fallen, crushing Lok-sha's chest.

She had been happy in the years she'd spent as his wife, certainly she was better off than she would have been as a refugee in the civil war that gripped much of China or as a prisoner of the Japanese. But as happy as she had learned to be, as safe as she had finally found herself, Anna never forgot her home, nor ceased to long for the day when she might return.

Now, her thoughts were interrupted by Shambe's appearance. "The plane is nearby," he said, "and there are two men."

Shambe was not only Lok-sha's best friend, but leader of the Ku-ts'a, the bodyguard of the *jyabo,* a carefully selected band of fighting men.

They rode now, side by side, Kulan, Shambe, and herself. "You will leave with the flying men?" Shambe asked. "And you will take the *jyabo* also?"

Startled, Anna Doone glanced at her son, riding quietly beside her. Of course . . . what had she been thinking of? Her son, Kulan, was *jyabo* now . . . king of six thousand tents, commander of approximately two thousand of the most dangerous fighting men in Asia!

But it was ridiculous. He was only fourteen. He should be in school, thinking about football or baseball. Yet fourteen among the Go-log was not fourteen among her own people. Lok-sha, against her bitter protests, had carried Kulan into battle when he was but six years old, and during long rides over the grasslands had taught him what he could of the arts of war and leadership.

Her son *jyabo*? She wished to see him a doctor, a scientist, a teacher. It was preposterous to think of him as king of a savage people in a remote land. Yet deep within her something asked a question: *How important would baseball be to a boy accustomed to riding a hundred miles from dawn to dusk, or hunting bighorn sheep among the highest peaks?*

"We shall regret your going," Shambe said sincerely, "you have been long among us."

And she would regret losing him, too, for he had been a true friend. She said as much, said it quietly and with sincerity.

When she heard of the plane, her thoughts had leaped ahead, anticipating their homecoming. She had taken notes of her experiences and could write a book, and she could lecture. Kulan was tall and strong and could receive the education and opportunities that he had missed.

Yet she had sensed the reproof in Shambe's tone; Shambe, who had been her husband's supporter in his troubles with Norba, a chief of a minor division of the Khang-sar Go-log.

Over their heads the sky was fiercely blue, their horses' hooves drummed upon the hard, close-cropped turf . . . there were few clouds. Yes . . . these rides would be remembered. Nowhere were there mountains like these, nowhere such skies.

When they came within sight of the plane, the two men sprang to their feet, gripping their rifles.

She drew up. "I am Anna Doone, and this is Kulan, my son."

The older man strode toward her. "This is amazing! The State Department has been trying to locate you and your family for years! You are the niece of Dr. Ralph Doone, are you not?"

"I am."

"My name is Schwarzkopf. Your uncle and I were associated during his work at the Merv Oasis." He glanced at Shambe, and then at Kulan. "Your son, you said?"

She explained the crashed plane, her marriage to Lok-sha, his death, and her wish to escape. In turn, they told her of how they had seized the plane and escaped from the Communist soldiers. Their landing had been made with the last of their fuel.

"If there was fuel, would you take us with you?"

"Take you? But of course!" Schwarzkopf's eyes danced with

excitement that belied his sixty-odd years. "What an opportunity! Married to a Go-log chieftain! So little is known of them, you understand! Their customs, their beliefs ... we must arrange a grant. I know just the people who—"

"If it's all the same to you, Doc," his companion interrupted, "I'd like to get out of here." He looked up at Anna Doone. "I'm sorry, ma'am, but you mentioned fuel. Is there some gas around here somewhere?"

"Several months ago my husband took a convoy bound for an airfield in Tibet. He captured several trucks loaded with gasoline. They are hidden only a few miles away." She paused. "I can drive a truck."

Yet, first she must return to the Go-log encampment to meet with the elders and the fighting men of the Khang-sar. Kulan, as *jyabo,* must be present. It would be improper and even dangerous if she were not present also, for a decision was to be made on the move to new grazing grounds, and there might also be some question as to leadership.

The time had come for the Khang-sar to return to their home in the Yur-tse Mountains, and the thought brought a pang, for these were the loveliest of mountains, splendid forests and lakes in a limestone range near the head of the Yellow River.

"Whatever you do," she warned, "you must not leave the vicinity of the plane. Start no fires, and let no metal flash in the sun. When our meeting is over, Shambe will remain near you until Kulan and I can come."

She swung her horse around. "If you are found, neither Kulan nor I could protect you."

"Kulan?" The younger man looked at the boy in surprise.

Kulan sat straight in the saddle. "I am now *jyabo,*" he replied sternly, "but our people think all outsiders are the enemy."

When they had gone some distance, Kulan sighed and said, "The machine is small. There will be no room for Deba."

She knew how much he loved the horse. "No, Kulan, there will be no room, but you would not wish to take him away. He was bred to this country, and loves it."

"I love it, too," Kulan replied simply.

She started to speak, but the horse herd was before them, and beyond were the felt yurts of the camp. Tsan-Po awaited them before their own tent. With Lok-sha gone, the Khang-sar Go-log would have need of the old man's shrewd advice.

Kulan waved a hand at the encampment. "How would we live in your country?"

"Life is very different there, Kulan, and much easier. You might become a fine scholar and lead a good life."

"If that is what you wish. I shall do my best, for both you and my father have taught me obedience. Only sometimes," his voice tightened, "sometimes I shall think of Deba and these grasslands, and of Amne Machin, the God Mountain."

For the first time she felt doubt, but quickly dismissed it. Of course she was doing the right thing. Once he was adjusted to life in civilization, he would be as happy there. True, he was mature for his years, as boys were apt to be among the Go-log. It was natural that he would miss Deba, and he would miss Shambe, as she would. Shambe had been a second father to him, even as Tsan-Po had been. The old lama had taught Kulan much that was beyond her.

Yet, how long she had dreamed of going home! Of luxuriating in a warm tub, conversing in English for hours on end, and the good, fireside talk of people who were doing things in the larger world of art, science, and scholarship. She longed for a life where she did not have to live with the fear that her son might die from something as silly as a tooth infection or as serious as the bullet from the rifle of a Communist soldier.

She was thirty-six, soon to be thirty-seven, and if she ever wanted a relationship with another man, it could not be here, where she had once been the wife of a king. Nor could she wait for too many years after the rough life on the steppes, a life that had been good to her so far, but was bound to leave her a windburned and arthritic old woman.

What Dr. Schwarzkopf had said was true. Her experience was unique. A book might sell ... she could make a contribution to anthropology, and even to geographical knowledge. As for Kulan, he would do well in America. He was tall and wide-shouldered, and would be a handsome man with his olive skin, his dark, curly hair and truly magnificent dark eyes. There was a touch of the exotic about him that was romantic, and at fourteen he was already stronger than most men.

As SHE ENTERED the yurt, she sensed trouble in the air. Shambe was beside her, but when had he not been present when she needed him?

All of the Khang-sar Go-log chieftains were there. Tsemba was the chief of two hundred tents and an important man whose opinion counted for much. Beside him were old Kunza, Gelak, and of course, Norba.

Norba was a towering big man with one muscular shoulder bare, as was the custom, his broad-bladed sword slung in its scabbard between his shoulder blades. His coterie of followers was close around him, confident now that Lok-sha was dead.

Norba had both hated and feared Lok-sha, but had no heart for a fight with the *jyabo*. Yet had Lok-sha left no heir, Norba would have become chief.

The impending shift to new grazing grounds promised trouble. A faction of the Khang-sar led by Norba wished to go to Tosun Nor, but Lok-sha had decided, under the present circumstances, it was better to graze far from the caravan trails and let a season go by without raids. The new soldiers from the east were not the undisciplined rabble of old. Something was afoot in China proper, and Lok-sha had thought it best to gather more information before testing fate. Moreover, there had been rumors of serious drought around Tosun Nor, and drought meant losses from the herds.

She seated herself beside Kulan, with Tsan-Po beside her, and Shambe seated on the other side of her son. Norba had moved to take the seat of *jyabo,* but Kulan was before him. Norba's face flushed angrily when he saw the boy take the seat where he wished to sit.

"Move, boy. Go play with the children."

Kulan sat very straight. "Unless it is decided otherwise, I am *jyabo,*" he replied. "Until then, take your place."

For an instant there was utter stillness, then a mutter from the followers of Norba, but Kulan ignored them. Glancing at her son, Anna Doone was astonished. Truly, he looked every inch the young king. There was strength in him, of that there would be no doubt, strength and courage.

Norba hesitated, then reluctantly took a seat. Anna could see his repressed fury and knew there was trouble to come. It was well that they were leaving. The thought of escape from all this sent a little tremor of excitement through her, excitement tinged with relief.

The yurt filled and the air was stifling. Anna studied the faces of the chieftains, but they were expressionless. Would they follow Kulan, or would they demand an older, more experienced leader?

Tsan-Po whispered to her that most of those within the tent were supporters of Norba, and Anna Doone felt inside her coat for the pistol she was never without.

Their very lives might depend on the selection of Kulan as *jyabo,* for if Norba were able to take power, he would at once seek to rid himself of his rival. It would not be without precedence if Norba attempted to kill Kulan here, now. Her hand on her pistol, Anna suddenly knew that if Norba even moved toward her son, she would kill him.

She accepted some tea, drinking from a bowl that had come to Tibet from India in the dower of a princess, more than a thousand years before. In those years, Tibet had controlled most of western China, as well as part of India and Kashmir.

Abruptly, without waiting for the others to assemble, Norba declared himself. "Tomorrow," he said, "we will move to Tosun Nor to pasture upon the old lands."

There was silence as he looked around the yurt. That silence held for a slow minute, and then Kulan said one word.

"No."

The word was definite, the tone clear, the challenge accepted.

Norba's face flushed with anger, but Kulan spoke before Norba could frame a word.

"There is drought at Tosun Nor. The grass lies yellow and dead, the air is filled with dust. The beds of streams are cracked earth. We must go to the mountains, to the Yur-tse."

Again Norba prepared to speak, but Kulan interrupted. "My father is dead, but I am my father's son. We rode upon the high grass together and he taught me what I must do."

For the first time, he looked at Norba. "You are *deba* of two hundred tents. You may ride with us or go to Tosun Nor. I would advise you to come with us."

Norba looked around at his followers. "We are men, and not to be led by a boy. It is I who shall lead the Khang-sar. When you are of an age to lead," he added slyly, "you may lead."

Tsan-Po spoke. "The boy is his father's son. Leadership falls upon him."

Norba got to his feet. "Enough! I say that I shall lead. I say it, and my men say it."

Kulan arose, and Shambe and Anna arose with him. Anna held her gun in her hand. "The Ku-ts'a stand without," Shambe said, "and they follow Kulan ... Unless all the chieftains say otherwise."

Norba's lips flattened against his big teeth, and for an instant Anna thought he would strike Kulan despite the fact that the bodyguards surrounded the tent. The Ku-ts'a numbered fifty-eight chosen men, the hereditary guard of the *jyabo*. Norba had not expected the Ku-ts'a. With the *jyabo* dead, he had believed they would accept the situation.

He slammed his sword back into its scabbard. "We will go to Tosun Nor," he said. "You are fools."

"Go, if you will," Kulan replied, "and those who survive are welcome to return. Our herds will be fat upon the long grass of the limestone mountains."

With a pang, Anna realized that Kulan was no longer a boy. The discipline had been strict and the training harsh, but he was every inch a king. Yet she was impatient, for their time was short, and if the plane were discovered, the fliers would be killed and they would be condemned to more fruitless, wasted years.

Alone at last, she said to him, "What was all that about the drought at Tosun Nor?"

"It had been rumored, so while you talked to the old man of your people, I asked the other. He spoke of dense clouds of dust high in the heavens, and of sheep and horses lying dead from starvation and thirst."

He paused. "It is well that Norba goes, for when he returns, if he returns, his power will be broken."

He glanced at her slyly, his face warming with a smile. "My mother taught me to listen, to question when in doubt, and to keep my thoughts until the time for speaking."

After Kulan was asleep, she went outside the yurt and stood alone under the stars. There was moonlight upon the snows of the God Mountain, reflected moonlight that seemed born from some inner glory within the mountain itself.

She thought of home, of the quiet college town and the autumn leaves falling. It had been almost twenty years, but tomorrow they would fly over the mountains to India. To a fine hotel, a room of her own, a hot bath, and a real bed ... it was impossible to imagine such things still existed.

For fifteen years she had been virtually a prisoner. True, Lok-sha had treated her well, and she had been respected among the Go-log, but their ways were strange, and her nights had been given up to dreaming of home.

The thought of Norba returned. If Kulan was gone, he would be in control, and would probably lead the Khang-sar Go-log to disaster. Lok-sha had always said he was a stubborn fool.

No matter. It was now or never. It was impossible that another opportunity would occur, for travel was restricted. No Europeans or Americans would be flying over this country. It was her last chance.

She looked around at the sleeping encampment. She would miss it. Lok-sha, despite their differences of background, had been a superior man. If he had been slow to appreciate her feelings, there had been no cruelty in him.

The icy peak was austere in its bath of moonlight; it was taller than Everest, some said, yet it gave an impression of bulk rather than height. It was no wonder the Go-log called it the God Mountain.

Tsan-Po was walking toward her. "Do you go tomorrow?"

She had ceased to be startled by his awareness of things. "Yes."

"You have been long away ... does someone await you there?"

"No."

"We will miss you, and we will miss Kulan."

"He goes to a great land. He will do well, I think."

"Here he is a king. Ours is a small king, but even a small king is still a king."

She felt the reproof of his tone, and together they watched the moonlight on Amne Machin. "He will make a strong man," the lama said, "a stronger man and a better leader than Lok-sha."

She was surprised. "Do you really believe that?"

"You have taught him much, and he has character. We Go-log face a trying time, for as the world changes, even we must change.

"Kulan has a sense of the world. You taught him of your land and of Europe, and I have told him of India, where I worked as a young man. He is schooled in the arts of war and statecraft, and I believe it is in him to be a great leader."

He was silent, then added, "Your country could use a friend here."

"Do you believe I am wrong to take him away?"

"We need him," Tsan-Po replied simply, "and he needs you. For several years yet, he will need you."

The lama turned away. "It is late." He took a step, then paused. "Beware of Norba. You have not finished with him."

When morning dawned, they rode swiftly to the hidden trucks. What Lok-sha planned to do with the trucks, she did not know, but presumably he intended to use them as a trap for Chinese soldiers.

She started the truck with difficulty for the motor was cold. There was no road, but the turf was solid, and she had driven on the prairie during her childhood in Montana. The old Army six-by-six was no problem.

Kulan followed, holding off to one side and leading her horse.

Keeping to low ground and circling to avoid gullies or patches of rock, she needed all of an hour to reach the plane.

The pilot and Dr. Schwarzkopf rushed to the tailgate and started to unload the cans. As soon as the truck was empty, Anna drove back for a second truck, and by the time she had returned, the cans of the first had been emptied into the tanks of the plane.

Yet they had scarcely begun on the second load when Shambe came down off the ridge where he had been on watch. Kulan, also watching from a quarter of a mile away, wheeled his mount and raced back at a dead run, drawing his rifle from its scabbard.

"Norba comes," Shambe said, "with many men."

Schwarzkopf dropped his jerry can and started for his rifle, but Anna's gesture stopped him. "Finish refueling," she said, and when he hesitated, "Doctor, put that gun down and get busy!"

Kulan swung his pony alongside her as she mounted, and Shambe drew upon the other side. They sat together, awaiting the oncoming riders.

Norba's horse reared as he drew up, a hard pleasure in his eyes. "So . . . you are traitors. I shall kill you."

Anna Doone's heart pounded heavily, yet she kept all emotion from her face. Her son's life, as well as her own, was at stake.

"These men are our friends. We help them on their way," she said.

"And I shall decide who is and is not a traitor," Kulan added.

From behind them the pilot said, "One more can does it."

Anna's heart lifted. Behind her was the plane that could take her home, the rescue of which she had dreamed for fifteen years. The time was here, the time was now.

The sky beckoned, and beyond the mountains lay India, the threshold to home.

"Go with them, Mother." Kulan's eyes did not turn from Norba. "I cannot, for these are my people."

Her protest found no words. How often had she taught him that kingship was an obligation rather than a glory?

Her eyes swung around the semicircle of savage faces, and then for one brief instant the dream remained, shimmering before her eyes: a warm quiet house, a hot bath, meals prepared from food from a market, life without fear of disease or crippling disfigurement, life without war.

"Dr. Schwarzkopf," she said, "you will leave your rifles and ammunition, they are in short supply here."

"If you are going," Kulan said, "you must go now."

"If these are your people, Kulan, then they are my people also."

The winding caravan of Norba's people appeared, heading north toward Tosun Nor. She should have remembered they would come this way.

Dr. Schwarzkopf brought the weapons and the ammunition. "You will not come with us, then?"

"I can't. This is my son."

"You will die," Norba said. His eyes flickered over the three he hated—the wife of Lok-sha, the leader of the Ku-ts'a, and the boy who stood between him and the kingship.

Norba's rifle started to lift, and Shambe's started up with it, but Kulan put out a hand to stop the movement, then stepped his horse toward Norba and looked into his eyes.

"I am *jyabo*," he said. "I am your king."

For an instant Norba's rifle held still, then slowly it lowered. With an oath, Norba whirled his horse and dashed away, followed by his men.

Behind them the motors broke into a roar, and throwing up a vast cloud of dust, the plane rolled off, gathered speed, then soared up and away, toward India, toward home.

"You should have let me kill him," Shambe said.

"No, Shambe," Kulan replied, "many go to die, but those who remain will remember that I spoke truth."

Three abreast, they rode to the crest of the ridge and halted. The caravan of Norba's followers moved north toward the great lake known as Tosun Nor, moved toward drought and death.

Anna Doone, born in Montana, looked beyond them to a bright fleck that hung in the sky. Sunlight gleamed for an instant on a wingtip ... then it winked out and was gone, leaving only a distant mutter of engines that echoed against the mountains.

May There Be a Road

Tohkta looked at the bridge suspended across the gorge of the Yurung-kash. After four years, the bridge hung again, and now, at last, he could go to his betrothed, to Kushla.

At this point the gorge was scarcely a hundred feet wide, but black cliffs towered into the clouds above it, even as they fell sheer away hundreds of yards below. Down those cliffs came the trails that approached the bridge on either side. From where the bridge came into view from above, it seemed the merest thread . . . a thin line for which the eye must seek and seek again.

Scarcely four feet wide, the bridge was built of their handmade rope, of slats cut from pine forests, and of thin planks laid across the slats. With every gust of wind the bridge swayed, but those who had built it hoped that it would be their lifeline to the outside world.

Tohkta's people were of the mountains, yet once each year they had descended to the oasis towns at the desert's edge, taking the furs, the wool and hides, for which they were known. The gold they sometimes took was a secret thing. In the timeless kingdom of their mountain valleys the bridge was their link to the future.

Only once in all the years their tribal memory encompassed had the bridge not been there, hanging five hundred feet above the tumbling white water. And for too long had Tohkta's people been isolated by its loss.

Four . . . almost five years before there had come a great shaking of the earth when the mountains raised higher, and steam and hot water gushed from newly made cracks. There had been a grinding of rock when the teeth of the earth were gnashed together. In the midst of it, the pinnacle that supported their bridge had toppled from the far side of the Yurung-kash into the gorge below.

There followed years of struggle against the high rocks and the torrent, years of terrible work to replace their bridge. Fields still had to be tilled and flocks tended, but two men had been dashed to death on the jagged rocks below when they fell from their ropes. Yet now the bridge was done.

The Kunlun Mountains rim the northern edge of Tibet, hanging above the deserts of Sinkiang, and are among the loneliest of the world's mountain ranges. Long, long ago when Tohkta's grandfather was a boy, a rare caravan still ventured along the ancient track that led from Sinkiang across Tibet and through the Himalayas to India itself, passing close to Mount Kailas, sacred to Buddhists.

For centuries that ancient track had been almost abandoned. Only yak hunters, as wild and strange as the creatures they hunted, used it now, or an occasional herdsman taking his flock to secret pasturage in the high mountain valleys.

Tohkta sat his horse beside his grandfather, Batai Khan, chieftain of their small tribe of fifty-six tents. This was a proud day, for today Tohkta rode to claim his bride from her father, Yakub, a wealthy Moslem trader. He glanced at his grandfather with pride, for the old man sat his horse like a boy despite his almost one hundred years. Fierce and fiery as always, the Khan was the oldest among a people known for their great age and their great strength.

Few outsiders ever came to know the mountain Tochari, remnants of a proud, warlike race that had ruled most of eastern Turkestan and much of western China. In ages past they had carried their banners against Mongol and Chinese, against Tungan and Turk, against the Tatar and Hun.

Slowly the column of twenty riders and their pack animals crossed the swinging bridge, and Batai Khan did not start up the trail until all were safely across.

"*Yol Bolsun!*" he called out, waving to the people of the village who lined the switchback trail on the other side of the gorge. It was an old greeting to those who rode the mountain trails: "May There Be a Road!"

And now, for the first time in four long years, there *was* a road. The home of the Tochari was an island in mountains, cut off by the deep gorges of the Yurung-kash and the Keriya, and at its ends by impassable slopes. Within there lay more than one hundred square miles of grassy valleys, forest glades, waterfalls, and grass-covered mountain pastures. It was an isolated paradise among the snow-covered peaks, but now it was isolated no longer.

TOHKTA WAS IMPATIENT. Kushla awaited in the ancient oasis town of Kargalik, and how many were the nights he had remained awake to dream of her? Batai Khan and Yakub had arranged the match, but since their eyes first met, neither Tohkta nor Kushla had thoughts for another.

Yet four full years had gone by when no word could be received from her, nor sent to her.

"She will have forgotten me," Tohkta said gloomily. "It has been forever."

"She was a child," Batai Khan replied, "now she will be a woman, and so much the better. You are not forgotten, believe me." He glanced around at his handsome grandson. "I, who know women, say it. You have been a dream to her, and who can forget a dream?"

In the days that followed the finishing of the bridge Tola Beg, an ancient yak hunter, had been the first to cross, and he brought strange news. Chinese soldiers of a new kind had come to Sinkiang and to Tibet. The Dalai Lama had fled to India, and soldiers were in Khotan and Kargalik as well as Lhasa. People had been driven from their farms and their flocks to work upon a new road, harnessed like yak or camels.

"Do not go, Batai Khan." Tola Beg peered across the fire from his ancient, rheumy eyes, his skin withered and weathered by wind and cold, darkened by wind and sun. "They will imprison you and seize your goods."

"It is the time for the marriage of Tohkta."

"There is danger. The Chinese seek the ancient track to India but it is not India they want; it is the men of our mountains they would enslave." Tola Beg gulped his yak-butter tea noisily, as was the custom. "They respect nothing and they have no God. The mosques and lamaseries are closed and the lamas driven to work in the fields. The prayer wheels are stilled and there is a curse on the land."

"I can go alone," Tohkta said. "I will take the gold and go for Kushla."

"We are Tochari." Batai Khan spoke with dignity. "Does a khan of Tochari go like a thief in the night to meet his betrothed?"

They were Tochari. That was the final word among them. Tohkta knew the history of his people, and much more had been told him by an Englishman. In ages past it was said some of his people had migrated from Central Asia, going westward to become the Greeks and the Celts. Others had gone into northern India, to settle there, driven by the Hiung Nu, known to western nations as the Hun.

The Englishman had dug in ancient refuse piles along the ruins of the Great Wall, searching for bits of wood or paper on which there was writing. He had told Tohkta these fragments would piece together the history of the area, and of the Tochari. He glanced at Tohkta's dark red hair and green eyes, a coloring not uncommon among these people of the mountains, and said the Tochari were a people who made history.

Batai Khan had rebuked him gently. "We know our past, and need not dig in dung piles for it. If you would know it, too, come sit by our fires and our bards will sing for you."

And now they rode to claim the bride of Tohkta, for a khan of the Tochari must ride with warriors at his back and gold to consummate the union. Raw and cold was the weather, for the season was late. Soon the high passes would be closed, and the mountain basins would brim full with snow.

IT WAS MIDNIGHT on the third day when they reached the outskirts of the ancient town, crossing the road by which silk had once been carried to Greece and Rome. They drew up in a grove of trees and waited as the moon set beyond the desert hills. Tohkta was impatient to push on to the town, for eagerness rode his shoulders with sharp spurs. But Batai Khan had the caution of years.

Old as he was, he sat erect in his saddle, and the broadsword he carried slung between his shoulders was a mighty weapon in his hands. "The town has a different smell," he said, "there is trouble here."

"I must go to the house of Yakub," Tohkta said. "Tola Beg can come. If help is needed, he can return for you."

The Khan paused a moment, then nodded.

The house of Yakub was the largest in the oasis, and Tola Beg led the way on foot. Wind rustled among the tamarisks as they skirted an irrigation ditch. Beside Tohkta the old yak hunter moved, silent as a *djinn*. Tohkta, who had stalked wild sheep upon the highest peaks, was hard put to keep pace with the old man.

Outside the nearby *Ya-men,* which was the government house, stood vehicles that smelled of greasy smoke and petrol. Tohkta had seen them before, in Khotan. There were soldiers there also, reflected light gleaming from their gun barrels. They were fine rifles that filled Tohkta's mind with envy.

"The old wolf was right," Tola Beg breathed in his ear, "the town stinks of danger."

The town was different, very different. The fires in the foundry were out and the alley of the bazaar was dirty and neglected. Everywhere there were horses and trucks and soldiers and supplies. Even in the violent days after the murder of the old governor, when the fighting between the Nationalists and the Moslem generals was at its worst, there hadn't been this many armed men in Kargalik.

"The forces of history are at work here," Tola Beg mumbled. "And that is something to avoid." They moved on through the darkness and then drew up.

Tohkta crouched in the shadows, listening. Before him was the wall of the compound of Kushla's father. Soon he would see her. His heart pounded with excitement.

Creeping like wild dogs to a sheepfold, they came into the yard. Here, too, they heard the language of the Han Chinese, and one voice that made Tohkta's hair prickle on his scalp . . . a voice with the harsh tone of command. Neither of them spoke Mandarin, for Sinkiang is a land of many tongues, Chinese the least of them, but both knew its sound.

The house of Yakub, yet filled with Han soldiers. Tola Beg tugged at his arm. They must steal away while they had the chance.

But where then was Yakub? And where was Kushla?

"We must go. They have taken it for their own use," Tola Beg whispered in his ear.

Tohkta moved back into the darkness, his thoughts racing over possible alternatives. Then it came to him, and he knew where they would be if they were alive and still in Kargalık.

IT WAS AN ANCIENT Buddhist temple, fallen to ruins, rebuilt, and ruined again. Sometimes Yakub had used it for a storehouse, and Kushla loved the ancient trees around it. There was shelter there, and a good spring nearby. They made their way through the dark town and approached with caution.

"Look!" Tola Beg caught his arm. "The spotted horse . . . it is the old one the girl loved. At least they left her that."

Why not? The horse was almost as old as Kushla herself, who would be eighteen this year.

Leaving Tola Beg, he moved swiftly, glancing each way, then listening. Like a wraith, Tohkta slipped past the yak hide that hung over the door.

In the vague light from the charcoal brazier he saw her, and on the instant he entered she looked up. She stood swiftly, poised like a young deer, ready for flight. And then she looked into his eyes and came into his arms without shame.

Yakub got to his feet. He was in rags. The one room of the temple that still possessed a roof held only a few sacks and some bedding. Yakub had been a proud and wealthy man, but was so no longer.

"Go, Tohkta! Go, quickly! If you are found here—!"

From his shirt, Tohkta drew the sack of gold. "The marriage price," he said. "I claim my bride."

How lovely she was! Her dark eyes glowed, her figure under the thin garments was so lithe and eager. The years he had waited had brought her to womanhood, and to a loveliness he could scarcely believe. He tried to say all this.

"If you think I am beautiful after all that has happened, then our parents have chosen well," she said.

"Please go!" Yakub seized his elbow. "For the sake of my daughter, take her and go. The gold also. If they find it they will take it, anyway."

"What has happened here?"

"The Red soldiers, the ones that we heard of but who never came, they have come at last. They take everything and say it is for the future. Whose future? What future? I do not understand them, for until they came, we were happy. All we wished was to tend our flocks in peace. Now they are moving into the mountains, more soldiers arrive every day."

"Batai Khan awaits us. Come, we will gather your flocks as we go, and you can live among us. I would not have my bride mourning her father on her wedding night."

Kushla handed him her bundle and they turned swiftly to the door. Then Kushla caught a cry in her throat, and Tohkta felt rage and despair crowding within him.

The man who stood in the doorway was small with square shoulders and a neatly perfect uniform. Slender, he seemed to have that whiplike strength that resists all exhaustion. His cold eyes inspected Tohkta with careful attention.

"Greetings." He stepped into the ruins of the room, and behind him were two soldiers armed with submachine guns. "Greetings to Yakub and his lovely daughter. Greetings to you, hillman. That is what you are, am I correct?" He spoke Tungan, and spoke it well. Tohkta said nothing.

"Answer me . . ." He pulled a small automatic from a holster. "Or I will shoot Yakub in the foot." He flicked the gun's safety off.

"Yes," said Tohkta. "I am from the hills."

"Very good. I am Chu Shih." He said this as if it were a fact that explained itself. "We have been waiting for you. Waiting quite awhile. We knew that this woman was betrothed to a young man from the Kunlun. I could have sent her and her father to a labor camp, but I wanted to meet you. Our destinies are intertwined, you see. Would you like to know how?"

Tohkta quietly assented. He was listening, listening to Chu Shih and listening for sounds from outside the building. There were more men out there, but how many he didn't know.

"You can have the opportunity of serving the people of China. I'm sure you do not care . . . but you will. There is a secret track over the mountains to India. It is the track used by Abu Bakr in the sixteenth century when he fled from Khotan. It is also my gateway to the mountain people. Do you know this track?"

"It is idle talk . . . bazaar talk. There is no track. There are only a few mountain pastures and fewer people. All you will find in the mountains are granite and ice, glaciers and clouds."

"If you were to show me the track, which is important to my future plans, I might permit you to keep your bride, and would let her father go free."

"Such stories are the talk of fools," Tohkta said. "They are the idle talk of goatherds."

To know men, Batai Khan had taught him, is the knowledge of kings. Tohkta looked into the eyes of Chu Shih and saw no mercy, only ruthless ambition. To refuse would mean torture and death. Torture he could stand; what he feared was torture for Kushla, or for her father.

"I do not believe," Chu Shih said, "that stories of the ancient route are talk. If you wish to go free, you will show me the track. If you do not show me, another will."

"I will show you what is there, but it may not be to your liking."

This man, Tohkta told himself, must die. I must kill him or return to kill him. If he lives our mountains will never be free. If need be Tohkta's people could wait for years before they came again to the oasis towns, and by that time, these might be overthrown, or their ideas changed. Young though he was, Tohkta had learned all things change; the Tochari had learned patience from their mountains.

Chu Shih's command brought in two more soldiers. Tohkta had a moment of sharp panic when he saw them, wanting to plunge at the door and fight his way free, but he fought down the feeling. He must think of Kushla and her father, who might be killed. Escape they must . . . somehow.

Out upon the street, the bridge of his wishing fell into the gorge of despair, for they had Tola Beg also. Two soldiers gripped the arms of the old yak hunter, and there was blood welling from an ugly cut on his cheekbone.

Turning, the Chinese colonel strode away. Kushla and Yakub being pushed ahead, Tola Beg and Tohkta followed surrounded by the six soldiers.

The Chinese who had searched them were coastal Chinese, unfamiliar with the customs of mountain Tochari. It was the custom in the hills to wear their hair long and their beards also. Tohkta's hair was wound about his head under his sheepskin hat, and into the hair was thrust a thin-bladed knife, as was also the custom.

Soldiers loitered before the *Ya-men,* several hundred yards away, but the street led through a narrow avenue of darkness bordered by a double row of tamarisks. In this darkness, Tohkta halted, and when the soldier behind him ran into him, Tohkta turned and drawing his knife, struck upward into the softness of the man's stomach.

Tohkta's hand drew Kushla behind him. Yakub, with more courage than Tohkta expected, seized the rifle of the soldier next to him, and then with a rush like a sudden gust of wind, Batai Khan and his riders swept through the tamarisks.

The horses were among the soldiers and all was confusion, pounding hooves, and flashing blades. Several of the soldiers had their rifles slung and Chu Shih was knocked sprawling by the shoulder of the horse of Batai Khan.

Lifting Kushla to the saddle of a lead horse, Tohkta leaped into his own saddle. A soldier slipped a rifle to his shoulder, but Tohkta rode him down, grasping the man's weapon as he fell. Then they were away in the darkness and riding hard for freedom and the hills.

There was shouting and a wild shot, but the attack had been sudden and with broadswords, the ancient Tochari way of fighting. In the darkness the soldiers had no chance against the charging horses and flashing blades. And it was only now that the force at the *Ya-men* was alerted.

Tohkta glanced back. Behind them there was confusion but no roaring of motors coming to life, yet remembering the eyes of Chu Shih, Tohkta knew pursuit would come soon, and it would be relentless.

FALSE DAWN WAS CRESTING the peaks with gold when they reached the Valley of Rain where Yakub's last herd was held. This was the only one the Chinese had not seized, for, as yet, they had not discovered it. The people of the oasis were secretive about their pastures, as his people were about the mountain tracks.

Tohkta checked his captured rifle in the vague light. How beautiful it was! How far superior to their ancient guns! Six rifles had been captured, and two men had even taken bandoleers of cartridges. They shared them among the others.

"We must go," Batai Khan said. "The flock we drive will cause us to move slowly."

Tohkta watched the yaks and fat-tailed sheep bunched for the trail. The Tochari were men of flocks and herds, and could not easily leave behind the wealth of a friend.

He looked up at the mountain peaks, and in the morning light, streamers of snow were blowing like silver veils from under a phalanx of cloud. Now fear seized at his vitals. They must hurry. If snow blocked the passes, none would escape.

Hours ago they had left the desert and the threat of pursuit by trucks or cars. Only mounted men or those on foot could follow them now. But the Chinese had horses; Tohkta had seen many of them in town and they would follow, he knew that as well. Whether they liked it or not they were leading Chu Shih into the mountains, just as he had wished.

Hunched in their saddles against the wind, they pushed on, skirting black chasms, climbing around towering pinnacles, icy crags, and dipping deep into gorges and fording streams, until at last they came to a vast basin three miles above the desert. Here they rested into the coming night.

Far away to the west lay a magnificent range of glacier-crested mountains, their gorges choked with ice, splendid in the clear air that followed the snow of the morning and afternoon. Though the setting sun lit the peaks and ridges, close over them hung a towering mass of cloud like the mirror image of the mountains below.

Long before dawn they were moving again. Batai Khan pushed onward, fearful of the storms that come suddenly at high altitudes where there was no fodder for man or beast. Pushing up beside him, Tohkta noted that the old man's face was drawn by cold and weariness. Batai Khan was old . . . older even than Tola Beg.

"Batai Khan," Tohkta asked, "now that we are among our mountains we must fight the soldiers. They must not be allowed to return with knowledge of this trail. Their leader, most of all, must be killed." He explained what Chu Shih had wanted.

"Tohkta," the old man paused, "you will await them in the pass. You are right and the beasts move slowly; we must have time. These fifty yak and many fat-tailed sheep will mean wealth to your wife's father and food and comfort for our people. But do not fight so hard that you do not return to us. Let the mountains do their work and if these soldiers come to the Yurung-kash we will be waiting for them."

"I shall remain with him," Tola Beg spoke up.

All those with modern rifles stayed beside Tohkta, eager to test them on their former owners. Two others remained, hopeful of obtaining more rifles for themselves. The pass was a natural point for a surprise attack, and so the Tochari set their trap where it would be unexpected, in its narrowing approach.

Though they had little ammunition, each fired several ranging shots to check the sights of their new weapons. They then concealed themselves, all but two, along the walls of rock before the deep cleft that was the pass. There they waited, waited for their enemies to come.

AND THEY CAME, the Chinese soldiers did. But they came slowly because of the great altitude, which bothered horses as well as the men.

Tohkta watched them from far across the elevated basin, and it began to snow once more. One of the horses slipped and fell, but the soldiers helped it up and came on.

How many were there? A hundred or more. But they were not dressed or provisioned for the high mountains. Tohkta could tell this because, though all were mounted, they had few packhorses, and these seemed to carry only weapons and ammunition.

At three hundred yards Tohkta and his hidden men opened fire. Instantly there was confusion. A milling of horses and men. For a moment only sporadic fire was returned, then Chu Shih rode into the midst of them on a tall gray horse and suddenly there was order. Soldiers dropped to the ground and sought cover, the bullets striking the rocks around Tohkta and his men were no longer random; it now seemed that the fire was seeking out each of them as separate targets.

"Be ready!" Tohkta called out as under the covering fire a group of soldiers swarmed forward. "Now, run!"

Tohkta turned and ran himself. Before him, Basruddin spun and fired one last shot before entering the pass. The others followed as rifle fire cracked and whined off the rocks around them. Tohkta had known that they couldn't stand off a concerted attack, but he also knew that in the thin air of the mountains he and his men could outrun any lowland soldier.

Chu Shih's men paused in their rush to fire at the fleeing Tocharis, but their breath came too hard at fourteen thousand feet and their shots went wild. At a signal from their leader, soldiers on horseback charged into the pass to pursue the retreating tribesmen, but this was exactly what Tohkta had been planning for.

Tola Beg and a strong young boy had made their way up the steep walls of the pass and together they had found a precariously balanced boulder that the yak hunter had spotted years before. With their shoulders braced against the cliff behind them and their feet on the huge rock they waited. They waited until they heard the sound of firing stop and the sound of horsemen entering the pass. Then they pushed.

Nothing happened.

They eased up and Tola Beg looked at the boy and they pushed together then released and pushed again. Suddenly the boulder was rocking and Tola Beg pushed hard, pushed with all the strength he had in his old body and with all the strength he had in his mind. Something gave inside of him, something in his back, but he pushed on through the blossoming pain and then the boulder was rolling. It dropped from sight, and Tola Beg could feel its impact further down the mountain, then he heard the roar of other rocks falling with it and the screams of men and horses.

TOHKTA, IBRAHIM, AND BASRUDDIN turned and threw themselves back into the maelstrom of dust and flying rock that now choked the pass.

They had seen little of it, for they had been running for their lives not only from the soldiers but from the landslide that nearly took them as well. It had only been the fast thinking of Ibrahim that had saved them, for as soon as they cleared the pass he had forced the running tribesmen into a corner of the hillside protected from the crashing torrent of rock.

Now they pushed their way back through the slide, and while Ibrahim mercilessly stripped the dead and wounded soldiers of guns and ammunition, Tohkta and Basruddin poured fire into the oncoming Chinese. Their lines wavered and fell back, the impact of this double ambush overcoming even Chu Shih's leadership. As soon as the soldiers had taken cover Tohkta and his followers fled back through the pass to where the others had brought up the horses.

Under a sky dense with cloud they started down the rocky slope. The men were excited by their victory, but Tohkta saw the look on the face of Tola Beg and knew that he was in pain. In the trees far below the pass they waited to see what the Han Chinese soldiers would do.

Chu Shih was taking no chances. After some time had passed there was activity around the mouth of the pass: a scouting party who had, no doubt, worked their way carefully through the rockfall alert for additional trouble. Then they watched as a squad moved into position on the hillside beside the entrance to the pass and set up a position with a machine gun unlimbered from one of the packhorses. Then, the area totally secure, mounted troops began to file out into the area controlled by the gun. Soon they would be ready to continue the pursuit.

Tohkta and his men filtered silently back into the trees. They had been very successful, counting many enemy dead or wounded, and Tola Beg was their only casualty. The old man had torn something in his back and could barely ride, being in constant pain.

BY AFTERNOON they were back up out of the trees and on a vast tilted plateau of snow and barren rock. The trail left by Batai Khan and his party was easily visible. The old warrior was pressing along as quickly as was possible, but Tohkta could tell that they were not far ahead. At the far edge of the plateau, just beyond their sight lay the beginnings of the trail down to the bridge. Remembering that trail and the bridge itself, Tohkta was suddenly frightened. However quickly his grandfather had been able to move the animals, once on the narrow trail their pace would slow to a crawl, and at the head of the bridge the beasts must be carefully managed or they would balk and panic. It might have been better to have turned them out into one of the mountain valleys on this side of the river, but as Tohkta galloped his horse along the path left by the horsemen and animals, he could see that was not the course that the old chieftain had taken.

Batai Khan was counting on the gorge of the Yurung-kash to protect the village. Since the beginning of time the approach to the bridge had been their village's greatest defense. The descending trail was exposed in every way, while the trail to the bridge from the side of the village wound between trees and rocks, the cover allowing the tribesmen to pour rifle and arrow fire into any attacker unlucky enough to start down the path.

Even though Tohkta had managed as successful an ambush as he could imagine in the pass, Chu Shih's management of the situation had been impressive. He had acted with courage, and once the officer had realized the danger he had carefully covered his men with the machine gun and then organized his column before proceeding. Even on the exposed approaches of the bridge trail Tohkta feared the effect that the rapid firer would have. Chu Shih must not be allowed to cross the gorge to their village and pastures, but he must not be allowed to return to report of this mountain route either. Something had to be done and it had to be done soon.

At the edge of the plateau the dark canyon of the Yurung-kash became visible in the distance. Looking back, Tohkta could see the first of the Han Chinese scouts fanning out as they discovered themselves facing open ground. There was one more thing that the young Tochari could see and it was this that gave him hope. The high ridges behind the soldiers were invisible ... invisible because of falling snow. The storm was headed toward them, but what was more important was the amount of snow that would build up in the pass. At fourteen thousand feet it wouldn't take long for the way back to Sinkiang to be closed for the season. Perhaps the weather would take care of one of their troubles.

He reined around and whistled to his men. "The invaders must not be allowed to return to the desert," he told them. "God brings a storm to answer our prayers, but they will try to reach our village. Even now Batai Khan may be crossing with Yakub's herds. We must hold the Chinese here to give our men time to clear the bridge, and we must hold them here to give the father of storms time to fill the pass."

They tied their horses where the trail dipped into the gorge. The bridge was a long way down and beyond a bend, but through the trees and rock Tohkta could see animals straggling up the trail on the other side. Good. If they could hold out for an hour Batai Khan would have the resistance organized and the trail to the bridge would become a trail of death for the Chinese. All Tohkta would have to do is get down the trail and across the bridge with fourscore soldiers at his heels.

Tohkta called for the boy who had helped Tola Beg and one other. He gathered up the nine rifles that Ibrahim had taken from the fallen troops in the pass; he weighed them heavily with ammunition also.

"Go to Batai Khan," he said. "Have him give these rifles to the best marksmen among our people. We must guard the bridge like in the stories of old, he will know what to do. Now go!"

He turned to the remaining men. "Go with them and prepare. Basruddin, Ibrahim, and Loshed; these I would keep with me."

"And I," said Tola Beg. When Tohkta began to protest he raised a hand. "Do not tell me I am hurt. It is only pain, I can still shoot farther than any man here and my hands are steady."

"All right." Tohkta shook his head but smiled. "Let us go see at what distance your lightning can strike."

BASRUDDIN AND IBRAHIM CRAWLED, flat to the ground, into the plain of ice and boulders. Tohkta, Loshed, and Tola Beg found their way to a group of rocks and carefully prepared a shooting position for the old hunter. Just over a hundred yards behind them they set up another position at the head of the Yurung-kash trail.

Though the plateau was flat, it angled downward away from them. The oncoming Chinese were clearly visible, and while they had some cover available, they could not use it and advance at the same time.

When they were nine hundred yards off, Tola Beg squeezed off his first shot. It struck at the ground just before the first horse, which reared and panicked.

"It was low. Six or seven feet." Tohkta, watching through the hunter's spyglass, advised him.

The rider had fallen from the horse even as the others scattered out, dismounting. As the fallen rider got to his feet, Tola Beg shot him through the thigh.

"The leg . . . two feet low."

The fallen rider, the man shot through the leg, was lucky, for Tola Beg now had their range. The yak hunter's next three targets died instantly, felled by bullets they didn't even hear.

Soldiers dove for cover; in moments the top of the plateau was empty but for standing horses. Tohkta had spotted where Chu Shih had gone to ground, and from that shallow depression he saw a flicker of movement and, a moment later, could hear the distant sound of a barked order. The hand of Chu Shih went up and gestured right and left. Instantly, six soldiers moved the one way, and six the other, advancing to flank Tohkta's small party.

But Tohkta had planned for this. He opened up on the men to the right and Loshed joined him. While they lacked the practice of the old hunter, both had good eyes, and soon they forced their targets further off down the top of the plateau, out of range.

Occasionally shots clattered in the rocks around them, but their cover was good and the range extreme. Several of the main party had pushed the advance and were struggling to set up a machine gun. "They have come far to die," Tola Beg said, and squeezed off two shots.

Out upon the granite a man screamed and died. And then the six flankers to the left ran into Ibrahim and Basruddin, belly down in the snow. Tohkta could not see all that happened, but within a moment five of the Chinese were dead; the last shot down as he ran panic-stricken back toward the main body.

Tohkta and Loshed cheered . . . and then the machine gun opened up. Tracers flew, like flickering meteors, the snow and earth around Basruddin shredded, the bullets throwing up gouts of mud then blood as the gun crew expertly worked their weapon. The heavy throbbing of shots ended, then the bullets were striking around them!

Tracers flashed toward the rocks. Loshed howled, a bright red line appearing on the back of his hand. Tola Beg twisted out of the way, grimacing as his back spasmed. Three times dust jumped from his heavy sheepskin coat and then there was blood on his lips. Tohkta dropped behind a rock trembling. He glanced at Loshed.

"The old hawk is dead." Scattered flakes of snow drifted from the dark sky.

"Basruddin, too, and maybe Ibrahim," Tohkta said. Behind them the machine gun lashed the rock, and ricochets whined off into the clouds like banshees. Then the fire tore high into the air to drop down and the end of its arc spattering like heavy rain inside their fort of rock. The gunner worked the falling bullets back and forth.

How can you fight this weapon? Tohkta damned himself for a fool. You couldn't raise your head, you couldn't even take cover. It took the random inaccuracy of rifle ammunition at long range and used that to its advantage, peppering a whole area with fire. Under its protection Chu Shih's soldiers would be advancing.

"Run to the horses," Tohkta commanded. "Our other position is useless. Get to the bridge. We will put our trust in God and Batai Khan. Let us hope that one or the other is ready for us."

They ran. First Loshed, then Tohkta, who paused a moment to scoop up the ammunition of Tola Beg and to touch his cold form once on the back. They ran with bullets hitting all around them, but the light was going and with the oncoming storm, snow filled the air. Then a rifle opened up seeking out the oncoming soldiers from the rocks at the head of the trail, covering them as they ran. They came to the horses, sliding down the hillside, landing in trampled snow. Ibrahim was waiting for them. He grinned. "I killed two more. They will be Basruddin's servants in heaven!"

Stepping into the saddle, Tohkta could clearly see the advancing Chinese, spread out in a skirmish line. The squad with the machine gun was struggling forward with the heavy weapon, the altitude weighing them down as much as the ammunition and tripod. Behind them, almost hidden by the swirling veils of snow, Chu Shih was bringing the horses up.

They came on, relentlessly. They had passed the point where they could retreat through the pass; in the time it would take to get back to that notch in the mountains it would be too late. Chu Shih's only hope for either victory or survival was to press on, find the Tochari village with its warm felt tents, its supplies of fuel and food. Nothing could survive upon the high plateaus. Tohkta knew then that he hated them, hated them with a wild hatred mingled with fear, for that slender, whiplike man was relentless as a hungry wolf, fierce as a cornered tiger. His men might whimper and wish to go back, but he drove them on.

A group of mounted soldiers thundered forward, through a gap in the line of advancing troops. Tohkta wheeled his horse, and the three of them plunged down the switchbacked trail. The horses skidded on the icy gravel; Ibrahim's mount slid and its shoulder struck Tohkta in the leg, sending both horses and riders into a painful collision with the rock wall.

Then the firing began from the head of the trail. With a wild glance thrown back up the slope Tohkta saw a knot of soldiers gathered there, rifles aimed almost vertically down at them. Flame stabbed from the gun muzzles, but then the soldiers were pushed aside and a squad of Han horsemen with Chu Shih in the lead took to the trail.

Tohkta, Ibrahim, and Loshed clattered through a straight stretch. The bridge was only one hundred yards off to their right, but it was still far below them. A bullet snapped past him and, looking up, Tohkta saw the first switchback lined with kneeling soldiers all firing down at them. Closer still, Chu Shih and his band of horsemen came on, less than a half-dozen switchbacks above.

Bullets ricocheted off the rocks. One caught Loshed across the top of the arm and he laughed, smearing his wounded hand with blood and waving it at Tohkta as they turned their horses into another level. Then a bullet caught him in the side and another pierced the spine of his horse and he was falling, the horse was falling, from the narrow trail and disappearing into the rocks hundreds of feet below.

At that moment a fusillade of rifle fire exploded from concealed points along the trail leading up to the Tochari village. Soldiers fell from the top of the trail, and in a moment the Chinese and the villagers were pouring volley after volley into each other in the thundering confines of the gorge.

Reaching the shelf where the bridge stanchions had been fastened to the rock, Tohkta dropped from his horse and was met by Batai Khan and four warriors armed with old rifles. Ibrahim turned his horse tightly in the narrow space.

"They follow us closely, Grandfather!" Tohkta pointed up the trail. But the four men had pressed forward, and as the first of Chu Shih's horsemen came into sight they fired, sending the first horse screaming over the cliff edge, its rider still astride, and collapsing two more in a struggling mass, blocking the trail.

Above, the machine gun opened up, forcing the defenders on the trail to cover and allowing soldiers to crowd their way onto the trail again. In the gray light of the gorge tracers whipped like hellfire, streaking in all directions as the burning bullets bounced from the rock and whirled away into the oncoming night.

The nearest soldiers were advancing again; using the dead horses as cover, they rained fire on the shelf, leaving few areas of even partial safety. Chu Shih was, whatever else he might be, a leader. Yet better than any of them he knew how desperately he must cross the bridge and take the village.

Tohkta nestled the stock of the rifle against his cheek, measuring the distance. He squeezed off his shot, and the man at whom he fired froze, then fell. The snow fell faster. Blown particles stung like bits of steel upon their cheeks. The Chinese above moved in. One paused to crouch against the rock wall. Ibrahim shot him, and he rolled down the trail to their feet.

At the top of the trail more soldiers made their way down the switchbacks, covered by the machine gun. They came in short, quick dashes, utilizing the slightest bits of cover. Ever they drew closer. Occasionally there would be the crack of one of the captured rifles or the dull boom of a muzzle-loader from the villager's side of the gorge and often a soldier would fall, but always this would instantly attract a lash of resumed fire from the machine gun.

"WE MUST GO, Batai Khan," said Tohkta. "We cannot hold out here."

"Yes," agreed the old man, and motioned to his companions to cross the bridge. He dropped into their place and, as they ran into the open, dropped the first soldier to raise a rifle. Ibrahim shot and Tohkta was beside him firing and reloading, but the second Tochari on the bridge was down and as the others bent to pick him up another was shot and fell into the crevasse. Then Ibrahim ran, pounding across the swaying bridge.

The old man put his hand on Tohkta's arm. "Go," he said. "Go, Tohkta Khan. I will stay."

It was not lost on Tohkta that Batai Khan had used the leader's title. He shook his head.

"No," Tohkta protested. "Our people need you."

"Go, I say!" He glared at Tohkta from his fierce cold eyes. Then in a softer voice, he said, "Would you have me die as an old horse dies? I cannot stop them," he said, "but the bridge can."

Tohkta stared at him, uncomprehending. Then it came to him, and he was astonished. For an instant he was filled with despair as he realized what tremendous cost had gone to the building of this bridge, the long struggle with the mountain and the river, the backbreaking toil. "You would destroy our bridge? It cost four years to build!"

"What are four years of work against four thousand years of freedom. In time, you can build another bridge." Even as his grandfather spoke, he knew it was what they must do. The despair left him.

Together they knelt and fired, retreated a few steps, then fired again. An icy wind roared down the tunnel of the gorge, and the bridge swayed before it. Down the cliff trail they could see them coming now, many dark figures, blossoming with fire. Bullets struck about them.

Batai Khan was hit, and he fell, losing his grip upon the rifle, which fell into the void. Tohkta bent to lift him but there was a gleam in the old man's eye. "Leave me here! You must destroy the bridge and silence the devil gun."

"Yes, Grandfather."

"Tohkta Khan, go with God!"

Batai Khan tore loose and fell to the stone. Snow drove down the gorge, obliterating all before them. And Tohkta ran though his heart was crushed.

On the bridge the howling wind caught him. The ropes flexed and jumped with every step and bullets tore through the rope and wood around him. Soldiers depressed the muzzle of the machine gun, holding the tail of the tripod high, and tracers tore at him. One left a smoldering hole in his sheephide jacket, another left a slice like that of a knife upon his calf.

Then he was across, he fell, and was struggling to rise when he felt small hands lift him. It was Kushla. Ibrahim was there, reloading his Chinese rifle.

"Go!" He grabbed her by the shoulders. "Have men bring axes. We must cut the bridge!"

Ibrahim was next. "Come on!" Tohkta said. "We must stop the machine gun!"

The three of them ran. They ran up the narrow trail, and though there was cover it was scant enough. Bullets flew. Tocharis fired back from behind rocks or trees. Men on both sides of the gorge died.

As he went Tohkta gathered up the few men with stolen rifles, and when he could wait no longer they took cover behind a boulder. There were five of them.

"We must destroy the devil gun!" Tohkta ordered them. "We must kill those who use it and any who are close, we must keep firing though we all may die. With that gun, the Hans can take the bridge before we can cut it. Are you ready?"

Together they rose and as one fired up and across the crevasse and into the group of soldiers around the gun. Several fell, and as Tohkta worked the bolt on his rifle, the gunner began to swing the muzzle. Fire sliced toward them and they fired again and again. Bullets bounded into the rock, into Ibrahim, tore Tohkta's rifle from his grasp and ripped his thigh. But as he fell so did the Chinese gunner, and the two tribesmen left standing shot the next nearest man, too.

Tohkta lurched to his feet. The gun was silent, the crew a struggling mob of the dead and dying. He lifted Ibrahim's rifle and shot a man who lifted himself from the trail near the gun. The man fell, clutched at the edge of the trail and, as the rock crumbled in his fingers, clutched at the barrel of the machine gun.

A moment later the man was spinning down into the gorge and the gun was falling fast behind him. Tohkta felt like crying out in triumph, but the day had been too expensive in lives and a dozen or more soldiers had poured onto the shelf where the stanchions of the bridge were fastened. Chinese and Tochari defenders alike were firing into each other at near point-blank range.

Then the roar of guns dropped to an occasional shot as tribesmen fled up the trail toward Tohkta. Across the river, at the turn of the last switchback, a slim figure astride a gray horse moved. Chu Shih rode forward. His mount leaped the mound of dead horses and men as if they were a low gate and not sprawled bodies on a narrow trail with a sheer drop on one side.

The soldiers parted as their commander rode amongst them; then, with riflemen in the lead, he started out onto the bridge.

Tohkta boiled with rage. He would never let them cross! He stumbled into a prone position and taking careful aim at Chu Shih's head squeezed the trigger.

The rifle clicked on an empty chamber. He was out of ammunition!

Down on the shelf there was flickering movement. The form of Batai Khan stood and drew the broadsword from the scabbard across his back. The razor-sharp blade flashed as he brought it down on one of the two ropes that held the right side of the bridge. The blade bit and bit again. Then the rope gave way and suddenly the bridge sagged and swung.

Chu Shih turned in his saddle, the horse rearing as the weakened bridge bucked and twisted like a living thing. There was a shot and Batai Khan jerked. More soldiers came running down the trail, firing their rifles.

The first of these skidded to a stop, working the bolt of his gun, and Batai Khan's great sword struck, disemboweling the man. Suddenly Han soldiers on all sides were firing. The men on the tilting, swaying bridge, the soldiers on the trail, all fired as the ancient Tochari leader turned, his massive body pierced by a half dozen bullets, and brought his blade down on the other right-hand rope.

The ends of the second tether, not cut through, spun and twisted as they unraveled. There was a frozen moment, then the soldiers ran panic-stricken back toward the rock shelf. For a moment the eyes of the Tochari chieftain and the Chinese officer locked, then Batai Khan raised his sword and bellowed, *"Yol Bolsun!"*

A single shot brought him down. The sword clattering to the rocks beside him. A single shot from an unknown trooper on the bridge ... a shot that did no good at all, for the primitive rope shredded and the floor of the bridge peeled away, hanging twisted almost a thousand feet over the roaring waters.

Chu Shih's horse fell, sliding, taking four soldiers with it. The officer grabbed for one of the ropes on the high side of the bridge, held for a moment, then tumbled toward the river far below.

Tohkta struggled to stand as two villagers ran past him, axes at the ready. In a moment the villagers reformed their positions along the trail and, with scathing fire, drove the remaining Han soldiers up the switch-back trail. Following them down to the bridgehead Tohkta watched as the axmen cut the bridge away. It collapsed with a crash against the far wall of the gorge. On the rock shelf above it lay the body of Batai Khan.

"Yol Bolsun," Tohkta whispered as Kushla came to stand beside him.

"What was that, my love?" she said.

"It means good-bye or good luck ... May There Be a Road." After a moment Tohkta laughed. For even though Batai Khan had destroyed their bridge he had bought them time. Time to live, to raise another generation in freedom, time to plan ... if necessary time to escape. This, in its own way, was as much of a road as that once joined by their bridge. He had a vision of a Buddhist's spinning prayer wheel. Even as they had once been connected to their future by the bridge, now they were connected to the future by the lack of it. A season? A year? A decade? Who could tell, but, as the Tochari know, nothing but the mountains lasts forever.

By torchlight, Tohkta Khan gathered his dead and returned to the village with his bride. The future given them by Batai Khan would begin tomorrow, and there was much to do.

By the Waters of San Tadeo

The dozen shacks that made up the village of San Esteban huddled, dwarfed and miserable, below the craggy ramparts that walled them away from the world. The lofty circle of mountains, with their ice-choked ravines and thick tangles of beech forest, formed an enclosing wall as impassable as the mountains of the moon. Only in one direction was escape from the village possible ... through the narrow mouth of the inlet, eight miles from the village.

Julie Marrat had thought of all that many times in the last few weeks, and each time she had come to the same conclusion, and each time that conclusion was just as hopeless. There was but one way of escape ... by boat.

There were three boats at the inlet, and all of these belonged to Pete Kubelik. One was the schooner that he used for infrequent trips up the coast and to bring in supplies. There were also two fishing boats, not much more than dinghies, far too small in which to brave the sea that lay outside. Yet escape she must, and immediately.

Returning to the bedside, she looked down at the dying man who was her father. Lovable, impractical, and a dreamer with an always restless heart, George Marrat had never been able to remain still. Now, this lonely inlet far south on the coast of Chile had trapped him, and once there he could not leave.

Two things ensured that. One was his own health, which failed rapidly in the cold, dreary world of San Esteban, where the sun rarely shone and the sky was overcast nearly three hundred days of the year. Yet had it been his health alone, Julie could have managed. The other element was Pete Kubelik.

From the moment they drew their ketch up to the jetty and Julie turned to look into the piglike eyes of the big trader, she had been frightened.

Right then she asked her father to leave, knowing that this was not a place they should stay.

He was amazed. "Why, Julie? We've only just come! We can at least look around, can't we?"

"No, Father, please! Let's go find somewhere else."

Her father had turned to face Kubelik, and the big man's brown face wrinkled in a smile. "I'm afraid my daughter doesn't like it here," he confessed.

"Well," Kubelik had replied, "it ain't much of a place for women, that's true, but there's gold here, plenty of it!"

"Gold?" Her heart sank at the eagerness in her father's voice. What would he do if he found it? she wondered. No man ever cared less for money, but in her father's mind the concept of gold was so much more than money. It was the reward that he was searching for, the last reward that would somehow repair the life that luck had deserted. But, ironically, that life without luck was not his . . . it was hers. "There's gold here?"

"Yes, sir!" Kubelik had turned and waved a hand at the long spit of black sand that pointed into the inlet from a nearby island. "We've washed many a good stake out of that beach! Best beach placer I ever saw! Was that why you came here?"

Had there been anxiety in the big man's voice? Julie had looked at him again, and felt such revulsion that she could scarcely stand to be near him.

Plodding along beside her father, Kubelik had dwarfed him with his huge body. His face was round and moonlike under the thick black beard. Wrinkles ran out in a network of tiny lines from the corners of both eyes, eyes that were small and cruel. His hands were dirty, the fingernails black and broken. And then, for the first time, she'd seen the gun. It was in a holster under his sheepskin coat.

Not until later did Julie wonder that none of the others came near them. An Indian woman standing in the door of a driftwood cabin hurriedly stepped back and closed the door when Julie started toward her. Despite the inhospitable gesture, Julie had not been alarmed, taking it for granted that the woman was naturally shy.

By midnight, when they moved into the inner room at Kubelik's station and to bed, they had met only one other man. He was a pasty Austrian named Rudy, and seemed to be Kubelik's shadow. He rarely spoke, but whenever Kubelik and Rudy shared a look, Julie realized there was some silent communication. She saw other people moving among the shacks, but they did not come near the store.

That inner room had been Pete Kubelik's suggestion. She had wanted to return to the boat, hoping that her father could be talked into leaving, but Kubelik laughed at her and waved her objections away with an impatient hand. He would take it as an insult, he said. By all means, they should stay. Entranced by his stories of the coast, her father listened, and they remained. And in the morning, their boat was gone.

She had just gotten out of bed when she saw through the small window the empty pier where the ketch had been left. Fear gripping her heart, she awakened her father. George Marrat's face went pale, and for the first time, he was afraid.

They rushed down to the beach, but the ketch was nowhere to be seen.

Kubelik had come from the house, rubbing his eyes. "What's the matter. Something wrong?"

"Our boat's gone!" Marrat exclaimed. "Lord, man! What will we do? What could have happened to it?"

"Wind, maybe," Kubelik suggested, "or some thief. No use standing here. Come in an' let's fix breakfast. Then we can take one of my boats an' look around."

Yet when her eyes happened to meet those of Kubelik, his had been triumphant.

Her father, despite his interest in the gold, was genuinely worried. He knew the mountains were impassable, that the forests were undergrown with thick moss, laden with moisture, and a man could sink to his waist in trying to struggle through. And by the end of the day, they realized that the boat was gone and they knew they would not find it.

"How about taking us to Puerto Montt?" Marrat had suggested. "You have the schooner, and we can't stay here. I have money in the bank back in Santiago. Take us out, and I'll pay your price."

"All right," Kubelik had said thoughtfully. "But you'll have to wait until I'm ready to go for supplies. A week or so, maybe."

Yet when the week had passed, he said nothing about leaving. Her father had been placer mining on the beach and caught a severe cold. By that time, they had moved to a small shack, refusing to accept more of Kubelik's hospitality.

"I'm sorry, Julie," George said. "When I get well, we'll get out of here and I'll make it up to you." He coughed, the breath rattling deep in his lungs.

"Get some rest," she said. He nodded and relaxed, breathing more easily. She sat there in the dark, a twenty-six-year-old woman who had failed in life, failed in marriage, who had fled back to her father, a ne'er-do-well adventurer, and ended up here, in a narrow fjord at the end of the earth.

Her grandfather had been a Chilean who migrated north with his son to fish the waters of British Columbia and Alaska. Her father had spent much of his life in Canada, and she was born there, schooled there, and had been wed there.

Like many young girls, Julie had thought that marriage would change her life, and indeed it had. But she discovered that the qualities in a man that had appealed to her when she was being courted were not the qualities that made a good partner for life.

Her husband had been a dashing young bohemian who could quote enough Spencer, Marx, or Freud to prove any point. Unfortunately, for all his obsession with the working man, he could not seem to hold a job. What she had mistaken for intensity turned out to be self-obsession, and the wild ways that she once thought were delightfully liberated proved to be simple self-indulgence.

After six months he had disappeared to prowl the bars and jazz clubs of San Francisco by himself, and she fled back to her father in shame. Julie hid herself away from the world on her father's boat, ashamed because she had not been wise enough to choose the right man and hadn't been strong enough to confront that man about their problems.

George Marrat had never questioned her. Although he had made many a poor choice himself, and life had dealt him many a blow, he still met the morning with a smile and fixed his eyes on the horizon. He planned a trip south to show his daughter his homeland, to take her mind off her problems. They would prospect on the southern coast. If they could find a cannery and take on a crew, they would fish the southern waters as he had in Ketchikan and Port Albion.

But now they were here in this dismal settlement. And George Marrat was very sick. Julie put her father to bed and hurried to the store for medicine.

Pete Kubelik shook his head. "Medicine?" he said. "Ain't got much. Aspirin, an' some cold tablets. Anything more I can do, let me know."

He came around the counter and leaned against it. Despite her fear, she forced herself to stand still, but couldn't look him in the eye.

"You know," he said, "we could get along, you an' me. Gets mighty lonesome here, of a winter." In the corner, Rudy stifled a whispering laugh.

"I'm sorry, Mr. Kubelik. I couldn't do that. When Father gets well, we will leave."

"Suppose he doesn't get well?"

Cold fear welled up within her. "Oh, he will," she said firmly. "He often has touches of cold like this. He'll get well, and then we'll leave."

Kubelik grinned at her, his teeth yellow and broken. "Well, maybe," he said. "*If* I decide to take you up the coast. Then again, I may just keep you here, sort of company for me."

"That's ridiculous!" She looked up at him for the first time. "You couldn't get away with anything like that! What about the authorities?"

"The Chileans? The army? The police?" He laughed with genuine amusement. "They don't come here. Know why these folks don't come near you? Because I told 'em to stay away, that's why. Know why they stay here? Because they can't get away, either! They are pilin' up gold for me. Me an' Rudy, here!"

He chuckled. "Why, the government thinks this place is abandoned. Nobody ever comes here, at least," his voice dropped to a whisper, "no-body that goes out again."

Two days later her father died.

He died suddenly, in the night. Only for a moment was he rational, and seemed to realize there was little time left. He called her to him. "Julie ..." His voice was hoarse. "I ..." He fumbled for words. "I know what happened to the boat. He ... Kubelik ... he towed it away. He hid it over at Rio San Tadeo. One of the others told me, that last day, workin' on the spit."

"It's all right, Dad," she said gently, "we'll manage!"

The long gray miles of cold sea and the towering cliffs that flanked it filled her with horror. In all the world, there could be no more desolate place than this coast north of Magellan. "We'll manage," she whispered, but she knew he was dying.

They buried her father at the foot of a huge rock three hundred yards up the canyon from San Esteban. Several of the villagers were out for the funeral, but had she ever hoped for help from them, she gave up now. They were a thin, woebegone group, obviously afraid of Kubelik, who towered above them.

There were six men in the village, she discovered, four of them Chileans and two Yahgans, natives from the Beagle Channel area. The four women were all Yahgans but one, an Ona woman from Tierra del Fuego.

After the funeral, she talked with them while Pete Kubelik and Rudy ignored her. They had the only weapons among the group, and aside from the pistol which he always carried, Kubelik possessed two shot-guns and a rifle. He had killed a man only a few days before their ketch arrived.

Recalling Kubelik's anxiety over their discovery of the place, she realized that was his greatest fear. Here in his little kingdom, he ruled supreme while they slaved for him and lived in abject fear of his rages. As he controlled the only means of escape as well as the only source of food, tobacco, and liquor, he was firmly in the saddle.

"But what about the boats?" she said to Aleman, one of the villagers. "Couldn't you steal one and get away?"

"Not a chance!" he told her. "His schooner has an auxiliary engine, and he'd have us before we made a dozen miles. Besides, where could we go on the supplies we'd have? We are a long way from the nearest port."

During the afternoon preceding her father's burial, she tried to recall exactly what the chart had pictured. The inlet was in the southeast corner of the Gulf of San Esteban, and the Rio San Tadeo was to the north. Although the chart indicated little of the nature of the country back of the coast, she knew it was rugged mountain and glacier. Of the beech forests, she knew only by hearsay, but they were pictured as dark, fearsome places, well-nigh impenetrable.

It was raining when they finished the funeral service. She started away when the grave had been filled, but Pete Kubelik overtook her. "Get your stuff, whatever you got," he ordered, "an' move over to my place."

It didn't take much to bring her to tears, but she intentionally pushed her sorrow and terror to the forefront. "Oh, not now! Please!" She sobbed hysterically, fell to her knees moaning, "My father ... my father ..."

She made the most unappealing spectacle of herself possible. Finally, in disgust, he shrugged it off. "All right, tomorrow, then," Kubelik said, and trudged away.

She was rolling up her father's jacket when she found the knife. Evidently, he had planned to use it himself, yet it was no knife she had ever seen aboard the boat. That meant he had acquired it since coming ashore, either finding it or getting it from one of the others.

The thought filled her with excitement. Perhaps ... if one of the men had given the knife to her father, she might have a friend out there. How could she know who he was?

Holding the coat so anyone peeking through the window could not see the knife, she examined the blade. It was bright and gleaming, and obviously had not been lying out in the weather.

The knife gave her courage. At least she could kill herself. The thought of killing Kubelik came first, but she dismissed the idea at once. He was too big, too strong, and he wore too many thicknesses of clothing. She would never have strength enough to drive the knife home.

Then she remembered the tobacco. Her father had come ashore prepared to trade, carrying a small sack filled with plugs of tobacco, some large packages of smoking tobacco, and a few cartons of cigarettes. In this place, it was a veritable fortune.

She had seen how avidly the men clutched the tiny packets of tobacco that Kubelik passed out. Maybe that was how her father got the knife.

For a long time she thought, wondering about the mountains and the inlet itself. If she could manage to steal a boat, she might get to the San Tadeo at least, and from there perhaps she could find her father's ketch. She would need neither food nor water to go that far. The thought of the eight miles against the engine of the schooner changed her mind. The river was out of the question.

Julie got up and put out her light, yet scarcely had the cabin become dark when there was a scratching at the window. Going to it, she stood to one side and peered out. In the vague light she could see a figure crouching in the darkness. Gently, she lifted the window.

"Missy? This Cuyu ... you got tobac' ... sí?"

Cuyu was one of the Yahgans. She remembered him at the funeral. He had been one of those who carried her father's body to the grave and helped fill it in. She remembered his eyes as she'd turned away, how they had seemed strangely gentle and compassionate.

"Yes! Yes, I have tobacco! Come to the door!"

"No door! He watch. He watch alla time! You speak me here!"

"Cuyu, can you get me away from here? Can you? Please!"

The Yahgan was silent. What sort of man was he? Would he be even worse than Kubelik? She dismissed that idea at once. Nobody could be worse.

"Can you get me to our ketch? My father was told it was anchored over on the San Tadeo!"

"San Tadeo? Sí. The boat, it there." There was sudden eagerness in Cuyu's voice.

She was almost frantic with excitement. "Oh, Cuyu! Take me to it and I'll give you all this tobacco! Yes, and more, too. Can we steal a dinghy?"

"No." The finality of his voice ended that possibility. "Maybe mountain." His voice was doubtful. "You strong? Walk fast? Climb?"

"Yes, oh yes!" Suddenly he hissed, and then like a shadow, he was gone.

Outside, in front of the cabin, she heard a crunch of boots on gravel. Had Kubelik changed his mind? Was he coming *now*? Or was he suspicious?

Instantly, she slipped off her shoes and got into bed, hunching the blankets around her. He came to the door, and she heard her latch lift, but the bar was in place. He hesitated, and there was no sound. Fear welled up within her. Suppose he broke down the door? Certainly, it would be little effort for a man of his brute strength. Praying she could make it sound right, she turned in the bed, as though in sleep.

Footsteps crunched around the house, and she felt rather than saw his head at the window. She had been unable to close it in time, and hoped he would believe she'd left it open for the air. He stood listening, and she kept her breathing deep and regular, hoping he would not look beneath the window for tracks. Suddenly, a light flashed on her face. After a minute of examination, he turned and walked away. Julie lay rigid, listening to the retreat of his footsteps on the coarse gravel.

It could have been no more than a minute before she heard the Yahgan again. Instantly, she was at the window. "I take," he whispered, "you bring tobac', sí?"

Swiftly, she dressed. She pulled on her boots and thrust the knife into the capacious pocket of her coat. It took her only a moment to climb through the window. She passed the tobacco to the Yahgan, but he returned it to her. "You keep—for now," he whispered.

Tugging at her sleeve, he moved off and away. Almost before she realized it, they were working their way through the gray trunks of ancient, long dead trees, and then into the timber itself. Her feet tangled in a soft, sinking bed of moss and she almost fell.

Cuyu caught her sleeve again and guided her in the darkness to a deadfall. She perceived his purpose; by walking on the fallen tree, they could keep out of the moss. Yet it was only a short distance, and then they were struggling in the knee-deep moss again. It was heavy with moisture, and before they had gone fifty yards she was soaked from the knees down. Yet Cuyu seemed to have eyes like a cat, for he found one deadfall after another.

How long they struggled and fought against the clinging, wet fingers of the forest she had no idea. Time and again she fell. She scratched her hands and face, but she kept going, fighting with the strength of desperation for every inch of distance. Suddenly, they emerged from the forest.

She was amazed. Before them, white and wide in the night, lay a glacier! Overhead, the clouds had momentarily parted and a few friendly stars shone through, but the Yahgan was looking at neither the stars nor the glacier. He was moving swiftly out over the icy surface, and the measure of his fear was the measure of her own. From time to time he glanced back. Was he expecting pursuit so soon?

Yet they made better progress now. Nor did Cuyu waste time. He led off swiftly and she almost had to run to keep up. That the Yahgan was frightened was obvious.

Leaving the glacier, they went up a steep, rocky trail along an icy black cliff, then down through a ravine. It was growing gray in the east, and despite all their travel, she had the feeling they had gained little ground. From time to time now, Cuyu stopped. He kept staring ahead, then listening.

L O U I S   L ' A M O U R

Something worried him. She was fighting exhaustion now, for they had not only encountered the roughest possible travel, but had kept up a pace far beyond her strength. Yet the Yahgan showed no evidence of tiring and no intention of slowing down. It was plain that he knew that if they were caught, while she might be taken back to the inlet, he would be killed on the spot.

Cuyu turned now, changing his course to proceed more directly north, but his eyes continued to watch toward his left. Once, through a break in the curtain of trees shrouding the cliff on her left, she thought she saw water.

Was the fact that they must go down to the water what Cuyu feared? Kubelik, guessing their route or seeing their tracks, might use the boat to come around the point and head them off. It would be pitifully easy, and in a matter of an hour he could render useless their night of struggle.

The dim game trail they had been following dipped sharply down into a fantastically rugged gorge. Here the moss was scarce, but the trees were laden with snow, and there was an occasional patch of ice. They went down the steep side, passing themselves from tree trunk to tree trunk to keep from sliding or falling all the way to the bottom.

A brawling stream roared along over stones, and Cuyu dropped on his stomach and drank. Julie followed suit, then got to her feet and looked around.

The gorge curved sharply right before them, and the course of the stream led down toward the north. While the direction was perfect for them and would make travel easier, it must also lead to the inlet she thought she had seen. Now she comprehended the reason for Cuyu's hurry. He hoped to get to the mouth of the river before they could be headed off.

He started again, with only a glance at her, nearly running wherever the path was smooth enough to permit it. At times they had to climb down over great tumbled masses of white boulders, or walk gingerly across slippery rocks, some of them covered with encroaching peat moss from the forest.

They came out of the trees and into the open delta of rocks and sand where the inlet met the mouth of the San Tadeo River. There was no boat in sight, but they ran now, trying to cover the exposed area as quickly as possible. They reached the woods where the river poured forth, a wide course of dark water rushing down from the mountains, and Cuyu paused to let her catch her breath. For a brief moment he grinned at her.

"Almos' to boat . . . you'll see."

Slowly, they started upstream along the watercourse, and soon, through the branches of the trees ahead, she could see the white of the ketch's hull. It was only a matter of minutes to reach the vessel. The trim craft was tied up in a deep backwater out of the main flow of the river. A good anchorage, Julie realized, but a difficult one for her to maneuver out of even with Cuyu's help. The ketch would have to be carefully backed and turned into the river, with most of the backing being into the current.

Without bothering to pull the boat in to shore, she climbed out on a low hanging branch and dropped to the deck. Cuyu followed as she made her way to the pilot house.

"You take us away?" he asked.

She could see that he was more terrified than ever, now that they had reached their destination. Terrified because, unlike the stretches of forest and glacier, this was a place where Kubelik would have to come on any search for them that he might make. She thought of the difficult job of fighting the river's current with a reversed engine, of how the ketch would slip sideways even as it moved back, and feared what roots or rocks lurked beneath the black waters of the San Tadeo. Sometime toward morning there would be a tide, and that would make her job much easier, but high tide was hours away and she was sure they didn't have an hour, let alone hours.

"I can try," she mumbled. The thought of the miles of gray, whitecapped water frightened her. She had spent many months at sea, but never without her father. She took a deep breath and reached out for the switch that activated the pumps. Nothing happened. She tried again.

But the moment she touched the console, she heard it. Off in the distance, but not distant enough, was the low *thot-thot* of an auxiliary engine. It could only belong to Kubelik's schooner. She turned, and through the open hatchway could see a movement through the trees that blocked her view of the river.

"Quick!" she said to Cuyu. "We must get off the boat and hide." But the native was already headed across the deck. He jumped for a branch and pulled himself up. Julie, desperate to know the full extent of her troubles, flipped up the cover and glanced into the electrical console. The battery cable had been removed, and the deck boards were scarred where Kubelik had yanked it up through the narrow channel. He had made sure that no one was going to be taking the ketch out of the river, at least not without winching it out of the backwater and upriver against the current. She dropped the cover and ran.

Back on deck, she saw Cuyu motioning frantically from the bank. She'd started for the branch when a shot rang out.

The Yahgan fled. The schooner was drawing into the backwater, and standing in the bow, a rifle in his hands, was Pete Kubelik!

"Cuyu!" Her cry seemed lost in the space between the trees. *"Look out!"*

She saw the Yahgan glance back, and then he left his feet and dove into the brush and in that instant the rifle barked. Did he stumble? Or was he already falling of his own volition?

The rifle barked again, but she heard no whine of bullet nor was she hit. Cuyu must have still been alive then, and another shot had been sent to finish the job. She heard Kubelik shout, and turned back to the companionway. Dropping down the ladder, she ran for her father's cabin. Just as she unlatched the door she both heard and felt Kubelik's schooner bump up alongside the ketch.

Hanging from leather loops attached to the side of the bunk was George Marrat's old Mannlicher carbine. Julie jerked it free and grabbed up the leather cartridge wallet that hung with it. Footsteps pounded overhead. She had no time to load and barely time to think. Kubelik was coming down the ladder. As she ducked into the companionway she could see the back of his legs as he descended. She slid through the galley door and threw the lock, although that would hold him only an instant.

Scrambling onto the mess table and pushing open the skylight, she tossed the rifle through and started to crawl out herself. Behind and beneath her, the door splintered open. She rolled through the hinged skylight as Kubelik roared, charging across the cabin.

Julie grabbed the carbine and plunged overboard. The icy water hit her like a fist, a cold, solid hammer in her stomach. Down she went, striking out toward the shore but still sinking. Her clothes, heavy shoes, and seven pounds of rifle carried her to the muddy bottom. Her ears popped and she pushed off, hitting the surface and gulping air. She saw a vague shape to her left and grabbed out, her hand scraping along the side of Kubelik's schooner. Her eyes cleared, and looking past the bow, she saw Kubelik stalking along the rail of the ketch, rifle in hand.

Julie Marrat took a deep breath and sank away from the boat. A couple of strokes and she felt the bottom again, and then the dirt and roots making up the side of the backwater. A submerged branch hit her in the face, and she grabbed at it, pulling herself up and along a fallen log to the shore. She stumbled up and water poured from her clothes in a rush.

There was a whip of air by her body and then the slam of a rifle shot. Pete Kubelik jacked another round into the chamber of his rifle, the spent case bouncing off the deck of the ketch. On the schooner, Rudy came running forward, shotgun in hand. She fell, rather than ran, into a dark space between the trees.

"You come back here!" Kubelik roared. "You come back or I'll kill you!"

Now it was the air that was a freezing fist closing on her lungs. Her sopping clothes clung to her as she slogged, almost knee deep in moss, deeper into the forest. Even as she ran she was sobbing with fear. Soon she slowed, realizing that she was leaving a trail even a blind man could follow, and found a deadfall like Cuyu had used. She worked her way deeper and deeper into the immense stand of beeches, and finally, shivering, collapsed from exhaustion.

Her breath came in shuddering gasps, but as she slowly caught her wind she became aware of the silence. There was no noise of pursuit ... there was almost no noise at all. For the moment she was safe.

Except the cold would kill her. It was still in the mid-forties, but her wet clothes would rapidly give her hypothermia, and in the night the temperature would drop another ten or fifteen degrees. She tried to hold herself still and quiet her chattering teeth. There were still no sounds of pursuit. She crawled around behind a fallen log and pulled off some chunks of bark, but they seemed too damp to burn. A long crack in the fallen tree, however, gave her access to the inside of the trunk, hollowed out by heart-rot, and from there she used the knife to scrape out some light, dry, strips of wood.

Using a box of safety matches that she had taken from the shack in San Esteban, she struck match after match with no answering flame; they had become too wet. Finally, she tried holding the match head against the striking area with the ball of her thumb as she rasped it along. The match flared but the pain in her hand made her drop it in the moss, where it went out. Blowing on her burned thumb, she was not surprised to find herself cursing in a manner befitting a sailor or dockhand. Gritting her teeth, she struck another match. There was the smell of burning sulfur, and even as she pulled her thumb away she knew she'd blistered it again; however, she lit her tiny fire and slowly fed the flames. Then she stripped the achingly cold clothes off, wrung them out, and laid them out across the log near the fire.

Shuddering, half frozen, and naked, she huddled by the log and prayed for her clothes to dry. In the dark and silent wood, exposed in every way, Julie was sure that this was when Kubelik would find her. He would follow her tracks, even where she had tried to make it hard for him. He would smell her fire. He would find her and ...

She turned and, fumbling with the cartridges, loaded the gun. She put a round in the chamber and set the safety. "Damn you," she whispered. "Damn you, if you come here, I'll kill you!"

Then she laughed.

She laughed at the picture of herself, stark naked and freezing in a primitive forest, clutching a rifle and daring a man like Pete Kubelik to come and get her. What made it funny was the thought of her husband, champion of the working class, seeing her now. That her often drunk, ineffective coffeehouse bolshevik could never even imagine this, which made her cough out a hard, mean laugh from lips that were set in a snarl.

"Come on, damn you."

From somewhere inside her there came a deep swell of emotion. Some of it was the loss of her father. Some of it was fear of this terrible man. Some of it was anger, finally not with herself, but with her no-good husband.

But most of it was an emotion that had no name, something ancient and primal, the feeling that a tiny animal might have when, after being pursued to the end of its endurance, it turns and bares its teeth. Not only does it have to fight, but something inside it has changed ... now it *wants* to fight.

MORNING FOUND Pete Kubelik painfully awake in his room at the San Esteban trade store. He had clumsily fallen off one of the deadfalls that Julie Marrat had skillfully negotiated in her escape the previous day. Kubelik had sprained his ankle, and now the swelling had become serious and excruciating. He took a swallow from a bottle of vodka he had half finished the night before and limped to the front door of the store. Throwing off the heavy bar, he stepped out into the gray and drizzling dawn.

Today he and Rudy would have to finish up what that damn girl had started. Regardless of the pain that shot through him every time he took a step, regardless of the hangover pounding in his temples, he'd find Julie Marrat, and if he couldn't make her come back with him, he'd kill her. He'd kill her anyway, but there'd be more pleasure for him if he brought her back alive.

He surveyed the long beach and the high cliffs. Time to get moving. He shook his head, trying to clear it, but that movement made his vision blur with pain.

Maybe he'd just kill her.

An invisible club knocked Pete Kubelik's bad leg out from under him. He went face-first into the sand, gasping in shock. He lurched around, trying to sit up even as the crack of the gunshot echoed back from the cliffs. Looking down, he saw blood welling from a hole dead center in his knee. He clawed for the pistol behind his hip.

Down on the beach, less than one hundred yards from the door of his store, the dark sand moved and shook. Julie Marrat stood up from the place where she had lain, half buried, through the night, the sights of her father's old carbine trained on Kubelik's front door. She worked the bolt on the rifle, and when Rudy came charging out of the building, shotgun in hand, she shot him in the stomach. Then she started forward.

Kubelik half raised the .45, but she spoke before he could bring it to bear.

"Don't! I won't kill you if you throw it away."

He was tempted to try, but the barrel felt heavy, too heavy, and down in his leg the pain was starting to rise like a giant comber. He dropped the gun and began to curse, a long quiet stream of the foulest language Julie had ever heard.

She picked the gun up. "I came back for my battery cable," she said. "You shouldn't have taken it ... or stolen our boat." She went up to the store and took the bolt from Kubelik's rifle. Then, using a rock, she beat the hammers from the trader's shotguns. The cable she eventually found lying on the deck of the schooner.

She fired up the schooner's auxiliary and threw off the lines. Several of the other inhabitants of the station had come down to the water and were watching her curiously. She called out to them.

"I'll leave this boat in the mouth of the San Tadeo River if you want it." They looked at her as she turned and headed down the inlet and toward the gulf. The last time she looked back, they had walked over to where Pete Kubelik lay in the sand. They had all taken up sticks or rocks, but were not striking him. They were just standing there. Finally, they slipped out of sight as she rounded the headland and started down to the sea.

Meeting at Falmouth

Night, and the storm ... howling engines of wind roared over the Lizard and above the slate roofs of Falmouth. Volleys of rain rattled along the cobblestones like a scattering of broken teeth.

Shoulders hunched against the wind and rain, the rider stared through the darkness toward a bend in the road ahead. It was January of 1794, and the worst storm of the winter was raging over the Atlantic, screaming above Land's End and lashing Mount's Bay with its fury.

Suddenly, a woman darted from the rocks beside the road and lifted her hand. Startled, the man drew up sharply, one hand dropping to his greatcoat pocket.

"Oh, sir! Sir!"

He looked down into the white, rain-wet face of a girl. She was shabbily dressed, with an old piece of sailcloth serving as a shield from the rain.

"What are you doing out here, girl?" he demanded. "You'll get a nasty bit of cold!"

"Sir, beggin' your pardon, but are you Mr. Talleyrand?"

"Talleyrand?" He was puzzled. "No, I'm not Talleyrand, and what would a serving wench like you be wanting with him?"

"It's up ahead, sir. I'm maid at the Bos'n's Locker, sir. The inn, it is. There's a bad lot there, a-plottin' they are, a-plottin' against Mr. Talleyrand."

"And you came out here to warn him?"

"I did, sir. I'd want no man murdered by them, not even a Frenchman, sir."

"And what makes you think Talleyrand will be here tonight? Only yesterday he sailed from England for America."

"I know that, sir. They talked of it. But they think he will be coming, sir."

"Thank you, girl. Now you'd best get inside before they find you're gone—" His voice broke off sharply as two men came running through the rain.

Both were roughly dressed, and in a momentary lull in the storm, he saw one of them wore a black patch over his eye. A tall, lean man he was, with the face of evil on him.

"So here you are!" His voice sounded shrill in the storm. "What are you doin' out here on the road, wench?" He grabbed at her shoulder and the girl stepped back.

Instantly, the rider pushed his horse between them. In his hand was a drawn saber. "Get back there, man! Leave the girl alone! She came to bring me a message, and it will be none of your affair!"

"Who're you?" The man with the patch peered up at him from the rain, careful to keep free of the saber point. He blinked his eyes, then drew back, smiling suddenly, almost leering. "Ahhhh, Tom! It's the Yank! It's that American who's been about the tavern. He's no bit of trouble for us, let's be back inside."

Without another word, they turned and hurried back through the rain.

When they had gone, the rider glanced down at the girl. "Put your foot in my stirrup, girl, and we'll have you back to the inn in no time."

When she had her foot in his stirrup, he put an arm about her waist to steady her. "Say nothing of this now, not to anyone. You understand?"

"Oh, yes sir! I'll not speak, sir!"

Dropping her to the ground, he then rode around to the stable. A hard-faced man with a wooden leg limped toward him, peering through the rain. "Oh, it's you?" He accepted the bridle. "Don't you worry, sir. I'll be carin' for the mare."

The American stamped his feet to shake off some of the water, then walked swiftly across the worn cobbles to the side door of the inn. There he repeated his stamping, and opened the portal.

Wind almost tore the door from his hand, and the candles gasped and went out. He stood stock-still, listening carefully until the lights were glowing again. The inn shutters rattled and, on the hearth, the flames guttered and spat.

The man with the black patch over his eye was hunched over a table with two other men. "I tell you, Tom, they will never pass the Lizard this night!"

"What then?" Tom was a burly man in a shabby cloak.

"Then it's here they will come! Only this morning, Brynie sighted their ship, and fighting a head wind she was! They'll put in here or be blown miles off their course."

"And if they come, we can still earn our guineas."

The American gave them no second glance, walking to a table near the fire and stripping off his rain-wet cloak. He removed his saber and placed it beside the cloak, but within easy grasp.

A compact, well-built man he was, but not large. Obviously a gentleman, but more than that. His was a strong, handsome face, his hair silvering at the temples. With it he wore the air of one born to command, yet it was a face that showed suffering, and was marked by some deep tragedy.

Drawing a book from his pocket, he opened it. He glanced up at the innkeeper. "Sherry," he said, "and if you have it, a bit of bread and cheese."

He glanced at the pages of the book, then at the three men. Slovenly rogues they were, if he had ever seen them. Scum, but a bloody, dangerous sort of scum, and plotting no good to anyone.

"Simple," Tom said then, waving a dirty hand, "they will come ashore, and if they come ashore, it's here they must come. So then, we have them."

"You speak of *them* . . . it is *him* we want."

"Garnet will know him."

"A tall man, he is, a tall man with a limp, a fair bit of nobleman and church."

The American turned a page of his book. The plotters had spoken in low tones, but their voices carried to him. Still, they had said nothing to be noted . . . had he not been warned by the maid.

Talleyrand . . . he knew the name well. A refugee from the French revolution now living in England, but about to leave for America. His was the reputation of a shrewd diplomat, cool but charming. He had a narrow escape from the guillotine, but evidently had not left all his enemies when he fled from France. These rogues were British if he had ever seen them, the sort of scum that can be had to kill for hire. But Garnet—that name had a French sound.

Obviously, the plotters were correct. No ship could beat past the Lizard on such a night, and if by some chance she did pass, then she could never hope to get beyond Land's End in the face of such a wind.

Tom jerked his head toward the American. His voice lowered, but could still be heard. "Who's that one? What . . . ?"

One of the others whispered a name, and all their faces turned toward him. The American felt shame mingled with anger send hot blood creeping up his neck and face. He turned a page of the book and the print blurred before his eyes. Dimly he heard the words, "Not him. He'll not interfere, not the likes of him."

So they thought him a coward as well, did they? Many things, but never that. He had been no coward at Saratoga, he—

On the hearth, the flames hissed as a drop of water fell down the chimney. The host, seeing his empty glass, crossed the flags to him. "Yes, Salem, if you please," the American said. "It's a foul night and the wine warms a man. They bottle with this, I think, some of the sunshine of Spain."

"That they did, sir. Would you have me leave the bottle?"

"If you will . . ."

Battalions of wind threw their weight against the shutters, then withdrew, rattling them with angry fingers.

So they would never forget? A man made one mistake . . . but it was the worst mistake. The worst of all.

The maid moved about the room, frightened and pale. From time to time she darted a glance at him, but the American continued to read.

Finally, the three arose, drew their cloaks about them and left the tavern. The innkeeper moved to stoke the fire, then placed a heavy chunk on the coals. He threw a glance at the American, then jerked his head after the departing trio. "A bad lot that, sir. Gallows bait for sure."

"They are staying here?"

"The night only, sir. I'd not have them longer if I had to call the watch from Falmouth."

"A good idea." The American turned a page of his book, then picked up his glass and drained it. "Salem?"

"Sir?"

"There will be some Frenchmen coming alone. One will be named Talleyrand. Would you tell him, from a friend, to have a care? To be on his guard?"

"From *them,* sir? There's that in the wind?"

"More than we know, I'm thinking. You'll tell him?"

"Of course, sir. But—"

"As a precaution only. I'll be back."

The maid started to speak, then stopped. Yet she hurried to the door and looked up at him, her eyes frightened. He chucked her gently under the chin. "You worry too much," he said.

He opened the door then, stepped out and drew it behind him. Falmouth was a cluster of roofs several hundred yards away. The Bos'n's Locker stood on the harbor road away from the town. Overhead the sign creaked dismally in the wind.

Drawing his collar tighter, the American bent his head into the wind and turned down the road in the direction of the docks. There was no trusting the men he had seen. It would be like them not to wait for Talleyrand to come to the inn, but to murder him along the coast and throw his body in the sea.

It was not in him to sit idly by while a man was attacked without warning. Or was it in part because he was irritated with inaction?

Rain whipped his face and pounded at him with tiny, angry fingers. He could see the men ahead of him along the road, and when they stopped near some dark buildings along the wharf, he drew back into the shadows himself.

From the darkness nearby a man stepped. "Followin' 'em, are ye? Now Dick'll be proud to know that. He——"

The American stepped quickly from the shadows and one hand grasped the newcomer by the throat, the other by the shoulder. Fiercely, he slammed the man back against the building, took a twist of the man's collar and let up only when he became afraid unconsciousness would keep the other from understanding his words. "Open your mouth," the very calmness of the American's voice was more frightening than rage would have been, "and I'll have the heart out of you. Get away from here now, and be glad that I haven't opened you up with my saber."

Gagging and pawing at his bruised throat, the man staggered back, then turned and hurried away into the storm. The American watched him for a few minutes, then glanced back to where the others waited in the darkness. Far away down the channel he thought he saw a light, and he moved along the building, well back in the darkness, his saber in his hand.

"Bloody awful night!" It was the man the others had called Dick.

"It is that."

"Any sign of her?"

"I be'ant lookin'. Soon enough when they put down a boat. If she comes, she'll come soon, you can mark that."

"Where then, Dick? Where'll we do't?"

"We've got to see him, first. Garnet will show us the man."

An hour passed on heavy feet. The wind did not abate, but the ship came. Her sails rolled up slowly, and the sailors at the canvas were unseen in the howling dark. They heard the rumble of her anchor going down, and later the chunk of oars, a sound caught only at intervals when the wind hesitated to gather force.

The American shifted his saber and dried his palm on his trousers beneath his greatcoat. Then he clutched the sword again.

He did not hear the boat come alongside, only suddenly there were men walking and he heard the sound of them speaking French. It was a language he knew, and he listened. He learned much of what he knew in

Quebec, and this was but little different. But no names were called, and the three men went by, two tall men and one short, stout, and slipping as he walked. At times he ran a few steps to keep up, and puffed when he slowed down.

Dick and his companions fell in behind, and the American followed them. And so they came again to the inn.

By then he was before them. He had run, and gotten around them and into the back door as from the stable. When they entered, he was again at his table, a glass of sherry poured, and engrossed in his book. They entered, and he glanced up.

"You are from the port?" the American asked.

"From the sea." The man who replied was tall, cold of eyes, and walked with a slight limp. The American knew him from description to be Talleyrand. "We are for America," the man said.

"It is my country."

Talleyrand glanced at him with quick interest. "Then you can tell us of your country. We go there as strangers. What can you tell of America? Is it a fair land?"

The American closed his book carefully. "A fair land? Yes, it is. If I were to tell you of it as I think of it, you would think me a poet rather than a soldier. And I do think of it, I think of it always."

The newcomers warmed themselves at the fire and the American went on, speaking to them but to himself also. "You will find it colder there than here, but the houses are strong and tight and warm. There will be less talk of art and more of the frontier, less of books and more of land, but there will be good food, and good drink. You will find it a land of strong men, of full-breasted women, fit to mother a race of kings."

"And this man Washington? Have you met him? We in France have heard much of him."

The American hesitated, glancing at his wineglass. "Washington? Yes, I knew him. He is a great man, a greater man than most of us believed. Though he does not, you might say, have a flair. He is a shrewd, thoughtful, considering man, but he has a temper."

"So I have heard." Talleyrand clasped his hands behind his back. "It needs a great man to retreat when all around him are demanding a victory. He knew the important thing was not to risk his army, to keep his fighting force intact."

The American gestured to the table. "Will you join me, gentlemen? With the wind as it is, you must plan to stay for hours, perhaps for days. You are Monsieur de Talleyrand?"

"I am. And this is Monsieur de Fougier. And our companion, Paul Garnet."

The American looked around at the name. Garnet had a hard face with cold eyes and a tight-lipped mouth. So this was the traitor? He hesitated over that thought.

"You will like my country," he said gently. "It is a fine, strong land. The earth will be frozen now, beneath the snow. The rooftops will be white, and a thousand chimneys will lift their fingers of smoke toward the sky, but soon after you are there, the spring will come. The trees will bud and the fields grow green, and the men will plow the earth and you will hear the heavy wagons along the dirt roads. It is a young land, monsieur, a growing, raw, wonderful land, and ... and ..."

Talleyrand smiled slightly. "And it is your country."

"Yes," the American said quietly, "it is my country. It will always be my country, the only one for me. I have only learned that now ... and now it is too late."

Suddenly, he looked up and saw that Dick was in the doorway. Tom was moving nearer, and Garnet suddenly arose and stepped back.

The American's hand was beneath his coat. "Talleyrand, watch yourself, sir. I have been waiting to warn you. Your life is in danger."

Talleyrand did not move from the table. His eyes flickered over the faces, came to rest on that of Garnet. If he was surprised, he gave no evidence of it. This man, who was for many years to be Europe's master of intrigue, who was to think always of his country and not of its ruler, was never to be surprised.

"You are clumsy, Paul. Had it not been for the storm, we would have gotten away from you."

"It does not matter. There was the storm!"

"But we are warned."

"And unarmed," Garnet replied coolly, triumphant now.

"I am not."

Their eyes turned to the American. He had drawn a pistol from beneath his dress coat. In his right hand he held the hilt of the still-sheathed saber.

There was something in that still, cold, handsome face that sent a shiver of apprehension through Garnet. This man ... this man would not be afraid to die. He would die hard, and not alone.

De Fougier lurched backward, his face white. The three men faced the assassins. One pale and cowering, one tall and straight and cool, one the mysterious soldier, with a pistol in his hand.

"Well, gentlemen," Talleyrand said coolly, "what is it to be? Are you ready to die, or will you retire quietly?"

Garnet was furious. He glared at the American. "He has but one shot, and there are four of us!"

The American smiled. "One shot, for *you*. And then the saber. I fancy the saber, my man. I was of the cavalry before this."

Dick spoke up angrily. "Belay the gab! It's him you want, ain't it?" He pointed an outstretched finger at Talleyrand. "Then by the ...!" He lunged, a dagger suddenly gripped in his fist.

The American's pistol exploded and Dick halted in mid-stride, his mouth falling open. At the same instant there was a second explosion and Garnet turned half around, then fell across the corner of the table. The table tipped, crashed on its side, and the wine bottle rolled off, struck the fallen man on the back, then rolled off onto the floor. The American stood with drawn saber. But the two others fled into the storm, the wind slamming closed the door behind them.

The second shot had been fired by Talleyrand, who held a small pistol. There was a flicker of irony in the Frenchman's eyes. "Yes, my American friend, even a diplomat knows that words must occasionally be backed with force." He glanced at the fallen man. "Very likely you've saved my life."

The American bent and retrieved the bottle from the floor. "And we did not break the wine."

Talleyrand glanced at the bodies of the two men. "It would be just as well if we went to some other place. There'll be trouble here soon."

"Monsieur?"

Talleyrand turned to face the American. "Yes?"

"If you will take the advice of one who is gone from his own country— go back to France. If that is not politically possible now, then go back when you can, as soon as you can. Believe me, monsieur, far better than any other, I know there is no country like one's own, and you will not be happy serving another."

"It is good advice, but now we go to America. Could you give me letters of introduction to someone there? It would be a great favor."

The American shook his head regretfully. "I am sorry, that I cannot do. I am perhaps the only American who cannot."

Their eyes held. Talleyrand hesitated. "Then, your name, sir? You can tell me that."

The American stiffened. His face was resigned and cold with pride and tragedy. "My name is Benedict Arnold."

Crash Landing

Dyea was the first to speak. "Don't anyone move." His voice was quiet, and its very calm destroyed the moment of rising panic. "The plane seems to be resting insecurely, we must act carefully and with intelligence. I will investigate."

With infinite care, he straightened himself from his seat, glancing briefly at the wreckage of the nose. There was no possibility that pilot or co-pilot were alive. The stewardess was sitting in the aisle, where she had been thrown by the crash. She looked toward him uncertainly.

"Miss Taylor," he said, recalling her name from the tab above her breast pocket, "I was an officer in the Army, and I have some experience with this sort of thing. If all will cooperate, I'm sure we will be all right."

He could see the relief in her eyes, and she nodded quickly. "Sit still," he said, before she could rise. "I'll only be a moment. The plane is resting, I believe, on a mountainside. Its position seems to be precarious."

The crashed commuter plane lay on the mountain, and could be no more than a dozen feet from the crest of the ridge. Balancing his weight, his body leaning against the slant, he eased down the incline to the door in the back of the cabin. Fortunately, it had not jammed. The wind, which had been blowing hard, seemed to have lulled, and he stepped carefully from the door.

Snow swirled around him as he took a few steps back, along the fuselage, and then he looked down into an awful void that dropped away beneath the very tail of the plane. For a long moment he stared, awed by what he could sense rather than see. The slightest gust of wind or concerted movement could start the ship sliding, and in an instant it would fall off into the black void.

Yet, where he stood, the rock was solid, covered only by a thin coating of ice and snow blown by the wind. Moving carefully, he checked the position of the cliff edge and the area nearest the crashed plane. Then he returned to the door.

Dyea stood outside and looked within. Five faces had turned to stare at him. "You must move one at a time, and at my direction. The ship is in an extremely dangerous position. If there is any confusion or hurry, it may start sliding. You, in the right front seat, rise carefully. If you're not sure you can move under your own power, please tell me now."

A voice came from that seat where no face showed. "I cannot move. You must all go first."

"Thank you." Dyea looked at a fat man who clutched a briefcase and was near the door. "You, sir, will begin. Rise carefully and cross to the door. Bring your blanket with you. Be sure the blanket will catch on nothing."

As if hypnotized, the man rose from his seat. Patiently, he gathered the blanket, and with extreme economy of movement, he folded it; then, with the blanket under his arm, he moved to the door. As he stepped to the snow, Dyea pointed. "Walk ten steps forward, then three to the left. There is a rock there that will protect us from the wind."

The man moved away, and Dyea turned to the next person. Only when the five who were capable of moving had been removed from the plane did Dyea look to the hostess. "Miss Taylor, get to your feet," he said, "move carefully and gather all the remaining blankets and pass them to me."

"What about this man?" She indicated the seat from which the voice had come.

"He must wait. All our lives are in danger. Free of the plane, they may still die of cold and exposure. We must think first of the greatest number. Furthermore," he added, "the gentleman's courage has already been demonstrated.

"When you've given me all the blankets and coats, get your first aid kit and as much food as you can. Move very carefully and slowly. The ship is resting upon the very lip of a cliff that looks to be more than six hundred feet high."

As the stewardess began her collecting of blankets, Dyea looked toward the seat back where the remaining occupant sat. "My friend, moving you is going to be extremely dangerous. Do not suggest that we shouldn't attempt it, for we shall. However, I'll move you myself. Miss Taylor will be out of the ship at the time. We may both die. Therefore, think of any message you may want to send to anyone who survives you. Also, if there is any identification, pass it to the stewardess."

"And you?" The voice from the seat was calm, yet seemed tightly held against some pain, or fear. "What of you?"

"There is no one," Dyea said quietly, "I am a man alone."

Steadily, the stewardess made her trips; a dozen blankets, food, then medicine. One of the men appeared out of the darkness and accepted an armful of blankets. "One per person," Dyea said to him, "then a second as far as they go. The same for the coats. Then move this food and the medicine kit into the shelter."

"May I help?" the man asked, nodding toward the plane.

"Thank you, no. The added weight and movement would only increase the risk." He turned toward the stewardess. "Are any others alive?"

She looked into several of the seats, then stopped at one where he saw only a thin hand. "Yes, this girl is alive!"

"Good. We will proceed as planned. Come out."

Miss Taylor tiptoed carefully to the door and stepped out into the snow. Dyea turned to her, and she saw his strong, harshly cut face in the glow of the moon.

"If the plane carries us away," he advised, "you will keep these people huddled together until daylight." He glanced at the luminous dial of his wristwatch. "It is now three o'clock in the morning. It will begin to grow light shortly after six, possibly a little before. When it has become gray, make a stretcher of a couple of coats, load anyone who may not be able to walk, and move eastward along the ridge.

"When you've gone perhaps a quarter of a mile, away from this precipice, angle down the mountain toward the trees. Once there, build a fire and build a shelter. You have matches?"

"Yes." She hesitated. "Good luck."

"Thanks. I'll move the injured man first."

"I'll wait."

"No. Please don't." Dyea's voice was flat. "Now," he lifted his voice to the man in the plane, "your name and address, please? And any message for the stewardess?"

There was a moment of silence. "I am Victor Barclay, of Barclay and Paden, attorneys. My wife and children are living in Brentwood, California." He hesitated. "Only my love to them."

Miss Taylor turned her dark, serious eyes to the big man beside her. "And you, sir?"

"No message," Dyea said.

"Your name?"

"It does not matter."

"But isn't there someone?"

"No."

"I would like to know."

He smiled. She saw it clearly in the moonlight. The dark seriousness of his face changed. "My name is Dyea. Spelled D-Y-E-A. My family pronounced it dee-ah, the accent on the first syllable."

He hunched his shoulders against the cold. "Go now. Stay clear of the plane. I believe the wings are both gone, but some part might be under the snow and might drag you over. The rock will give you shelter."

When the woman was gone, Dyea stepped into the ship. With the decrease of weight, the situation was even more precarious. He walked carefully to the seated man. A blanket was over his legs, but obviously, both were broken. No other injuries were apparent. "All right, Barclay," Dyea said, "I'm going to pick you up. It may hurt like the devil. Despite that, you must hold yourself very still. If you move, you'll overbalance me on this incline and I'll fall. A fall would start the plane sliding."

"Very well. I'm ready."

Dyea's eyes flickered for the first time. He looked down the plane toward the tail, then at the door. He touched his lips with his tongue and, setting his feet carefully, stooped and picked up the injured man. As he straightened, he felt a sickening sensation of movement beneath him. He stood stock-still, holding the lawyer as if he were a child. The movement stopped with a faint grating sound; turning, Dyea took his first step. As he put down his foot with the combined weight of nearly four hundred pounds, he felt the ship shift beneath him. A queer sensation went up his spine, such a feeling as he had known but once before, when ice cracked beneath his feet out on a lake, a half mile from shore.

He took another step. There was no further movement, and he climbed down into the snow and walked over to the dark huddle of figures waiting in the lee of the rock.

Placing the lawyer on a coat spread out for him, Dyea straightened. "I think both thighs are fractured. I did not examine him. Possibly the lower part of the left leg, also. Keep him very warm and set the legs if you can."

Barclay looked up through the sifting flakes. His eyes were large with pain. "Don't go back," he said, "that little girl may not be alive by now."

"She was unconscious," Miss Taylor said.

"It's no matter. I'm going back."

"Don't be a fool, man!" Barclay burst out. "That plane almost went with us. It won't stand any more moving around. You know it and I know it. There's no use losing two lives when the one may go anyway."

Dyea did not reply. He turned, chafing his hands together. Then he walked quietly and stopped beside the plane. He looked around him, feeling the bitter cold for the first time. Then he glanced back to where the survivors were gathered, obscured by the swirling snow. The wind was rising. It would be a bitter night and a miserable tomorrow. Rescue parties might be days in coming but, with luck, the group could survive.

He balked at the door, and the thought that the girl must be dead by now flashed through his mind. Maybe, but probably not. He knew that was his fear of returning to the plane sneaking up on him. He shook his head and chuckled. The sound of it revived him, and he put a hand on each side of the plane door, a foot on the edge.

He stepped inside the plane and moved, gently as possible, to the girl's seat. As he bent to look at her, she opened her eyes and looked right into his.

"Don't move," he said, "there has been an accident."

She looked at him very carefully, at his eyes, his face, and his hair. In the plane, the moonlight shone through the windows, bright between scudding clouds. "I know," she said. "Who are you?"

"It does not matter. Think of this. Several of the passengers were killed, but six have been removed and are safe. If you and I can get out, we will be safe, too, and we're the last."

Her eyes were wide and gray. They bothered him, somehow. They reminded him of other eyes. "Where are we?"

"On a very high mountain. It is very cold and the wind is blowing hard. We're on the edge of a high cliff. When I pick you up, the plane may slip. It did with the last person I carried, but he was very heavy. So you must hold very still."

"Maybe I can walk. Let me try."

"No. If you stumbled or fell, the shock would start us moving. I must carry you."

"You're very brave."

"No, I'm not. Right now I'm scared. My stomach feels empty and my mouth is dry. I'll bet yours is, too, isn't it?"

"You're risking your life for me."

"You're a romantic child. And believe me, the risk is much less than you might suppose."

He had been on one knee, talking to her. Now he slid an arm beneath her legs and another around her body, under her arms. An arm slid trustfully around his neck and he got carefully to his feet. After Barclay's weight, she seemed very light. He stood still, looking toward the door. It was seven steps, every step an increasing danger.

She looked toward the door, too, then at him. "Isn't it strange? I'm not afraid anymore."

"I wish I could say I wasn't."

He took his first step, placing his foot down carefully, then, shifting his weight, he swung the other leg. Then the right and again the left. Nothing happened. He took a deep breath, looked at the black rectangle of the door, then took another step. As if moved by the added weight, the

ship quivered slightly. The movement was only a tremor, but Dyea immediately stepped again, and then again.

Under his feet the plane started to move, and he knew that this time
it was going all the way. He lunged at the door and shoved the girl out into
the snow. He saw her land, sprawling. The nose of the plane was sliding
down while the tail held almost still, the body rotating. Fortunately, it was
swinging in an arc opposite from where the girl had fallen. Then the
whole plane slid in one section over the edge of the cliff. As it fell free,
Dyea, with one agonized, fear-driven snap of his muscles, sprang upward
and outward into the blackness and swirling snow.

There was one awful instant when, hands spread high and wide, he
seemed to be hanging in space. He hit a steep slope partially covered with
snow. He slid, then felt his lower body going over ... he clutched, grabbing a fingerhold just as he began to fall. His arms gave a frightful jerk but
he held himself, swinging in black, swirling snow over a vast, cold emptiness.

The moon emerged from under a cloud, and he started upward. He
was no more than four feet below the edge, the cliff before him not as
sheer as he'd thought. The brow sloped steeply back, and on the very
edge was the girl, peering over at him.

"I'll get help," she said.

"No." He knew his fingers would not retain their hold. "Can you
brace yourself against something? Can your heels dig in?"

She glanced around, then nodded. "Then slip out of your coat and
lower the end toward me. Hang on tight, but if you feel yourself going,
just let go."

His fingers were slipping in their icy crack, already so numb he could
scarcely feel them. Snow swirled in his face and the wind whipped at his
mouth, stealing his breath away. He gasped, then the coat slapped him in
the face. He let go with one hand and swung it around and up, grasping
the suede coat. He felt the weight hit her, but she held it. Carefully, he
drew himself up, hand over hand. When his feet were in the crack where
his fingers had been, he climbed over and lay beside her in the snow.

"I never was an Army officer," he whispered. "I never was anything."

His arm was stretched out and his cuff pulled back. He could see the
dial on his watch. It was just eleven minutes past three.

With These Hands

He sat bolt upright in his seat, hands clasped in his lap, eyes fixed in an unseeing stare upon the crushed shambles of the forward part of the plane. His mind without focus, fixed in the awful rigidity of shock.

Awareness returned slowly, and with it a consciousness of cold. Not a shivering cold, not even the icy edge of a cutting wind, but the immense and awful cold of a land of ice, of a land beyond the sun. Of frigid, unending miles lying numb and still under the dead hand of the Arctic.

No movement ... no life. No sound of people, no hum of motors, no ticking of clocks; only silence and the long white miles where the lonely wind prowled and whispered to the snow.

He had survived. He alone had survived. That thought isolated itself in his consciousness and with it came the dread of living again, the dread of the necessity for struggle.

Yet he need not struggle. He could die. He need only sit still until the anesthesia of shock merged without pain into the anesthesia of death. He need only remain still. He need only wait ... wait and let the cold creep in. Once he moved the icy spell would be broken and then he must move again.

He was alive. He tried to shut away the thought and find some quiet place in his brain where he could stuff his ears and wait for death. But the thought had seeped into consciousness, and with it, consciousness of cold.

It was a cold where nails break sharply off when struck with a hammer; a cold where breath freezes and crackles like miniature firecrackers; a cold that drove needles of ice into his nose and throat ... there was no anesthesia, no quiet slipping away, this cold would be a flaying, torturing death.

Icy particles rattled against the hull of the plane; a wind sifted flakes across the hair of the sitting dead. Of them all, he alone had survived. Curtis who had believed so much in luck, Allen who had drilled for oil in the most inhospitable deserts and oceans of the world, of the seven men returning to Prudhoe Bay, he alone had survived.

He slumped in his seat.

That was it. He had moved. To live he must move again, he must act. What could he do? Where could he go? Outside lay the flat sweep of a snow-clad plain and beyond the dark edge of forest, black and sullen under a flat gray sky.

Movement had broken the rigidity of shock. With that break came the realization; there must be no panic, for panic was the little brother of death.

"Sit still," he said aloud, "you've got to think."

If he was to survive it must be by thinking. To think before he moved and then to waste no movement. This power had enabled men to survive. Reason, that ability to profit by experience and not only from their own meager experience, but from the experience of others. That was the secret of man's dominance, of his very survival, for he not only had learned how to control heat, flood, and wind, but how to transmit to future generations the knowledge of harsh experience.

This was an ancient enemy, this cold. Men had survived it, held it away with walls and fire, and if he, Drury Hill, oil company executive and once a citizen of the air-conditioned city of Dallas, Texas, was to survive, it must be by brains, ingenuity, and perhaps through those shared experiences.

He would need matches, he would need fuel. Shelter first, then fire. Fire here was out of the question. There would be spilled gasoline from ruptured tanks. And this plane was his lodestone for rescuers. His only beacon to the outside world. Very well, then, the forest. He had matches and a lighter, recently filled. He would need tools or a tool. He would need a blanket or another heavy coat.

Carefully, he straightened to his feet. He moved to the body of Curtis, avoiding looking at his face. He searched his pockets and found a lighter, more matches, and a nail file. One by one he searched those he could reach, but it was "Farmer" Peterson whom he blessed.

Peterson came from Minnesota and had trapped his way through college. An astute geologist, he was still a country boy at heart. His pockets yielded a waterproof matchbox filled with wooden matches and a large clasp knife of the type carried by sailors, the blade all of five inches long.

In the back of the plane he found several Army blankets and some cans of C rations. Making a bundle of one blanket, he then took along a roll of blueprints for the new tank and distribution complexes to use as tinder to start a fire.

Pausing to think, he remembered that he must not allow himself to perspire, for when activity ceased the perspiration would turn to ice and then his clothing would become a chilling hull in which death could come quickly.

He sorted through the debris where the lockers had broken open, finding a cup and several other useful utensils. He stuffed them into the blanket along with the food and Curtis's coat, and dropped down from the ruins of the plane.

The black battalions of the forest were a dark fringe where sky and snow had a meeting place. With curious reluctance, he stepped away from the plane and, leaving behind his last link with civilization, comfort, and tangible evidence of man, he walked off over the snow.

It was cold ... his boots crunched on the snow ... his breath crackled lightly. The all-pervading chill seemed to penetrate the thickest clothing. Yet the movement warmed him and he paused, glancing back. The distance to the plane frightened him, but he turned, and face down from the raw wind, he walked on.

He floundered into the black and white silence of the tree line. This was the ragged fringe of the forest and the growth was not tall ... white snow, gray and barren sky, the spidery undergrowth and the solemn columns of the trees.

Then he saw, scarcely fifty feet into the trees, a deadfall. This had been a greater tree than most, uprooted and flung down, black earth clinging to the root mass and making a solid wall against the northeast.

Lowering his blanket pack into the hollow where the roots had been, he gathered four thick branches for a foundation, and then with some of the blueprint paper for tinder, he built a small pyre of twigs. The tiny flame leaped up, hissed spitefully at the cold, and then reached warily for the paper. It caught ... edges of flame crept along the folds, then the flame began to eat hungrily into the tiny stack of fuel. He watched with triumph as the flames increased and twined their hot fingers about the cold pile of twigs.

He had achieved a fire ... a minor victory won. Man's first companion against the cold and dark, his first step forward from the animal. It was a simple thing, but it was the first thing.

Yet as the flames sank their eager teeth into his small stack of fuel, he realized with quick fear that he could well become the slave of the fire, devoting all of his time to serving it. He must keep his fire small and remain close or all his strength would be required to feed the insatiable flame.

The root mass of the deadfall was more than seven feet of solid wall with a web of extending roots. Taking his time, Hill gathered evergreen boughs for a thick bed against the very base of the protecting wall, which supplied him not only with a windbreak, but with a reflector for his fire. Through the straggling roots, which extended out and down from the root mass, he wove other evergreen boughs, and into the roots overhead he did the same thing. Soon he had a cuplike hollow with an open face toward the fire.

After gathering more fuel, he banked his fire, placed sticks close at hand, then rolled up in his blankets on the bed of spruce boughs. He slept almost at once, awakening from time to time to replenish the flames, warned by the searching fingers of increasing cold.

At daybreak, he awoke in pain. The muscles of his back and neck were a tightly knotted mass. He had been hurt in the crash, and he was just now realizing it. The night in the cold and his odd sleeping position on the ground seemed to have turned his entire body into an assortment of seized and overstretched muscles. He moved and it hurt, but that wasn't the worst part. It was the sense of fragility that scared him, the sense that if he was called upon to use his body, it would fail him.

He moved close to the fire and, slowly, carefully, began to stretch, trying to loosen his knotted muscles. In two hours he felt slightly better, he made hot, strong black tea, and while the wind moaned among the icy branches overhead he ate one of the boxes of rations, and listened to the cracking and complaining of the trees. Out across the open field, the wind lifted tiny ghosts of snow and floated them eerily along.

Each day he must think ... he must plan. He must go farther afield for fuel, for later he might become weak and must depend upon that which was close by. He must add to his shelter and he must return to the plane to search for whatever else might be useful. And he must keep the plane clear of snow.

During that first day, he thought little beyond his work. He brought more blankets from the plane. He located two more deadfalls that he could draw upon for fuel. He built a framework of evergreens that could be shifted to whatever angle to protect him from the wind. He added more boughs to his bed.

By now they would know the plane was down ... a search would have already begun. Drury Hill believed their ship had been off course when it crashed, and with the present overcast, there was small hope of immediate rescue.

That night, he took stock of his situation. With no more exertion than was needed to live, his food supply would last three days. From his experience flying from Fairbanks to Prudhoe and back, he knew three days was simply not enough. In the vast area they must search, he could not gamble on them finding him in less than a week.

He must find other sources of food. He was too far from the coast for seals. There were caribou, but he had no rifle nor had he yet seen their tracks. There were lichens that could be eaten. That was what he had read. Hovering over his fire in the darkness and cold, he strove to remember every iota of information culled from his reading, listening, and living.

On the second morning he awoke in a black depression. The pain was back in full force. He had slept fitfully through the awful cold and now he lay staring into the fire. It was no use. He was a fool to expect rescue. He was one man in all this vast waste. They would never find him. He stared at his grimy hands, felt the stubble on his jaws, and then stiffly, he pushed himself to a sitting position and stoked the fire.

His head ached and his mind was dull ... was he becoming ill? Had he overworked? It had been twenty years since he had done anything like this ... twenty good years of living and leisure and seeing all the world held.

This could be a miserable way to die ... on the other hand, suppose he lived? A fire of optimism blazed up within him ... it would be something ... they had said he was past his prime ... that he should take it easy. He cursed. He made tea and ate several crackers. He must find food.

With a stout stick cleaned of bark, he started out, keeping to crusty patches of snow or ground swept bare by wind. He found, growing on some damp soil, a patch of Idelana lichen and gathered a bundle of it to take along. He searched for berries, having heard that some low-growing bushes held their berries all winter long. His back hurt as he walked but soon he was standing straighter and as he warmed up he felt less and less like a crippled old man.

Twice Arctic hares bounded away over the snow and once he saw a herd of caribou in the distance.

Nothing moved in the forest when he started back. The trees were more scattered. He crossed two streams frozen hard by the subzero cold. The branches of trees creaked in the wind. He cupped a gloved hand over his nose and tried to breathe slowly, his exhalations warming the incoming breath.

Wind picked up the snow ... he should improvise some snowshoes ... a gust of wind whined in the trees ... he glanced at the sky. A storm was blowing up.

Darkness came suddenly and he found himself floundering through soft drifts. Feeling his way back to solid ground, he started on, then caught a whiff of wood smoke and then saw the black blob of his shelter. He started toward it, collecting wood as he went. His fire was almost gone, and he nurtured it carefully back to life.

With some meat from a can and some of the lichen, which he soaked to remove the acid, he made a thick stew. Huddled in his shelter of boughs, Dru Hill of Dallas, Abu Dhabi, and Caracas ... all places that were warm and populated ... added fuel to his fire and slowly ate the stew. He ate, and found it good.

Around him the walls of his shelter became suddenly friendly and secure. The wind caught at his fire and flattened the flame. It would use a lot of fuel tonight. He grinned as he leaned back against the root mass. He had plenty of fuel. Here he was, a lone man in an uncharted wilderness, yet he had created this little bit of civilization, it was a long way from being a building, even a crude one, but it was shelter nonetheless. He thought of the buildings he had ordered built, the oil and gas wells he'd drilled, the tank complexes and pipelines. All had been a natural outgrowth of this same simple need. Shelter and fuel. At one end of the spectrum it demanded a wood fire and a windbreak, at the other cracking plants and parking lots. He saw in himself an extension of the natural order of things. Man against the elements. Man triumphant against the elements. The third night coming and he was still alive. He could win. He could beat this racket. Old Dru Hill wasn't dead yet.

Tomorrow he would make some snares and catch a few Arctic hares or snowshoe rabbits. Maybe he could make a net and trap some birds. He would have meat and there were more lichens. East through the woods, there might be berries. He might even improve his shelter.

At seven in the morning, he heard the throbbing motors of a plane. The sky was heavily overcast but he rushed out, shouting loudly, uselessly. He heard it overhead, heard it pass on ... at least they were trying. Hope mounted, then died. He considered a dozen unreasonable doubts, worried over fifty objections. They might never return to this locality.

Yet he did not despair, for they would continue to search. He worked through the fourth day at his usual tasks, a man below medium height, inclined to be fat, but he hurt less ... in some strange way his body seemed to be stronger. To the west he found a vast stretch of tundra broken by only occasional outcroppings of rock and by the stalks of some plant. Intrigued, he dug into the snow and frozen ground and got out the fattish sulfur-yellow roots. They tasted sweet and starchy. He collected enough to fill his pockets.

No more planes came over ... by nightfall he was dead tired and glad for sleep. On the fifth morning, two snowshoe rabbits were in his snares ... on the sixth morning a third rabbit. He had no luck with the larger and more cautious Arctic hares. On that day, he ate nothing but food he had gathered himself, except for tea.

He had avoided the plane except to clean off the snow ... only once after his first leaving had he entered, but the motionless bodies of his former companions had filled him with gloom. Instead he collected debris from the crash, pounding sheets of aluminum into a crude stove and reflector.

On the seventh morning, his snares were empty and for the first time he failed to add to his supply of food. On the eighth day, they were again empty . . . he struggled to the tundra for more of the yellow roots. Returning, he found a patch of black crowberries and, sitting there in the open, he ate all he could find.

Since that one time he had heard no planes . . . had the search been abandoned? Had it been a searching plane at all?

On the ninth morning, he found a small snowshoe rabbit in a snare and made a rich stew using lichen and the yellow roots. But still he heard no planes. He no longer listened for them nor looked for them. He went on about the business of survival . . . he gathered lichen and roots, he checked his snares . . . the rabbits were more cautious now . . . he added to his supply of fuel.

Returning to the plane, he found his bag, forgotten until now. Back at his fire, defying the cold and the loneliness, he shaved. Almost at once he felt better. The smooth feel of his cheeks under his hand was better than the scraggy beard. He concealed the bag under the trunk of the tree.

His clearing had taken on a lived-in look. The snow was trodden down, there was a huge stack of fuel, the lazy smoke of the fire. There were the skins of the rabbits he had staked out. He added fuel to his fire, including a chunk of birch, and walked away.

Alone on the edge of the tundra, he looked across the flat white sea of snow . . . what lay beyond? Just a vast space, or perhaps a settlement? A trapper's cabin? He was slogging along over the snow, head down, when he smelled smoke. A lot of smoke . . .

His head came up—then he broke into a clumsy run. From the site of his shelter rose a bright column of flame!

Heart pounding, he lunged across the snow. Twice he fell, plunging headlong, facedown in the snow. He had been almost a mile away . . . he stumbled into the clearing and stopped, blank with despair.

His shelter was gone. His blankets were gone. The other coat was gone. Only charred, useless masses remained. More than half his fuel was gone and the rest still burned.

In a panic, he tore at the pile of fuel, pulling the pieces back, rubbing the fire away in the snow. A spark blowing into the dry, resinous stuff of the shelter must have set it off. A low wind whined among the bare boughs overhead, moaned in the evergreens, stirring the blackened ashes of his fire, rattling the dead fingers of the birch, whispering out over the tundra, a lonely reminder of the cold and the night to come.

Soon it would be dark ... it would be colder. Wind would come ... his clothing would turn to ice now for he had perspired freely ... his strength was burned out from the running and the work ... he would die ... he would freeze.

He stared around him ... what to do? Where to begin again? Begin again? He was a fool to begin again. Begin again ... ? He laughed hysterically. His little corner of civilization was gone. But what had it been? A pitiful shelter. An almost irreplaceable pile of wood. Some junk that he had used to survive. Before the crash he probably would never have recognized it as a camp, he might have thought it trash collected by the wind. Before the crash he never would have recognized what had burned as being the difference between life and death. He never realized how little it took, never realized how simple the things were ... as long as they were the right things.

He had to do something....

With his knife he made rawhide strips of the rabbit skins. It was growing dark, the wind was increasing. Another storm was coming. He must contrive something new ... there was a patch of willows no more than two hundred feet away. He went there, scanned a thick clump a dozen feet around, and then going into the clump he broke off all the central trees, none of them in the center being over two inches in diameter, mostly less. Then he drew the tops of the outer ones down and tied them together with the rawhide strips. When he had several of them with their tops tied at the center, he went out and wove others among them, using some willows but mostly evergreens. As the dark closed in he was making a strong, hivelike shelter with a hole in the top for smoke to escape. A shelter strong because it was made of living trees.

Trampling down the snow, he dug a hole with his knife and built a small fire there. He carried boughs within and scattered them around, then made a bed near the fire. Outside he threw more evergreens on the house, then gathered fuel. One of the deadfalls was close by, and working until long after dark, he carried as much of it to the door as he could, and several armsful inside.

Finally he made a door of woven boughs and pulled it across the entrance. Outside the snow was falling, the wind was blowing with hurricane force. Inside his wigwam of willow and evergreen, its framework rooted in the ground, he was secure.

His blankets were gone and his food was gone ... including the precious tea ... but outside the snow fell and packed tighter and thicker about his shelter. Inside it grew warmer. A drop from overhead fell and hissed gently in the flames. Reclining on the boughs, he considered the situation again. This storm would end hope of rescue ... everything would be shrouded in snow and he doubted if he would have the strength to un-cover the plane . . . and for days he would not have the time. He must find food again, set snares, gather more fuel.

If he could only trap a caribou! Sitting up suddenly . . . there was that book about China . . . what had its name been? It had told how they trapped deer in the Altin Tagh . . . a hole about eight to twelve inches in diameter and a couple of feet deep . . . less could do . . . and a ring of sharp sticks, the sharp ends pointing toward the center. When the deer stepped into the hole, the sharp sticks would prevent it being withdrawn. Then he could rush in with his knife . . . he grinned at himself. What pre-posterous thing would he think of next?

Awakening in the dark, icy cold of morning, he rebuilt his fire and this time the shelter grew quickly warm, testifying to the thick outer cov-ering of snow. He squatted beside the fire, dreading the outer cold but dreading more the cold his leaving would let into his shelter.

He must have food, and unless the snow had buried the snares com-pletely, he might have something. There had been a few more stalks of the yellow root not too far away on the tundra. The idea of the previous night returned. If he could kill a larger animal his food problem would be solved for days on end . . . and if trapped, he might kill it with a sharp stick or his knife. Banking his fire carefully, he went out of the hut, clos-ing the door and covering it with snow.

All was white and still, but with a strange difference. Suddenly, almost with shock, he realized why. The sky was clear!

Now, if ever, a plane might come. But were they still searching? Had they given up? Then he remembered . . . the crashed plane was shrouded in snow and would be invisible from the sky!

He started toward it, then stopped. The chance of rescue was a wild gamble and he needed food. In this country, one's strength need wane only a little for the cold to kill. Weakness and exhaustion were fatal. Turning, he walked toward the snares. Two were buried and useless . . . the third had been tripped and the rabbit had escaped. He reset them and went through the woods to the tundra and found two stalks of the yellow-rooted plant. The roots were pitifully small.

Circling back, he stopped suddenly. In the snow before him were the tracks of a herd of caribou. The tracks were fresh and the herd must have passed within a few minutes! He was following them when suddenly he heard the roar of a plane!

Wheeling around, he ran from under the trees and stared up at the sky . . . it was there, big and silver and beautiful! It was low enough to see him. But it was also low enough to be quickly out of sight. He sprang into the air, shouting hoarsely. It disappeared off over the trees to the north. Rushing toward his shelter, he could only think that the crashed plane had been covered with snow. He went past the shelter and finally got to the plane. He had no more than reached it when he heard the ship returning.

It was coming too fast ... he could never make it. Desperately, he began trying to uncover some part, the silver of a wing, to the sunlight. But the snow was heavy and he was too late, the plane soared off to the south and its sound died rapidly away.

Glumly, he started to turn back and then went to work and cleaned the snow from the one undamaged wing and the fuselage. It was a slow, heavy task and noon had come and gone before he completed it. He was physically exhausted and ravenously hungry.

A plane had come, crossed over the area and gone. He must, he told himself, appreciate the significance of that. It meant his last chance for rescue was gone. They would not cover the same ground twice. As he prepared his meal, he considered that, using the two yellow roots and his prize ... an Arctic hare found in a snare set that very morning.

All right then. No rescue. If he was to survive until spring and then walk out, he must do it on his own. Dru Hill was surprised to find that he did not view the situation with alarm. He could survive ... he had proved that ... and if he could trap a caribou, he would have a good supply of meat. He could trap two if he could trap one. He could dry or smoke the meat and so build supplies for spring. He could make a pair of snowshoes and, now that hope of rescue was abandoned, he could afford to go further afield for food, not needing to remain near the crashed ship.

He took a deep breath and thought of the miles of wilderness that surrounded him. He didn't have much but the woods could provide, they had shown him that. He no longer thought of this Arctic forest with fear. It was beautiful, the trees comforting, the vast expanse of tundra a wonder and a challenge. His hearing had become supernaturally acute, his sense of smell delicate. He could survive.

This was something he never could have imagined two weeks ago. A man needed lights, an automobile, the complex comforts of the modern world. He, in his chosen profession, had provided the electricity, the gasoline, and the plastics to provide those comforts.

He grinned to himself. Farther afield there might be better hunting grounds, berries, perhaps more game. He thought of something else ... of the change in himself. Here he was, calmly and with confidence considering surviving the entire winter where a few days before he had doubted his ability to survive a few hours. But he was right. His doubts were gone, and justly so. This place was warm and could be made warmer.

He could take some metal from the plane for heads for a spear and for arrows. He could ... he heard voices.

He pushed aside the door and thrust his head out. Three men, two of them in Canadian Air Force uniforms, and the third was Bud Robinson, were slogging down the path.

He stood there and they stared at him, and then Robinson said, "By the Lord Harry! It's Dru Hill!"

Robinson looked around curiously. "We never dreamed anyone would be alive, but when we flew over this morning, Gene thought he saw a black spot on the snow. Only it was not on the snow, but where the snow had melted off the trees over your fire, here."

"We flew clear back to the post," Gene explained, "but it kept nagging me. There shouldn't be anything black after all that snow falling, so we took a chance and came back. It's lucky for you that we did."

Hours later the plane dropped down onto the runway of an airfield surrounded by warehouses and industrial buildings. Nearby a pipeline ran toward the distant sea. Dru Hill was hustled across the field and into a waiting ambulance. He insisted on sitting in front with the driver and at the hospital they gave him a clean bill of health, something he had not doubted.

They left him alone finally, the reporters, and doctors, company representatives, and police, in a brand-new motel room near the airfield. The walls and roof seemed strangely close. He paced the odd green carpeting far into the night. To Dru Hill the room smelled of cleansers and cigarettes and wallpaper glue. It was uncomfortably warm. He opened the window, letting in the cold night air and a small shard or two of ice. Beyond the parking lot was a line of scraggly pines obscuring a set of trash bins and the highway. The sound of engines and tires on the asphalt filled his ears. The air outside smelled like gasoline. Gasoline and garbage.

But then the wind blew and after a moment it carried away those smells, replacing them momentarily with the smell of the great Alaska beyond. Beyond the suburbs, the trailers, the gravel pits, and oil wells. He remembered how, as the plane lifted itself from the snow, he had looked back. The trees at the edge of the forest were only a dark line. The place where he had built his hut, staked his furs, and piled the wood for his fire could no longer be seen.

But he knew it was there.

The Diamond of Jeru

The Penan people of Borneo say that the forest and the earth will provide for you if only you will let them. I hadn't exactly found that to be true, but what did I know? I was an American, stopping briefly in their land and ignorant of their ways.

I WAS DOWN to my last few coins when John and Helen Lacklan arrived in Marudi. I'd come down from Saigon to make my fortune but luck had not been with me. For over a year I'd been living like a beachcomber who had accidentally found his way inland. There was a longing in me to make my way back home but no money to do it with. I'd told myself it was better to stay where I was and wait for an opportunity. Around Sarawak, in those days, a white man could go a long way just on confidence and the color of his skin.

My luck paid off in this way: a friend in the government office offered to send me some tourists, Mr. and Mrs. John Lacklan. He had set me up, time and again, with minor engineering and construction jobs and was responsible for my having been able to keep body and soul together over the last few months. The Lacklans were an American couple, in from Singapore. They were recently married and, most importantly, they were looking for a diamond.

Now they find diamonds around Bandak, around Kusan, and near Matapura, to name only a few places. They also find some rare colors in the Sarawak River. Most so-called "fancy" stones are found in Borneo, for diamonds come in a variety of colors, including black. But after looking over the possibilities they had come up the Baram River to Marudi or Claudtown, as some called it, and Vandover was going to send them to me.

It was late in the day and the wind picked up slightly, coming in over the river to where we sat on his porch near the old fort. "I told him about you." Vandover poured cold beer into my glass. "He wants to go up the Baram. You want enough money to get you home and ..." He eyed me mischievously. "I suspect that you wouldn't mind having one more go at the river yourself. All the better if Mr. Lacklan is paying."

We toasted my good fortune and I let the beer slide back down my throat. Cold beer had been a rare and precious luxury in my world for too long. If everything worked out I would soon be done with Borneo and on my way back ... back to the land of cold beer.

IT WAS DARK by the time I got home. I navigated my way across the room to the bed. Without lighting a lamp I undressed and lay back under the mosquito netting. Above my head fireflies cruised lazy circles against the ceiling, flickering, on ... off ... on ...

Money to go home. A buck or two to help get my feet back under me at the worst. At the best ...?

I, too, had come to Borneo hunting diamonds. If you were lucky you washed them out of a river just like panning for gold. I had found a fortune of them, in a pool just below a dried-up waterfall. I had spent a month in the bush digging them from the river, but ultimately, the river had taken them back.

Eager to return with my treasure and careless, I'd put my canoe into a rapid at the wrong angle and almost lost my life. As it was I lost the boat, the diamonds, and most of my kit. A family of Iban pulled me from the water and took care of me until I was on my feet again. I was seven weeks getting back, nursing broken ribs and a persistent fever.

What money I had left had slowly trickled away; paid out to Raj, my houseboy, and for food, drink, and quinine. I've heard it said that, in the tropics, you rented your life from the devil malaria and quinine was the collector. After my disaster on the Baram the disease had become a most demanding landlord.

But now I would have another chance. We would go upstream of the pool where I found my diamonds, closer to the source, the find would be better this time and I'd have Lacklan's fee even if we didn't locate a single stone. With the good feeling of money in my pockets I drifted off to sleep.

MY PLACE WAS a deserted bungalow that I'd adopted and repaired. When Lacklan and his wife appeared, I was seated on the verandah idly reading from Norman Douglas's *South Wind*.

They turned in the path, and I got to my feet and walked to the screen door. "Come in," I called out, "it isn't often I have visitors."

As they came up on the porch, I noticed that Helen's eyes went at once to the book I had been reading. She glanced up quickly, and smiled. "It's rather wonderful, isn't it?"

She was tall and lean, with fine thin limbs and dark blue eyes that shone in the shadow of her wide-brimmed straw hat. She had a face like that of a model from one of those fashion ads but with more character, faint friendly lines around the corners of her eyes and mouth, no makeup. Her nose was large but perfectly shaped and her jaw betrayed strength, a strength that also was apparent in her body, beautifully formed but built for a lifetime of swimming and skiing. Her skin, where it disappeared under the fabric of her sundress, looked like it was taking on a healthy shade of copper from the equatorial sun.

She had commented on my book. . . . "It's an old friend," I said, smiling.

Lacklan looked from one to the other of us, irritated. "You're Kardec?" he demanded. "I'm John Lacklan." He was tall and slightly stooped. A thin blue vein pulsed in one of his temples as he peered at me from behind glasses with round, nearly black lenses. Vandover had told me he was an administrator at one of the big government labs back in the States. Atom bombs or something.

Lacklan pushed ahead, up the stairs. "I understand you're the authority on diamonds?" The way he said "authority" indicated that he doubted it.

"Well"—I hesitated because I was well aware of all that I didn't know—"maybe. Will you sit down? We'll have a drink."

Raj was already at my elbow. He was a Sea Dyak, not over sixteen, but his mind was as quick and intelligent as anyone I've ever encountered.

"Scotch," Helen said, "with soda . . . about half."

Raj nodded and glanced at Lacklan, who waved a careless hand. "The same," he said.

When Raj returned with our drinks, Helen sat there sipping hers and watching me. From time to time, she glanced at her husband, and although she said nothing, I had an idea that she missed nothing.

"You've been up the Baram, above Long Sali?" he asked.

"Yes." I saw no reason for explaining just how far I had gone. Marudi was a rough sixty miles from the mouth and Long Sali was a village a hundred fifteen miles farther upriver.

"Are there diamonds up there? Gemstones?"

"There are," I agreed, "but they are scattered and hard to find. Most of the stones are alluvial and are washed out of creeks back up the river. Nobody has ever located their source."

"But you know where diamonds can be found, and you can take us to them. We're not wasting our time?"

In this part of the world I had become used to the cultures of Chinese and Malay, Muslim and British, all of these groups had a sense of politeness or patience bred into them. In comparison the directness and force of Lacklan's questions was like an attack.

"You are not wasting your time," I assured him. "I've found diamonds. I can't promise, but with luck, I can find more. Whether they are bort or gem quality will be anyone's guess."

"You speak the language?" he asked.

"I speak marketplace Malay," I said, "and a scattering of Iban. Also," I added dryly, "I know that country."

"Good! Can you take us there?"

"Us?" I asked cautiously. "Your wife, too?"

"She will go where I go."

"It's our project, Mr. Kardec," Helen Lacklan said. She stretched out a long, firm hand to show me the ring on her finger. An empty setting stared up at me like a blind eye. "John gave me this ring five years ago. We're going to find the stone together."

It was a wonderful, romantic notion but far easier said than done.

"You know your business best," I said carefully, "but that's no country for a woman. It's jungle, it's miserably hot, and there are natives up there who have never seen a white man, let alone a white woman. Some of them can't be trusted."

I was thinking of one nefarious old codger in particular.

"We'll be armed." His manner was brusque and I could see his mind was made up. I suddenly had a vision that both amused me and made me very nervous: John Lacklan as Henry Stanley blasting his way through the forests of central Africa. His chin was thrust out in a way that told me he was primed for an argument ... I knew to never come between a man and his weapons, especially when he's a client. I turned to her.

"I don't want to offend you, Mrs. Lacklan, but it is very rough country, bad enough for men alone, and with a woman along ..." I could see I was going to have to give her a better argument. "There will be snakes and leeches. I'm not trying to scare you, it's just a fact. We'll be on the water and in the water all day, every day, and with the humidity we'll never get dry, not until we get back. We'll be eating mostly fish we catch ourselves and rice. There is the risk of infection from any cut or scrape and an infection while you're upriver can kill you."

She was quiet for a moment. "I believe I'll be all right," she said. "I grew up in Louisiana, so the heat and humidity ... well, they are only a little bit worse here." She laughed and her teeth were white and perfect. "Really, Mr. Kardec, I'm quite strong."

"I can see that," I said, and then wished I'd said nothing at all.

Lacklan's head snapped up and for a moment he glared at me. This man was deeply jealous, though Helen didn't seem the kind of person who would give him reason. Of course, that very fact made her all the more attractive.

She caught his reaction to me and quickly said, "Perhaps it would be better if I stayed here, John. Mr. Kardec is right. I might make trouble for you."

"Nonsense!" he replied irritably. "I want you to go."

His eyes narrowed as they turned back to me and burned as they looked into mine. I couldn't tell if he was disturbed about my appreciation of his wife or because I'd made her consider not going upriver with him or, and I only thought of this later, because I'd made her consider staying in Marudi where she would be on her own while we were gone.

"We will both go, Mr. Kardec. Now what will it cost me and when can we leave?"

I explained what they would need in the way of clothing and camping gear. Warned them against wearing shorts, no reason to make life easy for the mosquitoes and leeches. And then told them my price.

"I get a thousand, American. The canoes, Raj, and four Iban crewmen will run you six-fifty. Kits, food, first-aid and mining supplies, maybe another three to three-fifty. Depends on whose palm I have to grease."

"Is that the best you can do?" he objected. "You're taking more than half for yourself!"

"Look, Mr. Lacklan, I've been where you need to go. I've found diamonds . . . lots of diamonds. I lost them all but I know where they were. If it was easy, or cheap, I'd be back there working that streambed right now instead of trying to make a deal with you."

I could see something behind his glasses. A calculation taking place, like in one of the computers he probably used at work, punch cards feeding in data, tubes glowing with orange light. "All right," he said. "But how are we going to split up our take? After all, I'm paying for this expedition. I should get a piece of whatever you dig out."

I guess I recoiled a bit. Anyway, Helen looked at me in concern and Lacklan leaned back in his chair smugly. I hadn't really given it much thought. I'd figured that I'd take them there and they'd work the river in one area and I'd find somewhere else. I could see that this might lead to problems, especially once he realized that he could enlist the boat crews in the digging and panning.

"We'll split what we find, fifty-fifty," I said. "With the best stone to be for Mrs. Lacklan's ring." He was still gazing at me, one eyebrow arched above the round steel rim of his dark glasses. I gave in a little more. "I'll give Raj and the boat crews a bonus from my share."

Helen Lacklan turned to him. "That's fair, darling, don't you think?"

"Yes, I suppose it is."

We settled on a date, ten days from then, to leave. They went to the door and Helen hesitated there. "Thank you," she said graciously. "I enjoyed the drink."

They walked away toward the town.

It's maybe only once in a lifetime that a man sees such a woman, and I confess I looked after them with envy for him. It made my throat dry out and my blood throb in my pulses just to look at her, and it was that as much as anything else that made me worry about taking the job. A man needed all his attention on such a trip as this . . . and no man could remain other than completely aware of such a woman when she was near him.

Nothing moves fast in the tropics, yet despite that I had lined up the boats, boatmen, and equipment within a week. Raj was instrumental in bringing everything together as always. Even when I had no money he stuck with me. "You make better job, boss," he'd say when I pushed him to look for work elsewhere. "We don't work much but we make lots money!" I'm not sure that I'd have liked the irregular pay if I had been in his place. But Raj seemed to come alive when trying to figure out something he'd never done before and the jobs we got were always a challenge of one kind or another.

Around Marudi I caught sight of John and Helen once or twice, it wasn't a big place. He was not one to take his attention from whatever he was doing to nod or say hello but once or twice I got a smile from her. Then for several days in a row I didn't see either of them.

The day before we were supposed to leave I spotted the Lacklans coming up the path from town. And something—their postures, the way they walked?—told me the plan had gone wrong.

"Kardec?" There was a bluster in his manner that seemed ready to challenge any response that I might have. "We've made other arrangements. I'll pay whatever expenses you've incurred so far." Helen did not meet my eyes.

"Other arrangements?" The answer was evasive. "You've decided not to go?"

"We'll be going, but with someone else. How much do I owe you?"

Frankly, it made me angry. The deal had been all set, and now . . . I stated my price and he paid me. Helen merely stood there saying nothing, yet it seemed she was showing a resentment or anger that I had not seen before.

"Mind telling me how you're going?"

"Not at all. But it doesn't really matter, does it?"

His very arrogance and coolness angered me, and also to have all my

THE DIAMOND OF JERU

excellent planning go for nothing. "It matters a great deal," I told him. "There's one other man that would take you upriver who is trustworthy, a native named Inghai, and he's down with a broken leg. If you go back in there with another native, you're a fool!"

"You're calling me a fool?" He turned on me sharply, his eyes ugly. For a minute I thought he was going to swing on me and I'd have welcomed it. I'd have liked nothing so much as to help him lose a few teeth.

Then I had an awful premonition. Jeru was up to his old tricks again. "Look," I asked, "is it a native? Did he show you a diamond? A big stone? Something about twenty carats?"

They were surprised, both of them. "And what if he did?"

"You tried to buy it and he wouldn't sell. Am I right?"

"So what?"

"If I am right, then this was the same fellow who guided two parties up the Baram before, one group from Kuching, one came over from Sibu. None of them ever came back."

"You're implying that he had them killed? For what reasons? For the diamonds they found?"

"Diamonds mean nothing to him. I believe he used the one stone he has to lure them upriver so he could murder them for their possessions."

"Nonsense!"

"He was an old man, wasn't he? With a deep scar on his cheek?"

Their expressions cleared. "No." Lacklan was triumphant. "He was a youngster. No older than your houseboy."

So they had switched, that was all. The trick was the same. The stone was the same. And they were not the first to do it. It had been done by the Piutes in Colorado, eighty or ninety years ago, with gold nuggets for bait.

"Have it your own way, Lacklan. It wouldn't matter if you were going alone, but you're taking your wife along."

His face flamed and his eyes grew ugly. "My wife is my own concern," he said, "and none of your affair."

"You're right, of course, only I'd do a lot of thinking before I'd let bullheadedness risk my wife's life. Risk your own all you like."

"Nonsense!" Lacklan scoffed. "You're just trying to scare us to keep our business."

So they walked away and I could see Helen talking with him as they went up the road toward town. Whatever she said, I heard him answer angrily.

WHAT THE LACKLANS were getting into had a certain smell to it. It was the smell of an old reprobate named Jeru who was hidden out upriver with a small band of renegades. Jeru was reputedly the last of the old-time Sea Dyak pirates and the story was that he had fled upriver from the Brook militia and was living like a tribal chief with a group of followers who had been outcasts from their own longhouses. No one really knew if this was true but it was known that Jeru had appeared in the cities along the coast and lured people, usually foreigners, into the backcountry. And once they disappeared they never returned.

It had been years since the last time this had happened and the story had been spreading that Jeru might be dead ... nonetheless, it had me worried.

THAT NIGHT there were four of us there on the verandah of the resident officer's bungalow. Van apologized for the deal with the Lacklans falling through. "There's no accounting for people, I suppose."

I didn't mention John Lacklan's hair-trigger jealousy and the fact that I might have helped arouse it.

"I've got another possibility for you though," he said. "There's a canal job. It cuts through from one of the creeks about a mile above town. Hasn't been used in years but Frears wants it open again. I told him you could do it, bossing a native crew. It'll pay almost what Lacklan would but it will take longer. We'll get you home yet."

"Van," I said, "I'm worried. Their story sounded so familiar. Remember Carter? That was two years before my time, but he came down from Hong Kong on a vacation. He met some native on the coast who had a big diamond and wouldn't sell it. The native agreed to show him where there were more. He went upriver and was never heard of again.

"A few months later, the same thing happened to Trondly at Kuching. There was also that story about the two who went up-country from Sibu and Igan, and another from Bintulu."

"That was old Jeru. Word has it he's dead."

"Maybe. But this sounds like the same come-on. And it sounds like the same diamond. Huge thing, high quality, native won't sell but he will take them to where he found it. If it's not Jeru then it could be someone else playing the same game. If a native finds a gemstone and sells it, he spends the little he got, and that's the end of it. This way that stone represents a permanent income. Rifles, ammo, blankets, trinkets, food, clothing, tools, and trade goods ... and every few months a new supply."

"Fantastic idea." Vandover rubbed his long jaw. "It sounds like that old blighter of a Jeru, or his ghost. Maybe he figured he was getting too well known to keep doing it himself."

"It could be," Fairchild agreed. "You'd better call Kuching on it. Sounds to me like a police matter."

My scotch tasted good, and the furniture on the verandah was com-
fortable. Turning the glass in my fingers, I looked over at Fairchild.
"Using your outboard? It is a police matter but I don't think it can wait.
That fathead can fry in his own juice for all I care, but I'd not like to see
Helen Lacklan trapped because of him."

"Use it," Fairchild assented. "If Rector wasn't due in tomorrow I'd go
with you."

BY DAYLIGHT the native huts and banana and rubber plantations were behind us. Only Raj accompanied me. Although a Sea Dyak of the coast,
his mother was Penan, one of the forest people. His uncles had occasionally taken him off on long migrations following the wild sego harvest and
he spoke a number of the inland dialects. He knew of old Jeru as well and
liked none of what he'd heard. From a *blotto,* the hollowed-out tree trunk
that is the native boat, he learned from three natives that the boy and his
two white clients were six hours ahead of us.

Raj sat up in the bow of the canoe, on the other side of my quickly
loaded supplies. The strong brown stream was muddy and there were occasional logs, but this outboard was a good one and we were making better time than Lacklan would be making. I did not attempt to overtake
them because I neither wanted them to think me butting in nor did I
want their guide to know I was following.

I was carrying a Mauser big-game rifle, a beautiful weapon. It gave
me a comforting feeling to have the gun there as I watched the boat push
its way up the Baram. The river trended slightly to the south-southeast
and then took a sharp bend east, flowing down from among a lot of
eight-thousand-foot peaks. Mostly jungle, yet there were places where
stretches of tableland waved with grass. This was wild country, rarely visited, and there were small herds of wild pigs and a good many buffalo.

We avoided villages as the necessary social activity that would accom-
pany our stopping would slow us down considerably. I made camp on a
small island cut off from shore by a few yards of rushing water. We slung
our hammocks, draped mosquito netting over them, and slid into our dry
clothes to sleep.

AS WE PRESSED ON the river narrowed and grew increasingly swift. We
were well into the Kapuas Mountains, the rugged chain that is the spine
of Borneo and terminates in the thirteen-thousand-foot dome of Kina-
balu. The air was clear and the heat less oppressive at the increased altitude. At times we pushed through patches of water flowers miles long
and so thick it looked like we could have gotten out of the boat and
walked.

I put on a bit more speed for the motor would soon be useless in the rocks and shallower rapids and I wanted to be able to catch up when necessary. We ascended cascades, the easier ones with the outboard howling at full throttle, the more difficult by shoving and hauling the boat through torrents of water streaming between the rocks and over low falls.

I wondered how the Lacklans were making out; I couldn't really imagine John Lacklan in chest-deep water pushing a canoe ahead of him. And though she might be willing to try, I couldn't imagine him allowing Helen to do such a menial job. How they were negotiating the river was a question that worried me because if neither of the Lacklans were doing the physical work, then there had to be more natives helping out besides just the one guide. The crew of the *blotto* had not mentioned the number in the crew and I'd heard no mention of an outboard like mine ... that meant oarsmen and probably two boats to split the weight of both the men and supplies into manageable amounts. So that meant four to eight natives, I hesitated to guess at their tribe and if they were from Jeru's group, that was probably a moot point.

"Raj," I called forward, "how many boats do you think they have?" We were stopped in a shallow sandy part of the stream at the top of a rocky cascade. I was bailing the water from the canoe and Raj was carefully wiping off our equipment. We were both soaking wet.

"Two, boss."

"And how many men on paddles, four?"

"Six. Two paddle in each boat, one rests."

I looked up at him narrowly. "How the hell do you know that?"

"I can see them!" He grinned at me and pointed ...

In the distance, through some trees and across the river, two boats were turning into the shore. I sloshed around for a better look. It was midafternoon and it looked like they were going to camp. There were two big dugouts each with four people in them and as I watched the men in the bows jumped out and dragged the hollowed-out logs up onto the shore. In one boat was a slender figure in a wide straw hat, that must be Helen, and in the other sat John Lacklan, wearing a cork sun helmet. For an instant his glasses flashed in the sun as he rose from the boat.

"We'd better pull out here and camp ourselves. I don't want to be seen."

We hauled the boat to shore, built a smoky fire to keep the sand flies away, and as Raj began to make camp I took my field glasses and crept along the bank to a spot across the river from the Lacklan camp. I slid in behind a decomposing log covered in plates of bracket fungus and focused my binoculars on the beach across the river.

Two of the tattooed natives were cooking a pot of what had to be rice and another had walked upstream and dropped a line into the water, patiently waiting for a fish to strike. The three others had vanished into the forest. Lacklan was sitting on the sand jotting notes in a book or journal and Helen was tying up their hammocks. I put down the glasses and glanced around. My spot was back within the tree line and relatively dry, even so it wouldn't be long before the leeches got at me. The air over the river was thick with brightly colored butterflies, some as big as my hand. They fluttered in and out of patches of sunlight like continuously falling leaves. I squinted through the lenses again. Lacklan looked comfortable on his small crescent of beach. The fisherman and one of the cooks looked to be in their mid-thirties, hard capable men, though small. Each had a *parang* at his side and near the kit of one of the natives that I assumed had gone into the jungle was an old single-barreled shotgun, its stock held together with copper wire.

The fisherman looked up suddenly and the two other members of the boat crews came wandering back into camp. With them was a slight younger man whose posture was somehow more assertive than the older men, tough as they might be. This would be the boy I'd been told about. He wore a button-down shirt that was missing most of its buttons and was tucked into an old pair of dungarees. The clothes were castoffs from someone down in the settlements but he wore them with a certain flair. Unlike the others, he did not have the traditionally pierced ears. Over his eyes he had on a set of sunglasses, the type that aviators tended to wear. The returning men sat close around the rice pot and the fisherman returned to his chore.

I was getting set to pull back into the trees and make my way back to our camp when I saw Helen walk away from the spit of beach across the river. She had obviously been waiting for the other men to come back, because as soon as they sat down she walked over to the place where Lacklan was sitting and spoke to him, then she picked up a small pack and walked away.

She headed downriver and in a moment was out of sight, lost in a tangle of vines and tree trunks. I slid back a ways, then moved through the forest on my side of the river, trying to catch up. If she went too far I was afraid she'd see our camp. Unless the two of them ran into trouble I was not of a mind to try explaining what I was doing there to a paranoid little tyrant like John Lacklan. I moved downstream as quickly as I could without being seen. Noise wasn't a problem here because the river would drown out anything short of a gunshot.

I dodged back toward the water and crouched down. I couldn't see anything. Then, I noticed some movement on the bank upstream of where I had been looking. It was a piece of fabric moving in the breeze. The khaki blouse that Helen Lacklan had been wearing hung from a branch near a calm backwater. Now, what ...?

Alarmed, I almost stood up. Then there was a bursting spray of silver as Helen's head appeared above the surface and shook the water from her hair. She swam for the bank and I would like to say that I was gentleman enough to avert my eyes when she climbed out but that in all honesty would not be true.

She fumbled with a pile of gray fabric on the sand that I now realized was the pants that she had been wearing, and then splashed back into the water with a bar of soap in her hand and began to wash.

The idea of a bath reminded me that I might not get one myself until I got back to Marudi, unless I could share Helen Lacklan's soap. An entertaining but not very realistic thought. Before I was tempted to watch when Helen climbed out again and got dressed, I slipped away from the riverbank and made my way back to camp.

THE NEXT DAY, travel was harder. We had to creep our way slowly upriver, cautiously coming around every bend, always alert for the chance that John Lacklan's canoes had stopped or that there would be a stretch of river long enough for them to look back and see us trailing them. To make matters worse, although they were heavily loaded, there was an extra man to switch off paddling in each of their boats and in the rougher spots all of them, including John and Helen, helped out. We had the outboard but I was afraid to start the damned thing because of the noise. It had enabled us to catch up but now we merely had its weight to contend with.

Mountains loomed up around us and the way was narrower. Somewhere, hidden in these peaks, I had heard there were huge caves. We were nearing the place where I had originally found my diamonds, a long day or two and we'd be there.

That gave me an idea. What would happen if I dropped into the Lacklan camp some afternoon and let them know my old diamond placer was nearby? John would almost certainly object but I wondered if he wouldn't be tempted to take a day or two out to see what might be found there. With luck I could derail the whole plan, if there was a plan at all. I leaned forward to speak to Raj. "Jeru's camp, does anyone know where it is?"

"No, boss. Very far upriver." He paused for a moment. "If I was Jeru I would not be on river. Policemans, they do not like to get out of the boat. They do not like jungle because their rifles are no good."

He was right, the limited light, limited range, and plentiful cover in the forest did reduce the effectiveness of firearms considerably.

"I have heard on the coast that the pirate Jeru went to a longhouse where all mans dead of sickness. He took longhouse for those who follow him. They are all very bad. They take heads, even now they take heads."

If Borneo is famous for one thing it is its native headhunters. As romantically gruesome as the practice is, it had been dramatically curtailed in recent years, at least along the coast. In the interior, the severed heads of tribal enemies are still kept for their magical power, and a freshly taken head has the most power.

The sun was just touching the rim of the mountains when Lacklan's boats tucked into the shore and Raj and I stopped paddling and let the current carry us back downstream about half a mile before finding a place to camp.

As was becoming my habit I took my field glasses and started upriver, out of camp. At the last moment Raj's voice stopped me for a moment.

"Boss?" I turned to where he was standing by the fire. "If there no trouble, we hunt for diamonds, okay?"

"Sure, Raj," I said. "We're up here, might as well." He was right. I'd given up the canal job to come after the Lacklans; we were using up the supplies I'd bought for them and nothing lucrative awaited us back in Marudi. On the day after tomorrow I would drop in on my favorite tourists and find out if I could get them away from their guides. Then we'd see if we could dig some diamonds. I didn't want to return from this fool's errand with nothing. On top of it all I had a sixteen-year-old Dyak kid who thought I was just enough off my rocker that he had to remind me occasionally to keep my eyes on the target.

THE RIVER WAS WIDE HERE, and though I was farther away than the first time I had spied on the Lacklans, the water was slow enough that I could hear some of what was going on in their camp. There was a clank of pots as one of the older men laid out his cooking supplies, the hard bark of an ax as someone back in the forest chopped wood.

Helen Lacklan sat in a patch of sunlight reading a book. From its bright red cover and small size I recognized it as a popular guidebook on Indonesia and Malaysia. John Lacklan sat in the boat cleaning his gun. It looked from this distance to be a bolt-action Winchester; with an ebony cap on the forestock I figured that it was one of the fancier models. From its long barrel and scope and the fact that the Lacklans came from New Mexico I assumed that it was his prized gun for deer or bighorn sheep . . . whichever, it wasn't the best weapon for the jungle. This was a place where speed and maneuverability counted most. As I watched he carefully depressed the stop and slid the bolt back into the rifle, then pressed five long cartridges back into its magazine. For the first time I was glad he was armed.

He tucked his cleaning supplies into a small pack and then stalked over to a mound of supplies and set the rifle down. He paused and made a comment to Helen but she barely looked up. He stood there, tension building up in him, for a moment, but then broke off and went to the other end of the camp. I realized that I was witnessing an argument or the aftermath of one.

Over the wash of the river, slow and quiet at this point, I heard a man's voice raised in anger. Then John Lacklan was standing over Helen yelling and gesticulating wildly. His thin face was turning a dark red under the fresh burn he'd been getting, and although I couldn't understand the words, his voice was hoarse. Suddenly, Helen threw her book at him and leaped to her feet. The red-covered guidebook bounced off of his shoulder and he backed up a step. She advanced toward him and it almost looked like she was daring him to hit her. They paused and he backed away. In some way, she had called his bluff.

I squirmed back into the shadows of the forest. At the last minute as I headed back to my camp I noticed the flamboyantly dressed Iban boy and two of the men from the boat crew standing in the tree shadows across from me. The older crewmen had averted their gazes with expressions of shock and embarrassment on their faces; such outbursts of emotion as they had just witnessed were not considered at all acceptable in Malaya, but the boy studied them carefully and with a knowing smirk from behind his dark glasses.

I LAY IN MY HAMMOCK that night wondering what would happen tomorrow afternoon when I faced them again. It was going to be awkward and I was going to have to act like there was never any problem between us. I didn't know if they would accept the story I was going to make up about deciding to use their supplies to look for diamonds, but it probably made more sense than what I was actually up to.

Had I really followed them hoping for the worst so that I could step in and rescue Helen Lacklan and make her husband look the fool that I took him to be? And if that was true how much of a fool was he? He had chosen another guide to keep his wife and I apart. I had thought the idea amusing at the time, then I'd thought it dangerous. I had had one short opportunity to appreciate Helen Lacklan and I doubted if she had given much thought, if any, to me. But here I was, following them through the bush and rapidly developing a case that would do a sophomore proud on a married woman I hardly knew. Paranoid he might be but I was beginning to guess few people called John Lacklan stupid.

Well, I would follow along for one more day, until we reached my old diamond placer, then I would do my best to divert them from whatever this Iban boy had planned. If they didn't want to follow me I would leave them to their destiny.

For better or for worse, I thought, I was back upriver. Even though it had cost me all the supplies that Lacklan had paid for, supplies that I might have sold, and losing the canal-cleaning job. I realized I'd better make the best of it. This was what I'd wanted all along: another chance at the diamonds. I drifted off to sleep as a soft rain began tapping at the shelter half strung over my mosquito net. Somehow I'd gotten what I'd wanted all along.

A HIGH-PITCHED CRACK of thunder brought me awake just before dawn. I lay listening, waiting for the echoes to roll back from the mountains or down the river canyon. Through some trick of the rain or the forest vegetation the echo didn't come. I thought about returning home with the money from a diamond find in my pocket ... I thought about returning home with enough to explain my having disappeared into the Far East for almost two years.

An hour later when the gibbon monkeys began to noisily greet the sun, Raj rolled out of his hammock and made up some breakfast. We didn't take long to get packed. I walked up the riverbank, the water running slightly higher because of last night's rain, just far enough to see if the Lacklans had left camp yet. Their boats were gone so we pushed out into the stream and dug our paddles in against the current.

Around us the forest released great plumes of steam as the sun's heat cut into the trees. Trunks, some two hundred feet tall, leaned out over the water leaving only the narrowest slot of sky overhead. In the jungle itself one rarely could see more than sixty yards without the view being blocked by the growth. Even the tops of the trees were obscured by a much lower canopy with only the massive trunks hinting at the true size of the forest giants.

We pushed past the Lacklans' campsite from the night before. They must have had an early start because their fire was cold, not even a thin line of smoke rising from behind the piled-up rocks they had used as a hearth. The shadows between the boles of the trees behind their camp were black as night, the few penetrating rays of the morning sun overshooting this area to glance off the emerald leaves of the higher forest.

Suddenly I stopped paddling. The canoe lost momentum and Raj looked around quickly.

"Boss? What's wrong?"

Hidden under the trees, deep within the shadows but not quite deep enough to keep the morning light from revealing it, was the stern of a *blotto.*

"Turn in!" I commanded, and we made for the shore.

Leaving Raj to haul our boat out of the water I grabbed up my gun and splashed up onto the rocky beach. I hit the darkness of the forest and froze, letting my eyes adjust.

The two dugouts rested in narrow lanes between the trees, back along the shore were drag marks from where they had been pulled out of the water and across the mud flat to the jungle. Everything, supplies, mining equipment, camping gear, everything but the paddles were gone!

Could they have headed away from the river to a legitimate place to placer for diamonds? Had they hidden the canoes or just pulled them away from the rising waters of the river? I walked back out to their campsite.

The fire was dead and there was no sign it had been doused with water. They had not had breakfast.

Then I saw it. Shining brightly in a patch of sunlight; the answer to my questions ... the worst answer to my questions. A long thin cylinder of brass. I picked it up and turned it over. It was stamped .30-06. The empty cartridge casing smelled powerfully of gunpowder even in this dampness. It had not been thunder I had heard just before dawn. It had been John Lacklan's rifle!

I HAD TRACKED animals while hunting in Arizona and Nevada but following a trail in the jungles of Borneo was a different experience altogether. Luckily, the Lacklans and their captors had left camp after the rain stopped and they were not trying to hide their trail. The fact that there were ten of them heavily laden with the goods from the canoes helped also.

Raj and I were burdened only with water, light packs, our *parangs*— Raj's being more along the lines of a traditional headhunting sword, thus larger than mine—and my rifle.

They left occasional slip marks in the mud, breaks or machete cuts on protruding branches and vines. The trail was not hard to follow. But another problem soon became apparent.

Away from the river we found ourselves climbing a tall ridge cut by many small streams. The trail then followed the top of the ridge as it switchbacked along between the Baram River on one side and a deeply cut canyon on the other. Visibility was so limited and the landscape so broken that although I could easily follow the trail or backtrack my own path I had no idea which direction was north, south, east, or west. I could barely tell which way was up- or downriver unless I could see the water close up and by now we were hundreds of feet above the banks. To make matters worse it was dark, dark as deep twilight, and the humidity had increased tremendously. I was overheated, slick with sweat, and making far too much noise as I pushed along the trail.

Raj was doing better than I and it wasn't only because of his youth. Although he had lived his life in Marudi he often went with his uncles to the forest and had some of the natural ease of the jungle peoples. He seemed to be able to instinctively place his feet in the most solid spots whether we were climbing over rocks covered with wet moss or skirting a deep bog of leaf mold. I dropped our pace to the point where I could follow him more exactly, and in relative silence, we pressed on.

By noon we seemed no closer to our quarry and I was down to the last of my canteen. We stopped by a brook that cascaded down the dim mountainside and had some dried pork while I boiled water on a tiny gas stove I had bought for the Lacklans. I didn't always purify my water when I was in the bush but this would be a disastrous time to get sick so we waited while the stove hissed and the pot finally boiled. Raj harvested a vine growing nearby and after pounding it with a rock he made a paste that we rubbed on our legs. *"Kulit elang,"* he said. "Will help a couple hours, leeches don't like." We pressed on.

THE DIM LIGHT under the tree canopy was fading and the black cicadas had started their rasping, throbbing chorus when we reached what seemed to be our destination. We were on another river, much smaller than the Baram, and tucked back in the trees at the edge of a gravel bank was a decrepit longhouse. Dugouts were pulled up on the bank and all around the main dwelling stretched a wasteland of squalor such as I had only seen in the native villages that had become ghettos because of their closeness to the large coastal cities.

The last of the sunlight was striking the overgrown slopes of the nearby mountains and the river valley was in shadow but I could barely make out overgrown fields and collapsed farm huts behind the ring of trash that had been ejected over the years from the longhouse. In most cases a Dyak longhouse is a fascinating structure; built up, off the ground and out of the floodplains on stilts, sometimes as much as twenty feet high, the interior of the building is twenty feet from floor to ceiling and often over one hundred feet long. Its roof and sides are made of a kind of native thatch or sheathed in tin, where available. Although surrounded by farming huts and storehouses it is the communal dwelling for the entire village.

This longhouse was one of the smaller ones and obviously very old. One corner was drooping dangerously on poorly repaired stilts and in this and other areas the verandah had all but given way. Across the distance I could hear harsh laughter and a slight strain of *sapeh* music on the wind, lights could be seen coming on through the doors and breaks in the walls.

Raj edged closer, he seemed jumpy, his fingers toyed with the hilt of his *parang*.

"You were right, boss." He whispered, although we were a good half mile away. "This is the longhouse of *Tuan* Jeru."

I was surprised by his use of the term *"Tuan,"* which indicates respect, and by his nervous whisper. I had seen Raj stand calmly by and thrust the same *parang* he was now nervously tapping deep into the side of a boar that attacked one of our workmen on a construction job. He had then pivoted like a matador and finished the enormous animal off when it turned to attack him instead. He had been barely fifteen at the time.

"Are you afraid of going in there? Tell me why?" I wasn't feeling too good about it myself but I figured I better know as much as possible.

Raj's chin came up and the dying light in the sky glinted in his eyes. "I am not afraid of any man!" he stated flatly. "But it is said that *Tuan* Jeru is a *bali saleng,* a black ghost, that he has killed many mans and taken their blood to bless the buildings of the English and Dutch and now for the oil companies."

"Do you believe that?" I demanded. "You've worked with me on many buildings. Have you ever seen a foreigner take the time to make a sacrifice of blood or anything else?"

"No . . ."

I wasn't sure that this was really the right argument to use and I actually had a fair amount of respect for the beliefs of Raj and his people, but if he went in there scared, witch doctor or not, Jeru would take advantage of the situation.

"How many do you think are down there?"

"If the stories are true, twenty mans, maybe ten womans, maybe more."

"What else do the stories say?" I asked.

"The mans of *Tuan* Jeru are *sakit hati;* they are killers and rapists from the oil camps and towns on the coast. No village would have them. They are collectors of blood and they take heads to make magic."

"Do you want to stay here, guard our backs?" I gave him a chance to get out with honor.

"I will go with you, boss," the boy said.

"Good. Now, what do you think is going on down there?"

"I think they have big *arak* party. Everyone get very drunk. They have all new trade goods, shotgun shell, fancy rifle. I think we wait."

"What about the Lacklans? Will they be all right?"

Raj paused, he wanted to tell me what he thought I wanted to hear but he knew I would press him for the truth. "I don't know, boss," he said. "I think maybe they cut off man's head. The woman, I don't know ... These people, they not Iban, not Kayan, not Kelabit," he named off the three major tribal groups, "they something different now ... outlaws, you know. I bet they get drunk like Iban though, you'll see."

I hoped so, because outlaws or not I was betting that just like a normal village they had plenty of dogs and roosters. The typical longhouse celebration in Sarawak was a roaring drunk and I hoped that was what they were building up to because otherwise we weren't going to get in there without raising an alarm.

I wanted to be ready when the moment came, so we moved in closer, carefully waded through the rushing waters of the stream, and circled away downwind of the skeletal silhouette of the longhouse. We settled down just inside the secondary tree line and waited to see what would happen. The noise from inside was getting louder and I was sure that Raj had been right about them working themselves up to an all-night drunk. I just wasn't sure what was going to happen to John and Helen ... or when.

They might be dead already and I couldn't wait much longer without trying to find out. I decided to split the difference; wait another hour but if I heard a commotion I'd go in with the rifle and hope for the best. If there were twenty men in the longhouse, at least five would have the cheap single-shot shotguns that were common in the backcountry of Borneo. Someone in there had possession of Lacklan's deer rifle and certainly there would be a full complement of spears, blowpipes, and machetes. My only hope was to get in and get as many of them covered as possible before anyone thought to grab a weapon. It wasn't much of a plan; get in fast, get out fast, and put my confidence in the local *arak*'s potency.

Now, in my experience, *arak* has the punch of the best (or worst, depending on your expectations) moonshine. It seemed to have the chemical properties of torpedo fuel or the infamous "Indian whiskey" that was made in the old days in Oklahoma. One shot would make you stagger, a couple more would make you stupid. Imbibing further could leave one blind or even dead. Waiting for a level of intoxication that would give me an edge was a risky business.

About a half hour later two men staggered out on the verandah and hung over the railing. They alternated between what sounded like telling jokes and laughing hysterically with being violently ill. After three or four rounds of this odd combination of social interaction they parted, one going back into the light and noise of the longhouse, the other slumped, snoring, against the railing. The sound of the crowd inside had taken on a harsher tone and I figured I'd better move in before something bad happened ... if it hadn't already.

Touching Raj on the shoulder I slipped past him and made my way down toward the river. We crept in past the outer circle of trash and one of my worst fears came suddenly true.

Three dogs rushed us out of the darkness under the longhouse. Barking and snarling they rushed through the moonlight like dark missiles, low to the ground ... missiles with pale flashing teeth.

I took a swipe at the first with my rifle butt and connected heavily. It backed off yelping. Raj moved quickly, snatching up the smallest of them by grabbing a fist of flesh on either side of the dog's neck just below the ears. He spun in a tight circle with the frantic beast snapping in his outstretched arms and let go, hurling the dog far out into the river. I clubbed with my rifle again, and drawing his *parang,* Raj swatted an animal with the flat of the blade. The two remaining dogs backed up, growling but no longer willing to attack. I was just beginning to curse our luck and wonder if we should either hide or charge the ladder to the longhouse when a door above us slammed open and a man staggered out onto the verandah and called out into the night in what sounded like Iban.

Instantly Raj answered in an angry adult tone I'd never heard him use before. The man above us muttered something and then whistled sharply and called out some kind of command. We stood frozen in the darkness as he wandered back inside and closed the door.

Raj heaved a sigh of relief and I turned to peer into the darkness where he was standing. "What, in the name of God, was that all about?" I demanded.

He laughed, a giddy, semihysterical cackle. "I told him to call off his damn dogs!"

WE WERE A MOMENT getting our wind back, then we worked our way under the longhouse and edged toward the back where, because of the slope of the gravel, the stilts were not so long. The ground beneath the building stank from garbage and worse. Above us feet tramped rhythmically on the ancient plank floor and shrill voices cried out. Toward the back the floor was low over our heads and then I was boosting Raj onto the verandah, and swinging up myself. Moving carefully on the weathered boards we eased up to a crack in the wall and peered in.

The light was probably dim, but with our pupils dilated by hours in the darkness it was blinding. Raj backed up for a moment and I blinked and squinted. In the center of a seated group a dancer leaped and whirled, his moves theatrically depicting ... something, I couldn't tell what. There were men and women in the room, but fewer women than I had thought.

Bottles, mostly old beer and wine, were lying about. Some were obviously empty, others still in use. I knew from past experience that they no longer held beer or wine; they had been filled and refilled time and again with *arak*.

The dancer disappeared from view and another took his place. He was a thin old man but he moved with an energy that, while not youthful, was surprisingly vigorous. He whirled and stomped, spinning a *parang* over his head with a glittering flash of steel. I suddenly saw that the dark area that I had noticed on one side of his face was not a shadow or a tattoo but a deep and twisted mass of scar tissue. He mimed climbing onto something higher than himself, something that moved unsteadily. He fought, he carried something away. He was raiding a ship or a boat . . . this must be Jeru! Not only was he here, still alive after all these years, but he was telling his story in a dance.

I bent to Raj's ear. "Is that him?"

The boy nodded; his body alive with fear and excitement.

"You watch our backs," I told him. I didn't want him working up a scare by watching this man that he believed to be a witch and I didn't want both of us to be night blind.

When I turned back to the crack Jeru was hacking his way through the forest and then something . . . he mimed men marching and everyone laughed. He was showing them he'd been chased by soldiers, paddled up a river, cut off men's heads with his *parang*. He stepped out of sight for a moment and came back with a long Japanese military rifle. He shook it in the air and then after handing it to someone, mimed cutting off what I surmised to be the Japanese soldier's head. He pointed to the roof with a harsh cry and, crouching, I could see a cluster of dark spheres hanging from the rafters. Severed heads. No doubt the unfortunate Jap was one of them.

The story continued with Jeru finding something in a stream. He held the imaginary something up to the light, turning it this way and that. He reached for his neck and pulled a leather strap off, over his head. In a setting or basket of leather there gleamed a stone.

This was it. The huge diamond that he had used for many years to lure men upriver, never to return. A diamond of fabulous size and quality, so the story went; from where I was all I could tell was that it was large and wrapped in braided strings of leather. It glowed rather than flashed, for this was a raw stone with none of the facets of a cut one, but there was a white fire hiding deep within it.

The old man took on a posture of humility, he moved stiffly, portraying a sense of age that obviously was not his natural state. Again, he got a laugh. He was showing the stone to someone, offering it, walking away as

if disinterested, then leading them on. He took an old stove-in pith helmet from the place it hung on the wall and wore it for a moment as he
paddled an imaginary boat. Then he was himself again and, beating his
companion to the ground, he drew his *parang* and cut off the man's head.

The audience was silent now and a sense of tension penetrated the
wall and clutched at my heart. Even Raj, eyes turned to the night, could
feel it and he moved closer to me, his hand on his knife.

JOHN LACKLAN STAGGERED into view, pushed along by the rough shoves
of the boy who had been his guide. His hands were tied, his clothing
torn, his body scratched and bruised. How badly he had been treated I
didn't know; the trip through the jungle might have left him in the condition that he was in. I admired him in that moment, though, for he held
his head high, in his eyes was the hollow look of fear but he didn't beg, or
cry, or even tremble. He was keeping himself together although I thought
I could tell that it was a near thing.

Without looking away I ran a shell into the chamber of my rifle and set
the safety. I wasn't at all sure about my original plan of barging in and spirit-
ing them away; there were easily as many shotguns in the room as I had
expected plus the Japanese rifle and the boy carried Lacklan's Winchester
over his shoulder. Not only were there more guns than I would have liked
but several were cradled in the hands of Jeru's outlaws, held casually but
ready for use.

The boy stepped in behind Lacklan and kicked the back of his left
knee, knocking him to a kneeling position. Lacklan started to get back up
but the boy unlimbered the rifle and poked him hard in the kidney with
the muzzle. John Lacklan gave a choking cough of pain and collapsed
back to the floor. Old Jeru whirled his *parang* and then tested the edge
against his thumb.

"Find me a door!" I whispered to Raj. "Damn quick!"

Now there was a commotion somewhere in the room. "Get off me!"
I heard Helen call out. Then she lurched into view, a portly Iban trying to
drag her down by one arm. She shook him off; he was surprised, I think,
by that same physicality that had caught my attention. She was bigger
than he was and lithely powerful.

"Stop it! You stop this!" she yelled at them. Raj was back tugging at
my sleeve but the boy, sunglasses pushed up on his forehead, stepped in
quickly and pressed the rifle barrel against Helen's throat . . . even if John
Lacklan got his head cut off I wasn't going in there if it risked Helen's
getting killed.

The boy yelled at her in Iban, then in English. "Sit, missy. You sit or

I kill you." He jabbed at her with the gun barrel. "Everybody die, you don't sit down."

She didn't even move.

"You can't kill him. Take our things, our money. You can't kill him!" she cried.

"We're Americans, damn it. Let us go or you'll regret this." John's voice wavered.

In my travels around the world I've noticed that identifying yourself as an American never helps, it just makes the locals get violent or want more money.

The boy shrugged, "We kill Englang, Dutch . . . America, who cares." He suddenly spoke in his own tongue for a moment and everyone laughed. Old Jeru the hardest.

"You don't want John's head." Helen spoke in a manner that let me know she wanted all to hear. "I know that Dyak tribesmen only take the heads of powerful enemies, of warriors. The head of a strong man is magic but a weak man . . . a weak man is nothing. My husband is not a warrior, he's not even a strong man. Did he walk here? No. You had to carry him over the last hill . . ."

"Be quiet, Helen!" John hissed. "Don't make this any worse than it is."

But she ignored him. "He's a scholar. What are you going to say? There are the heads of the Japanese soldiers, we fought their machine guns with knives but we won. There is the head of the man who read books, aren't we brave!"

The boy turned to Jeru and they spoke quietly for a moment. Others in the crowd seemed a bit nervous. The bottles started being passed around again but with them there started a low mutter of conversation.

Jeru spoke and the boy turned to Helen with a smirk. He spoke in Iban to the crowd and there was scattered laughter but it sounded forced. He said to her, "We cut off head; see what happens. No magic, we throw out!"

"No!" she cried and started to say something else but John bellowed at her.

"Helen, shut up! Just shut up!" He was almost crying in fear or frustration. He lurched to his feet and the boy smashed the butt of the rifle into the pit of his stomach. I was ready to move and Raj was even tugging me toward the door when Helen threw herself on the boy. Jeru knocked her to the floor but John charged him. With his hands tied all he could have done would have been to knock Jeru down but the old man deftly rapped John Lacklan on the head with the butt of his *parang* and Lacklan went to the floor, out cold.

Jeru hawked and spat. Then with a further growl of disgust he dragged Lacklan into a corner and dropped him. He motioned to the boy and the young man led the quietly sobbing Helen to the same spot, then they both stepped forward to the seated group and took up *arak* bottles.

I got the feeling that there had been a reprieve of sorts and I'd better make the best of it. Pulling myself away from the scene beyond the crack in the wall I let my eyes readjust to the darkness. When my vision started to come back I motioned Raj ahead of me. "Let's get on the ground, we've got to get to work."

We dropped down under the longhouse and I made my way back to the spot where the broken floor sagged toward the mud. This whole corner of the building was ready to collapse and I figured that it would be unlikely that anyone would be using it for anything. I shrugged out of my pack and dug out my mountaineer stove. I pumped up the pressure and fired it. Using the light from the flame I found a place where several broken logs and a piece of the *attap* thatch wall all lay together. I wedged the stove into the broken wood just under the thatch and let the plume of fire bite into the thatch.

I grabbed Raj and led him back to the spot where we had climbed onto the longhouse verandah.

"You stay here. When I come back I'm going to be coming fast, if anyone needs help getting off the porch you help. If you run into any of Jeru's people . . ."

"I know what to do, boss." He tapped the hilt of his *parang*.

"Right. If I'm not with you, go straight up the hill and follow the crest east, okay?"

I pulled myself up onto the aging boards again, and careful to walk along a crosspiece so as to make less noise, I slid up to the wall and took a fast glance through the crack. Heavily tattooed bodies moved back and forth, momentarily obscuring my vision. Nothing much was going on but more people were up and around. Well, that couldn't be helped.

I moved along the wall to the door that Raj had found. I breathed deep and waited for the fire to catch. Suddenly there was an excited burst of Iban from inside the building, the sound of running feet and a breaking bottle. It was only then that I smelled smoke. There was a rush of feet and a door in the front of the place crashed open. I couldn't see what was happening but I figured someone was going for water. I didn't move until I heard the crash of the floor giving way.

I HIT THE DOOR and came into the big room with the Mauser up, sling around my left arm. The long room was filled with smoke and the back, where I had started the fire, was listing. Flames were beginning to take the roof. An older man stood right in front of me with a bottle in his hand, he seemed to be standing back, bemused, while the main crowd moved toward the blaze. I dropped the rifle from my shoulder and clipped him on the side of the head as I went past.

A woman tore by me and in the confusion didn't even notice that I was there. Someone seemed to have fallen through the burning floor and that was fine with me. I dropped beside the Lacklans pulling my knife.

Lacklan twisted around in panic and kicked at me with both feet as I reached for his arms. Helen got it first.

"John, stop! It's help."

I grabbed one of the kicking feet and cut off the ropes that bound them, when they had tied his feet I didn't know. She extended her hands to me and I quickly swiped the blade between them catching the bindings by luck. Then there was the roar of an explosion and a scattering of bird shot tore into my boot and ankle like a swarm of angry bees. I dropped the knife and turned, bringing the rifle up.

A short, tattooed native struggled to reload his crude shotgun. Others stood behind him frozen, but they were all looking at me. Suddenly one of the men in back came up with the Japanese rifle, I didn't even know I had him in my sights until I squeezed the trigger.

The concussion in the long room was even louder than the shotgun. The rifleman went down and all hell broke loose. Men and women scattered, two shotguns belched fire in the light of the roaring flames, throwing huge plumes of white smoke. I wasn't hit but burning paper and powder smoldered in my clothes. I put three shots into the crowd as fast as I could work the bolt and then I was pushing Lacklan toward the door and praying that Helen was following. In my last look the room was an inferno of flame, burning thatch falling from the ceiling. Around the cluster of heads hanging from the rafters wasps swarmed in panic, driven from their nests in the empty eyes and mouths by the heat and smoke.

We crashed out into the fire-streaked night. Lacklan stumbled and a man dropped a bucket of water and came at me with a knife. I deflected it with my rifle barrel and kicked him hard on the hip. He fell and I gave him another in the face. The gun was empty and I had no time to reload.

I pulled Helen past me, pointed to the end of the verandah, and yelled, "Go! Find Raj!"

I turned, knowing that to run at that moment would be the end of me. Three men rushed forward in the shifting light and I went to meet them. I clubbed and punched and kicked and bit. One cut me across the back. Then I was on the wooden floor slamming my knee into his midsection. My rifle flopped uselessly, its sling still entwined with my arm.

There was a flare of light and an explosion of wood. One of my attackers threw himself off of me and there was Jeru, standing over me
holding a pistol so ancient it must have come to Sarawak with the first
white rajah. I twisted sharply, Jeru fired again, missing. He struggled to
cock the enormous relic, twisting the cylinder by hand. I scrambled sideways, put a knee into someone's stomach; suddenly I was fighting with
one of the men who attacked me again. We struggled, turned, and then
hit the railing of the verandah. With a splintering crash at least twenty
feet of it let go and we were falling.

In midair I pushed away from the man I was fighting, hit the ground,
and rolled. My rifle, still bound to my arm by a twist of the sling, rapped
me on the back of the head. My vision went gray but I heard Jeru's gun
bellow and the hard bite of black powder hit my nostrils. He was leaning
over the railing peering into the darkness, the torn side of his face a dark
knot of rage. I grabbed my rifle and ran underneath the burning longhouse.

Flames licked along the floor above me. The structure groaned as
walls twisted and buckled. In back, the corner where I had started the fire
was dark. Someone had managed to put out the flames, a futile gesture for
the fire had spread to the rest of the building.

I made it to the darkness and looked back. The dim forms of Jeru's
men began to appear in the firelight. Some ran off toward the river,
probably for more water, but four or five of them started forward under
the building, coming after me.

I'd had just about enough. I snapped four fresh cartridges into the
magazine of the Mauser and dropped a fifth into the chamber. I backed
up farther into the darkness and brought the rifle up. I took aim at the
first man, then shifted to one of the pilings beside him. I fired and splinters flew. They dropped to the ground but then came on, worming their
way forward through the debris under the longhouse. The first had a
shotgun and the second man carried a long blowpipe with a spear blade
bound to one end. I squinted, fired, and the heavy bullet took the blowpipe man along the top of the shoulder as I had intended, then burned
the back of his calf. He screamed, and I ran, blindly, uphill into the jungle.

I NEARLY TOOK a header into some kind of hole, leaves whipped my face,
and I slowed down. I cursed myself for not killing both of the men I'd
shot at under the longhouse. I had a total of nine bullets left, three in the
gun and six jingling in my pocket, I couldn't afford to waste them.

I had to find Raj and the Lacklans. If they hadn't made it out I'd have
to go back ... I wasn't looking forward to suicide.

I cut left along the hillside, heading in the direction they would have taken if they had gone straight up the hill. I stopped to catch my breath and found I couldn't keep my knees from shaking. I squatted down, sucking air, and felt the prickles of adrenaline recede from my limbs. I had shot a man. Several actually, but one of them I had killed for sure. Unbidden, a phrase that my father had used came to mind, "If you fool around with a bandwagon, you're liable to get hit with a horn." It wasn't as amusing as it had been but I was realizing that it didn't only apply to me getting into this situation, it applied to those poor chaps I'd shot, too.

Those men down there had lived as traditional Iban and Kayan or whatever. Some, perhaps many, had traveled to the cities and oil fields to try a different kind of life. But somewhere, something had gone wrong. Instead of staying on to collect their paychecks, instead of returning home to farm and fish, they had come here. In a country that was virtually without violent crime they joined with a man who made a living robbing tourists and diamond hunters. A man who was continuing to take heads not of his enemies in war, a practice, if not what I would call civilized, then at least honored by Iban tradition, but of people he had lured into a trap.

Helen had thought quickly back there. She'd confronted that old witch doctor with his own hypocrisy, given other circumstances it might have been funny. It was something else, too, though. Some of those men in there had believed in what she'd said. There was magic in the head of a brave enemy. To take a man's head was, in a strange way, actually an honor. If you had a vision of yourself as a warrior you didn't kill tourists. Helen might have planted a seed of doubt in a few of the men down there. Either old Jeru might have fewer followers come morning or they'd all be coming after me, the more honorable enemy.

I started up the hill again, going slowly in order to make as little noise as possible. In the dark phosphorescent mushrooms glowed dimly. The sounds of insects and animals filled the night, covering the noises that I made but also covering the sounds of anyone who might be following me. It felt like hours since Raj and I had the fight with the dogs but I could still occasionally see the moon through gaps in the trees; I didn't know what time it was but it had been headed down as we approached the longhouse. Higher and higher I climbed, pulling myself along using the trunks of the smaller trees and rocks and handfuls of undergrowth. I was exhausted, my legs were shot, and my arms and lower legs were covered with leeches.

Finally I reached the bare crest of the ridge and looked out across a vast panorama, dimly lit by the setting moon. I turned east and started climbing again.

When the landscape was left in blackness, when the last of the silver light had faded from the sky, I rested. I carefully cleaned the leeches off by

feel. One leg was puckered with bird shot but most of it had not penetrated my boot. I stopped myself from touching it. I knew Borneo, it was
going to get infected and the less I scared myself the better. I got up and
pressed on and it was only a few hundred yards farther when I heard voices
ahead.

It was Raj and the Lacklans, and they had collapsed at the foot of a
rock outcropping, half dead from exhaustion. "Raj?" I called out; I didn't
want him taking a swipe at me in the dark.

"Boss?"

"Yeah. Hold on, I'll be over there in a minute." I picked my way
across the rocks toward them.

It was a subdued reunion. We were all dead tired from running and
climbing over a thousand feet of mountain. I'm not sure that Helen and
John had realized what was going on yet. They were just happy to be
away from Jeru's longhouse and all in one piece.

Not long after I got my breath back, I began to notice that it was
cold. Now, there's not too many places on the island of Borneo where
you could say that but we were well over eight thousand feet and we were
all dressed for the heat. To make things worse we were worn-out and the
clouds were beginning to pile up against the mountain range, I could feel
the moisture on my cheek and lips and when I looked up the stars were
dimmer. Raj's teeth were chattering and the Lacklans were huddled together strangely; though Helen was curled up close to him, John was positioned almost as if he was trying to pretend she wasn't there. Well,
whatever they were going through was their problem. I was worried about
the cold.

"Let's get up," I told them. "We're going to go on a bit farther."

They looked at me uncomprehendingly, but Raj stumbled to his feet
and picked up our packs; he had brought mine along from the longhouse
somehow.

"Mr. Kardec?" Helen was sitting up. "I don't know if my husband
can . . . he hurt his leg before we got to that village."

"Let me see it," I said. "We have to go on. We need some shelter or
at least a fire and some food."

Lacklan pulled away from me as I squatted down beside him. "I can
make it. I don't need help." Then he said, "I don't need your help."

WE HELD TO THE RIDGE and we kept climbing. I needed someplace to
camp and this was probably not the place to find it but the slopes on either side of us were too steep to negotiate in the dark, especially given
our condition. I was beat, every muscle hurt, and my body begged to stop
moving. John had turned his ankle and could walk only with difficulty

but he and Helen were managing the altitude the best; after all, they lived near Santa Fe, over a mile above sea level. Raj was cold and something else was bothering him but he wasn't ready to talk about it. He helped John Lacklan along and kept his mouth shut.

Something was going on between John and Helen; she had tried to help him at first but he was having none of that. Finally, she gave up and he was on his own for a while but then, because he was stumbling badly, Raj offered to help and he'd accepted. Helen came up to me in the dark; she took my hand and pressed the haft of my knife into it. I returned it to its sheath.

"Thank you," she said. After that she walked with me more and more, and while I liked that in some ways, it disturbed me, too.

During a pause to rest I got Raj aside and questioned him on what went on before I joined them. "Nothing," he said. "They just act like they having big fight but they don't fight, they don't talk."

"Did they ask what we were doing here?"

He laughed softly. "Oh, yes. I tell them that you come to save them from the *bali saleng*."

For a Dyak, a people who tend to tell you only what you want to hear, Raj is sometimes too straightforward.

We came to the rocky upthrust of another peak, its blackness vaguely defined in the starlight, but there was shelter here, a bowl of rocks and, within it, the black mouth of a cave. From the sounds in the jungle below I could tell it was still a couple of hours until dawn. Huddled just inside the entrance we rested and I emptied my rucksack onto a rock. I used some peroxide on my leg and poured some across the cut in my back, then got up. With the empty bag I headed back into the night.

"Mr. Kardec, where are you going?" Helen's voice spoke out of the darkness.

"To find some fuel, I'll have to go down into the forest a ways."

"Are we still in danger?"

"I don't know. Come morning I expect they'll be after us."

"And they'll find us, too," Lacklan mumbled softly.

"But will they come up here?" she asked. "I read that many of the tribes feel that there are spirits in the mountains, especially the peaks, and will never go there."

I had heard the same. The natives were very aware of the *Toh*, the spirits of the forest and mountains. An area that was rarely visited was often considered to have dangerous *Toh* and was therefore avoided. It was Sarawak's version of our own self-fulfilling fear of the unknown. The high mountains were reputed to be the home of powerful *Toh*.

I didn't reply as I thought about it. I hoped she was right.

"So, maybe this place is safe. At least that's what I read." She was look-ing for some reassurance but she didn't get it from her husband.

"You and that confounded guidebook," he snapped. "We don't know that will work!"

"Well if that confounded guidebook is where she learned about headhunting, it probably saved your life." I said I'd had enough of Lacklan's attitude and he wasn't a potential client anymore. "Jeru wasn't even going to sharpen his *parang*."

"I'm glad you enjoyed that at my expense. I'll have you know that the weapons I've made could blow this miserable island off the map."

I was amazed. He was fuming because she had told that bunch of renegades he wasn't a warrior. He was an egomaniac and a fool. Or maybe just a brilliant man who was so small inside that he had become lost in the forest.

"Mr. Lacklan," I told him. "I don't know if you're suicidal or exactly what your problem is but I look at life this way—an adventure is some-thing you return home to tell about. If you don't make it back, it's just an exotic funeral. Be happy Helen did what she did. I am. If she hadn't I might have died because I was stupid enough to try and help you."

"And why did you come after us? Because you are the good Samaritan? Or because you are after my wife?"

"John!" Helen flinched and I could see that he'd aimed that barb more at her than me.

"I don't know," I said, "but this late in the game I'd be a fool to try to figure it out." I grabbed up the knapsack and headed out into the dark-ness. I started down the slope and Raj came scrambling after me. I hadn't planned on his coming but was just as happy; I knew he would be very uncomfortable if the Lacklans decided to continue the fight.

The purple light of predawn was just coming to the sky as we made our way along the mountainside about one hundred feet above the forest. I was headed toward an area below us that I had glimpsed from the ridge; it was lighter in color and I was sure it was a rock slide. Where it had hit the trees we might find some downed wood.

Sure enough, it was a slide. A huge lip of rock had flaked off and gone crashing down into the jungle. Underneath the scar were the dark mouths of several caves, probably connected to the cave above where the Lacklans waited. Thirty feet into the tree line we found all the wood we wanted, picking out the dry pieces was easy for little of it was damp. I fig-ured that we were so high that we were above most of the rain that soaked the lower elevations, either that or we were just lucky.

We gathered as much wood as we could fit in our packs and turned to go back up the mountain. For an instant Raj froze and so did I. Between ourselves and the brightening sky was a moving, flickering black cloud. There were bursts of darkness against the sky, a sound like water rushing up a shallow sandy beach; wings, thousands and thousands of wings. The dawning sky was darkened with bats. A thin cloud rising over the jungle, they coalesced into a dense riot of swooping, dodging confusion directly over us. Their wings cupping the thin air they streamed toward the mountainside. Under the scar of the fallen brow of rock, they flew, pouring into the cave mouths just above us.

Then from above us I heard a thin scream. Raj and I looked at each other, then I grabbed up my rifle and took off up the hill. The gun and the wood and the previous twenty-four hours of clambering up and down hillsides slowed me down. However, we made it to the top without having to ditch our loads and I eased around the rocks, rifle at the ready.

The Lacklans were well out of the circle of rocks and away from the cave, crouched behind the rocks and harried-looking. I almost laughed but couldn't summon the energy; a miniature tornado of bats fluttered and turned around the tunnel entrance, the last stragglers of the mass from below using the back door.

I'd had enough alarms for one day. Leaving Raj to start a fire in a small pocket in the rocks I went back into the cave and refilled my pack with its supplies. I ducked and shook my head as the last of the bats flew past but I got my rope, stove fuel, first-aid kit, and most importantly the little food I'd been able to bring along.

We warmed ourselves silently around the fire; the Lacklans didn't seem to feel like talking and I didn't feel comfortable conversing with them either. I shared our dried pork and heated two cans of condensed soup over the fire. It wasn't much and it wasn't very good but it was all I had and we needed anything we could get. When we were done I put out the fire. I hated to do it as we were all chilled but the sun was coming up and our smoke might have been visible. In the treetops below us the gibbons began their whooping cries, staking out their territory for the day.

"We're going to have to keep going," I said. "We're not safe until we're back on the river and we won't be safe even then." I looked in their eyes and was afraid of what I saw.

John, with his leg barely capable of bearing his weight, was nearly finished. Helen would go on without complaining but she couldn't go farther without rest. Raj could do what was necessary, he'd shut his mind down and go at it like a Chinese coolie, he'd survive if he could, regardless of the suffering. I hoped I could do the same but I wasn't sure.

"We'll be okay," I said, standing up. I looked out across the high ridge and the forest and clouds that swept away in both directions and I realized we weren't going to make it.

All we needed was rest. All we needed was to move slowly and accommodate John's injury. All we needed was time and I saw then that we were out of time.

Off down the backbone of the mountains, three miles away but plainly visible as the sunlight poured across a low shoal of clouds to the east, was a group of men. They were coming up the ridge toward us and there was an easy dozen of them ... more men than I had bullets, more men than I cared to engage even with my pockets full of ammunition.

"Raj!" I called. "I think we've got trouble." Instantly he was beside me, John and Helen not far behind. I pointed. "Is that Jeru?"

"Yeah, boss."

"What are we going to do?" This question was from Helen but there was no panic in her voice. She stood there, dirty, clothing torn, having had no sleep, and little rest ... it was an honest question, she was ready to get started.

"I hold them off as long as possible. You get out of sight; retreat into the cave. Take my rope, I believe there's a way out down below."

"You believe?" John was belligerent.

I shrugged. "With any luck they'll be satisfied with me and they won't know where you've gone."

"You'll be killed!" Helen grabbed my arm and turned me toward her. Her eyes searched mine, for what I didn't know; it was one of those moments when men and women have different things in mind.

"I might be. With luck I can kill enough of them that they decide I'm not worth it."

John shifted on his bad leg. "How much ammunition have you got?"

"Nine rounds."

"She's right, you'll be killed."

"You got a better idea?"

Nobody said anything. The men on the distant ridge were getting closer.

I turned. "Let's start by getting out of sight." I ripped open my pack and pulled out the bottle of stove fuel. Going to where we'd had our fire I picked up a fair-sized branch and blew on the white coals at one end. Ash flew away on my breath and deep in the darker cracks flickers of red glowed. I poured a bit of the fuel on the branch right up near the sparks and I blew again. In a minute I had a flaming torch.

The cave angled down, turned, and then dropped off abruptly, a black shaft corkscrewing downward. It would be a nasty climb but that in itself might save us. Bats skittered nervously on the ceiling, they didn't like the smoke from my torch.

"Raj," I called. "Get me my rope." He wasn't behind me, only the distant forms of the Lacklans peering in from the entrance. "Raj?"

I cursed and tossed my torch down the shaft. It fell, bounced, flared, and went out. In the darkness I could see reflected daylight deep in the shaft. Well, the lower cave *was* a way out, that was something in our favor. We could run, or they could. It wouldn't be much of a lead, but it would hold off the inevitable an hour, three? It would hold off the inevitable for them, not me. I headed back out of the cave. "Damn it, Raj, where's my rope?"

When I got to the entrance he was holding it in his hands but that was all. He looked at me strangely.

"Come on!" I insisted. We had to get him and the Lacklans started or this would all be for nothing.

"I stay with you, boss."

"This is no time for loyalty or bravery or whatever it is, Raj. If you don't go with them they'll never find the boats. Get going!"

He shuffled forward, hesitated . . . he was scared! Scared of the cave. I moved over to him and spoke softly, "What's wrong?"

"I go. But this not good. You think *Toh* big joke. I hope you right."

Suddenly I had an inkling of an idea. Maybe we could get out of this, all of us. If it worked it was going to take brains, and luck, and courage. But I'm better at courage when I think I've got a chance.

"Raj, if you're worried about the spirits, what about them?" I pointed out at the ridge. Jeru and his men were out of sight, negotiating a low spot, but I doubted we had more than half an hour. "Is Jeru afraid of *Toh*?"

He frowned. "Maybe . . ." Then he looked up at me, squinting. "His mans, they afraid, I think. Jeru he make *obat,* a spell, he say he *bali saleng.* He say what he does okay, but all mans still afraid."

"Good," I said. "Come with me." I snatched the coil of rope out of his hand and I ran to get my stove fuel.

"What's going on?" John Lacklan grabbed at me but I avoided him.

"I've got an idea!" I said and tossed him my rifle. "If they get within five hundred yards shoot once, I'll be back."

"Tell me what you're up to, damn it!"

I didn't tell him, I was already headed down the slope toward the mouth of the lower caves. I hoped he would show good judgment because as soon as I was over the edge I could no longer see the oncoming men.

RAJ AND I put our backs into it. We pulled three big partly rotten logs up the hill to the caves, both of us straining like a team of oxen on the rope. We laid a fire just inside where the tunnels converged and got it burning, then tossed every branch we could find up into a pile alongside it. We worked, getting everything into position and doing a fair job of it until I heard the boom of the Mauser.

I tossed the fuel bottle to Raj and took off running. "Don't do anything until you hear me whistle," I yelled back. I hit the mountainside and scrambled, arms and legs tearing at the earth and rock. I must have had my second wind but my muscles felt strange and hollow, it was not a good feeling.

I paused just under the lip to get a lungful of air then, hugging the ground, my leg throbbing, I slipped over the top. John was down inside the pocket of rocks where we'd had our fire and Helen was right behind him.

"What's happened?" I whispered.

"They're close. I shot and they went to ground."

"Okay. Give me the rifle. Stay clear of the cave mouth but if anything happens to me get back in the cave and stay there no matter what happens."

"What are you going to do?"

"Put on a show," I said and taking a deep breath, I stepped out.

"*TUAN* JERU! Come out and face me!" I stood there, the Mauser slung diagonally across my back. I would have rather left it with Lacklan but if they hadn't seen it on me they would have suspected an ambush. As it was I'd be lucky not to get a bullet or a blowgun dart.

After a moment there was a motion in the brush and the slight form of Jeru appeared with the boy in the aviator glasses at his side. They started for me across the last few feet of the rocky ridge. Jeru wore a wood-sheathed *parang* on one hip and the ancient pistol on the other. The boy carried Lacklan's rifle. They stopped a short distance away.

"You speak poorly," sneered Jeru, commenting on my fragmentary Malay.

"I speak this language no better than I have to," I said loudly, my main audience was Jeru's followers, "but I speak the language of the spirits well. My *obat* is as good as yours in this place. Go away from here. Go and leave us to ourselves. The gods of this mountain do not want you!" I pinched my fingers together, placed them between my lower lip and upper teeth, and whistled as loud as I could.

The boy took a step back and shook his head in shock. He brought up the long rifle but I didn't move. I tried to calmly stare him down . . . I was sure I was going to die.

Then there came a sound from the cave like a sudden rush of wind.

In the boy's glasses I saw reflected a momentary flash of orange flame in the tunnel mouth. Raj, on my signal, had poured the entire bottle of stove fuel on the fire.

With a rush like a great wave crashing on a reef the bats vomited from the cave. They came piping and flapping blindly into the morning sunlight driven by the smoky fire that Raj was now stoking with all the wood he could find. With the lower entrances to the tunnels blocked by smoke and flame they sought the upper opening in numbers that were terrifying to behold. They were a great disoriented black cloud that shot from the hole in the mountaintop as if from a high pressure hose. They fluttered and dove and poured into the sky above our heads.

Jeru crouched in surprise and I stepped in and before the boy could pull the rifle's trigger I slapped the barrel aside and kicked him in the groin. He went down, leaving me with the gun, and I saw two of Jeru's men racing away down the ridge, their tattooed backs glistening with the sweat of exertion and fear.

I turned to the old man and with a whining growl he drew his *parang*. He cut at me with such speed that I barely could move in time, shoving the rifle sideways into the blade. There was a ringing of steel and Lacklan's gun was torn from my grasp, falling to the rocks at my feet. Jeru reversed and I leaped back, the blade slicing air near my belly. He was fast; for an old man he was awfully fast.

I got my knife out and took a cut at him but he thrust along my arm, his blade leaving a trace of fire and a line of blood . . . he was better at this than I was. Better by a long shot.

He stabbed and cut. We fought back and forth there on that high ridge with a clear sweep of forest below us on one side and the white glare of the clouds beneath us on the other. And then he cut me, the knife grazing my chest, the blade momentarily catching on the Mauser's leather strap, and it was all over. His blade snagged and I caught his arm and was behind him in one movement. It was my fight then and for him it was hopeless. As good as he was with a knife, he was an old man. I was stronger than he was and I was heavier, too. I broke his arm but there was no give in him so I clipped him on the jaw, a punch that would have put away a much bigger man, and I'm not proud to say that I broke that, too.

He was unconscious. I was down, the world spinning around me, my chest bloody, my arm bloody, too bloody. The boy scrambled away, sobbing. There was the sound of gunfire. Helen was standing over me working the bolt on John's fancy rifle. Brass flew, bright against the sky. Men fled downhill, disappearing into the trees.

They broke open the first-aid kit, poured something in my wounds that hurt more than the knife had. Raj was getting me on my feet and my head was clearing; I had never really been out, just gray for a while, like I'd held my breath too long.

We were at the edge of the slope when I remembered. I pulled away from Raj's hands and went back. Jeru moaned when I turned him on his back. He looked at me, eyes no longer full of anger but neither was there fear. He waited for me to do whatever I had to do. It took only a moment.

"Thank you, *Tuan* Jeru," I told him. "Go to a village where no one knows you, live your days as an old man should. Cross my path again and I'll take *your* head and hang it on my porch."

I left him there, bats circling above, and I staggered off after the others. We went down past the cave where the fire still burned but was now low and dying. Then we were in the jungle and soon it was darker and hotter.

IT WAS TWO DAYS back to the boats. Two days of struggle and pain. John Lacklan and I setting our pitiful pace. His leg was swollen and my cuts and the places where the buckshot hit me had become infected. As much as I disliked the man he had a certain kind of toughness. It was the toughness of the littlest kid on the team or perhaps the brainy child that nobody liked . . . but he wasn't going to let that leg stop us. I had to make myself keep pace with him.

The boats were intact. In this I was surprised for I was sure that even if we got to the river without another fight I thought they would have stolen or destroyed the boats. I guess with their burned longhouse, several dead, and wounded leader they had enough to deal with. Raj took us downriver in the bigger dugout with Fairchild's motor jury-rigged to the stern. On the trip downriver I got sicker and they tell me when I arrived in Marudi I was unconscious and running a high fever. For the second time in two years I had returned from upriver barely alive. But this time I had the difference.

I LAY IN BED and got better. Vandover came down and brought the doctor. He shot me with penicillin, cleaned my wounds and dusted them with sulfa, then they sat on the verandah and drank the last of my scotch. I stared at the peeling paint on the ceiling.

She came to visit me an hour before the mail boat left for Singapore. The room was closed and dark but sunlight blazed through every crack in the shutters. She was dressed in a white traveling outfit and as she stood in the doorway she was a vague figure beyond the patched mosquito netting. I sat up.

"Mr. Kardec?" She came into the room, taking off a large pair of dark glasses. "I just came to thank you. You saved our lives." I could see that the wedding ring, with its empty socket, was missing from her finger.

I wanted to make some kind of smart comment but I didn't really know what it would be. "How's your husband?" I asked.

"He's got a bad sprain. All that walking we did made it worse. We're leaving today . . ." She stopped for a moment, holding on to some kind of feeling, I couldn't tell what.

"He won't talk to me," she said. "It's like I did something unforgivable back there but I don't see that I really had a choice."

"I think he's trying too hard to be a strong man." I thought this was right, it felt right. "Something inside of him is desperate. He's barely holding on to something but I don't know what it is. He'd of rather died back there than be saved by you."

"John was so brilliant. You should have seen him when we met. They all listened when he spoke, Dr. Teller, even General LeMay."

"This is a different world, Helen. You knew that, I could see it. Sometimes when there is nothing between you and nature you find out things you wish you didn't know . . . sometimes when you look at yourself you are smaller in the scheme of things than you thought you were." I shifted, sitting up a little farther, leaning back against the headboard. "There's been a time or two when I found myself in the middle of a dark forest praying for God to save me. You have to accept your fear and survive. It's not about your image of yourself, it's just about getting back in one piece."

"I guess so," she said.

We were both silent for a moment. Then she straightened up, all business.

"We should pay you, at least what we were going to for guiding us. We owe you that, and more."

I carefully moved the mosquito net aside and swung my feet to the floor. The cut under my bandages pulled tightly and it burned, but it was a healing pain.

"I don't want any money," and then before I could take it back, I said, "I did it for you. I don't want to lose that."

She crossed the room and bending down, she kissed me. For just a moment she held my face in her hand. "What will you do?" she asked. "How will you ever get home?"

I didn't really wonder how she knew this, I expect Vandover or Fairchild must have told her . . . it didn't matter. I sat straighter, trying to feel the strength in my body. It was there, not much, but coming back. I opened the nightstand drawer.

"Never underrate a man who has lived as I have, Helen. Just as a man who has lived as I have would never underrate a woman like you." I grinned. "I'm not proud and I do what it takes to survive." I held out my hand and opened it to show her. It was ironic, when I had gone into the forest for personal gain I had returned with nothing, but when I had gone intending to help others somehow I had been rewarded.

On my palm lay, in a setting of woven leather, the thong broken from when I had torn it from his neck ... *the diamond of Jeru!*

Death, Westbound

It was nearly dark when the westbound freight pulled out of the yards, and two 'boes, hurrying from behind a long line of empties, scrambled into one of the open doors of a boxcar about halfway between the caboose and the locomotive.

There were two more men in the car when they crawled in after their bundles. One of these was sitting at one side of the door where he could see without being seen, a precaution against any shack that might drift along or be standing beside the track. Joe had had experience with shacks, and much worse, with railroad dicks, he knew their kind. Sometimes the shacks were pretty good guys, but a railroad dick is always a louse.

The other occupant of the car lay in the shadow apparently sleeping.

The newcomers, two hard-faced young fellows carrying bundles, looked around.

Joe's curiosity got the better of him. "Westbound, fellas?"

"Yeah—you?"

"Uhuh. L.A., if we can make it."

"We?"

"Yeah, me an' the kid over there."

"Chee, I never even see 'em. S'matter, 's he asleep?"

"Naw, he's sick I guess, we been on this train t'ree nights now, an' he's been sick all the while. I don't know what's the matter. He coughs a lot, maybe he's a lunger."

"Chee, that's kinda tough, ain't it? Sick as a goddam drag when the bulls is all gettin' tough."

"The Santy Fe is the toughest line of 'em all, 'member hearin' 'bout Yermo Red?"

"Aw hell, Yermo was on the U.P. I made it thru there once on the bum with a coupla Polacks, he was plenty tough, that guy."

"Naw, he just t'ought he was tough, them guys is mostly yellow when there is a showdown."

Joe walked over to look at the kid. The boy's face was damp with perspiration and he looked bad. One of the others, a flat-nosed young fellow with heavy shoulders, walked over.

"Cheesus, he looks bad, don't he? 'At kid should aughta have a doctor!"

"Yeah."

The other young fellow walked over. "S'matter, Heavy? Is he bad off?" Then seeing the kid's face, he murmured: "Gawah!"

All three returned to a spot near the door. A heavy silence had descended upon the group. Joe rolled a cigarette and complied in silence to the others dumb request for the makin's.

Heavy looked glumly out at the night. "Cheesus, that's a helluva place to get sick in! Wonder if he'll croak?"

The slight youngster with the pale face who answered to the name of Slim, grunted: "Naw, he'll pul t'ru, a guy that has to live like this is too tough to die like anybody else."

Heavy looked at Joe and with a jerk of his head toward the kid: "Known him long?"

"Two weeks I guess. He had a coupla bucks and split 'em with me when I was bad off. He's a good kid. We been hunting jobs ever since, but this depression finished the work, seems like they ain't nothing left to do anymore."

"Wait'll we get a new president, what's Hoover care for us laborin' stiffs?"

Slim snorted derisively: "The next one won't be a bit better. One way or the other we get it in the neck!"

Heavy moved into a corner of the car and carefully arranging a roll of newspapers to form a place to lie, he lay down and drew his coat over his head to sleep. A few minutes later his snores gave ample proof of his success.

Slim jerked his head toward the sleeper: "Will he bother the kid, d'ye think?"

Joe shook his head: "Naw, the kid's out of his head, I guess he's about all in. When this train stops I'll try and find somebody to give him some dope or somethin'."

They lapsed into silence broken only by the steady pound and rattle of the swiftly moving freight train and the snores of the sleeper. At intervals the kid would move and talk indistinctly for a minute or so and then once more fall into silence. Outside the car the night was quite moonlit and they could see the fields flickering by in monotonous rotation. The countless cracks in the old car made it cold and dismal. Slim dosed off against the door, knees drawn up to his chin. Joe sat silent watching the fields outside and thinking.

It had been over a year since he had worked more than a few hours at a time, over a year of living in boxcars, cheap flophouses and any dump he could find to crawl into. But after all, what had it been before? Just a round of jobs, a few months and then a long drunk, or maybe a short one, if he got himelf rolled in some bawdy house. The kid here, he'd been the only pal he'd ever had that played square, an' now he was sicker'n hell. Life didn't mean much to a guy when he was just a workin' stiff. Sure, he'd boozed a lot, but what th' hell? Didn't he have a right to have a little fun? Well, maybe it wasn't fun, but at least a guy wasn't thinkin' about the next shift or how much ore he had to get out. Joe dozed off, but came to with a start as a red light flashed by and the freight began to slow for a station.

Slim and Heavy both woke up with the awareness that a hobo acquires when travelling.

"What kind of a burg is this we're comin' into, Joe? Looks like a damned jerk-water!"

"Yeah—I know the place. Just a water tank and a general store. Better keep outa sight, from now on, there's a bad bull in this next town if I remember right!"

The long drag slowly pulled to a bumping, groaning stop, and Slim, watching his chance when the shack was at the other end, dropped off.

Up ahead they could hear the shouts of the train crew as they worked about the engine, and once a shack went by, his lantern bobbing along beside the train. He just casually flashed it into the door as he passed, and as all three were out of sight, they were passed unnoticed.

A whistle up forward, more groaning and bumping and jarring, and the train slowly gathered momentum.

Heavy's forehead wrinkled anxiously: "Wonder what's become o' Slim? He should've made it by now!"

And a minute later, as the train gathered speed in the shadow of several oil tanks, he did make it, swinging into the car with a dark object in his hand.

"Whatcha got Slim?" Heavy leaned forward curiously.

"Aw, pull in your neck, Hefty, I just grabbed the kid a cuppa java an' a orange at that lunch counter!"

"But Cheesus, Slim, you only had a nickel!"

"Sure, I got the guy to gimme a cuppa java for the nickel and I swiped the orange when the lunch-counter girl wasn't lookin'. If he wants his cup back he'll have to pick it up in the next town!"

Joe rolled the kid over on his back and slowly raised him to a sitting position: "Here, kid, it's a cuppa coffee, try an' get it down, it'll do you good."

The kid tried to drink, but ended in a coughing spell that left flecks of blood on his lips. Joe laid him back on the floor and returned to the others near the door.

Slim looked helplessly at the orange: "Cheesus, guess he couldn't tackle this, he seems pretty far gone." He raised his hand as if to throw the orange away and then on second thought shoved it into his coat pocket.

Once more the train bumped along, the moon had gone down now and the night was black outside the door. Heavy was once more asleep, and Slim, chin resting on his knees, was dozing off. Joe still sat looking out into the night, his face grimy from cinders and dust, his beard graying in spots. At last he too dozed off into a half-sleep.

The freight was slowing for the next town when a swiftly bobbing flashlight awakened them. Joe was the first to comprehend.

"Cheesus, Guys, we're sunk, it's that railroad dick!"

Heavy cursed and jumped for the door to swing out when a harsh voice broke in: "Alright, Bo, stay where y'are or I'll shoot yer guts out! Come on, you, all of ya! Get 'em up in the air!"

"Alright, pile out on the ground an' less look you guys over. Keep 'em up, now!" The railroad dick's voice was harsh and his face ugly in the half-light. His companion, a weasel-faced fellow, glided up and started frisking them with the question: "Got anythin' on ya bigger'n a forty-five?"

Slim spoke agrievedly: "Aw why don't you guys leave us alone? We're just huntin' a place to work. What would we doin' packin' rods!"

The big fellow stepped forward beligerently: "Shut up, Bum, I'll do the talkin' an' you'll answer when yer spoken to, get me?"

Slim said nothing. The weasel-faced man pulled their personal effects from their pockets smirking over the few odds and ends a man carries about. A couple of jackknives, a piece of soiled string, a dirty handkerchief or two, a pocketbook containing a pair of poll tax receipts, a card for a hod-carriers union two years old, a few letters. The weasel-faced man read the letters with an occasional glance at Slim's angry face. Finally from one of them he extracted a picture of a girl which he held out for the big man to see with an insulting remark.

Slim's eyes swiftly calculated the distance, he jumped and struck viciously, his fist striking the weasel-face on the point of the chin, knocking him flat, the big man sidestepped and struck with the gun barrel felling Slim to the ground. Then stepping toward Heavy and Joe he snapped: "Got tough, did he? Well, suppose you guys try it, I killed a couple of guys fer tryin' to get tough with me!"

Joe's tired voice spoke slowly: "Uh-uh, I heard 'bout that, both of 'em unarmed. You said they got tough, some people said they had thirty bucks on 'em."

"What was that?" The big man whirled toward Joe. "What d'you say?"

"Me? I didn't say nothin', just clearin' my throat."

"Well, ya better be careful, get me? Or I'll slam you like I did him!" He waved his hand toward Slim's fallen figure.

He called to Weasel-face: "Look in that damned car, maybe they left some junk in there worth lookin' over!"

"Okay, Boss!"

Weasel-face scrambled into the car. Then: "Hey, Boss, here's another bum in here sleepin'!"

"D'hell there is! Well, roll the bastard out an' less look him over."

Voice from the car: "Come on, you, crawl outa that! Hey, what's the matter? Get up or I'll boot the hell outa ya!"

A moment later, Weasel-face dragged the kid to the door and dumped him out to the ground.

"Here he is, Boss, playin' sleepy on us!"

The Boss walked up determinedly and kicked the kid forcibly in the ribs, Joe's shout halted him, a frown on his face.

"Hey, Skipper, watch yerself, the kid's sick, he's got the consumption or somethin'!"

"He won't play sick with me; I'll boot his head off: get up, d'ye hear?" He grabbed the kid by the shoulder and jerked him to his feet where the kid hung in a slump. For a moment the Boss gazed into his face, his own growing white: "God! The son-of-a-bitch is dead!" He dropped the kid and turned around.

In the moment of detachment following his discovery, unable to help the kid, the remaining two, supporting the now conscious Slim, had slipped off into the surrounding darkness leaving the two dicks behind, and the crumpled form of the kid lying beside the freight, which slowly moving was once more westbound.

Old Doc Yak

He was a man without humor. He seemed somehow aloof, invulnerable. Even his walk was pompous and majestic. He strode with the step of kings and spoke with the voice of an oracle, entirely unaware that his whole being was faintly ludicrous, that those about him were always suspended between laughter and amazed respect.

Someone began calling him Old Doc Yak for no apparent reason, and the name stayed with him. He was a large man, rather portly, wearing a constantly grave expression and given to a pompous manner of speech. His most simple remark was uttered with a sense of earthshaking import, and a listener invariably held his breath in sheer suspense as he began to speak, only to suffer that sense of frustration one feels when an expected explosion fails to materialize.

His conversation was a garden of the baroque in which biological and geological terms flowered in the most unexpected places. Jim commented once that someone must have thrown a dictionary at him and he got all the words but none of the definitions. We listened in amused astonishment as he would stand, head slightly tilted to one side, an open palm aslant his rather generous stomach, which he would pat affectionately as though in amused approbation of his remarks.

Those were harsh, bitter days. The waterfronts were alive with seamen, all hunting ships. One theme predominated in all our conversations, in all our thoughts, perhaps even in the very pulsing of our blood—how to get by.

No normal brain housed in a warm and sheltered body could possibly conceive of the devious and doubtful schemes contrived to keep soul and body together. Hunger sharpens the wits and renders less effective the moral creeds and codes by which we guide our law-abiding lives. Some of us who were there could even think of the philosophical ramifications of our lives and of our actions. The narrow line that divides the average young man or woman from stealing, begging, or prostitution, is one that has little to do with religion or ethics but only such simple animal necessities as food and shelter. We had been talking of that when Old Doc Yak ventured his one remark.

"I think," he said, pausing portentously, "that any man who will beg, who will so demean himself as to ask for food upon the streets, will stoop to any abomination no matter how low."

He arose, and with a finality that permitted of no reply, turned his back and walked away. It was one of the few coherent statements I ever heard him make, and I watched his broad back, stiff with self-righteousness, as he walked away. I watched, as suddenly speechless as the others.

There was probably not a man present who had not at some time panhandled on the streets. They were a rough, free-handed lot, men who gave willingly when they had it and did not hesitate to ask when in need. All were men who worked, who performed the rough, hard, dangerous work of the world, yet they were men without words, and no reply came to their lips to answer that broad back or the bitter finality of that remark. In their hearts they felt him wrong, for they were sincere men, if not eloquent.

Often after that I saw him on the streets. Always stiff and straight, he never unbent so far as to speak, never appeared even to notice my passing. He paid his way with a careful hand and lived remote from our lonely, uncomfortable world. From meal to meal we had no idea as to the origin of the next, and our nights were spent wherever there was shelter from the wind. Off on the horizon of our hopelessness there was always that miracle—a ship—and endlessly we made the rounds in search of work. Shipping proceeded slowly, and men struggled for the few occasional jobs alongshore. Coming and going on my own quest, I saw men around me drawn fine by hunger, saw their necks become gaunt, their clothing more shabby. It was a bitter struggle to survive in a man-made jungle.

The weeks drew on, and one by one we saw the barriers we had built against hunger slowly fall away. By that time there were few who had not walked the streets looking for the price of a cup of coffee, but even the ready generosity of a seaport town had been strained, and shipping seemed to have fallen off.

One morning a man walked into the Seaman's Institute and fainted away. We had seen him around for days, a quiet young man who seemed to know no one, to have no contacts, too proud to ask for food and too backward to find other means. And then he walked in that morning and crumpled up on the floor like an empty sack.

It was a long moment before any of us moved. We stood staring down at him, and each of us was seeing the specter of his own hunger.

Then Parnatti was arrested. He had been hungry before, and we had heard him say, "I'm going to eat. If I can make it honest, I'll make it, but I'm going to eat regardless." We understood his feelings, although the sentiments were not ours. Contrary to opinion, it is rarely the poor who steal. People do not steal for the necessities but for the embellishments, but when the time came, Parnatti stole a car from a parking lot and sold it. We saw the item in the paper without comfort and then turned almost without hope to the list of incoming ships. Any one of them might need a man; any one of them might save us from tomorrow.

Old Doc Yak seemed unchanged. He came and went as always, as always his phrases bowed beneath a weight of words. I think, vaguely, we all resented him. He was so obviously not a man of the sea, so obviously not one of us. I believe he had been a steward, but stewards were rarely popular in the old days on the merchant ships. Belly robbers, they called them.

Glancing over the paper one afternoon, searching for a ship that might need men, I looked up accidentally just in time to see Old Doc Yak passing a hand over his face. The hand trembled.

For the first time I really saw him. Many times in the past few days we had passed each other on the street, each on his way to survival. Often we had sat in the main room at the Institute, but I had paid little attention. Now, suddenly, I was aware of the change. His vest hung a little slack, and the lines in his face were deeper. For the moment even his pompous manner had vanished. He looked old and tired.

In the ugly jungle of the waterfront the brawl for existence left little time for thinking of anything except the immediate and ever-present need for shelter and food for the body. Old Doc Yak had been nothing more than another bit of waterfront jetsam discarded from the whirl of living into the lazy maelstrom of those alongshore. Now, again, as on that other night, he became an individual, and probably for the first time I saw the man as he was and as he must have seen himself.

Tipped back against the wall, feeling the tightness of my leather jacket across my shoulders, I rubbed the stubble on my unshaved chin and wondered about him. I guess each of us has an illusion about himself. Somewhere inside of himself he has a picture of himself he believes is true. I guess it was that way with Doc. Aloof from those of us who lived around him, he existed in a world of his own creation, a world in which he had importance, a world in which he was somebody. Now, backed into a corner by economic necessity, he was a little puzzled and a little helpless.

Some of us had rented a shack. For six dollars a month we had shelter from the wind and rain, a little chipped crockery, a stove, and a bed.

There was a cot in the corner where I slept, and somebody had rustled an old mattress that was stretched out on the deck—floor, I should say. For a dime or perhaps three nickels, if he was good for them, a man could share the bed with three or four others. For a nickel a man got an armful of old newspapers with which he could roll up on the floor. And with the money gathered in such a way we paid another month's rent.

It wasn't much, but it was a corner away from the wind, a place of warmth, and a retreat from the stares of the police and the more favored. Such a place was needed, and never did men return home with more thankfulness than we returned to that shack on its muddy hillside. Men came and went in the remaining weeks of our stay, the strange, drifting motley of the waterfront, men good, bad, and indifferent. Men were there who knew the ports and rivers of a hundred countries, men who knew every sidetrack from Hoboken to Seattle. And then one night Old Doc Yak walked up the path to the door.

There was rain that night, a cold, miserable rain, and a wind that blew it against our thin walls. It was just after ten when the knock came at the door, and when Copper opened it, Old Doc walked in. For a moment his small blue eyes blinked against the light, and then he looked about, a slow distaste growing on his face. There was a sailor's neatness about the place, but it was crude and not at all attractive.

He looked tired, and some of his own neatness was lacking. He might have been fifty-five, but he looked older then, yet his eyes were still remote, unseeing of us, who were the dregs. He looked around again, and we saw his hesitation, sensed the defeat that must have brought him, at last, to this place. But our shack was warm.

"I would like," he said ponderously, "a place to sleep."

"Sure," I said, getting up from the rickety chair I'd tipped against the wall. "There's room in the double bed for one more. It'll cost you a dime."

"You mean," he asked abruptly, and he actually looked at me, "that I must share a bed?"

"Sorry. This isn't the Biltmore. You'll have to share with Copper and Red."

He was on the verge of leaving when a blast of wind and blown rain struck the side of the house, sliding around under the eaves and whining like a wet saw. For an instant he seemed to be weighing the night, the rain and the cold against the warmth of the shack. Then he opened his old-fashioned purse and lifted a dime from its depths.

I say "lifted," and so it seemed. Physical effort was needed to get that dime into my hand, and his fingers released it reluctantly. It was obviously the last of his carefully hoarded supply. Then he walked heavily into the other room and lay down on the bed. It was the first time I had ever seen him lie down, and all his poise seemed suddenly to evaporate, his stiff-necked righteousness seemed to wilt, and all his ponderous posturing with words became empty and pitiful. Lying on the bed with the rain pounding on the roof, he was only an old man, strangely alone.

Sitting in the next room with fire crackling in the stove and the rattling of rain on the windows, I thought about him. Youth and good jobs were behind him, and he was facing a question to which all the ostentatious vacuity of his words gave no reply. The colossal edifice he had built with high-sounding words, the barriers he had attempted to erect between himself and his doubt of himself were crumbling. I put another stick in the stove, watched the fire lick the dampness from its face, and listened to rain beating against the walls and the labored breathing of the man on the bed.

In the washroom of the Seaman's Institute weeks before we had watched him shave. It had been a ritual lacking only incense. The glittering articles from his shaving kit, these had been blocks in the walls of his self-esteem. The careful lathering of his florid cheeks, the application of shaving lotion, these things had been steps in a ritual that never varied. We who were disciples of Gillette and dull blades watched him with something approaching reverence and went away to marvel.

Knowing what must have happened in the intervening weeks, I could see him going to the pawnshop with first one and then another of his prized possessions, removing bit by bit the material things, those glittering silver pieces that shored up his self-vision. Each time his purse would be replenished for a day or two, and as each article passed over the counter into that great maw from which nothing ever returns, I could see some particle of his dignity slipping away. He was a capitalist without capital, a conqueror without conquests, a vocabulary without expression. In the stove the fire crackled; on the wide bed the old man muttered, stirring in his sleep. It was very late.

He did not come again. Several times the following night I walked to the door, almost hoping to see his broad bulk as it labored up the hill. Even Copper looked uneasily out of the window, and Slim took a later walk than usual. We were a group that was closely knit, and though he had not belonged, he had for one brief night been one of us, and when he did not return, we were uneasy.

It was after twelve before Slim turned in. It had been another wet night, and he was tired. He stopped by my chair where I sat reading a magazine.

"Listen," he said, flushing a little, "if he comes, Old Doc, I mean, I'll pay if he ain't got the dime. He ain't such a bad guy."

"Sure," I said. "Okay."

He didn't come. The wind whined and snarled around the corners of the house, and we heard the tires of a car whine on the wet pavement below. It is a terrible thing to see a man's belief in himself crumble, for when one loses faith in one's own illusion, there is nothing left. Even Slim understood that. It was almost daybreak before I fell asleep.

Several nights drifted by. There was food to get, and the rent was coming due. We were counting each dime, for we had not yet made the six dollars. There was still a gap, a breach in our wall that we might not fill. And outside was the night, the rain, and the cold.

The *Richfield,* a Standard tanker, was due in. I had a shipmate aboard her, and when she came up the channel, I was waiting on the dock. They might need an A.B.

They didn't.

It was a couple of hours later when I climbed the hill toward the shack. I didn't often go that way, but this time it was closer, and I was worried. The night before I'd left the money for the rent in a thick white cup on the cupboard shelf. And right then murder could be done for five bucks. Accidentally I glanced in the window. Then I stopped.

Old Doc Yak was standing by the cupboard, holding the white cup in his hand. As I watched, he dipped his fingers in and drew out some of our carefully gleaned nickels, dimes, and quarters. Then he stood there letting those shining metal disks trickle through his thick fingers and back into the cup. Then he dipped his fingers again, and I stood there, holding my breath.

A step or two and I could have stopped him, but I stood there, gripped by his indecision, half guessing what was happening inside him. Here was money. Here, for a little while, was food, a room, a day or two of comfort. I do not think he considered the painstaking effort to acquire those few coins or the silent, bedraggled men who had trooped up the muddy trail to add a dime or fifteen cents to the total of our next month's rent. What hunger had driven him back, I knew. What helplessness and humiliation waited in the streets below, I also knew.

Slowly, one by one, the coins dribbled back into the cup, the cup was returned to the shelf, and Old Doc Yak turned and walked from the door. For one moment he paused, his face strangely gray and old, staring out across the bleak, rain-washed roofs toward the gray waters of the channel and Terminal Island just beyond.

Then he walked away, and I waited until he was out of sight before I went inside, and I, who had seen so much of weariness and defeat, hesitated before I took down the cup. It was all there, and suddenly I was a little sorry that it was.

Once more I saw him. One dark, misty night I came up from the lumber docks, collar turned up, cap pulled low, picking my way through the shadows and over the railroad ties, stumbling along rails lighted only by the feeble red and green of switch lights. Reaching the street, I scrambled up the low bank and saw him standing in the light of a street lamp.

He was alone, guarded from friendship as always by his icy impenetrability but somehow strangely pathetic with his sagging shoulders and graying hair. I started to speak, but he turned up his coat collar and walked away down a dark street.

It's Your Move

Old Man White was a checker player. He was a longshoreman, too, but he only made his living at that. Checker playing was his life. I never saw anybody take the game like he took it. Hour after hour, when there was nobody for him to play with, he'd sit at a table in the Seaman's Institute and study the board and practice his moves. He knew every possible layout there could be. There was this little book he carried, and he would arrange the checkers on the board, and then move through each game with an eye for every detail and chance. If anybody ever knew the checkerboard, it was him.

He wasn't a big man, but he was keen-eyed, and had a temper like nobody I ever saw. Most of the time he ignored people. Everybody but other checker players. I mean guys that could give him a game. They were few enough, and with the exception of Oriental Slim and MacCready, nobody had ever beat him. They were the best around at the time, but the most they could do with the old man was about one out of ten. But they gave him a game and that was all he wanted. He scarcely noticed anybody else, and you couldn't get a civil word out of him. As a rule he never opened his face unless it was to talk the game with somebody who knew it.

Then Sleeth came along. He came down from Frisco and began hanging around the Institute talking with the guys who were on the beach. He was a slim, dark fellow with a sallow complexion, quick, black eyes, and he might have been anywhere from thirty to forty-five.

He was a longshoreman, too. That is, he was then. Up in Frisco he had been a deckhand on a tugboat, like me. Before that he had been a lot of things, here and there. Somewhere he had developed a mind for figures, or maybe he had been born with it. You could give him any problem in addition, subtraction, or anything else, and you'd get the answer just like that, right out of his head. At poker he could beat anybody and was one of the best pool shots I ever saw.

We were sitting by the fireplace in the Institute one night when he came in and joined us. A few minutes later, Old Man White showed up wearing his old pea jacket as always.

"Where's MacCready?" he said.

"He's gone up to L.A., Mr. White," the clerk said. "He won't be back for several days."

"Is that other fellow around? That big fellow with the pockmarked face?"

"Slim? No, he's not. He shipped out this morning for Gray's Harbor. I heard he had some trouble with the police."

Trouble was right. Slim was slick with the cards, and he got himself in a game with a couple of Greeks. One of the Greeks was a pretty good cheat himself, but Oriental Slim was better and cashing in from the Greek's roll. One word led to another, and the Greek went for a rod. Well, Oriental Slim was the fastest thing with a chiv I ever saw. He cut that Greek, then he took out.

Old Man White turned away, growling something into his mustache. He was a testy old guy, and when he got sore that mustache looked like a porcupine's back.

"What's the matter with that guy?" Sleeth said. "He acts like he was sore about something?"

"It's checkers," I said. "That's Old Man White, the best checker player around here. Mac and Slim are the only two who can even make it interesting, and they're gone. He's sour for a week when he misses a game."

"Hell, I'll play with him!"

"He won't even listen to you. He won't play nobody unless they got some stuff."

"We'll see. Maybe I can give him a game."

Sleeth got up and walked over. The old man had his book out and was arranging his men on the board. He never used regular checkers himself. He used bottle tops, and always carried them in his pocket.

"How about a game?" Sleeth says.

Old Man White growled something under his breath about not wanting to teach anybody; he didn't even look up. He gets the checkers set up, and pretty soon he starts to move. It seems these guys that play checkers have several different openings they favor, each one of them named. Anyway, when the old man starts to move, Sleeth watches him.

"The Old Fourteenth, huh? You like that? I like the Laird and Lady best."

Old Man White stops in the middle of a move and looks up, frowning. "You play checkers?" he said.

"Sure, I just asked you for a game!"

"Sit down, sit down. I'll play you three games."

Well, it was pitiful. I'm telling you it was slaughter. If the old man hadn't been so proud, everything might have been different, but checkers was his life, his religion; and Sleeth beat him.

It wasn't so much that he beat him; it was the way he beat him. It was like playing with a child. Sleeth beat him five times running, and the old man was fit to be tied. And the madder he got, the worse he played.

Dick said afterward that if Sleeth hadn't talked so much, the old man might have had a chance. You see, Old Man White took plenty of time to study each move, sometimes ten minutes or more. Sleeth just sat there gabbing with us, sitting sideways in the chair, and never looking at the board except to move. He'd talk, talk about women, ships, ports, liquor, fighters, everything. Then, the old man would move and Sleeth would turn, glance at the board, and slide a piece. It seemed like when he looked at the board, he saw all the moves that had been made, and all that could be made. He never seemed to think; he never seemed to pause; he just moved.

Well, it rattled the old man. He was sort of shoved off balance by it. All the time, Sleeth was talking, and sometimes when he moved, it would be right in the middle of a sentence. Half the time, he scarcely looked at the board.

Then, there was a crowd around. Old Man White being beat was enough to draw a crowd, and the gang all liked Sleeth. He was a good guy. Easy with his dough, always having a laugh on somebody or with somebody, and just naturally a right guy. But I felt sorry for the old man. It meant so much to him, and he'd been king bee around the docks so long, and treating everybody with contempt if they weren't good at checkers. If he had even been able to make it tough for Sleeth, it would have been different, but he couldn't even give him a game. His memory for moves seemed to desert him, and the madder he got and the harder he tried, the more hopeless it was.

It went on for days. It got so Sleeth didn't want to play him. He'd avoid him purposely, because the old man was so stirred up about it. Once Old Man White jumped up in the middle of a game and hurled the board clear across the room. Then he stalked out, mad as a wet hen, but just about as helpless as an Armenian peddler with both arms busted.

Then he'd come back. He'd always come back and insist Sleeth play him some more. He followed Sleeth around town, cornering him to play, each time sure he could beat him, but he never could.

We should have seen it coming, for the old man got to acting queer. Checkers was an obsession with him. Now he sometimes wouldn't come around for days, and when he did, he didn't seem anxious to play anymore.

Once he played with Oriental Slim, who was back in town, but Slim beat him, too.

That was the finishing touch. It might have been the one game out of ten that Slim usually won, but it hit the old man where he lived. I guess maybe he figured he couldn't play anymore. Without even a word, he got up and went out.

A couple of mornings later, I got a call from Brennan to help load a freighter bound out for the Far East. I'd quit my job on the tug, sick of always going out but never getting any place, and had been longshoring a little and waiting for a ship to China. This looked like a chance to see if they'd be hiring; so I went over to the ship at Terminal Island, and reported to Brennan.

The first person I saw was Sleeth. He was working on the same job. While we were talking, another ferry came over and Old Man White got off. He was running a steam winch for the crew that day, and I saw him glance at Sleeth. It made me nervous to think of those two guys on the same job. In a dangerous business like longshoring—that is, a business where a guy can get smashed up so easy—it looked like trouble.

It was after four in the afternoon before anything happened. We had finished loading the lower hold through No. 4 hatch, and were putting the strong-backs in place so we could cover the 'tween decks hatchway. I was on deck waiting until they got those braces in place before I went down to lay the decking over them. I didn't want to be crawling down a ladder with one of those big steel beams swinging in the hatchway around me. Old Man White was a good hand at a winch, but too many things can happen. We were almost through for the day as we weren't to load the upper hold 'til morning.

A good winch-driver doesn't need signals from the hatch-tender to know where his load is. It may be out of sight down below the main deck, but he can tell by the feel of it and the position of the boom about where it is. But sometimes on those old winches, the steam wouldn't come on even, and once in a while there would be a surge of power that would make them do unaccountable things without a good hand driving. Now Old Man White was a good hand. Nevertheless, I stopped by the hatch coaming and watched.

It happened so quick that there wasn't anything anyone could have done. Things like that always happen quick, and if you move, it is usually by instinct. Maybe the luckiest break Sleeth ever got was he was light on his feet.

The strong-back was out over the hatch, and Old Man White was easing it down carefully. When it settled toward the 'tween decks hatchway, Sleeth caught one end and Hansen the other. It was necessary for a man to stand at each end and guide the strong-back into the notch where it had to fit to support the floor of the upper hold. Right behind Sleeth was a big steel upright, and as Old Man White began to lower away, I got nervous. It always made me nervous to think that a wrong move by the winch-driver, or a wrong signal from the hatch-tender spotting for him, and the man with that post at his back was due to get hurt.

Sleeth caught the end of the strong-back in both hands and it settled gradually, with the old winch puffing along easylike. Just then I happened to glance up, and something made me notice Old Man White's face.

He was as white as death, and I could see the muscles at the corner of his jaw set hard. Then, all of a sudden, that strong-back lunged toward Sleeth.

It all happened so quick, you could scarcely catch a breath. Sleeth must have remembered Old Man White was on that winch, or maybe it was one of those queer hunches. As for me, I know that in the split second when that strong-back lunged toward him, the thought flashed through my mind, "Sleeth. It's your move!"

And he did move, almost like in the checker games. It was as if he had a map of the whole situation in his mind. One moment he was doing one thing and the next . . .

He leaped sideways and the end of that big steel strong-back hit that stanchion with a crash that you could have heard in Sarawak; then the butt swung around and came within an eyelash of knocking Hansen into the hold, and I just stood there with my eyes on that stanchion thinking how Sleeth would have been mashed into jelly if he hadn't moved like Nijinsky.

The hatch-tender was yelling his head off, and slowly Old Man White took up the tension on the strong-back and swung her into place again. If it had been me, I'd never have touched that thing again, but Sleeth was there, and the strong-back settled into place as pretty as you could wish. Only then could I see that Sleeth's face was white and his hand was shaking.

When he came on deck, he was cool as could be. Old Man White was sitting behind that winch all heaped up like a sack of old clothes. Sleeth looked at him then, grinned a little, and said, sort of offhand, "You nearly had the move on me that time, Mr. White!"

And Proudly Die

We were all misfits, more or less; just so much waste material thrown out casually at one of the side doors of the world. We hadn't much to brag about, but we did plenty of it, one time or another. Probably some of us had something on the ball, like Jim, for instance, who just lacked some little touch in his makeup, and that started him off down the odd streets. We weren't much to look at, although the cops used to come down now and again to give us the once-over. As a rule they just left us alone, because we didn't matter. If one of us was killed, they just figured it was a break for the community, or something. And probably they were right.

Maybe Snipe was one of us after all, but he didn't seem to fit in anywhere. He was one of those guys who just don't belong. He couldn't even find a place with us, and we had about hit rock bottom. Maybe in the end he did find a place, but if he did, it wasn't the place he wanted.

He had sort of drifted in, like all the rest. A little, scrawny guy with a thin face and a long nose that stuck out over the place where his chin should have been. His chin had slipped back against his neck like it was ashamed of itself, and he had those watery blue eyes that seemed sort of anxious and helpless, as though he was always afraid somebody was going to take a punch at him.

I don't know why he stayed, or why we let him stay. Probably he was so much of a blank cartridge nobody cared. We were a pretty tight little bunch, otherwise, and we had to be. It was a matter of survival. It was the waterfront, and times were hard. Getting by was about all a guy could do, and we did it and got along because each of us had his own line and we worked well together. Snipe didn't belong, but he seemed to like being around, and we didn't notice him very much. Whenever Sharkey and Jim would get to talking, he'd sit up and listen, but for that matter, we all did.

He seemed to think Sharkey was about the last word in brains, and probably he was.

Snipe was afraid to die. Not that there's anything funny about that, only he worried about it. It was like death had a fascination for him. He was scared of it, but he couldn't stay away. And death along the waterfront is never nice. You know what I mean. A sling breaks, maybe, and a half-dozen bales of cotton come down on a guy, or maybe his foot slips when he's up on the mast, and down he comes to light on a steel deck. Or maybe a boom falls, or the swing of a strong-back mashes him. But no matter how it happens, it's never pretty. And Snipe was scared of it. He told me once he'd always been afraid to die.

Once, I'd been down along the docks looking for a live wire to hit up for the price of coffee, when I saw a crowd on the end of the wharf. Guys on the bum are all rubbernecks, so I hurried along to see what was doing. When I got closer, I could see they were fishing a stiff out of the water. You know what I mean—a dead guy.

Well, I've seen some sights in my life, and death is never pretty along the waterfront, like I've said, but this was the worst. The stiff had been in the water about two weeks. I was turning away when I spotted Snipe. He was staring at the body like he couldn't take his eyes off it, and he was already green around the gills. For a minute I thought he was going to pull a faint right there on the dock.

He saw me then. We walked away together and sat down on a lumber pile. Snipe rolled a smoke from a dirty-looking sack of Bull Durham, and I tossed little sticks off the dock, watching them float lazily on the calm, dark water.

Across the channel one of the Luckenbach boats was loading cargo for her eastern trip, and the stack of a G.P. tanker showed over the top of a warehouse on Terminal. It was one of those still, warm afternoons with a haze of heat and smoke hanging over Long Beach. Another tanker was coming slowly upstream, and I sat there watching it, remembering how I'd burned my knees painting the white S on the stack of a tanker like it. I sat there watching, kind of sleepy-like, and wishing I was coming in with a payoff due instead of kicking my heels in the sun wishing for two bits. But all the time, way down deep, I was thinking of Snipe.

I felt in my pockets hoping for a dime I'd overlooked, but I'd shook myself down a dozen times already. Out of the corner of my eye I could see Snipe staring out over the channel, that limp-looking fag hanging from his lip, and his damp, straw-colored hair plastered against his narrow skull. His fingers were too long, and the nails always dirty. I felt disgusted with him and wondered what he wanted to live for. Maybe he wondered, too.

"That stiff sure looked awful, didn't it?" he says.

"None of them look so good t' me."

"I'd hate to look like that. Seawater is nasty stuff. I never did like it."

I grunted. A shore boat was heading for the Fifth Street landing, and I watched it as the wake trailed out in a widening V, like the events that follow the birth of a man. Then we could hear the slap of water under the dock.

"I'd sure hate to die like that. If a guy could die like a hero now, it wouldn't be so bad. I wonder what Sharkey meant the other night when he said when it was no longer possible to live proudly, a man could always die proudly?"

"What the hell difference does it make how you die? A corpse is a corpse, no matter how it got that way. That stuff about a life after death is all hooey. Like Sharkey said, it was an invention of the weak to put a damper on the strong. The little fellow thinks that if the big guy is worried about the hereafter, he'll play it fair in this one, see? A dead man don't mean anything, no more than a rotten potato. He just was something, that's all!"

"But what became of the life that was in him? Where does that go?"

"Where does the flame go when the fire goes out? It's just gone. Now, forget it, and let's find the gang. I'm fed up, talking about stiffs."

We started for the shack. A few clouds had rolled up, and it was starting to drizzle. Out on the channel the ripples had changed to little waves with ruffles of white riding the crests. There was a tang in the air that smelled like a blow. I looked off toward the sea and was glad I was ashore. It wasn't going to be any fun out there tonight. Snipe hurried along beside me, his breath wheezing a little.

"I'm a good swimmer," he said, reaching for a confidence I could tell he didn't have. "Well, a pretty good swimmer."

Where did a runt like him ever get that hero idea? From Sharkey, I guess. Probably nobody ever treated him decent before. Looking at him, I wondered why it was some guys draw such tough hands. There was Sharkey, as regular a guy as ever walked, a big, fine-looking fellow with brains and nerve, and then here was Snipe, with nothing. Sharkey had a royal flush, and Snipe was holding nothing but deuces and treys in a game that was too big for him.

His frayed collar was about two sizes too large, and his Adam's apple just grazed it every time he swallowed. He didn't have a thing, that guy. He was bucking a stacked deck, and the worst of it was, he knew it.

You see a lot of these guys along the waterfronts. The misfits and the also-rans, the guys who knew too much and those who knew too little. Everything loose in the world seems to drift toward the sea and usually winds up on the beach somewhere. It's a sort of natural law, I guess. And here was Snipe. It wouldn't have been so tough if he'd been the dumb type that thought he was a pretty swell guy. But Snipe wasn't fooled. Way down inside he had a feeling for something better than he was, and every time he moved he knew it was him, Snipe, that was moving.

You could see him seeing himself. It gave you kind of a shock, sometimes. I had never quite got it until then, but I guess Sharkey had from the first. You could see that Snipe knew he was Snipe, just something dropped off the merry-go-round of life that didn't matter.

Instead of going on with me, he turned at the corner and walked off up the street, his old cap pulled down over his face, his funny, long shoes squidging on the sloppy walk.

It was warm and cheery inside the shack. Sharkey had had the guys rustle up some old papers and nail them over the walls as insulation. When you couldn't do anything else, you could read the latest news of three months back or look at pictures of Mae West or Myrna Loy, depending if you liked them slim or well upholstered. Most of them looked at Mae West.

The big stove had its belly all red from the heat, and Tony was tipped back in a chair reading the sports. Deek was playing sol at the table, and Jim was standing by in the kitchen watching Red throw a mulligan together. Sharkey had his nose in a book as usual, something about the theory of the leisure class. I had to grin when he showed it to me. We sure were a leisure class, although there wasn't one of us liked it.

It was nice sitting there. The heat made a fellow kind of drowsy, and the smell of mulligan and coffee was something to write home about. I sat there remembering Snipe walking off up the street through that first spatter of rain, and how the wind whipped his worn old coat.

He was afraid of everything, that guy. Afraid of death, afraid of cops, scared of ship's officers, and of life, too, I guess. At that, he was luckier than some, for he had a flop. It would be cold and wet on the streets tonight, and there would be men sleeping in boxcars and lumber piles, and other guys walking the streets, wishing they had lumber piles and boxcars to sleep in. But we were lucky, with a shack like this, and we only kept it by working together. In that kind of a life, you got to stick together. It's the only answer.

Windy Slim was still out on the stem. He never came in early on bad nights, it being easier to pick up a little change when the weather is wet and miserable. Copper was out somewhere, too, and that was unusual, him liking the rain no better than a cat. The drizzle had changed now to a regular downpour, and the wind was blowing a gale.

We all knew what it would be like at sea, with the wind howling through the rigging like a lost banshee and the decks awash with black, glassy water. Sometimes the shack sagged with the weight of the wind, and once Sharkey looked up and glanced apprehensively at the stove.

Then, during a momentary lull, the door jerked open and Slim stomped in, accompanied by a haze of wind and rain that made the lamp spit and almost go out. He shook himself and began pulling off his coat.

"God have pity on the poor sailors on such a night as this!" Jim said, grinning.

"Say—" Slim stopped pulling off his wet clothes and looked at Sharkey. "Brophy and Stallings picked up Copper tonight!"

"The devil they did!" Sharkey put down his book. "What happened?"

"Copper, he bums four bits from some lug down on the docks where he used to work an' goes to the Greek's for some chow. He has a hole in his pocket but forgets it. After he eats he finds his money is gone. The Greek hollers for a bull, an' Brophy comes running, Cap Stallings with him.

"Snipe, he was with Copper when he raised the four bits, but when the bull asks him did Copper have any money, the little rat is so scared he says he don't know nothing about it. He always was scared of a cop. So they took Copper an' throwed him in the can."

"The yellow rat!" Tony said. "An' after all the feeds Copper staked him to!"

"Why have him here, anyway?" Red said. "He just hangs around. He ain't any good for anything!"

Me, I sat there and didn't say anything. There wasn't anything you could say. Outside the wind gathered and hurled a heavy shoulder against the house, the lamp sputtered and gulped, and everybody was quiet. Everybody was thinking what I was thinking, I guess, that Snipe would have to go, but there wasn't any place for him to go. I tried to read again, but I couldn't see anything but that spatter of falling rain and Snipe walking away up the street. Red was right, he wasn't any good for anything, not even himself.

The door opened then, and Snipe came in. It was all in his face, all the bitter defeat and failure of him. That was the worst of it. He knew just what he'd done, knew just what it would mean to that tough, lonely bunch of men who didn't have any friends but themselves and so had to be good friends to each other. He knew it all, knew just how low he must have sunk, and only felt a little lower himself.

Sharkey didn't say anything, and the rest of us just sat there. Then Sharkey took a match out of his pocket and handed it to Snipe. Everybody knew what that meant. In the old days on the bum, when the crowd didn't like a fellow, they gave him a match as a hint to go build his own fire.

Sharkey picked up the poker then and began to poke at the fire. Out in the kitchen everything was quiet. Snipe stood there, looking down at Sharkey's shoulders, his face white and queer. Then he turned and went out. The sound of the closing door was loud in the room.

The next morning Sharkey and a couple of us drifted down to the big crap game under the P.E. trestle. Everybody was talking about the storm and the ferry to Terminal Island being rammed and sunk during the night. About a dozen lives lost, somebody said.

"Say, Sharkey," Honolulu said, looking up from the dice. "One of your crowd was on that ferry. That little guy they called Snipe. I saw him boarding her at the landing."

"Yeah?"

"Yeah."

Sharkey looked down at the dice and said nothing. Slim was getting the dice hot and had won a couple of bucks. The lookout got interested, and when all at once somebody hollers "Bull," there were the cops coming up through the lumberyard.

Two or three of our boys were in the inner circle, and when the yell came, everybody grabbed at the cash. Then we all scattered out, running across the stinking tideflat east of the trestle. I got a fistful of money myself, and there was a lot left behind. I glanced back once, and the cops were picking it up.

The tide wasn't out yet, and in some places the water was almost knee deep, but it was the only way, and we took it running. I got all wet and muddy but had to laugh, thinking what a funny sight we must have made, about twenty of us splashing through that water as fast as we could pick 'em up and put 'em down.

I was some little time getting back to the shack, and when I did get there, Sharkey was sitting on the steps talking to Windy and Jim. They looked mighty serious, and when I came up, they motioned me to come along and then started back for the trestle.

Thinking maybe they were going back after the money, I told them about the cops getting it, but Slim merely shrugged and said nothing. He had a slug of chewing in his jaw and looked serious as hell.

Finally we got to the mud flat, and though it was still wet, Sharkey started picking his way across. We hadn't gone far before I could see something ahead, partly buried in the gray mud. It looked like an old sack, or a bundle of dirty clothes. When we got closer I could see it was a body—probably washed in by the tide.

It sort of looked as if the man had been walking in and, when the mud on his feet got too heavy, just laid down. Even before Sharkey stooped to turn his head over, I could see it was Snipe. He had on that old cap of his, and I couldn't have missed it in a million.

He looked pretty small and pitiful, lying there in the mud mingled with the debris left by an outgoing tide. Once in a while even yet, I think of how he looked, lying there on that stinking mud flat under a low, clouded sky, with a background of lumberyard and trestle. There was mud on the side of his face, and a spot on his nose. His long fingers were relaxed and helpless, but somehow there wasn't a thing about him that looked out of place. We stood there looking at him a minute, and none of us said anything, but I was thinking: "Well, you were afraid of it, and here it is—now what?"

We left him there and said nothing to anybody. Later, Red saw them down there picking him up but didn't go near, so we never knew what the coroner thought of it, if anything. I often wonder what happened when that ferry went down. She was hit hard and must have sunk like a rock, with probably fifty or sixty people aboard. It was Snipe's big chance to be a hero, him being such a good swimmer. But there he was.

As I said to Sharkey, it was a hell of a place to be found dead.

Survival

Tex Worden shoved his way through the crowd in the Slave Market and pushed his book under the wicket.

The clerk looked up, taking in his blistered face and swollen hands. "What'll you have, buddy? You want to register?"

"Naw, I'm here to play a piano solo, what d'you think?"

"Wise guy, eh?"

Tex's eyes were cold. "Sure, and what about it?"

"You guys all get too smart when you get ashore. I'm used to you guys, but one of these days I'm going to come out from behind here and kick hell out of one of you!"

"Why not now?" Worden said mildly. "You don't see me out there running down the street, do you? You just come out from behind that counter, and I'll lay you in the scuppers."

At a signal from the man behind the wicket a big man pushed his way through the crowd and tapped Tex Worden on the shoulder. "All right, buddy, take it easy. You take it easy, or you get the boot."

"Yeah?"

"Yeah!"

Tex grinned insultingly and turned his back, waiting for the return of his book. The clerk opened it grudgingly, then looked up, startled.

"You were on the *Raratonga*!"

"So what?"

"We heard only one of the crew was saved!"

"Who the hell do you think I am? Napoleon? And that saved business, that's the bunk. That's pure malarkey. I saved myself. Now come on, get that book fixed. I want to get out of here."

The plainclothes man was interested. "No kiddin', are you Tex Worden?"

"I am."

"Hell, man, that must have been some wreck. The papers say that if it wasn't for you none of them would have gotten back. Dorgan was on that boat, too!"

"Dorgan?" Tex turned to face him. "You know Dorgan?"

"*Knew* him? I should say I did! A tough man, too. One of the toughest."

Worden just looked at him. "How tough a man is often depends on where he is and what he's doing." He was looking past the plainclothes man, searching for a familiar face. In all this gathering of merchant seamen hunting work, he saw no one.

Times were hard. There were over seven hundred seamen on the beach, and San Pedro had become a hungry town. Jobs were scarce, and a man had to wait his turn. And he didn't have eating money. Everything he had had gone down with the *Raratonga*. He had money coming to him, but how long it would be before he saw any of it was a question.

Near the door he glimpsed a slight, bucktoothed seaman in a blue pea jacket whose face looked familiar. He edged through the crowd to him. "Hi, Jack, how's about staking a guy to some chow?"

"Hey? Don't I know you? Tex, isn't it?"

"That's right. Tex Worden. You were on the *West Ivis* when I was."

"Come on, there's a greasy spoon right down the street." When they were outside, he said, "I don't want to get far from the shipping office. My number's due to come up soon."

"How long's it been?"

"Three months. Well, almost that. Times are rough, Tex." He looked at Worden. "What happened to you?"

"I was on the *Raratonga*."

The sailor shook his head in awe. "*Jee-sus!* You were the only one who came back!"

"Some passengers made it. Not many, but some."

"How's it feel to be a hero? And with Hazel Ryan yet. And Price! The actress and the millionaire! You brought them back alive."

"Me an' Frank Buck. If this is how it feels to be a hero, you can have it. I'm broke. There's a hearing today, and maybe I can hit up the commissioner for a few bucks."

The other seaman thrust out a hand. "I'm Conrad, Shorty Conrad. Paid off a ship from the east coast of South America, and I lied to you. It didn't take me three months because I've got a pal back there. I'll say a word for you, and maybe you can get a quick ship-out."

They ordered coffee and hamburger steaks. "This is a tough town, man. No way to get out of this dump unless you can take a pierhead jump or get lucky. If you know a ship's officer who'll ask for you, you got a better chance."

"I don't know nobody out here. I been shipping off the East Coast."

A burly Greek came along behind the counter. He stared hard at them. "You boys got money? I hate to ask, but we get stiffed a lot."

"I got it." Shorty showed him a handful of silver dollars. "Anyway, this is Tex Worden. He was on the *Raratonga*."

"You got to be kiddin'."

The Greek eyed him with respect. "That where you got blistered?" he motioned toward Worden's hands. "What happened to them?"

"Knittin'," Tex said. "Them needles get awful heavy after a while."

He was tired, very, very tired. The reaction was beginning to set in now. He was so tired he felt he'd fall off the stool if he wasn't careful, and he didn't even have the price of a bed. If he hit the sack now, he'd probably pass out for a week. His shoulders ached, and his hands were sore. They hurt when he used them, and they hurt just as much when he didn't.

"It was a nasty blow, Shorty. You never saw wind like that."

"She went down quick, eh? I heard it was like fifteen minutes."

"Maybe. It was real quick. Starb'rd half door give way, and the water poured in; then a bulkhead give way, and the rush of water put the fires out. No power, no pumps—it was a madhouse."

They were silent, sipping their coffee and eating the greasy steaks. Finally Shorty asked, "How long were you out there?"

"Fifteen days, just a few miles off the equator. It rained once—just in time."

Faces of men he knew drifted by the door. He knew some of them but could not recall their names. They were faces he'd seen from Hong Kong to Hoboken, from Limehouse to Malay Street in Singapore or Grant Road in Bombay, Gomar Street in Suez, or the old American Bar on Lime Street in Liverpool. He'd started life as a cowboy but now he'd been at sea for fifteen years.

It was a rough crowd out there on Beacon Street, but if he did not know them all, he knew their kind. There were pimps and prostitutes, seamen, fishermen, longshoremen, and bums, but they were all people, and they were all alive, and they were all walking on solid ground.

There were gobs there from the battle wagons off Long Beach and girls who followed the fleet. There was an occasional drunk looking for a live wire who might spring for another bottle, and he liked it.

"Maybe I'll save my money," he said aloud, "buy myself a chicken ranch. I'd like to own a chicken ranch near Modesto."

"Where's Modesto?"

"I don't know. Somewhere north of here. I just like the sound of it."

Tex Worden looked down at his hands. Under the bandages they were swollen with angry red cracks where the blisters had been and some almost raw flesh that had just begun to heal. In the mirror he saw a face like a horror mask, for tough as his hide was, the sun had baked it to an angry red that he could not touch to shave. He looked frightening and felt worse. If only he could get some sleep!

He did not want to think of those bitter, brutal days when he rowed the boat, hour after hour, day after day, rowing with a sullen resignation, all sense of time forgotten, even all sense of motion. There had been no wind for days, just a dead calm, the only movement being the ripples in the wake of the lifeboat.

He got up suddenly. "I almost forgot. I got to stop by the commissioner's office. They want to ask me some questions. Sort of a preliminary inquiry, I guess."

Shorty stole a quick look at him. "Tex—you be careful. Be real careful. These aren't seamen. They don't know what it's like out there. They can't even imagine."

"I'll be all right."

"Be careful, I tell you. I read something about it in the papers. If you ain't careful they'll crucify you."

THERE WERE SEVERAL MEN in business suits in the office when they entered. They all looked at Tex, but the commissioner was the only one who spoke. "Thank you, son. That was a good job you did out there."

"It was my job," Tex said. "I done what I was paid for."

The commissioner dropped into a swivel chair behind his desk. "Now, Worden, I expect you're tired. We will not keep you any longer than we must, but naturally we must arrive at some conclusions as to what took place out there and what caused the disaster. If there is anything you can tell us, we'd be glad to hear it."

Shorty stole a glance at the big man with the red face. A company man, here to protect their interests. He knew the type.

"There's not much to tell, sir. I had come off watch about a half hour before it all happened, and when I went below, everything seemed neat and shipshape. When the ship struck, I was sitting on my bunk in the fo'c'sle taking off my shoes.

"The jolt threw me off the bench, an' Stu fell off his bunk on top of me. He jumped up an' said, 'What the hell happened?' and I said I didn't know, but it felt like we hit something. He said, 'It's clear enough outside, and we're way out to sea. Must be a derelict!' I was pulling on my shoes, and so was he, an' we ran up on deck.

"There was a lot of running around, and we started forward, looking for the mate. Before we'd made no more than a half-dozen steps, the signal came for boat stations, and I went up on the boat deck. Last I saw of Stu he was trying to break open a jammed door, and I could hear people behind it.

"We must have hit pretty hard because she was starting to settle fast, going down by the head with a heavy list to starb'rd. I was mighty scared because I remembered that starb'rd half door, and—"

"What about the half door, Worden? What was wrong with it?"

"Nothing at all, commissioner," the company man interrupted. "The company inspector—"

"Just a minute, Mr. Winstead." The commissioner spoke sharply. "Who is conducting this inquiry?"

"Well, I—"

"Proceed with your story, Worden."

"The half door was badly sprung, sir. Somebody said the ship had been bumped a while back, and I guess they paid no mind to repairs. Anyway, it wasn't no bother unless they was loaded too heavy, and—"

"What do you mean, Worden? Was the ship overloaded?"

Winstead scowled at Worden, his lips drawing to a thin, angry line.

"Well, sir, I guess I ain't got no call to speak, but—"

"You just tell what happened at the time of the wreck, Worden. That will be sufficient!" Winstead said, interrupting.

"Mr. Winstead! I will thank you not to interrupt this man's story again. I am conducting this inquiry, and regardless of the worth of what Worden may have to say, he is the sole remaining member of the crew. As a seafaring man of many years' experience, he understands ships, and he was there when it happened. I intend to hear *all*—let me repeat, *all*—he has to say. We certainly are not going to arrive at any conclusions by concealing anything. If your vessel was in proper condition, you have nothing to worry about, but I must say your attitude gives rise to suspicion." He paused, glancing up at the reporters who were writing hurriedly. "Now, Worden, if you please. Continue your story."

"Well, sir, I was standing by number three hatch waiting for the last loads to swing aboard so's I could batten down the hatch, an' I heard Mr. Jorgenson—he was the mate—say to Mr. Winstead here that he didn't like it at all. He said loading so heavy with that bad door was asking for trouble, and he went on to mention that bad bulkhead amidships.

"I don't know much about it, sir, except what he said and the talk in the fo'c's'le about the bulkhead between hatches three and four. One of the men who'd been chipping rust down there said you didn't dare chip very hard or you'd drive your hammer right through, it was that thin.

When I was ashore clearing the gangway, I saw she was loaded down below the Plimsoll marks."

"Weren't you worried, Worden? I should think that knowing the conditions you would have been."

"No, sir. Generally speaking, men working aboard ship don't worry too much. I've been going to sea quite a while now, and it's always the other ships that sink, never the one a fellow's on. At least that's the way it is until something happens. We don't think about it much, and if she sinks, then she sinks, and that's all there is to it."

"I see."

"Yes, sir. There was trouble with that half door before we were three days out. Me an' a couple of others were called to help Chips caulk that half door. You know—it's a door in the ship's side through which cargo is loaded. Not all ships have 'em. That door had been rammed some time or another, and it didn't fit right. In good weather or when she carried a normal load it was all right.

"But three days out we had a spot of bad weather; some of that cargo shifted a mite, and she began to make water, so we had to recaulk that door.

"To get back to that night, sir. When I got to my boat station, I saw one of the officers down on the deck with his head all stove in. I don't know whether he got hit with something or whether it was done by the bunch of passengers who were fighting over the boat. Ever'body was yellin' an' clawin', so I waded in an' socked a few of them and got them straightened out.

"I told them they'd damn well better do what they were told because I was the only one who knew how to get that lifeboat into the water. After that they quieted down some. A couple of them ran off aft, hunting another boat, but I got busy with the lifeboat cover.

"All of a sudden it was still, so quiet it scared you. The wind still blowing and big waves all around but ghostly still. You could hear a body speak just like I'm speakin' now. It was like everything quieted down to let us die in peace. I could tell by the feel of her that we hadn't long. She was settlin' down, and she had an ugly, heavy feel to her.

"Mister, that was a tryin' time. All those people who'd been yellin' an' fightin' stood there lookin' at me, and one little fellow in a gray suit—he had a tie on, an' everything. He was Jewish, I think. He asked me what he could do, and I told him to get to the other end of the boat, to loose the falls and lower away when I did.

"I got the boat cover off, and we got the boat into the water, and the ship was down so far and canted over—a bad list to her—that it was no problem gettin' those few folks into the lifeboat.

"I took a quick look around. The boat 'longside was already in the water, and there were two A.B.s with it, Fulton an' Jaworski, it was. They had maybe thirty people in that boat, and I saw one of the stewards there, too. There was nobody else in sight, but I could hear some yelling forward.

"Just then she gave a sort of shudder, and I jumped into the boat and told the Jew to cast off. He had trouble because she was rising and falling on the water, but a woman helped him. I didn't know who she was then, but later I found out it was that actress, Hazel Ryan.

"We shoved off, and I got oars into the water, and we started looking for others. When we got out a ways, I could see Sparks—one of them, anyway, in the radio shack.

"Then the ship gave a kind of lunge and went down by the head. She just dipped down and then slid right away, going into the water on her beam ends with all the port-side boats just danglin' there, useless, as they couldn't be got into the water. At the last minute, as she went under, I saw a man with an ax running from boat to boat cutting the falls. He was hoping they'd come up floating, and two or three of them did.

"All of a sudden I see a man in the water. He was a pleasant-looking man with gray hair, and he was swimming. He looked so calm I almost laughed. 'Cold, isn't it?' he says, and then he just turns and swims away, cool as you please. You'd have thought the beach wasn't fifty feet away.

"It's things like that fairly take your wind, sir, and there I was, trying to pull the lifeboat away from the ship and hopin' for the best.

"I turned my head once and looked back. Mostly I was trying to guide the boat through wreckage that was already afloat. When I looked back—this was just before she went under—I glimpsed somebody standin' on the bridge, one arm through the pilot-house window to hang on, and he was lighting his pipe with his free hand.

"It just didn't seem like it could be happening. There I was just minutes before, a-comin' off watch, all set for a little shuteye, and now here I was in a lifeboat, and the ship was goin' down.

"There must have been nearly a hundred people in the water and not a whisper out of any of them. Like they was all in shock or somethin' of the kind. Once a guy did yell to somebody else. Then something exploded under water—maybe the boilers busted. I wouldn't know. Anyway, when it was over, a lot of those folks who'd been in the water were gone. I fetched the bow of my boat around and rowed toward something white floating in the water. It was a woman, and I got her into the boat."

"Was that Hazel Ryan?" a reporter asked.

"No, it was Lila, a stewardess. Then I held the boat steady whilst another man climbed in. He pointed out three people clingin' to a barrel. I started for them.

"The sea was rough, and folks would disappear behind a wave, and sometimes when you looked, they weren't there anymore. Those people were havin' a time of it, tryin' to hang to that barrel, so I got to them first, and folks helped them aboard. The Ryan woman was one of them.

"I'll give her this. First moment she could speak, she asked if there was anything she could do, and I said just to set quiet and try to get warm. If I needed help, I'd ask for it.

"It was funny how black everything was, yet you could see pretty well for all of that. You'd see a white face against the black water, and by the time you got there, it was gone.

"One time I just saw an arm. Woman's, I think it was. She was right alongside the boat, and I let go an oar an' grabbed for her, but her arm slipped right through my fingers, and she was gone.

"Some of those we'd picked up were in panic and some in shock. That little Jewish fellow with the necktie and all, he didn't know a thing about the sea, but he was cool enough. We moved people around, got the boat trimmed, and I got her bow turned to meet the sea and started to try to ride her out."

"What about the radio?"

"We didn't think about that for long. At least I didn't. There hadn't been much time, and the chances were slim that any message got off. It all happened too fast.

"Sparks was in there, and he was sending. I am sure of that, but he hadn't any orders, and most shipmasters don't want any Mayday or SOS goin' out unless they say. If he sent it, he sent it on his own because the old man never made the bridge."

"The man you saw lighting his pipe?"

"Jorgenson, I think. He was watch officer, but they were changing watch, so I don't know. He wasn't heavy enough for the old man.

"Anyway, I'd no time to think of them. The sea was making up, and I was havin' the devil's own time with that boat. She'd have handled a lot easier if we'd had a few more people aboard.

"Lila, she was hurting. Seemed like she was all stove up inside, and the shock was wearing off. She was feeling pain, turning and twisting like, and the Ryan woman was trying to help. She and that little Jew, they worked over her, covering her with coats, trying to tuck them under so she'd ride easier. The rest just sat and stared."

"No other boats got off?"

"I don't know—except that boat with Fulton and Jaworski. They were good men, and they'd do what could be done. The ship had taken a bad list, so I don't think many of the boats on the topside could be launched at all."

"How was the weather?"

"Gettin' worse, sir. There was nobody to spell me on the oars because nobody knew anything about handling a boat in a heavy sea. I shipped the oars and got hold of the tiller, which made it a mite easier.

"Lila had passed out; spray was whipping over the boat. I was hanging to that tiller, scared ever' time a big one came over that it would be the last of us. There was no way to play. You just had to live from one sea to the next."

"How long did the storm last?"

"About two days. I don't rightly remember because I was so tired everything was hazy. When the sea calmed down enough, I let Schwartz have the tiller. I'd been gripping it so hard and so long I could hardly let go."

"You were at the tiller forty-eight hours without relief?"

"Yes, sir. Maybe a bit more. But after that she began to settle down, and the sun came out."

"The boat was provisioned according to regulations?"

"Yes, sir. We'd some trouble about water later but not much."

"How about the crew and the officers? Were they efficient in your opinion?"

"Sure. Yes, they were okay. I've been going to sea quite a spell, and I never have seen any seaman or officer shirk his job. It ain't bravery nor lack of it, just that he knows his job and has been trained for it.

"Sometimes you hear about the crew rushing the boats or being inefficient. I don't believe it ever happens. They're trained for the job, and it is familiar to them. They know what they are to do, and they do it.

"Passengers are different. All of a sudden everything is different. There's turmoil an' confusion; there's folks runnin' back and forth, and the passengers don't know what's going on.

"Sometimes one of them will grab a crewman and yell something at him, and the crewman will pull loose and go about his business. The passenger gets mad and thinks they've been deserted by the crew when chances are that seaman had something to do. Maybe his boat station was elsewhere. Maybe he'd been sent with a message for the engineer on watch below.

"Maybe those crewmen you hear about rushing the boats are just getting there to get the boat cover off and clear the falls. This wasn't my first wreck, and I've yet to see a crewman who didn't stand by."

"How long before she sank?"

"Fifteen minutes, give or take a few. It surely wasn't more, though. It might have been no more than five. We'd made quite a bit of water before the cargo shifted and she heeled over. With that half door underwater—well, I figure that door gave way and she just filled up and sank."

"Mr. Commissioner?" Winstead asked. "I'd like permission to ask this man a few questions. There are a few matters I'd like to clear up."

"Go ahead."

"Now, my man, if you'd be so kind. How many were in the boat when you got away from the scene of the wreck?"

"Eight."

"Yet when you were picked up by the *Maloaha* there were but three?"

"Yes."

"How do you account for that?"

"Lila—she was the stewardess—she died. Like I said, she'd been hurt inside. She was a mighty good woman, and I hated to see her go. Clarkson—he went kind of screwy. Maybe he didn't have all his buttons to start with. Anyway, he got kind of wild and kept staring at a big shark who was following us. One night he grabbed up a boat hook and tried to get that shark. It was silly. That shark was just swimmin' along in hopes. No use to bother him. Well, he took a stab at that shark and fell over the side.

"Handel, he just sat an' stared. Never made no word for anybody, just stared. He must've sat that way for eight or nine days. We all sort of lost track of time, but he wouldn't take water, wouldn't eat a biscuit. He just sat there, hands hanging down between his knees.

"I'd rigged a sort of mast from a drifting stick and part of a boat cover. The mast this boat should have carried was missing. Anyway, the little sail I rigged gave us some rest, and it helped. Late one day we were moving along at a pretty fair rate for us when I saw a squall coming. She swept down on us so quick that I gave the tiller to Schwartz and stumbled forward to get that sail down before we swamped. With the wind a-screaming and big seas rolling up, I'd almost reached the sail when this Handel went completely off his course. He jumped up and grabbed me, laughing and singing, trying to dance with me or something.

"Struggling to get free, I fell full length in the boat, scrambled up and pulled that sail down, and when I looked around, Handel was gone."

"Gone?" Winstead said.

"You mean—over the side?" the commissioner asked.

"That's right. Nearest thing I could figure out was that when I fell, he fell, too. Only when I fell into the bottom, he toppled over the side.

"Rain and blown spray was whipping the sea, and we couldn't see him. No chance to turn her about. We'd have gone under had we tried.

"For the next ten hours we went through hell, just one squall after another, and all of us had to bail like crazy just to keep us afloat."

"So," Winstead said, "you killed a passenger?"

"I never said that. I don't know what happened. Whatever it was, it was pure accident. I'd nothing against the man. He was daffy, but until that moment he'd been harmless. I figure he didn't mean no harm then, only I had to get free of him to save the boat."

"At least, that is your story?"

"Mister, with a ragin' squall down on us there was no time to coddle nobody. I didn't have a straitjacket nor any way to get him into one. It was save the boat or we'd all drown."

"Yet even with your small sail up, you might have lasted, might you not?"

Worden considered the matter, then he shrugged. "No way to tell. I was the only seaman aboard, and it was my judgment the sail come down. I'd taken it down."

"All right. We will let that rest for the moment. That accounts for three. Now what became of the other two?"

"The Jew—Schwartz, he come to me in the night a few days later. We were lyin' in a dead calm, and most of our water was gone. Sky was clear, not a cloud in sight, and we'd a blazin' hot day ahead. He told me he was goin' over the side, and he wanted me to know because he didn't want me to think he was a quitter.

"Hell, that little kike had more guts than the whole outfit. I told him nothing doing. Told him I needed him, which was no lie. It was a comfort just to have him there because what he didn't know he could understand when I told him. He wouldn't accept the fact that I needed him.

"It even came to the point where I suggested I toss a coin with him to see who went over. He wouldn't listen to that, and we both knew I was talkin' nonsense. I was the only seaman. The only one who could handle a boat. It was my job to bring that boat back with as many people as possible. I ain't goin' for any of that hero stuff. That's all baloney. Sure, I wanted to live as much as any man, but I had a job to do. It was what I signed on to do. At least when I signed on, it was to do a seaman's job. I ain't done nothing I wouldn't do again."

"I see. And what became of the other man?"

"He was a big guy, and he was tough. He tried to take charge of the boat. There's a lot happens in an open boat like that when everybody is close to shovin' off for the last time. People just ain't thinkin' the way they should. This big guy, he had more stamina than the rest of them. Most of them tried to take a hand in rowin' the boat.

"We'd no wind, you see, and I was hopin' we could get out of the calm into the wind again, but he wouldn't do anything. He just sat. He said I was crazy, that I was goin' the wrong way. He said I drank water at night when they were all asleep. Twice when I passed water forward for somebody else, he drank it.

"Then one night I woke up with him pourin' the last of our water down his damn throat. The Ryan woman, she was tuggin' at his arm to try to stop him, but hell, it was too late.

"It was her callin' to me that woke me up, and I went at him. He emptied the cask and threw it over the side. I tried to stop him, and we had it out, right there. He was some bigger than me and strong, but there was no guts to him. I smashed him up some and put him between the oars. I told him to row, that he'd live as long as he rowed. First we had to circle around and pick up the cask."

"An empty cask?" Winstead asked incredulously. "What in God's world did you do that for?"

"Mister, it's only in the movies where some guy on the desert an' dyin' of thirst throws away a canteen because it's empty. Shows how little some of those screenwriters know. Supposin' he finds water next day? How's he goin' to carry it?

"You throw away an empty canteen in the desert an' you're committin' suicide. Same thing out there. We might get a rain squall, and if we did, we'd need something to hold water. So we circled and picked up that cask."

"And what happened to Dorgan?"

Tex Worden's face was bleak. "He quit rowin' twenty-four hours before we got picked up."

Winstead turned to the commissioner. "Sir, this man has admitted to killing one passenger; perhaps he killed two or three. As to his motives— I think they will appear somewhat different under cross-examination.

"I have evidence as to this man's character. He is known along the waterfronts as a tough. He frequents houses of ill fame. He gets into drunken brawls. He has been arrested several times for fighting. His statements here today have cast blame upon the company. I intend to produce evidence that this man is not only a scoundrel but an admitted murderer!"

Tex sat up slowly.

"Yes, I've been arrested for fighting. Sometimes when I come ashore after a long cruise I have a few too many, and sometimes I fight, but it's always with my own kind. After a trip on one of those louse-bound scows of yours, a man has to get drunk. But I'm a seaman. I do my job. There's never a man I've worked with will deny that. I'm sorry you weren't in that boat with us so you could have seen how it was.

"You learn a lot about people in a lifeboat. Me, I never claimed to be any psalm singer. Maybe the way I live isn't your way, but when the time comes for the men to step out, I'll be there. I'll be doin' my job.

"It's easy to sit around on your fat behinds and say what you'd have done or what should have been done. You weren't there.

"Nobody knows what he'd do until he's in the spot. I was the only guy in that boat knew a tiller from a thwart. It was me bring that boat through or nobody. I'd rather lose two than lose them all. I wasn't doin' it because it was swell of me or because they'd call me a hero. I was bringin' them in because it was my job.

"Handel now. He wasn't responsible. Somethin' happened to him that he never expected. He could have lived his life through a nice, re-spected man, but all of a sudden it isn't the same anymore. There's no-body to tell to do something or to even ask. He's caught in a place he can't see his way out of. He'd never had just to endure, and there was nothing in him to rise to the surface and make him stand up. It sort of af-fected his mind.

"Hazel Ryan? She has moxie. When I told her it was her turn to row, she never hesitated, and I had to make her quit. She wasn't all that strong, but she was game. A boatload like her an' I could have slept halfway back.

"Dorgan was a bad apple. The whole boat was on edge because of him. He'd been used to authority and was a born bully. He was used to takin' what he wanted an' lettin' others cry about it. I told him what he had to do, and he did it after we had our little set-to."

"Who did you think you were, Worden? God? With the power of life and death?"

"Listen, mister"—Worden leaned forward—"when I'm the only sea-man in the boat, when we have damn' little water, an' we're miles off the steamer lanes, when there's heat, stillness, thirst, an' we're sittin' in the middle of a livin' hell, you can just bet I'm Mister God as far as that boat's concerned.

"The company wasn't there to help. You weren't there to help, nor was the commissioner. Sure, the little fat guy prayed, an' Clarkson prayed. Me, I rowed the boat."

He lifted his hands, still swollen and terribly lacerated where the blis-ters had broken to cracks in the raw flesh. "Forty hours," he said, "there at the end I rowed for forty hours, tryin' to get back where we might be picked up. We made it.

"We made it," he repeated, "but there was a lot who didn't."

The commissioner rose, and Winstead gathered his papers, his fea-tures set and hard. He threw one quick, measuring glance at Worden.

"That will be all, gentlemen," the commissioner said. "Worden, you will remain in port until this is straightened out. You are still at the same address?"

"Yes, sir. At the Seaman's Institute."

Shorty glanced nervously out the window, then at Winstead. Tex turned away from the desk, a tall, loose figure in a suit that no longer fit.

Winstead left, saying nothing, but as Worden joined Shorty, the commissioner joined them.

"Worden?"

"Yes, sir?"

"As man to man, and I was once a seaman myself, Mr. Winstead has a lot of influence. He will have the best attorney money can hire, and to a jury off the shore things do not look the same as in a drifting lifeboat.

"The *Lichenfield* docked a few minutes ago, and she will sail after refueling. I happen to know they want two A.B.s. This is unofficial, of course. The master of the vessel happens to be a friend of mine."

They shook hands briefly.

There was a faint mist falling when they got outside. Tex turned up his coat collar. Shorty glanced toward Terminal Island. "You got an outfit? Some dungarees an' stuff?"

"I'd left a sea bag at the Institute." He touched the blue shirt. "This was in it. I can draw some gear from the slop chest."

"They got your tail in a crack, Tex. What's next, the *Lichenfield*?"

"Well," he said shortly, "I don't make my living in no courtroom."

Show Me the Way to Go Home

It was the night the orchestra played "Show Me the Way to Go Home," the night the fleet sailed for Panama. The slow drizzle of rain had stopped, and there was nothing but the play of searchlights across the clouds, the mutter of the motors from the shore boats, and the spatter of grease where the man was frying hamburgers on the Fifth Street landing. I was standing there with a couple of Greek fishermen and a taxi driver, watching the gobs say good-bye to their wives and sweethearts.

There was something about the smell of rain, the sailors saying good-bye, and the creak of rigging that sort of got to you. I'd been on the beach for a month then.

A girl came down to the landing and leaned on the rail watching the shore boats. One of the gobs waved at her, and she waved back, but didn't smile. You could see that they didn't know each other; it was just one of those things.

She was alone. Every other girl was with somebody, but not her. She was wearing a neat, tailored suit that was a little worn, but she had nice legs and large, expressive eyes. When the last of the shore boats was leaving she was still standing there. Maybe it wasn't my move, but I was lonely, and when you're on the beach you don't meet many girls. So I walked over and leaned on the rail beside her.

"Saying good-bye to your boyfriend?" I asked, though I knew she wasn't.

"I said good-bye to him a long time ago."

"He didn't come back?"

"Do they ever?"

"Sometimes they want to and can't. Sometimes things don't break right."

"I wonder."

"And sometimes they do come back and things aren't like they were, and sometimes they don't come back because they are afraid they won't be the same, and they don't want to spoil what they remember."

"Then why go?"

"Somebody has to. Men have always gone to sea, and girls have waited for them."

"I'm not waiting for anybody."

"Sure you are. We all are. From the very beginning we wait for somebody, watch for them long before we know who they are. Sometimes we find the one we wait for, sometimes we don't. Sometimes the one we wait for comes along and we don't know it until too late. Sometimes they ask too much and we are afraid to take a chance, and they slip away."

"I wouldn't wait for anyone. Especially him. I wouldn't want him now."

"Of course not. If you saw him now, you'd wonder why you ever wanted him. You aren't waiting for him, though—you're waiting for what he represented. You knew a sailor once. Girls should never know men who have the sea in their blood."

"They always go away."

"Sure, and that's the way it should be. All the sorrow and tragedy in life come from trying to make things last too long."

"You're a cynic."

"All sentimentalists are cynics, and all Americans are sentimentalists. It's the Stephen Foster influence. Or too many showings of 'Over the Hill to the Poorhouse' and 'East Lynne.' But I like it that way."

"Do people really talk like this?"

"Only when they need coffee. Or maybe the first time a girl and a man meet. Or maybe this talk is a result of the saying good-bye influence. It's the same thing that makes women cry at the weddings of perfect strangers."

"You're a funny person." She turned to look at me.

"I boast of it. But how about that coffee? We shouldn't stand here much longer. People who lean on railings over water at night are either in love or contemplating suicide."

We started up the street. This was the sort of thing that made life interesting—meeting people. Especially attractive blondes at midnight.

Over the coffee she looked at me. "A girl who falls in love with a sailor is crazy."

"Not at all. A sailor always goes away, and then she doesn't have time to be disillusioned. Years later she can make her husband's life miserable telling him what a wonderful man so-and-so was. The chances are he was a fourteen-carat sap. Only he left before the new wore off."

"Is that what you do?"

"Very rarely. I know all the rules for handling women. The trouble is that at the psychological moment I forget to use them. It's depressing."

"It's getting late. I'm going to have to go home."

"Not alone, I hope."

She looked at me again, very coolly. "You don't think I'm the sort of girl you can just pick up, do you?"

"Of course not," I chuckled. "But I wished on a star out there. You know that old gag."

She laughed. "I think you're a fool."

"That cinches it. Women always fall in love with fools."

"You think it is so easy to fall in love as that?"

"It must be. Some people fall in love with no visible reason, either material, moral, or maternal. Anyway, why should it be so complicated?"

"Were you ever in love?"

"I think so. I'm not exactly sure. She was a wonderful cook, and if the way to a man's heart is through his stomach, this was a case of love at first bite."

"Do you ever take anything seriously?"

"I'm taking you seriously. But why not have a little fun with it? There's only one thing wrong with life: people don't love enough, they don't laugh enough—and they are too damned conventional. Even their love affairs are supposed to run true to form. But this is spontaneous. You walk down where the sailors are saying good-bye to their sweethearts be-cause you said good-bye to one once. It has been raining a little, and there is a sort of melancholy tenderness in the air. You are remembering the past, not because of him, because his face and personality have faded, but be-cause of the romance of saying good-bye, the smell of strange odors from foreign ports, the thoughts the ocean always brings to people—romance, color, distance. A sort of vague sadness that is almost a happiness. And then, accompanied by the sound of distant music and the perfume of fry-ing onions, I come into your life!"

She laughed again. "That sounds like a line."

"It is. Don't you see? When you went down to the landing tonight you were looking for me. You didn't know who I was, but you wanted something, someone. Well, here I am. The nice part of it is, I was look-ing for you."

"You make it sound very nice."

"Why not? A man who couldn't make it sound nice while looking at you would be too dull to live. Now finish your coffee and we'll go home."

"Now listen, I . . ."

"I know. Don't say it. But I'll just take you to the door, kiss you very nicely, and close it."

THERE HAD BEEN another shower, and the streets were damp. A fog was rolling from the ocean, the silent mist creeping in around the corners of the buildings, encircling the ships to the peaks of their masts. It was a lonely, silent world where the streetlights floated in ghostly radiance.

"You were wondering why men went to sea. Can't you imagine entering a strange, Far Eastern port on such a night as this? The lights of an unknown city—strange odors, mysterious sounds, the accents of a strange tongue? It's the charm of the strange and the different, of something new. Yet there's the feeling around you of something very old. Maybe that's why men go to sea."

"Maybe it is, but I'd never fall in love with another sailor."

"I don't blame you."

We had reached the door. She put her key in the lock, and we stepped in. It was very late, and very quiet. I took her in my arms, kissed her good-night, and closed the door.

"I thought you said you were going to say goodnight, and then go?" she protested.

"I said I was going to kiss you good night, and then close the door. I didn't say on which side of it I'd be."

"Well . . ."

The hell of it was my ship was sailing in the morning.

Thicker Than Blood

He had it coming if ever a man did, and I could have killed him then and nobody the wiser. If he had been man enough, we could have gone off on the dock and slugged it out, and everything would have been settled either way the cat jumped. There's nothing like a sock on the chin to sort of clean things up. It saves hard feelings and time wasted in argument. But Duggs was the chief mate, who wasn't man enough to whip me and knew it.

Bilge water, they say, is thicker than blood, and once men have been shipmates, no matter how much they hate each other's guts, they stand together against the world. That's the way it is supposed to be, but it certainly wasn't going to be that way with Duggs and me. I decided that in a hurry.

From the hour I shipped on that freighter, Duggs made it tough for me, but it wasn't only me but the whole crew. You don't mind so much if a really tough guy makes you like it, but when a two-by-twice scenery bum like Duggs rubs it in to you just because he has the authority, it just naturally hurts.

If we'd gone off on the dock where it was man to man, I'd have lowered the boom on his chin and left him for the gulls to pick over. But we were aboard ship, and if you sock an officer aboard ship, it's your neck.

Sometimes I think he laid awake nights figuring ways to be nasty, but maybe he didn't have to go to that much effort. I suspect it just came naturally. He made it rough for all of us but particularly me. Not that I didn't have my chances to cool him off. I had three of them. The first was at sea, the second in Port Swettenham, and the third—well, you'll hear about that.

Every dirty job he could find fell to Tony or me, and he could think of more ways to be unpleasant without trying than you could if you worked at it. Unless you have been at sea, you can't realize how infernally miserable it can become. There are a thousand little, insignificant things that can be done to make it miserable. Always something, and it doesn't have to be anything big. Often it is the little things that get under your skin, and the longer it lasts, the worse it gets.

Of course, the food was bad, but that was the steward's fault. Curry and rice and fried potatoes for three straight weeks. That was bad enough, but Duggs kept finding work for us to do after we were off watch. Emergencies, he called them, and you can't refuse duty in an emergency. There were men aboard that ship who would have killed Duggs for a Straits dollar. Me, I'm an easygoing guy, but it was getting to me.

One morning at four o'clock I was coming off watch. It was blowing like the bull of Barney, and a heavy sea running. Duggs had just come on watch, and he calls to me to go aft with him and lend a hand. The log line was fouled. Back we went, and the old tub was rolling her scuppers under, with seas breaking over her that left you gasping like a fish out of water, they were that cold.

We reeled in the log line, hand over hand, the wind tearing at our clothes, the deck awash. He did help some, I'll give him that, but it was me who did the heavy hauling, and it was me who cleared the little propeller on the patent log of seaweed and rope yarns.

Right there was the perfect opportunity. Nobody would have been surprised if we'd both been washed over the side, so it would have been no trick to have dumped him over the rail and washed my hands of him. Duggs had on sea boots and oilskins, and he would have gone down quick.

I finished the job, tearing skin from my hands and getting salt into the raw wounds, the ship plunging like a crazy bronco in a wild and tormented sea. Then, in the moment when I could have got him and got him good, he leaned over and shouted to be heard above the wind, "There! I'm sure glad *I* managed to get that done!"

And I was so mad I forgot to kill him.

The next time was in Port Swettenham. Duggs knew I had a girl in Singapore, but instead of letting me go ashore, he put me on anchor watch. All night long I stood by the rail or walked the deck, looking at the far-off lights of town and cussing the day I shipped on a barge with a louse-bound, scupper-jumping, bilge-swilling rat for mate. And my girl was ashore expecting me—at least, I hoped she was.

We sailed from Singapore, called at Baliwan and Penang, and finally we crawled up the river to Port Swettenham.

It was hot and muggy. Keeping cool was almost impossible, and I had only two changes of clothes for working. One of them I managed to keep clean to wear off watch; the other was stiff with paint and tar. When time allowed I'd wash the one set and switch. The mate deliberately waited one day until I'd changed into clean clothes, and then he called me.

We were taking on some liquid rubber, and down in the empty fuel-oil tank in the forepeak was a spot of water about as big as a pie plate. He told me to climb down fifteen feet of steel ladder covered with oil slime and sop up that water. Aside from being a complete mess before I'd reached the bottom, there was almost an even chance I'd slip and break a leg.

Forward we went together, then down in the forepeak, and stopped by the manhole that let one into the tank. He held up his flashlight, pointing out that dime's worth of water. I had a steel scraper in my hand, and when he leaned over that manhole, I thought what a sweet setup that was.

I could just bend that scraper over his head, drop him into the tank, put the hatch cover on, then go on deck and give them the high sign to start pumping rubber. There'd be a fuss when the mate turned up missing, but they'd never find him until they emptied the tank, and if I knew the old man, I knew he'd never pump the rubber out of that tank for a dozen mates. And just then Chips stuck his head down the hatch and yelled for Duggs.

Time passed, and we tied up in Brooklyn. I drew my pay and walked down the gangway to the dock. Then I turned and looked back.

From beginning to end that voyage had been plain, unadulterated hell, yet I hated to leave. When a guy lives on a ship that long, it begins to feel like home no matter how rough it is, and I had no other.

Six months I'd sailed on that packet, good weather and bad. Around the world we'd gone and in and out of some of the tiniest, dirtiest ports in the Far East. I'd helped to paint her from jack staff to rudder and stood four hours out of every twenty-four at her wheel across three oceans and a half-dozen seas. She was a scummy old barge, but as I stood there looking back, I had to cuss just to keep from feeling bad. Then I walked away.

After that there were other ships and other ports, some good and some bad, but I never forgot Duggs and swore the first time I found him ashore, I'd beat the hell out of him. Every time I'd see that company flag, and they had thirty-odd ships, I'd go hunting for Duggs. I knew that someday I'd find him.

One day in Portland I was walking along with a couple of guys, and I glimpsed that house flag over the top of a warehouse at the dock. Thinks I, now's my chance to get that mug; this will be him.

Sure enough, when I walked down the dock, there he was, giving the last orders before casting off and standing right at the foot of the gangway ready to board. It was now or never. I walked up, all set to cop a Sunday on his chin, and I say, "Remember me?"

He sized me up. "Why, sure! You're Duke, aren't you?" There'd been a time they called me that—among other things.

"That's me. And you—!"

"Well, well!" He was grinning all over. "What do you know about that? We were just talking about you the other day, and we were wondering what had become of you!

"Remember Jones? He's skipper on the *Iron Queen* now, and Edwards— he was third, you'll remember, he's with the *Bull Line*. They're all scattered now, but that was a good crew, and we came through a lot together. I'll never forget the night you hit that Swede in the Dato Kramat Gardens in Penang! Man, what a wallop that was! I'll bet he's out yet!

"Well," he says then, "I wish we could talk longer. It's like old times to see somebody from the old ship, and we came through, didn't we? We came through some of the roughest weather I ever did see, but we made it! And they say bilge water is thicker than blood. Well, so long, Duke, and good luck!"

Then Duggs stuck out his mitt, and I'll be damned if I didn't shake hands with him!

The Admiral

After I finished painting the hatch-combing, I walked back aft to the well deck where Tony and Dick were standing by the rail looking down into the Whangpoo. The sampan was there again, and the younger woman was sculling it in closer to the ship's side. When she stopped, the old woman fastened a net on the end of a long stick and held it up to the rail, and Tony put some bread and meat into it.

Every day they came alongside at about the same time, and we were always glad to see them, for we were lonely men. The young woman was standing in the stern as always, and when she smiled, there was something pleasant and agreeable about it that made us feel better. The old woman gave the kids some of the bread and meat, and we stood watching them.

Probably they didn't get meat very often, and bread must have been strange to them, but they ate it very seriously. They were our family, and they seemed to have adopted us just as we adopted them when they first came alongside at Wayside Pier. They had come to ask for "bamboo," which seemed to mean any kind of lumber or wood, and for "chow-chow," which was food, of course. The greatest prize was "soapo," but although most of the Chinese who live like that sell the soap or trade it, our family evidently used it—or some of it.

That was one reason we liked them, one reason they had become our family, because they were clean. They wore the faded blue that all the Chinese of that period seemed to wear, but theirs was always newly washed. We had thrown sticks of dunnage to them or other scrap lumber and some that wasn't scrap, but then the mate came by and made us stop.

There were five of them, the two women and three young ones, living in a sampan. Tony had never seen the like, nor had I, but it was old stuff to Dick, who had been out to the Far East before.

He told us lots of the Chinese lived that way, and some never got ashore from birth to death. There is no room for them on China's crowded soil, so in the seemingly ramshackle boats they grow up, rear families, and die without knowing any other home. There will be a fishnet on the roof of the shelter of matting, and on poles beyond the roof the family wash waves in the wind. Sometimes the younger children have buoys fastened to their backs so they will float if they fall over the side.

Two of the children in our family were girls. I have no idea how old they were. Youngsters, anyway. We never saw them any closer than from our rail to the sampan. They were queer little people, images of their mother and the old woman but more serious. Sometimes we'd watch them play by the hour when not working, and they would never smile or laugh. But it was the Admiral who was our favorite. We just called him that because we didn't know his name. He was very short and very serious. Probably he was five years old, but he might have been older or younger. He was a round-faced little tyke, and he regarded us very seriously and maybe a little wistfully, for we were big men, and our ship was high above the water.

We used to give them things. I remember when Tony came back from a spree and brought some chocolate with him. When he was painting over the side on a staging, he dropped it to the Admiral, who was very puzzled. Finally he tasted it and seemed satisfied. After that he tasted everything we dropped to him.

Tony had a red silk handkerchief he thought the world of, but one day he gave it to the Admiral. After that, whenever we saw the Admiral, he was wearing it around his head. But he was still very serious and maybe a little prouder.

Sometimes it used to scare me when I thought of them out there on the Whangpoo in the midst of all that shipping. Partly it was because the Chinese had a bad habit: they would wait till a ship was close by and then cut across her bows real sharp. Dick said they believed they could cut off evil spirits that were following them.

There were wooden eyes painted white with black pupils on either side of the bow of each sampan or junk. They were supposed to watch for rocks or evil spirits. Those eyes used to give me the willies, always staring that way, seeming to bulge in some kind of dumb wonder. I'd wake up at night remembering those eyes and wondering where the Admiral was.

But it got Tony more than me. Tony was a hard guy. He was said to have killed a cop in Baltimore and shipped out to get away. I always thought the old man knew, but he never said anything, and neither did the rest of us. It just wasn't any of our business, and we knew none of the circumstances. Something to do with payoffs, we understood.

Tony took to our family as if they were his own flesh and blood. I never saw a guy get so warmed up over anything. He was a tough wop, and he'd always been a hard case and probably never had anybody he could do for. That's what a guy misses when he's rambling around—not somebody to do something for him but somebody to think of, to work for.

One day when we were working over the side on a staging, the sampan came under us, and Tony turned to wave at the Admiral. "Lookit, Duke," he says to me, "ain't he the cute little devil? That red silk handkerchief sure sets him off."

It was funny, you know? Tony'd been a hard drinker, but after our family showed up, he began to leave it alone. After he gave that red silk handkerchief to the Admiral, he just quit drinking entirely, and when the rest of us went ashore, he'd stay aboard, lying in his bunk, making something for the Admiral.

Tony could carve. You'd have to see it to believe how good he was. Of course, in the old days of sail, men aboard ship carved or created all sorts of things, working from wood, ivory, or whatever came to hand. Tony began to carve out a model of our own ship, a tramp freighter from Wilmington. That was the night we left for Hong Kong and just a few hours after the accident.

We had been painting under the stern, hanging there on a plank staging, and it was a shaky business. The stern is always the worst place to paint because the stage is swinging loose underneath, and there isn't a thing to lay hold of but the ropes at either end.

Worse still, a fellow can't see where the ropes are made fast to the rail on the poop deck, and those coolies are the worst guys in the world for untying every rope they see knotted. One time at Taku Bar I got dropped into the harbor that way. But this time it was no trouble like that. It was worse.

We were painting almost overhead when we heard somebody scream. Both of us turned so quickly we had to grab the ropes at either end to keep from falling, and when we got straightened around, we saw the Admiral in the water.

Our family had been coming toward our ship when somehow the Admiral had slipped and fallen over the side, and now there he was, buoyed up by the bladder fastened to his shoulders, the red handkerchief still on his head. Probably that had happened a dozen times before, but this time a big Dollar liner was coming upstream, and she was right abeam of us when the Admiral fell. And in a minute more he'd be sucked down into those whirling propeller blades.

Then the plank jerked from under my feet, and I fastened to that rope with both hands, and I felt my heart jump with sudden fear. For a minute or so I had no idea what had happened, and by the time I could pull myself up and get my feet on the staging again, Tony was halfway to the Admiral and swimming like I'd seen nobody swim before.

It was nip and tuck, and you can believe it when I say I didn't draw a breath until Tony grabbed the Admiral just as the big liner's stern hove up, the water churning furiously as she was riding high in the water. Tony's head went down, and both he and the Admiral disappeared in the swirl of water that swept out in a wake behind the big liner.

There was a moment there when they were lost in the swirl of water behind the steamer, and then we saw them, and Tony was swimming toward the sampan towing the Admiral, who had both hands on Tony's shoulder.

That night when we slipped down the Whangpoo for Hong Kong, Tony started work on his boat. For we were coming back. We had discharged our cargo and were heading south to pick up more, and by the time we returned, there would be cargo in Shanghai for us.

You'd never guess how much that boat meant to us. All the time we were gone, we thought about our family, and each of us picked up some little thing in Hong Kong or Kowloon to take back to them. But it was the carving of the boat that occupied most of our time. Not that we helped because we didn't. It was Tony's job, and he guarded it jealously, and none of us could have done it half so well.

We watched him carve the amidships house and shape the ventilators, and we craned our necks and watched when he fastened a piece of wire in place as the forestay. When one of us would go on watch, the mate would ask how the boat was coming. Everybody on the ship from the old man to the black cook from Georgia knew about the ship Tony was carving, and everyone was interested.

Once the chief mate stopped by the fo'c'sle to examine it and offer a suggestion, and the second mate got to telling me about the time his little boy ran his red fire engine into the preacher's foot. Time went by so fast it seemed no time at all till we were steaming back up the Whangpoo again to anchor at Wayside Pier. We were watching for our family long before they could have seen us.

The next morning the boat was finished, and Chips took it down to the paint locker and gave it a coat of paint and varnish, exactly like our own ship; the colors were the same and everything. There wasn't much of a hold, but we had stuffed it with candy. Then we watched for the sampan.

Dick was up on the crosstree of the mainmast when he saw it, and he came down so fast it was a crying wonder he didn't break a leg. When he hit the deck, he sprinted for the rail. In a few minutes we were all standing there, only nobody was saying anything.

It was the sampan. Only it was bottom up now and all stove in. There wasn't any mistaking it, for we'd have known that particular sampan anywhere even if it hadn't been for the red silk handkerchief. It was there now, a little flag, fluttering gallantly from the wreckage.

Shanghai, Not Without Gestures

She came in from the street and stood watching the auction, a slender girl with great dark eyes and a clear, creamy complexion. It was raining outside on Kiangse Road, and her shoes were wet. From time to time she shifted uncomfortably and glanced about. Once her eyes met mine, and I smiled, but she looked quickly away, watching the auction.

There was always an auction somewhere, it seemed. One day it might be on Range Road or somewhere along the Route Frelupt, tomorrow in Kelmscott Garden. Household effects, usually, for people were always coming or going. The worlds of international business, diplomacy, and the armed services are unstable, and there is much shifting about, from station to station, often without much warning.

I knew none of these people, being an outsider in Shanghai and contented to be so, for a writer, even when a participant, must also be the observer. As yet I was not a writer, only someone wishing to be and endlessly working toward that end.

There were beautiful things to be seen, Soochow curtains, brass-topped tea tables, intricately carved chests of drawers, even sometimes swords or scimitars with jeweled hilts or the handmade guns of long ago. I used to imagine stories about them and wonder what sort of people had owned them before. It wasn't much of a pastime, but they were dark days, and it was all I could afford.

The girl interested me more. Reading or thinking stories is all right, but living them is better. This girl had obviously not come to buy. She had come to get in out of the rain, to find a place to sit down. Probably it was cold in her rooms.

Rooms? No—more likely just one room, a small place with a few simple things. Some worn slippers, a Japanese silk kimono, and on the old-fashioned dresser would be a picture—a man, of course. He would be an army or naval officer, grave and attractive.

By the way she seemed to be moving her toes inside her shoes and bit her lower lip from time to time, I knew she was tired of walking and her feet were sore.

When I tried to move closer to her, she noticed it and got up to go. I was persistent. There was a story here that I knew well. I had often lived it. When she stepped into the rain, I was beside her.

"Wet, isn't it?" I said, hoping to hear her voice, but she hurried on, turning her face away and ignoring me.

"Please," I said, "I'm not being fresh. I'm just lonely. Weren't you ever lonely?"

She started to walk slower and glanced at me. Her eyes were dark and even larger than I had thought. She smiled a little, and she had a lovely mouth. "Yes," she said, "I am often lonely."

"Would you like some coffee?" I suggested. "Or tea? What does one drink in Shanghai?"

"Almost everything," she said, and laughed a little. She seemed surprised at the laugh and looked so self-conscious I knew she was hungry. Once you have been very hungry you know the signs in someone else. It makes you feel very different. "But I would like some coffee," she admitted.

We found a little place several blocks away run by a retired French army officer and his wife. We sat down and looked across the table at each other. Her dark suit was a little shabby but neat, and she was obviously tired. I have become sensitive to such things.

There was the slightest bit of an accent in her voice that intrigued me, but I could not place it. I have heard many accents, but I was younger then, and that was the other Shanghai before the guns of Nippon blasted Chapei into smoking ruins and destroyed the fine tempo of life.

"You are new here?" she asked. "You don't belong here?"

"I have just come," I said, "but I belong nowhere."

"Then you must be at home. Nobody belongs in Shanghai. Everyone is either just going or just arriving."

"You?" I suggested.

She shrugged a shoulder. "I am like you. I belong nowhere. Perhaps Shanghai more than anywhere else because it is a city of passersby. Not even the Chinese belong here because this city was started for Europeans. It was only a mud flat then."

She moved her feet under the table, and I heard them squish. She had been walking a long time, and her feet were soaked.

"I'm part Russian, but I was born in Nanking. My grandfather left Russia at the time of the Revolution, and for a time they lived in Siberia. There was an order for his arrest, and he escaped over the border with his wife and children. She was French. He met her in Paris when he was a military attaché there.

"I am told he had a little money, but he could never seem to find a place, and the money disappeared. My father was an interpreter in Peking and then in Nanking."

She sipped her coffee, and we ordered sandwiches. This time there was money enough, and for once I had more in prospect. "He knew nothing about the Revolution or the tsar's government and cared less. Everyone talked politics in Peking—all the Russians did, at least. So he came to Nanking where I was born."

"An interesting man. I thought only grand dukes left Russia. What did he do then?"

"My grandfather died and left him whatever there was. For a time we lived very well, and my father drank."

The sandwiches came, and it was several minutes before she touched one, then a small bite only, which she took a long time chewing. I knew the signs, for when one is hungry, it is the taste one wants. In the movies, when they portray a hungry man, he is always gulping down his food, which is entirely false. It is not at all that way, for when one has been truly hungry for some time, the stomach has shrunk, and one can eat but a little at a time. Only in the days after that first meal can one truly eat, and then there is never enough.

"What did he drink?" I asked.

"Fine old Madeira at first. And port. He would sit in the cafes and talk of Tolstoi and Pushkin or of Balzac. He was a great admirer of Balzac. Father had always wished to become a writer, but he only talked of it. He could never seem to sit down and do it."

"There are thousands like him. If one wishes to be a writer, one shouldn't talk about it, one should do it."

"Then he could not afford such wines. He drank vodka then, and finally samshu or Hanskin."

The decline and fall of a refined palate. "And then he died?"

She nodded, but I had known that it had to be. For a man to sink from fine old Madeira to Hanskin—after that there is nothing to do but die.

Our coffee was finished. I looked into the cup, made a mental calculation, and decided against ordering another. "Shall we go?" I suggested.

The rain had resolved itself into a fine mist, and streetlights were glowing through the fog that was coming in off the river. It would be this way all night. She hesitated, glanced quickly at me, and held out her hand. "I'd better go."

I took her hand. "Why not come with me? It's going to be an unpleasant night." Her eyes met mine, and she looked quickly away. "Why not?" I said. "It isn't all that much of a place, but it's warm."

"All right," she said.

We walked rapidly. It was not going to be a nasty night; it was already one. A taxi skidded around a corner throwing a shower of spray that only just missed us. A rickshaw passed, going the other way, its curtains drawn. I was glad when we reached the door.

For myself it did not matter. Sometimes I walked for hours in the rain, but she was not dressed warm, and the rain was cold and miserable. The Shanghai streets were not a place to be at night and alone.

My place was warm. My boy was gone. I called him my "number-only" boy. I told him when he took the job he couldn't be the "number-one" boy because there would not be a number two, three, or four.

It was not just a room but a small apartment, pleasant in a way. Drifting men have a way of fixing up almost any place they stop to make it comfortable. Seamen often fix things up like any old maid might do and for much the same reason.

Yet the apartment was not mine. I'd been given the use of it by a Britisher who was up-country now. His name was Haig, and he came and went a good deal with no visible means of support, and I was told that he often stayed up-country months at a time. He had been an officer in one of the Scottish regiments, I believe. I had a suspicion that he was still involved in some kind of duty, although he had many weird Asiatic connections.

Some of the books were mine, and it pleased me when she went to the books immediately. It always makes a sucker out of a man who truly loves books to see someone taking a genuine interest in them.

Later, when she came out of the shower wearing my robe, her eyes were very bright. I hadn't realized she was so pretty. We sat by the fire, watching the coals.

"Lose your job?" I asked finally.

"Two weeks ago, and it came at a bad time. My rent was up last week, and there is always a demand for lodgings here. This morning they said not to come back unless I could pay."

"That's tough. What's your line?"

"I've done a lot of things. A secretary, usually. I can handle five languages very well and two others a little. I worked for Moran and Company in Tientsin, and then here for a transport firm, but lately there has been so little business, and the owner has been gambling. I don't know what I'm going to do."

Outside was China. Outside was Shanghai, the old Shanghai when it was an international city. Outside were the millions, of all nationalities. French, English, Japanese, Dutch, German, Sikh, Portuguese, Hebrew, Greek, Malay, and of course, Chinese. Outside was the Whangpoo, a dark river flowing out of China, out of old China and into the new, then down to the sea. Outside rivers of men flowed along the dark streets, men buying and selling, men fighting and gambling, men bargaining and selling, loving and dying. Millions of men, women, and children, opening countless doors, going into lives of which I knew nothing, eating the food of many countries, speaking in tongues I had never heard, praying to many gods.

Listening to her as she spoke of China, I remembered the shuffle of feet in the noontime streets. There was nothing I could do. It was bad for a man to be broke but so much worse for a woman. Especially for such a girl as this.

Perhaps I was a fool, but I, too, had been hungry. Soon there would be a ship, and I would go to Bombay or Liverpool or New York, while she—

"You wouldn't have come had there been any other place to go, would you?"

"No."

A lock of her dark hair had fallen against my robe. It looked good there. So black against the soft white of her throat.

"But I am grateful. What could I have done?"

Well, what? I had a feeling I was going to make a fool of myself. Americans are a sentimental lot, and every cynic is a sentimentalist under the skin. I knew enough about women to be skeptical but had been hungry enough to be human.

A wind moaned about the eaves, and rain dashed against the window.

"Listen," I said, "this isn't quite the sporting thing, is it? To have you come here because there was nowhere else to go and because I bought you a cup of coffee? Or maybe because of breakfast in the morning? I don't like the sound of it.

"Well, hell, I'm going to sleep on the sofa, and you can have the other room."

After the door closed, I stood looking at it. If she hadn't been so damned lovely it would have been easier to be gallant. Probably right now she was thinking what a sap I was. Well, she wouldn't be the only one.

I had a feeling I was going to be sorry for this in the morning.

The Man Who Stole Shakespeare

When I had been in Shanghai but a few days, I rented an apartment in a narrow street off Avenue Edward VII where the rent was surprisingly low. The door at the foot of the stairs opened on the street beside a moneychanger's stall, an inconspicuous place that one might pass a dozen times a day and never notice.

At night I would go down into the streets and wander about or sit by my window and watch people going about their varied business. From my corner windows I could watch a street intersection and an alleyway, and there were many curious things to see, and for one who finds his fellow man interesting, there was much to learn.

Late one afternoon when a drizzle of despondent rain had blown in from the sea, I decided to go out for coffee. Before reaching my destination, it began to pour, so I stepped into a bookstore for shelter.

This store dealt in secondhand books published in several languages and was a jumble of stacks, piles, and racks filled with books one never saw elsewhere and was unlikely to see again. I was hitch reading from Sterne when I saw him.

He was a small man and faded. His face had the scholarly expression that seems to come from familiarity with books, and he handled them tenderly. One could see at a glance that here was a man who knew a good book when he saw one, with a feeling for attractive format as well as content.

Yet when I glanced up, he was slipping a book into his pocket. Quickly, with almost a sense of personal guilt, I looked toward the clerk, but he was watching the rain. The theft had passed unobserved.

Now there is a sort of sympathy among those who love books, an understanding that knows no bounds of race, creed, or financial rating. If a man steals a necktie, he is a thief of the worst stripe. If he steals a car, nothing is too bad for him. But a man who steals a book is something else—unless it is my book.

My first thought when he slipped the book into his pocket was to wonder what book he wanted badly enough to steal. Not that there are only a few books worth stealing, for there are many. Yet I was curious. What, at the moment, had captured his interest? This small, gentle-seeming man with the frayed shirt collar and the worn topcoat?

When he left, I walked over to the place where the book had been and tried to recall what it might have been, for I had only just checked that shelf myself. Then I remembered.

It had been a slim, one-play-to-the-volume edition of Shakespeare. He had also examined Hakluyt's *Voyages,* or at least one volume of the set, Huysmans's *Against the Grain,* and Burton's *Anatomy of Melancholy.*

This was definitely a man I wished to know. Also, I was curious. Which play had he stolen? Was it the play itself he wished to read? Or was it for some particular passage in the play? Or to complete a set?

Turning quickly, I went to the door, and barely in time. My man was just disappearing in the direction of Thibet Road, and I started after him, hurrying.

At that, I almost missed him. He was just rounding a corner a block away, so he had been running, too. Was it the rain or a feeling of guilt?

The rain had faded into a drizzle once more. My man kept on, walking rapidly, but fortunately for me, he was both older than I, and his legs were not as long.

Whether he saw me, I do not know, but he led me a lively chase. It seemed scarcely possible for a man to go up and down so many streets, and he obviously knew Shanghai better than I. Yet suddenly he turned into an alley and dodged down a basement stairway. Following him, I got my foot in the door before he could close it.

He was frightened, and I could understand why. In those wilder years they found several thousand bodies on the street every year, and he perhaps had visions of adding his own to the list. Being slightly over six feet and broad in the shoulder, I must have looked dangerous in that dark passageway. Possibly he had visions of being found in the cold light of dawn with a slit throat, for such things were a common occurrence in Shanghai.

"Here!" he protested. "You can't do this!" That I was doing it must have been obvious. "I'll call an officer!"

"And have to explain that volume of Shakespeare in your pocket?" I suggested.

That took the wind out of him, and he backed into the room, a neat enough place, sparsely furnished except for the books. The walls were lined with them.

"Now see here," I said, "you've nothing to worry about. I don't intend to report you, and I'm not going to rob you. I'm simply interested in books and in the books people want enough to steal."

"You're not from the bookstore?"

"Nothing of the kind. I saw you slip the book into your pocket, and although I did not approve, I was curious as to what you had stolen and why." I held out my hand. "May I see?"

He shook his head, then stood back and watched me, finally taking off his coat. He handed me the book from his pocket, which was a copy of *Henry IV,* bound in gray cloth with a thin gold line around the edges. The book was almost new and felt good to the hands. I turned the pages, reading a line or two. "You've a lot of books," I said, glancing at the shelves. "May I look?"

He nodded, then stepped back and sat down. He certainly was not at ease, and I didn't blame him.

The first book I saw was Wells's *Outline of History.* "Everybody has that one," I commented.

"Yes," he said hesitantly.

Ibsen was there, and Strindberg, Chekhov, and Tolstoi. A couple of volumes by Thomas Hardy were wedged alongside three by Dostoevsky. There were books by Voltaire, Cervantes, Carlyle, Goldoni, Byron, Verlaine, Baudelaire, Cabell, and Hume.

The next book stopped me short, and I had to look again to make sure the bookshelf wasn't kidding. It was a quaint, old-fashioned, long-out-of-date *Home Medical Advisor* by some Dr. Felix Peabody, published by some long-extinct publisher whose state of mind must have been curious, indeed.

"Where in the world did you get this?" I asked. "It seems out of place stuck in between Hegel and Hudson."

He smiled oddly, his eyes flickering to mine and then away. He looked nervous, and since then I have often wondered what he must have been thinking and what went through his mind at that moment.

Scanning the shelves to take stock of what his interests were, I came upon another queer one. It was between Laurence Sterne's *Sentimental Journey* and George Gissing's *Private Papers of Henry Ryecroft.* It was *Elsie's Girlhood.*

After that I had to sit down. This man was definitely some kind of a nut. I glanced at him, and he squirmed a little. Evidently he had seen my surprise at the placement of some of the books or the fact that he had them at all.

"You must read a lot," I suggested. "You've a lot of good books here."

"Yes," he said; then he leaned forward, suddenly eager to talk. "It's nice to have them. I just like to own them, to take them in my hands and turn them over and to know that so much that these men felt, saw, thought, and understood is here. It is almost like knowing the men themselves."

"It might be better," I said. "Some of these men were pretty miserable in themselves, but their work is magnificent."

He started to rise, then sat down again suddenly as though he expected me to order him to stay where he was.

"Do you read a lot?" he asked.

"All the time," I said. "Maybe even too much. At least when I have books or access to them."

"My eyes"—he passed a hand over them—"I'm having trouble with my glasses. I wonder if you'd read to me sometime? That is," he added hastily, "if you have the time."

"That's the one thing I've plenty of," I said. "At least until I catch a ship. Sure I'll read to you."

As a matter of fact, he had books here to which I'd heard all my life but had found no chance to read. "If you want, I'll read some right now."

It was raining outside, and I was blocks from my small apartment. He made coffee, and I read to him, starting with *The Return of the Native* for no reason other than that I'd not read it and it was close at hand. Then I read a bit from *Tales of Mean Streets* and some from Locke's *Essay Concerning Human Understanding*.

Nearly every day after that I went to see Mr. Meacham. How he made his living, I never knew. He had some connection, I believe, with one of the old trading companies, for he seemed very familiar with the interior of China and with people there.

The oddity of it appealed to some irony in my sense of humor. A few weeks before I'd been coiling wet lines on the forecastle head of a tramp steamer, and now here I was, reading to this quaint old gentleman in his ill-fitting suit.

He possessed an insatiable curiosity about the lives of the authors and questioned me about them by the hour. That puzzled me, for a reader just naturally acquires some such knowledge just by reading the bookjackets, and in the natural course of events a man can learn a good deal about the personal lives of authors. However, he seemed to know nothing about them and was avid for detail.

There was much about him that disturbed me. He was so obviously alone, seemingly cut off from everything. He wasn't bold enough to make friends, and there seemed to be no reason why anybody should take the trouble to know him. He talked very little, and I never did know where he had come from or how he happened to be in such a place as Shanghai, for he was a contradiction to everything one thinks of when one considers Shanghai. You could imagine him in Pittsburgh, St. Louis, or London, in Glasgow or Peoria, but never in such a place as this.

One day when I came in, I said, "Well, you name it. What shall I read today?"

He hesitated, flushed, then took a book from the shelf and handed it to me. It was *Elsie's Girlhood,* a book of advice to a young girl about to become a woman.

For a minute I thought he was kidding, and then I was sure it couldn't be anything else. "Not today," I said. "I'll try Leacock."

When I remembered it afterward, I remembered he had not seemed to be kidding. He had been perfectly serious and obviously embarrassed when I put him off so abruptly. He hesitated, then put the book away, and when I returned the next day, the book was no longer on the shelf. It had disappeared.

It was that day that I guessed his secret. I was reading at the time, and it just hit me all of a sudden. It left me completely flabbergasted, and for a moment I stared at the printed page from which I was reading, my mouth open for words that would not come.

Yes, I told myself, that had to be it. There was no other solution. All the pieces suddenly fell into place, the books scattered together without plan or style, with here and there books that seemed so totally out of place and unrelated.

That night I read later than ever before.

Then I got a job. Dou Yu-seng offered to keep the rent paid on my apartment (I always suspected he owned the building) while I took care of a little job up the river. I knew but little about him but enough to know of affiliations with various war lords and at least one secret society. However, what I was to do was legitimate.

Yet when I left, I kept thinking of old Mr. Meacham. He would be alone again, with nobody to read to him.

Alone? Remembering those walls lined with books, I knew he would never actually be alone. They were books bought here and there, books given him by people moving away, books taken from junk heaps, but each one of them represented a life, somebody's dream, somebody's hope or idea, and all were there where he could touch them, feel them, know their presence.

No, he would not be alone, for he would remember Ivan Karamazov, who did not want millions but an answer to his questions. He would remember those others who would people his memories and walk through the shadows of his rooms: *Jean Valjean, Julien Sorel, Mr. John Oakhurst,* gambler, and, of course, the little man who was *the friend of Napoleon.*

He knew line after line from the plays and sonnets of Shakespeare and a lot of Keats, Kipling, Li Po, and *Kasidah*. He would never really be alone now.

He never guessed that I knew, and probably for years he had hidden his secret, ashamed to let anyone know that he, who was nearly seventy and who so loved knowledge, had never learned to read.

The Dancing Kate

It was a strip of grayish-yellow sand caught in the gaunt fingers of the reef like an upturned belly except here and there where the reef had been longest above the sea. Much of the reef was drying, and elsewhere the broken teeth of the coral formed ugly ridges flanked by a few black, half-submerged boulders.

At one end of the bar the stark white ribs of an old ship thrust themselves from the sand, and nearby lay the rusting hulk of an iron freighter. It had been there more than sixty years.

For eighteen miles in a northeast and southwest direction the reef lay across the face of the Coral Sea. At its widest, no more than three miles but narrowing to less than a mile. A strip of jagged coral and white water lost in the remote emptiness of the Pacific. The long dun swells of the sea hammered against the outer rocks, and overhead the towering vastness of the sky became a shell of copper with the afternoon sun.

At the near end of the bar, protected from the breaking seas in all but a hurricane, a hollow of rock formed a natural cistern. In the bottom were a few scant inches of doubtful water. Beside it, he squatted in torn dungarees and battered sneakers.

"Three days," he estimated, staring into the cistern, eyes squinting against the surrounding glare. "Three days if I'm careful, and after that I'm washed up."

After that—thirst. The white, awful glare of the tropical sun, a parched throat, baking flesh, a few days or hours of delirium, and then a long time of lying wide-eyed to the sky before the gulls and the crabs finished the remains.

He had no doubt as to where he was. The chart had been given him in Port Darwin and was worn along the creases, but there was no crease where this reef lay, hence no doubt of his position. He was sitting on a lonely reef, avoided by shipping, right in the middle of nowhere. His position was approximately 10°45' S, 155°51' E.

The nearest land was eighty-two miles off and it might as well be eighty-two thousand.

It started with the gold. The schooner on which he had been second mate had dropped anchor in Bugoiya Harbor, but it was not fit anchorage, so they could remain only a matter of hours. He was on the small wharf superintending the loading of some cargo when a boy approached him.

He was a slender native boy with very large, beautiful eyes. When the boy was near him, he spoke, not looking at him. "Man say you come. Speak nobody."

"Come? Come where?"

"You come. I show you."

"I'm busy, boy. I don't want a girl now."

"No girl. Man die soon. He say *please,* you come?"

Dugan looked at his watch. They were loading the last cargo now, but they would not sail for at least an hour.

"How far is it?"

"Ten minutes—you see."

A man was dying? But why come to him? Still, in these islands odd things were always happening, and he was a curious man.

The captain was coming along the wharf, and he walked over to him. "Cap? Something's come up. This boy wants to take me to some man who is dying. Says not to say anything, and he's only ten minutes away."

Douglas glanced at the boy, then at his watch. "All right, but we've less than an hour. If we leave before you get back, we'll be several days at Woodlark or Murua or whatever they call it. There's a man in a village who is a friend of mine. Just ask for Sam. He will sail you over there."

"No need for that. I'll be right back."

Douglas glanced at him, a faint humor showing. "Dugan, I've been in these islands for fifty years. A man never knows—never."

Misima, although only about twenty miles long and four or five miles wide, was densely wooded, and the mountains lifted from a thousand to three thousand feet, and as the south side was very steep, most of the villages were along the northern shore.

The boy had walked off and was standing near a palm tree idly tossing stones into the lagoon. Taking off his cap, he walked away from the wharf, wiping the sweat from his brow. He walked back from the shore and then turned and strolled toward the shade, pausing occasionally. The boy had disappeared under the trees.

At the edge of the trees Dugan sat down, leaning his back against one. After a moment a stone landed near his foot, and he glimpsed the boy behind a tree about thirty yards off. Dugan got up, stretched, and hands in his pockets, strolled along in the shade, getting deeper and deeper until he saw the boy standing in a little-used path.

They walked along for half a mile. Dugan glanced at his watch. He would have to hurry.

Suddenly the boy ducked into the brush, holding a branch aside for him. About thirty yards away he saw a small shanty with a thin column of smoke lifting it. The boy ran ahead, leading the way.

There was a young woman there who, from her looks, was probably the boy's mother. Inside, an old man lay on an army cot. His eyes were sunken into his head, and his cheeks were gaunt. He clutched Dugan's hand. His fingers were thin and clawlike. "You must help me. You are with Douglas?"

"I am."

"Good! He is honest. Everybody knows that of him. I need your help." He paused for a minute, his breathing hoarse and labored. "I have a granddaughter. She is in Sydney." He put his hand on a coarse brown sack under his cot. "She must have this."

"What is it?"

"It is gold. There are men here who will steal it when I die. It must go to my granddaughter. You take it to her, and you keep half. You will do this?"

Sydney? He was not going to Sydney; still, one could sell it and send the money to Sydney. He pressed a paper into his hand. "Her name and address. Get it to her—somehow. You can do it. You will do it."

"Look," he protested, "I am not going to Sydney. When I leave Douglas, I'm going to Singapore and catch a ship for home—or going on to India."

"You must! They will steal it. They have tried, and they are waiting. If they think you have it, they will rob you. I know them."

"Well." He hesitated. He had to be getting back. Douglas's appointment at Woodlark was important to him. He would wait for no man in such a case, least of all for me, who had been with him only a few weeks, the man thought. "All right, give me the gold. I've little time."

The woman dragged the sack from under the cot, and he stooped to lift it. It was much heavier than it appeared. The old man smiled. "Gold is always heavy, my friend. Too heavy for many men to bear."

Dugan straightened and took the offered hand; then he walked out of the shack, carrying the gold.

It *was* heavy. Once aboard the schooner it would be no problem. He glanced at his watch and swore. He was already too late, and the tide—

When he reached the small harbor, it was too late. The schooner was gone!

He stood, staring. Immediately he was apprehensive. He was left on an island with about two dozen white people of whom he knew nothing and some fifteen hundred natives of whom he knew less. Moreover, there was always a drifting population, off the vessels of one kind or another that haunt Indonesian seas.

Woodlark was eighty miles away. He knew that much depended on the schooner being there in time to complete a deal for cargo that otherwise would go to another vessel. He had been left behind. He was alone.

A stocky bearded man approached. He wore dirty khakis, a watch cap, and the khaki coat hung loose. Did he have a gun? Dugan would have bet that he had.

From descriptions he was sure he knew the man.

"Looks like they've gone off and left you," he commented, glancing at the sack.

"They'll be back."

"Douglas? Don't bet on it. He calls in here about once every six months. Sometimes it's a whole year."

"It's different this time," he lied. "He's spending about three months in the Louisiades and Solomons. He expects to be calling in here three or four times, so I'll just settle down and wait."

"We could make a deal," the man said. "I could sail you to the Solomons." He jerked his head. "I've got a good boat, and I often take the trip. Come along."

"Why? When he's coming back here?"

Deliberately he turned his back and walk away. Zimmerman—this would be Zimmerman.

At the trade store they told him where he could find Sam, and he found him, a wiry little man with sad blue eyes and thin hair. He shook his head. "I have to live here."

"Douglas said—"

"I can imagine. I like Douglas. He's one of the best men in the islands, but he doesn't live here. I do. If you get out of here, you'll do it on your own. I can tell you something else. Nobody will take the chance. You make a deal with them, or you wait until Douglas comes back."

Twice he saw the boy, and he was watching him. He lingered near the trees where he'd been when he first followed him, so he started back. He'd have to see the old man, and packing that gold was getting to be a nuisance.

When he got back to the shack, the woman was at the door, mashing something in a wooden dish. "He's dying," she said. "He hasn't talked since you left."

"Who is it?" The voice was very weak.

He went inside and told the old man he would have to leave his gold. The schooner was gone, and he had no way to get to Woodlark and overtake her.

"Take my boat," he said.

His eyes closed, and nothing Dugan said brought any response. And Dugan tried. He wanted to get away, but he wanted no more of his gold. From Sam's manner he knew Zimmerman was trouble, very serious trouble.

The woman was standing there. "He is dying," she said.

"He has a boat?"

She pointed and he walked through the trees to the shore. It was there, tied up to a small dock. It wasn't much of a boat, and they'd make a fit pair, for he wasn't much of a small-boat sailor. His seamanship had been picked up on freighters and one tanker, and his time in sail was limited to a few weeks where somebody else was giving orders. He'd done one job of single handing with a small boat and been shot with luck. On one of the most dangerous seas he had experienced nothing but flying-fish weather all the way. Still, it was only eighty miles to Woodlark, and if the weather remained unchanged, he'd be all right. If—

The boy was there. "Three of them," he said, "three mans—very bad mans." And then he added, "They come tonight, I think."

So how much of a choice did he have? He left at dark or before dark, or he stayed and took a chance on being murdered or killing somebody. Anyway, the sea was quiet, only a little breeze running, and eighty miles was nothing.

The best way to cope with trouble was to avoid it, to stay away from where trouble was apt to be.

The only thing between where he was and Woodlark were the Alcesters. He had sailed by them before and would know them when he saw them.

He glanced down at the boy. "I'll leave the boat on Woodlark."

The boy shrugged. "Wherever."

He had shoved off at sundown with a good breeze blowing, and even with his caution he made good time, or what was good time for him. He had the Alcesters abeam before daybreak, but there was a boat behind him that was coming on fast. His silhouette was low, so he lowered the sail a little to provide even less and gradually eased the helm over and slid in behind one of the Alcesters.

It was nearing daylight, but suddenly it began to grow darker, and the wind began blowing in little puffs, and there was a brief spatter of rain. He was running before the wind when the storm came, and from that time on it was sheer panic. On the second or third day—he could not remember which—he piled up on the reef, a big wave carrying the boat over into the lagoon, ripping the hull open somewhere en route.

When daylight came again, the storm was blowing itself out; the boat was gone but for a length of broken mast and a piece of the forward section that contained a spare sail, some line, and some odds and ends of canned goods. And the gold.

He had saved the gold.

Dawn was a sickly thing on that first morning, with the northern sun remote behind gray clouds. He made his way along the reef, avoiding the lacerating edges of the coral until he reached the bar.

The old freighter, one mast still standing and a gaping hole in her hull, was high and dry on the sandbar. A flock of gulls rose screaming into the air as he approached, and he walked over the soft sand into the hole.

The deck above him was solid and strong. Far down there was a hatch, its cover stove in, which allowed a little light at the forward end. Here all was secure. Sand had washed in, making a hard-packed floor. Dugan put down a tin of biscuits and the few cans he had brought along and went back outside.

It was just one hundred and fifty steps to the water of the lagoon and the hollow in the reef where rain had collected in the natural cistern. The hollow in the reef was just three feet deep and about the size of a washtub. It was half full, and the water, although fresh, was warm.

For the moment he had food, shelter, and water.

Gathering driftwood, of which there was a good bit, he built a shade over the cistern that would prevent a too rapid evaporation but could be removed when it rained.

There would be fish, shellfish, and crabs. For a time there might be eggs, and the first thing he must do would be to cover the reef, as much of it as he could reach, and see what he could find that was useful. Then he must get a fragment of that torn canvas and make a pennant to fly from the mast of the wrecked ship.

The work kept him busy. Scrambling over the reef, careful not to slip into a hole or break an ankle on the rough, often slippery rock, he gathered driftwood. Slowly the several piles grew.

At night he sat beside his fire in the hulk and ate fish and a biscuit.

After a while he lost all awareness of the sea. It was there, all around him, and it was empty. Occasionally, when his eyes strayed that way, he saw distant smoke. He rarely looked at the sack of gold.

For the first time he deliberately faced his situation. From his pocket he took the worn chart, but he did not need it to face the fact. The reef was a lonely, isolated spot in the Coral Sea, in an area where ships came but rarely. Aside from the sandbar itself there was only the ruffled water and a few black stumps of coral rising above it.

This was no place for a man. It was a place for the wind and the gulls, yet there was a little water, there was a little food, and while a man lived, there was always a chance. It was then that he looked up and saw the schooner.

It was tacking, taking a course that would bring it closer to the reef. He shouted and waved a hand, and somebody waved back. He turned and walked toward the wreck.

When the dinghy came in close to pick him up, he waded out and lifted his bag of gold into the boat. Then he climbed in. There were two men in the dinghy, and they stared at him. "My—my water—it was about gone. You came just in time."

The men stared at the sack, then at him. The place where the sack rested against the thwart had dented the sack. Only sand or flour or something of the kind would make such an impression. And the sack had been heavy. He couldn't say it was shells or clothing. They'd know he lied.

Yet it was not until he came alongside the schooner that he realized how much trouble he had bought for himself. He glanced at the schooner's name and felt a chill.

The *Dancing Kate*.

Bloody Jack Randall's schooner. Of course, he was never called Bloody Jack to his face, but behind his back they knew him by that name. He had killed a man in a saloon brawl at Port Moresby. There'd been a man shot in Kalgoorlie, but insufficient evidence released Randall. He was reported to have broken jail in New Caledonia after killing a guard.

After he was aboard, it was Randall's mate, a lean, wiry man with haggard features, who kicked the sack. "Hey? What you got in there? It looks mighty heavy."

"Gold."

It was a sullen, heavy day with thick clouds overhead and a small sea running. Kahler's eyes went to the sack again. "Gold?" He was incredulous.

"Yes." He slid his knife into his hand, point toward them, cutting edge uppermost. "This weighs about a pound. I measured the weight by this, and it is more than they thought."

"They?"

"A man in Misima asked me to deliver it to his granddaughter in Sydney."

"What kind of a damned fool would do that?" Kahler asked.

"A man who knew who he could trust." He glanced at Randall. "Where you bound?"

Randall hesitated. "East," he said finally. "We been scouting around."

"How about Woodlark? I'll pay my passage."

"All right." Randall walked forward and gave the change of course to the Bugi seaman. There were four of the Bugis, some of the best sailors among the islands; there was Randall himself, Kahler, and the big man who rowed the boat. That would be Sanguo Pete, a half-caste.

Taking his sack, he walked forward and sat down with his back against the foremast.

Kahler came forward. "We'll have chow pretty quick. One of those Bugis is a first-rate cook." He glanced down at him. "How'd you survive on that reef? You must be tough."

"I get along."

"By this time they probably figure you're dead," Kahler said.

"Maybe."

He knew what they were thinking. If something happened to him now, no one would know any better. Well, he promised himself, nothing was going to happen. He was going to meet Douglas at Woodlark.

When they went below to eat, he let them go first. He paused for a moment near one of the Bugi seamen. His Indonesian was just market-place talk, but he could manage. He indicated the sack. "It is a trust," he said, "from a dying man. He has a granddaughter who needs this." He gestured toward the reef. "The sea was kind," he said.

"You are favored," the Bugi replied.

"If there is trouble—?"

"We are men of the sea. The troubles of white men are the troubles of white men."

He went below. There was a plate of food at the empty place. Randall had not begun to eat. Coolly, before Randall could object, he switched plates with him.

"What's the matter?" Randall demanded. "Don't you trust me?"

"I trust nobody," he said. "Nobody, Mr. Randall."

"You know me?"

"I know you. Douglas told me about you."

They exchanged glances. "Douglas? What do you know about him?"

"I'm his second mate. I'm joining him at Woodlark. Then we'll arrange to get this"—he kicked the sack—"to that girl in Sydney."

"Why bother?" Kahler said. "A man could have himself a time with that much gold."

"And it will buy that girl an education."

"Hell! She'll get along—somehow."

The food was good, and when supper was over, he took his gold and went on deck. Randall was a very tough, dangerous man. So were the others, and it was three to one. He could have used Douglas or Hildebrand. Or Charlie—most of all, Charlie.

The sails hung slack, and the moon was out. There was a Bugi at the wheel, another on lookout in the bow. These were tricky, dangerous waters, much of them unsurveyed. He settled himself against the mainmast for a night of watching.

The storm that had wrecked his boat had blown him east, far off his course. It could be no less than a hundred miles to Misima and probably a good bit more.

The hours dragged. A light breeze had come up, and the vessel was moving along at a good clip. The moon climbed to the zenith, then slid down toward the ocean again. He dozed. The warmth of the night, the easy motion of the schooner, the food in his stomach, helped to make him sleepy. But he stayed awake. They, of course, could sleep by turns.

At one time or another there had been a good bit of talk about Randall, Sanguo Pete, and Kahler. They had a hand in more than one bit of doubtful activity. He was half asleep when they suddenly closed in on him. At one moment he had been thinking of what he'd heard about them, and he must have dozed off, for they closed in quickly and silently. Some faint sound of bare feet on the deck must have warned him even as they reached for him.

He saw the gleam of starlight on steel, and he ripped up with his own knife. The man pulled back sharply, and his blade sliced open a shirt, and the tip of his knife drew a red line from navel to chin, nicking the chin hard as the man drew back.

Then he was on his feet. Somebody struck at him with a marlin spike, and he parried the blow with his blade and lunged. The knife went in; he felt his knuckles come up hard against warm flesh, and he withdrew the knife as he dodged a blow at his head.

The light was bad, for them as well as for him, and one might have been more successful than three; as it was, they got in each other's way in the darkness. The man he had stabbed had gone to the deck, and in trying to crawl away, tripped up another.

He had his gun but dared not reach for it. It meant shifting the knife, and even a moment off guard would be all they would need.

One feinted a rush. The man on the deck was on his feet, and they were spreading out. Suddenly they closed in. The half-light was confusing, and as he moved to get closer to one man, he heard another coming in from behind. He tried to make a quick half turn, but a belaying pin caught him alongside the skull. Only a glancing blow, but it dazed him, and he fell against the rail. He took a cut at the nearest man, missed but ripped into another. How seriously, he did not know. Then another blow caught him, and he felt himself falling.

He hit the water and went down. When he came up, the boat was swinging. The Bugi at the wheel was swinging the bow around. As the hull went away from him, the bow came to him, and there were the stays. He grabbed hold and pulled himself up to the bowsprit.

For a moment he hung there, gasping for breath. He could see them peering over the rail.

"Did you get him, Cap?"

"Get him? You damned right I did! He's a goner." He turned then. "You cut bad, Pete?"

"I'm bleedin'. I got to get the blood stopped."

"He got me, too," Kahler said. "You sure we got him?"

Randall waved at the dark water. "You don't see him, do you? We got him, all right."

After a moment they went below, and the tall yellow seaman at the wheel glanced at the foremast against the sky, lined it up with his star. His expression did not change when he saw Dugan come over the bow and crouch low.

There was no sound but the rustle of bow wash, the creak of rigging, and a murmur of voices aft. He moved aft, exchanging one glance with the Bugi, and when he was close enough, he said, "Thanks." Not knowing if the man understood, he repeated, *"Terima kasi."*

He knew the Bugi had deliberately put the rigging below the bowsprit in his way. The wonder was that even with the distraction of the fighting Randall had not noticed it.

His gun was still in the side pocket of his pants, and he took it out, struggling a bit to do so, as the dungarees were a tight fit. He put the gun in his hip pocket where it was easier of access. He did not want to use a gun, and neither did they. Bullet scars were not easy to disguise and hard to explain when found on rails or deck houses.

Sanguo Pete loomed in the companionway and stood blinking at the change from light to darkness. There was a gash on his cheekbone that had been taped shut, and there was a large mouse over one eye. He hitched up his dungarees and started forward, a gun strapped to his hips. He had taken but two steps when he saw Dugan crouched close to the rail.

Pete broke his paralysis and yelled, then grabbed for his gun. It was too late to think about the future questions. As Pete's hand closed on the butt, Dugan shot him.

Randall loomed in the companionway, but all he saw was the wink of fire from Dugan's gun. He fell forward, half on deck.

Pete lay in the scuppers, his big body rolling slightly with the schooner. The Bugi looked at Dugan and said, "No good mans."

"No good," Dugan agreed.

One by one he tilted them over the side and gave them to the sea.

"My ship is waiting at Woodlark Island," Dugan said.

The Bugi glanced at him. "Is Cap'n Douglas ship. I know." Suddenly he smiled. "I have two brother on your ship—long time now."

"Two brothers? Well, I'll be damned!"

Kahler was lying on the bunk when he went below. His body had been bandaged, but he had lost blood.

"We're going to Woodlark," Dugan said. "If you behave yourself, you might make it."

Kahler closed his eyes, and Dugan lay down on the other bunk and looked up at the deck overhead. The day after tomorrow—

It would be good to be back aboard, lying in his own bunk. He remembered the brief note in the Pilot Book for the area.

This coral reef, discovered in 1825, lies about 82 miles east-northeast of Rossel Island. The reef is 18 miles in length, in a northeast and southwest direction. The greatest breadth is 3 miles, but in some places it is not more than a mile wide. At the northeastern end of the reef there are some rocks 6 feet high. No anchorage is available off the reef.

Wreck. The wreck of a large iron vessel above water lies (1880) on the middle of the southeastern side of the reef.

If they wanted to know any more, they could just ask him. He'd tell them.

Off the Mangrove Coast

There were four of us there, at the back end of creation, four of the devil's own, and a hard lot by any man's count. We'd come together the way men will when on the beach, the idea cropping up out of an idle conversation. We'd nothing better to do; all of us being fools or worse, so we borrowed a boat off the Nine Islands and headed out to sea.

DID YOU EVER cross the South China Sea in a forty-foot boat during the typhoon season? No picnic certainly, nor any job for a churchgoing son; more for the likes of us, who mattered to no one, and in a stolen boat, at that.

Now, all of us were used to playing it alone. We'd worked aboard ship and other places, sharing our labors with other men, but the truth was, each was biding his own thoughts, and watching the others.

There was Limey Johnson, from Liverpool, and Smoke Bassett from Port-au-Prince, and there was Long Jack from Sydney, and there was me, the youngest of the lot, at loose ends and wandering in a strange land.

Wandering always. Twenty-two years old, I was, with five years of riding freights, working in mines or lumber camps, and prizefighting in small clubs in towns that I never saw by daylight.

I'd had my share of the smell of coal smoke and cinders in the rain, the roar of a freight and the driving run-and-catch of a speeding train in the night, and then the sun coming up over the desert or going down over the sea, and the islands looming up and the taste of salt spray on my lips and the sound of bow wash about the hull. There had been nights in the wheelhouse with only the glow from the compass and out there beyond the bow the black, glassy sea rolling its waves up from the long sweep of the Pacific . . . or the Atlantic.

In those years I'd been wandering from restlessness but also from poverty. However, I had no poverty of experience and in that I was satisfied.

It was Limey Johnson who told us the story of the freighter sinking off the mangrove coast; a ship with fifty thousand dollars in the captain's safe and nobody who knew it was there anymore ... nobody but him.

Fifty thousand dollars ... and we were broke. Fifty thousand lying in a bare ten fathoms, easy for the taking. Fifty thousand split four ways. A nice stake, and a nice bit of money for the girls and the bars in Singapore or Shanghai ... or maybe Paris.

Twelve thousand five hundred dollars a piece ... if we all made it. And that was a point to be thought upon, for if only two should live ... twenty-five thousand dollars ... and who can say what can or cannot happen in the wash of a weedy sea off the mangrove coast? Who can say what is the destiny of any man? Who could say how much some of us were thinking of lending a hand to fate?

Macao was behind us and the long roll of the sea began, and we had a fair wind and a good run away from land before the sun broke upon the waves. Oh, it was gamble enough, but the Portuguese are an easygoing people. They would be slow in starting the search; there were many who might steal a boat in Macao ... and logically, they would look toward China first. For who, they would ask themselves, would be fools enough to dare the South China Sea in such a boat; to dare the South China Sea in the season of the winds?

She took to the sea, that ketch, like a baby to a mother's breast, like a Liverpool Irishman to a bottle. She took to the sea and we headed south and away, with a bearing toward the east. The wind held with us, for the devil takes care of his own, and when again the sun went down we had left miles behind and were far along on our way. In the night, the wind held fair and true and when another day came, we were running under a high overcast and there was a heavy feel to the sea.

As the day drew on, the waves turned green with white beards blowing and the sky turned black with clouds. The wind tore at our sheets in gusts and we shortened sail and battened down and prepared to ride her out. Never before had I known such wind or known the world could breed such seas. Hour by hour, we fought it out, our poles bare and a sea anchor over, and though none of us were praying men, pray we did.

We shipped water and we bailed and we swore and we worked and, somehow, when the storm blew itself out, we were still afloat and somewhat farther along. Yes, farther, for we saw a dark blur on the horizon and when we topped a wave, we saw an island, a brush-covered bit of sand forgotten here in the middle of nothing.

We slid in through the reefs, conning her by voice and hand, taking it easy because of the bared teeth of coral so close beneath our keel. Lincoln Island, it was, scarcely more than a mile of heaped–up sand and brush, fringed and bordered by reefs. We'd a hope there was water, and we found it near a stunted palm, a brackish pool, but badly needed.

From there, it was down through the Dangerous Ground, a thousand-odd miles of navigator's nightmare, a wicked tangle of reefs and sandy cays, of islands with tiny tufts of palms, millions of seabirds and fish of all kinds ... and the bottom torn out of you if you slacked off for even a minute. But we took that way because it was fastest and because there was small chance we'd be seen.

Fools? We were that, but sometimes now when the fire is bright on the hearth and there's rain against the windows and the roof, sometimes I think back and find myself tasting the wind again and getting the good old roll of the sea under me. In my mind's eye, I can see the water break-ing on the coral, and see Limey sitting forward, conning us through, and hear Smoke Bassett, the mulatto from Haiti, singing a song of his island in that deep, grand, melancholy bass of his.

Yes, it was long ago, but what else have we but memories? For all life is divided into two parts: anticipation and memory, and if we remember richly, we must have lived richly. Only sometimes I think of them, and wonder what would have happened if the story had been different if an-other hand than mine had written the ending?

Fools ... we were all of that, but a tough, ruddy lot of fools, and it was strange the way we worked as a team; the way we handled the boat and shared our grub and water and no whimper from any man.

There was Limey, who was medium height and heavy but massively boned, and Long Jack, who was six-three and cadaverous, and the power-ful, lazy-talking Smoke, the strongest man of the lot. And me, whom they jokingly called "The Scholar" because I'd stowed a half-dozen books in my sea bag, and because I read from them, sometimes at night when we lay on deck and watched the canvas stretch its dark belly to the wind. Smoke would whet his razor-sharp knife and sing "Shenandoah," "Rio Grande," or "High Barbaree." And we would watch him cautiously and wonder what he had planned for that knife. And wonder what we had planned for each other.

THEN ONE MORNING we got the smell of the Borneo coast in our nos-trils, and felt the close, hot, sticky heat of it coming up from below the horizon. We saw the mangrove coast out beyond the white snarl of foam along the reefs, then we put our helm over and turned east again, crawl-ing along the coast of Darvel Bay.

The heat of the jungle reached out to us across the water and there was the primeval something that comes from the jungle, the ancient evil that crawls up from the fetid rottenness of it, and gets into the mind and into the blood.

We saw a few native craft, but we kept them wide abeam wanting to talk with no one, for our plans were big within us. We got out our stolen diving rig and went to work, checking it over. Johnson was a diver and I'd been down, so it was to be turn and turn about for us ... for it might take a bit of time to locate the wreck, and then to get into the cabin once we'd found it.

We came up along the mangrove coast with the setting sun, and slid through a narrow passage into the quiet of a lagoon where we dropped our hook and swung to, looking at the long wall of jungle that fronted the shore for miles.

Have you seen a mangrove coast? Have you come fresh from the sea to a sundown anchorage in a wild and lonely place with the line of the shore lost among twisting, tangling tentacle roots, strangling the earth, reaching out to the very water and concealing under its solid ceiling of green those dark and dismal passages into which a boat might make its way?

Huge columnar roots, other roots springing from them, and from these, still more roots, and roots descending from branches and under them, black water, silent, unmoving. This we could see, and beyond it, shutting off the mangrove coast from the interior, a long, low cliff of up-raised coral.

Night then ... a moon hung low beyond a corner of the coral cliff ... lazy water lapping about the hull ... the mutter of breakers on the reef ... the cry of a night bird, and then the low, rich tones of Smoke Bassett, singing.

So we had arrived, four men of the devil's own choosing, men from the world's waterfronts, and below us, somewhere in the dark water, was a submerged freighter with fifty thousand dollars in her strongbox.

Four men ... Limey Johnson—short, powerful, tough. Tattooed on his hands the words, one to a hand, *Hold—Fast*. A scar across the bridge of his nose, the tip of an ear missing ... greasy, unwashed dungarees ... and stories of the Blue Funnel boats. What, I wondered, had become of the captain of the sunken ship, and the others who must have known about that money? Limey Johnson had offered no explanation, and we were not inquisitive men.

And Long Jack, sprawled on the deck looking up at the stars? Of what was he thinking? Tomorrow? Fifty thousand dollars, and how much he would get of it? Or was he thinking of the spending of it? He was a thin, haggard man with a slow smile that never reached beyond his lips. Competent, untiring . . . there was a rumor about Macao that he had killed a man aboard a Darwin pearl fisher . . . he was a man who grew red, but not tan, with a thin, scrawny neck like a buzzard, as taciturn as Johnson was talkative. Staring skyward from his pale gray eyes . . . at what? Into what personal future? Into what shadowed past?

Smoke Bassett, powerful tan muscles, skin stretched taut to contain their slumbering, restless strength. A man with magnificent eyes, quick of hand and foot . . . a dangerous man.

And the last of them, myself. Tall and lean and quiet, with wide shoulders, and not as interested in the money. Oh, yes, I wanted my share, and would fight to have it, but there was more than the money; there was getting the money; there was the long roll of the ketch coming down the China Sea; there was the mangrove coast, the night and the stars . . . there were the boat sounds, the water sounds . . . a bird's wing against the wind . . . the distant sounds of the forest . . . these things that no man can buy; these things that get into the blood; these things that build the memories of tomorrow; the hours to look back upon.

I wanted these more than money. For there is a time for adventure when the body is young and the mind alert and all the world seems there for one's hands to use, to hold, to take. And this was my new world, this ancient world of the Indies, these lands where long ago the Arab seamen came, and where the Polynesians may have passed, and where old civilizations slumber in the jungles; awaiting the explorations of men. Where rivers plunge down massive, unrecorded falls, where the lazy sea creeps under the mangroves, working its liquid fingers into the abysmal darkness where no man goes or wants to go.

What is any man but the total of what he has seen? The sum of what he has done? The strange foods, the women whose bodies have merged with his, the smells, the tastes, the longings, the dreams, the haunted nights? The Trenches in Shanghai, Blood Alley, Grant Road in Bombay, and Malay Street in Singapore . . . the worst of it, and the best . . . the temples and towers built by lost, dead hands, the nights at sea, the splendor of a storm, the dancing of dust devils on the desert. These are a man . . . and the solid thrill of a blow landed, the faint smell of opium, rubber, sandalwood, and spice, the stink of copra . . . the taste of blood from a split lip.

Oh, yes, I had come for things other than money but that evening, for the first time, no man gave another good night.

Tomorrow there would be, with luck, fifty thousand dollars in this boat . . . and how many ways to split it?

No need to worry until the box was aboard, or on the line, being hoisted. After that, it was every man for himself. Or was I mistaken? Would we remain friends still? Would we sail our boat into Amurang or Jesselton and leave it there and scatter to the winds with our money in our pockets?

That was the best way, but with such men, in such a place, with that amount of money . . . one lives because one remains cautious . . . and fools die young.

AT THE FIRST STREAKS of dawn, I was out of my blankets and had them rolled. While Smoke prepared breakfast, we got the diving outfit up to the side. We were eating when the question came.

"I'll go," I said, and grinned at them. "I'll go down and see how it looks."

They looked at me, and I glanced up from my plate and said, "How about it, Smoke? Tend my lines?"

He turned to me, a queer light flicking through his dark, handsome eyes, and then he nodded.

A line had been drawn . . .

A line of faith and a line of doubt . . . of the three, I had chosen Smoke Bassett, had put in him my trust, for when a man is on the bottom, his life lies in the hands of the man who tends his lines. A mistaken signal, or a signal ignored, and the diver can die.

I had given my life to Smoke Bassett, and who could know what that would mean?

JOHNSON WAS TAKING soundings, for in these waters, chart figures were not to be trusted. Many of the shores have been but imperfectly surveyed, if at all, and there is constant change to be expected from volcanic action, the growth of coral, or the waves themselves.

When we anchored outside the reef, I got into the diving dress. Limey lent me a hand, saying to me, "Nine or ten fathoms along the reef, but she drops sharp off to fifty fathoms not far out."

Careful . . . we'd have to be careful, for the enemies of a diver are rarely the shark or the octopus, but rather the deadline and constant danger of a squeeze or a blowup. The air within the suit is adjusted to the depth of the water and its pressure, but a sudden fall into deeper water can crush a man, jamming his entire body into his copper helmet. Such sudden pressure is called a squeeze.

A blowup is usually caused by a jammed valve, blowing a man's suit to almost balloon size and propelling him suddenly to the surface where he lies helpless until rescued. While death only occasionally results from a blowup, a diver may be crippled for life by the dreaded "bends," caused by the sudden change in pressure, and the resulting formation of nitrogen bubbles in the bloodstream.

When the helmet was screwed on, Limey clapped me on the top and I swung a leg over to the rope ladder. Smoke Bassett worked the pump with one arm while he played out the hose and rope. Up—down. *Chug-chug.* A two-stroke motion like a railroad hand car. It didn't take much energy but each stroke was a pulse of oxygen . . . like a breath, or the beating of your heart. The big mulatto grinned at me as he worked the handle.

Clumsy, in the heavy shoes and weighted belt, I climbed down and felt the cool press of water rise around me. Up my body . . . past my faceplate.

It was a slow, easy descent . . . down . . . down . . . and on the bottom at sixty feet.

In the dark water, down where the slow weeds wave in the unstirring sea . . . no sound but the *chug-chug-chug* of the pump, the pump that brings the living air . . . down in a green, gray, strange world . . . cowrie shells . . . a big conch . . . the amazing wall of the reef, jagged, broken, all edges and spires . . . a stone fish, all points and poison.

Leaning forward against the weight of the water, I moved like some ungainly monster of the deep, slowly along the bottom. Slowly . . . through the weeds, upon an open sand field beneath the sea . . . slowly, I walked on.

A dark shadow above me and I turned slowly . . . a shark . . . unbelievably huge . . . and seemingly uninterested . . . but could you tell? Could one ever know?

Smell . . . I'd heard old divers say that sharks acted upon smell . . . and the canvas and rubber and copper gave off no smell, but a cut, a drop of blood in the water, and the sharks would attack.

Chug-chug-chug . . . I walked on, turning slowly from time to time to look around me. And the shark moved above me, huge, black, ominous . . . dark holes in the reef where might lurk . . . anything. And then I saw . . . something.

A blackness, a vast deep, opening off to my right, away from the reef. I looked toward it, and drew back. Fifty fathoms at some places, but then deeper, much deeper. Fifty fathoms . . . three hundred feet.

A signal . . . time for me to go up. Turning, I walked slowly back and looked for the shark, but he had gone. I had failed to hold his interest . . . and I could only hope that nothing in my personality would induce him to return.

When the helmet was off, I told them. "Probably the other way. But when you go down, Limey, keep an eye open for that shark. I don't trust the beggar."

ON THE THIRD DAY, we found the hulk of the freighter. At the time, I was below, half asleep in my bunk. Bassett was in the galley cooking, and only Long Jack was on deck, handling the lines for Limey. Dozing, I heard him bump against the vessel's side and I listened, but there was nothing more, only a sort of scraping, a sound I could not place, as if something were being dragged along the hull.

When I heard the weighted boots on the deck, I rolled over and sat up, kicking my feet into my slippers. Johnson was seated on the rail and his helmet was off and Long Jack was talking to him. When they heard my feet on the deck, they turned. "Found it!" Limey was grinning his broken-toothed smile. "She's hanging right on the lip of the deep. She's settin' up fairly straight. You shouldn't have much trouble gettin' the box."

THERE WAS A full moon that night, wide and white; a moon that came up over the jungle, and standing by the rail, I looked out over the lagoon and watched the phosphorescent combers roll up and crash against the outer reef. When I had been standing there a long time, Smoke Bassett walked over.

"Where's Limey?"

"Fishin'," he said, "with a light."

"Tomorrow," I said, "we'll pick it up."

"Anson Road would look mighty good now. Anson Road, in Singapore ... an' High Street. You know that, Scholar?"

"It'll look better with money in your pocket."

"Look good to me just anyway." Smoke rolled a cigarette. "Money ain't so important."

We watched the moon and listened to the breakers on the reef. "You be careful down there," Smoke Bassett told me suddenly. "Mighty careful." He struck a match and lit his cigarette, as he always did, one-handed.

Lazily, I listened to the sea talking to the reef and then listened to the surf and to the jungle beyond the line of mangroves. A bird shrieked, an unhappy, uncanny sound.

"Them two got they heads together," Smoke Bassett said. "You be careful."

Long Jack ... a queer, silent man around whom one never felt quite comfortable. A taciturn man with a wiry strength that could be dangerous. Only once had we had words and that had been back in Macao when we first met. He had been arrogant, as if he felt he could push me around. "Don't start that with me," I told him.

His eyes were snaky, cold, there were strange little lights in them, and contempt. He just looked at me. I didn't want trouble so I told him, "You could make an awful fool of yourself, Jack," I said.

He got up. "Right now," he said, and stood there looking at me, and I know he expected me to take water.

So, I got up, for this was an old story, and I knew by the way he stood that he knew little about fistfighting, and then a fat man, sitting in a dirty singlet and a blue dungaree coat, said, "You *are* a fool. I seen the kid fight in Shanghai, in the ring. He'll kill you."

Long Jack from Sydney hesitated and it was plain he no longer wanted to fight. He still stood there, but I'd seen the signs before and knew the moment was past. He'd had me pegged for a kid who either couldn't or wouldn't go through.

That was all, but Long Jack had not forgotten, I was sure of that. There had been no further word, nor had we talked much on the trip down the China Sea except what was necessary. But it had been pleasant enough.

The next morning when I got into the suit, Limey came up to put on the copper helmet. There was a look in his eyes I didn't like. "When you get it out of the desk," he said, "just tie her on the line and give us a signal."

But there was something about the way he said it that was wrong. As I started into the water, he leaned over suddenly and stroked his hand down my side. I thought he wanted something and turned my faceplate toward him, but he just stood there so I started down into the water.

When I was on the deck of the freighter, I started along toward the superstructure and then saw something floating by my face. I stepped back to look and saw it was a gutted fish. An instant, I stood there staring, and then a dark shadow swung above me and I turned, stumbled, and fell just as the same huge shark of a few days before whipped by, jaws agape.

On my feet, I stumbled toward the companionway, and half fell through the opening just as the shark twisted around and came back for another try.

And then I knew why Limey Johnson had been fishing, and what he had rubbed on my arm as I went into the water. He had rubbed the blood and guts of the fish on my suit and then had dumped it into the water after me to attract the shark.

Sheltered by the companionway, I rubbed a hand at my sleeve as far around as I could reach, trying to rub off some of the blood.

Forcing myself to composure, I waited, thinking out the situation.

Within the cabin to the right, I had already noticed the door of the desk compartment that held the cash box stood open to the water. That meant the money was already on our boat; it meant that the bumping I'd heard along the side had been the box as it was hoisted aboard. And letting me go down again, rubbing the blood and corruption on my sleeve had been a deliberate attempt at murder.

Chug-chug-chug ... monotonously, reassuringly, the steady sound of the pump reached me. Smoke was still on the job, and I was still safe, yet how long could I remain so under the circumstances?

If they had attempted to kill me they would certainly attempt to kill Smoke, and he could not properly defend himself, even strong as he was, while he had to keep at least one hand on the pump. Outside, the shark circled, just beyond the door frame.

Working my way back into the passage, I fumbled in the cabin, looking for some sort of weapon. There was a fire ax on the bulkhead outside, but it was much too clumsy for use against so agile a foe, even if I could strike hard enough underwater. There was nothing ... suddenly I saw on the wall, crossed with an African spear of some sort, a whaler's harpoon!

Getting it down, I started back for the door, carefully freeing my lines from any obstructions.

Chug ... chug ... chug ...

The pump slowed, almost stopped, then picked up slowly again, and then something floated in the water, falling slowly, turning over as I watched, something that looked like an autumn leaf, drifting slowly down, only much larger.

Something with mouth agape, eyes wide, blood trailing a darkening streamer in the green water ... it was Long Jack, who had seen the last of Sydney ... Long Jack, floating slowly down, his belly slashed and an arm cut across the biceps by a razor-edged knife.

An instant I saw him, and then there was a gigantic swirl in the water, the shark turning, doubling back over, and hurling himself at the body with unbelievable ferocity. It was my only chance; I stepped out of the door and signaled to go up.

There was no response, only the *chug-chug-chug* of the pump. Closing my valve only a little, I started to rise, but desperately as I tried, I could not turn myself to watch the shark. Expecting at any moment that he would see me and attack, I drifted slowly up.

Suddenly the ladder hung just above me although the hull was still a dark shadow. I caught the lower step and pulled myself slowly up until I could get my clumsy feet on the step. Climbing carefully, waiting from moment to moment, I got to the surface and climbed out.

Hands fumbled at the helmet. I heard the wrench, and then the helmet was lifted off.

Smoke Bassett had a nasty wound over the eye where he had been struck by something, and where blood stained his face it had been wiped and smeared. Limey Johnson was standing a dozen feet away, only now he was drawing back, away from us.

He looked at the harpoon in my hands and I saw him wet his lips, but I said nothing at all. Bassett was helping me out of the helmet, and I dared not take my eyes from Johnson.

His face was working strangely, a grotesque mask of yellowish-white wherein the eyes seemed unbelievably large. He reached back and took up a long boat hook. There was a driftwood club at my feet, and this must have been what had struck Bassett. They must have rushed him at first, or Long Jack had tried to get close, and had come too close.

When I dropped the weight belt and kicked off the boots, Smoke was scarcely able to stand. And I could see the blow that had hit him had almost wrecked the side of his face and skull. "You all right? You all right, Scholar?" His voice was slurred.

"I'm all right. Take it easy. I'll handle it now."

Limey Johnson faced me with his new weapon, and slowly his courage was returning. Smoke Bassett he had feared, and Smoke was nearly helpless. It was Limey and me now; one of us was almost through.

Overhead the sun was blazing ... the fetid smell of the mangroves and the swamp was wafted to the ketch from over the calm beauty of the lagoon. The sea was down, and the surf rustled along the reef, chuckling and sucking in the holes and murmuring in the deep caverns.

Sweat trickled into my eyes and I stood there, facing Limey Johnson across that narrow deck. Short, heavy, powerful ... a man who had sent me down to the foulest kind of death, a man who must kill now if he would live.

I reached behind me to the rail and took up the harpoon. It was razor sharp.

His hook was longer ... he outreached me by several feet. I had to get close ... close.

In my bare feet, I moved out away from Smoke, and Limey began to move warily, watching for his chance, that ugly hook poised to tear at me. To throw the harpoon was to risk my only weapon, and risk it in his hands, for I could not be sure of my accuracy. I had to keep it, and thrust. I had to get close. The diving dress was some protection but it was clumsy and I would be slow.

There was no sound ... the hot sun, the blue sky, the heavy green of the mangroves, the sucking of water among the holes of the coral ... the slight sound of our breathing and the rustle and slap of our feet on the deck.

He struck with incredible swiftness. The boat hook darted and jerked back. The hook was behind my neck, and only the nearness of the pole and my boxer's training saved me. I jerked my head aside and felt the thin sharpness of the point as it whipped past my neck, but before I could spring close enough to thrust, he stepped back and bracing himself, he thrust at me. The curve of the hook hit my shoulder and pushed me off balance. I fell back against the bulwark, caught myself, and he lunged to get closer. Three times he whipped the hook and jerked at me. Once I almost caught the pole, but he was too quick.

I tried to maneuver . . . then realized I had to get *outside* of the hook's curve . . . to move to my left, then try for a thrust either over or under the pole. In the narrow space between the low deckhouse and the rail there was little room to maneuver.

I moved left, the hook started to turn, and I lunged suddenly and stabbed. The point just caught him . . . the side of his singlet above the belt started to redden. His face looked drawn, I moved again, parried a lunge with the hook, and thrust again, too short. But I knew how to fight him now . . . and he knew, too.

He tried, and I parried again, then thrust. The harpoon point just touched him again, and it drew blood. He stepped back, then crossed the deck and thrust at me under the yard, his longer reach had more advantage now, with the deckhouse between us, and he was working his way back toward the stern. It was an instant before I saw what he was trying to do. He was getting in position to kill Bassett, unconscious against the bulwark beside the pump.

To kill . . . and to get the knife.

I lunged at him then, batting the hook aside, feeling it rip the suit and my leg as I dove across the mahogany roof of the deckhouse. I thrust at him with the harpoon. His face twisted with fear, he sprang back, stepped on some spilled fish guts staining the deck. He threw up his arms, lost hold of the boat hook, and fell backward, arms flailing for balance. He hit the bulwark and his feet flew up and he went over, taking my harpoon with him . . . a foot of it stuck out his back . . . and there was an angry swirl in the water, a dark boiling . . . and after a while, the harpoon floated to the surface, and lay there, moving slightly with the wash of the sea.

THERE'S A PLACE on the Sigalong River, close by the Trusan waters, a place where the nipa palms make shade and rustle their long leaves in the slightest touch of wind. Under the palms, within sound of the water, I buried Smoke Bassett on a Sunday afternoon . . . two long days he lasted, and a wonder at that, for the side of his head was curiously crushed. How the man had remained at the pump might be called a mystery . . . but I knew.

For he was a loyal man; I had trusted him with my lines, and there can be no greater trust. So when he was gone, I buried him there and covered over the grave with coral rock and made a marker for it and then I went down to the dinghy and pushed off for the ketch.

SOMETIMES NOW, when there is rain upon the roof and when the fire crackles on the hearth, sometimes I will remember: the bow wash about the hull, the rustling of the nipa palms, the calm waters of a shallow lagoon. I will remember all that happened, the money I found, the men that died, and the friend I had . . . off the mangrove coast.

Glorious! Glorious!

The four men crouched together in the narrow shadow of the parapet. The sun was setting slowly behind a curtain of greasy cloud, and the air, as always at twilight, was very clear and still. A hundred and fifty yards away was the dirty gray earth where the Riffs were hidden. The declining sun threw long fingers of queer, brassy light across the rise of the hill behind them.

On their left the trench was blown away by artillery fire; here and there a foot or a shoulder showed above the dirt thrown up by explosions. They had marched, eaten, and fought beside those men, dead now.

"Better keep your head away from that opening, kid, or you'll get it blown away."

Dugan pulled his head back, and almost on the instant a spout of sand leaped from the sandbag and splattered over his face.

Slim smiled wryly, and the Biscayan looked up from the knife he was sharpening. He was always sharpening his knife and kept it with a razor edge. Short, thick-bodied, he had a square-jawed, pock-marked face and small eyes. Dugan was glad they were fighting on the same side.

"You got anything to eat?" Slim asked suddenly, looking over at Dugan.

"Nothing. I ate my last biscuit before that last attack," he said. "I could have eaten forty."

"You?" Slim looked at the Irishman.

Jerry shrugged. "I ate mine so long ago I've forgotten."

He was bandaging his foot with a soiled piece of his shirt. A bullet had clipped the butt of his heel the day before, making a nasty wound.

Somewhere down the broken line of trenches there was a brief volley followed by several spaced rifle shots, then another brief spatter of firing.

Slim was wiping the dust from his rifle, testing the action. Then he reloaded, taking his time. "They're tough," he said, "real tough."

"I figured they'd be A-rabs or black," Jerry said, "and they ain't either one."

"North Africa was never black," Dugan said. "Nearly all the country north of the Niger is Berber country, and Berbers are white. These Riffs—there's as many redheaded ones as in Scotland."

"I was in Carthage once," Slim said. "It's all busted up—ruins."

"They were Semitic," Dugan said. "Phoenicians originally."

"How you know so much about it?" Slim asked.

"There was a book somebody left in the barracks all about this country and the Sahara."

"You can have it," Jerry said. "This country, I mean."

"Book belonged to that colonel—the fat one." Dugan moved a small stone, settled himself more comfortably. "He let it lay one time, and somebody swiped it."

"Hey!" Jerry sat up suddenly. He held the bandage tight to survey the job he was doing, then continued with it. "That reminds me. I know where there's some wine."

Slim turned his long neck. "Some *what?*"

He looked gaunt and gloomy in his dirty, ill-fitting uniform. One shoulder was stained with blood, and the threads had begun to ravel around a bullet hole. He had been hit nine times since the fighting began, but mostly they were scratches. He'd lost one shoe, and the foot was wrapped in canvas. It was a swell war.

Jerry continued to wrap his foot, and nobody said anything. Dugan watched him, thinking of the wine. Then he looked across at the neat row of men lying side by side near the far parapet. As he looked, a bullet struck one of them, and the body jerked stiffly. It did not matter. They were all dead.

"Over there in the cellar," Jerry said. He nodded his head to indicate a squat gray stone building on the peak of a conical hill about a quarter of a mile off. "The colonel found a cellar the monks had. He brought his own wine with him and a lot of canned meat and cheese. He stored it in that cellar—just like in an icebox. I helped pack some of it in not over two weeks ago. He kept me on patrol duty three days extra just for breaking a bottle. He brought in a lot of grub, too."

The Biscayan glanced up, mumbling something in Spanish. He pulled a hair from his head and tested the edge of the blade, showing his teeth when the hair cut neatly.

"What's he say?"

"He says it may still be there." Jerry shifted his rifle and glanced speculatively at the low hill. "Shall we have a look?"

"They'd blow our heads off before we could get there," Slim protested, "night or no night."

"Look," Jerry said, "we're liable to get it, anyway. This is going to be like Anual, where they wiped them all out. Look how long we've been here and no relief. I think they've written us off."

"It's been seventy-five days," Dugan agreed.

"Look what happened at Chentafa. The officer in command saw they'd had it and set fire to the post; then he died with his men."

"That's more than these will do."

"Hell," Jerry said, "I think they're already dead. I haven't seen an officer in a week. Only that corporal."

"They pick them off first. Those Moors can shoot." Slim looked at Dugan. "How'd you get into this outfit, anyway?"

"My ship was in Barcelona. I came ashore and was shanghaied. I mean an army patrol just gathered in a lot of us, and when I said I was an American citizen, they just paid no attention."

"Did you get any training?"

"A week. That was it. They asked me if I'd ever fired a gun, and like a damned fool I told them I had. Hell, I grew up with a gun. I was twelve years old before I found out it wasn't part of me. So here I am."

"They wanted men, and they didn't care where or how they got them. Me, I've no excuse," Slim said. "I joined the Spanish Foreign Legion on my own. I was broke, hungry, and in a different country. It looked like an easy way out."

Far off to the left there was an outburst of firing, then silence.

"What happened to the colonel? The fat one who had all that wine brought in?"

"Killed himself. Look, they tell me there's a general for every twenty-five men in this army. This colonel had connections. They told him spend a month over there and we'll promote you to general, so he came, and then we got pinned down, and he couldn't get out. From Tetuan to Chaouen there's a whole line of posts like this one here at Seriya. There's no way to get supplies, no way to communicate."

The talk died away. It was very hot even though the sun was setting.

A big Russian came up and joined them. He looked like a big schoolboy with his close-cropped yellow hair and his pink cheeks. "They come," he said.

There was a crackle of shots, and the four climbed to their feet. Dugan lurched from weariness, caught himself, and faced about. The Russian was already firing.

A long line of Moors was coming down the opposite slope, their advance covered by a barrage of machine-gun fire from the trenches farther up the hill. Here and there a captured field gun boomed. Dugan broke open a box of cartridges and laid them out on a sandbag close at hand. Slowly and methodically, making each shot count, he began to fire.

The Biscayan was muttering curses and firing rapidly. He did not like long-range fighting. Jerry leaned against the sandbags, resting his forehead on one. Dugan could see a trickle of sweat cutting a trail through the dust.

Somewhere down the parapet one of their own machine guns opened up, the gray and white line before them melted like wax, and the attack broke. Slim grounded his rifle butt and leaned against the sandbags, fumbling for a cigarette. His narrow, cadaverous features looked yellow in the pale light. He looked around at Dugan. "How d'you like it, kid? Had enough?"

Dugan shrugged and reloaded his rifle, then stuffed his pockets with cartridges. The powder smoke made his head ache, or maybe it was hunger and the sound of guns. His cheek was swollen from the rifle stock, and his gums were sore and swollen. All of them were indescribably dirty. For seventy-five days they had held the outpost against a steady, unrelenting, consistent, energy-draining attack that seemed to take no thought of men lost. Their food was gone; only a little of the brackish water remained, and there would be no relief.

"They've written us off," Slim said. "We're dead." He was hollow eyed and sagging, yet he was still a fighting man. He looked at Jerry. "How about that wine?"

"Let's go get it. There's a machine gun there, too, and enough ammo to fight the battle of the Marne."

"Does the sergeant major know?"

"He did." Jerry indicated the line of dead bodies. "He's over there."

"Who's in command?" Dugan asked.

"Maybe nobody. The lieutenant was killed several days ago, shot from behind. He was a fool to hit that Turk. He slugged one guy too many."

The sun was gone, and darkness was falling over the low hills. There was no movement in the trenches across the way. The Russian stood up, then sat down abruptly, his throat shot away. He started to rise again, then just sat back down and slowly rolled over.

Slim picked him up as though he were a child and carried him to the line of bodies, placing him gently on the ground. Then he unbuckled his cartridge pouches and hung them around his own waist. Dugan looked through an opening in the sandbagged parapet at the broad shoulders of shadow along the slope. A dead Moor hung head down over the barbed wire about fifty feet away, and a slight breeze made his burnoose swell.

When it was dark, the corporal came along the trench. He looked old. His thin, haggard face was expressionless. He said what they all knew.

"There won't be any relief. I think everything behind us is wiped out, too. We wouldn't stand a chance in trying to get away. They're out there waiting, hoping we try it.

"There'll be at least one night attack, but with daybreak they'll come. There's thirty-eight of us left. Fire as long as you can, and when they get through the wire, it's every man for himself."

He looked around vacantly, then started back up the line. His shoes were broken, and one leg was bandaged. He looked tired. He stopped suddenly, looking back. "If any of you have the guts to try it, go ahead." He looked from Jerry to Slim, then at Dugan. "We're through."

Slim walked over to the dead officer and took his automatic, then the cartridges for it. He took some money, too, then dropped it into the sand. Having a second thought, he picked it up.

"If a man could get away," he said, looking over at Dugan, "this would pay a boatman. Gibraltar—that would be the place."

Dugan sat down, his back to the parapet. He glanced along the trench. Far down he could see movement.

Thirty-eight left! There had been 374 when they occupied the post. He tilted his head back and looked at the stars. They had looked the same way at home. How long ago was that?

Jerry got up. He glanced at Slim, and the Texan shrugged. "Let's go," he said. And they went.

Jerry pointed. "We'll go down that shallow place, and there's a ditch. Follow that to the right and it takes you right up to the building. If we get into that ditch, we've got it made."

There was no moon, but the stars were bright. The rear parapet had been partly knocked down by the explosion of a shell. They went over fast, Jerry first, then Dugan. Flat on their faces, they wormed across the dark ground, moving fast but silently. The ground was still hot. In the darkness his hand touched something warm. It was a gun, an automatic. He thought of Slim and felt suddenly sick; then he remembered the sergeant who had been killed out here a few days before. He took the gun but turned at right angles. The Biscayan was close behind him, his knife in his teeth, his rifle lying across his forearms.

Dugan heard a slight movement and looked up suddenly into the eyes of a Moor. For a split second they both stared, and then Dugan jerked his rifle forward, and the muzzle struck the Moor right below the eye. The Moor rolled back and then came up, very fast, with a knife. Dugan kicked him on the kneecap, then hit him with the butt and followed with the barrel. He went down, but another loomed up.

There was a scream as the Biscayan ripped one up, and then Slim broke into the fight with an automatic. Then there was a roar of shots from all along the parapet. It was the expected night attack, sooner than believed and almost successful.

Dugan came up running, saw a Moor loom up before him, and shot without lifting the rifle above his belt line. The Moor spun out of the way and fell, and Dugan fell into the ditch just one jump ahead of the Biscayan. Then Slim and Jerry joined them. Jerry was carrying three rifles and a bandoleer of cartridges.

They went along the ditch at a stumbling run. Dugan slipped once and almost fell, but when he straightened up, the stone house was looming above them. Jerry led them to the trap door at the end of the ditch.

The room was empty except for a desk and a couple of chairs. One chair was tipped on its side, and there were papers scattered about. The room had a musty smell, as the door and windows were heavily shuttered and barred. Both openings could be covered by rifles from the trenches below, and as the position was not a good one, the Moors had not taken it.

Jerry dragged the heavy desk aside and struck a match to find the iron ring concealed in a crack. With a heave he opened the cellar. In the flare of the match Dugan saw that Jerry's scalp was deeply lacerated and dried blood matted his hair on one side.

Slim slid into the hole and a moment later was handing up bottles. Then he sent up a magnum of champagne, and the Biscayan came up with some canned fruit and cheese.

"This guy had a taste for knickknacks," Slim said. "There's everything down here that you could get into a can."

"He took three hot ones right through the belly on the first day," Jerry said. "He was scared and crying like a baby. I don't believe he'd ever done a day's duty in his life."

Dugan took a bottle of Château Margaux and a can of the cheese. The wine tasted good. After a bit he crawled into a corner, made a pillow of some cartridge pouches, and went to sleep. When he awakened, light was filtering into the room from around the shutters. Jerry was sitting wide legged near the cellar door, and he was drunk. Slim was at the desk.

"Kid," Slim said, "come here."

He had a map laid out. "See? If you get the chance, take the ditch to here, then down along that dry creek. It's not far to the coast, and most of those boat guys will give you a lift for money. You got any money?"

"About twenty bucks. I've been hiding it in case."

"Here." Slim took the money he'd taken from the dead officer. "You take this."

"What about you?"

"I ain't goin' to make it, kid. I got a hunch. If I do, we'll go together. If you board that boat, they may take your rifle, but you keep your side-arm, you hear? Keep it hidden. You may need it before you get across."

He turned to look at Dugan. "How old are you, kid?"

"Twenty-two," Dugan said, and he lied. He was just past sixteen.

"You look younger. Anyway, go through their pockets, whoever's dead. They won't mind, and you'll need whatever there is.

"Don't go near the army or a big town. Head for the seacoast and stay out of sight. Anybody you meet out here will try to stop you. Don't let it happen. You get away—you hear?"

Jerry lifted the bottle in a toast. "Tomorrow we die!" he said.

"Today, you mean," Slim said.

The Biscayan came up from the cellar with a machine gun. It was brand-spanking-new. He went down again and came up with several belts of ammo, then a box of them. He set the machine gun up at a shuttered window and fed a belt into it.

Dugan looked at the automatic he had picked up. It was in good shape. He found another in the cellar and several spare clips. He loaded them.

Scattered shooting broke into a steady roar. A shell exploded not too far away.

Slim had found two Spanish versions of the Colt pistols and loaded them. He strapped them on, pleased. "You know what I'm going to do? I'm going to get good and drunk, and then I'm going to open that door and show them how we do it down in Texas!"

He emptied half a bottle of the wine and looked at Dugan. "You ever been in Texas, kid?"

"I worked on a ranch there—in the Panhandle."

"I grew up on a ranch," Slim said. "Rode for a couple of outfits in New Mexico before I started out to see the world. I knew this would happen sometime. Just never figured it would be here, in a place like this."

He picked up the bottle of wine and looked at it. "What I need is some tequila. This here is a she-male's drink! Or some bourbon an' branch water."

Dugan took his rifle and walked to the window. He helped the Bis-cayan move the machine gun to a more advantageous position, a little closer, a little more to the left. He checked his rifle again and loaded two more and stood them close by. From a crack in the shutters he studied the route he might get a chance to take. It must be done before the whole country was overrun by the Moors.

Suddenly Jerry moved, the dried blood still caked in his stubble of beard. He crawled on hands and knees to the edge of the trapdoor from the ditch. Then he stopped, breathing hoarsely, waiting.

Dugan had heard nothing above the occasional rattle of distant rifle fire as the Riffs began to mop up. Suddenly the trapdoor began to lift, very cautiously, then with more confidence. When it had lifted about a foot, a big Riff thrust his head up and stared into the room. All the occupants were out of his immediate range, and he lifted his head higher, peering into the semidarkness. In that instant Jerry swung the empty magnum. The solid *bop* of the blow was loud in the room, and the man vanished, the door falling into place. Jerry jerked it open, slammed it back, and leaped down into the hole. There was a brief scuffle, and then Jerry came back through the trapdoor, carrying a new rifle and a bandoleer.

Now the crescendo of firing had lifted to a loud and continuous roar, and Slim started to sing. In the tight stone room his voice boomed loudly.

Glorious! Glorious!
One keg o' beer for the four of us!
Glory be to heaven that there isn't
Ten or 'leven,
For the four of us can drink it all alone!

The Biscayan took down the bar and threw the shutters wide. Below them and away across the tawny hill the Riffian trench was suddenly vomiting up a long line of men. From behind the parapet before them a scattering fire threw a pitiful challenge at the charging line.

Dugan wiped the sweat from his eyebrows and leaned against the edge of the window. He was sagging with incredible exhaustion, and his body stank from the unwashed weeks, the sweat and the dirt. He lifted the rifle and held it against his swollen cheek and began to fire.

Behind him Jerry and Slim were singing "Casey Jones." Dugan looked down at the Biscayan, a solid chunk of man who lived to fight. Hunched behind the machine gun, he waited, watching the line as an angler watches a big fish approaching the hook.

Suddenly the firing stopped, waiting for a killing volley at close quarters. Dugan had stopped, too. One man, a tall Moor on a fine-looking horse, had ridden out on a point a good six hundred yards away, watching the attack. He stood in his stirrups, lifting a hand to shout a command, unheard at the distance. For what seemed a long minute Dugan held his aim, then squeezed off the shot, and the man stood tall in his stirrups, then fell from the saddle to the dust and lay there. Then the Biscayan opened fire.

Dugan looked down at him, aware for the first time that the Biscayan was drunk. The gray line melted before him, and the Biscayan lifted the bottle for another drink.

The unexpected fire from the stone house, cutting a wide swath in their ranks, paralyzed the attack. Then a bunch of the Riffs broke away from the main attack and started toward the stone house. Jerry was up, firing slowly, methodically. Suddenly the machine gun swung, fired three short bursts, and the bunch of attackers melted away. From behind the parapet came a wavering cheer. Dugan winced at the few voices. So many were gone!

Dugan squinted his eyes against the sun, remembering the line of silent men beside the parapet and the big Russian with the schoolboy pink in his cheeks.

The Biscayan lifted his bottle to drink, and it shattered in his hand, spilling wine over him. With a lurid burst of Spanish he dropped the neck of the bottle and reached for another. And he had never been a drinking man.

Slim sat on the floor, muttering. "I'm goin' to get damn good an' drunk an' go out there and show 'em how we do it down in Texas."

He started to rise and sat down hard, a long red furrow along his jaw. He swore in a dull, monotonous voice.

Dugan saw the line of Moors sweep forward and across the parapet. There was scattered shooting, some rising dust, then silence. He blinked, feeling a lump in his throat. He had known few of them, for they had been together too short a time. Only weeks had passed since he lay in his bunk aboard ship, feeling the gentle roll as it steamed west from Port Said.

The sunlight was bright and clear. Outside, except for the scattered bodies of the slain, all was quiet and peaceful under the morning sun. Dugan looked across the valley, thinking of what he would do. There was little time. Perhaps time had already run out.

The afternoon was waning before they attacked again. This time they were careful, taking advantage of the slight roll of the hill to get closer. The last hundred yards was in the open, and they seemed unaware of the ditch, which would be hidden from them until they were almost fallen into it.

Dugan's face was swollen and sore from the kick of the rifle. He was hot and tired, and he switched rifles again.

A single shot sounded, lonely against the hills, and something gasped beside him. He turned to see Jerry fall across the sill. Before he could pull him back, three more bullets chugged into his body.

"Kid," Slim said, "you better go. It's time."

He took the bar down from the door and looked down the sunlit hill.

A knot of Moors was coming toward him, good men, fighting men, dangerous men. Slim stepped out with a pistol in each hand and started down toward them.

He was drunk. Magnificently, roaring drunk, and he had a pistol in either hand. "I'm a-goin' to show them how we do it down in Texas!" He opened fire, then his body jerked, and he went to his knees.

Dugan snapped a quick shot at a Moor running up with a rifle ready to fire, and then Slim got up. He had lost one gun, but he started to fire from waist level. His whole left side was bloody.

Dugan turned to yell at the Biscayan, but the man was slumped across his machine gun. He had been shot between the eyes.

Dugan pushed him away from the gun and swung it toward the front of the house. In the distance, against the pale-blue sky, above the heat waves dancing, a vulture swung in slow circles against the sky. Slim was down, all sprawled out, and the enemy was closing in.

He pointed the gun toward them and opened up, singing in a hoarse, toneless voice.

> Glorious! Glorious!
> One keg o' beer for the four of us!
> Glory be to heaven that there isn't
> Ten or 'leven,
> For the four of us can drink it all alone!

His belt went empty, and the hill was bare of all but the bodies. He got up and closed the heavy plank door.

He caught up a bandoleer and another pistol. Then he dropped through the trapdoor.

All was still. He stepped over the dead Moor and went out into the shadowed stillness of the ditch.

And then he began to run.

By the Ruins of "El Walarieh"

From the hillside above the ruins of El Walarieh one could watch the surf breaking along the shore, and although the grass was sparse, thin goats grazed among the occasional clumps of brushwood high on the hill behind me. It was a strange and lonely coast, not without its own wild beauty.

Three times I had been there before the boy approached. He was a thin boy with large, beautiful eyes and smooth brown skin. He squatted beside me, his shins brown and dirty, looking curiously toward the sea, where I was looking.

"You sit here often?"

"Yes, very often."

"You look at something?"

"I look at the sea. I look at the sea and the shore, sometimes at the clouds." I shifted my position a little. "It is very beautiful."

"Beautiful?" He was astonished. "The sea is beautiful?" He looked again to be sure that I was not mildly insane.

"I like the sea, and I like to look at those ruins and to wonder who lived there, and what their lives were like."

He glanced at the ancient, time-blackened ruins. "They are no good, even for goats. The roofs have fallen in. Why do you look at the sea and not at the goats? I think the goats are more beautiful than the sea. Look at them!"

I turned my head to please him. There were at least fifty, and they browsed or slept upon the hillside above me. They were white against the green of the hill. Yes, there was beauty there, too. He seemed pleased that I agreed with him.

"They are not my goats," he explained, "but someday I shall own goats. Perhaps as many as these. Then you will see beauty. They shall be like white clouds upon the green sky of the hillside."

He studied the camera that lay on the grass near my feet. "You have a machine," he said. "What is it for?"

"To make pictures. I want to get pictures of the sea and the ruins."

"Of the goats, too?"

To please him, I agreed. "Yes, also of the goats."

The idea seemed to satisfy him, yet he was obviously puzzled, too. There was something he did not understand. He broached the idea to me, as one gentleman to another. "You take pictures of the sea and the ruins ... also of the goats. Why do you take these?"

"To look at them. To catch their beauty."

"But why a picture?" He was still puzzled. "They are here! You can see them without a picture. The sea is here, the sky, the ruins ... the goats, too. They are always here."

"Yes, but I shall not always be here. I shall go away, and I want them to remember, to look at many times."

"You need the machine for that? I can remember. I can remember all of the goats. Each one of them." He paused, thinking about it. "Ah! The machine then is your memory. It is very strange to remember with a machine."

Neither of us spoke for a few minutes. "I think you have machines for many things. I would not like that."

The following day I was back on the hillside. It had not been my plan to come again, yet somehow the conversation left me unsatisfied. I had the feeling that somehow I'd been bested. I wanted the goatherd to understand.

When he saw me sitting there, he came down the hillside. He saluted me gravely, then sat down. I handed him a cigarette, and he accepted it gravely. "You have a woman?" he asked.

"No."

"What, no woman? It is good for a man to have a woman."

"No doubt." He was, I thought, all of thirteen. "You have a woman?" I asked the question gravely.

He accepted it in the same manner. "No. I am young for a woman. And they are much trouble. I prefer the goats."

"They are no trouble?"

He shrugged. "Goats are goats."

The comment seemed to explain much. He smoked in silence, and I waited for him to speak again. "If I had a woman, I would beat her. Women are good when beaten often, but they are not so productive as goats."

It was a question I did not wish to debate. He seemed to have all the advantage in the argument. He undoubtedly knew goats, and spoke of women with profound wisdom. I knew neither goats nor women.

"If you like the hillside," he said at last, "why do you not stay? The picture will be no good. It will be the sea and the ruins only at one time, and they are not always the same. They change," he added.

"My home is elsewhere. I must go back."

"Then why do you leave? Is it not good there? I think you are very restless." He looked at me. "Have you goats at home?"

"No." I was ashamed to admit it, feeling that the confession would lower me in his esteem. "I have no goats."

"A camel?" He was giving me every chance.

"No," I confessed reluctantly, "no camel." Inspiration hit me suddenly. "I have horses. Two of them."

He considered that. "It is good to have a horse, but a horse is like a woman. It is unproductive. If you have a horse or a woman, you must also have goats."

"If one has a woman," I ventured, "one must have many goats."

He nodded. I had but stated a fact.

Where There's Fighting

The four men were sprawled in a cuplike depression at the top of the pass. From where the machine gun was planted it had a clear field of fire for over four hundred yards. Beyond that the road was visible only at intervals. By a careful watch of those intervals an enemy could be seen long before he was within range.

A low parapet of loose rock had been thrown up along the lip of the depression, leaving an aperture for the .30-caliber gun. Two of the men were also armed with rifles.

It was very still. The slow warmth of the morning sun soaked into their bones and ate the frost away, leaving them lethargic and pleased. The low rumble as of thunder in the far-off hills were the bombs over Serbia, miles away.

"Think they'll ever come?" Benton asked curiously.

"They'll come," Ryan said.

"We can't stop them."

"No."

"How about some coffee? Is there any left?"

Ryan nodded. "It'll be ready soon. The part that's coffee is done, the part that's chicory is almost done, and the part that's plain bean is doing."

Benton looked at the two who were sleeping in the sun. They were mere boys. "Shall we wake them?"

"Pretty soon. They worry too much. Especially Pommy. He's afraid of being afraid."

"Sackworth doesn't. He thinks we're bloody heroes. Do you?"

"I'd feel heroic as blazes if I had a shave," Ryan said. "Funny, how you like being shaved. It sets a man up somehow."

Pommy turned over and opened his eyes. "I say, Bent? Shall I spell you a bit? You've been there hours!"

Benton looked at him, liking his fresh, clean-cut look.

"I could use some coffee. I feel like I was growing to this rock."

The young Englishman had risen to his feet.

"There's something coming down there. A man, I think."

"Couldn't be one of our men. We didn't have any over there. He's stopped—looking back."

"He's coming on again now," Sackworth said after a moment. He had joined them at the first sign of trouble. "Shall I try a shot?"

"Wait. Might be a Greek."

The sun climbed higher, and the moving figure came slowly toward them. He seemed to move at an almost creeping pace. At times, out of sight of the pass, they thought he would never show up again.

"He's carrying something," Pommy said. "Too heavy for a rifle, but I saw the sun flash on it back there a way."

The man came into sight around the last bend. He was big, but he walked very slowly, limping a little. He was wearing faded khaki trousers and a torn shirt. Over one shoulder were several belts of ammunition.

"He hasn't carried that very far," Ryan said. "He's got over a hundred pounds there."

Benton picked up one of the rifles and stepped to the parapet, but before he could lift the gun or speak, the man looked up. Benton thought he had never seen a face so haggard with weariness. It was an utter and complete weariness that seemed to come from within. The man's face was covered with a stubble of black beard. His face was wide at the cheekbones, and the nose was broken. His head was wrapped in a bloody bandage above which coarse black hair was visible.

"Any room up there?" he asked.

"Who are you?" Benton demanded.

Without replying, the big man started up the steep path. Once he slipped, skinning his knee against a sharp rock. Puzzled, they waited. When he stood beside them, they were shocked at his appearance. His face, under the deep brown of sun and wind, was drawn and pale, his nose peeling from sunburn. The rags of what must have once been a uniform were mud stained and sweat discolored.

"What difference does it make?" he asked mildly, humorously. "I'm here now."

He lowered the machine gun and slid the belts to the ground. When he straightened, they could see he was a half inch taller than Benton, who was a tall man, and at least thirty pounds heavier. Through his shirt bulging muscles showed, and there was blood clogging the hair on his chest.

"My name's Horne," he added. "Mike Horne. I've been fighting with Koska's guerrillas in Albania."

Benton stared, uncertain. "Albania? That's a long way from here."

"Not so far if you know the mountains." He looked at the pot on the fire. "How's for some coffee?"

Silently Ryan filled a cup. Digging in his haversack, Horne produced some Greek bread and a thick chunk of sausage. He brushed the sand from the sausage gravely. "Want some? I salvaged this from a bombed house back yonder. Might be some shell fragments in it."

"You pack that gun over the mountains?" Ryan asked.

Horne nodded, his mouth full. "Part of the way. It was surrounded by dead Greeks when I found it. Four Italians found it the same time. We had trouble."

"Did you—kill them all?" Pommy asked.

Horne looked at him. "No, kid. I asked them to tea an' then put sand in their bearings."

Pommy's face got red; then he grinned.

"Got any ammo for a .50?" Horne looked up at Benton. "I got mighty little left."

"They put down four boxes by mistake," Benton said.

Ryan was interested. "Koska's guerrillas? I heard of them. Are they as tough as you hear?"

"Tougher. Koska's an Albanian gypsy. Sneaked into Valona alone a few nights ago an' got himself three dagos. With a knife."

Sackworth studied Horne as if he were some kind of insect. "You call that bravery? That's like animals. One can at least fight like a gentleman!"

Horne winked at Ryan. "Sure, kid. But this ain't a gentleman's fight. This is war. Nothing sporting about it, just a case of dog eat dog, an' you better have big teeth."

"Why are you here?" Sackworth demanded.

Horne shrugged. "Why am I any place? Think I'm a fifth columnist or something?" He stared regretfully into the empty cup. "Well, I'm not. I ran a gun in the Chaco a few years ago; then they started to fight in China, so I went there. I was in the Spanish scrap with the Loyalists.

"Hung around in England long enough to learn something about that parachute business. Now that's a man's job. When you get down in an enemy country, you're on your own. I was with the bunch that hopped off from Libya and parachuted down in southern Italy to cut off that aqueduct and supply line to the Sicily naval base. Flock of 'spiggoties' spotted me, but I got down to the water and hiked out in a fishing boat. Now I'm here."

He looked up at Benton, wiping the back of his hand across his mouth. "From Kalgoorlie, I bet. You got the look. I prospected out of there once. I worked for pearls out of Darwin, too. I'm an original swag man, friend."

"What's a swag man?" Pommy asked.

Horne looked at him, smiling. Two of his front teeth at the side were missing.

"It's a bum, sonny. Just a bum. A guy who packs a tucker bag around looking for whatever turns up."

Horne pulled the gun over into his lap, carefully wiping the oil buffer clean. Then he oiled the moving parts of the gun with a little can he took from his hip pocket and slowly assembled it. He handled the gun like a lover, fitting the parts together smoothly and testing it carefully for head space when it was ready for firing.

"That a German shirt you have on?" Sackworth asked. His eyes were level, and he had his rifle across his knees, pointed at Horne.

"Sure," Horne said mildly. "I needed a shirt, so I took it out of a dead German's outfit."

"Looting," Sackworth said with scorn. There was distaste and dislike in his gaze.

"Why not?" Horne looked up at Sackworth, amused. "You're a good kid, so don't start throwing your weight around. This sportsmanship stuff, the old school tie, an' whatnot—that's okay where it belongs. You Britishers who play war like a game are living in the past. There's nothing sporting about this. It's like waterfronts or jungles. You survive any way you can."

Sackworth did not move the rifle. "I don't like him," he said to Benton. "I don't trust him."

"Forget it!" Benton snapped. "The man's all right, and Lord knows we need fighting men!"

"Sure," Horne added quietly. "It's just you an' me are different kind of animals, kid. You're probably Eton and then Sandhurst. Me, I came up the hard way. A tough road kid in the States, then an able seaman, took a whirl at the fight game, and wound up in Chaco.

"I like to fight. I also like to live. I been in a lot of fights, and mostly I fought pretty good, an' I'm still alive. The Jerries use whatever tactics they need. What you need, kid, in war is not a lot of cut an' dried rules but a good imagination, the ability to use what you've got to the best advantage no matter where you are, and a lot of the old moxie.

"You'll make a good fighter. You got the moxie. All you need is a little kicking around."

"I wish we knew where the Jerries were," Ryan said. "This waiting gets me."

"You'll see them pretty quick," Horne said. "There's about a battalion in the first group, and there's only one tank."

Benton lowered his cup, astonished. "You mean you've actually seen them? They are coming?"

Horne nodded. "The main body isn't far behind the first bunch."

"Why didn't you say so?" Sackworth demanded. His face was flushed and angry. "We could have warned the troops behind us."

"Yeah?" Horne did not look up from wiping the dust from the cartridges. "Well, we couldn't. You see," he added, looking up, "they broke through Monastir Pass two days ago. Your men back there know more about it than we do. This is just a supporting column to polish off any leftovers like us."

"Then—we're cut off?" Pommy asked.

Horne nodded. "You have been for two days. How long you been here?"

"Just three days," Benton said. He studied Horne thoughtfully. "What are you? A Yank?"

Horne shrugged. "I guess so. When I joined up in Spain, they took my citizenship away. It was against the law to fight fascism then. If it was wrong then, it's wrong now. But me, I feel just the same. I'll fight them in China, in Spain, in Africa, or anywhere else.

"In Spain when everything was busting up, I heard about this guy Koska. One of his men was with us, so when he went back, I trailed along."

"They're coming," Sackworth said. "I can see the tank."

"All right," Benton said. He finished his coffee.

"Did you fight any Germans in Spain?" Pommy asked.

"Yeah." Mike Horne brushed invisible dust from the gun and fed a belt of cartridges into it. "Most of them aren't much better than the Italians. They fight better—the younger ones try harder—but all they know how to do is die."

"It's something to know that," Sackworth said.

"Nuts. Anybody can die. Everybody does. And dead soldiers never won any battles. The good soldier is the one who keeps himself alive and fighting. This bravery stuff—that's for milksops. For pantywaists. All of us are scared, but we fight just the same."

"The tank's getting closer," Sackworth said. He was plainly worried and showed it.

"I got the .50," Horne said. He settled himself comfortably into the sand and moved his gun on the swivel. "Let it get closer. Don't fire until they are close up to us. I'll take the tank. You take the first truck with the other gun, I'll take the second, an' so on. Get the drivers if you can."

They were silent. The rumble of the tank and heavy clank of the tread drew nearer. Behind them rolled the trucks, the men sitting in tight groups. They apparently expected no trouble.

"I'd have expected them to send a patrol," Benton said, low voiced.

"They did," Horne replied.

They looked at him, startled. His eyes were on the gray-green column. He had sighted the fifty at the gun aperture on the tank.

"All right," he said suddenly.

His gun broke into a hoarse chatter, slamming steel-jacketed bullets at the tank. Then its muzzle lifted suddenly and swept the second truck. Soldiers were shouting and yelling, spilling from trucks like madmen, but the two first trucks were smashed into carriers of death before the men could move. The Germans farther back had found their enemy, and steel-jacketed bullets smashed into the parapet. Pommy felt something like a hot whiplash along his jaw.

They were above the column and out of reach of the tank. Mike Horne stood up suddenly and depressed the gun muzzle. The tank was just below. The gun chattered, and the tank slewed around sideways and drove full tilt into the rock wall as though to climb it.

Horne dropped back. "The older ones have a soft spot on top," he said.

The men of the broken column ran for shelter. Some of them tried to rush the steep path, but the fire blasted them back to the road, dead or dying. Others, trying to escape the angry bursts from the two guns, tried to scramble up the walls of the pass but were mowed down relentlessly.

It had been a complete and shocking surprise. The broken column became a rout. Horne stopped the .50 and wiped his brow with the back of his hand. He winked at Ryan.

"Nice going, kid. That's one tank that won't bother your pals."

Ryan peered around the rocks. The pass was empty of life. The wrecked tank was jammed against the rock wall, and one of the trucks had plunged off the precipice into the ravine. Another was twisted across the road.

A man was trying to get out of the first truck. He made it and tumbled to the road. His coat was stained with blood, and he was making whimpering sounds and trying to crawl. His face and head were bloody.

"Next time it'll be tough," Horne said. "They know now. They'll come in small bunches, scattered out, running for shelter behind the trucks."

Rifle fire began to sweep over the cup. They were low behind the parapet and out of sight. It was a searching, careful fire—expert fire.

Benton was quiet. He looked over at Horne. Officially in charge, he had yielded his command to Horne's superior knowledge.

"What d'you think?" he asked.

"We'll stop them," Horne said. "We'll stop them this time, maybe next time. After that—"

Horne grinned at Pommy. "First time under fire?"

"Yes."

"Take it easy. You're doing all right. Make every shot count. One cinch is worth five maybes."

Pommy crowded his body down into the gravel and rested his rifle in a niche in the rocks. He looked at Mike Horne and could see a thin trickle of fresh blood coming from under his bandage. The wound had opened again.

Was it deep, he wondered, or just a scratch? He looked at the lines about Horne's mouth and decided it was deep. Horne's sleeve was torn, and he had a dragon tattooed on his forearm.

They came with a rush. Rounding the bend, they broke into a scattered line; behind them, machine guns and rifles opened a hot fire to cover the advance.

They waited, and just before the men could reach the trucks, swept them with a steel scythe of bullets that mowed them down in a row. One man tumbled off the brink and fell into the ravine; then another fell, caught his fingers on the lip, and tumbled head over heels into the ravine as the edge gave way.

"How many got there?" Horne asked.

"A dozen, I think," Ryan said. "We got about thirty."

"Fair enough." Horne looked at Sackworth. The young Englishman was still resentful. He didn't like Horne. "Doing all right?" Horne asked.

"Of course." Sackworth was contemptuous, but his face was drawn and gray.

"Ryan," Horne said, "you and Pommy leave the main attack to the machine guns. Watch the men behind the trucks. Pick them off as they try to move closer. You take the right, Pommy."

The German with the bloody face had fallen flat. Now he was getting to his knees again.

Then, suddenly, three men made a concerted rush. Ryan and Pommy fired instantly, and Ryan's man dropped.

"I missed!" Pommy said. "Blast it, I missed!"

There was another rush, and both machine guns broke into a clattering roar. The gray line melted away, but more kept coming. Men rounded the bend and split to the right and left. Despite the heavy fire a few of them were getting through. Pommy and Ryan were firing continuously and methodically now.

Suddenly a man broke from under the nearest truck and came on in a plunging rush. Both Ryan and Pommy fired, and the man went down, but before they could fire again, he lunged to his feet and dove into the hollow below the cliff on which their pit rested.

"He can't do anything there," Sackworth said. "He—"

A hurtling object shot upward from below, hit the slope below the guns, rolled a few feet, and then burst with an earth-shaking concussion.

Horne looked up from where he had ducked his head. Nobody was hit. "He's got grenades. Watch it. There'll be another in a minute."

Ryan fired, and a man dropped his rifle and started back toward the trucks. He walked quite calmly while they stared. Then he fell flat and didn't get up.

Twice more grenades hit the slope, but the man was too close below the cliff. They didn't quite reach the cup thrown from such an awkward angle. "If one of those makes it—" Benton looked sour.

Pommy was shooting steadily now. There was another rush, and Benton opened up with the machine gun. Suddenly another grenade came up from below, traveling an arching course. It hit the slope, too short. It rolled free and fell. There was a terrific explosion.

"Tough," Ryan said. "He made a good try."

"Yeah," Horne said. "So have we."

Hours passed. The machine guns rattled steadily now. Only at long intervals was there a lull. The sun had swung over and was setting behind the mountain.

Horne straightened, his powerful body heavy with fatigue. He looked over at Ryan and grinned. Ryan's face was swollen from the kick of the rifle. Benton picked up a canteen and tried to drink, but there was no water.

"What now?" Pommy said.

Horne shrugged. "We take it on the lam."

"What?" Sackworth demanded. "What does that mean?"

"We beat it," Mike Horne said. "We get out while the getting is good."

"What?" Sackworth was incredulous. "You mean—run? Leave our post?"

"That's just what I mean," Horne said patiently. "We delayed this bunch long enough. We got ours from them, but now it doesn't matter anymore. The Jerries are behind us now. We delayed them for a while. All around through these hills guys are delaying them just for a while. We've done all we could here. Now we scram. We fight somewhere else."

"Go if you want to," Sackworth said stubbornly. "I'm staying."

Suddenly there was a terrific concussion, then another and another.

"What the deuce?" Benton exclaimed. "They got a mortar. They—"

The next shell hit right where he was sitting. It went off with an ear-splitting roar and a burst of flame. Pommy went down, hugged the earth with an awful fear. Something tore at his clothes; then sand and gravel showered over him. There was another concussion and another.

Somebody had caught him by the foot. "Come on, kid. Let's go."

They broke into a stumbling run down the slope back of the nest, then over the next ridge and down the ravine beyond. Even then they ran on, using every bit of cover. Once Pommy started to slow, but Horne nudged him with the rifle barrel.

"Keep it up," he panted. "We got to run."

They slid into a deeper ravine and found their way to a stream. They walked then, slipping and sliding in the gathering darkness. Once a patrol saw them, and shots rattled around, but they kept going.

Then it was night, and clouds covered the moon and the stars. Wearily, sodden with exhaustion, they plodded on. Once, on the bank of a little stream, they paused for a drink. Then Horne opened the old haversack again and brought out the remnants of the sausage and bread. He broke each in half, and shared them with Pommy.

"But—"

Pommy's voice caught in his throat. "Gone?" he said then.

Horne nodded in the darkness. "Yeah. Lucky it wasn't all of us."

"But what now?" Pommy asked. "You said they were behind us."

"Sure," Horne agreed. "But we're just two men. We'll travel at night, keep to the hills. Maybe they'll make a stand at Thermopylae. If not there, they might try to defend the Isthmus of Corinth. Maybe we can join them there."

"But if they don't? If we can't?"

"Then Africa, Pommy, or Syria or Suez or Russia or England. They'll always be fighting them somewhere, an' that's where I want to be. It won't stop. The Germans win here, they win there, but they got to keep on fighting. They win battles, but none of them are decisive. None of them mean an end.

"Ever fight a guy, kid, who won't quit? You keep kicking him, and he keeps coming back for more, keeps trying. You knock him down, but he won't stay down? It's hell, that's what it is. He won't quit, so you can't.

"But they'll be fighting them somewhere, and that's where I want to be."

"Yeah," Pommy said. "Me, too."

The Cross and the Candle

When in Paris, I went often to a little hotel in a narrow street off the Avenue de la Grande Armee. Two doors opened into the building; one into a dark hallway and then by a winding stair to the chambers above, the other to the café, a tiny bistro patronized by the guests and a few people of the vicinity.

It was in no way different from a hundred other such places. The rooms were chill and dank in the morning (there was little heat in Paris, even the girls in the Folies Bergère were dancing in goose pimples), the furnishings had that added Parisian touch of full-length mirrors running alongside the bed for the obvious and interesting purpose of enabling one, and one's companion, to observe themselves and their activities.

Madame was a Breton, and as my own family were of Breton extraction, I liked listening to her tales of Roscoff, Morlaix, and the villages along the coast. She was a veritable treasure of ancient beliefs and customs, quaint habits and interesting lore. There was scarcely a place from Saint-Malo to the Bay of Douarnenez of which she didn't have a story to tell.

Often when I came to the café, there would be a man seated in the corner opposite the end of the bar. Somewhat below medium height, the thick column of his neck spread out into massive shoulders and a powerful chest. His arms were heavy with muscle and the brown hands that rested on the table before him were thick and strong.

Altogether, I have seen few men who gave such an impression of sheer animal strength and vitality. He moved in leisurely fashion, rarely smiled, and during my first visits had little to say.

In some bygone brawl, his nose had been broken and a deep scar began over his left eye and ran to a point beneath a left ear of which half the lobe was gone. You looked at his wide face, the mahogany skin, and polished

over the broad cheekbones and you told yourself, "This man is dangerous!" Yet often there was also a glint of hard, tough humor in his eyes.

He sat in his corner, his watchful eyes missing nothing. After a time
or two, I came to the impression that he was spinning a web, like some
exotic form of spider, but what manner of fly he sought to catch, I could
not guess.

Madame told me he was a *marin,* a sailor, and had lived for a time in
Madagascar.

One afternoon when I came to the café, he was sitting in his corner
alone. The place was empty, dim, and cold. Hat on the table beside him,
he sat over an empty glass.

He got up when I came in and moved behind the bar. I ordered *vin
blanc* and suggested he join me. He filled the two glasses without comment, then lifted his glass. *"À votre santé!"* he said. We touched glasses and
drank.

"Cold, today," he said suddenly.

The English startled me. In the two months past, I had spoken to him
perhaps a dozen times, and he replied always in French.

"You speak English then?"

He grinned at me, a tough, friendly grin touched by a sort of wry
cynicism. "I'm an American," he said, "or I was."

"The devil you say!" Americans are of all kinds, but somehow ...
still, he could have been anything.

"Born in Idaho," he said, refilling our glasses. When I started to pay,
he shook his head and brought money from his own pocket and placed it
under an ashtray for Madame to put in the register when she returned.
"They call me Tomas here. My old man was an Irish miner, but my mother
was Basque."

"I took it for granted you were French."

"Most of them do. My mother spoke French and Spanish. Picked
them up around home from her parents, as I did from her. After I went to
sea, I stopped in Madagascar four years, and then went to Mauritius and
Indochina."

"You were here during the war?"

"Part of the time. When it started, I was in Tananarive; but I returned
here, got away from the *Boche,* and fought with the maquis for a while.
Then I came back to Paris."

He looked up at me and the slate-gray eyes were flat and ugly. "My
girl was dead."

"Bombs?"

"No. A Vichy rat."

He would say nothing more on the subject and our talk drifted to a strange and little known people who live in and atop a mountain in Madagascar, and their peculiar customs. I, too, had followed the sea for a time so there was much good talk of the ways of ships and men.

Tomas was without education in the accepted sense, yet he had observed well and missed little. He had read widely. His knowledge of primitive peoples would have fascinated an anthropologist and he had appreciation and understanding for their beliefs.

After talking with him, I came more often to the café, for we found much in common. His cynical toughness appealed to me, and we had an understanding growing from mutual experiences and interests. Yet as our acquaintance grew, I came to realize that he was a different man when we talked together alone than when others were in the room. Then his manner changed. He became increasingly watchful, talked less and only in French.

The man was watching for someone or something. Observing without seeming to, I became aware the center of his interests were those who came most often to the café. And of these, there were four that held his attention most.

Mombello was a slender Italian of middle years who worked in a market. Picard was a chemist, and Leon Matsys owned a small iron foundry on the edge of Paris and a produce business near The Halles. Matsys was a heavy man who had done well, had educated himself, and was inclined to tell everyone so. Jean Mignet, a sleek, catlike man, was supported by his wife, an actress of sorts. He was pleasant enough to know, but I suspected him of being a thief.

Few women came to the café. Usually the girls who came to the hotel entered by the other door and went to the chambers above, and after a period of time, returned through the same door. To us, they existed merely as light footsteps in the dark hall and on the stairs.

Madame herself, a friendly, practical Breton woman, was usually around and occasionally one of the daughters Mombello would come in search of their father.

The oldest was eighteen and very pretty, but businesslike without interest in the men of the café. The younger girl was thin, woefully thin from lack of proper food, but a beautiful child with large, magnificent dark eyes, dark wavy hair, and lips like the petals of a flower.

Someone among these must be the center of interest, yet I could not find that his interest remained long with any one of the four men. For their part, they seemed to accept him as one of themselves. Only one, I think, was conscious of being watched. That one was Jean Mignet.

On another of those dismal afternoons, we sat alone in the café and talked. (It always seemed that I came there only when the outside was bleak and unhappy, for on the sunny days, I liked being along the boulevards or in St. Germaine.) The subject again arose of strange superstitions and unique customs.

There was a Swede on one of my ships who would never use salt when there was a Greek at the table; an idea no more ridiculous than the fear some people have of eating fish and drinking milk in the same meal.

Tomas nodded. "I've known of many such ideas," he said, "and in some of the old families you will find customs that have been passed along from generation to generation in great secrecy for hundreds of years.

"I know of one"—he hesitated, describing circles on the dark tabletop with the wet bottom of his glass—"that is, a religious custom followed so far as I know by only one family."

He looked up at me. "You must never speak of this around here," he said, and he spoke so sharply and with so much feeling, I assured him I'd never speak of it anywhere, if he so wished.

"In the family of my girl," he said, "there is an ancient custom that goes back to the Crusades. Her ancestor was a soldier with Saint Louis at Saint-Jean d'Acre. No doubt you know more of that than I do. Anyway, when his brother was killed in the fighting, there was no shrine or church nearby, so he thrust his dagger into a log. As you know, the hilts of daggers and swords were at that time almost always in the form of a cross, and he used it so in this case, burning a candle before the dagger.

"It became the custom of a religious and fighting family, and hence whenever there is a death, this same dagger is taken from its wrappings of silk and with the point thrust into wood, a candle for the dead is burned before it.

"Marie told me of this custom after her mother's death when I came hurriedly into her room and surprised her with the candle burning. For some forgotten reason, a tradition of secrecy had grown around the custom, and no one outside the family ever knew of it.

"That night in the darkened room, we watched the candle slowly burn away before that ancient dagger, a unique dagger where on crosspiece or guard was carved the body of Christ upon the cross and the blade was engraved with the figure of a snake, the snake signifying the powers of evil fallen before God.

"I never saw the dagger again while she lived. It was put away among her things, locked carefully in an iron chest, never to be brought out again until, as she said, she herself died, or her brother. Then, she looked at me, and said, 'Or you, Tomas, for you are of my family now.'"

He looked at me, and underneath the scarred brows, there were tears in his eyes.

THE CROSS AND THE CANDLE

"She must have been a fine girl," I said, for he was deeply moved.

"She was the only thing in my life! Only a madman, a mad American, would return to France after the war broke out. But I loved her.

"Look at me. I'm not the kind of man many women could love. I'm too rough, too brutal! I'm a seaman, that is all, and never asked to be more. A good man at sea or in a fight, but I have no words with which to say nice things to a woman, and she was a beautiful girl with an education."

Tomas took out his wallet and removed a worn photograph. When I looked at it, I was frankly astonished. The girl was not merely a pretty girl, she was all he had said, and more. She *was* beautiful.

Furthermore, there was something in her eyes and face that let you know that here was a girl who had character, maybe one who knew what loyalty was.

"She is lovely," I said sincerely. "I never saw anyone more beautiful!"

He was pleased, and he looked at me with his face suddenly lighter. "She was magical!" he said. "The best thing in my life. I came first to her house with her brother, who had been my shipmate on a voyage from Saigon. She was a child then, and I thought of her as nothing else.

"So, when next I came to the house, I brought her a present from Liverpool, and then others from Barcelona and Algiers. Simple things, and inexpensive, the sort of things a sailor may find in almost any port, but they had romance, I suppose, a color.

"I gave them simply because I was a lonely man, and this family had taken me as one of them, and because the giving of things is good for a lonely heart.

"One day, she was twelve then, I think, she had gone to a theater in the Boulevard de Clichy with her brother, and when they came out, she saw me with a girl, a girl from a café in the Pigalle. She was very angry and for days she would not speak to me.

"Her brother teased her, and said, 'Look! Marie thinks already she is a woman! She is jealous for you, Tomas!' "

He smiled at the memory. "Then, I was gone again to sea, and when I came again to the house, Marie was fourteen, taller, frightened, and skinny. Always she stared at me, and I brought her presents as before. Sometimes I took her to the theater, but to me she was a child. She was no longer gay, full of excitement and anger. She walked beside me very seriously.

"Four years then I was gone, and when I returned . . . you should have seen her! She was beautiful. Oh, I tell you, she was a woman now, and no doubt about it.

"I fell in love! So much that I could not talk for feeling it, but never did I think for a moment that it could matter.

"But did I have a choice? Not in the least! She had not changed, that one. She was both the little girl I knew first and the older one I knew later, and more besides. She laughed at me and said that long ago she had made up her mind that I was to be her man, and so it was to be whether I liked it or not! Me, I liked it. She was so much of what I wanted that she frightened me.

"Can you imagine what that did to me, m'sieu? I was a lonely man, a very lonely man. There had been the girls of the ports, but they are not for a man of soul, only for the coarse-grained who would satisfy the needs of the moment. Me, I wanted love, tenderness.

"I know." He shrugged. "I don't look it. I am a sailor and pleased to be one, and I've done my share of hard living. More than once, I've twisted my knife in the belly of a man who asked for it, and used my boots on them, too. But who is to say what feeling lives in the heart of a man? Or what need for love burns inside him?

"My parents died when I was young and the sea robbed me of my country. In such a life, one makes no close friends, no attachments, puts down no roots. Then, this girl, this beautiful girl, fell in love with me.

"Fell in love? No, I think the expression is wrong. She said she had always loved me even when she was a child and too young to know what it meant.

"Her mother and brother approved. They were good people, and I had lived long among them. Then the mother died, Pierre was away in the colonies, and Marie and I were to be married when he returned. So we lived together.

"Is this wrong? Who is to say what is right and what is wrong? In our hearts we understood and in France, well, they understand such things. What man is to live without a girl? Or a girl without a man?

"Then away I went to sea on my last trip, and while I was gone, the war came, and with it the Germans. When I returned, I joined the maquis to get back into France. Her letters were smuggled to me.

"Marie? She was a French girl, and she worked with the underground. She was very skillful, and very adept at fooling the *Boche*. Then, something happened.

"One of the men close to her was betrayed, then another, finally, it was her brother who was killed. The Gestapo had them, but they died without talking. One night I came to her to plead that she come away with me, it had been three years that I had fought in the underground, for her, almost six. But she told me she could not go; that someone close to her was working with the Nazis, someone who knew her. She must stay until she knew who it was.

"Yet try as she could, there was no clue. The man was shrewd, and a very devil. He finally came to her himself, after her brother was caught. He told her what he knew of her underground activities and of mine. He told her unless she came to live with him that I would be tortured and killed.

"He had spied upon her. He had even discovered her burning the candle before the dagger for Pierre after he was killed. He told her of it, to prove how much he knew—to prove he knew enough to find me—and she had admitted the reason.

"In the letter in which all this was told, she could not tell me who he was. He had friends in the underground, and she was fearful that learning who she was writing about, they would destroy the letter if they saw his name, and then she would be cut off from me and from all help.

"She would give me his name, she said, when I came next to Paris. He had not forced himself on her, just threatened. We had to plan to do away with him quickly. Marie said, too, that she was afraid that if the invasion came, he would kill her, for she alone could betray him; she alone knew of his activities for the Nazis.

"The invasion a secret? Of course! But when orders began to come for the underground, come thick and fast, we knew it was coming. Then, the landings were made, and for days we were desperately busy.

"We rose in Paris, and they were exciting, desperate days, and bitter days for the collaborators and the men of Vichy. Their servitude to the Nazis had turned to bitterness and gall; they fled; and they begged, and they died.

"When I could, I hurried to the flat where Marie lived. It was near here, just around the corner. I found her dying. She had been raped and shot by this collaborator two days before and she had crawled to her apartment to wait for me. She died telling me of it, but unable before her last breath to give me his name."

"And there was no way you could figure out who he was?" I asked.

"How?" He spread his hands expressively. "No one suspected him. His desire for her was such that he had threatened her, and in threatening her he had boasted of what he had done. That was a mistake he rectified by killing her.

"Only one thing I know. He is one of our little group here. She said he lived in this neighborhood, that he was waiting here more than once when he accosted her. He thinks himself safe now. My girl has been dead for some time and her body buried. She is never mentioned here.

"Mombello? He is an Italian. Picard is a chemist, and has had traffic with Germany since the twenties. Matsys? An iron foundry owner who retained it all through the war, but who was active in the underground as were Picard and Mignet."

We were interrupted then by some others coming into the café, yet now the evening had added zest. Here was a deadly bit of business. Over the next two hours, as they trooped in, I began to wonder. Which was he?

The slender, shrewd Mombello with his quick, eager eyes? That lean whip of a man, Mignet? The heavy Matsys with blue and red veins in his nose, and the penchant for telling you he'd seen it all and done it all? Or was it dry, cold Picard who sipped wine through his thin lips and seemed to have ice water for blood?

Which man was marked to die? How long would Tomas sit brooding in his corner, waiting? What was he waiting for? A slip of the tongue? A bit of drunken talk?

None of these men drank excessively. So which one? Mombello whose eyes seemed to gloat over the body of every woman he saw? Mignet with his lust for money and power and his quick knife? Or big affable Matsys? Or Picard with his powders and acids?

How long would he wait? These five had sat here for months, and now . . . now there were six. I was the sixth. Perhaps it was the sixth to tip the balance. Here they were caught in a pause before death. Yet the man who killed such a girl, and who betrayed his country, should not go free. There was a story in this, and it had an ending, somewhere.

Over the following gray days, several in a row, the conversation ebbed and flowed and washed around our ears. I did not speak privately to Tomas again but there seemed an ongoing, silent communication between us. Then, in a quiet moment of discussion, someone mentioned the bazooka, and it came to me then that another hand had been dealt . . . mine.

"A strange weapon," I agreed, and then moved the tide of conversations along the subject of weapons and warfare. I spoke of the first use of poison gas by soldiers of Thebes when they burned sulfur to drive defenders from the walls of Athenian cities, then to the use of islands of defense; a successful tactic by the Soviets in this war, previously used by the Russians defending themselves against Charles XII of Sweden.

Then other weapons and methods, and somehow, but carefully, to strange knives.

Tomas ignored me, the spider in his web, but he could hear every word and he was poised, poised for anything.

Mignet told of a knife he had seen in Algiers with a poisoned barb in the hilt near the blade, and Mombello of a Florentine dagger he had once seen.

Tomas stayed silent, turning his glass in endless circles upon the table before him, turning, turning, turning. We locked eyes for a moment and before he looked away he seemed to sigh and give a nearly imperceptible nod.

"There was a knife I saw once," I said suddenly, "with engraving on it. A very old knife, and very strange. A figure of Christ on the cross rose above a fallen snake. The religious symbolism is interesting. I'd never seen its like before, the worksmanship was so finely wrought."

A moment passed, a bare breath of suspended time . . .

"It was not the only one, I think," Leon Matsys said. "Odd things, they were used in some custom dating back to the Crusades."

He looked up, about to say more, then slowly the life went from his face. He was looking at Tomas, and Tomas was smiling.

Jean Mignet's eyes were suddenly alive. He did not know, but he suspected something. He was keen, that one.

Leon Matsys's face was deathly pale. He was trapped now, trapped by those remarks that came so casually from his lips. In the moment he had certainly forgotten what they might imply, and could not know that it would matter. He looked to one side and then the other, and then he started to take a drink.

He lifted the glass, then suddenly put it down. He got up, and his face was flabby and haunted by terror. He seemed unable to take his eyes from Tomas.

I glanced at Tomas, and my muscles jumped involuntarily. He had the ancient knife in his hand and was drawing his little circles with its point.

Matsys turned and started for the entrance, stumbling in his haste. The glass in the tall door rattled as it slammed closed, leaving only a narrow view of the dimly lit street.

After a moment Tomas pushed his chair back and got up and his step was very light as he also went out the door.

A Friend of the General

It began quite casually as such things often do, with a group of people conversing about nothing in particular, all unsuspecting of what the result might be.

My company was quartered in the château of the countess, as during the war she had moved into what had once been the gardener's cottage. It was the sort of place that in Beverly Hills would have sold well into six figures, a warm, cozy place with huge fireplaces, thick walls, and flowers all about.

The countess was young, very beautiful, and clever. She had friends everywhere and knew a bit of what went on anywhere you would care to mention. I was there because of the countess, and so, I suppose, was everybody else.

Her sister had just come down from the Netherlands, their first visit since the German occupation. There was a young American naval attaché, a woman of indeterminate age who was a Russian émigré, a fragile blond actress from Paris who, during the war, had smuggled explosives hidden under the vegetables in a basket on her bicycle. There was a baron who wore his monocle as if it were a part of him but had no other discernible talents and an American major who wanted to go home.

The war was fizzling out somewhere in Germany, far from us, and I wondered aloud where in Paris one could find a decent meal.

They assured me this was impossible unless I knew a good black-market restaurant. Due to the war there was a shortage of everything, and the black-market cafés had sprung up like speakeasies during the Prohibition era in the States—and like them you had to know somebody to get in.

Each had a different restaurant to suggest, although there was some agreement on one or two, but the countess solved my dilemma. Tearing a bit of note paper from a pad, she wrote an address. "Go to this place. Take a seat in a corner away from the windows, and when you wish to order, simply tell the waiter you are a friend of the general."

"But who," somebody asked, "is the general?"

She ignored the question but replied to mine when I asked, "But suppose the general is there at the time?"

"He will not be. He has flown to Baghdad and will go from there to Chabrang."

I could not believe that I had heard right.

"To *where*?" the naval attaché asked.

"It is a small village," I said, "near the ruins of Tsaparang."

"Now," the Russian woman said, "we understand everything! Tsaparang! Of course! Who would not know Tsaparang?"

"Where," the naval attaché asked, "are the ruins of Tsaparang?"

"Once," I began, "there was a kingdom—"

"Don't bother him with that. If I know Archie, he will waste the next three weeks trying to find it on a map."

"Take this"—she handed me the address—"and do as I have said. You will have as fine a meal as there is in Paris, as there is in Europe, in fact."

"But how can they do it?" Jeannine asked. "How can any café—"

"It is not the restaurant," the countess said, "it is the general. Before the war began, he knew it was coming, and he prepared for it. He has his own channels of communication, and being the kind of man he is, they work, war or no war.

"During a war some people want information, others want weapons or a way to smuggle escaped prisoners, but the general wanted the very best in food and wine, but above all, condiments, and he had them."

The general, it seemed, had served his apprenticeship during Latin American revolutions, moving from there to the Near and Middle East, to North Africa, and to China. Along the way he seemed to have feathered his nest quite substantially.

A few days later, leaving my jeep parked in a narrow street, I went through a passage between buildings and found myself in a small court. There were several shops with artists' studios above them, and in a corner under an awning were six tables. Several workmen sat at one table drinking beer. At another was a young man, perhaps a student, sitting over his books and a cup of coffee.

Inside the restaurant it was shadowed and cool. The floor was flagstone, and the windows hung with curtains. Everything was painfully neat. There were cloths on the tables and napkins. Along one side there was a bar with several stools. There were exactly twelve tables, and I had started for the one in the corner when a waiter appeared.

He indicated a table at one side. "Would you sit here, please?"

My uniform was, of course, American. That he spoke English was not unusual. Crossing to the table, I sat down with my back to the wall, facing the court. The table in the corner was but a short distance away and was no different from the others except that in the immediate corner there was a very large, comfortable chair with arms, not unlike what is commonly called a captain's chair.

"You wished to order?"

"I do." I glanced up. "I am a friend of the general."

"Ah? Oh, yes! Of course."

Nothing more was said, but the meal served was magnificent. I might even say it was unique.

A few days later, being in the vicinity, I returned, and then a third time. On this occasion I was scarcely seated when I heard footsteps in the court; looking up, I found the door darkened by one who could only be the general.

He was not tall, and he was—corpulent. He was neatly dressed in a tailored gray suit with several ribbons indicative of decorations. The waiter appeared at once, and there was a moment of whispered conversation during which he glanced at me.

Embarrassed? Of course. Here I had been passing myself as this man's friend, obtaining excellent meals under false pretenses. That I had paid for them and paid well made no difference at all. I had presumed, something no gentleman would do.

He crossed to his table and seated himself in his captain's chair. He ordered Madeira, and then the waiter crossed to my table. "Lieutenant? The general requests your company. He invites you to join him."

A moment I hesitated, then rising, I crossed over to him. "General? I must apolo—"

"Please be seated." He gestured to a chair.

"But I must—"

"You must do nothing of the kind. Have they taught you nothing in that army of yours? Never make excuses. Do what has to be done, and if it fails, accept the consequences."

"Very well." I seated myself. "I shall accept the consequences."

"Which will be an excellent meal, some very fine wine, and I hope some conversation worthy of the food and the wine." He glanced at me. "At least you are soldier enough for that. To find a very fine meal and take advantage of it. A soldier who cannot feed himself is no soldier at all."

He filled my glass, then his. "One question. How did you find this place? Who told you of me?"

Of course, I could have lied, but he would see through it at once. I disliked bringing her into it but knew that under the circumstances she would not mind.

"It was," I said, "the countess—"

"Of course," he interrupted me. "Only she would have dared." He glanced at me. "You know her well?"

It was nobody's business how well I knew her. "We are friends. My company is quartered in her château, and she is a lovely lady."

"Ah? How pleasant for you. She is excellent company, and such company is hard to come by these days. A truly beautiful woman, but clever. Altogether too clever for my taste. I do not trust clever women."

"I rather like them."

"Ah, yes. But you are a lieutenant. When you are a general, you will feel otherwise."

He spent a good deal of time watching the court, all of which was visible from where he sat. He had chosen well. The court had but one entrance for the public, although for the fortunate ones who lived close there were no exits, as I later discovered.

Not only could he not be approached from behind, but anyone emerging from the passage was immediately visible to him, while they could not see him until they actually entered the restaurant.

On our second meeting I surprised him and put myself in a doubtful position. I was simply curious, and my question had no other intent.

"How did you like Chabrang?"

He had started to lift his glass, and he put it down immediately. His right hand slid to the edge of the table until only his fingertips rested there. His tone was distinctly unfriendly when he replied, "What do you mean?"

"When I asked the countess if you would be here, she said you were in Baghdad—on the way to Chabrang."

"She said *that*? She mentioned Chabrang?"

"Yes, and I was surprised. It isn't the sort of place people hear of, being in such an out-of-the-way place, and only a village—a sort of way station."

His right hand dropped into his lap, and his fingers tugged at his trouser leg, which clung a bit too snugly to his heavy thigh. "You know Chabrang."

It was not a question but a statement. His right hand hitched the pant leg again. Suddenly I realized what was on his mind, and I almost laughed, for I'd been away from that sort of thing too long and had become careless. The laugh was not for him but simply that it seemed like old times, and it was kind of good to be back.

"You won't need the knife," I told him. "I am no danger to you."

"You know Chabrang, and there are not fifty men in Europe who know it. Am I to believe this is pure coincidence?"

He had a knife in his boot top, I was sure of that. He was a careful man and no doubt had reason to be, but why that was so I had no idea and told him as much.

"It was my only way out," he said. "They found me, but they were looking for a man who was carrying a great lot of money, and I had nothing but food, weapons, and some butterflies. They let me go."

"I believed it was a way out for me, too," I said, "but I was not so lucky. I had to turn back."

He turned to look at me. "When were you in China?"

"It was long ago." I have never liked dates. Perhaps because I have a poor memory for dates in my own life. "It was in the time of the war lords," I said.

He shrugged. "That's indefinite enough."

We talked of many things. He gestured widely. "This is what I wanted," he said. "I wanted time—leisure. Time to read, to think, to see. Some people make it some ways, some another. Mine was through war."

"It is no longer regarded with favor," I suggested.

He shrugged again. "Who cares? For ten thousand years it was the acceptable way for a man to make his fortune. A young man with a strong arm and some luck could go off to the wars and become rich.

"All the old kingdoms were established so. All the original 'great families' were founded in just such a way. What else was William the Conqueror? Or Roger of Sicily? Or their Viking ancestors who first conquered and then settled in Normandy? What does Norman mean but Northmen? Who were Cortés and Pizarro? They were young men with swords."

"Ours is a different world," I suggested. "Our standards are not the same."

"Bah!" He waved his fork. "The standards are the same, only now the fighting is done by lawyers. There is more cunning and less courage. They will sell you the arms—"

"Like Milton," I said.

He stopped with his fork in the air and his mouth open. "You know about Milton," he said. "I am beginning to wonder about you, lieutenant."

"Everybody in China knew that story. Perhaps I should say everybody in our line of business or around the Astor Bar. It was no secret."

"Perhaps not. Perhaps not."

Such stories are repeated in bars and tearooms, over bridge tables as well as in the waterfront dives. Milton had been a well set up man in his early forties, as I recall him. A smooth, easy-talking man, somewhat florid of face, who played a good game of golf, haunted the Jockey Club, and owned a few good racehorses, Mongolian ponies brought down for that purpose. He had been a dealer in guns, supplying the various war lords with rifles, machine guns, mortars, and ammunition. As a machine gun was worth its weight in gold and as some European nation was always liquidating its stores to replace them with more modern weapons, Milton did well.

He reminded me of a first-class insurance salesman, and in a sense that was what he was. The weapons he sold were the kind of insurance they needed.

He might have become enormously wealthy, but he had an urge to gamble, and he had a blonde. The blonde, some said, was none too bright, but she had other assets that were uniquely visible, and nobody really inquired as to her intelligence, least of all Milton.

A day came when too much blonde and too much gambling left him nearly broke, and she chose that moment to say she wanted to go to Paris. She pleaded, she argued, and he listened. He was willing enough, but the problem was money.

At that moment an order came for six thousand rifles, some machine guns and mortars, with ammunition for all. Milton had only six hundred rifles on hand and insufficient cash. Such deals were always cash on the barrel head. He agreed to supply what was needed.

Long ago he had arranged a little deal with the customs officials to pass anything he shipped in a piano box, and as a piano salesman he seemed to be doing very well indeed.

Knowing the kind of people with whom he dealt, he also knew the necessity for absolute secrecy in what he was about to do, so with one German whom he knew from long experience would not talk, he went to his warehouse, and locking the doors very carefully, he proceeded to pack the cases with old, rusted pipe and straw. Atop each case, before closing it, he put a few rifles to satisfy any quick inspection. Yet the greatest thing he had going for him was his reputation for integrity. He supervised the loading of the piano boxes on a Chinese junk and collected his down payment of three hundred thousand dollars.

He had taken every precaution. Through a close-mouthed acquaintance he had bought two tickets on a vessel that was sailing that very night.

"Pack an overnight bag for each of us," he said. "Nothing more. And be ready. Say nothing to anyone and I'll buy you a completely new wardrobe in Paris."

Now, his rifles loaded on the junk, he drove at once to his apartment on Bubbling Well Road. He ran lightly up the steps carrying the small black bag. "Come! We've got to move fast! There's not much time to catch the boat!"

This, you must remember, was before World War II, and there were no airlines as such.

"Where are the tickets?" he asked.

She came to him, her blue eyes wide and wonderful. "Oh, Milt! I hope you're not going to be angry, but the Funstons are having a party tonight, and they are always such *fun*! Well, I turned in our tickets and got tickets on another boat, a much faster one, that leaves tomorrow!"

No doubt there was a moment of sheer panic; then what he hoped was common sense prevailed. It would take that junk a week to get to its destination. Well—four days at least. There was nothing to be done, and why not one more night?

The next morning was one I would never forget. I'd known Milton only to speak to, although we did have a drink together once. When a friend banged on my door at daybreak and told me he had something to show me, I went along.

What he showed me was what Milton might have expected, for the men with whom he did business did not play games.

There, standing upright in the parking lot outside his place on Bubbling Well Road, was a piece of the rusty pipe he had so carefully packed. On top of it was Milton's head. His complexion was no longer florid.

"Everybody knew that story," I repeated. "At least everybody of our sort. I heard it again a few days ago in the Casual Officers' Mess on Place St. Augustine."

"But you know about Chabrang," the general said.

The wine was excellent. "I see no connection," I said.

He gave me a sidelong glance, filled with suspicion. Why the mention of Chabrang disturbed him, I could not guess, as it was but an unimportant village on one of the routes out of Sinkiang to Ladakh. It was in no way noteworthy except that it was near the ruins of Tsaparang. The ruins represented about all that remained of a long-ago kingdom.

"Did you know Milton?" I asked.

"I knew him. If the Chinese had not killed him, I would have. Those munitions were consigned to me."

"To *you*?"

"They were consigned to me for the war lord, and the fraud put my head on the block. I was suspected of complicity."

"What happened?"

"I acted. Perceiving that I was suspected, and knowing the gentleman concerned was not one to dillydally, I made my move. You see, he already owed me money, a considerable sum. By disposing of me, he could make somebody atone for the fraud and liquidate his debt at the same time."

He fell silent while the waiter brought a steaming platter of seafood. When he had gone, the general resumed. "It was the time to move, so I acted. Remember that this is the first principle—*act*! Remember that, my young friend! Do not deliberate! Do not hesitate! Do not wait upon eventuality! *Act!* It is always better to do something, even if not quite the right thing, than to do nothing. *Action! Decision!* Only these are important!"

He toyed with an oyster, glancing from under his brows. "My mind, at such times, works quickly. He needed a scapegoat to save face. Not in Shanghai but there, before his men! At once! Instantly I perceived it was I who must pay."

He ate the oyster, and taking a bit of bread, buttered it lavishly. Many of the good people of France had not seen so much butter in months.

"You see, the commander himself did not yet know of the fraud, but immediately the discovery was made, an officer had left to report to him. He could reach him in not less than an hour, then an hour to return.

"The captain of the junk had seen none of what went on, so I went to him immediately, put money in his hand, and told him to sail to such and such a point upriver. The cargo would be received there.

"Then I went to the telegraph station, which was closed. I broke in to it and sent a message to another, rival war lord up the river, offering the guns to him for a fancy price. He was desperately in need of them, and I told him I could promise delivery if the money was paid to me in gold. A place of payment was mentioned.

"There was a charter plane at the field. You knew him, I think? Milligan? He would fly you anywhere for a price and land his plane on a pocket handkerchief if need be. Moreover, he could be trusted, and there were some, in those days, who could not. I placed five hundred dollars in his hand and said I wished to leave for Shanghai at once.

" 'After I gas up,' he said.

" 'Now,' I told him. 'Right now. There is petrol at—' I took his map and put my finger on the place. 'And you can land there.'

" 'If you say,' he replied doubtfully. 'I never heard of—'

" 'The petrol is there,' I promised him. 'I had it placed there for just such an emergency.' "

The general looked around at me. "You are young, lieutenant, and wise as you may be, you are still learning, so remember to trust no one!

Prepare for every eventuality no matter how remote! Not even a mouse trusts himself to one hole only. That is an old saying, but it has remained in my mind, and can I be less wise than a mouse?

"We took off at once. Within twenty minutes of my realization I *acted*! And that night I was in Shanghai with *her*!"

"Her?" He had lost me.

"Of course! With Milton's blonde. What was her name? I've forgotten. No matter. I was there, consoling her.

"Of course"—he glanced at me—"I was younger then and not so— so—well, I am a little overweight now. But then, ah, I was handsome then, lieutenant! I was handsome, and I was, of course, younger.

"I found her in tears. She was weeping for him. For Milton. Or perhaps she was weeping for that lost trip to Paris. About women, lieutenant, one never knows. No matter.

"There on the floor was the black bag. It was out of the way, back against the sofa's end, but I recognized it at once. True, I'd never seen it before, but I'd seen others of the kind. In it would be the money! All that delightful, beautiful money! And she was crying? Well, as I have said, she was a woman, and about women one never knows.

"I consoled her. What else could I do? What does one do with a pretty woman who is sad and has a quarter of a million dollars, give or take a few? I told her she must not worry, that I—*I* would take her to Paris! And who knew Paris better? Who knew the nightspots, the cafés, the bordel—Well, who knew the town better than I? Even its history!

"Oh, I was marvelous that day! I told her exciting and glamorous tales of what the city was like, of living there, and I dropped names, names of all the famous and infamous. As a matter of fact, I actually did know some of them.

"She was consoled! She rested her head on my shoulder. As you have seen, they are very broad. She dried her tears; then she smoothed her dress, she touched up her makeup, and she said, 'I still have the tickets. We could go at once. I—there is nothing more for me here! Nothing!'

" 'I know.' I took her two hands. 'It is tragic. But in Paris, my dear, you can forget. In Paris there is music, there is dancing, there is love, and there is beauty! And we shall be there—together!' "

He paused, refilling his glass. "She listened, her blue eyes very wide and wondering. She was a dear girl, no question of it. The black bag was at my feet. 'Look!' I took from my pocket a packet of bills and stripped off several of the thousand-dollar denomination. 'Take this! I shall meet you in Paris! Go to this place—' I wrote out the name of a small, discreet hotel—'and wait for me. I shall not be long.'

"Then I picked up the black bag and walked out. Once beyond the door with the bag I did not wait for the lift, but ran down the stairs. I had it, did I not? I had the black bag with the quarter of a million, and more to come from my own sale of the munitions! Ah, it was exciting, my friend, most exciting! It is always exciting when one is making money! And such delightful sums! Into my car then and away to the field where Milligan awaited me.

"Racing out on the field, I leaped from the car. Milligan was there, beside his plane, but he was not alone.

"Three men were with him, and one of them was the old marshal. He was the last person I expected in Shanghai, where he had many enemies, but here he was. One of the men stood guard over Milligan, and the other had a pistol directed at me.

"My eyes caught those of Milligan. He was a man I knew—a tough man, a ready man. Did I tell you that he was from Texas? Anyway, a lift of the brows, a small hand gesture—he knew what was coming. There was no doubting that he wished to be away as much as I.

" 'Ah, Marshal Chang! How delightful to see you! And what a surprise to find you in Shanghai of all places! Once I knew what happened I flew here at once! At once, Marshal. It was my duty as your aide, your confidant, and your friend to rectify this error!'

"You see, one does what one can, and I had already given up on this money. True, what I was about to do would *hurt*! Hurt, lieutenant! But it was my only way out. The old marshal would be in no mood for games, and every second here was filled with danger for him, so he was desperate. As for me, it is a wise soldier who knows when to retire from the field.

"Anyway, did I not have money awaiting me at the other end? From my sale of the arms?

" 'When I realized what had happened, Marshal, I flew to recover your money! It was the least I could do for one who has been my friend, my adviser, almost a second father!'

" 'Recover?' he asked, puzzled.

" 'Of course! It is here! In this bag! Now if you would like to fly back with me?'

" 'Let me see the money,' he demanded.

" 'Of course,' I said, and yielded the bag to his grasp. Yielded it reluctantly, you understand, for I had hoped to have that money somehow, someway. If I could just get the marshal into the plane—

"He gestured to one of his men, he who had been covering me, to open the bag. He did so. The marshal leaned over and peered inside; then he looked up at me, and his face was dark with anger.

"Looking into the bag, I knew why, knew that we had been cheated, that—

"The bag was filled with old newspapers, and there was a novel there to give it weight. And *that* novel? How could it have had weight enough? It was by a writer I have never liked—never!

"The old marshal was trembling with anger. 'You!' he shouted. 'You—!'

"It was a time, lieutenant, a time for decision! Never have I been more pleased with myself than what I did then! In an instant I should have been killed! And Milligan, also! It was a time for *action,* and like the old soldier I was, I *acted*!

"He who guarded me had lowered his pistol while he opened the bag, and for that reason he was holding the pistol but loosely. I struck down at the base of his thumb with the edge of my hand, and as the pistol fell from his hand, I seized it and fired!

"Not at the man I had disarmed but at the man guarding Milligan.

"Turning swiftly, I shoved the old marshal. He was a heavy man, and he tottered back off balance and fell. Milligan had leaped into the plane, and the man I had disarmed leaped at me. My pistol exploded, and he fell; then I leaped into the plane, and we were off—gone!

"Once again, lieutenant, I had snatched victory from the jaws of defeat. I do not wish to appear smug, but it is only the truth.

"In Kansu I received payment for the guns and told them where the junk would be. Then once more we took off. In the air I changed clothing, changed to such a costume as an English scientist might wear in the field. I had it always with me, for you know how the English are—one is apt to find them anywhere, in any out-of-the-way, godforsaken place, doing God knows what.

"I was to be a hunter of butterflies and a bit vague about all else. You see? It was an excellent cover.

"We landed—I shall not say where, for it is a field I have often used and may well use again. I have such places here and there. One never knows, does one?

"There I paid Milligan. Ten thousand dollars, more than he had ever seen before at one time, and there I left him, but with regret. He was a man, that one!

"I bought horses, and in a small town I found some equipment abandoned at some time by a scientific scholar before he attempted the Karakoram Pass. Have you tried it? If not, do not. It is—anyway, there is another older pass not far from there that is useful if one does not mind swinging bridges over gorges with roaring water beneath.

"It is a very remote country, yet it seemed by far the best and far from troublesome officials. Who would expect to find anyone in such a place. Yet when we reached Chabrang—"

"Yes?"

"We went to a place where we might find food, and I heard a merchant, a Kirghiz, complaining in a loud voice against the government! He had been stopped, searched, questioned. It seemed there were soldiers there looking for someone with a great deal of money. As if any merchant dared carry any money at all in such a place!

"You can see my problem. But again I refused to be defeated! It is my decision that counts! I decided, and I acted! Promptly!

"I inquired, and in a voice just loud enough that all might hear, as to the ruins of Tsaparang and which road must I take?

"I knew the road, and I had seen the ruins. Who could forget them, high in that yellow cliff? Built into the very face of it like some of your cliff dwellings.

"Of course I knew where the ruins lay, and we went to them. The men I had hired to travel with me and who owned the horses were only too glad to lie in the shade and rest. I took a pack from a horse, some scientific instruments, and of course the money. Then I made my way up the steep slope. One too curious fellow chose to follow me, but I found heavy stones that must be moved from my path, so he soon lost interest.

"I hid the money, hid it securely, in a place only I shall find, and in its place I packed some broken bits of pottery, a few blue beads, bits of carnelian and such. I took measurements, and took pictures with an old camera I had wheedled from Milligan, and then returned to my horses.

"We were stopped, of course, and questioned. We were searched, and they found the shards of pottery, some butterflies collected long ago by that traveler, whoever he was, and some very smelly bottles.

"I had donned thick-lensed glasses with which I peered at them—I had to peer to see anything at all—and there, where they think much of the evil eye, they were pleased to be rid of me."

"And now you have been back? Did you pick up the money?"

He smiled. "One does what one must, lieutenant. Now I live here in Paris, and, I might say, I live well." He patted his stomach affectionately. "Even very well."

He sipped his wine. "Of course one must be careful when one has enemies. The old marshal—yes, he is alive and well—too well, altogether. He dislikes me for some reason. He would have me shot if he could. And regrettably there are others."

"What of the blonde? Milton's girlfriend? Did you ever see her again?"

"See her?" He smiled complacently. "In fact, I shall see her tonight. I see her quite often, in fact."

"And the money? Milton's money?"

"She had taken it out of the black bag and hidden it. But she was a fool! Did she spend it on beautiful clothes? Did she buy jewels and wine? She did not. She *invested* it, every centime! Invested it, can you imagine?"

He emptied his glass. "She invested in the black market. Somewhere she found truckloads of American cigarettes and tanks of petrol."

"So the quarter of a million is forever beyond your reach?"

"Did you say a quarter of a million? It is more than a million now, and only the good Lord knows where it will end! Given time, that stupid girl will own half of Paris."

I stood up. After all, I had things to do even if he did not, and as I turned to pick up my cap from an adjoining chair, there was a spiteful little snapping sound from beside me and a loud report from the door. Turning quickly, I saw the student, he who had been drinking coffee and working his sums at the outside table. The student had a Luger pistol that was slipping from his fingers, and as if by magic, the gendarmes were running into the court.

"Sit down, lieutenant." The general caught my arm, and holding it out from my body a little, guided me to a chair. "You cannot leave now. There will be questions."

Glancing out the door, I saw the student, or whatever he was, lying as he had fallen. Evidently he had spun when hit, for he lay face down almost in the doorway but headed the other way.

"Relax, lieutenant. It is nothing. The poor man! It is terrible, the kind of help one gets today! So inefficient!"

The police were there, questioning everybody, but of course nobody knew anything. We were the last.

The general spoke excellent French. "I am General—"

"We know, *mon général,* we know. Did you, by any chance, see what took place?"

"I did not, but you know how it is. The Free French are still finding pockets of resistance, and of course they are hunting collaborators. When they find them—" He held up his forefinger and thumb like a pistol. "When they find them—*ping*! And they deserve no better."

He stood up. "If you would like to search—?"

"Oh, no!" The gendarme was appalled. "Of course not, *mon général*! Of course not!"

When I reached my quarters that night, it was with some relief that I pulled off my tie and then started to shed my trench coat. Something bumped my side, and I slid my hand into the pocket—an automatic, small, neat, and very deadly.

It was not easy to be a friend of the general.

Author's Tea

"I've been reading your work, Mr. Dugan, and like it tremendously! You have such *power,* such *feeling!*"

"Thank you," he heard himself saying. "I'm glad you liked it." He glanced toward the door where several women were arriving. They weren't young women. He sighed and glanced hopelessly toward the table where one of those faded dowagers who nibble at the crusts of culture was pouring tea. Now if they only had a steak—

"Mr. Dugan," his hostess was saying, "I want you to meet Mrs. Nowlin. She is also a writer."

She was so fat she had almost reached the parting of the stays, and she had one of those faces that always reminded him of buttermilk. "How do you do, Mrs. Nowlin?" He smiled in a way he hoped was gracious. "It is always a pleasure to meet someone in the same profession. What do you write?"

"Oh, I'm not a *regular* writer, Mr. Dugan, but I do so love to write! Don't you find it simply fascinating? But I just never have been able to get anything published. Sometimes I doubt the publishers even *read* my manuscripts! Why, I believe they just *couldn't!*"

"I imagine they are pretty busy, Mrs. Nowlin. They get so many stories, you know."

"Why, I sent one of my poems away not long ago. It was a poem about James, you know, and they wouldn't take it. They didn't even *say* anything! Just one of those rejection slips. Why, I read the poem at the club, and they all said it was simply *beautiful!*"

"Was—was James your husband?" he asked hopefully, glancing toward the tea table again. Still no steak.

"James! Oh, goodness no! James is my dog! My little Pom. Don't you just *adore* Poms, Mr. Dugan?"

Then she was gone, fluttering across the room like a blimp escaped from its moorings.

He sighed again. Every time chance caught him at one of these author's teas, he would think of Frisco Brady. He could imagine the profane disgust of the big Irish longshoreman if he knew the guy who flattened him in the Harbor Pool Room was guest of honor at a pink tea.

Dugan felt the red crawling around his ears at the thought, and his eyes sought the tea table again. Someday, he reflected, there is going to be a hostess who will serve real meals to authors and achieve immortality at a single stroke. Writers would burn candles to her memory, or better still, some of those shadowy wafers that were served with the tea and were scarcely more tangible than the tea itself.

He started out of his dream and tried to look remotely intelligent as he saw his hostess piloting another body through the crowd. He knew at a glance that she had written a book of poetry that wouldn't scan, privately published, of course. Even worse, it was obvious that in some dim, distant year she had seen some of Garbo's less worthy pictures and had never recovered. She carried her chin high, and her neck stretched endlessly toward affected shoulders.

"I have so *wanted* to meet you! There is something so deep, so spiritual about your work! And your last book! One feels you were on a great height when you wrote it! Ah! . . ."

She was gone. But someone else was speaking to him, and he turned attentively.

"Why do so many of you writers write about such *hard* things? There is so much that is beautiful in the world! All people aren't like those people you write about, so why don't you write about *nice* people? And that boy you wrote about in the story about hunger, why, you know perfectly well, Mr. Dugan, that a boy like that couldn't go hungry in this country!"

His muscles ached with weariness, and he stood on the corner staring down the street, his thoughts blurred by hunger, his face white and strained. Somehow all form had become formless, and things about him took on new attitudes and appearances. He found his mind fastening upon little things with an abnormal concentration born of hunger and exhaustion. Walking a crack in the sidewalk became an obsession, and when he looked up from that, a fat man was crossing the street, and his arms and legs seemed to jerk grotesquely. Everything about him seemed to move in slow motion, and he stopped walking and tried to steady himself, conscious it was a delirium born of hunger.

He had been standing still for a moment trying to work his foot free from the sock where it was stuck with the dried blood from a broken blister, and when he moved forward suddenly, he almost fell. He pulled up sharply and turned his head to see if anyone noticed. He walked on then with careful attention.

He was hungry.

The words stood out in his consciousness, cold and clear, almost without thought or sensation. He looked at them as at a sign that had no meaning.

He passed a policeman and tried to adopt a careless, confident air but felt the man looking after him. Passing a bakery, the smell of fresh pastry went through him like a wave, leaving a sensation of emptiness and nausea.

"You've had such an *interesting* life, Mr. Dugan! There must have been so many adventures. If I had been a man, I would have lived just such a life as you have. It must have been so *thrilling* and romantic!"

"Why don't you tell us some of the *real* stories? Some of the things that actually happened? I'll bet there were a lot you haven't even written."

"I'm tellin' you, Dugan. Lay off that dame, see? If you don't, I'll cut your heart out."

The music moved through the room, and he felt the lithe, quick movements of the girl as she danced, and through the smoky pall he heard a chair crash, and he looked down and smiled at the girl, and then he spun her to arm's length and ducked to avoid the first punch. Then he struck with his left, short and hard. He felt his fist thud against a jaw and saw the man's face as he fell forward, eyes bulging, jaw slack. He brought up his right into the man's midsection as he fell toward him and then stepped away. Something struck him from behind, and it wasn't until he got up that the blood started running into his eyes. He knew he'd been hit hard, and heard the music playing "In a little Spanish town 'twas on a night like this, stars were shining down . . ."

He was speaking then, and he heard himself saying, "There is only the personal continuity. The man we were yesterday may not be the man we are tomorrow. Names are only trademarks for the individual, and from day to day that individual changes, and his ways and thoughts change, although he is not always himself aware of the change. The man who was yesterday a soldier may be a seller of brushes tomorrow. He has the same name, but the man himself is not the same, although circumstances may cause him to revert to his former personality and character. Even the body changes; the flesh and blood change with the food we eat and the water we drink.

"To him who drifts about, life consists of moving in and out of environments and changing conditions, and with each change of environment the wanderer changes, also. We move into lives that for the time are very near and dear to us, but suddenly all can be changed, and nothing remains but the memory.

"Only the innocent speak of adventure, for adventure is only a romantic name for trouble, and when one is having 'adventures' one wishes it were all over and he was elsewhere and safe. 'Adventure' is not nice. It is more often than not rough and dirty, cruel and harsh . . ."

Before they screwed on the copper helmet, Scotty stopped by, his features tight and hard. "Watch yourself, kid, this is bad water and too many sharks. Some say there are more octopi and squids here than anywhere else, but usually they're no trouble. We'll try to hold it down up here." He slapped his waistband as he spoke. Scotty moved, and Singapore Charlie lifted the helmet.

"Don't worry, skipper, I'll keep your lines clear, and I can handle any trouble." Then Dugan was sinking through the warm green water, feeling it clasp him close so that only the copper helmet protected him. Down, down, still farther down, and then he was standing on the sandy floor of the ocean, and around him moved the world of the undersea. There was silence, deep, unfathomable silence, except for the soft hiss of air. He moved forward, walking as though in a deep sleep, pushing himself against the water, turning himself from side to side like some unbelievable monster that haunted the lower depths.

Then he found the dark hull of the old ship and moved along the ghostly deck, half shrouded in the weed of a hundred years, moving toward the companionway where feet no longer trod. He hesitated at the door, looking down into darkness, and then he saw it moving toward him, huge, ominous, frightening. He tucked his warm-blooded hands into his armpits to leave only the slippery surface of the canvas and rubber suit. It came toward him, only vaguely curious, and inquiring tentacles slipped over and around him . . . feeling . . . feeling . . . feeling.

He sipped his tea and avoided the eyes of the woman who had the manuscript she wanted him to comment on, nibbled impotently at those infinitesimal buttons of nourishment, and listened to the ebb and flow of conversation about his ears. Here and there a remark swirled about, attracting his momentary attention. He heard himself speaking, saying how pleasant it had been, and then he was out on the street again, turning up his collar against the first few drops of spattering rain.

East of Gorontalo

Ponga Jim Mayo leaned against the hogshead of tobacco and stared out at the freighter. His faded khaki suit was rumpled, his heavy jaw unshaven. The white-topped cap carried the label "Captain" in gold lettering, but Ponga Jim looked like anything but a master mariner, and felt even less like one.

Being broke was a problem anywhere. In Gorontalo it became an emergency of the first water. Everything he owned in the world was on him, from the soft, woven-leather shoes on his feet to the white-topped cap to the big Colt automatic in its shoulder holster.

Jim pushed his cap back on his head and glanced at Major Arnold, sitting on a bitt at the edge of the wharf. In his neat white drill and military mustache he could have been nothing but a British officer.

"Tell me, William," Jim said, "just what brings a big-shot intelligence officer to Celebes? Something in the wind?"

"You get around a lot, don't you?" Major William Arnold lighted a cigarette and glanced up at Jim.

"Yeah, when I can." Ponga Jim grinned. "Right now I'm on the beach, and it looks like I'm not getting off for a while. But there isn't much in the Indies I don't know."

Arnold nodded. "I know. You might do me some good, Jim. If you see anything suspicious, give me a tip, will you? There's a rumor around that while England's busy in Europe, there will be a move to pick up some of her colonies in the Far East. This is a Dutch colony, but we're cooperating."

"Then," Mayo said thoughtfully, nodding his head toward the broad-beamed, battered tramp freighter, "you might add her to your list of suspects."

"That's the *Natuna* out of Surabaya, isn't it? Didn't you used to be her skipper?"

"Yeah." Ponga Jim shifted his position to let the breeze blow under his coat. He was wearing a gun, and the day was hot. "Then the company sold her to Pete Lucieno, and I quit. I wouldn't work for that dope peddler on a bet. I'm no lily of the valley, and frankly, I'm not making any boasts about being above picking up a slightly illegal dollar—I've made some of your British pearl fisheries out of season before now, and a few other things—but I draw the line at Pete's kind of stuff."

"No love lost, I guess?" Arnold squinted up at Jim, smiling.

"Not a bit. He'd consider it a privilege to cut my heart out. So would Dago Frank, that majordomo of his, or Blue Coley. And I don't fancy them."

Major Arnold soon left, walking back up toward the club. Ponga Jim lighted a cigarette and stared thoughtfully at the *Natuna*. Then his eyes shifted to the other ship in port, a big white freighter, the *Carlsberg*. Although there were three or four schooners, and a scattering of smaller craft, it was the two freighters that held his attention.

"Now, William," he said whimsically, "you should never miss a bet. Being an old seafaring man, it strikes me as being somewhat phony for that native scow to be shoving herself around in circles. Especially, when she goes behind the *Carlsberg* riding high and comes out with darn little freeboard. Then she wanders around, gets behind the *Natuna,* and comes out riding high in the water again.

"Now the only *Carlsberg* I ever knew sailed out of Bremen, not Copenhagen." Mayo's eyes flickered to the sleek white *Carlsberg*. "So, putting a possibility of registry changed from Bremerhaven to Copenhagen, some mysterious goings-on connected with the *Natuna,* a scow whose owners would frame their mothers for a dollar six-bits, a war, and William's rumors, what do you have?"

Ponga Jim Mayo straightened up and sauntered off down the dock. It was nearly sundown, and the seven guilders that remained in his pocket suggested food. After that—

JIM WALKED INTO Chino John's and stopped at the bar.

"Give me a beer," he said, glancing around. A man standing nearby turned to face Mayo.

"Well, if it isn't my old friend Ponga Jim!" he sneered. "On the beach again, no?"

Jim looked at Dago Frank coolly and then past him at Lucieno. The fat little Portuguese glistened with perspiration and ill-concealed hatred.

"Yeah," Jim said. "Anytime to keep out of the company of rats."

"I disdain that remark," Lucieno said. "I disdain it."

"You'd better," Jim said cheerfully. "If you took it up, I'd pull your fat nose for you!"

Dago Frank's eyes narrowed. He stepped closer.

"Then maybe you pull mine, eh?" he challenged.

Ponga Jim's right fist snapped up in a jarring right that knocked every bit of wind from Dago Frank's body.

Then jerking him erect, Mayo jolted another six-inch punch into his midsection and dropped him to the floor. Coolly, he picked up his beer and drank it, and then he turned and looked at Lucieno. The fat Portuguese began to back away, his face white.

Jim grinned. "Okay, pal," he said cheerfully. "It was just a little lesson to teach your boyfriend to talk nice to his superiors. Next time—" He shook his finger warningly and turned away.

Arnold was standing on the boardwalk as Jim strode through the swinging doors. He chuckled, clapping Jim on the shoulder.

"That was great! Everybody in the Dutch East Indies has been hoping to see that pair get called. But you've made an enemy, and a nasty one."

"That's just the fifth episode," Mayo said, shrugging. "I beat them out of a cargo of copra and pearl shell down in the Friendly Islands about three years ago. About six months later they tried to kidnap old Schumann's daughter over in the Moluccas. They were going to sell her to some native prince. I put a stop to that, and a couple of their boys got tough."

"What happened to them?"

"You know, William," Jim said seriously, "I was trying to remember the other day. They had an accident or something."

He straightened his tie, and gave the automatic a hitch into a better position.

"By the way, William," he asked carelessly, "where's the *Natuna* bound this trip?"

"To Port Moresby, with general cargo."

Ponga Jim walked down the street, and when he turned at the corner, glanced back. Major Arnold, his neat, broad-shouldered, compact figure very casual, was standing in front of Chino John's. Jim grinned, and turned the corner carelessly. Then, suddenly alert, he wheeled and darted down an alley, turned into a side street, and cut through the scattering of buildings toward the dock. The British Intelligence was convenient at times, at others, a nuisance.

There was no one in sight when he reached the dock. He let himself down the piling and crawled into a skiff moored there in the dark. Quickly, he shoved off.

Overhead there was a heavy bank of clouds. The night was very still, and the skiff made scarcely a shadow as it slipped through the dark water. Staying a hundred yards off, Ponga Jim avoided the lighted gangway and cautiously sculled the boat around to the dark side of the *Natuna*. There was no one in sight, so with painstaking care he drifted the boat nearer and nearer to the silent ship. When he came alongside he laid his paddle down and stood up, balancing himself.

Fortunately, the sea was still. Picking up the heaving line lying in the stern of the boat, Mayo tossed the monkey's fist around a stanchion of the taffrail, and catching the ball, he pulled it down.

Once aboard that ship he would be practically in the hands of his enemies and with no legal status. Ponga Jim grinned and settled the gun in its holster. Then taking two strands of the heaving line, he climbed swiftly—hand over hand.

There was no one in sight, and pulling himself through the rail, he rolled over twice and was against the bulkhead of the after wheelhouse. There was no movement aft. Forward, the light from a port glinted on the rail and the water, and he could see the watchman standing under the light near the gangway. It was Blue Coley.

Jim crawled into the shadow of the winch and then along the deck to the ladder. The well deck was empty, so he slipped down. Then he hesitated.

The passage was lighted, but it was a chance he had to take. The crew's quarters were forward, the officers' amidships. There was small chance of anyone being aft. He stepped into the passageway and hurried along, passing the paint locker. The rope-locker door was fastened, and he swore as he dug for his keys. Luckily, he still had them. Once inside, he closed the door carefully and locked it again.

There was a vague smell of paint and linseed oil. He felt his way along over coils of line, until he stopped abruptly. Then, cautiously, he struck a match. The paint had been shifted into the rope locker. Carefully, he snuffed the match and then paused in indecision. Then he crawled over the coils of line and found the door into number five hatch. He grinned. Luckily, he knew every inch of the *Natuna*. He hadn't commanded her for a year for nothing, and he liked to know a ship. He knew her better now than the man who built her. She'd changed a lot in twenty years, and there had been repairs made and some changes.

The door was stiff, but he opened it and crawled into the hold, carefully closing the door after him. He was on his hands and knees on a wooden case.

He struck a match, shielding it with his hands despite the knowledge that the hold was sealed tight and the hatch battened down and ready for the sea. The case was marked in large black letters, CANNED GOODS. Returning to the rope locker, Jim picked up a marlinespike and returned to the hold. Working carefully, he forced open the wooden case. Striking another match, he leaned over.

Then he sat back on his heels, smiling. The case was filled with automatic rifles.

"Well, well, Señor Lucieno!" he muttered to himself. "Just as I suspected. If there's dirty work, you'll be in on it."

Thoughtfully, he considered the open case. The match had gone out, but he could remember those cool barrels, the magazines. He rubbed his jaw.

"Contraband," he said. "And I'm broke. What was it Hadji Ali used to say? 'Lie to a liar, for lies are his coin; steal from a thief for that is easy; lay a trap for the trickster, and catch him at the first attempt; but beware of an honest man.' "

Taking one of the rifles from the case he began to assemble it in the dark.

"Well, Petey, old darling, you're a liar, a thief, and a trickster, and contraband is fair game for anyone—so here's where I move in."

Fastening the case shut, he carried the automatic rifle with him. Then he descended into the lower hold, and found a place near the shaft-alley housing where there was a space in the cargo. He had known it was there. Stowing cargo in that spot always necessitated it because of the ship's structure. There was also a small steel door into the shaft alley. So far as he knew it had not been used since he had ordered it cut there while making repairs. Opening another case he got some excelsior and made himself comfortable. Then crawling back into the 'tween decks, he felt his way over the cases until he was immediately under the hatch.

Listening, he heard no feet on the deck, so he opened a case. As he had suspected, this was really canned goods. He tried several cases, and with his coat for a sack, carried an armful back down to his hideout.

"If you're going to stow away, Jim boy," he told himself, "by all means pick a ship you know, and one carrying food."

Opening a can of pineapple he ate, speculating on the future. The *Natuna* was bound for Port Moresby. That would mean something like ten or twelve days. It might be more, depending on the weather. The *Natuna* was a temperamental old Barnacle Bill of a ship. She might stagger along at twelve knots, and she might limp at eight or nine. It was hot, too damned hot, but during at least part of the day he could stay in the 'tween decks under a ventilator.

Besides, there wasn't a chance of his being here ten days. Pete Lucieno wasn't one to spend a dime or a guilder he could save, and that would mean he wouldn't take this cargo a bit farther than he could help. If he was bound for Port Moresby, that meant he was discharging the contraband somewhere this side of there, and if he was going that far, it meant his point of discharge wouldn't be very much this side. Which meant that he was heading somewhere along the New Guinea coast, and probably the mouth of the Fly. There were islands there and easy access to the interior.

Obviously, whoever planned to use these rifles and the other munitions, intended to distribute them among the natives and then stir up trouble. By raiding Port Moresby, friction could be created and the entire Indies might be set aflame. Then it would require British action to protect her nationals and save her colonies.

DURING THE NEXT TWO NIGHTS, Ponga Jim Mayo searched the paint locker and the lamp locker. As he had suspected, both were stored with ammunition. He picked up some for the automatic rifle, and found some clips for his automatic, stuffing his pockets with them.

For water, he had to go to the gravity tank on the boat deck. Otherwise his only chance was to enter the crew's quarters forward or the galley or mess room amidships. Neither was practical. As for the boat deck, by crawling through the bulkhead door into number four and then into number three hatch, he could climb the ladder to the 'tween decks and from the top of the cargo, could scramble into the ventilator just abaft the cargo winches at number three hatch. From the ventilator cowl he had a good view of the deck without being seen, and it was simple to slip out and up the ladder to the boat deck.

On the fifth night, Mayo slipped out of the ventilator and walked across the deserted deck to the ladder, climbing to the boat deck. He drank, and then filled the can he'd carried with him.

Crouching near the tank, he could see the officer on watch pacing the bridge. By his thick shoulders and queer gait, Jim recognized him as Blue Coley. That would mean, he reflected, that Dago Frank would have the eight-to-twelve watch. Lucieno couldn't navigate and knew nothing of seamanship, so obviously someone else had the eight to four. Ponga Jim wrinkled his brow thoughtfully. Now who the devil?

Long ago he had discovered it was well to know the caliber of one's opponent. Dago Frank was a vindictive, treacherous, blood-hungry rascal who would stop at nothing. Blue Coley was a thick-headed, strong-armed thug without enough on the ball to carry through a job of this kind.

Suddenly Jim flattened out on the deck. Aft, near the ventilator he used for access to the deck, was a slight, square-shouldered figure. Even as he watched, the man came forward soundlessly, and as he moved across the ribbon of light from the starboard passage, he was clearly revealed for an instant. He was a lascar in dark green cotton trousers which flapped about his legs halfway between knee and ankle, and his head was done up in a red turban. There was a puckering scar on the man's face, and he was muscular. In his belt was an ugly-looking kris.

Now what's this? Jim felt himself getting irritated. Had the fellow seen him? And who was he? How did he figure in this deal? If one of the crew, he had no reason to be ducking or dodging around. Unless, that is, he was aft when he had no business to be.

Watching, Jim saw the native come forward stealthily and then suddenly dodge out of sight near the starboard rail. There was a walk forward along the rail outside the amidships house.

But scarcely had he disappeared when a shadow appeared in the lighted passage, and then a man walked out on deck. Jim's eyes narrowed.

It was a heavy, brutal head set down on massive shoulders with scarcely any neck at all. The shoulders were enormously wide and thick, the chest was deep, and when he walked his knees jerked queerly, like those of some wrestlers. When he turned, Jim could see a flattened nose above a mouth like a gash set in a wide, dark face. It was a face marked with brutality and strength, and the whole man radiated a sense of evil power that Ponga Jim had never seen in any other human thing.

When he lifted his hands, Jim could see they were thick and powerful with stubby fingers and backed by huge-boned wrists. A black beard darkened the man's jaw, and there was a mat of hair visible at his open shirt. Despite the brutality in the man's face, there was a shrewd sort of animal cunning, too.

Ponga Jim Mayo felt the hair prickle along the back of his neck, and he wet his lips thoughtfully. Without doubt this was the skipper, and he was something far different from Dago Frank or Blue Coley. When the man went back into the passage, Jim slipped down the ladder and aft to his ventilator, but he was no sooner inside than he heard footsteps approaching.

He hesitated, gun in hand. His jaw set hard. If they found him now, there would be nothing to do but shoot it out.

Two men stopped near the ventilator. Lucieno was speaking.

"We're making good time. The day after tomorrow we will drop the anchor in the mouth of the Fly. Gruber will be there to meet us."

"What about Borg?" Dago's voice was cautious.

"We let Borg alone," Lucieno said severely, "if we know what is good for us." He hesitated. "You know what he thinks? He thinks somebody's aboard—a stowaway."

Jim felt his heart pounding, and his mouth went dry.

"A stowaway?" Dago Frank broke in. "That is not possible, unless—"

"Jim Mayo, you think, eh? I think, too. Borg, he think he see somebody on the main deck. Two nights ago. The night we leave Gorontalo, he see an empty boat floating. Now somebody been in the chart room. He say that."

"What now?" Dago Frank asked. "I like to get hold of him, of that Ponga Jim."

The two walked off forward, and Jim slipped down into the 'tween decks and then down the ladder to his hideout. Once there, he checked the automatic and returning it to its holster, checked the automatic rifle. Then he pulled a case over the opening and stretched out.

It could only have been a few minutes when he was awakened suddenly. Every sense alert, he waited, listening. There was silence, then the scratching of a match. In the dim light thrown against the bulkhead he could see a shadow. It looked like a lascar turban, but he couldn't be sure. The gun slid into his hand, and crouching, breathless, he awaited discovery. None came.

There were soft movements and then a metallic sound, a short hard blow, and then another. And silence. He waited a long time, but there was no further movement. Crawling out of his concealment, he felt his way over the cases. In the top tier, a case of canned goods had been pulled aside. He knew every case from crawling over them so much. A faint scent of oil came to his nostrils, and shielding it carefully, he struck a match.

The end of one of the boards in the case had been saturated with oil and then forced open bit by bit, and more oil added, effectively quieting any possible screech from a nail!

But who? Ponga Jim returned to his hideout distinctly uneasy. He had a feeling that matters were getting out of hand: the unknown skipper, obviously a more dangerous and cunning man than either Frank or Lucieno, and now this mysterious searcher. Added to that was the problem of the lascar. Still puzzling over the problem, he fell asleep.

HE AWAKENED WITH A START, instantly conscious of two things. He had overslept, and something was definitely wrong. Crawling to his knees he slipped on his shoulder holster and then his coat. Putting on his cap, he waited, listening.

There was no sound. But suddenly he was conscious of a peculiar odor. He frowned, trying to place it. Then it struck him like a blow!

Formaldehyde! Evidently, while he slept too soundly, they had crept through the hold or at least looked in.

Not seeing him and fearing to stumble across an armed man, they were trying to smoke him out.

Lunging to his feet he hurriedly shifted the case over the entrance to his hideout. By that time the fumes were growing thick. Stumbling over the cargo, he found the door into number four.

His heart sank. The door was locked tight. Wheeling about, gasping and choking, he stumbled across to the rope-locker door. It, too, was locked. For an instant he hesitated, his mind desperately searching for a way out. Then he remembered the plate into the shaft alley. Stumbling back over the cargo, he tumbled into his hole and pulled the case back over the entrance; then he turned and felt for the plate. Finding it, he found the wrench he had thoughtfully stolen from the locker and started on one of the nuts.

It was stiff, rusty. Desperately, he tugged. The wrench came loose, and he skinned his knuckles on the nut below. Choking, eyes red and breath coming in gasps, he got one of the nuts loose and then another. He thought the final nut would never come off. Twice the wrench slipped loose. Then suddenly it was off, and he slid through the hole into the darkness of the shaft alley.

Coughing and spluttering, he struck a match. The great whirling metallic shaft loomed above him. He dropped the match, and taking the plate by a bolt through its center, he slipped it back on the bolts. Turning, he walked forward to the swing door, moving carefully. Beyond it, the shaft alley was lighted. Running now, he slipped the Colt from its holster. Amazingly enough, the shaft-alley door was open, and even as he plunged through and closed it after him, he was conscious of the bad seamanship. Now if he were still in command—

The engineer on watch didn't even look up, and the fireman was arguing with the oiler in the fire room. Crossing the floor plates in two jumps, Ponga Jim ran up the ladder to the orlop deck, then forward to the ladder to the main deck. Just as he reached it, a lascar came down the ladder, and his eyes went wide when he saw Mayo. Jerking up the spanner he carried, the lascar tried to strike, but Jim stiff-armed him with a left and knocked the native sprawling.

It was quiet on deck, and the sun was shining when Mayo stepped out of the passage. He realized then that he had overslept by many hours, for it was already late in the afternoon. Off on the port side was the long blue line of the New Guinea coast, and he stood there, letting his eyes grow accustomed to the sun. Aft, he could hear voices.

Then he started forward and ran up the ladder to the bridge.

As he stepped into the wheelhouse the lascar at the wheel gave a sharp cry. Dago Frank, evidently on watch while the skipper tried to smoke out the stowaway, wheeled. His face turned gray, and he grabbed at a gun. Then Ponga Jim slugged him.

Frank toppled forward, his jaw slack, and Jim slugged him again. Then he turned on the man at the wheel.

"Put her over to port about ten degrees," he snapped. "Quick now, or I'll spill your guts on this deck!"

His face white with fear, the lascar put the wheel over. A sudden sound from the chart room startled him, and he whirled to see Pete Lucieno standing in the door, pistol in hand.

"Drop it!" Mayo snapped.

Lucieno smiled—and dropped the gun. Then he bowed slightly.

"Of course, my friend. With the greatest of pleasure. I see you now where I have long wished to see you."

"Wha—?"

Then something crashed down on the back of his head, and a sharp arrow of pain stabbed through his consciousness as he felt himself falling.

WHEN PONGA JIM MAYO OPENED HIS EYES, his head was throbbing with pain. He tried to move, and surprisingly, he was not bound. He sat up, groaning.

"Comin' out of it?"

He looked up, blinking back the pain. Borg, his powerful legs braced to the roll of the ship, stood looking down at him. The man had a pair of field glasses in his right hand. He shifted them to his left.

"Get up."

Ponga Jim crawled unsteadily to his feet, facing Borg. The man stared at him.

"Ponga Jim Mayo, eh? Tough guy, are you?" He swung. His fist smashed against the angle of Jim's jaw, and Mayo went down. He got up, staggering, and Borg hit him again.

Then Borg laughed. "You may be tough around this bunch, but you ain't tough t' me."

He walked over to Jim and kicked him viciously in the ribs. Jim started to get up, and sneering, Borg swung a vicious kick at his head. Mayo rolled over and swung his ankle up behind Borg's leg, spilling the big man to the deck.

With a snarling oath, Borg scrambled to his feet, his face livid. He swung a terrific right, but Jim ducked and hooked a left to the body. Even as he threw it, he knew he didn't have the stuff. The punch landed, and then Jim hooked his right to Borg's head, but the man grabbed him and hurled him across the room.

Following him, Borg slammed a wicked right to the head that made Ponga Jim roll and grab at the shelf along the wall. Then Borg hooked him in the kidney and dug a wicked right into his body. As Jim started to fall, he felt a terrific blow crash against his jaw.

IT SEEMED HOURS LATER when he came to. He kept his eyes shut and lay very still, conscious that he was bound hand and foot now, and conscious that there were two men in the chart room, one at the wheel.

Opening his eyes to a slit, Jim saw the man at the wheel was a lascar, but not the one who had been there when he was fighting Borg. The two men came out of the chart room, and he saw one was Dago Frank, the other Lucieno.

"In about an hour he say," Lucieno said. "The submarine he come in about an hour."

"This one," Frank said, motioning toward Mayo, "I like to kill."

The two went out on the bridge, and Jim lay very still, resting, his desperate thoughts striving through the stabbing pain to find a way out. He stretched a little, but the ropes were tight. Borg was a seaman, and Borg had tied those ropes to stay.

Jim lay still, staring through his half-opened eyes at the helmsman's feet. Suddenly, his eyes lifted—green flapping trousers, a wide leather belt, an ugly kris, and then broad, muscular brown shoulders and a dark red turban. It was the lascar who had been prowling that night on deck! And the one, he felt sure, who had opened a box of rifles in number five hold.

There was something phony about this somewhere. He lay still, feigning unconsciousness. Another lascar came in, relieving the man at the wheel. Ponga Jim heard the course as they repeated it, and he started.

In the excitement, the lascars had continued to steer his course, ten degrees north and east of the proper one! He stirred a little, to get a better view of the room. Then in a far corner, among some signal flags, he glimpsed his gun! Evidently flying from his hand when he was struck from behind, it had fallen among those flags, unnoticed.

In an hour, Lucieno had said. At least fifteen minutes had passed, possibly more. He lifted his eyes. They stopped, riveted on a bit of red outside the starboard door of the wheelhouse. The lascar was standing on the ladder, concealed unless the man at the wheel noticed him, or unless Dago Frank walked along the bridge. The red turban came into sight and then the scar-puckered face.

The man at the wheel was daydreaming, staring off at the coastline to port. The lascar at the door lifted a knife into view, laid it carefully on the deck, and shot it slithering straight at Jim. Instinctively, he arched his body. The man at the wheel jerked around, staring.

The knife was safely under Jim's body, and the lascar in the doorway was gone. Outside the door an awning string rattled against the stanchion. The lascar peered, started to call to Frank, and then shrugged and was silent. Working carefully, Jim got the knife turned edgewise. It was razor sharp. Holding himself carefully, so as not to slice off a finger, he managed to use his hands enough to cut through a rope and then another. Swiftly, he freed himself and stood up.

The lascar turned, and found himself with a knife pressed against his stomach. His face gray, he stood very still, his mouth looking sick.

"One sound and I'll cut your heart out!" Jim snapped. "Get back to that wheel, and don't let a yelp out of you!"

Turning, he caught up the automatic and stepped to the door. Dago Frank was standing in the wing of the bridge, staring at the shoreline. It was suddenly very near, too near. He wheeled and started for the wheelhouse, and brought up suddenly.

"All right, Dago," Jim said coolly, "this is it. You wanted to kill me, now go for your gun!"

Frank's hand shot down, and Ponga Jim stood very still, canting to the roll of the ship. When Dago Frank's gun came up belching flame, he fired. He heard a bullet smack viciously into the wall of the wheelhouse, but that was all. Frank turned half around and fell headlong.

A white man rushed out on deck with a rifle, and Ponga Jim fired. The man ran three steps and then pitched headlong over the rail, the rifle clattering on the deck. Blue Coley started out of the passageway below, and Jim's gun coughed. The bullet smacked against a steam-pipe housing at his feet, and Blue stumbled back into the passage in a desperate hurry. Another shot chased him down the passage.

Leaping through the door, Jim was just in time to snap a shot at the lascar at the wheel as the man tried to throw a knife. The native dropped, coughing blood. Jim leaped past him to the engine-room telegraph and jerked it over to SLOW—then to STOP.

A BULLET WHISTLED by his head and smashed the chronometer, and he saw an oiler standing in the forecastle door. Jim fired, and the man jumped back inside. Another rifle shot crashed, and then Ponga Jim chanced a shot into the open doorway, and there was nothing further. He turned suddenly, snapping a shot at a gun in a forecastle port.

Borg had come up the other ladder and was standing in the doorway, staring at him. The man was unshaven, and his face was almost black.

Ponga Jim glanced down at the empty automatic, tossed it aside.

"I got something for you, big boy," he said. His left jabbed quickly, but Borg ducked and laughed, crashing right into a whipping right uppercut.

"Go ahead, Jim!" a voice shouted from the door behind him. "I'll hold this bunch!"

Mayo whirled, stepping back to watch the door and Borg at the same time. The lascar with the red turban stood in the doorway with an automatic rifle. He was grinning.

"William!" Ponga Jim shouted. "William, by all that's holy!"

"Righto, old chap!"

The cheery voice sounded in his ears as Borg rushed. Jim lashed out with another left, and this time stabbed Borg over the eye, splitting it to the bone. A ponderous fist crashed against the side of Jim's head, and a million stars sprang into the sky. Jim laughed suddenly, full of the lust to fight, and fired both hands into the big man's body furiously.

Borg hooked a hard left to his head and then grabbed him, but Ponga Jim jerked away, crossing a short right to the face, and hooking a left to the body. Borg rushed, clubbing with his right, but missing. Then suddenly Borg launched himself in a vicious flying tackle!

Ponga Jim's knee jerked up into the man's face, knocking him sprawling to the deck. But Borg was up, a wild right catching Jim in the body. He gasped, and a left slammed against his head, dropping him to his knees. Borg lunged, kicking, and Ponga Jim hurled himself at the one leg Borg had on the floor.

The big man came down with a crash, and then both men were on their feet. Jim walked in wide open, his eyes blazing with the joy of battle. Left right, left right, punch after punch he ripped into the big man's head and body, hooks, uppercuts, and swings, a battering volley.

Borg was powerful, but too slow. He started to back up, lifting his arms to get that blinding fury of punches out of his eyes and face only to catch a terrific right in the solar plexus. He gasped and Jim let him have another in the same place and then another. The man fell forward on his face, and turning, Jim heard the hoarse rattle of the automatic rifle.

Suddenly, Arnold's puckered scar twisted and his eyes widened.

"Jim!" he yelled. "The sub!"

Mayo sprang to the door. The sub had come up on the port bow, and the officer in the conning tower was staring at the ship in amazement. And it was no wonder. The *Natuna* was swinging idly on a flat sea, her deck a rattle of gunfire.

Arnold was yelling something about a sack, and Ponga Jim ran out on the bridge. Behind the corner of the wheelhouse was a canvas sack, and jerking it open, he saw it was full of hand grenades. The sub was closing in for a better view, and a gun crew had swung the gun around to cover the ship. They were launching a boat, and a dozen men were climbing into it.

PONGA JIM JERKED the pin and hurled the grenade. It hit the side of the submarine near the gun crew, and there was a terrific blast. But he had already thrown another. It fell short, but even as the gun crashed, he hurled another.

Their shot put a hole through the stack, but it was the only one they got a chance to fire. Arnold had rushed into the wing of the bridge and poured a stream of hot lead down at the conning tower and then clipped a couple of shots at the boat. Ponga Jim Mayo's next grenade lifted the boat out of the water, a blasted bunch of wreckage and struggling men.

The sub started to back off, but Jim hurled another grenade. The officer on the conning tower, apparently uninjured by Arnold's burst of rifle fire, had started down the ladder. In one horror-stricken moment his face showed white. Then there was a terrific concussion! The last grenade had fallen down the conning tower hatch.

William lowered his gun. His face was bleeding from a cut on his head.

"The marines have landed and have the situation well in hand!" he said.

"It wasn't a limey said that!" Mayo grunted. "That was an American."

"Righto!" William Arnold agreed.

Borg was getting to his feet. Mayo walked in and slugged him with the barrel of his automatic, which he'd retrieved and loaded.

"I'll tie this bird. He's wanted somewhere. Or we can kick him ashore in Sydney."

"Sydney?" Arnold said. "Why Sydney? This ship—"

"Listen, pal," Ponga Jim said patiently. "You're the British Intelligence or something, aren't you? Well, you want this activity stopped down here. You've prevented the landing of a lot of guns, and you've sunk an enemy submarine. Now I am informed that a certain gent high in official military circles at Sydney can buy arms and ammunition. For me, this represents profit, no loss. Now unless you want to stage the War of 1812 all over again, we go to Sydney!"

Major William Arnold grinned. "This is no time to sever diplomatic relations with Ponga Jim Mayo," he said cheerfully. "Let me get some pants while you muster the rest of this crew, and we're off!"

He started down the ladder.

"Hey!" Jim said. "You know any dames down there?"

"Just two," Arnold said. "Why?"

"Just two," Mayo said regretfully. "That's going to be tough. I'd hoped there would be enough for you, too!"

"Nuts!" Arnold said grimly, and walked down the ladder with his green pants flapping.

On the Road to Amurang

When he reached the road, Ponga Jim Mayo hesitated. Behind him, the wide, cool verandah of the Dutch Club echoed with soft laughter, the click of billiards, and the tinkle of glasses. There was a glow in the sky over Glandestan Way. But Ponga Jim's eyes turned toward the Punchar Wharves, where the *Semiramis* was tied.

His frown deepened. Balikpapan was no place for an empty ship. But it was better than having it at the bottom of the Molucca Passage, like the *Silver Lady.*

He hitched his shoulder to shift the heavy Colt automatic. Abruptly he faded into the shadows of the shrubbery, gun in hand.

"Jim," a voice called softly. "Hold it."

A drunken seaman was staggering down the road in stained dungarees and a grizzle of gray beard. He lurched closer, peering into Jim's face. Ponga Jim slipped the gun back into its holster.

"Damn you, William! If this is the way the British Intelligence works, the enemy will have to fumigate to get rid of you!"

Major Arnold chuckled. Then he grew serious.

"Jim, don't you own the *Semiramis* now?"

"If you call a down payment owning it. But the way things look, I'll never get a cargo for her. She's lying over at Punchar Wharves, as empty as my pockets will be tomorrow."

"What's the matter? Are the shippers afraid?"

Jim spat disgustedly. "Do you blame them? The *Arafura,* gone without a trace somewhere in the Sea of Celebes. The *Viti Queen,* last sighted off Flores. And now it's the *Silver Lady,* with a thousand tons of tin. In case you don't know, tin is valuable stuff. And a half-dozen sailing craft gone."

"I know, Jim. Japan has threatened for years to take all the Far Eastern

Dutch and British colonies if England went to war in Europe. There won't be a British or Dutch ship in the Indies within thirty days!"

Ponga Jim whistled. "Submarines?"

"We don't know. Subs demand a base."

Jim stared thoughtfully down the dark road. Thousands of islands, with lagoons, streams, and bays—

"You know all these damn islands, Jim. If you were going to hide a submarine base, where would you do it?"

"There's a lot of places on Halmahera, on Buru, or Ceram. But there are places along the coast of Celebes, too. Nobody really knows these islands yet, William. But if I were going to base subs, I'd pick a spot on the Gulf of Tolo."

"That's Celebes, isn't it?" Major Arnold asked.

"Yeah, an' not a track or clearing for miles and miles. A lonely country with cliffs and canyons six hundred feet straight up and down. Waterfalls and rapids that plunge over a wilderness of rocks. William, there's jungle back there that would turn a monkey's stomach sick with fear!"

"Listen, Jim," Major Arnold said slowly. "I'm going to do you a favor. In return you can do me one. Li Wan Fang has a consignment to deliver that means a contract for him. The *Silver Lady* was to handle it. The cargo goes to Amurang, Menado, and Wahai."

"What a pal you are! Between Menado and Wahai is the Molucca Passage. And on the bottom of the passage is the *Silver Lady*! You wouldn't put a guy on the spot, would you?"

The major grinned cheerfully. "You wanted a cargo, didn't you? All I ask is that you keep an eye open for a sub base."

"An' go prowling around the Gulf of Tolo and get my rudder shot off? Listen, you scenery bum. I'll keep my eyes open, but I'm not getting the *Semiramis* sunk running errands for you."

"Ssh!" Major Arnold whispered suddenly. His voice became querulous, whining. "I sye, Guv'nor. Let a chap 'ave the price of a beer?"

"A beer?" Jim snapped harshly. "Here's a guilder. That ought to get you off the streets."

Jim spun on his heel and strode down the road. A car swung around a bend behind him. For an instant, its headlights sharply revealed three men. Ponga Jim's breath came sharply, and his hands slid from his pockets. He walked toward them.

Everyone in the islands knew Pete Lucieno. Short, fat, and oily, he participated in everything crooked in the Indies. With him were Sag Dormie and a huge man with a great moonlike face. Sag Dormie was known all too well in the islands. He had done time in the States and

Australia. Some said he'd escaped from Devil's Island penal colony. He was kill crazy. The big man was new. Looking up into his face, Ponga Jim felt his hackles rising. The man's eyes were dead.

Years before, in the States, Ponga Jim had been climbing a mountain. Pulling his head over the edge of a great, flat rock, he had found himself staring into the ugly eyes of a rattlesnake. That snake's eyes had been blank like these.

Ponga Jim looked at Pete and grinned insolently.

"What are you doing in Borneo? I thought they were putting a bounty on rats."

Pete Lucieno's eyes narrowed. "At least my ships have cargoes," he said softly. "They don't lie rusting at the dock."

"Yeah? Some people will carry anything for money. But you can have that stuff. I've got my own cargo. Sailing tomorrow for Amurang, Menado, and Wahai."

"*Where?*" Sag Dormie leaned forward intently. Jim noticed that Pete's eyes were eager. "Taking the Molucca Passage?"

"You bet! Want to come along? There's always room for rats in the bilges." Even as Jim watched Sag, he sensed the real danger was in the placid, fleshy man beside him.

Sag's hatchet face twisted into a sardonic smile.

"Through the Molucca Passage? I want to live a few years yet!"

"You are too sure of yourself, Captain," Lucieno said, his beady eyes gleaming from under his brows. "What of the *Silver Lady*?"

"Cap Marlin was my friend," Ponga Jim said coldly. "He was sunk. I only hope the guys who got him come after me."

He brushed by them and strode along the road. There was work to do and a cargo to load before daybreak. Yet he was uneasy. It had been only a matter of weeks since he had thrown Pete Lucieno for a loss by preventing the landing of munitions on the coast of New Guinea. Lucieno would never forgive that. What was more natural than that he should know of this threat that hung over the masts of British and Dutch shipping? Who else would dare locate a submarine base in the islands?

Jim walked up the gangway. A slim, dapper young Chinese stepped from the shadows behind the companionway.

"Captain Mayo? I am Li Wan Fang. I have been informed you would transport some cargo for me. I took the responsibility of ordering it on the docks in readiness."

"Yeah—okay," Jim said, startled. "You surprised me. Chinese in these waters don't often speak good English. On second thought; neither do the white men."

"I went to the University of California for two years and took it very seriously. Then I went to the University of Southern California for two years. Now I take nothing seriously."

"We're going to get along," Ponga Jim grinned. "Do you know the chance we're taking?"

Li nodded. "But I must make delivery at once. And you have a reputation for getting results, Captain Mayo."

"It'll take more than that," Jim said crisply. He spun on his heel. "Mr. Millan! Get those hatches open and tell Haynes to power the winches."

It was hours later when he went below. The *Semiramis* was already dipping her bow into the heavy seas. The deck was still a confusion of lines and gear. It was going to be good to lie down. And he'd need all the rest he could get.

Opening the door, he stepped into his cabin. The wind caught the door, jerking it from his hand. He turned and pushed it shut.

When he looked around again, he stared into a gun muzzle. Beyond Sag Dormie, Pete Lucieno and the other man were sitting on a couch.

JIM HESITATED. It was only for the flicker of an eye, but he found there wasn't a chance to shoot it out. Sag had him covered, yet was out of the line of fire of Lucieno and the big man. Ponga Jim relaxed.

"Visitors, I see. Just where do you boys think you're going?"

"Dussel thought this would be a good way to go to—to Menado," Sag said. "So we moved in when you weren't looking. I've been wanting to see how tough you were." He struck suddenly, smashing the back of his hand across Jim's lips.

Ponga Jim felt something burst inside and then dribble away, leaving him cold with anger. But Sag Dormie's gun was steady, and he did not move. Lucieno had a gun out, too. Mayo tasted blood in his mouth. He started to lift his hand to his mouth. The gun butt was just inside his coat—

"He's got a gun, Sag," Lucieno said. "In a shoulder holster. He carries it so always."

Sag jerked the gun from Mayo's holster and stuck it in his belt.

"I'll handle this. You won't need a gun anymore, Captain Ponga Jim Mayo."

Dussel moved his big body, and the settee creaked.

"You are to proceed as if nothing has happened, Captain Mayo," he said. "You will go to Amurang, discharge cargo there, and then go on to Menado. I trust you will be discreet. Otherwise it might be necessary to take steps."

"You think you'll get away with this?" Jim queried casually. "You got to go topside sometime. What happens when the crew finds out?"

Dussel smiled, his pulpy flesh folding back like sodden dough.

"They know already. The last two cases you hoisted aboard contained my men. By now they have taken command. Your crew will do the work. My men will superintend it. Job Dussel does not make mistakes."

"I wonder about that. Do you think I'm going to take this lying down? And when this is over, what happens?"

"It is immaterial to me how you take this. When this is over, you and your ship will lie at the bottom of the Molucca Passage."

Dussel's voice was utterly final. For the first time in his life, Ponga Jim felt a rush of desperation. His eyes met Dussel's and fastened there. In the gross, white body before him was cold brutality, a ruthlessness almost reptilian. This man would stop at nothing.

Ponga Jim pushed the cap back on his head and slipped his thumbs behind the broad leather belt.

"Nothing to lose, eh?" he said. "I like it that way, Herr Dussel. You guys can pilot this ship. These are dangerous waters. But if I get knocked off anyway, what's it to me?"

Dussel's heavy-lidded eyes gleamed.

"I thought you would understand, Captain. You will obey orders carefully. You have heard of the Malay boot, Captain? It is child's play to some of the tortures I could use. If you don't obey—" He smiled. "But you will."

Ponga Jim shrugged. "You win."

Job Dussel's face remained folded back in a flabby smile.

Turning, Ponga Jim went topside. Daylight had come, and the sun was sparkling on the choppy sea. Thoughtfully he climbed the companionway to the wheelhouse.

Slug Brophy, his chief mate, was standing watch. His tough, hard-bitten features were surly. In either wing of the bridge lounged a man with a Luger automatic. There was another in the wheelhouse. When Jim walked into the chart room, the man followed to the door, standing aside to let Brophy enter.

"Keep everything quiet, Slug," Jim said. "We hold this course until we get out of the strait. We're calling at Amurang and Menado before we make the Molucca Passage, then south to Wahai."

Ponga Jim paused. The guard was still standing in the door. Jim's finger touched the chart.

"I expect Herr Dussel to take over after we get into the passage." Jim touched the chart again, and his voice was precise. "We'll have to be careful right here. It's a bad spot, where things usually happen. Until then it should be plain sailing."

Slug nodded. "Okay, Cap. I get it."

The days were bright and sunny. The old *Semiramis* rolled along over the sea, doing her ten knots without a hitch. The crew moved carefully. Ponga Jim slept on the settee in the chart room. No further words were spoken. Yet he knew the crew was ready and waiting. But they didn't get a chance. Herr Dussel remained below, usually in conference with Lucieno.

Sag Dormie was wearing two guns openly now, and there were ten armed white men. Slowly Ponga Jim's spirits ebbed, but he continued to watch. There was bound to be a break.

It was almost midnight, and he was to go on watch. He swung his feet down from the settee. Pulling on his woven-leather sandals, he heard the lookout sound the bells, warning of a ship to starboard.

Instantly he was on his feet. He could see the squat, powerful mate on the bridge. Not far away, the two guards engaged in low-voiced conversation. The guard in the wheelhouse was nodding against the bulkhead. It was one chance in a million, and Jim took it.

His hand groped for the switch controlling the light on the topmast. He began switching the light on and off, his eyes intent on the topmasts of the approaching ship.

LI WAN FANG, BALIKPAPAN, ENEMY ABOARD GET WORD M. W. A.

SIGNED MAYO.

He was sending the message the second time when one of the guards saw the flickering light. As the guard leaped from the deck of the wheelhouse, Jim slammed a vicious right to his chin. He toppled back. Just as the two guards jammed in the port door, Jim sprang out. A bullet shrieked after him. He went down the companionway and crashed into Herr Dussel, just issuing from the captain's cabin.

Mayo hurled a terrific right at Dussel, and missed. A smashing right sprawled him to the deck. He sprang to his feet, amazed at the huge man's astonishing speed. Jim stabbed out with a wicked left. He might as well have hit a wall. A powerful blow struck him on the chin, and he rolled back against the bulkhead. Before he could get in the clear, two more vicious punches hit him.

Staggering, Jim tried to crouch. An uppercut jerked him erect. A lightninglike right cross sent him spinning. Dussel followed, for a killing punch. Jim struggled to his feet, rolled away, and then circled warily.

He wanted to tear into the giant, battle him to the wall, and beat him down. But there was no time for that. Even if he won, there were the other men.

Job Dussel was crowding him into a corner. Jim backed away carefully.

Suddenly he reached back and grabbed the rail. He kicked out viciously. The blow caught Dussel in the chest, staggering him across the deck.

With the agility of a panther, Jim leaped over the rail to the main deck.

He landed running. A bullet smashed into the hatch coaming nearby. Another one whipped by his ears. He threw himself to the deck, landing on one shoulder. He rolled over to momentary safety behind a winch.

Something hard lay under his hand—a wooden wedge used for battening a hatch. The sky had clouded over, and a few spattering drops of rain were falling. In the glare of occasional lightning, he could see four men with rifles on the bridge. Two more were on the captain's deck, where he had battled Dussel.

Coming forward were Sag Dormie and three thugs. Behind him was the tightly battened number one hatch. Beyond that was the forecastle, and above it the forecastle head, and nothing else but a spare ventilator lashed to the steam-pipe housing and a small hatch into the forepeak. Of course there was the anchor winch. But he couldn't see a possible hiding place.

Instinctively Jim knew these men were out to kill him. Crawling to his feet, grasping the wedge, he waited. At a distant flash of lightning, he hurled the wedge. He had the satisfaction of hearing the solid smack of wood against flesh. A gun roared, but it was a chance shot. He knew he hadn't been seen.

He reached the forepeak and waited tensely. Aft, on the bridge, he heard Dussel roaring.

"Go ahead, you fools! He's not armed!"

It was only a matter of minutes. He was trapped. The forepeak was a hole without exit. Behind him was the bow, dipping slightly with the roll of the ship.

He crept close to the rail. He heard two men reach the forecastle head on the port side, not twenty feet away. Someone else was just stepping from the companionway, even closer.

Ponga Jim knew he could hesitate no longer. He crawled through the rail and lowered himself over the side of the ship. The bow dipped. For an instant he felt a wave of panic.

Clinging desperately, he grabbed through the hole of the bow chock. A slip meant a plunge into the dark waters below. He shifted his other hand to the chock and then lowered himself into the flukes of the anchor.

It was a wild gamble, but his only chance. He thanked all the fates that the *Semiramis* was blunt bowed. A light flashed on, off, and then on again.

"Chief!" Dormie shouted, his voice incredulous. "He's gone. He's disappeared!"

"Search the forepeak, you damned numbskull!" Dussel roared. "If that devil gets away, I'll kill you. Search the forecastle, too."

Crouching on the flukes of the anchor, Ponga Jim waited tensely. The old barge would soon be dipping her bows under. After that his time would be short. Feet pounded on the deck. He heard the men cursing.

"Maybe he slipped past," Dormie grumbled. "It's dark enough. He couldn't hide here."

A WAVE SPLASHED over Ponga Jim's feet. The bow dipped and black water swept over him. He clung to the anchor, shivering.

Minutes passed. Feet mounted the ladder again. He heard a man muttering. Then the fellow walked across the deck and stood by the bulwark overhead.

Another sea drenched Jim to the skin. He clung to the flukes, trying to keep his teeth still. The ship gave a sickening lunge. His feet fell clear, and for a moment he hung clear as the bow lifted. Then lightning flashed.

As he pulled himself up, he saw a man leaning over the bulwark. It was Longboy, one of his own crew.

With a roar, a huge sea swept over Jim. The *Semiramis* lifted her bow. "Psst!" he hissed sharply. Longboy looked down, startled. "Get a line," Jim whispered. "It's the skipper." The man wheeled around from the rail. In an instant, a line dangled in front of Jim's face. He went up, hand over hand. Just as the bow dipped under another big one, Jim tumbled on deck.

"Lookout!" a hoarse voice shouted. "Come to the bridge."

"Getting too rough here," Jim commented. "They'll have you stand watch there. Tell Brophy I'm safe, but be careful. Then you three stand by. I'm going to start something, and damned quick!"

As Longboy hurried aft, Ponga Jim went down the companionway, into the forecastle. What he wanted now was a weapon. It was dark inside.

Suddenly a cigarette glowed. It was a guard. In the faint glow of the cigarette he saw the glint of metal. The guard's head turned.

Ponga Jim swung. He had only the mark of the glowing cigarette, but it was enough. He felt bone crunch under his fist. The man crumpled. Jim struck a match.

A frightened face peered from the curtains of a bunk, then another.

"Out of those bunks now!" Jim snapped. "I'm taking over." He picked up the guard's Luger and fished two clips from his pocket. He turned on the powerful lascar behind him. "Where are these fellows? You just came off watch, didn't you?"

Abdul nodded. "Two mans in crew's mess. Two mans below. One man on poop deck. Three on bridge. Small fat man, he sleep. Two other mans sleep. Big fat man, he talk this Dormie."

"Right, Abdul, you get that man on the poop deck. Then you, Hassan, Mohamet, Chino, get the two men below. Chino, slip on this man's coat and cap. Go to the ladder an' call them. They'll come up."

"Yes, Tuan. We understand." The four men slipped out on deck, their naked feet soundless in the rising storm.

Ponga Jim turned to the two men who remained. They were short and powerful men, alike as two peas. Both wore green turbans.

"Sakim, you and Selim go aft. One of you tell Millan. Then meet me by the crew's mess."

Dampness touched his face. He stood grasping the rail. A wave, black and glistening, rolled up and then swirled by. A storm of spray swept across the deck. He tasted salt on his lips. Rain and spray beat against his face. The green starboard light stared down at him, a solitary eye. It was going to be a bad time before morning.

HE STARTED AFT, walking fast, his knees bending to the roll of the ship. Job Dussel wanted a showdown, and he was going to get it. Jim couldn't wait for Menado, not even for Amurang. Maybe his message would get to Li Wan Fang, maybe not. It was a chance he couldn't afford to take. Major Arnold had said that not a British or Dutch ship would arrive for days.

What the plan was, he could only guess. One thing he knew—they had done for Cap Marlin and the *Silver Lady*. Now they threatened peaceful vessels that carried no munitions, no soldiers, only traded quietly among the islands. Ponga Jim's jaw set hard, and his eyes narrowed.

Suddenly he laughed. He caught the rail of the companionway to the deck outside his cabin and swung up. His hand was on the door, the Luger ready. A light flashed across him from the bridge. The Luger snapped up and roared. The light crashed out. He heard the tinkle of falling glass and then someone moaned. There was a shout from the wheelhouse.

Ponga Jim jerked the door open.

"Get 'em up!" he roared. He stopped, amazed. The room was empty!

He sprang inside and rushed to the adjoining cabin. It was also empty. Wheeling, he raced for the door. From above came a shout, a shot. Aft, he heard sounds of confusion. He leaped to the deck outside his cabin door. A blast of wind and spray struck his face.

A guard stood in the opening of the amidships passage. Even as Jim's eyes caught the flash of movement, the rifle roared. A shot clipped by his head. Jim fired. The man staggered and then jerked up the rifle again. Jim fired again. The man dropped the rifle and grabbed his stomach with both hands.

Jim made the bridge in two jumps. He came face to face with Brophy. The Irishman was grinning.

"Everything under control, Cap! You got one, I got one, an' the other got away. Get Dussel, Dormie?"

Jim's brow creased. He was staring aft. Something had slipped up somewhere.

"No. They weren't in the cabin."

He strode into the wheelhouse, Longboy was standing there with a rifle. The man at the wheel was grinning.

"Steady as she goes," Jim said. He turned to Longboy. "Get in the chart room and open the port aft. Watch carefully. Shoot to kill."

Abdul appeared around the corner of the deckhouse. Behind him were Chino and Hassan. When they reached the bridge, Ponga Jim looked quickly from one to the other.

"Two we kill. Mohamet, he die, too."

Ponga Jim sighed wearily. "Chino, you stand by here. Brophy, keep this bridge. Don't let anybody but our men come up."

Jim slipped cartridges into the Luger. He started down the companionway. It was blowing a gale now. Every few minutes the sea came roaring over the bow and swept aft, gurgling in the scuppers.

Selim was standing in the door of the galley when they went aft. Sakim was just beyond. Both were watching the door of the crew's mess.

"How many?" Ponga Jim asked.

"Two. They stay still, Tuan. Something funny."

Ponga Jim stepped quickly to the mess room door. The two men sitting at the table were dead. One was the man he had shot in the passage. The other was probably one of those killed below. They had been propped up to delay pursuit.

FIVE MEN KILLED, and one of his own. Gunner Millan came running down the passage, gun in hand.

"Where'd they go? What the devil's happening?"

Ponga Jim shrugged grimly. "I wish I knew. We got five of them. There are five left, besides Dussel, Lucieno, and Sag Dormie. We got them outnumbered two to one, but half our boys are on duty."

"Listen, Cap," said Slug Brophy, running. "That guy Dussel radioed some ship. I heard him tell Lucieno they were going to meet us in Himana Bay."

"That's the answer," Jim cried. "Dussel decided to hole up until help comes. He doesn't want to waste his men."

"But where is he?" Millan asked.

"Somewhere aft. Either the poop or below." Ponga Jim turned to Brophy. "You better get back on that bridge. No traffic in here, but you never can tell. Swing north about thirty degrees. I'll give those guys at Himana something to think about."

Brophy went forward, teetering with the roll of the ship. Jim motioned to Selim.

"You and Sakim stand by with the rifles. If one of them shows his noggin, blast it off. Abdul, you and Hassan turn in and get some sleep. Gunner, radio Amurang, Gorontalo, or someplace. Get in touch with Major Arnold or Li Wan Fang. Try to get some dope on a converted merchantman."

"You don't think it's a sub?" Millan asked.

"If it was, they'd never pick Himana Bay. There's a native village, and a sub would attract too much attention. It's only a few hours across the peninsula to Gorontalo. An armed freighter could lay there a week."

Dawn broke, with the sun bright and the sea choppy. Ponga Jim was drinking coffee in the wheelhouse when Selim came up with a rush.

"Men gone!" he shouted. "He take boat off poop. All gone!"

"What?" Jim demanded. "Well, maybe it's good riddance."

He stood up and raised the binoculars.

"Selim! Get below and turn out the crew. Send Millan to me."

Gunner Millan came running. He was minus a shirt, but had strapped on a gun. Ponga Jim turned quickly.

"Go aft and jerk the cover off number five. Then hoist out that gun you'll find in the 'tween decks under canvas. I want it mounted aft. You know how to handle that. Lucky this damned old barge is a war veteran and still carries her gun mounting."

"Where'd you get the gun?" Millan asked.

Jim grinned. "I knocked over a load of munitions a few weeks ago. That gun looked good, so I kept it and sold the rest. Unless I'm mistaken, we're going to have the fight of our lives. I didn't get the idea until Selim told me Dussel and his boys got away—"

"Got away?" Millan cried.

"Yeah, they launched that lifeboat from the after wheelhouse. It was a gamble, but they took it. The weather broke about four bells. They'll contact that cruiser of theirs."

"It'll take them a couple of days to get to Himana," Millan exclaimed. "By that time we'll be in Amurang."

"No," Jim said. "There's a radio in that boat. Himana Bay isn't more than thirty or forty minutes from where they left us. Even if the radio wouldn't do it, they could sail with the breeze they've had since they started." He pointed with the hand that held the glasses. "There's smoke on the horizon. Unless I miss my guess, that will be them."

Millan clambered down, and Ponga Jim crossed to the wheel.

"Swing back to eighty degrees. At four bells, change her again to one hundred and thirty degrees."

Longboy mumbled the course back to him, and Jim walked back to the bridge. It was going to be a tight race. Changing course was going to bring them up on him faster. But it was going to take him in close to the coast, nearer Amurang, in waters he knew and where his shallower draft would be an advantage. The other ship was doing at least fifteen knots to the *Semiramis*'s ten.

Slug Brophy came up, looking tough.

"This is going to be good, Cap. Ever see Millan handle one of those big guns?"

"He used to be on the *Hood*. I never saw him work."

"That guy could knock the buttons off your shirt with a sixteen-inch gun." Brophy chuckled.

Ponga Jim glanced aft. "She's coming up fast. Looks like about forty-eight hundred tons."

"Yeah," Brophy muttered. "And riding fairly low. But she's not loaded by a damn sight."

Ponga Jim pointed to a spot on the chart.

"See that? That point is Tanjung Bangka. Right about here is a patch of reef. She lies in about a fathom and a half. Loaded the way we are, she will give us just enough clearance. You're taking her over."

"Maybe she's not so deep now, Cap. What if there ain't that much water?"

"Then it's going to be tough. We're going over, and I only hope that monkey back there follows us!"

Ponga Jim ran down and hurried aft. Selim, Sakim, Abdul, and Hassan were all standing by with rifles. Millan crouched at the gun with two men.

Smoke leaped from the bow of the other vessel. A shot whistled overhead. Another blasted off to starboard.

"Get that gun if you can," Jim said quietly. He picked up a rifle. "I want that monkey in the crow's nest."

Whipping the rifle to his shoulder, he fired three times. The man in the crow's nest slumped forward. His rifle slid from his hands.

Millan's gun roared. Jim saw the shell smash into the bulkhead of the forward deckhouse. The gun crashed again. At the same instant a shell blasted open number four hatch, ripping a winch and ventilator to bits.

"There goes my profit on this trip," Jim said. "I never did care for war."

Millan's gun crashed. They saw the shell shatter the enemy's gun. Millan fired again. A shot struck the *Semiramis* amidships. Mayo winced.

He ran to the rail and glanced at the faint discoloration of the reef.

"A fathom and a half is right," he said cheerfully. "I must report that to the Hydrographic Office. Get that after gun when she strikes the reef. When we swing alongside, let them board us. They will, because they'll be sinking!"

"Are you nuts?" Millan protested.

THERE WAS A terrific crash astern, a grinding scream as the bow of the pursuing ship lifted over the reef. With a tortured rending of steel plates, the big freighter slid over the reef, canted sharply to starboard. Ponga Jim turned and raced for the bridge.

"Hard to port!" he yelled at Brophy. "Swing around and come in alongside."

Millan's gun banged, then again. Someone was shouting from the bridge. Rifle shots swept the deck of the *Semiramis*. Back aft, Millan was coolly battering the larger ship to pieces. The shells were smashing the superstructure into a mountain of twisted steel.

The *Semiramis* slid alongside. Ponga Jim dived for the ladder, gun in hand. A bullet slammed by his head and went whining off over the sea. He snapped an effective shot at a big German sailor.

The main deck was a pitched battle. Abandoning his gun, Millan was leading the lascars to stem the tide of men leaping from the rail of the wrecked ship. From the bridge, Slug Brophy was working two guns, firing from the hips.

Ponga Jim fired twice. Something struck him a terrific blow on the head. He pulled himself erect, feeling the warm rush of blood down his face. Something smashed into the bulkhead beside him and he found himself staring at a mushroomed bullet. With an effort, he pulled himself around.

Sag Dormie was standing on the edge of the ruined number four hatch. Just as Jim looked up, Sag's gun blossomed fire. Miraculously, he missed. Ponga Jim's gun swung up, roaring a stream of fire and lead.

Blank astonishment swept over Sag's face. Still trying to lift his gun, he toppled back into the black maw of the hatch.

Shooting and slugging furiously, Ponga Jim leaped into the brawl on the main deck. Hassan was down, his body riddled. Big Abdul stabbed and ripped a heavy knife at a circle of enemies. Jim's shot cut one of them down. Another man wheeled to face him. Mayo slammed him with the barrel of the gun. The man wilted.

But where the hell was Dussel? Blood streaming down his face, Jim stared around. He saw him, standing on the bridge of the other ship. As he looked up, Job Dussel saw him and beckoned.

Jim cleared both rails at a leap. Job met him at the top, his white, pulpy face wrinkled in a smile. Then the big man leaped.

But this time Jim was ready. Rolling under a left, he slammed each fist into the big man's body. Dussel crowded him back, swinging. When he tried to duck he was caught with a wicked uppercut that knocked him back against the wheelhouse. There was no chance for boxing. It was a matter of standing toe to toe on the narrow bridge and slugging.

Dussel hooked a vicious right that knocked him to his knees and then shot out a kick that Jim barely evaded. Staggering to his feet, Ponga Jim was blinded by the blood from his scalp wound. He scarcely felt the terrific driving force of those blows that rained about his head and body. Driving in, he weaved and bobbed. He felt only the killing desire to batter that gross body against the bulkhead, to drive him back, back, back!

Ponga Jim stared. The huge, hard body, seemingly so soft, was impregnable, almost beyond injury. But the face—

Jim crowded closer, swinging both hands. A blow staggered him. But he went under and whipped up a left hook that bared Dussel's cheekbone. A terrific right knocked Dussel sprawling along the bridge.

Someone was shouting at Jim. He looked up, dazed. A slim white cutter had swept up, scarcely a half-dozen yards away. Standing on the bow was Major Arnold, immaculate in a white and gold uniform!

"Jump!" Major Arnold yelled. "That scow is sinking under your feet! Stop playing slap hands and move!"

"William," Jim gulped. He suddenly felt relaxed and empty inside. "You look sweet enough to kiss. Am I seeing stars or are those gold buttons?"

"Just jump, damn you!" Arnold roared. "If you don't, I'll come after you!"

Jim stared around. The water was creeping over the decking of the bridge!

Jim sprang to the rail of the bridge and off into the water. Dripping, he was hauled aboard the cutter. He could see the sturdy old *Semiramis* standing off.

"Look!" Major Arnold said suddenly.

On the bridge of the sinking freighter, Job Dussel had tottered to his feet. His wide, repulsive face was horribly smashed and bloody.

Staggering to the rail, Dussel toppled blindly into the water. With a grinding crash, as though it had waited for that instant, the freighter slipped down into deeper water. Only swirls of water marked the spot. . . .

PONGA JIM TURNED to Major Arnold.

"William," he said. "I got so busy there at last, I never did find out where your sub base was located."

"You said the Gulf of Tolo before you started," William grinned. "That gave me a lead. Then the *Valapa Bay* relayed the message you sent with the mast light. I knew if they were aboard the *Semiramis,* it was because they had to get to the Molucca Passage, or to some boat en route. That pointed in the same direction. We investigated and found the submarine base.

"You see, Dussel and Lucieno didn't dare show themselves on a British ship. The Dutch were watching for them, too. Then the boys found you were going to Amurang, Menado, and Wahai, so they slipped aboard. Job Dussel sank the *Silver Lady.* He also sank those other ships, sank them without a chance. He was aiming at paralyzing the entire trade of the islands—and he came damned near success. He was a brute, all right!"

Ponga Jim Mayo wiped the back of his hand across his bloody mouth.

"Yeah, he was a brute," he said. "But, William"—Jim pointed back at the reef, where the waters were stirring slightly over the rocks—"that guy could fight! Boy, how that guy could fight!"

From Here to Banggai

You know, William," Ponga Jim Mayo said drily, "I'm getting so I hate to see that handsome pan of yours showing itself around. Every time you come around me I end up getting shot at."

Major Arnold smiled blandly. "Never give it a thought, Jim. I don't. They can't shoot a man that was born to be hung."

"Huh!" Ponga Jim emptied his glass and reached for the bottle. "That's a swell crack from the guy whose bacon I've saved at least twice. If it wasn't for me you'd have lost the war right here in the East Indies. And you, a British Intelligence officer, razzing me. It pains me, William, it really pains me!"

"All of which," Major Arnold continued, ignoring him, "reminds me. How did you ever get that 'Ponga' tied to your name?"

Mayo grinned and settled back in his chair. "It's a long story, William. A story that will make your pink British ears pinker, and much too rough for your sensitive moral condition. However, over in Africa, there's a place called Gabon, and in Gabon is a town called Ponga-Ponga. Now a few years past over in Ponga-Ponga was a young man named Mayo, and—"

"Jim," Major Arnold whispered suddenly. "Who are those men at the next table?"

Ponga Jim chuckled. "I was wondering how long it would take you to wake up to those lugs," he said. Then he said guardedly, "Despite the obvious military bearing of at least two of them, those gents are merely innocent passengers on the good ship *Carlsberg*. You may remember the *Carlsberg* is from Copenhagen, but not so many days past her home port was Bremerhaven.

"The chap with the bulge behind his belt is a commercial traveler, even though he looks like a member of the Nazi Gestapo. The lean, hard-faced guy isn't a naval officer, but only a man traveling for his health. The—"

"Ssh!" Major Arnold whispered. "The fat one is coming over."

The man's face was rotund, and his round belly was barely controlled by a heavy leather belt. He looked jolly and lazy until you saw his eyes. They were small, and hard as bits of steel. Like the others, he wore whites and a sun helmet.

He stopped beside their table. "I beg your pardon," he said, smiling slowly, "but I accidentally heard your friend call you Ponga Jim. Aren't you master of the *Semiramis*?"

"Yeah," Jim acknowledged. "Have a seat."

The German seated himself between them, smiling contentedly. "And your friend?"

MAJOR ARNOLD WAVED a deprecatory hand, looking very much the neat, well-bred Englishman. "My name is Girard, William Girard," he said. "I'm trying my hand at pearl buying."

"And mine is Romberg," the fat man said. Then he turned to Jim. "Isn't it true, Captain, that you clear for Bonthain and Menado soon? Captain van Raalt, the pilot, told me your cargo was for those ports. My friends and I are interested, as we have some drilling machinery for shipment to Banggai."

"Banggai's on my route," Jim said. "You and your friends want to go along as passengers?"

Romberg nodded. "I can start the cargo moving right away, if you wish," he said.

"The quicker the better," Mayo said, getting up. "Alright."

Romberg, after shaking hands with each of them, rejoined his friends.

"Well, William," Jim said softly, when they had reached the street, "what do you make of it?"

"That cargo to Banggai looks like a load of trouble, if you ask me," the major said grimly. "Cancel it. I didn't know they were here yet, but I knew the Gestapo was out to get you. They know you messed up that New Guinea deal and their plans here."

Ponga Jim shrugged. "So what? Cargo doesn't lay around waiting for a guy. I'll take my chances and—" he smiled grimly, his eyes hard, "they'll take theirs!"

"Don't say you weren't warned," Arnold said resignedly.

"William," Ponga Jim said pointedly, "I need that money. Everything I got in the world is in that old tub down there by the dock."

He turned and walked rapidly down the street. Over six feet tall, Ponga Jim weighed two hundred pounds and carried it like a featherweight. In the officer's cap, the faded khaki suit, and woven-leather sandals he looked tough, hard-bitten. His jaw was strong, and his face was tanned by wind, sun, and brine.

Arnold shrugged. "Maybe," he said softly, "maybe he can do it. If ever a man could go through hell barefooted, that's the one!"

MAKASSAR WAS DOZING in the heat of a tropical evening. Like many tropical towns it can sleep for weeks or months and then suddenly explode with volcanic force, releasing all its pent-up violence in one mad burst and then falling quietly into the doldrums once more.

Now it was quiet, but with an uneasy stillness like the hush before a storm. Ponga Jim stopped on the end of the Juliana Quay, and Slug Brophy walked up.

"Been around the joints?" Jim asked him.

Brophy nodded. He was a short, thickset man with enormously broad shoulders and a massive chest. His head was set on a short, thick neck. His heavy jaw was always black with beard. He was wearing whites, with shirt-sleeves rolled up and his cap at an angle.

"Yeah," Brophy said, "but I came back. I don't like the looks of things. Everything is quiet enough, but some of the bad ones are looking wise. I saw Gunong, Stello, and Hankins. They've all been drinking a little, and they've got something up their sleeves."

"Crew aboard?" Jim asked.

"All but Li Chuang, the Chinese steward you picked up in Perth. He's ashore picking up something extra special for you."

Jim nodded. "I'm going to look him up. We're getting under way as soon as this new cargo gets loaded. The Gunner watching it?"

Brophy nodded. "Cap," he asked, "is there anything funny about this cargo?"

"Trouble. Those Nazis want me out of the picture. This whole deal is a trap. But they pay in advance."

Brophy grinned widely. "In advance, huh? Okay, Cap. Let's go!"

Ponga Jim turned and started back up the street. A month before, he had bought the *Semiramis* in Melbourne, a battered old tramp with too many years behind her. From the beginning, there had been trouble finding a steward. Then he had stumbled across Li in Perth and had shipped the Chinese at once.

Since then life aboard ship had improved. Li knew how and where to buy supplies, and he always managed to save money. In short, he was too close to a miracle to have running around loose, Jim thought.

Jim was passing the Parakeet Nest, a dive near the waterfront, when he heard a fist smack and a rattle of Chinese in vigorous expostulation.

His pulses jumped at the sound, and he wheeled, pushing through the swinging doors.

Hankins, a burly beachcomber with an evil reputation; Gunong, a Buginese; and Stello, a Portuguese Malay were gathered about, shouting. On the floor lay Li Chuang, his packages scattered about, his face livid with anger.

Hankins stood over him, kicking the slender Chinese in the ribs.

With one bound, Mayo was through the door. Gunong shouted and Hankins whirled, and even as he turned he unleashed a terrific right. It was a killing punch, and Jim Mayo was coming fast. It caught him full on the chin and sent him crashing against the wall. His head bounced, and he slid to the floor.

For just an instant, everyone stared, unbelieving. Then with a roar, Burge Hankins leaped to finish the job. But that instant had been almost enough, and Jim rolled his head away from the wild kick launched by the raging beachcomber.

Hankins's recklessness cost him victory. The kick missed, and Mayo lurched drunkenly to his feet. The room swam before him in a smoky haze. A punch slid off the side of his head, and he staggered forward, fighting by instinct while Hankins wasted his fury in a mad rain of blows when one measured punch would have won.

Ponga Jim Mayo was out on his feet. The room circled him dizzily, and through the haze he saw the horror-stricken face of Li squatting on the floor, blood trickling through his lips.

Ponga Jim was punch-drunk and he was still groggy, but suddenly he was a fighting man. With a growl like a wounded beast, he struck savagely. His left smashed into Hankins's face and knocked the surprised beachcomber against the bar with such driving force that his head bobbed, just in time to meet the sweeping right that lifted him off his feet and knocked him bloody and broken into a corner.

The startled crowd stared, and the giant Gunong ran a thin tongue over his parched lips. Feverishly, his eyes sought the door. Ponga Jim took a step forward, and then, with the speed of light, he leaped.

Gunong's knife slashed out. A half inch closer would have ripped Ponga Jim's stomach open. But it ripped his shirt from side to side and left a red slash across the skin. Then Jim was upon him with a hail of blows that swept down almost too fast for the eye to follow. In seconds Gunong was out cold.

But Ponga Jim was playing no favorites. He smashed out and knocked a Buginese cutthroat reeling. Someone leaped astride of his back and he grabbed the man by the head and threw him bodily over his shoulder into the wall. With a roar of fury Jim waded into the crowd. Blows rained about him. Men screamed with pain, and he felt hands grasping at his legs. He kicked back desperately, and somebody cried out.

With a leap, Jim reached the bar. He smashed a bottle over the head of the nearest man. Maddened faces, streaked with blood and sweat, massed around him. A fist struck his chin, staggering him. He came up with a broken chair leg.

The room was a riot of fighting and insane fury.

Suddenly Jim remembered the gun, and his hand jerked up and ripped open the holster. Then he cursed with fury. To hell with it! He slammed a fist into a face nearby, grabbed the man by the throat and jerked him to arm's length overhead, and heaved him out into the crowd. He was swaying dizzily, and suddenly he was conscious that his arms were heavy, that he was fighting with his back to the wall. Still they crowded around him.

The floor was littered with injured men, but still he didn't use the gun. For an instant, they drew back, staring at him with malevolence.

A big Dyak was down, his face a smear of blood. He tried to get up and then fell back. The pack sensed a kill. Like wolves about an injured bull, they circled warily. They were closing in now.

Ponga Jim Mayo crouched, waiting. He still had the gun, but like a true fighting man, he hated to use it. Guns were his business, but a fight was a fight, and gang fight or otherwise, Ponga Jim Mayo had always won. Desperate, bitter, bloody, but always he and his crew had come out on the top.

Stello, who had hung back, now came forward. He was clutching a kris, and his lips were parted in a sneer of hatred. Yet, even as Jim waited, knowing the next attack would be the last, he realized something was behind this, something more than a mere attack on his cook. These men were cutthroats, but they were organized cutthroats. They hadn't gathered here by accident. Even as he realized that, his mind leaped to his ship, to Romberg, to . . .

STELLO SMILED, his beady eyes gleaming maliciously. "You want beg now, Ponga Jim? You want die now?"

The big half-caste took a step forward. Behind him, the semicircle moved forward. In a split second they would attack!

Ponga Jim's hand, out of sight behind the bar, fell across the handle of the shot-filled hose that the bartender used in case of brawls. In that instant, Stello lunged. But as he lunged the loaded hose swept up and lashed him across the face!

Ponga Jim Mayo heard the bones crunch, saw the big man's nose flatten and his face turn blue with that vicious blow. And in the instant the doors burst open and Slug Brophy leaped in, followed by the crew of the *Semiramis*. What followed was a slaughter.

Somewhere outside a policeman stopped. He looked at the door. He saw a notorious cutthroat stagger outside, trying desperately to pull a knife from his chest. Then the officer turned and disappeared into the darkness. This was no place for an honest policeman.

The streets were silent and still very suddenly, as a silent body of men walked out on Juliana Dock and aboard the *Semiramis*.

The Gunner was standing by the gangway, pistol in hand. Ponga Jim came up, staggering. His face was smeared with dried blood and his shirt was gone. The holster with the gun was still hanging from his shoulder. As the men trooped slowly aboard, Ponga Jim turned to the Gunner.

"All aboard, Millan? If they are, get the anchor up. There'll be hell from here to Batavia for this night's work." He glanced across at the *Carlsberg*, her shadow looming large in the darkness.

He walked to his cabin and fell across the bed. There were things to be done, but they would have to wait. With a sigh Ponga Jim fell asleep.

It was morning when he awoke. He took a shower, washing away the dried blood from his face and hair. Gingerly, he bathed a swollen lip and hand. There was a bad gash on his scalp, too, and a lump under one eye. Casually, he dressed then and checked his gun.

The morning sun struck him like a blow, and he stood still for a moment, looking out over the sea. It was calm, with the wind about force two. Ponga Jim climbed the ladder to the bridge. The Gunner came out of the wheelhouse. He looked worried, but brightened when he saw Mayo.

"Hi, Cap. Glad to see you around."

Jim grunted. "Yeah, I'm glad to be around."

"That must have been some fight!" Gunner exclaimed.

"That fight was a plant, a put-up job!" Ponga Jim looked off over the sea astern. To the south loomed the heavy shoulders of a mountainous island. "Kabalena?" he asked Gunner. "That's Batu Sengia, isn't it?"

"Yeah," Millan agreed. "We're doing okay. You want to take over now?"

Jim shook his head. "Hold it till noon. I'll take the twelve to four."

Ponga Jim walked into the wheelhouse and stood staring down at the chart spread on the table. Major Arnold had been right. That effort in the Parakeet Nest had been the first attempt. That failing, there would be something else. The only question was when and where. Soon his ship would be in Tioro Strait, then Wowoni Strait and the Banda Sea. These islands, Muna and Butung, were little known, their inhabitants strange tribes of Malay-speaking people who kept to themselves.

Ponga Jim had taken the cargo with the full knowledge that it meant trouble, confident of his ability to cope with it. Remembering the icy flecks in Romberg's eyes his scalp tightened. He glanced at the passenger list lying on the desk. Romberg, Kessler, and Braunig. Kessler was the thin, hard-faced man, Braunig the burly, silent fellow.

The Gunner came in. "How's it look, Jim?" he asked softly. "We got some tough babies aboard?"

"Yeah," Ponga Jim said. "Keep your eyes on them, and tell your watch to do the same thing. Keep a rod handy."

The Gunner slapped his waistband. "I got one." His brow wrinkled. "I'm more scared of that damned orangutan than I am of any of them."

"That *what*?" Jim wheeled. "Did you say orangutan?"

"Sure, didn't you know?" Millan was astonished. "Braunig says it's a pet. Biggest one I ever saw. He feeds it himself, won't let anybody else get close."

"Pet, is it?" Ponga Jim's left eyebrow squinted and his eyes narrowed. "In a strong cage?"

Millan nodded. "Yeah, It would be a hell of a thing to tackle in the dark. Or in the daytime, for that matter."

Mayo shrugged. "It won't get out. Put an extra lock on it. And if Braunig kicks, send him to me."

He watched the blunt-bowed *Semiramis* plow through the seas. Old she might be, but she was dependable. Ponga Jim knew that peace in the East Indies might erupt into war at any moment. The war that had thrown all Europe into arms and that threatened at any moment to turn cities into a smoking shambles, was already eating at the shores of these lonely islands. Twice, Ponga Jim Mayo had been involved in attempts to create strife here, at this furthest limit of the British Empire.

An American adventurer and master of tramp freighters, Mayo preferred to mind his own business, settle his private fights, and stay out of international affairs. But following the sea in the Indies had never been a picnic, and he had come up from the brawling fury of a hundred waterfronts to a command that he meant to keep.

Jim's eyes narrowed angrily, and his jaw set. Once, he had deliberately butted in to avert more trouble. Now they were out to get rid of Jim Mayo as fast as possible.

Carefully, his fingers touched the swollen lump under his eye and felt his jaw. He felt stiff and sore from the brutal kicking and beating he'd taken.

Somewhere in the islands, perhaps still back in Makassar, Major William Arnold was waging an almost single-handed fight to keep peace in these East Indian waters. But it was a lonely, dangerous job. All over the world secret agents of the Gestapo were striking at the lifeline of the British Empire. All through the islands there was sabotage, propaganda, and undercover warfare.

Slug Brophy came up to the bridge. "Romberg was asking about you," he said, winking. "When I told him you were on the bridge, he seemed surprised. Those guys got enough guns to arm the U.S. Navy."

"Yeah?" Jim stroked his chin thoughtfully. "Let the Gunner handle this a bit longer. You come with me."

He wheeled and ran down the ladder. Sakim and Longboy were painting amidships.

"Drop those brushes," Jim snapped. "Slug, get them a couple of guns."

When they were armed he went amidships. The three Germans were sitting in the petty officers' mess, talking and drinking beer. Jim stopped in the doorway.

"I understand," he said crisply, "that you men have guns aboard. I want them. Nobody packs a rod on this boat but my officers and myself."

Romberg shrugged. "But in times like this maybe we need our guns," he said softly.

"You get them when you leave the boat," Mayo snapped. "All right, on your feet for a search."

Romberg's face whitened.

Kessler got to his feet, face flushing with anger.

"There will be no searching here!" he snapped. "This is insolence!"

"Yeah?" Ponga Jim chuckled without mirth. "You guys got a lot to learn. An' when you talk about insolence, sourpuss, remember you're not in the German army now. You're on my ship, and I'm in command here!"

Kessler started forward and then stopped. "So? You know, do you? Well, what of it?"

Mayo's gun slid into his hand. "You guys asked for transportation for yourselves and your cargo. You're getting it. Get tough, and you'll get a lot more. I said I'd get you there, but I didn't say I'd get you there alive." He shrugged. "Take their guns, Slug. The first one that peeps will have to digest some lead."

The three men stood very still, hands raised, while Brophy frisked them expertly. Once Romberg's eyes flickered to the port and he stared.

For outside was Sakim, with a rifle barrel resting on the edge. Longboy stood outside the other, his brown face eager.

Romberg's eyes swung back to Mayo, and there was a hint of admiration in them. "You'd have made a good German officer, Captain Mayo."

Jim snorted contemptuously.

Brophy passed out of the room with the guns tucked in his waistband. Then Ponga Jim slid his back into its holster.

"Sorry to have bothered you, Gents. Adios."

Day slid into night. Mayo was worried. Something had to break. There was a possibility that disarming them had also wrecked their plans, but he had no faith in the idea. There was something else, something more to be expected. At twelve he would go on watch, and by that time if everything went well they would be entering the Banda Sea with a straight shot for Bangkulu before turning east for Banggai Bay.

Night had fallen and the stars were bright when he turned aft for a last look around before his night watch. The passage amidships was empty, but he heard voices in Romberg's cabin.

For an instant, Ponga Jim hesitated outside the door. Kessler was talking. If Braunig was there he was not speaking. But that was usually the case. Jim walked aft to the sternpost and stood watching the wake, his back to the after deckhouse. Then he turned and started forward.

Sharp, fierce snarling and then a shrill, angry yapping shattered the still air. Puzzled, he hesitated. Something was bothering the orangutan. He went down the ladder to the storeroom beneath the after wheelhouse.

In the small space was the cage of the orangutan, a huge beast, almost as big as a gorilla. Foaming at the mouth, the big ape was screaming with fury and trying to get through the bars at Braunig, who was crouching before the cage. His wide, ugly face was contorted with sadistic frenzy as he stabbed at the ape with a pointed stick.

As Ponga Jim reached the foot of the ladder, the ape grabbed the stick and with a terrific jerk, ripped it from Braunig's hands. The stick broke and the ape hurled the pieces at Braunig. The burly German roared with laughter, until one of the sticks hit him on the shoulder. Then, with a snarl of rage, Braunig jerked up a boathook and stabbed at the ape with the sharp end.

"I'll show you!" Braunig snarled. "You slobbering beast!"

Jim crossed the intervening space in a leap, ripping the boathook from Braunig's hands. "I'll be damned if you will!" he snapped. "Get back to your cabin before I lose my temper."

"You! Why, you—!" Braunig's face purpled with fury.

Smack!

Jim's right smashed into the big German's mouth and knocked him skidding along the deck. The German sprang to his feet, crouched, and then lunged. Jim sidestepped.

"Better get on deck before I get peeved," he said again. "I don't want to hurt you."

Braunig was powerful. He wheeled and rushed at Ponga Jim. But Mayo stepped back quickly. The German plowed ahead. Jim crossed a right, hooked both hands to the body, and jerked up a hard right upper-cut. Braunig staggered, and Jim knocked him down with a hard left hook. He got up, and Jim floored him again. The big man lay there, groggy, but still conscious.

"All right," Jim said coolly, "now go on deck."

Slowly, heavily, the man climbed to his feet and staggered drunkenly up the ladder. Jim crossed to the cage where the big ape clung to the bars, staring.

"What's the matter, old fellow?" he asked softly. "Been treated pretty mean, haven't you?"

The orangutan stared back at him, its eyes bloodshot, ugly. Staring at the ape, Jim could see that the beast's mind had been warped into a seething caldron of hatred where nothing lived now but the lust to kill. Through the red hair on its body he could see countless scars. Why, Jim wondered? Just cruelty? But why cart the ape around and suffer the expense of keeping it for only cruelty? He shrugged and went up the ladder to the deck.

Brophy was standing in the wing of the bridge when Jim came on watch. "This kind of gets a guy," Brophy said softly. "Something's in the wind, and you don't know what or where it'll come from."

Mayo nodded. "Better get below and turn in," he said. "They won't wait much longer. They've got to strike between here and Banggai, because there's a destroyer there now."

He watched Brophy down to the main deck and then turned back. The visibility was good, for the night was clear and the stars were bright. Tupa, the Alfura seaman taken aboard in Bonthain, was at the wheel, Selim on watch in the bow.

His thoughts reverted to Romberg. There was more in the wind than a plan to eliminate him. That, he was certain, was only incidental to greater plans, and they must be plans with some bearing on the cargo below. Drilling machinery it might be, and some of it obviously was; but there were other supplies, also.

The sea was calm, just a light wind blowing. He took his glasses and scanned the sea thoughtfully. A sub? There hadn't been a sub sighted since the affair off the New Guinea coast. True, there were German agents in the East Indies; there had been efforts at sabotage, but most of it ineffectual.

Aside from the attempts to create revolt among native tribes in Papua and to destroy shipping, things had gone along smoothly. It was so obvious a tactic to attack the far-flung British Empire at many points, and as

Holland was supported by the British navy in the Indies, that included the Netherlands Indies.

Ponga Jim let one hand slip up to the gun butt in the shoulder holster. War couldn't come to the Indies without becoming a personal problem.

ROMBERG WAS A wily customer. Had the plot to kill him in the Parakeet Nest succeeded, he would have been safely out of the way, and still the cargo would have gone on to Banggai Bay, and whatever else remained of the plot would have proceeded without further delay.

Sparks walked out on the bridge. "Message for you, Cap," he yawned sleepily. "Just came in."

"Suppose you turn in, Sparks? You may get another long shift tonight. I'll listen in occasionally."

McVey turned and left the bridge. The message was brief and to the point. It said:

NO CARGO EXPECTED BANGGAI. ROMBERG, KESSLER, BRAUNIG UN-
KNOWN. HAVE YOU GOT YOUR NECK OUT!

WILLIAM.

Ponga Jim frowned thoughtfully. He had suspected that it was some point near Banggai, but that they intended to transship there. He paced the bridge, his mind weighing the possibilities. When Gunner Millan came up to relieve him at four o'clock, he was still far from a solution.

THE HOURS SLIPPED BY. The sun came up and the day warmed. The crew was under a strain. The men were jumpy. Several times Jim saw his three passengers gathered in serious conversations, but he ignored them until late in the afternoon. Braunig, his face battered and swollen, had just returned from feeding the orangutan, and the three were standing amidships. Jim came out of the passageway and strolled up to them.

"Suppose you guys let your hair down," he said slowly, "and tell me just where you think you're going? I know it isn't Banggai."

Romberg's lips tightened, and he glanced at Kessler. "Unfortunately, Captain Mayo, our plans have gone somewhat awry. However, it is true we don't have any great desire to land at Banggai. We intended to see the cargo was taken to Tembau."

"My deal says Banggai," Ponga Jim said sharply. "And to Banggai we go."

Romberg cleared his throat. "Captain Mayo, I know something of shipping conditions in these waters now and how difficult it is to keep busy. Suppose I offered you a bonus to carry us to Tembau."

Jim shrugged. "You know my terms: cash first. It'll cost you five thousand. If I don't get it, you go to Banggai and you can deal with the native rajah there." He grinned. "However, he has no love for Germans and is very pro-British."

Romberg hesitated, but Ponga Jim had seen triumph leap into his eyes.

"All right, Captain Mayo," Romberg said. "I'll see you in the salon at dinner. It will take all my available funds and those of my friends. But we'll manage."

On the impulse of the moment, Jim stepped into the radio room when he went forward. Picking up a pencil, he wrote rapidly.

"Tear that up after you send it, Sparks," he ordered. "And stand by." It read:

WILLIAM GIRARD,
HOTEL KONINGSPLEIN,
MAKASSAR, CELEBES, N. E. I.
DESTINATION TEMBAU. OUT OF THE FRYING PAN INTO THE FIRE.

MAYO.

The *Semiramis* pushed her bows into the seas, rolling easily on a changed course. Tembau lay on the edge of the Greyhound Strait. There was one anchorage, Ponga Jim Mayo was remembering. It was one he had never seen, but it had become almost a legend in the islands. Tukoh Bay wasn't a nice place, for it had become a resort for all the renegades in the islands. But if it was Tukoh Bay they wanted, to Tukoh Bay they would go.

Tupa was in the crow's nest when the *Semiramis* slipped through the outlying reefs to Tembau. The island lifted itself high out of the water, and from the sea there was no evidence of the village at Tukoh Bay. Slug Brophy came up to the bridge. He had two guns strapped on. Gunner Millan was standing by on the poop deck with several of the crew.

Slowly the old tramp wallowed into Tukoh Bay, and Jim Mayo gave the word to let go forward. A few minutes later, the three Germans went over the side into a native sampan and were taken ashore. Lighters came alongside, and with them, Kessler and Braunig to superintend the discharge of their cargo.

When the last sling was going over the side with its cases, Romberg came aboard.

"Well, Captain, you promised delivery, and here we are. I want to thank you for a pleasant voyage. But as the tide is out, you won't be leaving before daybreak. Perhaps I'll see you before then."

Daybreak! Ponga Jim felt himself turn cold inside. Night in Tukoh

Bay? That was something he'd overlooked. The town was full of cut-throats ready for anything that promised payment. He watched the three men go ashore and saw the lighters pull away.

Red Hanlon, the chief engineer, came up from below, wiping his hands. Jim motioned to him.

"Listen, Red, I want you to keep steam up all night. We can't get out of here until daybreak. And with that crowd ashore, anything may happen.

"Tell Slug and the Gunner I want to see them in my cabin, Li, and quick!" Jim ordered the steward.

IN A BUNGALOW BUILT back under the trees behind the little village of Tukoh Bay, the three Germans sat together. Behind a low table was another chair, and the man who sat there was thin and bald. He looked old, yet when he moved it was with a grace that proved him much younger than he appeared. His features were narrow, hawklike. A big man, powerfully built, lay on a divan nearby.

The man behind the table shuffled some papers on his desk. "How many men does he have?" he demanded harshly.

"Twenty-five in all," Romberg said. "The steward is a Chinese and can be discounted."

The man behind the desk stared at Romberg coldly. "A Chinese? Discounted? That was what the Japanese thought. Let us not make the same mistake." He paused. "Armament?"

Romberg hesitated. "I'm not sure. Each of the officers is armed. I believe they have two rifles for game, and a shotgun."

"You needn't worry, Herr Heittn," the big man on the divan said. "I've heard a lot of this Ponga Jim Mayo, and those boys of mine would like to take him."

"Don't forget, Petrel," Heittn replied drily, "that a submarine has failed, that this man almost single-handed captured a ship and destroyed a sub. This man is not to be trifled with. No doubt," he said, glancing at the discoloration on Braunig's eye, "that our friend could tell us a little about him."

Heittn glanced from one to the other. "We must not fail this time. The boat must be seized, the crew destroyed."

IT WAS DARK in the cabin when Li entered, but he flashed no light. "Captain Mayo?" he whispered. "They come now."

Silently, Ponga Jim got up and strapped on his guns. Then he took down the rifle. By the chronometer, which he struck a match to check, it was almost three in the morning. Another hour and it would be turning gray. He picked up the automatic rifle and walked to the bridge.

Brophy was leaning on the bulwark looking over the dodger. It was pitch-dark, but not far out there was a larger blob on the water.

"Tupa in the crow's nest?" Mayo asked.

Brophy nodded. "Yeah, everybody's at his station. What you going to do, Skipper? Hoist 'em aboard with the winches?"

"Wait and see. I'm going to give those boys a bellyful of war."

"I hope you know what you're doing. There's more than two hundred men out there. Selim slipped ashore, and he says they're armed to the whiskers."

The boats were nearer now. Ponga Jim walked back slowly to the wheelhouse.

"All right, Sparks," he commanded. "Lights!"

Suddenly the sea flashed into white brilliance under the rays of three great searchlights, and almost at the same instant, the whistle blew the fire drill signal. Hoses were strung out and connected. The boats swung alongside, and the attackers began swarming up the side.

"Steam!" Jim roared, firing a blast into the nearest boat.

In almost the same instant, a roar of steam belched from the fire hoses, full into the faces of the men swarming up the sides and clinging to the rail of the *Semiramis*!

One gigantic half-caste took the blast full in the face at scarcely a yard. His face vanished as if by magic, and screaming horribly, the man let go of the rail and tumbled back into the water.

It was all over in an instant. Screaming in agony, the attackers leaped into the sea. From the bridge, Ponga Jim waited, watching.

Unnoticed, a motor launch had slipped in close to the bow, and suddenly, there was a yell from forward. Ponga Jim spun around, firing as he turned. His shot knocked the gun from the hands of a big Swede he recognized as Hankins.

Then, with a rush, the group swept aft. Two of his own men went down. The others, caught from behind, rushed for shelter aft, unable to handle the hoses effectually without endangering others of the crew. The major attack was broken, but now, with dawn breaking and safety in sight, defeat swept down upon them behind a hail of lead. Jim ran down the ladder, and whirled at the foot of it to find himself face-to-face with Braunig.

The big German had rushed forward from the after part of the ship, and for an instant Jim failed to appreciate what it might mean. The German jerked up his gun and fired. Mayo dropped into a crouch, hammering a stream of slugs at Braunig. The first shot struck the man in the chest, but by some superhuman burst of strength he lunged forward, firing again.

A terrific blow slammed Mayo on the head, and he spun halfway around, but not before seeing Braunig topple over on his face, dead.

Romberg was nowhere in sight, but the battle had divided itself suddenly into a series of individual scraps. Kessler, leaping from the body of a Malay fireman, his knife red with blood, turned to see Ponga Jim, coming toward him. Kessler hurled the knife, but he missed. Then Jim leaped in a flying tackle, and they crashed to the hatch, rolling over and over.

Jim came up on top and leaped free. The German jumped up and landed a left that knocked Jim back on his heels. Kessler let go with another, but Mayo grappled with him and hurled the man back against a winch. As Kessler came at him, Mayo caught him with a short left hook that cracked against the German's chin with a pop like the report of a pistol. Kessler toppled forward, unconscious.

Grabbing up his fallen gun, Ponga Jim ran aft. In the passageway he stumbled over a body. And on number four hatch was another, but the battle seemed to have centered forward. And Jim Mayo could only recall that Braunig had come forward. What could he have done aft? And how did he get there?

Suddenly, a shrill scream of horror sounded from the poop deck, and Mayo reached the stern in two bounds, just in time to see Li come staggering out of the passageway, screaming with fear.

The Chinese steward staggered over a chock and fell headlong just as Jim leaped through the door. He stopped, dead still, feet spread wide.

Not six feet away, the huge orangutan was standing, its bloodshot eyes burning with hate. Its hands, arms, and face were stained with blood, and at its feet lay what was left of Romberg, a horror only to be recognized by the clothing. Then the ape sprang!

Mayo's gun jerked up, and the trigger slammed on an empty chamber. Quickly, Jim dropped the gun and hurled his closed fist at the creature's body. It landed solidly, and the beast gave a queer, gasping cry. Then one hand slapped across Jim's face, knocking him against the bulkhead. The ape sprang, ripping the shirt from his shoulders. But Mayo swung aside, and then leaped, swinging a barrage of blows that knocked the big ape head over heels.

Slowly, the orangutan crawled to its feet. The murderous fury still blazed in its eyes, but it was wary now. This was a different mode of attack, something new. Suddenly, it grabbed the pipes overhead and hurled itself bodily through the air, feet first!

Jim tried to duck, but those feet struck him full on the chest and he turned a complete somersault, sprawling on the deck outside, gasping for breath. The ape sprang at him, snarling and screaming; but Jim rolled over and caught the animal with a vicious kick as it leaped toward him. It toppled back, and Jim smashed a right to the face.

The orangutan dropped to the deck and began to whimper.

Cautiously, Jim got to his feet, and prodded the ape below and into its cage. Then he snapped the lock that Romberg had unfastened. Somehow, the big ape had got to him before he could escape. Trained to hate men and to kill, the beast had acted violently.

Ponga Jim Mayo staggered back to the deck. There were no sounds of fighting now, but when he raised his head he saw a seaplane at anchor nearby. He went toward it.

Major Arnold was leaning against the deckhouse amidships lighting a cigarette. He lifted an eyebrow as he saw how battered Jim was.

"Fighting again?" he asked wearily. "Such brutality! Tsk, tsk, tsk!"

Ponga Jim looked very astonished.

"Me? Fighting? I've done more battling in the last few days than the whole Allied army has done since the war started!"

Arnold nodded. "We got Kessler. What happened to Romberg and Braunig?"

Ponga Jim told him briefly.

"The worst one got away," the major said. "Heittn, his name was. We've been trying to get him for months."

"Have a drink?" Jim invited.

The major nodded. "What were they carrying in those cases, Jim?"

"Ammunition and guns," Jim replied. "It'd been chaos for us if they'd distributed them. I wasn't certain of their cargo until we reached Tembau. Then I knew."

"Well, here's how," said the major, downing his drink. Then, "Who-o-o-o! What was in that glass?"

"My own concoction. I call it a Barata Sling."

"Gad!" breathed Major Arnold. "What action!"

"Action?" said Ponga Jim Mayo, laughing. "You mean reaction. Wait until you try to get up!"

The House of Qasavara

Ponga Jim Mayo looked toward the dark blotch of Bam Island. "Easy does it," he said, his eyes swinging toward Cape Wabusi. "Port a little . . . hold it!"

Quickly, Jim Mayo stepped to the *Semiramis*'s engine-room telegraph and jerked it to stop. They had reached anchorage.

"All right, Mr. Brophy," he called. "Let go forward!"

He stood in the wing of the bridge of the freighter waiting to hear the splash of the anchor. Then he turned and went down the ladder.

Carol Sutherland got up quickly when he came into the ship's saloon. His white-topped cap was at a jaunty angle, but she thought that without the gleam of humor that was never far from his eyes his bronzed face would have been a little grim.

"Are we there?" she asked. "Is this Broken Water Bay?"

Ponga Jim nodded. In the glow of the light her red-gold hair was like a flame.

"Yes, this is it. But you can't go ashore tonight. It will be bad enough in the daytime."

"But my father's here, and—"

Her protest ended as he lifted a hand. The throb of engines down below had ceased, but there was another sound, the low, pulsing beat of drums rolling down from the dark, jungle-clad hills. She stopped, her mouth partly opened to speak, while the sound of the drums filled the room and seemed to pound with the same rhythm as the blood in her veins.

"Hear that?" he asked gravely. "Gets you, doesn't it?" He waited for a moment, listening. "And those fellows are headhunters or cannibals, Stone Age men living in a land that time forgot. Think of it," he said, waving a hand toward the lonely New Guinea shore. "Most of them have never seen a white man; thousands of them don't know there is such a thing. This is the jungle, Miss Sutherland. And this is a lonely coast, where few ships come."

"My father is here somewhere, Captain Mayo," she said simply. "I must go to him."

He shrugged. "If he's ashore we'll find him tomorrow. No boat leaves this ship before daybreak, I value my men too highly. Those boys ashore are stirred up. This whole country is throbbing with hate. There have been fifty-three natives who worked for white men killed within the past two weeks."

JIM WALKED into his cabin, and when he returned he wore a gun in his shoulder holster.

"You know," he said thoughtfully, "I can't figure what Colonel Sutherland would be doing on this coast. This Broken Water Bay is an unhealthy country in more ways than one, and certainly no spot for a plantation."

"But I know he came here," she protested. "I heard him mention the bay to this man who came to see him before he left. That man was coming, too. They were to land near the mouth of a small river, and I believe they were going to a village close by."

"That's impossible," he said decidedly. "There isn't any village near here. Those drums are fifteen miles from here at least."

"But I heard them talk about looking for someone, about finding the House of Qasavara."

"The House of Qasavara!" Ponga Jim stuck his thumbs in his belt. "Are you kidding me?"

"Why, no," she exclaimed in surprise. "I—"

"But you told me your old man was looking for a plantation location near Broken Water Bay, and now you spring this here Qasavara business on me."

"What's strange about that?" she demanded. "I heard Daddy and this man talking about it, and supposed it was a native village nearby."

Jim tossed his cap on the table and ran his fingers through his hair.

"Listen," he said, exasperated. "Qasavara is a cannibal-spirit living back in that steamy jungle somewhere. The House of Qasavara is where he takes his victims, and where the natives offer sacrifices to him.

"Until a couple of months ago he'd almost been forgotten, then several bodies were found bitten by five poisonous teeth. One was found at Salamoa while we were there, another at Madang, a couple outside of Port Moresby, and one near the airport at Lae. Every one of them was a native employed by white men. Then last week twelve were found at one time, all of them marked by the five teeth of Qasavara."

"But what can all that have to do with Father?" Carol asked. "I don't understand."

Jim shrugged. "You've got me, lady." He rubbed his jaw thoughtfully, and then he looked up, meeting her eyes. "Didn't you tell me your father came from Sydney? That he worked for the government in some inspection service or something?"

"That's right. And about six weeks ago he received a letter from Port Moresby that worried him, and decided to come up here. I came with him, but stopped in Port Moresby."

"How about this guy who came to see him? Was he a slender, well-built fellow with a blond mustache? Military walk and all that?"

She nodded, puzzled. "Do you know him?"

"Know him?" Jim chuckled. "He's the best friend I've got. And sometimes I wonder if that's saying anything at all."

AFTER CAROL SUTHERLAND RETURNED to her cabin, Ponga Jim walked out on deck. It was completely dark, the sky spangled with stars, but no moon. In the blackness a quarter of a mile away was the darker shoreline and a faint, silver gleam from a rustle of surf.

Jim rubbed his jaw thoughtfully. It would be a joke on Arnold to show up here when Arnold had left him in Menado. And it must be a tough job or Major William Arnold would never have sent to Colonel Sutherland for assistance in breaking the case.

Yet he had seen in the few ports he had touched that the natives were frightened and surly. Whispers had come to him that all whites were to be murdered, and all those who worked for whites; that Qasavara had returned to claim Papua and would kill all Dutch and British people.

There was a stirring of unrest throughout the islands, and an outbreak now, calling for ships, money, and men, would be a severe blow to England. Besides, the Indies were the richest prize on earth, and to countries thirsting for colonies and expansion, they represented a golden opportunity.

Several times, Ponga Jim and Major William Arnold had spiked the guns of the Gestapo and other foreign agents working in the Indies. But those had been attempts at sinking ships and at destroying commerce in the islands. The present effort would stir much more strife than the former attempts.

Then he looked up and saw the head.

A native, his face frightfully painted with streaks of white, was crawling over the rail. Even as Ponga Jim's eyes caught the movement, a dozen other bodies lifted into view and the rail was swarming with savages. Jim let out a yell and went for his gun.

At the first blast of fire three heads vanished. Another native, already on the deck, let out a wild yell and pitched over on his face. With a scream of rage a big savage hurled a spear that missed by an eyelash and then, jerking a stone hatchet from his belt, hurled himself at Jim, his face twisted with hatred.

Dropping into a crouch that sent the wild blow with the hatchet over his shoulder, Jim whipped a terrific left hook to the Papuan's belly. Then he jerked erect and slammed the man alongside the head with a wicked, chopping blow from the barrel of his automatic. Without a sound the native dropped to the deck.

From the bridge a machine gun broke into a choking roar as burst after burst swept the rail and the boats thronging out from shore. Jim snapped a quick shot at a big headhunter running aft, and wheeled around to see Selim wrest a spear from another and run him through.

Abo, one of the seamen, was down on the deck, writhing with agony, but Tupa had jumped astride his murderer's shoulders from the boat deck and buried a knife in the man's neck.

As swiftly as they had come, they were gone, and the rail was littered with bodies. Jim ran to the taffrail and snapped a couple of quick shots at the boats. He was rewarded by seeing one native jerk to his feet and topple over the side.

Slug Brophy came running aft with Red Hanlon and two of the crew. All carried rifles.

"That'll hold them," Jim said drily. "I wonder what started that?"

Slug grinned. "You can't chase all over the ocean mixing into trouble wherever you find it without getting guys after your scalp!" he said grimly. "These babies didn't tackle this boat because it's what they wanted, but because they were told to!"

"Yeah," Jim agreed. "You got something there."

Suddenly he thought of Carol and started forward on a run. He swung into the starboard passage and stopped dead still.

At the end of the passage her door swung idly with the slight roll of the ship, and the room beyond was lighted and empty. In the passage, a native woman lay on the floor, dead.

Jim swore viciously and leaped over the sprawled body. One glance told him that Carol was gone. Wheeling, he saw another native huddled in a corner, run through with his own spear. A groan startled him.

Whirling, gun in hand, he saw Longboy struggling to sit up, blood running from a gash on his scalp. Quickly, he knelt beside him.

"What was it, Boy?" he asked. "What happened?"

"Six, eight mans, they come overside while you fight. I see them. I hit one, knock him over. I throw marlinespike, get another one. Then pretty

soon I in here, mans grab Missee, I sock 'em. Stick him with spear. Somebody shoot—bang, I no know what happen."

Jim got to his feet. "Red, get this man to the steward, you hear? Slug,
we're going ashore. Those babies can't travel much faster than we can. I
brought that dame down here, and I'll see she gets to her old man in one
piece. Gunner stays here in charge. I'll take you, Selim, Tupa, Abdul, the
Strangler, and Hassan. We've got to move fast!"

When the boat touched the sand the moon was just lifting over the
horizon. Jim Mayo shifted his rifle to his left hand.

"Red, you and Fly Johnny take the boat back," he ordered. "I'll keep
Singo and Macabi with the rest of us. We might stumble into a tough
scrap. Tell the Gunner to get the hook up if I'm not back by daylight and
take her around to the Sepik. If we don't get them we'll pick you up
about two miles up off Sago Bar."

Turning quickly, he struck off at a rapid walk. The natives would be
traveling fast, as they would not expect pursuit before daylight and there
was little chance of an ambush near the bay. Giant ficus trees spread their
aerial roots beside the path, and there was heavy undergrowth, mostly
ferns and sugarcane. The jungle shut in suddenly, dark and ominous.

PONGA JIM SLOWED his pace. Just how many men were in the band ahead
he could not guess. Probably forty or fifty, for there had been nearly a
hundred in the attacking party, and fearful execution had taken place along
the rail and in some of the boats.

Slug hurried up alongside Jim. His short, powerful body moved as
easily and rapidly as any one of the long, lithe seamen behind. "Skipper,
I hate to think of them Guineas having Miss Sutherland. That girl was a
bit of all right."

"Yeah," Jim nodded gravely. "You bet she was. But I'm not worried
about them. That attack was planned by a white man for a purpose. You
know what I think, Slug? Somebody knew that girl was aboard!"

"You mean they jumped us just to get her?"

"That's just what I mean. At first, I thought it was some of the same
bunch we've had trouble with, and they recognized the boat. I thought
maybe they were afraid we were going to butt in again. But now I think
they had some spy who saw the girl come aboard in Port Moresby or
saw her at Salamoa. The attack was a blind so that under cover they could
get her."

"But what's the idea? What good would she be to them?"

"None, unless—" Jim hesitated, frowning.

"Unless what?"

"Unless they've got her father, and probably Arnold. They could use her to put pressure on Sutherland and Arnold, to make them give up a lot of information that both of them have."

Slug hitched his gun a little and swore under his breath. He knew only too well what fiendish tortures those savages could think of, but it wasn't the Papuans who would be worst, for the civilized men who led them would be most dangerous.

In the damp light of dawn they stopped for a hurried lunch. All the men were silent, grim. Jim scouted out along the trail with Tupa. Tupa knelt in the mud, pointing.

"See? They come this way," he said.

Jim studied the marks of high heels thoughtfully. Several times during the night his flashlight had picked them out along the trail among the tracks of other men. Now, in the growing light of day, they were plainer.

Ponga Jim swore suddenly.

"Slug!" he called. Brophy came running. "Look at those tracks! Carol Sutherland never made those! She'll weigh about a hundred and fifteen, and by now she'd be tired. Yet those steps are light. They've got a child or a girl wearing those shoes!"

Brophy scowled. "But where the hell—"

"The river!" Jim said suddenly. "They made for the river. Get that stuff out of the way and let's go!"

In a matter of minutes the packs were made, and Ponga Jim led off into the jungle at a rapid walk. As he walked, his mind worked rapidly. It could be either Heittn or Petrel, but somehow he believed this last attack was by someone new to him.

William, not so long since, had mentioned something about two German agents, Blucher and Kull, who had come into the Indies. Despite the loneliness of some sections of the New Guinea coast, it would be a poor place from which to operate. His common sense told him that the seat of the trouble would be in the dark and little-known interior. Legends placed the House of Qasavara somewhere in the unknown country at the headwaters of the Sepik.

They were following a well-beaten trail, and Jim paused from time to time to listen, but heard no sound. He was sure the trail would bring him out somewhere near Sago Bar, where he could intercept the *Semiramis*. Despite time and trouble, regardless of danger, it was up to him to follow the natives who had captured Carol Sutherland. Also, there was a chance Arnold was somewhere up the river and in terrible danger.

DAWN WAS JUST BREAKING when they came out on the bank of the river. About a mile wide, it rolled rapidly seaward, bearing here and there a giant tree or snag floated from the jungle upriver. The flood season was past, but the water was still high. The Sepik would carry a boat that didn't draw more than thirteen feet for at least three hundred miles. With a good deal of extra water, there was a chance he could go much farther than that.

Tupa glided to his side, moving soundlessly.

"Papua boy, he come!" he whispered, pointing up the bank.

Moving toward him in the early light of dawn he saw a dozen powerful savages.

"Wussi River boy," Tupa said softly. "They bad. Plenty mean."

The Wussi River was some distance west, and these warriors were far off their usual beat. Ponga Jim shifted his rifle to the hollow of his arm and waited. His dealings with the natives there had been friendly, but for the most part they were a surly bunch. Many of them understood a few words of German and called small coins "marks." Obviously, a remnant of the touch of civilization acquired when the Germans had owned that section, prior to the world war.

Jim stepped forward. "You see Papua man? White girl?"

The Wussi River men stared at him sullenly, muttering among themselves, but did not reply. Then one of them, a big man, stepped from the crowd and began a fierce harangue. His voice rose and fell angrily, and he made fierce gestures. Ponga Jim watched him warily.

"What's he say, Tupa?" he asked guardedly.

"He say you go away. You bad white man. Qasavara very angry. Pretty soon he call all white men, all who know or talk to white men. Mebbe so all people who no fight white men."

"Tell him that's a lot of hooey," Jim said coolly. "Tell him I'm a friend. Tell him Qasavara is dead, he was killed by Qat, the good spirit."

Tupa told him quickly, but the native shook his head stubbornly. Tupa's eyes widened.

"He say Qasavara has many men. Pretty soon he kill all English. He say Qasavara has dragons, two of them, with wings. Pretty soon take plenty heads."

"Yeah?" Jim said. He hooked his thumbs in his belt. "So they got some ships? You tell that monkey face I personally will take care of Qasavara. Tell him he swiped my woman."

Jim grinned and shifted the gun in his hands, watching the natives warily.

"Hey, Skipper!" Brophy said suddenly. "Here comes some more from the other direction! About twenty of them!"

PONGA JIM WHEELED, but as he turned, he caught a flicker of movement from the jungle trail along which they had come.

"All right, boys," he said casually. "We're in for a fight. So take it easy and back up to those snags on the bar. Brophy, you and the Strangler get over there behind those logs now. Just walk over, taking it easy. As soon as you get sheltered, cover our retreat. Get me?"

"Right down the groove, Skipper!" Brophy said cheerfully.

"Selim! Abdul! Hassan!" Jim snapped quickly. "Take that downriver bunch. Tupa, watch the jungle. You, too, Singo. Macabi, you follow Brophy back to those snags."

He had noticed the snags before they were scarcely on the bank of the river. A half dozen giant jungle trees of the ficus type had floated here and beached themselves on Sago Bar. Tumbled together, they formed a rude semicircle facing the jungle, open toward the river. They presented a natural fortress from four to six feet high.

"All right, Tupa," he said finally, "you tell that big walrus we're going out on the bar to cook some breakfast."

The big man spoke suddenly, fiercely, walking rapidly toward them. Tupa looked worried.

"He say you move, he kill!" he said.

"Yeah?" Jim grinned. He handed his rifle to Tupa. "All right, when I sock this lug, you guys leg it back on that bar. Get sheltered as quick as you can." The big native, a powerful man with huge muscles and an ugly face came closer. "Watch it, Brophy!" Jim said loudly. "Here comes the fireworks!"

The big native stepped close and grabbed at Jim's arm. Then Jim hit him a short, wicked right chop that laid the man's cheek open for four inches. A short left hook came up into the man's belly, and the savage pitched forward on his face. A howl of anger went up, and suddenly, they rushed.

Ponga Jim whipped out his automatic and fired rapidly as he backed up. Two natives spilled over on their faces, and then the rifles behind him began to crash. He turned and legged it for shelter. Something caught at his sleeve, but it wasn't until he was safe behind the log that he looked down. Slug's face was pale.

An arrow had gone through his sleeve near the wrist. One of those ugly, barbed arrows typical of the Papuans. Jim drew it out carefully.

"Would you look at that?" he said. "A yard long and six sharp bits of bone stuck in the shaft. If that got in a man they'd have to cut a six-inch hole to get it out. And those things are steeped in decayed meat. Starts septic poisoning." He tossed the arrow over the log. "Let that be a lesson to you guys. Don't any of you get hit."

Five of the natives were stretched out on the riverbank, and the rest had drawn back to the edge of the woods. There were at least a hundred savages inside the edge of that jungle by now, not over seventy yards away. Jim sat down and reloaded the clip in his automatic.

"You guys watch your step now," he said cheerfully. "There's nine rifles here and if we can't keep those guys from crossing that beach, we're a bunch of saps. Those boys can fight, but they haven't any belly for this stuff. If they start to come out, wait until nine of them are in sight. Then let them have it."

"HERE THEY COME!" Slug said suddenly, and Ponga Jim whirled to see a wave of savages break from the edge of the jungle. Coolly, carefully, his men began to fire, and the brown line wilted like wheat before a mowing machine.

The attack broke, and the remaining natives fled, with at least thirty men scattered on the beach.

"Now what do they think of Qasavara?" Ponga Jim muttered drily. "Get set, you guys! Here comes the *Semiramis!*"

The freighter was steaming up the river, and slowly the bow swung over in the channel, and a boat was lowered. On top of the chart house, Red Hanlon suddenly appeared and jerked the canvas jacket off the machine gun. He sat down behind it, and suddenly the gun began to rattle, drawing a thin line of steel along the jungle.

Red Hanlon met Jim at the rail as he came up the pilot ladder.

"We got a guy here says he knows right where the House of Qasavara is," he said.

Ponga Jim turned and looked at the powerful young native. Big, stalwart, and beautifully muscled, he carried a spear and a large knife in a wooden sheath. His head was shaven in front. Jim frowned.

"You're no Papuan," he said. "You're a Toradjas boy."

The big native nodded eagerly. "Me Toradjas. Me go Celebes, Banggai, Balabac, Zamboanga. Pretty soon me come Salamoa, come here."

"You get around, don't you?" Jim said, speculatively. "You know where the House of Qasavara is?"

"Me sabby. These boy," the Toradjas made a careless gesture that took in all Papua, "they afraid Qasavara. I see his house close by Ambunti. Five white man there, one hifty-hifty. Two white man tie up. One you friend."

"My friend?" Jim said, incredulously. "What makes you think so?"

"Me see you him Amurang one time. You go Qasavara?"

"Yeah," Jim said. "What do you call yourself?"

"Man in Makassar, he call me Oolyssus," he said proudly. "Now Lyssy."

"Ulysses?" Jim grinned. "Not far wrong at that, boy. You get around. All right, let's go!"

All day they steamed steadily up the Sepik. Here and there a cloud of herons flew up, or a flock of wild pigeons. Along the muddy banks crocodiles sunned themselves, great, ugly-looking fellows, many times larger than any seen downstream.

"What's the plan, Skipper?" Slug said, walking up from the main deck at eight bells.

Jim shrugged. "No plan. Ambunti is two hundred and sixty miles from the mouth. It will be nearly morning before we get there. I'm going to take Lyssy and go out to that House of Qasavara, and what happens after that will be whatever looks good."

"You're not leaving me, Skipper. There's going to be a mess back in those woods, and you know it. You can just figure Brophy in on that, or I quit!"

"Okay, Slug," Jim said. "I can use you. I think this Toradjas is on the level. Good men, those fellows, good seamen, fierce fighters, and they don't have a bit of use for other natives. Think they are superior. I've seen a lot of them, and they'd tackle their weight in mountain lions."

IT WAS PITCH-DARK when they dropped the anchor in the shelter of a river bend near Ambunti. The current was slack there, and the water sounded three fathoms. Silently, a boat was lowered, settling into the water with only a slight splash. Then the three men rowed ashore and slipped into the brush.

Ponga Jim stumbled along the path in the dark, following Lyssy and with Brophy bringing up the rear. They had made something more than two miles when suddenly Lyssy stopped dead still. In the same instant, a light flashed in Jim's eyes, and before he could move, a terrific blow crashed down over his head. He felt himself sinking as a wave of blinding pain swept over him, and he desperately tried to regain his feet. Then there was another blow, and he slid to his face in the muddy trail.

IT WAS A LONG TIME later when he came to. His lids fluttered open, but he lay still, without trying to move, but trying desperately to understand where he was. He realized suddenly that he was lying face down on a stone floor. He twisted, and an agonizing pain struck him like a blow. He turned over slowly.

"Ah!" said a voice sarcastically. "The sleeping beauty awakens!"

He struggled to sit up, but was bound hand and foot. Still, after a struggle, he managed it. Slowly, he glanced around.

"Well, well! What a pretty bunch this is!" he muttered.

Major William Arnold sat opposite him, his face dirty and unshaven. Beside him was Colonel Sutherland, a plump man with a round British face and calm blue eyes. Further away along the wall was Carol herself, her clothes torn, her face without makeup, but looking surprisingly attractive.

"William," Ponga Jim said slowly. "I never thought I'd see the time when I'd see you wrapped up like that."

There was a groan, and he turned slightly to see Slug Brophy coming out of it.

"You, too, eh? What happened to our Toradjas?"

"He got away," Slug grunted. "That guy has skin like an eel. They grabbed him, and then he was gone—just like that."

"Now what?" Carol said brightly. "All you brave and bold he-men should be able to get out of a little mess like this."

"I don't think you can depend on them, Miss Sutherland," a cool voice said in very precise English.

Jim turned his head stiffly and saw two men standing in the door. One was a thick, broad-shouldered man with a powerful neck and the arms of an ape. The other man was tall, obviously a man of some culture.

"Permit me, Captain Mayo," he said with exaggerated politeness. "My coworker, Wilhelm Blucher. I am Count Franz Kull."

As he spoke, two more men appeared in the door.

"Ah, yes! And this is Fritz Heittn, with whose brother you have already come in contact, and this," he indicated the tall, very dark man with massive, stooped shoulders, "is Torq Vokeo. You will know him well, very well, no doubt!"

"Vokeo is our expert in the matter of helping people to remember—you understand? He is, I might add, very efficient."

He turned abruptly. "No more of this horseplay. Major Arnold, you will give me copies of the codes I asked for at once. You will also tell me where your other men are located and what their tasks are. I want that information by noon tomorrow. If I do not have it then, Miss Sutherland will be tortured until you give it to us. I should dislike to leave her to the tender mercies of Torq, but that is a matter for you and her father to decide."

He looked down at Ponga Jim coldly. "As for you, Captain Mayo, there can be only one answer—death. We can't have you in our way further. Within twenty-four hours our bands of native warriors will strike Salamoa, Lae, Madang, Hollandia, and elsewhere. Two of our planes will bomb Port Moresby, and within a matter of hours, New Guinea will again be in our complete possession. Nevertheless, I shall deem it a great privilege to have the honor of wiping you off the slate. You've given us no end of trouble."

"Yeah?" Jim grinned insultingly. "And, Herr Kull. I'm going to give you a lot more. Do you think I came up here without reporting what I knew?"

Kull laughed. "We'll see about that! As for reporting what you knew, we had you under espionage until you were on the river. There has been no chance since then."

Turning, he motioned to the others. "We'll give them a little time to think matters over. Then you may have them, Torq."

When the heavy door closed and locked, Ponga Jim shrugged.

"Nice people!" he said expressively. "But if he thinks I'm going to lie here and wait, he's got another guess coming."

Just then the door opened softly, and Torq Vokeo stepped in. He held an iron spit, its end red hot and glowing. He smiled at Jim, baring his teeth wolfishly.

"You think is funny, eh? I show you!"

Quickly, Vokeo stepped across the room.

"Get set, Slug!" Jim said suddenly.

Throwing himself on his back, he kicked out viciously with his bound legs. Vokeo, caught with a terrific kick on the upper legs, stumbled and fell headlong. Instantly, Slug Brophy rolled over on top of the man.

Arnold, his eyes suddenly gleaming with hope, rolled over quickly three times, and rolled across Torq's legs. Then Sutherland rolled on his head. Cursing viciously, his oaths muffled by Sutherland's weight, Torq struggled to get free, but the three heavy bodies were too much for him.

Even as the man fell, Jim rolled over and pushed his tied wrists against the red hot spit. The smell of burning hemp filled the room. Time and again his wrists wavered, and burned him, but he persisted. Then, suddenly, he gave a terrific jerk, swelling his muscles with all his great strength. Slowly then, the rope stretched; another jerk, and it came apart!

With a leap, he was on his feet, and in a matter of seconds, he had untied Arnold. Then, as Arnold bent over Brophy's wrists, Jim grabbed Torq by the throat to stifle his shouts, and calmly slugged him on the chin. Then, while Arnold and Brophy freed Sutherland and his daughter, Ponga Jim bound the unconscious man and gagged him.

"Only one gun," Jim said, getting up. "You take it, Colonel. I'll have another in a minute."

He walked directly to the door and without a second's hesitation, pulled it open. The native guard turned, and Ponga Jim's fist met him halfway. Coolly, Jim dragged him inside, smacked him again, and then passed his rifle to Arnold and his knife to Slug.

Ponga Jim grinned. "Folks, it might be a good idea to wait here until they come back again, but I'm no hand to wait. Personally, I say we move right now. We make a break for the open, and once there, if attacked, it is every man—and woman—for himself. Make for the river at the big bend below. Ambunti. That's where the ship is."

He jerked open the door, and they started walking, fast. They had reached the end of a long, low stone hall before they were seen. A native guard half turned. Then he opened his mouth to scream. Jim sprang, but too late. A ringing yell awoke a million echoes in the hall. Then Jim slugged him.

But the native was big, and he was tough. With a yell of savage fury, he dove for Jim's legs. Jim tried to sidestep and then fell headlong.

"Run, damn you!" he yelled at the others.

Then he jerked to a sitting position and hooked a short left to the native's eye. It jarred the man loose, and Jim lurched to his feet and kicked him viciously in the stomach. With a howl of pain, the man rolled over on the floor.

In the yard outside there was a rattle of gunfire. And suddenly Fritz Heittn stepped into sight with a submachine gun. His eyes narrowed with eagerness as he saw the group clustered just beyond the door, and he lifted the gun. Then he saw Ponga Jim.

Concealed by a bend in the stair, Jim was slipping quickly and silently up the stairs. A dozen steps away when Heittn saw him, Jim leaped to his feet and lunged, even as Heittn brought the machine gun down and pulled the trigger!

But suddenly, even as Jim staggered erect, the gun slipped by him and went plunging down the stair. At the top of it, Fritz Heittn stood dead still, his eyes wide and staring. Then slowly, he leaned forward and fell face down on the steps. Sticking from between his shoulder blades was the haft of a big knife!

Startled, Jim stared along the stone platform where Heittn had stood. Coming toward him, at a rapid trot, was Lyssy. Grinning, he stooped over and retrieved his knife.

WITH A QUICK SLAP on the Toradjas's shoulder, Ponga Jim ran down the steep steps and grabbed up the fallen machine gun. Then he stepped to the door. Across the narrow landing field he could see Arnold and Brophy disappearing into the woods after the others. Following them were Blucher and a dozen renegades.

Ponga Jim took in the situation at a glance. The two planes, one a heavy bomber, the other a small amphibian, were not a hundred yards away. Without a second's hesitation, Jim made his decision. He started down the landing field, which was actually a wide stone terrace belonging to the temple of Qasavara, toward the planes. A bullet whizzed by his ear from behind and smacked viciously against the stones ahead of him. Wheeling around, Jim caught sight of two figures silhouetted against the sky on the temple roof. He swept the machine gun to his shoulder, fired a burst, and saw one of the men fall headfirst over the parapet and take a long plunge to the stone terrace below. The other man vanished.

Jim wheeled, and as he turned a gun crashed, almost in his ear it seemed, and a bullet smashed into the machine gun and glanced off, ripping a gash in his sleeve and tearing a ragged cut along his arm. Franz Kull was standing not ten feet away, a Luger aimed at Ponga Jim's stomach. The gun was pointed and the finger tightening on the trigger, and there wasn't a chance in the world of him missing at that distance.

Jim staggered, and slowly his knees buckled. He tumbled over on his face. Kull hesitated, lowering the Luger to cover Ponga Jim's still form.

"Got him," Kull whispered. "They got him after all!"

He glanced quickly around. Blucher was furiously directing his band of renegades in the pursuit of the escaped prisoners.

Kull smiled and slipped the gun into his waistband. He stood for a minute, staring down at Ponga Jim Mayo's body, at the slow pool of blood gathering under his left side.

"Almost," he said, "I am sorry."

He stooped and caught Jim by the arm, turning him over. He saw Jim's eyes flicker open and saw the right fist start, and in one panic-stricken moment, realized he had been tricked. Then that fist slammed against the angle of his jaw, and he staggered, grabbing for his gun.

Like a tiger, Jim was on his feet. A left knocked the gun from Kull's hand, and a right sent him reeling against the parked bomber. But Kull straightened, slipped Ponga Jim's left, and hooked a hard left to the head. He ducked a right, and sunk a left in Jim's body, then a right.

Ponga Jim grinned. "A boxer, eh?" he said.

He jabbed quickly, and the punch set Kull off balance. A right caught him in the midsection, and a sweeping left sent him to his knees. Coolly, Jim stepped back.

"Get up, Kull, and take a socking!" he ordered.

Kull straightened and then rushed, hooking hard with both hands. Jim staggered, grinned, and tied Kull up, whipping a wicked left to his head and body. The punches traveled scarcely six inches, yet they landed with sledgehammer force. Kull jerked away, and Mayo whipped up a right uppercut that knocked him back against the plane. Then Jim stepped in and crossed a short, hard right. Kull slipped to the stone pavement.

Ponga Jim wheeled and swung open the door to the cabin of the amphibian.

THE MOTOR SPUTTERED and then roared into life. Out of the corner of his eye, Jim saw Blucher turn, puzzled. Then he started, and gave her the gun. It was little room for a takeoff, but enough, and Ponga Jim cleared the trees at the other end of the terrace by a matter of inches. He banked steeply and came back flying low.

Blucher stared at him, puzzled, and a half dozen of the renegades stared upward. Then Jim cut loose with both machine guns, raking the terrace.

With a roar of rage, Blucher jerked up his gun, but the blast of leaden death was too much for him, and he broke and ran for the jungle. His men were less fortunate, and the machine guns swept the terrace like a bolt of lightning.

Then it was all over. Slowly he wheeled above the huge stone building, getting a good look at it for the first time, the great towers, the battlements, and the queer, fantastic architecture. Jim glanced over the side, and nothing moved on the terrace.

He turned the plane and flew for the distant masts of the *Semiramis*.

NIGHT HAD FALLEN when they met on the captain's deck of the tramp freighter. Above on the bridge, Slug Brophy paced casually, watching the channel as the dark jungle-clad banks slid by.

Ponga Jim leaned back in his deck chair, pushing back his cap.

"There goes your Qasavara trouble, William!" he said cheerfully. "Again Mayo comes to the rescue. It seems I have to save the British Empire about once every thirty days."

Arnold chuckled. "You aren't doing so bad. Picked up a nice amphibian plane, just like that."

"The fortunes of war, William, merely the fortunes of war! Hello! Here comes Ulysses!"

The big Toradjas stopped a few feet away and then stepped forward, handing Ponga Jim a thick wad of Bank of England notes. Colonel Sutherland gulped, and his eyes widened. "Me find him House of Qasavara," he said. "You take, eh?"

"You bet I'll take!" Jim said, winking at Arnold. "Ah, the sinews of war! Ulysses, you are now a member of my crew, a full-fledged member!"

"You betcha!" Ulysses said.

"That man," Major Arnold said positively, "has the makings of either a thief or a philosopher!"

Ponga Jim got up and offered his arm to Carol.

"Both, William, both! He's going to be a soldier of fortune!"

Well of the Unholy Light

Rain had fallen for three days, and the jungle dripped with it. The fourth day had begun with heavy showers and faded into a dense fog. Yet despite the rain, the drums had not stopped.

The path was a slide of mud between two solid walls of jungle, green by day, an impenetrable blackness by night. Three miles by trail they had said. It would be like Frazer to live in such a place. He walked slowly. The drums bothered him.

He knew as much about the interior of Halmahera as anyone did, which wasn't a great deal. Mostly, the natives lived along the coast, rarely going into the interior. But the drums were somewhere beyond Mount Sahu, apparently, and they might be as far away as Gam Konora.

The only way he could tell when he reached the clearing was by the sudden feeling of space around him. Then he glimpsed a light from the bungalow. He wondered again why Frazer had sent for him. The man had never been one to ask for help. He had been notoriously a lone wolf.

Suddenly he dropped to a crouch and then squatted down, listening. Someone was coming around the house! He dropped one hand to the gravel path to balance himself and waited. The footsteps stopped abruptly, and he realized the person had stepped off the path. He heard then the soft *swish* of receding steps through the grass. He started to call out, but then thought better of it and waited.

After a moment, he stepped up on the verandah and rapped softly. There was no reply. He pushed the door open and stepped in.

Then he stopped. The headless body of a man lay on the floor beside the desk! Staring, he stepped closer, noticing an old tattoo on the hand, between the forefinger and thumb. A faded blue anchor. Stepping carefully around the pool of blood, he glanced at the papers on the desk. He was just reaching to pick them up when a cold voice interrupted:

"So, we have a murderer!" The man's voice was flat. "Put your hands up."

Looking up he saw three men standing in the doorway. The speaker was a tall man with a cold white face, blue eyes, and blond hair. The others were obviously policemen.

"I'm afraid you've made a wrong guess," he said, smiling. "I came to pay Bent Frazer a visit and found things like this."

"Yes?" The man was icily skeptical. "Nevertheless, you will consider yourself under arrest. It so happens that Benton Frazer had no visitors. He was a recluse."

"You think I murdered this man?"

"What else am I to think when I find you standing over the body with bloody hands?"

Involuntarily, he glanced down. His right hand was bloody!

But mingled with the blood sticking to his hand were tiny bits of sand and gravel. The path, that was it! When he crouched he had put his hand down. Whoever had carried the head away had obviously gone that way or else was wounded himself. Then, he thought swiftly, the man he had heard had not been the murderer, unless he had returned on a second trip!

"Don't be dumb," he said sharply. "If I killed him, where's the head?"

The man scowled. "You could have disposed of that. Hans," he snapped, "keep an eye on the prisoner. Thomsen, you will search the house!" He turned to the prisoner. "I am Karl Albran, the resident official from Susupu. Now what is your name, and where are you from?"

"My name?" the prisoner echoed. "My name is Mayo—Ponga Jim Mayo. I'm skipper of the freighter *Semiramis,* of Gorontalo."

"Ponga Jim Mayo!" Albran's face blanched. Then slowly the expression faded, to be replaced with something like triumph. "So," he said softly, "Ponga Jim Mayo! I have heard of you, my friend." Albran turned slightly. "Hans, this fellow has made something of a record for escaping from tight corners. So shoot if he makes even one false move."

Hans smiled wolfishly. "This is one corner he won't get out of!" he said. "I hope he tries."

After Albran turned on his heel and left the room, Jim let his eyes rove around. There was still the problem of the murdered man. To the right of him, and near the window, was a pool of water. Remembering his own movements, he recalled that he had come around the other side of the blood, and none of the three recent arrivals had stood over there. Then, naturally, it had been someone else, who had arrived on the scene and surveyed it carefully and without interruption. Probably the man who had stepped from the path. But who?

A white man, Jim was sure. Bare feet don't make such a sound on a gravel path. And white men in Halmahera were few and all too easily traced. Albran? He considered that. Yet it was hardly probable. And why had the head been removed?

Albran and Thomsen returned to the room with two other men. One of them Jim recognized instantly as Doc Fife. The roving surgeon was known in all the islands. He glanced at Jim out of shrewd eyes.

"Albran tells me you killed Frazer," said Fife, smiling a little. "I told him he was crazy."

Jim shrugged, said nothing.

Albran's eyes were cold. "I found him here, starting to go through the papers on the desk. The body was still warm, and Jim had blood on his hand. Has it now. And I say he killed Frazer!"

Ponga Jim stared at Albran very thoughtfully. "Want a case pretty bad, don't you?" he said.

Albran smiled coldly. "This is a time of war. I shall not delay the progress of justice, but order you shot—immediately."

"What?" Fife demanded angrily. "You can't do that! Nothing has been proved—"

"Proved?" Albran demanded. "Am I to deny the sight of my eyes?"

"Wait a minute!" Jim snapped. "I'm getting sick of this nonsense! If the sight of your eyes was worth anything you'd know the dead man is not Bent Frazer!"

Albran whirled, consternation in his eyes. Fife looked startled.

"What do you mean?" Albran demanded.

"That faded blue anchor tattooed on the man's hand?" Jim said drily. "Frazer wouldn't let himself be tattooed. He was at least two inches taller than this man and not so heavily built. This is Kimberly Rinehart. He was a friend of Frazer's. I knew him well and recognized the body as soon as I came in."

"Then—then where's Frazer?" Albran exclaimed, "He must have murdered this man!"

"Nuts," Jim said drily. "Frazer wouldn't kill Rinehart. He is one of the few friends Frazer ever had. In fact, I think whoever killed this man thought he was killing Frazer. I think somebody wanted Bent Frazer dead. They sent a man to kill him, and he killed the wrong man."

"Perhaps you know more about that than we do!" Albran snapped. "We'll take you back to the village!"

"Okay." Jim shrugged.

Hans stepped toward him, and Ponga Jim started to follow Albran. But suddenly his foot slipped in the blood and he plunged forward, his head smashing into Albran's back and knocking him through the door into a sprawled heap on the path outside. Tumbling across him, Jim rolled over, scrambled to his feet and dove into the night and the jungle.

Thomsen snapped a quick shot into the night, and Ponga Jim grinned as it went yards from its object. After his first plunging run had carried him through the thick wall of jungle, Jim had stopped dead still. To move meant to make noise. He realized suddenly that he was clutching a bit of paper from the desk, picked up at the moment Albran discovered him. He thrust it in his pocket.

Back at the bungalow, Albran was shouting orders at Thomsen and Hans. Nearby, Doc Fife was talking in low tones with the man who had come up with him, a man whose face Ponga Jim could not distinguish.

Gradually Jim worked around a thick clump of ferns. Slowly, carefully, he worked his way back from the clearing. For a half hour he tried nothing but the most careful movement. Then he struck out, moving more boldly, and found the bank of a small stream. He stepped in carefully, found it shallow, and began to wade downstream toward the shore.

Walking in the water made travel faster, and Jim had time to think. He didn't know why Bent Frazer had written him after all this time. He had no idea what Kim Rinehart would be doing there or why he should be killed or, if his theory was right, and Kim had been killed by mistake, just why anyone should want to kill Frazer.

And where did Albran fit in? The Dutch resident was a recent appointee, although he had been in the islands for some time, despite frequent trips back to the Netherlands. Yet, somehow, Jim couldn't believe that he didn't know more than he had any right to know. How had he happened on the scene so soon? And where had Doc Fife come from? Who was the man with him? And who was the man who had passed Jim in the darkness?

He was glad when he got back to the shore and could use his flashlight to signal the nightwatch on the *Semiramis*. Yet when he turned in he was no closer to a solution....

PONGA JIM AWAKENED to a banging on his door. Then he heard Slug Brophy, his chief mate, roar:

"Skipper! Wake up, will you? A couple of Dutch coppers out here want to put the pinch on you. Shall I drop the anchor on 'em?"

Jim sat up on his bunk. "Let them come aboard," he said finally. "I'll see them in the saloon. And tell Li I want some breakfast."

Karl Albran, his lean face dark and ugly, was waiting in the saloon when Ponga Jim came out. With him was Doc Fife and another man whom Jim recognized instantly without giving any indication of it. A fourth man came in a moment later, and Jim's eyes narrowed slightly before he smiled. Essen, he thought.

He sat down. "Don't mind if I eat, do you? Nothing like a few ham and eggs to set a man up."

"I suppose you know," Albran said icily, "what you can get for resisting an officer?"

Jim chuckled. "Sure, but I also know what I could get walking down a trail ahead of a man who wanted me dead, too. And I don't want any."

"Are you insinuating that I—"

Jim nodded. "You're darned right I am." He took a mouthful of ham and eggs. "I'm not playing poker this time, Albran," he said. "That walk down the mountain last night in the wet didn't suit me a little bit. I don't know what this racket is all about, but your part of it smells."

"Why, you—" Albran's face turned crimson with anger. "I'll—"

"No, you won't," Jim said quietly. "And if you wanted to use the law, you can't use it on my ship. I've got a crew here, mister, a tough crew. So don't get any fancy ideas."

"I think," Fife said, interrupting, "that Mr. Bonner and I"—(so Colonel Sutherland of the British Intelligence was now Mr. Bonner, Jim thought)—"have convinced Mr. Albran that it is highly improbable that you would kill a man who had been your friend, and without reason. However, there must be an investigation, and Mr. Bonner here, who has had some business connections with Benton Frazer, is anxious the case be cleared up. We thought you might help us."

Jim shrugged and then told them of receiving a message from Frazer and of what followed. He told it casually, carelessly, eating all the while.

"How about the message?" Bonner asked. "Did that give you any information?"

Jim reached into his coat pocket and tossed it on the table. It read:

COME AT ONCE. SOMETHING RIGHT DOWN YOUR ALLEY. TELL NO ONE. IMPORTANT YOU ARRIVE BEFORE THE FIFTH.

FRAZER.

"You have no idea what he wanted?" Fife asked. "Had he said anything previously that would be a clue?"

"Listen," Jim said. "I hadn't seen Frazer or heard from him in ten years. We worked some together but we were never what you'd call friends."

"I'm sorry about last night," Albran said suddenly. "If I'd thought, I'd have realized the truth. A few days ago Frazer discharged a Papuan, a former headhunter. Obviously, he killed him for revenge and then fled to New Guinea with the head."

Ponga Jim chuckled. "No soap, pal."

"What do you mean?" Essen said. "Is it not obvious if the head is gone that a headhunter must take it? Who else had use for heads?"

Jim chuckled. "Whoever killed Kim didn't know I was going to come along so conveniently and be accused. He wanted Frazer out of the way, because Frazer knew something. But he didn't want any investigation or questions asked. So he took the head, thinking it would be passed off as a headhunter's job."

"Why couldn't it be?" Bonner asked.

"Simply because," Jim said drily, "headhunters do everything according to habit and custom. The removal of a victim's head follows a set pattern. Papuans always do it in the same manner, and rather neatly. Our friend who knocked off Kim just hacked off the head, not knowing his Papuan customs. As I said," Jim looked up, grinning at Essen, "the guy who figured that one out was a dumb cluck with a head like a cabbage."

"Then you believe Frazer, or rather, Rinehart, was killed by a white man?" Fife asked thoughtfully.

Ponga Jim nodded. "I sure do. Furthermore," he added, "Frazer is still around somewhere, still ready to tell what he knows. Find him and you'll blow the lid off more than Kim Rinehart's murder. And when you begin to get suspects, ask them one question."

"What?" Albran demanded.

"Ask them: 'What do you know about the Well of the Unholy Light'!"

Silence gripped the saloon, and Jim saw Fife watching Essen. The man's face was set and stiff. He was staring at Ponga Jim, his glance fairly ablaze with hatred.

"What do you mean?" Bonner asked. "What is the Well of the Unholy Light?"

"Back up on the slope of Gam Konora is a well that shows a peculiar, misty glow at night," Jim explained. "It is phosphorescent or something. You can't trace the origin of the light, either. There's a *batu paduran* there. In other words, a stone city. It isn't so very far from here. A day's travel if you know the trails."

"What does it have to do with this murder?" Fife asked.

Ponga Jim Mayo got up slowly, reaching for his cap.

"That's your problem," he said seriously. "But whoever killed Rinehart will answer to me. He wasn't my friend, but we fought a couple of wars together, and men who do that don't fail each other. So," Jim looked first at Essen and then at Albran, "I'm declaring myself in for the duration!"

After they had gone, Jim stood staring out the porthole thoughtfully. The rain had begun again, a cold, slanting rain. He looked toward the green shores of Halmahera, looming gray now. He had a sense of impending danger that left him restless and ill at ease. Unconsciously, his hand strayed to the butt of his heavy Colt.

Frazer had stumbled on something big, he knew. But what? The only clue he had that wasn't available to them all from the beginning was the slip of paper from the desk in Frazer's cabin. It had been torn, and just enough remained to tell him the words had been "Well of the Unholy Light." And Jim knew about the well, somewhere up on the slopes of Gam Konora, over five thousand feet of active volcano and a taboo region, rarely visited by anyone, native or white.

That Colonel Sutherland, masquerading as Bonner, was around, offered ample evidence that this was something international in scope. It also meant that somewhere in the vicinity Major William Arnold would be working on the problem.

PONGA JIM GRINNED. He and William were to brush elbows again. But where, he wondered then, did Kim Rinehart fit into the picture? How did he happen to be on the spot when the killer arrived for Frazer?

Yet whatever was in the wind was too big for Essen. The man was dangerous, but not the type to lead any action as big as this must be. Albran was Dutch but, like a scattering of his countrymen, was obviously pro-Nazi. Fife and Sutherland, he had learned, had been hunting near Mount Sabu and so had an alibi for being on hand. But what was the answer?

There seemed only one chance of finding out—to go to the Well of the Unholy Light.

THE RAIN HAD CEASED and the clouds were breaking up when Ponga Jim Mayo rounded the shoulder of Gam Konora and looked down on the steep canyon that separated him from the plateau where the well was supposed to be. He hesitated, staring down.

The canyon was a fearful gash in the earth and washed by a charging, plunging mountain stream. Across from him the wall of the mountain broke, and he could look past it to the plateau beyond. A huge stone column reared from the jungle, at least a hundred feet high, and beyond it was a square tower, half fallen to ruins.

It was then he saw the bridge, not more than a hundred feet away, but blending its color so easily with the rock as to be almost invisible, a swaying bridge of hemp rope, native-made, suspended across the three hundred feet of the canyon. Below it was the stream. Jim looked down and then started for the swaying bridge.

It trembled giddily at his first step, and he had taken no more than three steps before he had a feeling that he was being watched. Carefully, yet with seeming carelessness, his eyes searched the jumble of rocks he was approaching. There was nothing, no movement or indication of life.

He walked on quietly, but managing to weave just a little on the swaying bridge, enough to make the chances of hitting him with the first shot a little more difficult. But he had reached the end of the bridge and had his feet on the rock before anything happened. Then a cool, deep voice spoke suddenly from the rocks:

"You stand still now and answer me some questions."

Ponga Jim stopped. "Okay, pal. Let's have them."

"What's your handle, mister? What name you go by?"

"The name is Mayo," Jim said pleasantly. "They call me Ponga Jim."

"Where you get that 'Ponga' part?"

"From the village of Ponga-Ponga in French Equatorial Africa. Anything else?"

"If you was looking for a man you knew in Manchuria, and he was in Fez, where would you look? And if he was in Algiers?"

Jim's eyes narrowed, "In Fez, I'd look in the long room behind a leatherworker's stall in the street near the Green Mosque. In Algiers, I would go to the place of Mahr-el-din in the Kasbah."

A powerfully built black man came from behind a cluster of boulders and stepped down with his big hand outthrust. He wore a dark red shirt and a pair of blue dungarees. Two big guns were strapped to his hips, and a high-powered rifle was in the hollow of his arm. Two bandoleers of cartridges crossed his chest.

"How you, Captain Mayo?" he said cheerfully. "I'm Big London. A friend to Bent Frazer. He told me if anything happened to him I was to get down here and watch out for you, that you'd be along, and that you'd answer those questions. That way, I'd know you. But I'd have known you, anyway."

Jim shook hands, sizing up the mighty black man with appreciation.

"What's up?" he asked. "Where's Frazer?"

"They got him down there by the well. They got a couple of hundred men down there."

"How many?" Jim was incredulous. "Did you say two hundred?"

Big London nodded. "That's right. They've been bringing them in planes. Dropped twenty here last night from parachutes. But Frazer, he said to start nothing until you got here." Then he added, "Those men are Japanese, all but two or three."

Led swiftly by the big black man, Ponga Jim slipped through the rocks until they could get a good view of the city. It was scarcely that, just a temple. Now it was all in ruins, and a small circle of stone houses was surrounded by a fallen wall. The stone plaza had been cleared of debris, but was not large enough for a plane to land. But even as they watched they saw several men carrying rifles from one of the buildings. A cool voice behind them spoke:

"How do you do, Captain?"

Jim wheeled. Five men in a neat rank stood behind them. Four were Japanese soldiers, their rifles ready. The fifth was Heittn, a Nazi agent.

"See how easily a man is captured when he grows confident?" Heittn said, speaking over his shoulder to the soldiers. Then, to Jim, "We knew Frazer had communicated with you, so we were ready this time." Heittn's narrow, heavy-lidded eyes shifted to the black man. "We won't need you," he said and lifted his automatic. Without a second's hesitation, he fired.

Big London had started to leap, but his body turned slowly and plunged down the steep slope of shale. For sixty feet his body slid and then brought up against a boulder.

Ponga Jim's eyes went hard.

"That was a dirty stunt!" he said.

"Of course." Heittn shrugged. "We want you to use for bait. He would have been excess baggage."

It was an hour before they finished questioning him. Heittn had begun it when they got him safely below and in a stone room. Four bulky Germans, an Italian, and three Japanese had entered with him. The door was closed. His hands had been bound. Then Heittn had walked up and struck him in the mouth. Then he stepped back and kicked Jim across the shins.

Ponga Jim moved like lightning, kicking out himself. The kick caught Heittn in the pit of the stomach and rolled him across the room. Instantly, the five men hit Jim at once. He was knocked to his knees, jerked to his feet, and driven into the wall and battered. Then Heittn pushed his way through the crowd, his face a mask of fury.

He had a short length of rubber hose, and he slammed Jim wickedly across the shoulders with it. Then came a powerful blow over the head that drove Jim to his knees. Heittn hit him twice more before he could get up.

Ponga Jim was desperate. He knew what such a beating could do to a man. He had seen the Gestapo work before. But he lunged to his feet, determined to go down without a whimper, without whining. Heittn battered him, then the others. The Italian named Calzo took his turn at the hose.

"What's the matter?" Jim said drily. "Can't you hit a man unless he's tied?"

Calzo's face flamed with anger, and he dealt Mayo a terrific blow over the head that knocked him into oblivion.

When Jim opened his eyes he was conscious of pain. His body was afire with agony. He lay very still, staring up into darkness. Then he tried to move, but was bound hand and foot. His stirrings brought a voice from the abysmal darkness.

"Jim?" It was Frazer. "Are you all right?"

Jim groaned. "All right, nothing! Those rats used a hose on me."

"You're not the only one. What happened to London?"

"Heittn shot him. You alone here?"

"No!" It was a new voice. "They got me, too. Right after you stumbled onto Rinehart's body."

Jim was startled. "William?" he gasped. "Can't you keep out of trouble? What's the gag, anyway?"

Frazer said, "Remember the *Carlsberg*? She's down here with a cargo of eighteen-foot baby submarines. They are built to submerge to five hundred feet, and each one carries a torpedo. They plan on sewing a string of them clear across the Indies, with the *Carlsberg* as mother ship. She can carry about fifty of them without much trouble. Todahe Bay is the main base."

"It's a good spot," Major Arnold said. "An almost closed harbor, unseen until you're almost inside."

"Todahe Bay?" Jim said thoughtfully. "That's close by." He lay quiet a minute. "What are they doing here?"

"It's a torpedo plant," Frazer said. "They have natural heat here when they need it, they have power from that stream down below, and because of the well, no native will come near. The well is a big pool in the rock, opening to an underground lake, and the water is made phosphorescent by some growth in it. Like seawater."

"But how do they get the torpedoes down to the subs?" Jim asked.

Frazer shrugged. "I don't know. Rinehart tipped me off to all this. He was a German, you know. They rang him in on the deal, and he was smart enough to play along and keep his mouth shut. Then he came to me with the story. Somebody killed him. I picked that up from one of the guards this morning."

Jim lay very quiet. He knew now that something had to be done. Fifty pocket submarines could create havoc in the East Indies. With luck they might cut shipping in half in a matter of weeks.

There was a sound of feet. Then the door rattled and swung back on its hinges. Jim noticed then that the room was carved from solid rock. He was jerked to his feet and found himself facing Karl Albran, Essen, and the guard.

"So!" Albran sneered. "You are so smart, eh? You walk right into a trap. I knew it would happen!"

"Untie his feet," Essen told the guard. "Heittn would see you now. We are using you for bait. Bait to end the existence of the *Semiramis!*"

As the guard untied his feet, it was now or never, Jim thought. He felt the rope fall loose about his ankles and waited until the guard had drawn it clear. Then he kicked, short and hard.

The toe of his shoe caught the kneeling guard in the solar plexus. Then Jim lunged, smashing Essen full in the chest with his head, knocking him into the wall. Instantly Karl Albran sprang into the dark cell, his gun up. But momentarily blinded by the darkness he stood stock-still, staring. In that second, Arnold jerked his bound body to a sitting position and butted the Dutchman behind the knees. The man staggered, and before he could regain his balance, Arnold rolled against his ankles. The man hit the floor hard. Ponga Jim jerked the guard to his feet with the one hand he had managed to jerk free. Jim pushed him away and then hit him with the free hand. And as he fell, he grabbed the man's knife and cut himself loose just as Essen made a dive for the door. He leaped after him, but Albran had struggled free of the bound men and was on his feet. He swung a wild blow that hit Jim on the ear, and then charged in, punching wildly. At the same instant, Essen wheeled and tackled him from behind.

Then, suddenly, Big London dropped from somewhere above the door. Stepping into the room he grabbed Essen and smashed the Nazi into unconsciousness. Jim butted Albran and then hit him in the stomach. The Dutchman went down, and Jim wheeled to cut Arnold free as the black man freed Frazer.

"I thought you were dead," Jim managed to gasp.

"He shot as I fell, missed me, so I kept on falling," the black man explained. Then Big London sprang for the door, turned, and caught a ledge over the cell door, pulling himself up. Lost in the shadows above the cell door was a black tunnel. He pulled himself in, extended a hand to Frazer, and then to Arnold.

Jim glanced back into the cell; then he pulled himself up and followed Big London at a rapid trot down the floor of the tunnel. In a few minutes they came to another tunnel and crawling out, were in the clear.

Silently, Big London dug into a bunch of ferns and passed out guns.

"I stole them," he boasted. "Right from under their eyes."

"What now?" Frazer demanded. "Where do we go from here?"

"Back," Jim said grimly. "We're going back down there and blast thunder out of things."

"But there's two hundred of them!" Frazer protested.

"Sure," Ponga Jim agreed. "One of you is going to the *Semiramis* for men. Or rather, you're going back across the bridge and signal from the shoulder of the mountain. They'll be watching. I told them to."

Grabbing a rifle, Ponga Jim ran to a cluster of boulders overlooking the stone plaza below. Japanese soldiers were spilling from all the buildings, rifles in hand. Instantly, he threw his gun to his shoulder and fired. One of the soldiers stopped in midstride and plunged over on his face. Beside the Yank, Frazer, Arnold, and Big London were pouring a devastating fire into the square. But suddenly a machine gun broke loose from the tower, and they were forced back.

"You're it, London!" Jim said. "Beat it for the shoulder of the mountain. When you can see the *Semiramis,* flash the mirror you'll find there by the lightning-struck tree. Get it?"

The black man wheeled and was gone like a flash.

"Come on," Jim said grimly. "We're going back down the tunnel!"

"What?" Frazer demanded. "Are you crazy?"

"In a minute," Jim said, "this mountain here will be flooded with Japanese and Nazis. The bridge will be covered, and we won't have a chance. So we're going back down there where they would never expect us to be!"

IT WAS A SILENT GROUP of men that crept back along the tunnel. When they looked down into the passage outside their cell, it was empty. One by one they dropped down. Then, gun in hand, Jim led the way down the passage.

This passage must come out in one of the stone buildings, he thought, and must be close to the well. And that well was something he must see. Somehow the *Carlsberg* and her cargo of submarines must be stopped. Somehow this plant must be wrecked. The problem, he knew, was to find how they got torpedoes to the ships on Todahe Bay.

They emerged from the passage in a square stone building near the tower. Outside the door the square seemed empty, yet they knew there were men in the tower above and probably others around close. Eyes narrowed, Jim studied the square thoughtfully. The tracks of some sort of a cart or truck led from the tower toward a cluster of rocks under the overhang of the cliff. The tracks had cut through the layer of soil to the solid rock of the plateau. Whatever they had carried had been heavy.

"What next, Jim?" asked Arnold softly.

"Look!" Jim indicated the marks of the wheels. "They've wheeled their torpedoes in that direction. Well, that's the way we're going! From now on it's going to be a running fight until we reach the shelter of those rocks. Beyond that, I don't know what we'll find. But I've got fifty that says it's the Well of the Unholy Light!"

"Let's go!" Frazer said.

GUN IN HAND, Jim sprang through the door. A Japanese sentry was standing across the plaza. And before he could get his gun up, Jim shot him in the stomach. Then they started on a dead run for the rocks, just a hundred yards away. Abruptly then, a myriad of tiny spurts of dust jumped all around them. Jim heard a curse and knew someone was hit. He wheeled, fired, and then ran on. He was almost to the rocks when suddenly Essen sprang from behind them, holding a submachine gun. His eyes glinting with triumph, he jerked the gun to his shoulder.

Ponga Jim stopped dead still and lifted his own gun. The automatic bucked in his hand, then again. Essen backed up, astonished. Then slowly he pitched over on his face and lay still. But already Ponga Jim was beyond him, with Major Arnold at his side. It was only then that they saw Frazer. Bent was down on his knees, facing the opposite direction, his whole side stained with blood. He was firing slowly, methodically. Even as they saw him, Frazer's Luger spoke, and a Japanese on the tower toppled forward, dead. Then a burst of machine-gun bullets from the tower hit Bent Frazer, fairly lifting him from the ground.

Ponga Jim Mayo turned, his face hard, staring around him. They stood on a narrow ledge of rock around the well. The water did glow with a peculiar light, visible in the shadows of the pool under the overhanging cliff. But there was nothing, only the well, a pool probably fifty feet across.

"Well," Arnold said. "Here we are. Now what?"

"Keep your shirt on, William," said Ponga Jim grimly. "Maybe I've guessed wrong, but I don't think so."

"This is a fine time to be in doubt!" Arnold snapped. "I think—"

Suddenly the waters of the pool began to stir as with the heavings of some subterranean monster. Then a conning tower broke the surface, and after it—the deck of a submarine!

"William," said Jim, "watch outside. I'm taking this ship!" He turned quickly. "Don't let them see your face until they are out of there," he whispered hoarsely, "and for the love of Mike, don't shoot!"

Breathless, they heard the conning tower hatch open and the sound of feet on the rounded surface of the sub. Then they heard a second pair of feet. A guttural voice spoke harshly in German, and Ponga Jim turned.

The two men, one a Nazi, the other the Italian, Calzo, were standing on the sub, just about to step ashore. Arnold pulled the trigger of his gun, but it clicked on an empty chamber. Coolly, Ponga Jim shot the Nazi over the belt buckle twice. As the man fell forward, Jim pivoted and snapped a quick shot at Calzo, who was hurriedly aiming his gun. The bullet struck the Italian's gun, knocking it from his hand.

But Calzo was game. With a snarl of fury, he leaped ashore. Out of the corner of his eye Jim saw Arnold feverishly reloading his automatic and heard a wild yell from the plaza. Then Calzo sprang at him, swinging a powerful right. Jim ducked under the blow and hooked low and hard for Calzo's ribs. The punch smashed home with driving force. Then Jim stepped in with a sweeping right uppercut that knocked the Italian off the edge and into the well. He sank like a stone. Now Arnold was firing desperately.

"Quick, Jim!" he yelled. "Here they come! At least fifty of them!"

"We've got a sub. Come on!" Jim snapped.

ARNOLD SNAPPED ONE quick shot out of the conning tower and then slammed the hatch shut. In a minute he had swung into the engineer's compartment, and with Jim at the periscope they submerged slowly.

"You got any idea what this is all about?" Arnold snapped. "This isn't just a toy, you know."

"We're submerging," Jim said cheerfully. "We're going down around five hundred feet. Then we'll find a passage and get out of it into Todahe Bay. There we'll find the *Carlsberg* loaded with submarines, and we'll shoot her one in the pants—I hope."

"*You* hope!" Arnold said sarcastically. "You mean, *I* hope! And if something happens and you're wrong?"

"We wash out," Jim said simply and shrugged.

"Yeah?" William said. "That's okay for you, but I've got a date with a girl in Makassar."

Slowly the sub sank deeper and deeper. Ponga Jim wiped the sweat from his brow. After all, maybe it wouldn't work. Still, the sub had just come up. It had to come from somewhere.

"You mean Kitty, that dancer from Manila?" Jim asked, grinning.

Arnold was astonished. "How did you know?"

Jim chuckled. "She tells me about all the strange people she meets," he said. "Interesting girl, Kitty."

The sub was still sinking, and for a moment they were still.

"My friend," Arnold said suddenly, "are you sure these things will take five hundred? That's awful deep!"

Jim stared at the depth gauge as the needle flickered past 200. 250—300—350—

"Maybe we've missed the outlet," Arnold said.

"You would think of that," Jim growled.

The pressure was building up at a terrific rate. He tried to see something, but the water around was black and still.

Four hundred!

"If it's anywhere, it'll be pretty quick now, William," Jim said. "If it isn't, we're dead pigeons."

Four hundred and fifty!

"Do you suppose your crew got to that bunch upstairs?" Major Arnold asked.

"I'd bet my life on that. That bunch of fighting fools never misses."

Five hundred!

Nothing but blackness and the close, heavy heat of the sub. Then he saw it suddenly—the outline of an opening illuminated by the powerful light of the sub. Slowly, carefully, he eased the sub into the blackness.

"Like floating down a sewer," Jim said aloud.

"I wouldn't know," Arnold said. "I never floated down any sewers."

Suddenly they were out, and then they were rising.

"Thar she blows!" Ponga Jim said suddenly. "About two points on the bow. Stand by while I run this crate in a little bit, I'm going to give her both barrels. I thought these babies only carried one torpedo, but they have two!"

And with that he released both torpedoes.

All was quiet, then—

THE SHUDDERING IMPACT of the explosion made them gasp for breath. Then, a split second later, the second!

"Two strikes, William!" shouted Ponga Jim. "Come on, we're heading for the Ibu River and the *Semiramis* at top speed. We hit the *Carlsberg* one forward and one aft. She won't float ten minutes!"

Ponga Jim ran shaky fingers through his hair. Suddenly he realized that he was sitting in trousers soggy with blood.

"William," he said, "those Nazis clipped me. I'm shot."

"Where?" Arnold yelled.

Jim looked down. "Nuts! I was just sitting in a paint bucket!"

There was silence for a moment, and then Arnold spoke up:

"Honest, Jim. Have you been out with Kitty? What's she like?"

"Wonderful!" Ponga Jim said, grinning. "Why, Kitty is—" Red fluid cascaded over him. "Hey!" he roared, blinking. "What did you throw at me?"

"The rest of the paint bucket," Arnold said grimly.

West from Singapore

crisp voice at Ponga Jim's elbow said: "Captain Mayo?" Ponga
Jim turned. His white-topped cap with its captain's insignia was
pushed back on his dark, curly hair, and his broad, powerful
shoulders stretched the faded khaki coat.

Colonel Roland Warren could see the bulge of the .45 automatic in
its shoulder holster, and there was disapproval in his eyes. Front the woven
leather sandals to the carelessly worn cap, Ponga Jim Mayo was anything
but what he believed a ship's captain should be.

"I'm Mayo," Jim held out his hand, "and you'll be Colonel Warren?
Nice to have you aboard."

Warren nodded. "My men will be along directly. May I see their
quarters now? Will their cabins be amidships?"

"Sorry, Colonel, but they'll have to bunk in the 'tween decks. We don't
carry passengers as a rule and only have three cabins available. Two of them
are occupied. I'd planned to put you and Captain Aldridge in the other."

"The 'tween decks?" Warren was incredulous. "My men are officers,
I'll have you know, and—"

"Sorry," Jim repeated. "Officers, men, or gods, they ride the 'tween
decks or swim."

"Very well," Warren's blue eyes were frosty. "However, you had no
business taking passengers aboard for such a trip. The Admiralty won't approve. I suppose you know that?"

"Colonel Warren," Jim said quietly, "for all I care the Admiralty can
go to blazes. My first duty is to these passengers."

The flyers were coming aboard, a pink-checked, healthy lot, all except
two in their late teens or early twenties. These two turned toward the
bridge. Ponga Jim's eyes sharpened.

The men were both as tall as Ponga Jim himself and one of them was
as heavy. He was a powerfully built man with rusty-red hair, freckles, and

a scar along his jawbone. His nose was broken and slightly askew. His manner was cocky, aggressive.

He stepped up to Mayo with his hand out. "Hi, Jim!" he said, grinning. "Long time no see."

Mayo's eyes brightened.

"Ring Wallace! I haven't seen you since China!"

The second man watched them with interest. He was wiry, handsome in a dark, saturnine way, and there was something crisp and efficient in his manner.

"Captain Henry Aldridge," Warren said, "my second in command."

Aldridge bowed from the hips, smiling.

"How are you, Captain? I've been hearing some interesting things about you. That Qasavara affair, for instance."

"I hope," Warren said drily, "that you won't find it necessary to indulge in any of your freebooting expeditions on this trip. I can't say that we Britishers approve of pirates!"

"No?" Jim said quizzically. "Ever hear of Sir Francis Drake?"

Warren started as if struck, and his eyes blazed. Then his face flushed, and he spun on his heel and went below. Ring Wallace grinned and winked at Jim.

"He's all right. Just needs a little seasoning. He's a good man, Jim."

Aldridge studied them both carefully. "Colonel Warren *is* a good man. But I think we Englishmen and Australians have little to say about freebooting, eh, Mayo?"

Jim looked at him curiously. "Which are you? You don't have the lingo, somehow."

"Australian," Aldridge said. "From back in the bush, but educated on the Continent."

Slug Brophy and Gunner Millan came up to the deck. Jim turned to them.

"All set, Skipper. Number five battened down, all standing by fore and aft," reported Slug.

"Then send Selim up to the wheel and let's get out of here."

He watched his mates go, one forward, one aft. Selim, his dark, pockmarked, knife-scarred face cool and expressionless, came to the wheel.

"You've an odd crew," Aldridge said. "Quite a mixture."

Jim nodded. "Selim and Sakim are brothers. A strange contradiction themselves. Afridis from the Afghan hills who went to sea. Used to be smugglers on the Red Sea and down the coast of Africa. Big London is from the Congo. Lyssy is a Toradjas from the Celebes. Tupa and Longboy are Bugis. Boma is a Dyak. They are a mixture. And all fighting men.

"The Gunner there," he nodded aft, "did ten years in His Majesty's Navy. Brophy was in the American Marines, went to sea, and then was with me in the Chaco and in China."

"What about your passengers, Captain?" Aldridge asked politely. "I haven't seen them around."

"You won't," Ponga Jim replied shortly. He stood by with a megaphone, directing the movements of the ship. When the tug was cast off, he took her out himself, watching the endless panorama of Singapore harbor, the hundreds of ships of all sizes and kinds, the white houses, red islands, and dark green foliage.

Sakim came up the ladder with a yellow envelope. "A message, Nakhoda," he said, bowing.

Jim ripped it open. It was terse, to the point.

PROCEED WITH CAUTION. BELIEVE RAIDER INFORMED OF EVERY AC-
TION. ARMED MERCHANTMAN OF TEN THOUSAND TONS OPERATING
IN INDIAN OCEAN. YOU MAY HAVE ENEMY AGENT ABOARD. ORDERS
HAVE GONE OUT YOU ARE NOT TO REACH THE RED SEA. LUCK.

ARNOLD.

Jim passed the message to Brophy and Millan. "William's on the job," he said. "Looks like our work's cut out for us."

Millan looked aft thoughtfully. "I don't like that Warren," he said. "Could it be him?"

"Might be anybody," Jim replied. "Not necessarily a German. A lot of people who don't see beyond the surface think dictatorships are best. They forget their supposed efficiency is because they censor news of mistakes, or shoot them. Warren is British, but he might be that kind of person. On the other hand, there's Wallace."

"You and him have always been on opposite sides," Slug suggested, "maybe—"

"We've got to keep a weather eye on them all," Jim said. "But the main job will be getting to the Red Sea. At least one raider has us marked for sinking, and we've got thirty planes aboard and twenty-three flyers, to say nothing of two passengers and some munitions."

DAY IN AND DAY OUT the *Semiramis* steamed south by east, through Banko Strait, around Sumatra, and through the Straits of Sunda and into the wide waters of the Indian Ocean. On deck and on the bridge there was an endless watch.

On the after deck, the two 5.9s painted to resemble booms and further disguised with blocks hooked to their muzzles, were never without a crew. The gun crews slept on deck in the shadow of their guns, ready and waiting.

Still the *Semiramis* headed south and a little west. The shipping lanes for India and the Red Sea fell behind. The lanes for the Cape were further south. When they reached the tenth parallel, Ponga Jim changed the course to due west.

Twice, Ring Wallace came to the bridge. His face was grave and his eyes hard. He said nothing. Each time he looked pointedly at the sun, indicating to Mayo that he knew they were off the course for Aden, but Jim ignored him.

The tension mounted daily. Everyone watched the horizon now, when they weren't watching the blank, unspeaking doors of the two cabins. But the passengers remained unseen. The steward went to them with one guard, and neither man would talk.

Ring Wallace, pointedly wearing a gun, had taken to idling about the deck amidships. The R.A.F. men were uneasy. Only the crew of the *Semiramis* seemed undisturbed.

One night Ponga Jim got up, slipped on his coat, and casually checked the load in his automatic. It was habitual action, born of struggle and the need for a gun that was ready. Then he picked up his cap and stepped toward the door.

"Hold it."

Mayo froze. That would be Wallace. He turned slowly to face him. Ring was just inside the opposite door, his face grim. The gun in his hand was steady.

"Why the artillery?" Jim asked mildly.

"Mayo," Ring said slowly, "I've known you for about ten years. We ain't seen things eye to eye, but a good part of the time you have been nearer right than me. This time, I ain't so sure."

"You asking for a showdown, Ring?"

"Sure, I want to know what we're doing hundreds of miles off our course. I want to know who your passengers are. I want to know what your intentions are.

"For the first time in my life I'm doing something without thinking of money. I decided to go to the Near East to fight because I don't like dictatorships and I'd really like to make sure I arrive in one piece."

Wallace broke off to give Mayo a hard, direct glance and then plunged on in a flat-toned voice.

"I know a lot of this stuff is the old blarney. It's propaganda. England's leadership has been coming apart at the seams for years. Her people are all right, but at the top they're a lot of wealthy and titled highbinders. It's the same way in the States. When you look for pro-Nazis look in the higher brackets of income, not the lower. Well, I've fought for money, and I've fought for the heck of it. This time it's for an idea.

"So maybe I ain't so smart. But this cargo gets through or you go over the side—feet first. I'm not kidding, either."

"Put up the heater, Ring. This time it looks like we're pitching for the same club. Look!" He took him to the chart. "Somewhere in this ocean we're scheduled to be sunk. There's the route for low-powered steamers. Here's the route we could have taken. It's dollars to guilders both routes are covered. So what do I do? I stop the radio and then drop out of sight. To all intents and purposes we're lost!"

"Look here," Jim handed a message to Wallace. "Sparks picked this up last night."

S.S. *RHYOLITE* SUNK WITH ALL HANDS TWO DAYS OUT OF SINGAPORE.
S.S. *SEMIRAMIS* REPORTED MISSING. NO WORD SINCE LEAVING SUNDA.

"See? The Admiralty's worried. Intelligence is worried. But we're safe, and a third of the distance gone. Tonight, however, we change course. After that, anything can happen."

"So I'm a sucker," Ring said, grinning. "Be seeing you."

HOURS PASSED SLOWLY on the bridge. The night was dark and still. The air was heavy with heat. Along the horizon a bank of black clouds was building up, shot through from time to time with lightning. The barometer was falling, and Ponga Jim mopped his brow.

A sudden flash of lightning lit up a cloud like an incandescent globe. Mayo dropped his hands to the railing and stared.

By the brief glimpse he had seen something else. There, not even a mile away was the black outline of a ship! Instantly, Jim stepped into the wheelhouse.

"Put her over easy," he said quietly. "Put her over three points and then hold it."

Instinctively, he knew the long, black ship was the raider. But with any luck he was going to slip away. Obviously, the raider's lookout hadn't seen him.

The *Semiramis* swung until her stern was almost toward the raider. Ponga Jim glanced aft as they started to pull away. Then almost before his eyes, and on his main deck, a light flashed. From over the way came the jangle of a bell.

Swiftly, he stepped to the speaking tube. "Red," he snapped. "This is it. Give her all you've got."

He sounded the signal for battle stations, and still in complete darkness, felt his ship coming to life. Millan emerged from his cabin and dashed aft. Other men appeared from out of nowhere.

Catching a gleam from aft, Jim knew the two 5.9s were swinging to cover the raider.

A gun from the German belched fire. The shell hit the sea off to port. Then a huge searchlight flashed on, and they were caught and pinned to the spot of light.

A signal flashed from the raider, and Sparks yelled, "He says stop or he'll sink us!"

"Let 'em have it!" Jim roared. Grabbing the megaphone, he stepped into the wing of the bridge. "Gunner! Knock that light out of there!"

He took a quick glance around to locate the cloud. It was nearer now, a great, rolling, ominous mass shot through with vivid streaks. A shell crashed off to starboard, and then the 5.9s boomed, one-two.

A geyser of water leaped fifty feet to port of the advancing ship, and then the second shell exploded close off the starboard quarter.

"That rocked her!" Jim yelled. "Keep her weaving," he told the quartermaster.

"*Taiyib*," Sakim said quietly.

Despite the fact that the freighter was giving all she had, the raider was coming up fast. The guns were crashing steadily, but so far neither had scored a hit.

The black cloud was nearer now. Jim wheeled to the door of the pilothouse when there was a terrible concussion and he was knocked sprawling into the bulkhead.

Almost at once, he was on his feet, staggering, with blood running into his eyes from where his head had smashed into the doorjamb. The port wing of the bridge had been shot away.

Millan's guns crashed suddenly, shaking the deck, and both shots hit the raider.

The first pierced the bow just abaft the hawsepipe and exploded in the forepeak. The second smashed the gun on the foredeck into a heap of twisted metal.

"Hard aport!" Jim yelled. "Swing her!"

Then the storm burst around them with a roar, a sudden black squall that sent a blinding dash of rain over the ship.

A sea struck them and cascaded down over the deck, but the *Semiramis* straightened. Behind them a gun boomed. But struggling with a howling squall they had left all visibility behind them.

Slug Brophy came up the ladder. He was sweating and streaming with rain at the same time.

"Take her over," Jim directed briefly. "And drive her. Stay with this squall if you can."

Lyssy appeared on the deck below, his powerful brown body streaming with water.

"Go below and tell Colonel Warren I want all his men in the saloon—*now*!" Jim bawled.

For a few minutes he stayed on the bridge, watching the storm. Then he went down to the saloon. The flyers, their faces heavy with sleep, were gathered around the table. Only Warren and Aldridge appeared wide-awake. Aldridge was running a deck of cards through his long fingers, his dark, curious eyes on Mayo.

"What does this mean?" Warren asked. "Isn't it bad enough with a raider and a storm without getting us all up here?"

Ponga Jim ignored him. He looked around the table, his eyes glancing from one to the other.

"Before we left Sunda Strait," he began suddenly, "I had word there was an enemy agent aboard."

Warren stiffened. His eyes narrowed. Wallace let the legs of his chair down hard and leaned forward, elbows on his knees. Aldridge held the cards in his left hand and flicked the ash from his cigarette. His eyes shifted just a little, toward Wallace.

"Tonight," Jim went on, "I had concrete proof. We were slipping away in the darkness, unnoticed, when someone on the main deck flashed a light!"

"*What?*" Warren sat up straighter. "You've captured him?"

"No," Jim said. "I don't know for sure who he is. *But he's in this room!*"

Warren was on his feet, his face suffused with anger.

"I resent that!" he said sharply. "What about your own crew? These men are all mine. Why must one of them be the traitor? That's impudence! It's unfair!"

"It sounds like it," Mayo agreed, "but my crew have been with me a long time. Each of them has been in battle against Nazis. They have no love for them."

"Natives and renegades!" Warren protested angrily.

"But good men," Ponga Jim said quietly, his eyes dark and brilliant. "I've fought beside them. They aren't interested in ideologies. The traitor is."

He hesitated, looking around. "I wanted to warn you. One of you undoubtedly knows who the guilty man is. Just think. When you decide, no matter who it is, come to me.

"There are, as you know, raiders in this ocean looking for us. Our chances of reaching Aden without encountering one of them are small.

Every hour that spy is aboard makes our risk greater. But whatever he does, he will have to be alone to do it. So stay together. *And under no circumstances must any man be found on deck alone!*"

"And the passengers?" Aldridge asked softly. "What of them? Those very mysterious passengers who never appear on deck. Mightn't one of them be the spy?"

"No," Jim said quietly. "There is no possibility of that."

He turned and left the saloon, hurrying down the passage toward the two mysterious cabins. He tapped lightly on the door. There was a murmured word, and the door opened. Jim stepped inside, closing the cabin door softly.

Two people faced him, a man of perhaps fifty and a girl of twenty-five. The man was tall and finely built, with a dark, interested face and a military bearing. He got quickly to his feet, even as Jim's eyes met the girl's. General André Caillaux and his niece had been famous in the Paris that preceded the Nazi attack.

And for years in North Africa, General Caillaux had been one of the most loved and feared officers in the French army.

Known for daring and fair dealing as well, he had great influence among the men. So enormous was this influence that the wavering Pétain government sent him to a position in New Caledonia. Now, hoping that his prestige might swing the Foreign Legion and other powerful detachments to their side, the British were returning him to North Africa.

"How is it?" Caillaux asked quickly. "Is there trouble?"

"A brush with a raider." Jim's feet braced against the roll of the deck, and his knees bent slightly when it tipped. "We got away in a squall. Hit once, but no serious damage. We holed his bow enough to make trouble in this blow, and wrecked one of his guns."

"The Nazi agent?" Caillaux's voice was anxious.

Jim shrugged. "You got me. Wallace has always been the sort to do anything for money. But this time I doubt it."

"Warren?"

"I don't know. He may be just officious, overly conscious of his new rank. And it might be a clever disguise."

"Who else could it be?" Jeanne asked. Her voice was husky.

"It might be anyone of the twenty-three. It might be Aldridge. He's a deep one. Never says much. But don't open the door for anyone but me."

He stepped out into the dark passageway and started to pull the door shut. He saw the flicker of the shadows a second too late, and then something smashed him alongside the head. He felt himself falling. But with a mighty effort, struggling against a black wave of unconsciousness, he held himself erect and swung blindly with his free hand. He missed. Something struck him again. But his hand clung to the door, and now he fell forward, pulling it shut.

As the lock clicked there was a snarl of impotent fury from his attacker. The man leaped at him, striking viciously at his head and face with a heavy blackjack. The attack was entirely soundless, for neither man had made a noise aside from that brief but angry snarl. Ponga Jim, groggy from the first blow, never had a chance. The pounding continued. He struggled to throw off the blows, to protect himself, but was unable to get his hands up.

The passage was lost in abysmal darkness. Only half conscious of what he was doing, Jim tried to retreat. But his enemy pursued him, hitting him with jarring blows that left him numb and unfeeling. Finally, he slipped to the deck, even his great strength unable to endure more battering.

A LONG TIME LATER, he fought his way back to consciousness. He was sprawled on the cold steel of the deck, some distance from where he had fallen.

He caught a steampipe housing and pulled himself to a sitting position. His head throbbed with great waves of agony. When he moved, white-hot streaks of pain shot through his brain and something hammered against his skull with great force. He tried to turn his head, and his brain seemed to move like heavy paint in a bucket. A dim light was growing in the east. On the deck he could see the dark smear of his blood where he had been dragged. His attacker had planned to drop him overboard, but had been frightened away, evidently.

Ponga Jim staggered to his feet and reeled against the bulkhead, clutching his throbbing head with both hands. It was caked with blood. Stumbling, he reached the ladder and climbed slowly to the lower bridge. Somehow he got the door open and lunged into his cabin, the roll of the ship sending him sprawling to his knees.

He was still there when the door opened and Brophy came in.

"Skipper, what's happened?" His wide, flat face was incredulous.

"I'll get him now," Jim muttered, hardly aware of the other man. "I know how to find him."

For three days Jim stayed in his bunk except when on watch. His face was swollen, and there were cuts and abrasions on the sides of his head. He was remembering that. He had not been struck *over* the head. All the blows had struck *up*. The attacker had struck with peculiar, sidearm blows. It was unusual, and for the average man, unnatural.

His jaw ached, and the back of his head was bruised. However, when he came to the bridge on the fourth day, he was just in time to see the raft.

It was a point on the starboard bow, a crude raft with a man clinging to it. Even as they saw it, the man stirred, trying to rise.

"Pick him up," Jim said, and staggered into the wheelhouse to sit down.

He still sat there when the man was brought to him. Warren and some of the others crowded inside. The man's skull stood out, the skin like thin yellow paper drawn over it. His eyes were blazing pools of fever.

"Ile du Coin," he whispered hoarsely. "Hurry."

"What?" Jim asked. "What's on the Ile du Coin?"

"Sixty men, tortured, starving, dying. Prisoners from a raider. I escaped. They shot, hit me. Hit me." His fingers touched the scalp wound. "Ile du Coin," he muttered again, his wits straying.

"How many Nazis?" Jim asked, watching the man narrowly.

He looked up, blinking. "Fifty. A raider sunk, saved the crew. Other ship is due back." He stared at Jim. "They die there, horribly. Please hurry!"

WARREN HESITATED, looking from the man to Ponga Jim, for once uncertain.

"Might be a trap," he said, hesitantly.

"Yes," Jim said. "But no man looks that bad for a trap."

Aldridge gazed at the man. "We'd better go," he said. "We can get away before the other raider returns." He looked at Ponga Jim. "You know the island?"

"Of course," Jim assured him. "It's one of the Chagos group, not far off our course. We'll go."

The rescued man, his name was Lauren, described the island. Ponga Jim listened and then shook his head.

"A small, rocky island with some scrub and coconut palms? Uninhabited? That's not Ile du Coin. That's Nelson Island. It's in the same group."

Lauren nodded. "The prisoners are in a barbwire stockade beyond a big cluster of palms and well out of sight. The Nazis have a fortified position behind some low dunes and scrubs. You can't see it until you're close by. The cove is too shallow for a ship."

Mayo turned and went below. There was a word or two at Caillaux's cabin, and the door opened.

The general looked at his bandaged head, and Jeanne's eyes widened. "What happened?" she asked.

"Someone tried to get me before I could close the door when I was here last. I got the door shut, and then he tried to kill me."

Briefly, Jim explained. "You see how it is, General. You are my mission. I have no right to risk you or Mademoiselle, yet these men will die if they are not saved."

Caillaux studied Ponga Jim, pulling at his earlobe. Jeanne stepped over to her uncle and took his arm. The general smiled and said, "My niece and I feel the same. You believe you can do this?"

"I do."

"Then the best of luck. We want you to try."

A SHORT TIME LATER Ponga Jim studied the island through the glass.

"Half ahead," he said.

Brophy put the engine-room telegraph over and then back to half speed, watching the island.

"We'll drop the hook off the northeastern point," Jim murmured. "The bay has a sandy beach where you can effect a landing. I'll take you and a landing party of Lyssy, Big London, Tupa, Boma, Longboy, and Selim and Sakim.

"The Gunner will have to keep a very sharp lookout for subs and also for the raider."

Warren had come up to the bridge. Wallace and Aldridge were behind him.

"We insist on going," Warren said firmly. "I don't approve of this, but if there are some of our men ashore, we want to help."

"Suit yourself," Jim agreed. "But not all of you. You three can come, and bring five more. Too many men will be worse than none. I want a small party that will maneuver easily. And my men know this sort of fighting."

It wasn't until the prow of the lifeboat grated on the sand that there was any sign of life. Then it was the flash of sunlight on a rifle barrel.

"*Down!*" Jim snapped, and threw himself to the sand. The others flattened instantly, just in time to miss a raking volley.

Instantly, Ponga Jim was on his feet. He made a dozen steps with bullets kicking sand around him and then flattened behind a low hummock and hammered out three quick shots at the spot where he'd seen the rifle. There was a gasping cry and then silence.

No orders were necessary. The flyers hesitated and then took their cue from Lyssy and the crew of the *Semiramis*. They worked their way forward, keeping to shallow places and losing their bodies in the sand.

Jim touched Lyssy. "They are bunched right ahead of us. Slip over to the left and flank them. London, you take the right. Take no chances, and keep your fire down. I want them out of that position."

The two men disappeared, and Mayo looked at Warren. "This is war, friend," he said grimly.

THE NAZIS OPENED a hot fire that swept the dunes, a searching volley that covered the ground thoroughly.

Only the hollows saved the landing party.

Mayo scooped sand away and worked his body forward. A shot kicked sand into his face. He worked in behind a low bush and lifted his head slowly beside it.

He had been right. The low dunes behind which the Nazis were concealed ran across the island diagonally, but both flanks were exposed. He snapped a quick shot into the space ahead and then slid back in time to miss the answering volley.

The Nazis were shooting steadily, hammering each available screen with steady fire. But suddenly a rifle cracked off to the left, and there was a scream of pain. The rifle spoke again, and there was an answering volley. Another shot came from the right, and Jim yelled.

In a scattered line his men rushed forward firing from all positions. The Germans, although in superior numbers, retreated hastily. Ponga Jim stopped, braced himself, and fired. A Nazi stumbled and fell headlong. Two more were down in the hollow where they had taken shelter. Now another stumbled and collapsed as a bullet ripped into his body.

Jenkins, a flyer from Kalgoorlie, rushed up beside Jim, stopped suddenly, and dropped to his face in the sand.

Jim fired. The Nazi let his rifle slip from his hands, bowed his head and took two steps, and then toppled.

Mayo crawled behind a five-foot bank of sand and looked around. All of Warren's pomposity was gone. Under fire, the man had changed. Whatever else he was, he came of fighting stock.

Ring Wallace, an old hand at this game, was grinning. "Nice work, pal. Now what?"

"We're stuck," Jim said. "They've got a fortified position up there, and it will be tough to get them out of it. Listen to those machine guns. Those boys know their stuff, too."

Brophy had been grazed by a bullet, and Tupa had a flesh wound. Aside from the first flyer, there were no serious injuries.

Wallace nodded to Jim's comment. "Yeah, I could see the edge of a concrete abutment. It's in crescent form and backed by the cove."

"Let's rush them," Warren said. "Otherwise it's a stalemate until that raider gets back."

Ponga Jim shook his head. "We'd lose men in a rush. Wars aren't won with dead soldiers. There's always a way to take a position without losing many men, if you look for it." Suddenly his eyes narrowed. "Slug, do you recall what the chart said about the water in that cove?"

Brophy nodded. "There's a coral ledge topped with sand with about a fathom of water over it. Outside of that it slopes off gradually until at a hundred yards it's about three fathoms. Why?"

"You'll be in command here. I'll take Selim, Longboy, and Sakim with me. We'll bring the wounded aboard. Now scatter out and don't move either forward or back, get me?"

"What are you going to do?" Warren protested.

"Wait and see," Jim said. "If this works I'm one up on the Nazis for trying new angles. We're going to take that position in less than thirty minutes! Now listen. Keep up an intermittent fire. Pretty soon Millan will lay five shells in that fort, get me? Then you'll hear shooting over there. And when you hear shooting beyond the wall, come running. I'll need help."

Millan met them at the ladder. "What's up?" he demanded.

Jim indicated the cove.

"As the fort lays, the situation is impregnable from the island with our weapons. I want you to lay five shells behind that abutment. And they've got to be right on the spot. If you overshoot, you'll kill the prisoners. If you undershoot, you'll get our boys for sure."

THE GUNNER STUDIED the situation. Then he rolled his chewing in his jaw and spat.

"Yeah," he said, "I'll lay 'em right in their laps."

"Well, whatever you do," Ponga Jim added, "don't drop any shells in the cove, because if you do they'll be in my lap!"

"The cove?" Millan was incredulous. "You couldn't get in there with a boat! They'd riddle you!"

Ponga Jim grinned. "Break out those Momsen lungs, will you? I'll show those Jerries some tricks!"

An hour dragged by. The warm afternoon sun baked down on the little island. Ring Wallace took a swallow from his canteen and swore. Warren wiped the sweat from his face and kept his hands away from the hot rifle barrel. "I wonder what became of Mayo?" he asked.

"Darned if I know," Ring said. "But he's got something up his sleeve. Whatever it is, it better be good. That raider has me worried."

A gun crashed from the *Semiramis,* and a shell screeched overhead, bursting beyond the abutment with a terrific concussion. A fountain of sand lifted into the air. Another shell screeched, and there was another explosion.

"That Millan!" Brophy said admiringly. "That guy can put a shell in your pocket. Just name the pocket!"

Two more shells dropped beyond the abutment, then a fifth.

The water of the cove stirred and rippled. Up from the pondlike surface five weird heads appeared, five faces masked in Momsen lungs. Lowering themselves into the water beyond the point, they had walked around in ten feet of water. Now they stripped the waterproof jackets from their guns and walked on. They were within a hundred feet of the shore, in just four feet of water, before they were seen.

One machine-gun emplacement had been smashed to bits with the first shell. Two others had exploded on the abutment itself, and a third had landed in a gasoline supply that was burning furiously. The final shell had been shrapnel, and the devastation had been terrific. Seven men had fallen from that one shell alone.

Crawling from behind a pile of boxes, one of the defenders glanced at the cove. His jaw dropped. For a fatal second he stared, uncomprehending; then he jerked up his rifle. Too late. Ponga Jim shot him in the stomach. As the startled defenders turned, Jim ran up the last few feet, and his automatic opened with a roar like a machine gun.

In a scattered line the other men rushed up the beach. The Germans, caught off balance, were rattled. They fell back. And in that instant the frontal attack broke over them. Brophy, Wallace, Warren, and the others cleared the barrier. The two sides met in a deadly rush.

A German dove at Jim. He spun out of the way, clouting the man over the head with the barrel of his gun. Then he snapped a quick shot at a man leveling a rifle at Wallace and fired a burst into a group trying to swing the machine gun on the prisoners.

A terrific blow struck him over the ear, and he went down, grabbing at the man's legs. He upset his assailant and scrambled astride, swinging both hands for the fellow's jaw. Then he was on his feet again and grabbing up a rifle. He jerked the barrel up into a charging German's stomach and pulled the trigger. The man's mouth fell open, and with his back half blown away, he sagged limply to the ground.

As SUDDENLY AS it had started, it was over. Brophy released the prisoners, and Wallace herded the half-dozen Nazis still alive into a corner of the fort where Lyssy and Big London took them over.

Aldridge came up on the run.

"Nice going!" he said, clapping Mayo on the shoulder. "That attack from underwater completely demoralized them."

"Yeah," Wallace agreed. "Now if we only had the spy—"

"We have," Ponga Jim said shortly.

A silence fell over the crowd. Brophy's gun slipped into his hand, and he backed off a little, covering the group. Colonel Warren looked from one to the other, puzzled.

"What's the matter with your shoulder, Aldridge?" Jim said, unexpectedly. "Hurt it?"

"Oh, that?" Aldridge shrugged. "Years ago. Can't lift my arm overhead. But what about this spy?"

"So when you hit a man," Mayo continued, "you couldn't hit him over the head? It would have to be a swinging, sidearm motion? Then you were the guy who jumped me in the passage."

Aldridge smiled, but his eyes were cold, wary.

"Nonsense! You think I'm a spy? Me? I went to school with Warren, there, and—"

"Remember the first day I saw you?" Mayo said. "You mentioned the Qasavara affair. That business is lost in the files of the British Intelligence service. My own connection with it is known to only two Englishmen— Colonel Sutherland and Major Arnold, who were with me. If you knew of it, you had to learn from a Nazi source."

Mayo smiled. "I was suspicious of you for knowing that. Later, I checked on the location of the flyers during my attack. You could have been in your hammock. On the other hand, you could have slipped out. From the locations, no one else could have.

"So today I had you followed by Fly Johnny, one of my crew. In fact, for the past week he has never been more than a few feet from you.

"Today, when we first came ashore, Millan went through your quarters. He found the package of flashlight powder you used in making signals. He also found other evidence, so I think the case is clear."

Aldridge nodded, his face hard.

"Sounds conclusive," he agreed, "so I guess—"

He wheeled like a cat and jerked Warren's gun from his hand. Eyes blazing with hatred, the gun swept up. But he was too slow. Ponga Jim stepped forward in one quick stride, half turning on the ball of his foot. His right fist smashed upward in an uppercut that slammed Aldridge into the sand, the gun flying from his fingers.

Ponga Jim looked at him once. "Bring him along," he said, "we'll be going now."

"You know," Warren said seriously, "the more I think about it the more I believe Drake had something!"

Ponga Jim grinned. "Yeah, and he would have liked you!"

In the radio shack, Ponga Jim Mayo picked up the stub of a pencil, grinned, and scratched out a message.

MAJOR WILLIAM ARNOLD
RAFFLES HOTEL
SINGAPORE, S. I.

PROCEEDED WITH CAUTION AND A LOT OF GOOD IT DID. ARMED MERCHANTMAN OF TEN THOUSAND TONS NOW HAS HOLE IN HIS BOW AND DISABLED GUN. WE HAVE ENEMY AGENT ABOARD—IN IRONS. WE HAVE MET THE ENEMY AND YOU CAN HAVE THEM. WILL BE IN RED SEA FRIDAY. NUTS TO YOU.

MAYO.

South of Suez

CHAPTER I

The heavy concussion of the first shell brought Ponga Jim Mayo out of his bunk, wide-awake in an instant. He was pulling on his shoes when he heard the whistle in the speaking tube.

"Skipper?" It was Gunner Millan. "We're running into a battle! Can't see a thing but red flashes yet, about three points on the starboard bow. Sounds like a battlewagon."

"Put her over to port about four degrees," Ponga Jim said quietly. "Have the watch call Brophy and get the gun crews topside."

He got up, slid into his dungarees, and slipped on the shoulder holster with the forty-five Colt. There would be no need for it at sea, but he had worn the gun so long he felt undressed without it.

When Ponga Jim reached the bridge the sky was lit with an angry glow of flame. Two freighters of the convoy off to the starboard were afire, and something was lifted toward the sky that looked like the stern of a sinking ship. They could hear the steady fire of six-inch guns and then the heavy boom of something much bigger.

SECOND MATE MILLAN came toward him along the bridge, swearing under his breath.

"Skipper," he said. "I must be nuts, but I'd swear that gun wasn't smaller than an eighteen-inch, and there's nothing afloat carries a gun that big!"

"Sounds like it," Jim said briefly. "Might be a sixteen. The *Tirpitz,* maybe. But you wouldn't think they'd gamble a battleship in waters as narrow as the Red Sea."

The blazing wreck of one freighter was directly opposite them, and suddenly a low, ominous blackness moved between them and the blazing ship. For a few minutes it was clearly outlined against the red glow of flame.

Squat, black, and ugly, the monster glistened in the reddish light. It was built low and completely covered by what appeared to be a steel shell. Even as they looked they saw the muzzle of a heavy gun belch flame. A big freighter, almost a mile away, was attempting to escape. Even as they watched, the shell struck it amidships.

Suddenly, but with every move so perfectly detailed as to seem like a slow-motion picture, the distant freighter burst. The amidships vanished and the bow and stern seemed to lift away from it and then fell back into the flame-tinged water. Then there was a slow rain of black débris.

"Gun crews standing by, sir," First Mate Slug Brophy said, as he came up. He saluted snappily, but he was scowling as he looked off across the water. "What the devil kind of a craft *is that?*" he demanded. "Looks like she was a seagoing tank."

Ponga Jim nodded. "It's what I've been wondering why someone didn't do," he said crisply. "That's a new battleship. No elaborate super-structure, no basket masts or turrets. She's completely covered by a steel shell and probably bomb-proof. She's built along the lines of a stream-lined Merrimac."

"Lucky that fire's in her eyes and we're back here," Slug said. "One shell from her and we'd be blown so high we'd starve to death falling back."

"Yeah." Jim studied the warship through his glass and then glanced ahead. "Gunner, lay all five guns on that baby. I'm going to give her a broadside and then run for it."

"You're nuts!" Brophy exploded. "Why, Chief—"

"You heard me," Ponga Jim said sharply. "Get going."

He stepped into the wheelhouse.

"Selim," he said to the pockmarked, knife-scarred man at the wheel, "aren't we abreast of the old smuggler's passage through the reef? It gives us about five fathoms, doesn't it?"

Selim nodded, lifting his eyes from the compass.

"I take her through?" he asked.

Ponga Jim studied the mystery ship ahead thoughtfully and then the nearing bulk of a large rocky island.

"Yeah," he said. "We'll fire that barge a broadside and then slip around that island and through the reef passage. They can't follow us, and blacked out the way they have us these days, we'll be invisible against that rocky shore. We got a chance."

He stepped back to the bridge and lifted his megaphone.

"You may fire when ready, Gridley!" he said and grinned.

The crash of the five 5.9s left his ears momentarily dead and empty. The freighter heeled sharply over. With his glasses on the warship, Ponga Jim waited for the *Semiramis* to recover.

"All right, Gunner," he called. "Once more!"

He had his glasses on the warship when the salvo struck. He scowled and then spun on his heel.

"Hard over!" he snapped crisply. "Show them our stern, if anything." He stepped on the speaking tube. "Chief," he called, "give me all she's got! We're in a spot, so keep her rolling."

Slug Brophy and Gunner Millan had returned to the bridge. The squat first mate wiped his face with a blue handkerchief.

"You sure pick 'em big when you want trouble!" he observed. "See those five-point-nines slide off that shell? Like rice off a turtle's back! What kind of a ship is that, anyway?"

"That ship," Ponga Jim said quietly, "can destroy British and American naval supremacy! The United States has the biggest, best, and most efficient navy afloat, but we haven't anything as invulnerable to attack as that ship!"

Behind them a gun boomed, and off to the left a huge geyser of water lifted toward the sky. Ponga Jim glanced aft and then looked at the black bulk of the rocky island. Selim was cutting it close, but no one knew the Red Sea better than he did.

The *Semiramis* steamed straight ahead and then, at a low word from Selim, slowed to half speed as he turned the ship at right angles to her course. Ponga Jim stared into the darkness ahead, hearing the roll of the surf on the coral reef. He put his hand up to his forehead, to find he was sweating.

Brophy stood close beside him, staring down at the black, froth-fringed reef dead ahead.

"You sure this guy knows what he's doing?" Slug muttered. "If he doesn't—"

"He does," Mayo said quietly. "Selim was a smuggler in this sea for several years. He knows every cove and passage in the eleven hundred miles of it."

As if to prove his statement, the reef suddenly seemed to open before them, and an opening, invisible until they were close up, appeared in the reef.

In a matter of seconds they were through and in the clear water of the inside passage. . . .

TWO DAYS LATER the *Semiramis* steamed slowly into the harbor at Port Tewfik and moved up to the place at the dock that had been made ready for them.

"Mr. Brophy"—Ponga Jim turned to the chief mate—"get the hatches off and the cargo out of her as quick as you can. Take nothing from any- body, use any gear you need, but it must get out. Also, I want a man at the gangway every hour of the day and night. Nobody comes aboard or leaves without my permission. Also I want one man forward and one aft. All to be armed. Understand?"

"You must be expecting trouble," a cool voice suggested.

Ponga Jim turned to find himself facing a square-shouldered young man with a blond mustache and humorous blue eyes. He was a slender man with a narrow face, dark, immaculate, and with a military bearing, and had just boarded the *Semiramis* with a companion.

"William!" he exclaimed. "What in time are you doing in Egypt? Thought you were in Singapore?"

Major William Arnold shrugged his shoulders.

"Trouble here, too," he said. "Heard you were coming in, so thought I'd drop down and see you." His gaze sharpened. "Have any trouble com- ing up from Aden?"

"We didn't," Ponga Jim said drily, "but we saw a convoy get smashed to hell."

"You *saw* it?"

Ponga Jim was nodding as Major Arnold quickly added:

"Jim, let me present Nathan Demarest, our former attaché at Bucharest. He's working with me on this job."

"Glad to know you," Ponga Jim said, and then he looked back at Arnold. "Yes, we saw it," he said briefly, and went on, as his glance went back to Demarest. "Arnold will tell you that I don't run to convoys, so we were traveling alone. About six bells in the middle watch I got a call and got on deck to find a big warship blasting the daylights out of the convoy. Only one destroyer remained in action when we came up to them. And that not for long."

"A ship?" Arnold demanded. "Not submarines?"

"A ship," Mayo repeated. "A ship that couldn't have been less than forty thousand tons. She was streamlined and completely shelled over like a floating fort, and she mounted eighteen-inch guns."

"Your friend Captain Mayo is a humorist," Demarest suggested to Arnold, smiling. "There is no such ship."

"I'm not joking," Ponga Jim said stiffly. "There was such a ship, and we saw it."

Arnold looked at his friend thoughtfully.

"What happened, Jim?" he finally asked.

"We were coming up in the darkness and were unseen. I gave them two salvos from my guns, and then we slipped around an island and got away."

"You hit her?"

"Yes—direct hits—and they didn't even shake her. Just like shooting at a tank with a target rifle."

Demarest's face had hardened. "If this is true we must get in touch with the Admiralty," he said. "Such a ship must be run down at once."

"If you'll take my word for it," Mayo said slowly, "I'd advise being careful. This ship is something new. I don't believe bombs would have any effect on her at all. She looks like someone's secret weapon."

Ponga Jim Mayo glanced at the winches.

The booms were being rigged, and in a few minutes the cargo would be coming out of the freighter.

"Is this what brought you here, William?" he asked. "Or something else?"

"Something else," the major said. "Have you heard of Carter's death? Ambrose Carter, the munitions man? He was found shot to death in his apartment near Shepheard's in Cairo three weeks ago. Then General McKnight was poisoned, and Colonel Norfolk of the CID, who was investigating, was stabbed."

"McKnight poisoned?" Ponga Jim exclaimed. "I heard he died of heart failure."

"That's our story," Arnold agreed. "We mustn't allow anyone to know, Jim. But those are only three of the deaths. There have been nine others, all of key men. Some poisoned, some shot, one stabbed, two found dead without any evidence of cause of death, others drowned, strangled, or snake bit."

"Snake bit?"

"By an Indian cobra. The thing had been coiled in one man's bed. When it bit him he died before help could get to him. Jim, they called me here because these deaths can't be explained. Carter, for instance, was an acknowledged pro-Nazi, a former friend of Hitler's. If it weren't for that, it would seem logical the Nazis were starting a reign of terror, killing off the leadership for a major attack in the Near East."

"If not the Nazis," Jim protested, "then who could it be?"

"I wish I knew." Arnold's eyes narrowed. "But you'd better come along and tell this to Skelton. He's in charge here in Port Tewfik. The man who will have to know and to act."

CHAPTER II

Seated in the office of Anthony Skelton, two hours later, Ponga Jim Mayo repeated his story, quietly and in detail. Two other men were there besides Demarest and Arnold. One he was introduced to as Captain Woodbern, of the Navy. The other was General Jerome Kernan.

Before Ponga Jim's story was completed, Skelton was tapping his desk impatiently. Captain Woodbern was frankly smiling.

"Major Arnold," Skelton said abruptly, "I've heard a great deal of your ability. I've also heard of the work Captain Mayo has been doing in the Far East. Which makes me the more surprised at your taking our time, Major, with such an obvious cock-and-bull story. This Captain Mayo evidently has a peculiar sense of humor or is susceptible to hallucinations. Such a story as his is preposterous on the face of it!"

Arnold stiffened. "I know Captain Mayo too well, Mr. Skelton," he replied stiffly, "to doubt his word. If he says this story is true, then I believe it is true!"

"Then you're more credulous than any intelligence officer should be!" Skelton snapped.

"Captain Mayo evidently saw something," Captain Woodbern said, smiling, "but I'm afraid the darkness, the battle, the flames, and the general excitement caused his imagination to work a little overtime."

General Kernan turned slightly in his chair. He was a big man with a hard jaw, a cold eye, and a close-clipped mustache.

"Mayo isn't the type to be seeing things, Skelton," he said. "Major Arnold has known him for some time, and his work has been valuable. I want to hear more of his story."

Skelton glanced down at some papers on his desk. "We'll see that proper investigation is made," he said shortly. "In fact, we have already ordered two destroyers to the scene."

Ponga Jim leaned forward. "Then, Mr. Skelton," he said quietly, "you've sent two destroyers to destruction. Either they will return having found nothing, or they'll never come back." He got up abruptly. "Thanks for believing my story, General. As for you, Skelton, I'm not in the habit of having my word questioned. All I can say or do about that here and now, is to assure you that you are following the same trail of incompetence and smugness of others who didn't believe Hitler would attack Britain, did not believe in parachute troops, or that the Japanese would bomb Pearl Harbor and the Philippines while suing for peace. Well, do what you choose. I shall investigate further myself!"

Skelton's eyes blazed.

"No," he said sharply, "you won't! In the Far East your blunderings may have been occasionally convenient, but we want no civilian interference here. You make one move to investigate or to interfere and I'll have the *Semiramis* interned for the duration!"

Ponga Jim smiled suddenly. He leaned his big brown fists on the edge of the desk and looked into Skelton's eyes.

"Listen, pal," he said coldly, "you may have a lot of red tape around the throats of other men. But I'm not subject to your orders, and I'll sail when and where I please. If you want to intern my ship, I've got five-point-nines and plenty of ammunition. You'll think you've tackled something. When I get ready to sail, I'm sailing. Stop me if you feel lucky."

He glanced at Arnold.

"Sorry, William, but you can't help that. Be seeing you." He strode from the room.

Skelton's face was deathly white. "I want that man put under arrest and his ship interned!" he snapped.

General Kernan got to his feet.

"You're starting something with the wrong man, Skelton," he said smoothly. "If necessary Captain Mayo would shoot his way out of harbor or sink trying."

"Nonsense!" Skelton snapped.

"No." Kernan was looking after Mayo thoughtfully. "The man's a Yank, but I was doubting if they had any left like him. Now that I know they have, I feel a lot better. Mayo's another of the school of Perry, Farragut, Decatur, and Hull."

Nathan Demarest left the room quietly, glanced down the hall along which Mayo had gone, and then stepped into an empty office and picked up the telephone.

PONGA JIM WALKED SWIFTLY down the street and then stopped in a place for a drink. When he turned to leave, he saw a slim, wiry man sitting at a table near the door. The man did not look up, but something in the man's attitude made Mayo suspicious. He would almost have sworn it was the same man he had seen loitering outside Skelton's office as he left. He scowled. Who would want him followed in Suez?

The quay was a litter of piled barrels and cases, of gear and bales. Ponga Jim was just passing a huge crane whose bulk forced him to the edge of the dock, when a black body catapulted from the darkness and smashed him with a shoulder, just hip high. He felt himself falling and grabbed desperately, catching his attacker by the arm. They fell, plunging into the black water with terrific force, but even as they sank Ponga Jim felt his attacker's arm slip from his grasp, and the next instant the man had drawn a knife and lunged toward him.

Ponga Jim dived and felt the hot blade of the knife along his shoulder. His lungs all but bursting he slammed a punch into the man's belly. He saw his attacker's mouth open, but the man was a veritable fiend, and he lunged again with the knife, teeth bared. Ponga Jim pushed away, kicking the man in the belly. Then they broke water.

Instantly, the fellow took a breath and dived, but Ponga Jim went down with him. At one time Ponga Jim had been a skin diver for pearls. The swift thought flashed now that this fellow was good, and he had a knife, but—

The man swung in the water, his body as slippery as an eel's, and then he lunged at Ponga Jim with the knife. But Mayo was too fast. He dived again, catching the man's wrist. Turning the arm, he jerked it down across his shoulder with terrific force.

Then he pulled free, smashing a fist into the fellow's belly for luck. As he swam he could see the man sinking, his teeth bared, his mouth leaving a trail of bubbles. The arm was broken.

Ponga Jim swam to a small boat dock and scrambled from the water. For a moment he stood there, dripping and staring back, but there was nothing to be seen. He put his hand up, and it came away from his shoulder bloody.

"Somebody," he muttered softly, "doesn't like me!"

The dark shape of the *Semiramis* loomed not fifty feet away. He climbed the ladder to the dock and then moved warily toward the freighter. As he came up the gangway, a dark shape materialized from beside the hatch. He recognized the half-shaven head of the big Toradjas, one of his trusted crew.

"It's all right, Lyssy," he said. "It's me."

"Something happen astern, Captain. Somebody—" Lyssy saw Ponga Jim's dripping clothes, and his eyes widened. "Somebody try to kill you?"

"That's right." Mayo glanced back at the dock. "Keep your eyes open. Who else is on watch?"

"Big London, he forward. Longboy aft. Sakim, he around somewhere, too."

"Has anyone been here?"

"Yes, Captain. One man he come say he want to talk to you. He say very important. He say General Kernan send him."

"Where is he?" Ponga Jim demanded.

"In your cabin. You say no man come aboard, this man he worry to see you. We lock him in."

Ponga Jim grinned. "Okay. You stay here."

HE QUICKLY CLIMBED the ladder to his deck and then fitted his key in the lock of his door. He swung it open—and stopped dead in his tracks. The man sitting in Jim's chair, facing the door, had been shot above the left eyebrow.

Slowly, Ponga Jim reached behind him and drew the door to. He circled the body, studying it with narrowed eyes. Then he stepped behind the body and sighted across the dead man's head in line with the wound. The bullet had come through the open porthole. In line with the port was the corner of the warehouse roof. Whoever had fired the shot had stood on that corner and made a perfect job.

Ponga Jim went out to the deck and called Lyssy.

"Did you hear a shot?" he demanded.

"No, Captain, nobody shoot!" Lyssy said positively

That meant one thing to Ponga Jim. A silencer had been used.

"The man up there is dead," he said. "He was shot from that warehouse roof."

Sakim came up, and Ponga Jim hurriedly scratched a note.

"Take this message to Major Arnold at this address," he instructed. "Give it to no one else. Then return here."

He went back into his cabin and, closing the door, careful not to disturb the position of the body, he searched the murdered man's pockets. He spread everything he found on his desk and studied the collection carefully. There was a key ring with several keys, a billfold, a fountain pen, a gun, some odd change, mostly silver, and a ticket stub indicating that the victim had but recently arrived from Alexandria. Also, there was a magnificent emerald ring, the gem being carved in the form of a scarab.

Turning his attention to the billfold, Ponga Jim found a packet of money amounting to about eighty Egyptian pounds, around four hundred dollars. In one pocket of the billfold was a white card and on it, in neat handwriting, a name.

ZARA HAMMEDAN

After a few minutes thought, he pocketed the key ring, the card with the name, and the emerald ring. On second thought, he returned the ring to the table, retaining the other things he had chosen.

CHAPTER III

At a sudden rap on the door, Ponga Jim looked up. He opened the door to find Major Arnold, General Kernan, and Nathan Demarest awaiting him. They had come promptly in answer to Mayo's note.

Arnold crossed at once to the body and made a cursory examination.

"Then this man who has been killed never managed to talk to you?" General Kernan asked.

"No," Ponga Jim replied. "I was delayed myself. Someone tried to add me to your list of killings."

Arnold looked up quickly. "I noticed you were wet. Did they shove you in?"

Ponga Jim nodded. He was looking across the room at a mirror.

"Yes. Good attempt, too. But I don't kill very easy."

"What happened?" Demarest asked. "Did you   catch him?"

"No. I killed him. He cut me a little, but not much."

"But you were in the water," Demarest persisted. "How could you kill him?"

"I killed him," Ponga Jim said quietly, "in the water. He got his belly and lungs full of it."

Demarest's eyes narrowed a little, and then he glanced at the body. "That man was a half-caste," he said. "But his killers must have taken him for you."

"I don't think so," Ponga Jim said. "I think the killer knew who he was shooting."

"So do I," Kernan said. "This man who was shot came here with a message for you. He came to me first, learned you were here, and said he would talk to no one but you. Had some message for you."

Arnold straightened up. "Had you noticed something, Jim? No identification on this man. Not a thing. We can check on this ticket stub and the gun, but I'm sure they will give us nothing."

"What about the ring?" Ponga Jim asked.

"Old, isn't it?" Arnold said. "And odd looking. It might be a clue."

Ponga Jim picked up the ring. "Look at that again, William. Emeralds and rubies were carved into scarabs only for royalty. The emerald itself is big, the ring too heavy for ordinary wear. It's probably a funeral ring, and probably dates back three thousand years. That ring is museum stuff. But I'll bet it didn't come from any museum."

"Why?" General Kernan asked. He examined the ring curiously.

"Such prize archaeological specimens are too well cared for. And if anything as valuable as that were lost, everyone would have heard of it. No, this man, whoever he was, had found a tomb and had been looting it."

"He might have picked it up in some thieves' market," Demarest protested.

"What I'm wondering," Arnold said, "is how all this can tie in with your mysterious battleship? A thief with a stolen ring or one looted from a tomb could scarcely have anything to do with such a thing."

"That battleship," Ponga Jim suggested, "or even if I was crazy and it was only a submarine or two, must have a base. The first problem, it seems to me, is to locate that base. The fact that the ship is in the Red Sea gives us a chance to keep it here—if we can. My theory is that this dead guy may have known where the base is, and maybe that knowledge ties in with that ring."

MAJOR ARNOLD STAYED ON after the others had gone.

"Go slow, Jim," he advised. "Skelton doesn't approve of civilians' interfering in government affairs, and he persists in maintaining that you have no right to have an armed ship, that actually you're a pirate."

"Yeah?" Ponga Jim chuckled. "Maybe he's right. I'm an American, even though I've spent little time there. My shipping business is in war areas but I'm not asking America's protection. I protect myself. But seriously, William, this business has got me going in circles. Why the rush to kill me? Who knows, except you guys, that I saw that warship? Who knows that a shipowner and skipper like myself would ever dream of investigating the thing? Why should this guy with the ring come to me?"

Arnold nodded. "I've thought of that," he said. "Frankly, Jim, other people have, too. Skelton even hinted that you might have sunk that convoy."

"What?" Ponga Jim's face hardened. "Some day that guy's going to make me sore."

"But see his angle. You have guns. There were two destroyers with that convoy, but what would prevent you from giving one of them a salvo at close quarters when they expected nothing of the kind? And then the other?"

"There's something in that," Ponga Jim admitted. "But you and I know it's baloney. And where does this killing me come in? Only one way I can see it. These babies have an espionage system that reaches right to the top here in Egypt. They know about me coming through; they know about my plan to go on."

Arnold was thoughtful. "Jim," he said slowly, "I've got a hunch. You've knocked around a lot. Suppose you were right, and this isn't a Nazi deal? Who or what could it be? My hunch is that you know, and somebody knows you know, and is afraid you might talk."

Ponga Jim frowned. "I know? What d'you mean?"

"Suppose that while knocking around—you used to be in Africa—you stumbled across some person or place connected with this. You have forgotten, but someone in this plot hasn't."

Mayo nodded. "Might be something to it. But what?"

"Think it over. In the meanwhile, we'll have this body taken off your hands."

When Arnold had gone Ponga Jim walked out on deck and called Selim and Sakim.

"Listen," he said. "You boys used to be wise to everything that happened in the Red Sea. I want you to go out into the bazaars, anywhere, and I want the gossip. I want to know more about this warship we saw. I want to know about the guy that was killed in my cabin. Above all, I want to know something about a woman named Zara Hammedan!"

The two Afridis stiffened.

"Who, Nakhoda?" Selim said. "Did you say Zara Hammedan?"

"That's right."

"But, Nakhoda, we know who she is!" Selim hesitated. Then: "I will tell you, Nakhoda. This is a secret among Moslems, but you are our protector and friend. There is among Moslems a young movement, a sect of those who are fanatics who would draw together all Moslem countries in a huge empire. These men have chosen Zara Hammedan for their spiritual leader: She is scarcely more than a girl, Nakhoda, but she is of amazing beauty."

"Who is she? An Arab?"

Selim shrugged. "Perhaps. It is said she is of the family of the Sultan of Kishin, leader of the powerful Mahra tribe, whose territory extends along the coast from Museinaa to Damkut."

Slug Brophy came up as the two were leaving.

"Any orders, Skipper? We'll have her empty an hour after daybreak."

"Yeah."

Ponga Jim talked slowly for several minutes, and Slug nodded.

"Can you swing it?" he asked finally.

"Sure." Brophy hitched up his trousers. "This is going to be good. . . ."

A FEW MINUTES after daybreak, Ponga Jim went ashore and headed for Golmar Street. As he disappeared, Brophy stepped out on deck. With him was Big London.

"That's the lay," Slug said briefly. "The chief's going alone. You follow him, see? But keep that ugly mug of yours out of sight. I got a hunch he's sticking his neck out, and I want you close by if he does. He'd raise the roof if he knew it, so keep your head down."

The giant black man nodded eagerly and then went ashore. Brophy looked after him, grinning.

"Well, Skipper," he muttered, "if you do get into it, you can use that guy."

FOR THREE HOURS, Ponga Jim was busy. He dropped into various bars, consumed a few drinks, ate breakfast, and lounged about. In his white-topped peaked cap with its captain's insignia, his faded khaki suit, and woven leather sandals, he was not conspicuous. Only the unusual breadth of his shoulders and his sun-browned face somehow stood out. The bulge under his left shoulder was barely noticeable.

The streets of Suez were jammed. War had brought prosperity to the port, and the ships that came up from around the Cape of Good Hope were mostly docking here. Hundreds of soldiers were about the streets. Ghurkas, Sikhs, and Punjabis from India, stalwart Australians and New Zealanders, occasional Scotsmen, and a number of R.A.F. flyers. And there were seamen from all the seven seas, thronging ashore for a night or a day and then off to sea again. There was a stirring in the bazaars, and rumors were rife of new activity in Libya, of fighting to break out in Iraq once more, of German aggression in Turkey.

And the grapevine of the Orient was at work, with stories from all the Near East drifting here. To a man who knew his way around, things were to be learned in the bazaars.

Ponga Jim went on to Port Said, flying over and later flying back. At four in the afternoon, he presented himself at Skelton's office.

He was admitted at once. Demarest, Kernan, Arnold, Woodbern, and Skelton himself were there.

"Glad you dropped in, Mayo," Skelton said abruptly. "I was about to send for you. Our destroyers wirelessed that they could find only wreckage. Two more destroyers coming up from Aden effected a junction with the same report. What have you to say to that?"

"The warship could have hidden," Ponga Jim said quietly. "You would scarcely expect it to wait for you."

"Hidden? In the Red Sea?" Skelton smiled coldly. "Captain Mayo, a warship could not be concealed in the Red Sea. No ship could be."

"No?" Ponga Jim smiled in turn.

"No," Skelton said. "Furthermore, Captain Mayo, I have deemed it wise to order your ship interned until we can investigate further. I am a little curious as to those guns you carry. I also hear you carry a pocket submarine and an amphibian plane. Strange equipment for an honest freighter."

"The spoils of war," Mayo assured him, still smiling. "I captured them and have found them of use. And I hate to disappoint you, Skelton, but I'm afraid if you expect to intern the *Semiramis* you are a bit late."

"What do you mean?" Skelton snapped.

"The *Semiramis,*" Ponga Jim said softly, "finished discharging shortly after daybreak this morning. She left port immediately!"

"What!"

Skelton was on his feet, his face white with anger. The other men tensed. But out of the corner of his eye, Ponga Jim could see a twinkle in General Kernan's eyes.

"No doubt you'll find the *Semiramis,*" Ponga Jim said coolly, "since you say no ship can be concealed in the Red Sea. Good hunting, Skelton!"

He turned and started for the door.

A BUZZER SOUNDED, and behind him he heard Skelton lift the phone.

"What?" Skelton shouted. "Both of them?" The telephone dropped back into the cradle. "Gentlemen," Skelton said sharply, "the destroyers sent from this base to investigate Captain Mayo's report have both been sunk. A partial message was received, telling how they had been attacked. Captain Mayo, you are under arrest!"

"Sorry, gentlemen," Mayo said, "but I can't wait!"

He swung the door open and sprang into the hall.

"Stop him!" Skelton roared.

A burly soldier leaped from his position by the wall, grabbing at Mayo with both hands. Ponga Jim grabbed the big man by the wrist and hurled him over his back in a flying mare that sent the big fellow crashing into the opposite wall. Then he was down the hall, out into the street, and with one jump, was into the crowd.

Another soldier rushed from the building and started down the steps close on Ponga Jim's heels. A Herculean black man, lounging near the door, deftly thrust his foot in the way, and the soldier spilled head over heels into the crowd at the foot of the stone steps.

Rounding a corner, Ponga Jim slipped into a crowded bazaar. He stopped briefly at a stall, and when he left he was wrapped in a long Arab cloak, or aba, and on his head was a headcloth bound with an aghal. With his dark skin and his black hair he looked like a native.

He walked on, mingling with the people of the bazaar. Twice soldiers passed him, their eyes scanning the bazaar, but none looked at him.

But as Ponga Jim drifted slowly from the bazaar and out into the less crowded streets, a slim, hawk-featured man was close behind. And a little further back, Big London, his mighty muscles concealed by his own aba, trailed along, watching with jungle-trained cunning the two men in the crowd ahead.

CHAPTER IV

The marketplaces of the East teem with gossip, and stories are told over the buying of leather or the selling of fruit or in the harems.

To hear them, many an intelligence officer would pay a full year's salary.

During the morning, Ponga Jim had heard much. Now, in his simple disguise and with his easy, natural flow of Arabic, he heard more. A discreet comment or two added to his information.

Several points held his interest. If the Nazis were behind the mysterious killings of the key men who had been murdered here, and if they owned the mystery warship, why had Ambrose Carter been killed, known as he was to favor Hitler? And what had he been doing in Egypt?

Who was the man who had been shot aboard the *Semiramis*? Where had he obtained the scarab ring? Why did he want to talk to Ponga Jim and no one else? And what was his connection with the girl, Zara Hammedan?

And last but not least, what could Ponga Jim Mayo possibly know that the enemy might fear?

Whatever it was, it had to be something he had known before he left Africa, several years before. There seemed only one answer to that. He would have to go over all his African experience in his mind, recalling each fact, each incident, each person. Somewhere he would find a clue.

In the meanwhile, he would have to avoid the police and even more, the killers who would be sure to be on his trail. The card that had been found on the dead man, the card bearing the name of Zara Hammedan, was the only good lead Ponga Jim had, and to Zara Hammedan he would go.

He had already learned that she lived in the Ramleh section of Alexandria. So at eight o'clock, moving up through the trees, Ponga Jim looked up at the Moorish palace that was Zara Hammedan's home. There were no windows on the lower floor; just a high, blank wall of stucco. Above that, the second floor projected over the narrow alley on either side of the house, and there were many windows, all brilliantly lighted.

A limousine rolled up to the entrance, and two men in evening dress got out. For an instant the light touched the face of one of them. He was Nathan Demarest!

As other cars began to arrive, Ponga Jim studied the house thoughtfully. Had there been no crowd he would have shed his disguise, approached the house, and sent his own name to the lady. But now—

Keeping under the cypress trees, he worked down along the alley. At one place the branches of a huge tree reached out toward the window opposite it. Ponga Jim caught a branch and swung himself into the tree with the agility of a monkey. Creeping out along the branch, he glanced through the window into a bedroom, obviously a woman's room. At the moment, it was empty.

The window was barred, and the heavy bars were welded together and set into steel slides in the window casing. Ponga Jim crept farther along the branch, a big one that had been cut off when it touched the house. Balancing himself, he tested the bars. Almost noiselessly, they lifted when he strained.

They wouldn't weigh a bit under eighty pounds, and it was an awkward lift. Looking about, he found a fair-sized branch and cut it off with his seaman's clasp knife. Then, leaning far out, he worked the set of bars up and propped the stick beneath them.

It was quite dark, and in the dim light Ponga Jim could see nothing beneath him. Once, he thought he detected a movement, but when he waited, there was no more movement, no sound. He pushed the window open with his foot and slipped through the window.

Below, in the darkness, the jungle-keen ears of Big London, who had been watching Ponga Jim slowly working the bars up, had heard a soft step. He faded into the brush as softly as a big cat. A man slid slowly from the dark and glanced around, trying to place the black man, and then slid a knife from his sleeve. And as Ponga Jim leaned far out toward the window, he drew the knife back to throw.

A huge black hand closed around his throat, and he was fairly jerked from his feet. Struggling, he tried to use the knife, but it was plucked from his nerveless fingers by the big black. Before the man knew what was happening, he was neatly trussed hand and foot and then gagged.

Ponga Jim gently closed the window behind him and glanced around. There was a faint perfume in the room. He crossed to the dressing table and slid open a drawer. Inside were some letters. He had started to glance over them when a voice in the hall startled him. Instantly, he dropped the packet into the drawer and stepped quickly across the room and into a closet.

The door opened and a woman came in. Or rather a girl, followed by a maid. Her hair was black, and her eyes were large, and slightly oblique. Her white evening gown fitted her like a dream and revealed rather than concealed her slender, curved figure.

She wore a simple jade necklace that Ponga Jim could see was very old. Standing in the darkness, he watched through the crack of the closet door, fearful that the maid might come to the closet.

Zara Hammedan, for it was obviously she, glanced up once, straight at the door behind which he stood. Then the maid started across the room toward him.

"No, Miriam," Zara said suddenly, "just leave the things. I'll take care of them. You may go now. If anyone asks for me, tell them I'll be down shortly."

The maid stepped from the room and drew the door closed. Zara touched her hair lightly and then put her hand in a drawer and lifted a small, but businesslike automatic. Then she looked at the closet door.

"You may come out now," she said evenly, "but be careful! You should clean the sand from your shoes."

Ponga Jim Mayo pushed the door open and stepped out, closing it behind him.

"You," he said smiling, "are a smart girl."

"Who are you?" she demanded. Her face showed no emotion, but he was struck again by its vivid beauty.

"I am a man who found another man murdered in his cabin," Ponga Jim said quietly, "and that man had your name written on a card that was in his pocket. So I came to you."

"You choose an odd way of presenting yourself," Zara said. "Who was this man?"

"I do not know," Jim said. "He came to see me, and in his pocket was a ring with an emerald scarab."

She caught her breath.

"When did this happen?"

"Shortly after midnight. The man was shot by someone using a silencer from across the street. So far the police know nothing about the murder. Or about the ring or your name."

"Why did I not know of this?" she asked. "It seems—"

"One of your present guests knows," Ponga Jim said. "Nathan Demarest."

"He?" She stared at him wide-eyed. "But who are you?"

He smiled. "I'm Jim Mayo," he said.

"Oh!" she rose. "I have heard of you. You came here, then, to learn about the murdered man?"

"Partly." He sat down and took off the headcloth. "The rest is to find what he wanted to tell me, where he got that ring, and what you know about a certain warship now in the Red Sea. Also, what there is to this Moslem movement you're heading."

She smiled at him. "What makes you think all of these questions have anything to do with me?"

"I know they have," he said. "And I've got to know the answers, because somebody's trying to kill me. I was attacked last night, shoved in the harbor by a killer."

"You?" she exclaimed. "Was it a man with a scar across his nose?"

"Sure," Ponga Jim said. "That's him." He took a cigarette from a sandalwood box and lit it. Then he handed it to her. "A friend of yours?"

"No!" The loathing in her voice was plain. "But the man was a pearl diver from Kuwait. I don't see how——"

"How I got away? I've done some diving myself, lady, and a lot of fighting. Now give. What's this all about?"

"I can't tell you," Zara said. "Only—if you want to live, take your ship and leave Egypt, and don't ever come back!"

"That's not hospitality," he said, grinning, "especially from a beautiful girl. No, I'm not leaving. I've been warned before and threatened before. I've as healthy a respect for my own hide as the next man, but never have found you could dodge trouble by running. My way is to meet it halfway. Now somebody wants my hide. I'd like to see the guy. I'd like to see what he wants and if he knows how to get it."

"He does. And I'll tell you nothing but this—the dead man was Rudolf Burne, and you are marked for death because of three things. You beat a man playing poker once who never was beaten before or since, you know where the emerald ring came from, and you know where the warship is!"

"*I* do?" Ponga Jim stared. "But——"

"You'll have to go now!" Zara said suddenly, her eyes wide. "Quick! There's someone coming!"

He hurried to the window. She stood behind him, biting her lip. Suddenly he realized she was trembling with fear.

"Go!" she insisted. "Quickly!"

"Sure." He slid open the window and put a leg over the sill. "But never let it be said that Jim Mayo failed to say good-bye." Slipping one arm around Zara's waist, he kissed her before she could draw back. "Goodnight," said Ponga Jim. "I'll be seeing you!"

As the steel grate slid into place, he heard the door open. Then he was back in the foliage of the tree and in a matter of seconds had slid to the ground.

"Now," he told himself, "I'll——"

At a movement behind him he whirled, but something crashed down on his head with stunning force. There was an instant of blinding pain when he struggled to fight back the wave of darkness sweeping over him, then another blow, and he plunged forward into a limitless void.

CHAPTER V

When Ponga Jim's eyes opened he was lying on his back in almost total darkness. A thin ray of light from a crack overhead tried feebly to penetrate the gloom. He tried to sit up, only to find he was bound hand and foot and very securely.

His head throbbed with agony, and the tightly bound ropes made his hands numb. After an instant of futile effort, he lay still, letting his eyes rove the darkness. The place had rock walls, he could see—one wall at least. There seemed to be some kind of inscriptions or paintings on the wall, but he couldn't make them out.

The air was dry, and when he stirred a powdery dust lifted from the floor.

Lying in the darkness he tried to assemble his thoughts. Most of all there hammered at his brain the insistent reminder that he, himself, knew the answers to the puzzling questions that had brought him to this situation. Zara had told him that he knew the man behind the scenes, where the ship was, and where the ring had come from.

But there was something else—a memory he couldn't place, a sensation of lying in the bottom of a boat and hearing voices. Now he slowly pieced together that memory, scowling with effort to force the thought back to consciousness. In that swaying darkness he half remembered, with spray on his face and damp boards against his back, he seemed to have heard a guttural voice saying in triumph:

"That will be the biggest convoy of all! Forty ships, and they are helpless before the *Khamsin*."

Then another voice that had muttered, "And only two days to wait!"

Ponga Jim Mayo lay still, his head throbbing. For the first time in a life of fierce brawls, barroom brannigans, gunfights, and war on land and sea, he was helpless. Not only was he imprisoned somewhere far from civilization, he was sure, but he was bound so tightly that even to wriggle seemed impossible. The feeling came over him that he was not just imprisoned. He had been carried here to die.

His mind sorted out his memories. The warship was in the Red Sea. Zara had told him that something in his own past, something he had forgotten but another remembered, linked him with the base of the warship.

Carefully, trying to neglect nothing, he tried to recall that long, narrow, reef-strewn sea of milky, sickly water. He remembered the sandstorms sweeping across the sea from the desert, the days of endless calm and impossible heat when the thermometer soared past one hundred and thirty degrees.

He remembered rocky islets and endless, jagged coral teeth ready to tear the bottom from a ship, sandy shores where desert tribesmen lurked, ready to raid and pillage any helpless ship, pirates now as they had been ages ago in Solomon's time.

And along those mountainous, volcanic shores where no rain fell were ruins—ruins of the heyday of Mohammed, of Solomon, of Pharaohs; ruins whose names and origins were lost in the mists of antiquity. No like area in all the world has so many ruined cities as the shores of the Red Sea and the edge of Arabia where it faces the Indian Ocean.

Even in Mokha, once the center of the coffee trade, in 1824 a city of twenty thousand inhabitants with a shifting population that made it much larger, only two or three hundred Somalis, Arabs, and Jews now lived in ruined houses of stone, crawling like animals in rags from their lairs, cowardly and abject, but ready to fight like demons if need be. Mokha was now only a memory, with its streets heaped with debris, its stone piers crumbling into the stagnant, soupy sea.

Yet somewhere along the shores of the Red Sea was a base. A base that must be well equipped and fitted for at least minor repairs, with tanks filled with water and fuel oil. But where?

His memory searched around Hanish Island, around many a *Ghubbet* and *khor,* down the Masira Channel and past Ras Markaz, across the dreaded Rakka shoals and up to Jiddah town, where the Tomb of Eve with its wide, white dome stands among the old windmills.

Somewhere in that heat, sand, and desolate emptiness was the base for the battleship of mystery he had seen.

Now Europe, Asia, and even America were at war, and in the Near East the bazaars were rife with whispers of intrigue, with stories of impending rebellion, of the gathering desert tribes, of restlessness along the Tihama, of gatherings in the Druse hills. And then out of the night— murder.

Hard-bitten old General McKnight, who knew the East as few men did—murdered, poisoned with his own sherry. And Norfolk, shrewd criminal investigator, stabbed suddenly on a dark street. One by one the men who could fight this new evil, this strange, growing power, one by one they were dying, murdered by unseen hands at the direction of a man who sat far behind the scenes pulling the strings upon which puppets moved to kill.

Ponga Jim stirred restlessly. That was the horror of it, to know that he knew the clue, that somewhere down the chaotic background of his past was the knowledge that could end all this killing here.

Suddenly, he stiffened. There had been a movement, a sly, slithering sound. And for the first time, he became conscious of a peculiar odor in the place. His eyes had gradually grown accustomed to the dim light, and now, with a skin-crawling horror, he saw!

On a heap of broken stone and piled earthen jars was a huge snake, lifting its ugly flat head and looking toward him! His throat constricting with terror, Ponga Jim's eyes roved again. And now that he could distinguish things better and in the dim vagueness could see grotesque figures, of carts, animals, and workmen painted on the walls, he knew he was in a tomb! He was lying where a sarcophagus once had lain, on a stone table probably three or four feet above the floor.

TURNING HIS HEAD, he could see the dim outlines of great coils, more snakes. And still more.

He looked up, cold sweat breaking out on his forehead, and it dawned upon him what had been done. Above, a loosely fitted stone slab had been moved back, and his body had been lowered into this old tomb. Soon he would fall off the table to the floor, and the snakes would bite. Or he would die of thirst or of starvation.

Ponga Jim felt with his feet toward the edge of the stone table. He got his ankles over, and a thrill went through him as what he had hoped proved true. The edge of the stone slab on which he lay was clean-cut, sharp!

Hooking his ankles over the edge, he began to saw. It would take a long time, but it would have to be. A snake moved, rearing its head to stare, but he worked on as sweat soaked his clothing.

It seemed that hours passed, but still he worked, on and on. Above him, the light grew dim and darkness closed down.

Suddenly, dust spilled in his face, and above him he heard a grating as of stone on stone. He looked up, and above him was a square of sky and stars, blotted out suddenly by an enormous shape.

"Captain Jim?" The voice was husky with effort. "You down there, Captain?"

"You're right I am!" Ponga Jim's voice was hoarse with relief. "Watch it! I'm tied hand and foot, and this place is crawling with snakes. Get a line and rig a hook on it."

"Captain, they ain't no more line up here than there's nothin'! This here place is nothing but rock and sand. Ain't no fit place for no snake even."

"Wait!"

In desperation, Ponga Jim hacked viciously at the edge of the slab and suddenly felt the weakened strands give. He hacked again, kicking downward against the stone edge, sawing, jerking against the corner.

The snakes were stirring restlessly now. He knew what would happen if one struck him. Within an instant he would be bitten a hundred times. Snakes, like rats and men, can be gang fighters.

But the rope fell loose.

He crawled to his feet, staggered, and almost toppled from the table into the crawling mass below.

Ponga Jim's hands were bound, but even if they had not been it was a good ten feet to the hole above.

"London," he called, "scout around and find something to haul me out of here or I'll start knotting these snakes together. If I do I swear I'll toss you the hot end to hold!"

"Don't you be doing that!" Big London said hastily. "I'll see what I can find."

Ponga Jim bent over, working his slender hips between the circle of his arms and bound wrists. Once he had them down over his hips he stepped back through the circle and straightened up, his arms in front of him. Then he began working at the knot with his teeth. It was a matter of minutes until the knots were untied.

Shaking the ropes loose, he gathered up the pieces. He had about eight feet of rope; a bit less when he had knotted the two together with a sheet bend.

There was sound above him.

"Captain"—Big London's voice was worried—"I reckon you going to have to start working on them snakes. They ain't nothing up here like no rope."

"Lie down!" Ponga Jim said, "and catch this rope! I'll toss it up, you take a good hold, and then I'm climbing. And you better not let go!"

"You just leave it to London, Captain," the black man assured him. "I'll not let go!"

Big London caught the rope deftly. Then Ponga Jim went up, hand over hand. When he reached Big London's hands, he grabbed the big man's wrist. London let go of the rope and caught him. In a few seconds he was standing in the open air.

"Thanks, pal!" Ponga Jim said fervently. "I've been in some spots, but that one—"

"Captain," Big London said, "we better be going. This is clean across the Gulf of Suez and way down the coast. They spent the best part of the night and morning coming down here."

Ponga Jim looked around. It was bright moonlight.

"Is there a high cliff right over there?" He pointed toward the southeast. "One that drops off into the water? And is there a black hill right over there?"

"Sure is, Captain," Big London said. "I took me that black hill for a landmark. I smuggled myself away on their boat, hoping they'd leave one man alone so I could take over, but they never. Then I waited, hid out till they took you ashore. I wanted to follow, but they got clean away with three men with guns still on the boat. I had to slip over into the water when they started again, swim ashore, and then trail you up here."

"You did a good job." Ponga Jim chuckled. "The joke is on them. This place is the Ras Muhammed, the tip of Sinai Peninsula, and right over there, not three miles from here, in one of the neatest little bays in this area, is the *Semiramis!*"

An hour and a little more passed before they reached the shore of the little inlet surrounded by high cliffs. At a cleft in the rock they made their way down to a beach of black sand and decomposed coral. The freighter was anchored, a dark blotch, not a hundred yards offshore. At Ponga Jim's shout, a boat was hastily lowered.

No sooner had Ponga Jim reached the freighter than he called Brophy.

"Slug," he said, "get number five open and break out that amphibian. I want her tuned and ready to take off by daybreak This is going to be quick work."

He walked into the cabin, tossed off his clothes, and fell into his bunk. In seconds he was sound asleep.

CHAPTER VI

Four men and a woman sat in the spacious living room of Zara Hammedan's Ramleh residence. Zara's face was composed, and only her eyes showed a hint of the strain she was undergoing.

One of the men stood up. He was well over six feet and broad shouldered, and he moved with the ease of a big cat. There was a great deal of the cat about him—in his eyes, in the movements of his hands. His hair was black, but white at the temples, and his eyes were large and intensely black. His face was swarthy and his arched eyebrows heavy. There was about him something that spoke of a sense of power, of command, and in every word, every gesture, was an utter ruthlessness.

"You see, gentlemen?" he said lightly. "Our plans move swiftly. There was a momentary danger, but Captain Mayo has been taken care of. He was dropped into the Tomb of the Snakes this morning. By this time he has been dead for hours. By tomorrow noon the convoy will be well into the Red Sea. It carries fifty thousand soldiers, many planes, much petrol, and much ammunition. By tomorrow at dark that convoy will be completely destroyed. As always, there will be no survivors.

SOUTH OF SUEZ 363

"And tomorrow night? General Kernan and Major Arnold will be shot down. Within an hour a reign of terror will begin in Cairo, Alexandria, Port Said, Suez, Beirut, Damascus, Baghdad, and Aleppo. By tomorrow night at midnight, the British will be leaderless in the Near East. Rebellion will break out." The man paused. "Then we will take over."

"I do not like it." The man who spoke was slender and bald, and his small eyes were shrewd. "It is not practical. And that Ponga Jim was disposed of in too theatrical a manner. He should have been shot. I would never leave such a man alive."

"The man is just a man." The imperious words of the tall man were smooth, cold. "One would think, Herr Heittn, that you thought him supernatural."

Heittn smiled thinly. "I know this man," he said shortly. "Did I not use every means to dispose of him? Did he not kill my brother? Did he not handle Count Kull like he was a child?"

"Strength is not enough," the tall man said. "It takes brains!"

"You got something there, Chief," one of the other men said. His jaw was heavy, his nose flat. He looked like a good heavyweight boxer. "But I been hearing about this guy Mayo. He's a tough cookie."

"But I know how to handle 'tough cookies,' Mullens," the tall man assured. "You have only to handle your end. You have your men ready?"

"You bet," Mullens said. "I got four of the best rodmen that ever slung a heater. All of 'em with tommy guns. We'll mow your pals Kernan and Arnold down like they were dummies."

"Then we're all ready. You're sure about the time, Demarest?"

"Yes," said Demarest. "The time is right. Everything will move perfectly. The destruction of this convoy, the fourth consecutive convoy to be totally destroyed, will wreck the troops' morale. A whispering campaign has begun. Kernan cannot be replaced. He knows the East too well."

Heittn was watching the tall man steadily, his eyes curious.

"I don't understand your stake in this, Theron," he said abruptly. "What is it you want? You are not German. You are not just an adventurer. I do not understand."

"No reason why you should, Herr Heittn," the man called Theron snapped. "You have a task to do. You will do it. What you think or do not think is of no interest to me if your task is well done."

Zara arose and excused herself. Theron's eyes followed her as she left the room. They were cold, curious.

"What of her?" Demarest asked. "You are sure of her?"

"I will be responsible for her, Demarest. She has too much power among the Arabs not to be of value to us. But she must be kept with us always."

The group broke up. Heittn was first to leave. He took his hat and started for the door, then glanced swiftly around, and with surprising speed darted up the stairs toward Zara's room. There he tapped lightly on the door.

It opened at once, and before Zara could speak, Heittn slipped into the room. He looked at the girl narrowly.

"What do you want?" she demanded.

The German looked down at the small automatic in her hand.

"You will not need that, Fräulein," he said gently. "What I want is of interest to us both. I want to know about *him*." He pointed downward. "Can we trust him? What does he want? Who is he?"

Zara's face paled. She glanced toward the door. It was locked. She crossed to the window, started to close it, and then caught her breath. The steel bars were gone!

But when she turned, her face was composed.

"I know no more than you, Herr Heittn," she said calmly, "except he seems to have unlimited funds. Also, he is ambitious."

Heittn nodded. "Ah!" he said seriously. "That is what I have seen, Fräulein. Too ambitious. And he has power, too much power. Sometimes"—he shook his head worriedly—"I think he is beyond us all, that man. He is not a National Socialist, yet he is too strong with the party for me."

"But what could he do?" Zara protested.

"Do? A strong man with money, ambition, and courage—what can he not do in such times as these? Nations are rising and falling; men are discouraged, afraid. They will look anywhere for shelter. The weak admire the strong, and that one, he is strong. He is cruel. I admit it, Fräulein. I am afraid of him!"

Casually Zara Hammedan lighted a cigarette. Her eyes strayed toward the closet door, now closed. She frowned a little. The bars from the window had been slid up out of sight again, and that could mean but one thing. Ponga Jim Mayo was somewhere in the house.

She looked at the German shrewdly. "Herr Heittn, your government does not appeal to me, you know that. But I would even prefer the dictatorship of Nazi Germany to what would follow the success of these schemes in the Near East! I do not know more about that man than you do, but I do know that Captain Mayo knew, or knows, something that he does not wish anyone to know."

"And Mayo is dead," Heittn said slowly.

"Perhaps." Zara flicked the ash from her cigarette. "You had better go, Herr Heittn. It grows late."

The Nazi turned to the door and then glanced around.

"I go, but I have a plan to make our friend below be a bit more reasonable." He smiled. *"Guten Abend, Fräulein!"*

As Heittn walked swiftly down the hall he glanced over the stairs, but no one was in sight. With a quick smile, Heittn went down the carpeted stairs. He had reached the door when a voice froze him in his tracks. Something in the low, even tone sent a chill up his spine. He turned slowly.

Theron stood in the shadow near the door from the wide living room. The light fell across his face. There was something regal in his appearance. In his right hand, he held a Luger.

"I thought you left us, Herr Heittn?" he said coldly. "I do not like spies!"

"Spies?" Heittn shrugged. "Come, come, Theron! That is hardly the term. I went up to see Miss Hammedan about—"

"But searched my room in the meantime, is that it? Give me that blueprint, Herr Heittn. Give it to me, at once!"

"Blueprint?" the Nazi was puzzled. "I don't understand."

Above in the darkness, Zara slipped from her room and looked down. In her hand was an automatic. She hesitated and then lifted it slowly.

"Don't!"

A hand closed over her wrist, and the voice that spoke to her was low. Demarest stepped up beside her.

"Not now," he said. "Without him, nothing would work. He holds all the strings. The whole plot would be useless and we would be exposed."

In the silence they could hear the words that were being spoken at the front door.

"All right, Herr Heittn," Theron was saying. "It does not matter. But if the blueprint were to leave this house, it would matter."

The sound of the automatic was flat and ugly in the dim hallway. Heittn's face went sick, and the man stepped back, two short steps. Then he sat down, abruptly, with a thin trickle of blood coming from the hole over his heart.

Her face deathly pale, Zara Hammedan turned abruptly and went to her room. Nathan Demarest glanced after her and then returned to his own room.

Zara closed the door and then turned. In the dim light the man sitting on the bed was plainly visible. His peaked cap lay beside him, and he still wore the faded khaki suit and woven leather sandals. She could see the butt of his automatic under the edge of his coat.

"You—you must go quickly!" she protested. "He killed Herr Heittn. He will stop at nothing now!"

Ponga Jim lifted an eyebrow. "What I want to know is—who is he?"

"Theron," she whispered. "He will be coming up, too, wanting to know what Heittn said to me. Go—quickly!"

Ponga Jim's eyes were bright.

"Theron. That answers a lot of things!" He stepped to the window, put a foot over the sill, and reached for the thick branch. "So long, beautiful. Be seeing you!"

CHAPTER VII

Ponga Jim had reached the ground and was starting to slip back into the trees when he saw them. Four men closing in on him.

He knew what that meant, and he didn't hesitate. He jumped the nearest one, hooking a left short and hard to the man's head. It hit with a *plop,* and the man's head flew back. He dropped like a sack of meal.

A shot clipped by his head, and Ponga Jim dropped into a crouch as his own gun came out. The big automatic roared. Once—twice—three times.

Two men dropped, a third screamed shrilly and staggered back into the building. Holding his left shoulder, Ponga Jim ran. He dodged through the trees with bullets clipping the leaves about him, ducked into an alley, and then crossed into another street. A car was waiting with the motor running. He jumped in.

"Move!" he said, and Sakim let the car into gear and stepped on the gas.

Ponga Jim glanced at his watch. It was three A.M. At noon the convoy would be attacked, and he had until then, and until then only. It was going to be nip and tuck if he made it.

He felt sick. Fifty thousand soldiers coming up the Red Sea toward Suez, fifty thousand Anzacs to strengthen the Army of the Nile. He knew the plot now. What he had overheard and what he had found in his ransacking of Theron's room had told him the whole story.

Native mobs running riot in the streets, men dying by the thousand—Kernan, Arnold, all of them.

The car slowed up as it neared the American Export Line's office on the Rue Fouad. A man stepped from the shadows, and the car whined to a halt. Major Arnold hit the running board with a jump.

"Jim! What's happened?" Arnold's face was tense. "When Selim found me he said all calamity was to break loose today. What do you know?"

As the car raced across town, Ponga Jim told his story quickly and concisely.

"Ptolemais Theron is the man behind it all," he said. "He's a bad one, William! I've known of him for years. He and I played poker once with two other men in the place of Mahr-el-din in the Kasbah. Ring Wallace was there and Ski Jorgenson. Theron had just sidestepped a term on the breakwater for illicit diamond buying and was working on a deal to sell a lot of world war rifles to the Riffs. We were talking of the Red Sea, and Ski—"

Ponga Jim stopped short, and his face went blank.

"By heaven, William, I've got it!"

"Got what?" Arnold's face was tight, stiff.

"William"—Ponga Jim's voice was low with emotion—"Ski Jorgenson had been working a salvage job in the Gulf of Aqaba, near Tirān Island. He told us of finding some huge caverns under the cliffs of the islands— one room five hundred yards long, with a dozen chambers opening off from it, and water in that main chamber. He told us about what a swell smuggler's hangout it would be. And the entrance is deep. A ship could come and go—if it had no masts!"

"You mean that's the base of that mystery battlewagon?" Arnold's face lit up. "By the Lord Harry, if it is we'll blast the place in on them!"

"That's the base. Theron wanted me killed because I knew too much. When Ski told about the caverns he also told some stuff about the ancient tombs at Adulis, and the chances are Theron's been robbing them for the gold to put this deal over. That would be where Rudolf Burne got the emerald ring he had. Probably he was in on the deal, got cold feet, and came to me because he knew I wouldn't turn him over to the police. But he was shot before he could talk."

The car slid to a halt, and Arnold dropped out.

"Don't worry about us," he said drily. "We'll be all set."

"Wait!" Ponga Jim put a hand on Arnold's arm. "Don't say a thing about yourselves—I mean you and General Kernan. I've already arranged for that. I'm going to have Selim, Sakim, Big London, and Longboy standing by. They'll get the men who'll be sent to kill you.

"Don't trust anyone. Somebody high up is in this, somebody close to you." He paused. "Oh, yes! Remember Carter? He built the *Khamsin*. Built the plant for it for the Nazis."

"Okay." Arnold smiled suddenly and held out his hand. "I don't know what you've got up your sleeve, but good luck. And in case something slips up—it's been a grand fight!"

Ponga Jim grinned. "Listen, pal. Just to keep the record straight. Keep Zara Hammedan undercover. She means well, and—"

"Who?" William grabbed Ponga Jim's arm. "Why, you didn't mention her! Where did you—"

"Shh!" Mayo said, grinning. "It's late, William, and you'll wake up the neighbors. Zara? Oh, we're just like that!" He held up two fingers. "A honey, isn't she?"

Selim stepped on the gas.

"I hope you get shot!" Arnold yelled after him.

TIRĀN ISLAND, at the southern end of the Gulf of Aqaba, is six and a half miles long and in the south part is about five miles wide. Chisholm Point is steep and cliffy, but Johnson Point, the northwest tip of the island, is low and flat, of sand and dead coral. South of the point, two flat, sandy beaches afford good landing, but the coast elsewhere consists of undercut coral cliffs.

It lacked but a little of daylight when Ponga Jim Mayo stepped ashore on one of those sandy beaches. Slug Brophy scowled at him in the vague light.

"I don't like it, Skipper. I don't like shooting at no ship when you're aboard it. And if they catch you they'll fill you so full of lead you'll sink clean through to China."

"Forget it," said Mayo. "I've got my job to do—you've got yours. Have the boats and life rafts ready, alright? We've got one chance in a million that the *Semiramis* will come out of this, but a chance. All I'm figuring on is crippling the *Khamsin*—that's the name of the mystery battleship—so she can't move fast. Then maybe she can be kept busy until the convoy escapes. Have the sub over right away. Jeff and Hifty from the engine room can handle it."

The boat shoved off into the darkness, and Ponga Jim climbed the gradually shelving beach. He paused there, looking over the island: sand, decomposed coral, and rock, with here and there some grass. He was going on a memory of what Ski Jorgenson had said several years before, that there was an opening of the cave to the island itself, aside from the huge mouth that opened into the gulf.

He found it by sheer good luck, after he had looked for an hour. It was already daylight when he saw the small hole Ski had mentioned. Surprisingly, there was no one near it. He slid through and found himself in a passage where he could stand erect. He hurried, hesitated at a branching passage, and then chose the larger. It opened into the huge cavern so suddenly that he almost walked right out into the open.

Even so, he stopped in his tracks, staring. He stood in the darkness at one side of a huge cavern, its domed roof lost in the shadows overhead. But what held his gaze was the warship.

It was at least five hundred feet long, painted black, but glistening with metallic luster. The hull seemed to be built like that of any battleship, but above deck the ship was covered with a turtleshell covering. There were two turrets forward and one aft, each looking much like slightly less than half a ball where the rounded surface lifted above the shell. The turrets, obviously, could turn to cover any point from dead ahead to a complete right angle on either side.

Between, in three tiers, like guns in a fort, were smaller guns. Nowhere on the ship was there any exposed deck, any open space. The ship was completely covered with a steel housing from stem to stern.

There were lights around the ship, and men working. Ponga Jim could hear the clangor of metal and could see a great moving crane, and obviously the branch caverns were fitted with shops for the building and upkeep of ships.

Keeping in the shadows, Ponga Jim worked his way to a place where the cavern narrowed. His plan was to get aboard and keep the quarter pint of nitroglycerine he had intact—which meant keeping himself intact.

Dozens of men were working and sweating. Armed guards patrolled the area near the ship, and at any moment Ponga Jim knew he might be seen. Warily, he dodged behind a pile of oil drums, waiting.

The German who came around the corner of the pile came without any warning, and Ponga Jim looked up to see the man staring at him. He saw the man's eyes widen, saw his mouth open, and then Ponga Jim took a chance and smashed a right hand into the man's belly. If the fellow knocked him down with that nitro in his pocket—

The big German's breath was knocked out of him, but he swung a wicked punch while trying to yell. And somehow he got out a knife. Mayo ducked the punch, and smashed both hands into the man's wind, but then the knife came down in a vicious stabbing cut. Ponga Jim started to duck, but the knife struck him, and he felt the blade bury itself in his side. He smashed his fist into the German's throat, smashed and smashed again.

Fiercely, in darkness and silence, their breath coming in great gasps, the two fought. A terrific punch rocked Ponga Jim's head, and that smoky taste when rocked by a bad one came into his mouth. Then he smashed another punch to the Nazi's windpipe and hit him hard across the Adam's apple with the edge of his hand. The German went down, and Ponga Jim bent over him, slugging him again.

There was no choice. Even now if the man were found, they would search and Ponga Jim would die. And not only he would die, but fifty thousand soldiers would die, men would die in Alexandria, Cairo, and Port Said; for the news of the attacked convey was to be the signal for the beginning of the slaughter. Innocent people would die and brave men. Worse, a tyrant as evil as Hitler would come to power here in the Near East, a killer as ruthless as a shark of the sea, as remorseless as a slinking tiger.

The Nazi sank at Ponga Jim's feet. Behind the piled drums as they were, they had remained unseen. He picked the big German up and felt a white-hot streak of agony along his side.

Remembering a huge crack in the cavern floor back about fifty feet, he carried the man over to it and dropped him in. He did not hear the body strike bottom.

"Sorry, pal," he muttered, "but this is war. It was you or them."

Creeping back, he studied the ship. There was no activity in front of him. That meant a chance. He walked out of the shadow and calmly went up the gangway into the ship. A man glanced up, but at the distance Ponga Jim must have looked like any other officer, for the man went on with his work.

Ponga Jim found himself in an electrically lighted tunnel. He could see the amazingly thick steel of the ship's hull as he went forward, walking fast. He passed several doors until he got well forward. Then he went into a storeroom.

He found a place secure from observation, slipped off his coat, and taking a deep breath, twisted to look at the wound. It had gone into the muscle back of his ribs from front to back. He plugged the wound and then tried to relax.

CHAPTER VIII

It was the throb of engines that awakened Ponga Jim. Dimly he was conscious they had been going for some time. By the feel of the ship he knew they were in open water.

Timing was important. The convoy's attempted destruction would begin it. Ponga Jim rolled back the sacks and stepped out into the storeroom. He glanced at his wristwatch. It was early yet.

He went to a port and glanced out. The sea was calm, only white around the coral. The sun was hot and the air clear except for the dancing heat waves over the rocky shore.

He looked again, and his hands gripped the rim of the port. He felt his heart give a great leap. They were nearing Gordon Reef in the Strait of Tirān! He saw the small, iron ship plainly visible on the rocks of the reef; the wreck had been there so long it was hardly noticed anymore.

But today it meant more. Today, if all went well, a pocket submarine of a hundred tons would be lying there, waiting—the submarine he had captured in the Well of the Unholy Light, on Halmahera.

He was watching, yet even then he could just barely see the ripple of foam when the sub's periscope lifted. In his ears he could hear words as though he were there himself. He could hear Jeff speaking to his one-man crew: "Fire one!" Then, after a few seconds, "Fire two!"

Ponga Jim saw the white streak of a torpedo and heard someone sing out above; then he saw the second streak. The big warship was jarred with a terrific explosion and then a second or two later, with a second. A shell crashed in the water only dozens of feet from the tiny sub. But the periscope was gone now.

Ponga Jim gripped his hands until the fingernails bit into his palms. How much damage had been done? Would Jeff and Hifty get away? Thank God the warship had no destroyer screen to pursue and drop depth bombs.

There was shouting forward, and he could feel the ship slowing down. He set his jaw. Now it was up to him. Now he would do what he came for and end this scourge of the sea once and for all.

He found a uniform in the pile of junk in the storeroom and crawled into it. Then he stepped out into the passage again.

No one seemed to notice him. Men were running and shouting in the steel tunnel. He joined those hurrying men. He gathered that the first torpedo had hit right where he had wanted it to. From the stolen blueprint, he had known that the extreme bow and stern of the warship were but thinly armored. Elsewhere, twenty inches of steel protected the waterline. The second fish had wasted itself against that steel bulwark.

As he dashed forward, a man passed him, and Ponga Jim saw a startled look come into the man's face. The fellow stopped, and Ponga Jim ducked into the passage leading down. A moment later he heard a man yelling, and swore viciously. To be discovered now!

At a breakneck pace he went down the steel ladder. Water was pouring in through the side into one of the blisters below. Into two of them. He heard a petty officer assuring another that the damage was localized, that the *Khamsin* would be slowed a little, but was in no danger of sinking.

Above them, Ponga Jim heard a shouted order. He ducked toward a steel door in the bulkhead. The petty officer shouted at him in German, but he plunged through. Then he stopped and placed the bottle of nitro-gylcerine against the steel bulkhead.

THE DOOR SWUNG OPEN again, and Ponga Jim flattened against the bulkhead. Men dashed through. On impulse, Ponga Jim stooped, caught up the bottle and sprang back through the door and then ran for the ladder. A man shouted and grabbed at him, but he swung viciously and knocked the man sprawling into a corner. Another man leaped at him with a spanner, and Ponga Jim scrambled up the ladder and then wheeled and hurled the bottle down the hatch near the damaged side of the ship!

There was a terrific blast of white flame, shot through with crimson. Ponga Jim felt himself seized as though by a giant hand and hurled against the wall. He went down with a jangle of bells in his head, and above him he could hear the roar of guns, the sound of shells bursting, and a fearful roaring in his head. . . .

Ponga Jim fought back to consciousness to find himself lying on some burst sacks. Struggling to get to his knees, he realized the deck was canted forward.

There was blood all over him. He turned, and sickened at the sight that met his eyes. The deck was covered with blood, and a half dozen men lay around him, their bodies torn and bloody. He crawled to the wall, pulled himself up, and glanced down into the yawning chasm where he had thrown the nitro.

The compartment was full of water, and it was still rising, slowly but surely. He started aft, feeling his way along the steel tunnel in the dark.

His head throbbed, and something was wrong with one of his legs. He had an awful feeling that part of it was gone, but he struggled along, conscious of the steady burning in his side.

The world was full of thunder, and he could hear the heavy crash of the mighty eighteen-inch guns above him. He was thankful he had stuffed his ears with cotton before starting this. He had known there would be a battle. But were they shelling the convoy? He fought his way to a port and wiping the blood from his eyes, stared out.

In a kind of madness he saw, across the world of smoke and flame, the ugly stern of the old *Semiramis*. Her rusty sides were scarred with red lead, but the 5.9s were firing steadily.

With a stretch of coral reef between the *Semiramis* and the warship, and the freighter itself almost out of sight in the deep, high-walled inlet where it had been concealed, she presented a small target and one that called for careful firing. It was too close for the big guns and in an awkward position for the smaller guns. Gunner Millan, he saw, was doing just what he had been told to do. All of the 5.9s were aimed at one spot on the bow of the *Khamsin* and were pounding away remorselessly.

But the *Khamsin* was not staying to fight. The convoy was still to be attacked, and crippled though the mystery battlewagon was, she had only to get out into the sea to bring those big eighteen-inch guns to bear on that convoy. She was injured, but proceeding as scheduled.

Clinging to the port, Ponga Jim heard an ominous roaring. Then he saw a V-shaped formation of bombing planes. The first one dipped and then another, and then the warship was roaring with exploding bombs. He turned from the port and started aft again.

Dazed, he staggered from side to side of the tunnel. He had done what he could. What remained was for the navy to do. He staggered forward, saw a steel door in the hull, and fell to his knees, clawing at the dogs. He got one loose and then another.

Suddenly there was a wild shout. A man was rushing toward him, his face twisted with fury. Nathan Demarest! He sprang at Ponga Jim Mayo, clawing for a knife. Mayo caught the dogs, pulled himself erect, and then stuck out his foot. Demarest was thrown off balance and went to his knees, but then he was up. Ponga Jim jerked another of the dogs loose and spun around, bracing himself for Demarest's charge.

The man flung himself forward, and Mayo started a punch. It landed, but Demarest struck him in the chest with a shoulder. The door gave suddenly behind them, and both crashed through and fell, turning over and over, into the water!

Vaguely, Ponga Jim was grateful for the warmth of the water and then for its coolness. He felt someone clawing at him, pushed him away, and then caught hold and kept pushing. Darkness swam nearer through the water, and he lost consciousness once more.

WHEN HIS EYES OPENED he stared up at a sort of net of steel, and when he tried to turn his head his neck was stiff as though he had taken a lot of punches. He tried to move, and someone said:

"Take it easy, mister."

He managed to get his head turned and saw a man in a British naval uniform standing by.

"What happened?" he asked.

"Everything's okay," the seaman said. "You're on the *Markland,* of Sydney. This is one of the convoy."

The seaman stuck his head out the door. "Tell the old man this guy is coming out of it," he yelled.

Almost at once a big, broad-shouldered man came through the door with a hand outstretched.

"Mayo!" he exclaimed. "Sink me for a lubber if I didn't get a start when they brought you over the side. You and that black man of yours!"

"What happened?" Ponga Jim asked. "How's the *Semiramis*?"

"Huh, you couldn't sink that old barge!" the captain roared. "Sure as my name's Brennan, you can't! But she's lost the starboard wing of her bridge, two guns are out of commission, there's a hole through the after deckhouse, and about ten feet of taffrail are blown away, but no men killed. Some shrapnel wounds. The sub got back safe."

The door pushed open, and Major Arnold came in.

"Hi, Jim!" He gripped Mayo's hand, grinning. "You did it again, darn you!"

"The *Khamsin*?"

"Still afloat, but the navy's after her. They are fighting a running battle toward Bab el Mandeb. But she's down by the head and badly hurt. She'll never get away. Everything else is under control. We got Theron. Your boys wiped out Mullens and his gang when they tried to get Kernan and me."

Arnold turned toward the door.

"General Kernan is here," he informed, "with Skelton. They want to see you. Skelton says he owes you an apology."

"Yeah?" Ponga Jim lifted himself on an elbow. "Listen, you—"

The door opened and General Kernan and Skelton came in. Skelton smiled.

"Fine work, Captain! We'll see you get a decoration for this."

Ponga Jim stared at him, his eyes cold. For an instant there was silence, and then Skelton's smile vanished, his eyes widened a little, and his muscles tensed.

"William," Ponga Jim said carefully, "arrest this man. He is a traitor. He was working hand in glove with Theron, and I have documentary evidence to prove it!"

"What?" Kernan roared. "Why, man, you're insane!"

Skelton's eyes narrowed as he stared at Ponga Jim. Then he sprang back suddenly, and there was a gun in his hand.

"No," he said tightly, "Theron told me someone stole some papers. Of course it's true! I've made fools of you all! And if it hadn't been for this thick-skulled sailor with his fool's luck, we'd have won, too! He's a great man, Theron is, a great man! Do you hear?" His voice rose to a scream and then cut off sharply. "But you three will die, anyway. You three—"

Big London's powerful black arm slipped through the door and around Skelton's throat. Then London jerked, and there was an ominous crack. He dropped Skelton's body.

"I didn't mean for to kill him, Captain," he said sheepishly. "But his neck was so little!"

"Who got me aboard here?" Jim said, ignoring the body.

Arnold swallowed. "Big London. He was coming behind in the small boat with two others as you had suggested when you said you'd unload as soon as possible. He dived in after you."

"Demarest?"

"Was that who you were fighting with?" Arnold frowned. "I had been watching him. I had the dope on him, but before I could have him arrested, he slipped away." He hesitated. "By the way, when we flew down to join the convoy, we brought somebody with us. She wants to see you."

"She?"

"Yes."

Jim looked toward the voice. Zara Hammedan was standing in the door.

"Are you surprised?"

"Surprised?" Ponga Jim looked up at Arnold with a grin. "William, can't you see the lady wants to be alone with me?"

Arnold gave a snort and turned toward the door.

"And by the way, old chap," Ponga Jim added, "don't slam the door when you go out!"

"That guy!" Arnold said sarcastically. "Shoot him, drop him over the side, and he comes up with a blonde under one arm, and a brunette under the other! What can you do with a guy like that?"

Voyage to Tobalai

CHAPTER I

Vivid lightning burst in a mass of piled-up cloud for an instant, revealing a black, boiling maelstrom of wind-lashed waves. The old freighter rolled heavily as she took a big one over the bows. Ponga Jim Mayo crouched behind the canvas dodger and swore under his breath.

Slug Brophy, his first mate, ran down the steep, momentary incline of the bridge.

"That lightning will give the show away," he shouted above the storm. "If there's a sub around she'll spot us quick as an Irishman spots a drink!"

"I'm glad we cleared Linta before we hit this," Ponga Jim yelled back at him. "Even if we're seen, we'll be safe until this blows itself out. There's no sub in the Pacific that could hit us in this mess."

He stared over the dodger into the storm, pelting rain and blown spray beating against his face like hail. The storm might keep the subs below, and that was good. Even if their batteries were low and they had to run on the surface, effectively firing a torpedo or deck gun in these wildly pitching seas would be next to impossible. Once the storm was over, however, they would be back to carefully scanning the sea in all directions.

Out of Capetown with a cargo of torpedo planes, she was running for Balikpapan, and there wasn't a man aboard ship who didn't know how desperately those planes were needed now, in February of 1942. They were American planes, taken aboard from a crippled freighter in the harbor at Capetown. The original ship had been damaged by a submarine attack.

The *Semiramis* wasn't one of your slim, brassbound craft with mahogany panels, but a crusty old Barnacle Bill sort of tramp. She was rusty, wind-worried, wave-battered, and time-harried; in short, she had character.

Taking on the cargo for the East Indies, Ponga Jim pushed her blunt bows across the long, lonely reaches of the southern Indian Ocean, far from the steamer lanes where the submarines waited. Then, avoiding the well-traveled route through Sunda Strait, he held a course through the empty seas south of Mava and the Lesser Sunda Islands. Passing up Lombok, Alas, and Sapeh Straits one after the other, Mayo finally turned north through Linta Strait, a little-used route into the Java Sea.

Not merely content with using Linta Strait, he deliberately avoided the safe passage east of Komodo, and took the dangerously narrow opening between Padar and Rinja Islands.

When Brophy had come on deck and noticed Jim was taking the freighter through the narrow passage, he looked over, his expression grim.

"Cap," he said, "you better get the boys over the side and have them grease up the hull, otherwise you're going to scratch her paint job."

But they got through, and back along the routes they could have taken, ships were sunk. Waiting subs scored three times in one day at Sunda, twice at Lombok. Even off Linta, a schooner had been shelled and sunk, but the *Semiramis,* hull down across the horizon by then, had slipped away into the oncoming storm. Now, headed north for Balikpapan, lightning might spoil it all.

ANOTHER WAVE BROKE across the bows and water ran two feet deep in the stern scuppers. Slug Brophy grinned, his hard, blue-jowled face dripping with rain.

"God have pity on the poor sailors on such a night as this!" he chanted, in a momentary lull. "That's what the fishwives would be saying tonight along the chalk cliffs of England. How is it, Cap? Will we make it?"

Mayo grimaced. "We've got a chance."

In a flash of lightning, Brophy could see rain beating against Jim's lean, sun-browned face.

"I'm not taking her through Makassar Strait," Ponga Jim said suddenly, "it smells like trouble to me. That's ugly water for submarines."

"How you going?" Brophy asked quizzically.

"I'm taking her north around the east end of Mangola Island, then through Bangka Strait an' down the west coast of Celebes. From there to Balikpapan, we'll have to be lucky."

Brophy nodded. "It's twice as far, but there haven't been any sinkings over that way. Funny, too, when you think about it."

"Nothing much over there right now. A few native craft, an' maybe a K.P.M. boat. But the Dutch ships are off schedule now."

Jim pulled his sou'wester down a little tighter. He stared into the storm, shifting uneasily. He was remembering what Major Arnold had told him in the room at the Belgrave Hotel in Capetown.

"Jim," the major had said, "I flew down here from Cairo just to see you. You're going right into the middle of this war, but if there's anyone in this world knows the East Indies, it's you. After you deliver your cargo at Balikpapan, you'll be going to Gorontalo.

"I'd like you to go on from there, go down through Greyhound Strait. If you see or hear of any ship or plane concentrations, let me know at Port Darwin."

ON THE RAIN-LASHED BRIDGE Ponga Jim voiced his thoughts. "Slug, you could hide all the fleets of the world in these islands. Anything could happen down here, and most everything has."

"I'd feel better if we didn't have that woman aboard," Brophy said suddenly. "A woman's got no place on a freight ship. You'd think we were a bloody tourist craft!"

"Don't tell me you're superstitious, Slug," Jim chuckled. "Anyway, this scow runs on fuel oil, and you don't skim it off a lagoon, you've got to buy it with cash. As long as that's the way it is, anybody who can pay can ride."

"Yeah," Brophy said cynically, "but that gal isn't ridin' for fun. Something's going on!"

Jim laughed. "Take over, pal," he said, slapping the mate's shoulder, "keep her on the same course, an' don't run over any submarines! I'll worry about the woman!"

"Huh!" Brophy grunted disgustedly. "If you'd worry I wouldn't be gripin'!"

Ponga Jim swung down the ladder and started to open the door into the cabin. Instead, he flattened against the deckhouse and stared aft. There had been a vague, shadowy movement on the boat deck!

Swiftly and soundlessly, Ponga Jim slipped down the ladder and across the intervening space. Then he went up the ladder to the boat deck like a shadow, moving close against the lifeboats. Carefully, he worked his way aft toward the .50-caliber antiaircraft guns where he had seen the movement.

Lightning flared briefly, and he saw someone crouching over the machine gun. It was an uncertain, fleeting glimpse, but he lunged forward.

Some instinctive warning must have come to the crouching figure for even as Jim sprang, he saw the white blur of a face, then it melted into the darkness and was gone.

At the gun, nothing. In two steps, Jim was at the edge of the boat deck, his .45 poised and ready, but the afterdeck was empty. His eyes narrowed with thought, he retraced his steps to the cabin. Someone had been tampering with the guns, and that someone would not be satisfied with one attempt.

He stepped into the cabin, shedding his oilskins. He started to hang them up when a voice froze him immobile.

"I hope I'm not intruding . . . ?"

RAYNA COURCEL SAT at his desk smoking a cigarette. In slacks, he reflected, she was as seductive as in anything else. But then, her figure would give sex appeal to a shroud.

"Up early, aren't you?" he suggested. "What's on your mind? Don't you know it's four o'clock in the morning?"

"Of course. I wanted to ask a favor, and didn't want anyone to know . . . I want to go ashore. I have to go ashore."

"Ashore?" Ponga Jim's face was bland. "Why?"

"Because," Rayna said quietly, "this ship is going to be blown up."

"That strikes me as reason enough," Jim said, unbuttoning his coat. "When does the big event come off?"

"Tomorrow or the following day . . . when you're somewhere in the Spermonde Archipelago."

"Is there a crystal ball in your cabin? Maybe you should read my palms. . . ." He gave her a moment to understand his question.

"Oh, I know what I'm talking about, Captain. You have a spy on your ship. I was up on the lifeboat deck having a cigarette and I heard someone sending Morse code. I read Morse, learned it in the girl scouts. . . ."

Mayo arched an eyebrow. "I'll bet you did."

"Are you going to let me finish? Good. The message was being sent ahead to a submarine . . . that's all I got."

Ponga Jim leaned back in his chair. His dark blue woolen shirt was open at the neck, and just under the edge of his coat Rayna could see the butt of his .45.

"All right. You're a smart girl, aren't you?" Jim said. "If I put you ashore where will you go?"

"To Makassar. I have it all planned. I go to Makassar, and . . ."

"And we go ahead and be blown up," Jim chuckled. "Lady, you please me. The only thing wrong with the setup, besides the fact that I don't like being blown up, is that we're not going to be anywhere close to Makassar tomorrow. I'm not even going near Celebes."

Rayna Courcel's face turned a shade white.

"What do you mean?" she exclaimed sharply. "Your route takes you that way!"

"Honey," Ponga Jim stood up, running his fingers through his hair.

"I'm tired. You may not need beauty sleep, but I do. And don't worry about being blown up. Your spy may be trying to communicate but, in all likelihood, he has no idea where he is."

She started to speak, then bit her lip. At the door, she turned to face him, her hands behind her on the doorknob.

"I can't figure you out," she said, "but I'm afraid you're headed for a big surprise."

"Maybe," Ponga Jim said. "And maybe I won't be the only one."

CHAPTER II

Bright morning sunlight sparkled on the sea when Ponga Jim Mayo went on deck. Tam O'Neill and Ben Blue were leaning on the rail. Both were gunners taken on at Capetown.

"Better check those machine guns," Mayo said briefly.

"Beggin' your pardon, sir," Tam said, "but my guns are always ready."

"O'Neill," Ponga Jim said shortly, "I'm not doubting you. But I never give an order without adequate reason. Last night they were tampered with."

O'Neill's face flushed. "Thank you, Captain," he said. He wheeled and was up the ladder in two jumps.

It was barely eight o'clock, but his three passengers were already at the table when Jim sat down. Eric Frazer, his third mate, was also there. With Millan splitting his time as artillery officer, Jim had shipped an additional third mate.

Frazer had come aboard in Zanzibar. He was short, powerful, and without expression. He had been, he said, a mate on a Danish vessel running to Rio, Para, and up the Amazon until the war put him on the beach.

The two men who, with Rayna Courcel, made up the passenger list were Brace Lamprey, an engineer, and Ross Mallory. Both were South Africans with interests in New Guinea. Now Jim was beginning to wonder if everyone was what they first seemed to be.

"When should we sight the Spermonde Islands?" Lamprey asked casually, as Jim seated himself. "If I remember my East Indies, they are off the southwest corner of Celebes."

Rayna's hand tightened on her fork, but she did not look up.

"We'd be seeing them now," Jim said, "if we were going that way."

Mallory started violently, and stopped eating. He seemed about to speak when Lamprey interrupted.

"What do you mean, Captain?" he inquired. "Where are we going? Isn't that the route to Borneo?"

"Too many submarines that way," Jim said. "We're going north around Celebes."

Jim looked over at Frazer but the man was eating steadily, apparently ignoring the conversation.

Mallory straightened up. "See here, Captain!" he began angrily, "I don't propose to be dragged all over the ocean during a war. They are bombing the north coast of Celebes. I demand to be set ashore at once!"

"At once?" Jim asked. "That would mean the closest possible point, wouldn't it. I expect we can manage without much trouble. We're not quite a mile from land now."

They all looked up, surprised. Rayna's eyes strayed to the porthole.

"Not quite a mile?" Mallory was startled. "Where!"

"Straight down," Jim said.

Lamprey laughed, but Mallory's face grew red and angry.

"That isn't funny, Captain!" he growled. "I demand you put me ashore immediately!"

"What's the matter," Jim asked innocently, "afraid you'll be blown up with the ship?"

In the sudden silence that followed, they could hear the sea against the hull. Only Frazer was undisturbed. He ate in silence. Ross Mallory's eyes were suddenly wary.

"What do you mean?" he demanded.

"Mean?" Jim shrugged. "Well, it's one of the things that happen when a Japanese sub fires a torpedo at you."

HE GOT UP and walked out on deck. Mallory knew something, he decided. He began to feel better. Ever since the trip began, he had the feeling of trouble brewing. It was getting on his nerves. Now, at least, the trouble was beginning to show itself.

The girl had heard someone sending Morse code, she thought that they were going to be torpedoed ... a spy who wanted to be torpedoed ... that was a new one. Ponga Jim had no doubt that there were men out there who would give their lives for their country or cause but he doubted that destroying the small shipment of planes aboard the *Semiramis* was worth the ultimate sacrifice. Whatever was going on was something else ... something else entirely.

He was staring off over the sea, and had been watching a fleck in the sky for almost a minute before he realized it was a plane.

It was coming fast and low. The blunt arrows of bombs racked under its wings.

He yelled, and saw O'Neill swing his gun. The Mitsubishi swooped in but even as they saw it, the plane was turning. The nose lifted into a climb, and was still climbing when O'Neill followed it with a long burst from the double fifties. The range was extreme and the bullets had no effect. As men ran to the other guns the plane circled, just out of range. Then, climbing at a terrific rate, the aircraft seemed to disappear into the cloudless blue sky.

Red Hanlon, the chief engineer, stood by No. 3 hatch rubbing his cauliflower ear.

"Skipper," he said, "that guy wasn't shooting."

"Just getting a look at us," Jim said dryly, "after all, he has friends aboard."

"*What?*" Mallory stopped. "Spies aboard here? What kind of ship is this, anyway?"

Ponga Jim ignored him. If they wanted the ship blown up, why not bomb or torpedo it? That job would have been simple for the plane they had just seen.

The only reason there could be for sparing the ship would be if there were enemy agents aboard who planned to leave the ship, and probably blow it up on leaving. But what was going on that had caused an agent to board his ship ... and what was so important that the Japanese had sent out a plane to be sure of their location?

The *Semiramis* was on a course that would take her by the usual route through Makassar Strait. But he was just as sure that he no longer had any intention of going that way.

JIM TURNED and went up the ladder to the bridge. Frazer, immaculate in a white linen coat, turned to face him. He had been studying the horizon through his glasses.

"We're changing course," Jim said. He stepped into the wheelhouse where Tupa, an Alfur seaman, was at the wheel. "Put her over to fifty," Mayo said. "And hold her there."

Frazer joined him. "Then you aren't going through the strait?" he asked.

"After being spotted like that," Jim said. "Not a chance. We're going east. I may decide to put in at Buton."

Frazer hesitated, as though about to speak. Then he turned and walked back to the bridge.

TWICE DURING THE DAY, Ponga Jim changed course, but each time swung back to the neighborhood of fifty degrees. Once, standing on the bridge, he saw Lamprey looking at the sun's position with a thoughtful expression. Obviously, the man had noted the changes of course. Rayna was watching the sky, too, but with an altogether different expression.

Millan stopped beside him on the deck after dinner. His face was troubled.

"You reckon we've got a spy aboard, Skipper? Should I search their cabins?"

"No," Jim told him, "whoever it is wouldn't have anything incriminating around. But today, we've changed course, so the spy will make an attempt to communicate within the next twenty-four hours, and my bet is within the next six. Then maybe something will break."

Yet it was not until an hour later that he remembered his conversation with Rayna.

She had heard Morse code being sent ... but why from the lifeboat deck? It was nowhere near the *Semiramis's* radio room, which was occupied around the clock. Walking out to a spot on the bridge wing where he could see the spot where she stood, he realized she must have been standing just behind one of the ventilators!

Taking a flashlight from a drawer, Jim put on his faded khaki coat and picked up his cap. Silently, he stepped out on the lower bridge. There was no one in sight. He walked aft along the windward side of the main deck to avoid meeting anyone. His soft, woven-leather sandals made no noise on the steel deck. He halted in the shadows by the deckhouse. There was no sound but the rustle of water along the hull but somewhere out there were Japanese submarines, and the sleek, swift destroyers. North Borneo had fallen, Menado in Celebes had been shelled and bombed.

In a swift succession of raids, the Japanese had struck at Rabaul, in the Bismarcks, and at Sorong, a village on poles alongside the beach at Doom Island. Singapore had its back to the wall in a desperate, all-out battle for survival.

But closer another enemy waited, a more dangerous enemy because he was unknown. Yet an enemy who held in his hand not only the lives of those aboard, but the men for whom these planes and munitions were destined. And that enemy was here on this ship with them.

Ponga Jim moved past the crew's mess unseen, and entered the rope locker.

All was still, a haunting stillness that concealed some living presence. Yet he knew there was no one in the locker but himself, it was only that he was getting closer. There was a smell of new hemp and tarred lines, of canvas and of turpentine.

Crawling around a pile of heavy line, he softly loosened the dogs and opened the door concealed there. He felt with his foot for the steel ladder, and like a wraith, glided down into the abysmal blackness of the hold.

CHAPTER III

There the dark was something one could feel, something almost tangible. Ponga Jim hesitated, listening with every nerve in his body.

Down below, he could hear the sea much more plainly and he was conscious again, as he always was, of its dark power separated from him by only a thin partition of steel. There was a faint smell of old cargoes, of copra, rubber, tea and coffee, of sago, nutmeg, and tobacco. He waited an instant in the darkness listening.

Then he heard it, the faint tinkle of metal on metal. He felt the hackles raise on the back of his neck, and he moved forward on cat feet, feeling his way by instinct through the racked torpedo bombers and cases of ammunition. In his mind he was trying to locate whoever was in the hold, to locate the man by putting himself in the man's place.

Suddenly, he remembered. What a fool he had been! The amphibian, his own aircraft, had a two-way radio as well as a code sender!

Then he heard the clicking of the key Crouching in the darkness just forward of the tail assembly, he tried to make out the words, but the echoes made it difficult. He made out the name of the ship, *Semiramis*, and some numbers. . . . A compass heading!

Jim stepped closer, putting his foot out carefully. But even as he moved, the cabin door opened. He felt rather than saw the figure and instantly, he sprang!

Yet even as he leaped something rolled under his foot and he crashed to the deck.

He heard a smothered gasp, and reached out desperately, suddenly gripping an ankle. Then a heel kicked him viciously in the head. He let go and rolled over. A pistol barrel, aimed at his head, missed and smashed down upon his shoulder.

He fell back, grunting with the pain of it, and then the same pistol caught him a glancing blow on top of the head. Momentarily stunned, he struggled to climb to his feet, his head blazing with pain.

Staggering, he fell against a packing case, and froze, listening. Jim heard no sound of retreating footsteps. Whoever he was, the man was no fool. Jim could hear nothing, not even breathing. He crept along behind the cases. He put his hand out and was startled by the touch of human flesh. In a kind of instinctive panic, he rocked back on his knees and swung with everything he had. His fist smashed into a muscular shoulder, and the man grunted. An arrow of pain slithered down his arm from a knifepoint, and he lunged close.

A fist slammed against his jaw, and he twisted, trying to catch the man's knife-wrist. As in everything else, there is a knack to fighting in the dark, an instinctive gauging of position that comes with experience. But it was experience his opponent had as well.

He jammed a fist against a corded stomach, but took a jolting punch himself. He felt the man draw back his arm and shift balance to drive the knife home, but he fell away from the blade and hooking his toe behind his opponent's ankle, jerked the leg from under him.

They got up together, and he took a smashing blow to the mouth then hooked a hard one to the chin, feeling the man go down under the blow.

Instantly, he dropped, falling knees first at the spot where the man's stomach should have been, but the fellow rolled away quickly. Then there was a scuffle of feet. Sensing the spy was trying to get away, Ponga Jim grabbed for the flashlight, which had fallen from his pocket during the fray. He felt around, finding the light after a few moments. He snapped it on, his gun ready. The hold was empty. He shook his head to clear it. Was it one or two different people he had struggled with there in the dark?

Mayo swore under his breath and ran for the topside ladder. On deck, he came to a stop, groping for the rail as he waited for his eyes to adjust to the blinding sunlight. Squinting forward and aft he searched for the mysterious man from the hold. No one was nearby.

Ponga Jim stopped amidships. Brace Lamprey had come on deck and not far from him was Ross Mallory. Lamprey looked at Jim curiously.

"What happened to you, man?" he asked. "You look like you've been slugging it out with them!"

"I was," Jim said coolly. Lamprey's face was smooth, unmarked. Nor did Mallory show any signs of conflict. The two of them seemed all too cool to have participated in the fight below.

Ponga Jim went up the ladder to the bridge. Blore, one of the South Africans, came out of the wheelhouse.

"Are we changing course to go in to Buton?"

"No," Jim said shortly, "we're swinging wide. We're going east, through Kelang Strait."

Blore turned a little, his eyes intent. "That's a long way around, isn't it? What's in the wind, Skipper? Do you have some mission other than delivering these planes?"

Ponga Jim shoved his cap back on his head. "My only mission is minding my own business. These planes go where they were sent, and anything that gets in the way gets smashed, understand?"

Blore's eyes dropped a little, but his face was expressionless.

"Yes, sir," he said sullenly. "I understand you, Captain."

Ponga Jim Mayo walked back to the chart room. He was getting jumpy, he shouldn't have spoken so hard to the kid.

He glanced down at the chart. Due north from Kelang Strait would take him just west of the Ombi Islands. Something stopped him cold, and he stared down at the chart, caught by a sudden thought. As he stared down at the map, he felt himself chill through and through at the realization of what was about to happen.

IT WAS NO LONGER a vague premonition, no longer a few scattered acts and words fitting to the hint dropped by Arnold. He could see it all, and the realization struck him speechless for the moment.

In his mind, Jim was seeing an island, a high tableland near Obi Major. Thick, dank green jungle ran down to the sea. But Jim was not thinking of the jungle, he was thinking of that tableland.

He was remembering the day he had climbed the steplike mountain and stood looking out over the top, a flat, dead level field, waving with long grass. Eight hundred feet above the sea, it was. "Tobalai," he muttered, "Tobalai Island!"

From outside there was the shriek of an incoming shell followed by the deep concussion of a heavy cannon. Then ship's alarms blasted the signal for general quarters.

The waiting, it seemed, was over.

CHAPTER IV

Ponga Jim dived for the bridge. He saw, ahead of them, the low, dark profile of a submarine. In front of its conning tower a crew rushed to reload the deck gun.

"Starboard fifteen degrees," he called out and reached for the forward fire-control phone. But something was wrong. The sub had fired a warning shot, it had not tried to sink them, and Eric Frazer was standing in the door of the chart room, one side of his face a dark and purple bruise.

Even though he was ready for it, the punch almost nailed him. Frazer threw his right hand fast and hard. But Jim's left hook was harder.

"Never lead a right hand," he said, and knocked the third mate down. Frazer was up like a cat, but Jim fished out his pistol and covered him. Suddenly, the ship's heading started to swing, and Jim turned instinctively to the wheel. He was just in time to see the blow start, but too late to block it. Blore slugged him across the head with a blackjack.

Jim started to fall, and Frazer slugged him from behind. Then the blackjack fell again and Ponga Jim went to his knees, blinded with a sickening pain. He went down. Even then, his consciousness a feeble spark lost in a sea of blackness, he struggled. Someone must have hit him once more because he felt his knees slide from under him and he faded out in a pounding surf of agony.

WHEN HE OPENED his eyes, he was alive to nothing but the throbbing pain in his head. It felt heavy and unwieldy when he made an effort to move. His hands were tied, and his ankles also. He struggled to sit up and the pain wrenched a groan from his swollen lips.

"Skipper?" It was Brophy's voice.

"What happened?" Ponga Jim asked. "What in blazes happened?"

"They took over the ship," Brophy said. "They took us like Dewey took Manila. I woke up with a gun in my face, an' they got the Gunner when he came on watch."

"They?" Mayo puckered his brow, trying to figure it out.

"Yeah. Frazer, Lamprey, and Mallory. They had six of the South African crew with them. I heard some of them talking. I guess they are actually Boers who sympathize with the Nazis ... anyway, they're working with the Japs."

"Makes sense," Jim said, remembering. "I think we're headed for Tobalai."

"Why Tobalai?" Brophy asked.

"I'm guessing they've turned the top of the island into a landing field. From there they can cover any point in the East Indies, but particularly anywhere from where we are now to Mindanao."

"That's slick thinking ... you're probably right!"

"I don't feel so smart," Jim said bitterly. "A lot of good we can do, all wrapped up like premium hams."

The door opened, and Li came in with a tray of food. The Chinese put it down carefully for two armed men stood in the door, guns ready. One was a Japanese, the other the seaman, Blore.

"Wait until I get out of here," Ponga Jim said. "I'll see you guys swing for this."

"You will, eh?" Blore sneered. "You won't be getting out and tomorrow morning what is left of the United States fleet will come steaming up through Greyhound Strait from the Banda Sea."

Ponga Jim turned cold inside, but he kept up the sarcastic, skeptical manner.

"Yeah? So what?" he said.

A weasel-faced seaman leaned into the hatch. "Then a couple of cruisers will draw their fighters into a trap and these planes of yours attack the carriers ... the crews will think it's their own men coming back. There's two battleships lying behind Obi Major, an' a dozen submarines are waiting to clean up the job."

"Ah?" the voice was gentle, polite. "Are you being entertained, Captain Mayo?"

Weasel-face stopped, his mouth half open to speak. Slowly he turned a sickly yellow. Captain Toya Tushima stepped into view. The trim little Nipponese held his features in an expression of calm benevolence but Weasel-face turned as though fascinated with horror.

"I cannot say that it is good to see you again, Captain Mayo, but, in a war of strangers, I do feel a certain pleasure in an old acquaintance."

"It's been a long time since Manchuria, hasn't it?"

"Perhaps for you." The Japanese looked at him carefully, as he might at a piece of awkward furniture. Then indicating the weasely crewman he spoke to Frazer who had come up.

"Do we need this man?" he asked.

Eric shrugged. "He is one of the recruits from the Transvaal ... I don't think so."

"Good," Tushima said pleasantly. "Stand aside."

He unbuttoned his holster carefully and drew out a gun. The crewman drew away.

"No!" he begged hoarsely. "No! Please!"

The report of the gun was thunder within the steel walls. The seaman crumpled slowly, a round blue hole between his eyes.

Tushima looked at Blore.

"You really mustn't talk so much," he said. Without a backward glance, he walked away.

Blore, his hands shaking, picked up the dead man and carried him out. Brophy swallowed and looked at Li.

"I don't think I'm eating," he said. "I don't think I got the stomach for it."

"Better try," Jim said, "this isn't over yet."

After they had eaten and Li was gone, the two men remained in the half darkness of the rope locker. Millan and the others, they heard, were confined in the seaman's fo'c's'le. Remembering the door into No. 5 hold he had used before, Jim began to work at his bonds. The door was behind the stack of line and, apparently, unnoticed. If they could get free ...

For a long time, he worked in the darkness, twisting, tugging, and straining, but without success. And all the time, he carried a picture in his thoughts of the long gray ships of war coming up from the Banda Sea, taking the back door to the Philippines from their bases in Samoa and

Port Darwin. Once their air cover had been lured away, the torpedo planes, the same ones that the *Semiramis* carried, would approach and, appearing to be the American planes returning from the battle, would get close enough to the carriers to launch a crippling attack. It was a potentially devastating plan.

"We've got to get out of here!" Jim exclaimed suddenly. "If they get away with this, it will make Pearl Harbor look like a pink tea!"

He was thinking rapidly. If he could get his hands free, he could get down the ladder into the hold. Unless Lamprey had found it, or one of the others, there was a tommy gun in the Grumman. If he could get that gun and get on deck, he'd take his own chances.

Tugging at the ropes was a waste of time. Jim growled under his breath. Suddenly, an inspiration struck him.

"Slug?" he whispered. "Where did you put the gear from that smashed lifeboat? The one that was blasted in the Red Sea?"

"Over there, in the drawers," Slug said. "Why?"

"There's a couple of hatchets, an' all the other gear. What I'm thinking of is the matches."

Jim stretched out his legs and dug in his heels, dragging himself to the place where the smaller articles of gear were stowed. By getting his chin in the handhold on the drawer, he worked it open. Backing up to a pile of line, he worked himself up the pile until he was on his feet. He felt around carefully, and found the matches.

Their hands were tied behind them but Brophy struck a light and held the match so that Jim could slide back and hold his wrists over the flame. It burned his hand, burned his wrist, then went out. Brophy awkwardly struck another but dropped it trying to maneuver the match toward Jim's wrists. The third time, however, Jim used the heat from the flame as a guide and positioned the rope carefully. It charred slowly, caught fire and burned, then went out. Brophy tried again, but the match broke in striking. Finally they got the rope burning and with a surge of strength, the strands parted. In a matter of minutes, they were both free.

CHAPTER V

Rubbing his wrists to restore circulation, Jim got to his feet. Then picking up a couple of steel battens for fastening hatches, he slid them under the door handle, driving a couple of wooden wedges in place to hold them securely. Slug watched him curiously.

"You figure out the wildest things," he said. "What's the idea?"

"Keep them guessing awhile. Suppose somebody came in before we got out of the hold? We'd be killed before we could get anywhere close to the deck. As it is, they'll think we're just trying to keep them out in case they get an idea to bump us off."

Climbing over the rope, he grabbed the handle of the door to the hold, and twisted sharply. Nothing happened. The dismay on Brophy's face mirrored his own.

"Locked!" Jim said. "They locked it!"

The mate hesitated, then doubling a big fist he grinned at Jim.

"We can always jump them when they come in to feed us," he said.

"Won't do. They'd cut us down before we'd taken three steps."

"Then I guess you better start kicking a hole in the deck," Slug said dryly. "That's the only way out I can see."

"Wait a minute." Jim crawled over the lines to the one porthole. The paint was stuck, but cutting around the edge with the hatchet, he managed to get it open. "We'll have to wait until dark," he whispered, "but we're going out that port."

"Into the ocean?" Brophy asked. "Not me!"

Jim chuckled. "What's the matter? Getting chilly around the arches? You know blamed well you'll do it if there was a chance of getting a crack at those mugs."

Slug grinned. "Maybe, but I haven't got the build you have. I'm thicker in the middle and might not go through so easy."

Twice attempts were made to open the door, but they sat silent, listening. The Japanese weren't worried. Both exits were closed tight, and if the prisoners wanted to do without food, they had only themselves to blame, and were much less trouble.

As they waited, Ponga Jim was recalling what Weasel-face had said. Two battleships behind Obi Major. That would mean they would be inside the reef somewhere between Tanjongs Woko and Parigi, probably. More ships might be lying in the Roads at Laiwoei.

On the other side of Greyhound Strait, several ships could lie out of sight in Banggai Bay, and even more in the deeper, spacious waters of Bangkalang Bay. Scouting planes could only see them when almost over the bays themselves, but it would already be too late.

He was no nearer a plan. If he had a plane, he could fly over and warn the fleet before they were in danger. Once warned they could handle the situation. He had no doubt about that.

Before he realized, it was dark. Slug Brophy had been lying on the piled-up lines looking out through the porthole.

"We're not far offshore now," he said. "I thought I glimpsed moonlight on the tin roof of the storage shed at Laiwoei and I thought I recognized Mala Mala a while back."

"Then it's time for us to go into action." Jim got up quickly, thrusting a hatchet in his belt.

Picking up a heaving line he crawled to the port. He tossed the tail end of the line to Slug.

"Take a turn around some of that inch line," he said. "This all depends on whether anybody is near enough or not. If they see or hear, we're out of luck."

Putting one arm and shoulder out the port, he worked his broad shoulders through. Then, sitting in the port with Slug holding his legs, he leaned back and threw the monkey's fist.

The edge of the deck was just about eight feet above his head, and the ball of knotted rope went over the edge and under the lowest part of the rail. It hit the deck, rolled down with the roll of the ship, then back. He had missed.

Gauging the distance again, he tried another toss. But that time, too, he failed to make it roll down on the opposite side of the stanchion. On the seventh attempt, he was successful. It rolled back hard enough to come over the edge. Then by paying out line the weight of the monkey's fist brought it back down to him. Passing it on to Slug, he began hauling down on the line until the inch line was around the stanchion.

Sliding back into the port, he cut off the inch line while Slug unbent the heaving line.

"I'm going to take the piece we use with us, or drop it over the side," Jim said. "Let them think we're locked up. They'll find out too soon, anyway."

Pulling himself back to a sitting position in the port, he grasped the two lines in his hands and went up, hand over hand. As soon as he was over the ship's side, he dropped the rope close in front of the port so Brophy would see it.

He glanced around and was just in time to see the descending marlinspike, and jerked his head aside. The power of the blow jerked the man off balance and he almost fell over the rail.

Before he could cry out, Jim struck him. A driving right to the chin, and then another short one in the wind. Gasping for breath, the man struck wildly, and Jim almost lost balance and fell into the sea.

Clinging precariously to the rail, the two fought desperately and in silence. Then Ponga Jim's superior strength gave him an advantage. The man was slipping, and he let go of Jim and grabbed desperately at the rail, but Jim knocked his hands loose and as the man fell forward, Jim grabbed the back of his neck and tipped him over the side.

Brophy jerked back out of the way just as the man fell past, but there was no scream, only a splash, and no further sound. Brophy came up the rope and Jim helped him to the deck. Then he wiped the cold sweat from his brow.

"What do we do?" Slug said. "Turn the boys loose an' take over the ship?"

"It's too late," Jim said. "Look!"

The *Semiramis* was just coming into the Roads at Laiwoei. Ahead of them lay a long gray destroyer, beyond that a cruiser and another destroyer.

They drew back into the darkness between a cargo winch and the mainm'st. "Go below in the hold somewhere and watch your chance to turn the others loose. Then if you can slip out of the Roads somehow, do it."

"What about you?" Brophy demanded.

"I'm going ashore. Somehow I'm going to get word to the fleet, and somehow I'm going to get on Tobalai and see if I can throw a monkey wrench into this deal. Do what you can."

Silently, the two men gripped hands, then Ponga Jim dropped to his knees behind the hatch-coaming and worked his way forward. A dash to the walk along the lee rail got him to shelter. He climbed up on the rail, did a hand-over-hand up the stanchion, and crawled over the edge to the boat deck.

There he lay, catching a breath, and looking under the lifeboat to estimate the situation. If he ran for it and made a dive over the side, he would be seen and heard. Probably on the destroyer as well as his own ship. His only chance was to wait.

He lay still, studying the situation. The deck was stirring with movement. He heard them let go the anchor forward, and saw a fast motor launch coming alongside from the nearest warship. That would be for Tushima, as they must have signaled.

Crawling aft to the machine gun, a glance told him there was no ammunition. That was as he had expected. They had removed any chance of its use by any of the crew that might escape. Swiftly, he dodged down the ladder and into the lighted passage. Footsteps approached, and he opened the nearest door and stepped in.

THERE WAS A STARTLED GASP, and he wheeled to find himself facing Rayna Courcel. The girl's eyes were wide.

"You!" she exclaimed. "Where did you come from?"

"Me? Seemed like a nice night for a stroll, so I started out. Got a gun?"

She picked up her handbag, drew the gun, and pointed it at him.

"I'm glad you reminded me," she said. "You came in so quickly I forgot."

"Are you giving it to me?" he said. "Or am I taking it?"

"You won't try that, Captain Mayo," she said quietly. "If you do, I'll shoot, and I should very much dislike to do that."

"It will not be necessary, Miss Courcel," a voice interrupted.

Before Jim could turn he was seized from behind by a pair of powerful arms that were thrown about his body. Instantly, Jim dropped to one knee, at the same time grabbing his attacker's wrist and elbow and giving a hard jerk.

With surprising ease the man flopped over Mayo's shoulder and hit the deck hard. It was Eric Frazer. Before he could move, Jim hooked a short one to his chin, and slipped the man's .45 from his holster.

Wheeling, he jumped into the passage, kicked a surprised guard in the stomach, and ran for the rail. The motor launch was alongside, and Jim made the ladder running, and was halfway down before the two surprised Japanese seamen in the boat could act. One of them grabbed for a gun, and Ponga Jim fired. The man dropped the gun and spilled over on his face.

There was a sudden movement behind him, and Jim fired again. Then he wheeled. Big London and Lyssy had been under guard but now they were right behind him, and even as they dropped into the boat, Big London cast off.

Jim leaped to the controls and the idling motor roared into life. On deck there was confusion, shouting, jostling men rushed toward the rail, and Big London, balancing himself easily, lifted the automatic rifle the sailor had been about to use, and sprayed the rail.

Ponga Jim spun the launch in a turn that almost capsized the boat and with the motor roaring wide open, raced for the destroyer. Missing the bow by inches, and the starb'rd anchor hawser by less, he spun the wheel again and raced the boat down close under the lee of the warship. It was too close for accurate firing from the deck and the rocky islet of Kadera was just a bit over a hundred yards astern.

"Down!" Jim yelled. "Get down!"

Lyssy and Big London both dropped, but both opened fire on the destroyer. A gun roared from the stern, and a shell hit the waves twenty yards ahead of them. Jim swung the boat hastily toward the spot where the shell had landed, and with the motor wide open, water lifting in a roaring fan on either side of the bow, raced for the shelter of Kadera. A machine gun rattled, and a bullet glanced from the engine cowling and whined past his ear. He skidded the boat around a rock, and for an instant was sheltered by the islet.

Dodging and turning, he raced the boat for the coast beyond Tanjong Parigi. What he wanted wasn't at Laiwoei, but at Tobalai off the east end of Obi Major. But there wasn't a chance of retaining the launch. It was slower than other boats they soon would have in pursuit, and was unarmed except for the weapons they had themselves.

Lyssy came up beside him. The Toradjas's eyes were bright.

"Both yellow man dead," he said. "You shoot plenty good, Captain. Where we go?"

"Ashore," Jim said briefly. "You and London go through this boat. Get all the guns and ammunition you can find. Anything else that looks good. We're going to have a fight of it. They don't dare let us get away."

Cutting the motor for an instant, he listened, and hearing the roar of motors behind him, opened up again. Tensely, he crouched over the wheel. The pursuit was getting under way faster than he had believed. It would be nip and tuck now, and if they got away it would be sheer luck, nothing less.

The motor wide open, he rounded the Tanjong and headed off down the coast, his wake a streak of white, boiling water. Spray beat against his face, and the two widening fans of water cut away from the knife-like bow.

The water was black and glistening, the night speckled with stars. Behind him, Big London and Lyssy crouched in the stern, rifles ready. Beyond the boat he saw at a glance, the sea was empty to the point, and along the coast down which they were running the jungle crowded to the very water's edge.

Ponga Jim spun the wheel suddenly, and with his motor wide open, roared for the blackness of an opening under the mangroves. The launch shot through the hole like some insane monster of the sea, and hit the muddy shingle with such force that it ran halfway up the low bank before it stopped. Instantly, Jim cut the motor and leaped out.

"Grab the guns and let's go!" he said. "They won't find the boat for a while!"

CHAPTER VI

The launch was at least ten feet under the mangrove roots and out of sight from sea. They would have a good start, and fortunately, no two men in his crew were better bushmen than these two, Big London, who had grown up on the banks of the Congo, and Lyssy, the wandering warrior from the Toradjas' highlands of Celebes.

Lyssy took the lead, and with almost instinctive skill, led them into a game trail. They started off at a fast trot. The trail led steadily upward toward the interior mountains. If it had only meant escape, Ponga Jim thought, he could have kept alive and safe for years in this jungle with these two companions. But there was no time to lose.

Rounding a shoulder of cliff several miles back from the coast, Ponga Jim saw a searchlight sweeping the jungle. It would only be a few minutes now until they found the launch, and then the Japanese would be back on their trail.

Steadily, they kept on, weaving up into the mountains, but tending steadily toward the east and south. Once, crossing a stream, they saw the huge coil of a snake on the bank, later they walked into a herd of wild pigs that fortunately did not charge, but just wandered away, grunting stupidly.

"They come," Lyssy said suddenly.

In the moment of silence they could hear a shout as their trail was seen.

The moon had come up, and the jungle lay ominous and shadowy beneath the brightening sky. Ponga Jim hesitated. The country was too rough for fast travel, and he could see that his idea of crossing the island and seizing a boat at one of the three or four small villages along that coast was going to be a near thing. Already his ship would be arriving at Tobalai and the Japanese would be unloading the planes.

Keeping to the jungle trails, they waded down a stream, then cut back on another trail toward the coast. Then, suddenly, in the first open place they found, they saw beneath them, and some distance away, the climbing Japanese marines. Instantly, Jim lifted his rifle and all three fired at once. Two of the Japanese fell, and another staggered against the brush, clawing at his chest.

Confused, and not knowing where the shots came from, the soldiers fired randomly. But their shots were aimed south, up the trail. Ponga Jim gave the signal, and they fired another volley, then faded into the jungle. They moved at a fast trot, occasionally stopping to listen.

The moonlight was lost in the high upper branches of the mangroves, and the three slipped down to the coast unseen. Ponga Jim hesitated an instant, looking out over the water. A destroyer lay out there but here, within a hundred and fifty feet, were two patrol boats. Four men waited beside them, on guard.

"All right, here's where we take them," Jim said.

Working along the edge of the jungle, he got within sixty feet of the boats. Here was a small, sandy beach. Lyssy drew his knife, waited an instant, and then threw it.

The man facing the jungle grunted, and fell over on the sand. Startled, the three Japanese crowded about him. None of them had seen the knife, and they bent over to turn the fallen man on his back.

JIM RAN SWIFTLY and soundlessly. The nearest marine started to turn and straighten, but Jim's right hand smashed him on the point of the chin, knocking him to the sand.

Big London rushed in close, and a soldier grabbed at his extended left arm, but Big London was too quick, and he kicked viciously, his heel striking the man on the kneecap. With a low cry the man fell, and then Big London clamped on a headlock, twisted sharply, and sat down hard on the sand.

He got up quietly. The job was finished, and Jim sent the two men to one boat and he took the other. They started the motors and headed out to sea. Jim glanced at the destroyer. If they were challenged . . .

They were. They were just sheering off to bear away from the destroyer when a command boomed out over a loudspeaker. Big London and Lyssy were in the boat behind him. They kept on their path and instantly a shot plunged across their bows.

Without an instant's hesitation, Jim acted. Turning onto a course toward the destroyer, he opened the motor wide. With a roar, the boat almost leaped from under him. He slammed the two arming levers on the console down and punched every button he could see. Whirling, he leaped to the rear deck and dove off into the churning water.

The other boat was alongside, and Lyssy grabbed him by the shoulders. He was not quite in the boat when the first patrol boat was shelled by the destroyer. The bow went to fragments and the boat was dead in the water and sinking. Then there was an appalling crash, and the thunder of a terrific explosion. A burst of fire momentarily appeared alongside the Japanese warship.

Ponga Jim grabbed the wheel from Big London and sent the speedboat roaring out to sea, her bottom fairly skimming the waves.

"What was that explosion?" London asked, staring with wide eyes. "The destroyer, she all afire."

"The speedboat had two torpedoes in its tubes," Mayo said, "so has this one."

The black sea swept past underneath them, and in the distance a thin gray line began to grow above the horizon. Jim's face was set and hard as the boat roared down the coast heading for Tobalai. The patrol boat would do fifty miles an hour, and was doing it.

The fleet would be moving now, moving out across the sea toward the north. And on the tableland of Tobalai, his planes, the aircraft he had been entrusted with, would be warming up, waiting for the American aircraft of the carrier squadron to take the bait and fly to attack the Japanese battleships. The trap was set and the disguise was perfect.

Big London crouched low behind Jim, and Lyssy stared back at the glow where the destroyer burned. The sea raced by, and Jim's hands gripped the wheel. It was a long way, but they could make it, they might make it.

"What happen to our ship, I wonder?" Big London asked.

"I don't know," Jim said. "I just don't know."

He had been thinking of that, too. The *Semiramis,* all he owned in the world, and the crew, who were not only men who worked with and trusted him, but his friends.

DAY WAS JUST BREAKING when he ran into the cove on the shore of Tobalai. Dropping anchor in shallow water, the three went over the side and Mayo and Big London walked ashore.

"We're here," Ponga Jim grinned. "Now there's not much left to do."

"Excuse me, *Capitan* Mayo," a voice said politely, "I dislike to interrupt but I must ..."

Ponga Jim turned, unbelieving. "How ... ?"

Captain Tushima smiled. "I flew here. You see ..." He gestured with one hand to a line of soldiers with machine guns. "You two are my prisoners!"

Two? Mayo did not turn his head, but in his heart there was a sudden burst of elation.

"You're always around at the wrong time, Captain," he said coolly, "and this is the worst."

He turned carelessly. Big London, his black face sober, stood about a dozen feet away. Lyssy was gone. Evidently he had sensed trouble and stayed underwater after diving out of the boat.

Brace Lamprey and Mallory came down from the jungle. Lamprey looked around.

"Where's the guy with the trick haircut?" he demanded sharply.

"Who?" Ponga Jim asked innocently. "You mean the Toradjas?"

"I don't know what he is," Lamprey returned. "The big fellow with the front half of his head shaved."

"That's him. The Toradjas warriors all wear their hair that way. He left us back in the jungle on Obi Major. We scattered out, and he didn't get back with us."

Mallory said nothing, but stared at Jim, a curious light in his eyes. Eric Frazer came down out of the jungle. He was wearing a gun and his cheekbone was badly cut, one eye black.

Ponga Jim grinned at him, and Frazer's eyes blazed.

"I owe you one, Mayo, and I'm going to give it to you now!" He walked up, and drawing his gun, drew back to hit Jim with the barrel.

Ponga Jim made believe to duck, but instead, lunged forward and hit Frazer with his shoulder, knocking the man into the sand. His face red with anger, Frazer swung up the gun to kill Mayo, but Tushima spoke sharply, and he stopped.

"I thought you wanted him killed," Frazer said sullenly. "Why keep him alive?"

"Because," Tushima said slowly, "I want one American to see with his own eyes the destruction of the rest of their most powerful fleet."

Ponga Jim looked at him, but said nothing. Tushima turned, and motioning the guards to follow with him, started back up the steep path.

Jim thought rapidly. He was a prisoner, but there still was time if he could free himself, and Lyssy had escaped. There was no greater woodsman alive, and if anything could be done, he would do it.

TUSHIMA DROPPED BACK to walk beside Jim.

"This war has long been coming, *Capitan* Mayo," he said gravely, "but we shall win now that it is here."

"Yeah?" Jim shook his head. "If you'd been smart enough to see that getting bogged down in China proper wasn't a solution to getting bogged down in Manchuria you wouldn't be trying to take over more territory than you can ever hold. The situation gets worse with every island you take."

Tushima shrugged. "I am only responsible for delivering a victory here and now. Policy, I leave to others."

"Yeah? Well, someone hasn't studied their history and someday they are very likely to stick you with the problem."

THE MOUNTAIN ROSE toward the plateau in steplike formation, and on the topmost step before reaching the tableland itself, several houses and barracks had been constructed in the jungle.

Rayna Courcel came from a bungalow as Ponga Jim approached. Her eyes widened a little, but she said nothing. Once she glanced at Mallory, but Ross was silent.

Ponga Jim and London were put into a cell behind a barred door. Jim sat down on the cot. Only a few hours remained, probably less than that, and the only factor in the whole mess that promised anything at all was the fact that Lyssy was outside in the jungle.

Beyond the barracks and in the jungle on the edge of the tableland above were the two huge gasoline storage tanks with fuel for the planes. Already there was a bustle of movement around them as the planes were being readied for their big fight. The American torpedo bombers were being armed and serviced, crewmen were even freshening the insignias on their sides and wings to be sure that they couldn't be missed.

Excitement was in the air now, for all knew what was coming, and not one but knew that on this flight might rest the future of the Japanese empire. At one fell stroke, they might wreck the remaining naval power of the United States, sending the last of the Pacific Fleet into the dark turmoil of oil-slicked waves.

Ponga Jim stared thoughtfully at the fuel tanks. They weren't so far away at that. If he could rid himself of that guard he might be able to handle the door. He turned to examine it again and was surprised to see Rayna.

"You here?" he said. "I should think you'd be aloft watching the preparations."

Her expression did not change. "How long will it take the planes to get there? To the strait, I mean?"

He shrugged. "A bit less than half an hour, I think. But not much. If you're sticking around, you'd better keep out of the way. You wouldn't look very nice all mussed up, and I may take a notion to crash out."

"Would you?" Rayna looked at him curiously. "Why?"

"A lot of the usual reasons. I'm patriotic, I suspect. Then I wouldn't want to see all those kids in fleet getting ambushed by planes that I brought out here."

"But what could you do?" Rayna asked. "One man, against so many."

"As much as possible." He looked at her carefully. "I haven't got you placed, though, honey. Just where do you fit in?"

"Actually I'm assistant to the Canadian military attaché in Pretoria." She smiled. "We heard that something was up but I think I'm in over my head. . . ."

"Is there a radio around here?" Jim asked, keeping his eyes on her.

"Yes. It's in the barracks, on the upper floor."

"Then talk to the guard a minute." Jim had been looking at the door. It was a door of steel bars, but the hinges were set in a wooden frame. It had been hastily made, with a guard on duty, it didn't have to be that strong.

He turned to Big London. "Step up here, old fellow. This guard doesn't savvy American. I've been watching him. You and me are going out of this joint, and I mean now."

Big London grinned, showing his white teeth and flexing his muscles. "What do we do, Cap?"

Ponga Jim walked up to the door and took hold of the bars. The guard was standing in the door explaining something to Rayna in Japanese.

London took hold of the bars and looked at Jim. Mayo took a breath.

"Let's *go!*" he said, and heaved with all his strength.

The iron bars of the door broke away from the frame on the first heave, splintering the crudely hewn wood. The guard whirled, jerking up his gun, but as he started to take a step, Rayna tripped him.

The marine spilled over on his face, and as Big London gave another terrific heave, wrenching the door away from its flimsy, shanty framing, Jim lunged through. A blow with the rifle butt as the guard started to get up, and he was knocked completely cold.

"Come on!" Jim snapped.

CHAPTER VII

Ponga Jim picked up the rifle and started at a rapid walk for the barracks. They had made it almost halfway before someone noticed them. Then two Japanese soldiers stopped and stared at them.

Without a second's hesitation, Ponga Jim walked right up to the nearest one, smiling. Rayna said something he didn't follow in Japanese, and the man frowned, looking uncertainly from Jim's gun to the Negro. Jim was almost within arm's length of the man when the soldier made up his mind that something was wrong. He opened his mouth to yell, and Jim drove the barrel of the rifle into the soldier's solar plexus with terrific force.

Big London, who had been carrying a length of wood, sprang up and knocked the rifle from the second man's hand, then brought the club down over his head. Grabbing up the rifles they ran for the barracks.

Behind them was a startled yell, then a shot. Jim turned and fired three times, taking his own sweet time and dropping each man he shot at. Then they rushed into the empty barracks and slammed the door. London jerked a table in front of it, and they rushed on upstairs after Rayna.

A Japanese sat at the desk when they came in, and he reached for a gun. Big London whirled, smashing him across the back of the neck with the rifle butt.

"Get at the window," Jim said quietly. "Rayna, if you can shoot, take one of those rifles, but don't waste any shots."

The switch was open and he sat down and slipping on the headphones began to call:

"Calling U.S. Pacific Fleet, any ship ... calling Pacific Fleet ... you are running into danger ... you are running into danger!"

Almost instantly and so quickly it surprised him, a voice snapped in his ear, the tones sharp, incisive: "Come in, please ... identify yourself?"

"Captain James Mayo, master of the freighter *Semiramis* ... calling from Tobalai ... the enemy has planes waiting to take off ... battleships and submarines in vicinity of Greyhound Strait ... some planes bear American markings ..."

BIG LONDON'S RIFLE was firing steadily now, and outside shouts of anger could be heard. Above on the tableland a plane's motor broke into a roar. A hail of lead swept the room, but most of it was too high. Rayna was firing now.

Jim stayed at the instrument. "Check with Major Arnold, British Military Intelligence ... two battleships ..."

"Hold it!"

Jim turned his head, gun in hand, to see Ross Mallory in the hall.

"They've been holding me here," Mallory said. "Let me in on this!"

"Is this a double cross?" Jim demanded harshly. "Mallory, you start anything now and I'll kill you!"

"Nothing like that. They had me in a tight spot. I was supposed to do the broadcast that made them think the American planes were returning early." Mallory was sweating. "I can't do it, no matter what it costs me. Here ..." He handed Mayo a notebook.

Jim glanced down at the notebook, open at the page. "Those are the forces here," Mallory said. "Tell them."

Ponga Jim snapped into the mouthpiece: "Are you there?"

"Waiting," the voice was cool.

"Two battleships, *Nagato* class ... three cruisers of the *Myokos* class, one *Furutaka* ... at least ten submarines."

The firing was a steady roar now, and leaving the switch open, Jim jumped from the radio and grabbed up a rifle. Down below the men were trying to mount the stairs with Mallory holding it with bursts from a light machine gun.

They tried a rush, but the machine gun and Jim's rifle stopped it.

Then a single shot rang out and Mallory backed up, coughing. The long gun started to slip from his hands and Jim caught it, charging halfway down the stairs, the gun chattering.

The crowd of Japanese melted, and Jim raced back up the steps. He grabbed up more ammunition, stuffing it in his pockets. Then, he lifted the machine gun and fired a burst at the nearest gasoline storage tank.

The tracers hit the tank and there was a terrific blast of fire; a wave of heat struck them like a blow. The barracks sagged with the power of it, and then yells and screams lifted and were lost in the roaring inferno of the burning gasoline.

Catching Rayna by the hand, Jim yelled at Big London. Mallory was dead. Evidently, something crooked he had done in the past had given the spies a hold over him, but he had died a brave death in the end. The three raced down the stairs, forgotten in the roaring flames outside. Running, they started up a back trail to the plateau above.

Suddenly, from behind them there was a gigantic explosion that almost knocked them to their knees. "The other tank," Jim said.

They ran on, gasping for breath. The jungle had been showered with gasoline and flame, and burning and blackened shreds of foliage were falling around them. They reached the plateau in a dense cloud of smoke. Several Japanese saw them and ran forward. Ponga Jim opened up, firing a burst, then dashed for a plane.

Suddenly, from nowhere, Lyssy was beside them.

"The ship!" he yelled. Flames danced on his brown face and his staring eyes. "The ship, she come!"

Turning, Ponga Jim looked down. True enough, the old *Semiramis* was below, lying a half mile off shore. Even as they watched, her guns belched fire. She was firing on a Japanese submarine.

Jim wheeled, passing the machine gun to Big London.

"Go to the ship!" he shouted. "Hurry!"

"What about you?" Rayna cried, catching his sleeve.

"I'm going up there," he said.

Then he was gone, running for an idling plane. It was a captured fighter, probably taken from another supply ship taking American planes to the East Indies.

A Japanese was just getting into the seat, and Jim grabbed him, jerking him back. The flyer fell awkwardly, and a mechanic started to run around the plane, but Jim was already in, and in a matter of seconds the plane went roaring down the plateau. Just in time, he eased back on the stick and the fighter shot aloft.

Only a few planes remained on the field, for most of them had taken off just before the explosion of the first tank. Jim leveled off and opened the throttle wide, heading for Greyhound Strait.

What was happening up ahead he could only guess. There was a silence that worried him. Still, he had far to go. He swung wide, turning to go south of Taliabu.

Like a bullet from a gun, his ship roared through the sky at three hundred miles an hour.

Easing back on the stick, he climbed, reaching for more and more altitude. Then, through a break in the clouds, he saw it, the splendid majesty of the fleet, moving up the sea in formation, but no longer headed for a deadly surprise, now for a battle. Almost automatically, he had slipped into his 'chute.

Then, lower down and ahead of him, already swinging toward the fleet, he saw the flight of false American planes. The decks of the carriers were partially empty, indicating that they had launched aircraft in pursuit of the Japanese warships that had been intended as bait. Jim prayed that they would stay away from the coming battle and not add to the confusion and slaughter.

Ponga Jim looked down at the formation of planes, then at the fleet below them and ahead. With a grin and a wave to the gods who watch over fools and flyers, he pushed the stick forward. The nose went down and he opened the throttle wide. He was behind them, and with the sun behind him. A perfect start.

The heavy plane went into the roaring crescendo of a power dive, and he saw the air-speed needle climbing up 300 … 350 … 400 … 450, and then he was opening up with all six machine guns and the cannon. A fighter below him swerved and suddenly burst into flame. It crashed into another plane, and the two whirled earthward in a tangled mass of twisting metal. His guns were spewing flame again and in an instant he was in the middle of a dogfight, alone against a dozen enemy planes.

He saw a torpedo plane pull up and go whirling out of sight, then a fighter was in his sights, then he was past and the aircraft was a plummeting mass of wreckage. Ack-ack from the ships opened up and anti-aircraft machine-gun fire laced the sky.

Now that the formation had broken, the Japanese pilots couldn't locate him as quickly in the confusion of the battle. Every plane in the sky had American markings. Yet he knew that anything flying was his enemy. Fighting like a demon, and using the ship as though it were part of him, he circled, spun, dove, and climbed, fighting the ships with everything it had. In the middle of it, he glanced upward and saw something that made his heart jolt with fear. High above he saw a fighter ship peel off of a new formation and come shooting down toward them, and after it a long string of others. The American planes! The returning planes from the carriers!

Down below he could see the belching guns, and hear the mighty thunder of crashing cannon as the Japanese ships opened fire. But then he was shooting upward, climbing out and praying that he wouldn't be shot down by his own countrymen.

They fell upon the Japanese-piloted aircraft and suddenly Jim could see the method to their madness. Every American pilot had his cockpit canopy slid back. They were taking a horrible buffeting but, at close range at least, they could identify each other. Jim ripped the Perspex windscreen back and wheeled back into the fray.

A ship showed in his sights and he opened up, ripping a long line of holes down the side, and the plane suddenly turned into flame, and fell from sight.

How long he fought he didn't know, or how many ships he downed, but then suddenly, he saw a torpedo bomber headed toward a battleship, and he did an Immelmann and whipped around on the bomber's tail. The rear gunner opened fire on him, but he roared on into the blazing guns, his own, one steady stream of fire.

He was coming in from slightly below and suddenly, a shell from his cannon hit the torpedo on the enemy plane. There was a terrific blast of fire, and a crash like thunder, and then his own plane, hit by a barrage of flying fragments, dove crazily.

For an instant he righted it, but one wing was vibrating wildly and he knew he was finished. He struggled with the crash belts, a plane dove toward him, its guns roaring, and something struck him a terrific blow on the head.

In a blaze of pain lighted by the burning bomber, and accompanied by the rising crescendo of exploding shells, he turned back to the controls. He dropped toward the water, using his flaps to kill his speed and skipped across the ocean, like a stone. He saw sky and water, his body was pounded by forces he couldn't identify, whirled and slapped and was finally drenched with salty water laced with gasoline. He slipped out of the belts, gave thanks that the canopy was already open, and then lost consciousness.

IT WAS A LONG TIME later when he opened his eyes, and for an instant he could not remember what had happened. Around him were the familiar sights of his own cabin on the *Semiramis*. He tried to sit up, and pain struck him like a physical blow. For an instant everything was black, then he opened his eyes.

Major Arnold was standing over him, a look of concern on his face. Ponga Jim grinned, painfully.

"Always show up in time for the payoff, don't you?" he said.

Arnold smiled. "I showed up in time to fish you out of the water, and if I hadn't you would have been feeding the fish by now."

"What happened?" Jim asked.

Arnold shrugged. "What would happen? Once our boys knew what the score was they moved in and mopped up. Seven destroyers sunk, one battleship, and two cruisers. The fighting is over except for a few cleanup jobs.

"I was with your fleet, and they got planes off the carriers right away and hit the Jap ships from above before they were expecting it. They caught two of the cruisers inside the reef near Parigi and they never got out."

"How about this boat?" Ponga Jim asked.

Slug Brophy stepped up, grinning. He had a welt on his cheekbone and a long gash on his head.

"I got to the Gunner. Longboy had already got loose. They only left a few men aboard once they had the planes off. So we took over."

"Sounds like it was a swell scrap," Jim mumbled. He looked at Arnold. "I got a real crew, William. I got some good boys!"

"Right you are," Arnold agreed. "They handled it nicely."

"Did any of them get away?" Jim asked seriously.

"Only one," Brophy said. "But we got two submarines before they could dive, and laid a couple of shells aboard a battlewagon. The Gunner always wanted to shoot at a battlewagon," Brophy added.

"Here's somebody who wants to talk to you," Arnold said as Rayna appeared. "I don't get it, Mayo. Here I am, handsome, with a smooth-looking white and gold uniform, romantic eyes, and the figure of a Greek god, and yet you get all the women!"

"It's the poissonality, William!" Jim sighed, grinning. "It's the poissonality!"

Wings Over Brazil

CHAPTER I

Ponga Jim Mayo walked out on the terrace and stood looking down the winding road that led across the miles to Fortaleza and the Brazilian coast. Behind him the orchestra was rolling out a conga. Under the music he could hear the clink of glasses and the laughter of women.

His broad, powerful shoulders filled the immaculate white dinner coat, and as he walked to the edge of the terrace, he thrust his big, salt-hardened hands into his coat pockets, bunching them into fists.

"It doesn't make sense," he muttered, "something smells."

"What is it, Captain Mayo? What's troubling you?" He knew, even as he turned, that only one woman could have such a voice. Señorita Carisa Montoya had been introduced to him earlier, but he knew well enough who she was. She was visiting from São Paulo, and he had met her ships in a score of ports, knew of her mines and ranches. He had been surprised only that she was so young and beautiful.

He shrugged. "Troubling me? I'm curious why the skipper of a tramp freighter is invited here, with this crowd."

He glanced out over the spacious, parklike grounds. All about him was evidence of wealth and power. A little too much power, he was thinking. And the people dancing and talking, they were smooth, efficient, powerful people. They represented the wealth and ambition of all Latin America.

She smiled as he lit her cigarette. "You seem perfectly at home, Captain," she said, "and certainly, there isn't a more attractive man here."

"At home?" He studied her thoughtfully. "Maybe, but being invited here doesn't make sense. I had never met Don Pedro Norden before."

"Possibly he has a shipping contract for you," Carisa suggested. "With his holdings, shipping is a problem during a war."

"Might be." Ponga Jim was skeptical. "But with your ships and those of Valdes, he wouldn't need mine."

"You're too suspicious," she told him, smiling. She took him by the arm. "Why don't you ask me to dance?"

They started toward the floor. "Suspicious? Of course I am, this is wartime."

She glanced at him quickly. "But aren't you a freelancer? A sailor of fortune? I hear you take cargo wherever you choose to go, regardless of the war."

"That's right. But I'm still an American," he said simply. "Even sailors of fortune have their loyalties."

Three men stepped out of a door. One was Don Ricardo Valdes, a shipping magnate from the Argentine. The other two were strangers. One tall, slightly stooped, middle-aged. His gray face was vulpine, his eyes intent and cruel.

The other man was slightly over six feet, but so broad as to seem short. His blond hair was trimmed close in a stiff pompadour, and he had a wide, flat face with a broken nose. He looked like a wrestler, and had actually been a top-notch heavyweight boxer.

"Captain Mayo?" Valdes held out a hand. "I'd like to present Dr. Felix Von Hardt and Hugo Busch."

Von Hardt's hand was what Mayo expected, careful, dry, and without warmth. Busch had a grip to match his shoulders, and when Ponga Jim met the challenge, strength for strength, the German's face flushed angrily.

"If the señorita will excuse us?" Von Hardt's voice was smooth.

"Of course." Carisa looked at Ponga Jim. "But I'll be expecting you later, Captain. We must have our dance."

When she was gone, Valdes lit a cigarette. "Captain, we've heard you have an aircraft—an eight-passenger ship? We'll give you fifty thousand dollars for it."

The plane was stowed away on the Semiramis at Fortaleza. No one had been aboard but the crew and government officials, so how did these men know of the plane?

"Sorry." Mayo's voice was regretful. "It's not for sale."

Did they know where he got the plane, he wondered? He had taken it, as one of the fortunes of war, from Count Franz Kull, a German espionage agent and saboteur, in New Guinea. It was specially built, an amphibian with a few hidden surprises that the agent had paid dearly for.

"I'll double the price," Valdes said. "One hundred thousand."

"Sorry, gentlemen," Mayo repeated. "That plane is one of my most prized possessions."

"You'd better take what you can get," Busch said harshly, "when you can get it."

Ponga Jim measured the German. "I don't like threats, friend. Now, if you'll excuse me—"

Valdes halted him. "Think it over, Captain," he suggested. "We can turn a lot of business your way. Especially," he added meaningfully, "after the war."

Ponga Jim's fists balled in his coat pocket. "I'll take my chances, Valdes," he said coldly. "I don't like the odor of your friends."

SEÑORITA MONTOYA was dancing. For once Mayo would have liked to cut in. But it was a practice he had never cared for, and everywhere, but in the United States, was considered grossly impolite.

He had taken but a few steps when she was beside him. "Have you forgotten our dance, Captain?"

Ponga Jim looked at her and caught his breath. She was radiantly beautiful. Too beautiful, he thought, to believe. He remembered that again, a moment later.

"I hope you made the deal, Captain," she said, "it would be wise."

"Why?" Over his shoulder he saw Von Hardt talking to Don Pedro. The big Spanish-German was a powerful man physically with a domineering manner thinly veiled by a recent layer of polish.

"Because I like you, Captain," she said simply, "and these are dangerous times."

His eyes narrowed. Another threat? Or a warning? "Think nothing of it," he said, smiling again. "All times are dangerous in my business. I play my cards as they fall, the way I want to play them. I'll make my own rules and abide by the consequences."

He knew Busch, at least, was a full-fledged Nazi. Von Hardt probably was. Scanning the room, Mayo noticed at least a dozen others with a pronounced military bearing.

Don Ricardo, he knew, was hand in glove with the Falange. Just before the war, on a visit to Spain, the man had spent much time with Suner, the pro-Nazi foreign minister. If ever a room was filled with Nazi sympathizers, this was it.

He was startled from his meditations by a sudden stiffening of Carisa's body under his hand. Her eyes were over his shoulder, and turning, he glanced toward the French doors.

A slender, broad-shouldered man stood there alone. He was undeniably handsome, but was only a trifle over five feet tall. One hand touched the neatly waxed mustache, and the other was in his coat pocket. He surveyed the room with all the sangfroid of a ringmaster watching a group of trained horses perform.

A subtle change had come over the guests. Men had stopped talking. Faces had stiffened. Mayo glanced at Norden and saw the multimillionaire's face slowly change from rage to a cold, ugly triumph. All evening he had felt the charged atmosphere of danger at Castillo Norden. Now for the first time, it had centered on one object. However, the small man in the door was undisturbed.

Then Mayo saw something else. A dark form flitted past the French doors behind the man and faded into the shadows beside the window. Then another. Two more men, hard-looking customers in evening clothes, were walking toward the window, talking quietly. Another man left his partner and lit a cigarette.

They were coming, closing in. Slowly, casually, as in a well-rehearsed play. And the little man kept watching the room with an air of blasé indifference.

Carisa's face was deathly pale. "Please!" she whispered. "Let's go to the conservatory. I feel faint."

He was fed up with wondering who was on what side and pretending that he had an open, cosmopolitan attitude about such things. He had been invited here so that he could be conned into selling his aircraft by a bunch of Nazis and he was expected to politely not notice.

"Sorry," he said. "You go. I want to talk to that man." He was startled by the fear in her eyes.

"No!" she whispered. "You mustn't. There's going to be trouble."

He laughed at her. "Of course," he said, "that's why I'm going."

Casually, he walked over to the man standing by the windows. The musicians were playing another piece now, a louder one.

"Hi, buddy," Mayo said softly. "I don't know who you are, but you're right behind the eight ball. There are four or five men on the terrace and more here in the room."

The smile revealed amazingly white teeth. "Of course." The little man bowed slightly. "They do not like me here. I am Juan Peligro. Your name?"

"Mayo. Jim Mayo."

Peligro's eyebrows lifted. "So?" He looked at Ponga Jim thoughtfully. "I have heard of you, Captain. Have they made an offer for your amphibian yet?"

Ponga Jim glanced at Peligro quickly. "How did you know?"

"One learns much. They need planes, these men."

A burly man with a square, brutal face suddenly stood beside Mayo. "Captain Mayo? Don Ricardo wishes to speak with you."

"Why not let him come here?" Ponga Jim said. "I like it in this room."

The man's face darkened. "You'd better go," he insisted. "This man does not belong here. He is going to be dealt with."

Ponga Jim grinned suddenly. He felt amazingly good. "I like him," he said. "I like this guy. You deal with him, you deal with me."

The man hesitated. Obviously, they wanted no outward disturbance. "We don't want any trouble," the man said, "you—"

His right hand dropped to his pocket too slowly. Ponga Jim's left hand closed on his wrist, and his right moved also, in the form of a fist. That punch struck the man in the solar plexus and knocked every bit of wind out of him.

As he started to fall, Ponga Jim caught him by the shoulders and spun him around. Using the man as a shield, he started for the door. "Let's go," he said over his shoulder.

Don Pedro Norden and Dr. Von Hardt were standing at the door. Von Hardt's expression was stiff. Norden was purple with rage. "You fool," he snarled angrily. "I'll have you bullwhipped."

"Try it," Ponga Jim said, smiling.

At the outer door, the man Mayo was holding made a sudden lunge. Instantly, Mayo pushed him hard between the shoulders. As the man fell down the steps, the two made a dash into the shrubbery beyond the drive.

Running swiftly across the grass, Peligro spoke to Ponga Jim. "Gracias, amigo. But you make trouble for yourself."

"What would I do? That gang was tough."

Behind them Mayo heard running feet. Somewhere a motor roared into life, then all was still. But he was under no illusions. The pursuit would be swift, efficient, and relentless. Worst of all, it was more than ten miles to Fortaleza.

They had started across another curve of the drive when a car rounded a bend and they were caught dead in the headlights. Before they could get off the drive, the car swept alongside.

"Quickly!" It was Carisa Montoya at the wheel, and Ponga Jim did not hesitate. Peligro was in beside them and the car rolling almost as soon as she had spoken.

Miraculously, the gate was unguarded. The broad highway to the port lay open before them. Yet before they had been driving more than two minutes, Carisa slowed and sent the big car into a side road that led off down a steep grade through clumps of trees.

She slowed down. The car purred along almost silently. Huge boulders loomed up and were passed. Trees cast weird shadows over the road. Then they turned again and swung in a narrow semicircle back toward the hacienda.

"The highway is a trap," Carisa explained swiftly. "Don Pedro has five guards between the Castillo Norden and Fortaleza. No one can approach his place without permission."

"You'd better drop us and get back," Mayo warned. "This is all right for us, but for you it might be bad."

"Yes, please," Peligro said suddenly. "Let us out. The stable road will take you back without their knowledge. Then instantly to bed. We can go on from here."

The car slid soundlessly away. Ponga Jim Mayo looked after her. "That woman's got nerve," he said. "But not the best of friends."

Peligro was already moving, and before they had gone a hundred yards, Mayo knew that he was not walking blind. The little man knew where he was going.

"They will scour the country," Peligro said. "Don Pedro will be angry that I came here tonight."

"Will the señorita be able to get back all right?" Mayo asked.

Peligro shrugged. "She? But of course. The stable road, it is most safe. The peóns are there, but then, they see what they wish to see."

"Would Norden kill a woman?"

Peligro chuckled without humor. "He would kill anyone. He lives for power, that man."

"Is he a Nazi? Busch looked it."

"Sí, Busch was a storm trooper. Von Hardt is also a Nazi. But Don Pedro Norden? He is a Nordenista, amigo, and that is all. He uses the Nazis as they use him."

"What about you?"

"I?" Peligro chuckled. "Let us say I love what Don Pedro hates. Perhaps that is sufficient. But then, I am a Colombian."

"The fifth column is strong in Colombia." Mayo studied the figure ahead of him.

"Naturalmente. Everywhere. But my country could never be a Nazi domain. There are more bookshops in Bogotá than cafés. Think of that, amigo. Men who read are not Nazis."

Peligro stopped suddenly, then deliberately pushed through a thick wall of brush beside the path. After a few minutes, they stood in a small clearing. Under the arching branches was an autogyro, the outline of its rotating wing lost in the shadows.

Ponga Jim looked at the Colombian with respect. "Well, I'm stumped," he said. "You think of everything, don't you?"

Juan Peligro winked. "One does or one dies, my friend."

CHAPTER II

It was still dark when Ponga Jim Mayo came alongside the ship. Only a dim anchor light forward, and the faint glow over the accommodation ladder. He paid the boatman and watched him start for the Custom House Pier. For some reason, he felt uneasy.

He glanced forward at the bulking stern of the freighter that lay a ship's length beyond the *Semiramis*. She was a Norwegian ship, the *Nissengate*.

Mayo had mounted the ladder and was just stepping to the deck when a dark figure hurled itself from the blackness beyond the light. A shoulder struck him a terrific blow in the chest, and he was knocked off balance into the hand-line.

It caught him just at the hips, and overbalanced, he fell headfirst into the sea. He hit the water unhurt and went down, deep, deeper. He caught himself and struck out for the surface.

A dark body swirled by him, and a knife slashed. Avoiding it, he shot through the surface, and an instant later his attacker broke water not six feet away. Ponga Jim dived and grabbed the man's wrist, wrenching the knife from his grasp. Then closing with him, Mayo began to smash powerful blows into his body.

The man sagged suddenly. All the breath had been knocked from his body. The platform of the accommodation ladder seemed only a few feet away. Ponga Jim struck out, reached it, and crawled up. He dragged his prisoner with him.

He lay still, getting his wind. Then he got up and pushed the stumbling man ahead of him up the ladder.

"What iss?" A big man with a childlike pink face stepped out of the dark.

Instantly, Ponga Jim knew his mistake. Fighting and swimming, they had worked their way forward until alongside the Norwegian ship, boarding it by mistake. Glancing back toward the other ship, he could see they had swung nearer on the tide.

"Sorry," Mayo said. "This fellow jumped me as I came aboard my ship. I'll call a boat and we'll go back."

The seaman stared at him warily. He was carrying a short club and a gun. He looked like a tough customer. "How I know dat's true?"

The man who had attacked Ponga Jim came to life. "It's a lie," he burst out. "He attacked me."

"Aboard my own ship?" Mayo laughed. "Hardly." He swung the man into the light. He was short and thick, almost black. There was an ugly scar over one eye, another on his cheek. He glared sullenly at Mayo, then with a jerk, broke free.

Ponga Jim grabbed at him, but the watchman stepped between. "How do I know yet which iss lyin'?" he demanded.

"Ask the men aboard my ship." Ponga Jim gestured aft. "The *Semiramis.*"

The man peered at him. "Dot iss not der *Semiramis.* I neffer see no ship by dot name. Dot iss der *Chittagong,* of Calcutta."

"What?" Mayo stared aft. The dark loom of the ship was unfamiliar. Her bridge was too high, and there were three lifeboats along the port side of her boat deck, not two as on the *Semiramis.*

"You come aboard der wrong ship, mister," the seaman told him. "I t'ink you better go ashore now."

The man with the scarred face leered at him, his yellowish eyes triumphant. Ponga Jim looked from one to the other. Dripping with water, he turned and went down the gangway.

When he had hailed a harbor boat, he had himself sculled aft. The other ship was a flush-decker at least a thousand tons heavier than the *Semiramis.* There were four other ships in the harbor, all unknown to him.

Ponga Jim Mayo scowled and let his memory travel back for a moment. Shortly after eight-thirty that morning, he had walked down the accommodation ladder and been taken ashore. Slug Brophy and Gunner Millan, his first and second mates, had leaned on the rail as he went. Beyond, several of the crew had been working about the deck.

Back on the Custom House Pier, Mayo took stock of the situation. He had been through too much with his crew to doubt their loyalty. He knew Brophy would never consent to move without ample reason, for Brophy was not a man to be bluffed or imposed upon.

Somewhere in the background would be Norden and his Nazi friends. Fourteen hours earlier, Mayo had left the ship with a full crew. Now she was gone.

In the meantime, he had received an offer for his amphibian plane. Upon refusing the offer, he had been threatened. The affair of Juan Peligro had brought about an open break with his host.

The Spanish-German might have had the ship removed from the harbor. If so, he would have laid deliberate plans to conceal his action. He would be ruthlessly efficient. No doubt the officials in port were all in his pay.

Coolly, Ponga Jim went to a hotel, obtained a room, and went to bed. In the morning after a good breakfast, he sought out Duro the port captain. "What happened to the *Semiramis?*" Ponga Jim asked. "When I went ashore yesterday she lay aft of the *Nissengate.* When I returned she was gone."

The Brazilian looked at him thoughtfully. "The *Semiramis,* you say? I never heard of it."

"The pilot who brought me in was Du Silva," Mayo said.

Captain Duro studied Ponga Jim curiously, then shrugged. "I don't think so. Señor Du Silva has not come to work all week ... I believe he is sick."

"Now that's a bunch of ..." Then he stopped. "I see," he said warily.

"If I were you," the man told him lazily, leaning toward him, "I'd go home and get some sleep."

Ponga Jim's hand shot out and took the port officer by the throat. "And if I were you," he said coldly, "I'd figure out another story before the American consul and President Vargas begin to ask questions."

Duro's face paled, but he merely stared at Mayo, his eyes ugly.

"What could you tell them? That your ship, armed with a full crew, had been stolen from the harbor? It could be very amusing, señor."

Ponga Jim slammed the port captain back into his chair. "No," he said flatly, "I'd tell them Don Pedro Norden was a traitor, and that you were his tool."

He strode from the office. After all, Duro was right. It would be an utterly preposterous story. Ships of several thousand tons displacement do not vanish into thin air. As for witnesses, no doubt fifty people had noticed the *Semiramis,* but how many could see her name at that distance? The *Chittagong,* moored in the same place, would be considered the same ship. The few who knew better could be bribed or frightened.

Then, he was aware of the fact that his own reputation did not appeal to many government officials. He had been in action against the Japanese and Germans in the East Indies before the war began. That his aid had been invaluable to the Dutch and British was data burned deep into reports of their intelligence services. The fact that he had usually profited from those services would be enough to blacken his reputation with some people.

A man of Norden's strength could build a substantial case against a lone captain of a tramp freighter with a mixed crew. Even if he won in the end and proved his point, it would require months of red tape and argument. In the meantime, what of his ship and his men?

Just why Norden wanted planes Mayo did not know, but the presence of Nazis on the hump of Brazil boded no good for the Allies. It was too near the source of bauxite for American planes. It was a place of great wealth and poverty, two elements that were often unstable when combined.

What Ponga Jim Mayo wanted done he must do himself. No doubt the communications were controlled by Norden, and it was to be doubted if any message he might send would be allowed to leave Fortaleza.

No doubt the freighter had been moved to some nearby river mouth or minor port where the plane would be removed. Possible anchorages were few, but there was nothing he could do to search. For the moment, the *Semiramis* and her crew must get along on their own. Don Pedro would expect him to protest to the government. He would expect excited demands, protests, much noise. In that case, it would be very simple for Don Pedro to have him sent to an insane asylum. Certainly, a man claiming someone had stolen an unknown ship and its crew would be insane enough for most people.

Long ago, Ponga Jim Mayo had discovered that attack was the best defense. He had discovered that plotters like to take their own time. He knew that one man with energy and courage could do much. So he wasn't going to protest or demand, he wasn't going to argue. He was going to carry the fight to the enemy.

Jim bought a suit of khakis, and returning to the hotel, changed from the bedraggled suit. Castillo Norden was on a spur of Mount Jua, approximately ten miles from town. In the side street not far from the hotel was a disreputable Model A. Nearby a Brazilian loitered. He was a plump, sullen man with a mustache and round cheeks.

"How much to rent the car all day?" Mayo asked.

The Brazilian looked at him, bored. "You go to Castillo Norden, my friend," he replied, "you go to trouble."

Ponga Jim grinned. "Maybe I'm looking for trouble. Do we go?"

The Brazilian tossed his limp cigarette into the gutter.

"Why not?" he said with a shrug.

They rattled out of town and drove in silence for several miles. The man paid no attention to the main road, but took side roads toward Mount Jua. "I am Armando Fontes," he said, "always in troubles." He looked at Ponga Jim. "You have a gun?"

At Mayo's nod, he drew back his own coat and showed an enormous pistol stuffed in his waistband. "I, too!" he spat. "These men are bad. You better watch out. They got plenty stuff."

Leaving Fontes with the car, Ponga Jim walked up the stable road. He saw no one. It was easy to understand why Carisa and Peligro had been sure the road was safe.

It led through two rows of trees that would have allowed quick concealment in case of need.

Then he passed the stables and went on through the garden. He glanced back and saw a workman at the stables had straightened and was watching him, but when the *obrero* saw himself observed, he hastily bent over his work.

It was late afternoon when Ponga Jim slipped behind the boll of a palm, then behind a clump of hibiscus at the edge of the terrace where he had stood the night before.

He was waiting there when the French doors opened suddenly and

Don Pedro Norden came out, walking with Don Ricardo. "You will see," Norden was saying, "the planes will be here. The fields have been ready for months. As you know, there has been no passport control at Fortaleza and we've been importing technicians, army officers, engineers, all sorts of men, most of them Germans."

"What about the Japanese?" Valdes suggested.

"Ready. The colonies around Cananea and Registro will act simultaneously with those here in Ceará and those on the Amazon. Our men have been posted in key spots for weeks now, ready for the day. The transport planes will move them where they are needed."

Valdes smiled grimly and nodded.

"You will give the word?"

"Soon. There are approximately three million Germans, Japanese, and Italians in this country. Most, of course, want no trouble but our men will hide in those communities and when the time comes they will make sure that the right kind of incidents occur. I think we can count on a good many joining us once they are threatened by the government.

"First, seventy key men will be assassinated. To allow for mistakes, each man is covered by two groups. Vargas and Aranha are among the first, of course. Both are strong, capable men, and without them the army will have to step in.

"São Paulo will be seized—it is practically in our hands now. Also Manáos. The Amazon will be closed to traffic, all available shipping will be impounded. Our airfields here and at Teresina will be receiving and refueling planes. We will have Brazil before Vargas realizes we are moving."

Valdes nodded. "A good plan, and a careful one."

Norden snorted. "How did I make my money, Don Ricardo? By taking chances? I made it by planning. At all my properties in South America there are bases. Fuel is stored, the two ships in Fortaleza harbor are full of munitions for our cause, we are ready. This amphibian we picked up today—it will be priceless in getting about. We need many planes now, and they are hard to get."

"What of the United States?" Valdes asked. "Will they interfere?"

"The Germans believe so. I doubt it. The Axis backs this move because they want a diversion, something to divide the strength of the North Americans. The Yankees will send some forces here, but we can handle what they send. The Americans are soft—their own correspondents say so."

Valdes nodded. "Perhaps, but this Mayo, he took that situation over last night too fast to suit me."

"Him?" Norden sneered. "He will be telling people his wild story of a stolen ship. It is too preposterous!"

"Perhaps." Don Ricardo was uneasy. "You have been successful but perhaps you are too sure." Valdes hesitated, biting his lip. "Don Pedro," he said slowly, "I have been hearing stories. When the amphibian landed here one of the men recognized it. The plane is special, made to order for Count Kull, one of Germany's most dangerous secret agents. It was taken from him by an adventurer in the East Indies."

"You mean—Mayo?" Don Pedro was scowling.

"Just that. What I'm saying, Don Pedro," Valdes insisted, "is that Ponga Jim Mayo may be a very dangerous man."

Norden paused. "All right. I'll give the order that he be killed on sight. Now let us go in. I could use a drink."

CHAPTER III

Killed on sight. Ponga Jim watched them go. At least it was all in the clear now. The amphibian was here. If he only knew where the *Semiramis* was!

He stood still, staring out across the spacious grounds that surrounded the Castillo Norden. What a fool he was to believe he could cope with all this alone. Don Pedro Norden had stood upon the terrace like a king, a man who knew great power, yet thirsted for more. He was no petty criminal, no agent of a foreign power. He was playing the Axis off against the United States to win more power for himself.

Even to hope seemed foolish. The man was shrewd, he had power and held all the strings. Ponga Jim stood behind the hibiscus and knew that there was only one way out—right through the middle. Don Pedro had built well, but could the structure stand attack?

He glanced around. There was no one in sight. He caught the rack on which the wisteria grew and went up, hand over hand, to the balcony above.

He flattened against the building. He had been unobserved so far as he could see. He stepped to the window and pushed it inward. Carisa Montoya sat before a mirror in her robe, polishing her nails.

"Hello," he said cheerfully. "Did I come at the wrong time?"

She stiffened and swallowed a scream. "Jim, are you mad? If they find you here, they'll kill you. You've got to get away!" She caught him by the arm. "You must—now!"

"After all my trouble getting here? Anyway, why are you worried? And whose team are you on, anyway?"

"Not on theirs," she said. "But I have to be careful. And you're too good a dancer to die young."

He grinned. "Shucks, and I thought it was my boyish smile. All right, tell me one thing and I'll go. Where is Don Ricardo's room?"

Her face paled. "You mustn't. That would be insane."

"Tell me," he insisted. "The longer you stall, the greater the danger."

"Across the hall and the third door on your left."

He walked to the door, and turning the key, glanced out. The hall was empty. He stepped out and pulled the door shut softly. Then he walked quietly across the hall to the third door. He touched the knob, and it turned gently under his hand.

Ponga Jim Mayo opened the door and stepped in—and found himself looking into the business end of a Luger in the hands of Hugo Busch.

"So," the German said. "We meet again."

Jim said nothing. The German's left hand was holding the telephone handset which had evidently just been replaced on the cradle. Carisa! Could she—

The door opened behind him, and then he heard Valdes's crisp voice. "May I ask what this means?" he demanded.

"The American came in, I followed," Busch said, shrugging. "How he got here, I don't know."

"Don Ricardo," Ponga Jim said coolly, "do you think if he followed me in that I would be standing near the door? I came in and found him."

"He lies," Busch snapped. "What would I be doing in your rooms?"

Valdes looked at the German thoughtfully. "What, indeed? Nevertheless, Herr Busch, it will bear thought. Now, if you like, take him away. I must dress for dinner."

WITHOUT A WORD Busch marched Ponga Jim to a square building near the stables. The windows were heavily barred. A man working nearby glanced up and saw Jim, then went on repairing a wagon, uninterested.

Hugo Busch, keeping carefully out of reach, swung open a cell door and pushed Jim inside. Then, suddenly, and before Mayo could turn, Busch struck him over the head with the gun barrel.

Jim staggered and almost went to his knees, then Busch hit him again. Ponga Jim tottered against the wall, blood running into his eyes from a cut scalp, blinded by pain and the ruthlessness of the sudden attack. Calling a guard, Busch handed the soldier the gun. Then he turned around and walked up to Jim.

"So? You come to cause trouble, eh? We'll see about that. Maybe I'll give you all the trouble you want."

His left smashed Jim on the jaw, knocking him across the cell. Ponga Jim pawed blindly at his face to get the blood out of his eyes.

On the second jab, Jim went under it and smashed Busch under the heart with his right. Before Busch could clinch, Jim hooked a left to the jaw and jarred the German to his heels.

Bursting with rage, Hugo Busch rushed back. Using all the power and skill that had once carried him to the Olympics he went to work. Blinded by blood and pain from the two brutal blows with the gun, Jim could get no power into his blows. Busch came up with a sweeping hook that lifted Mayo bodily and knocked him against the wall. He hit hard, slipped to the floor, and his head banged against the steel cot.

In a bloody haze, he tried to get up, and slipped back. He felt a heavy kick in the ribs, then another, but consciousness slipped from him, and he lay still.

It was dark when he opened his eyes, pitch dark. He rolled over, his body one endless wave of pain. Struggling, he got his knees under him and straightened. His head felt heavy and rolled on his neck. Fumbling, he felt of his face. It was cut and swollen, and his head had two long gashes from the gun barrel, and a big lump from the blow against the cot.

How long he stayed on his knees he did not know, but suddenly, he came to himself and got up. Then he was suddenly sick, and going to the corner, retched violently. Feeling around, he found a bucket of water, took a long drink, then poured some in the basin and splashed it over his face and head.

Then he lay down on the cot and after a while, he fell asleep. It was morning when he awakened.

A FUMBLING OF a key in the lock awakened him, and he staggered to his feet to see Hugo Busch come in, stripped to the waist. The man was muscled powerfully, and he grinned at Mayo. There was a welt on his jaw, and a bit of a blue lump over one eye.

"Ready for a workout?" Busch grinned.

Unbelieving, Jim saw the man meant to beat him again. Busch walked up and swung his open hand at Jim's face. Bleary from the frightful beating of the night before, Mayo could barely roll his head out of the way, but Busch missed his careless slap, and it made him angry.

He jabbed a left at Jim's cut eye, and Jim started to go under it, but Busch was ready and dropped the left. The punch took Mayo between the eyes, and grabbing suddenly, he got Busch by the arm and jerked him into a right to the body. The punch lacked force, but had enough to hurt.

Busch tried to get loose, but Ponga Jim clinched and hung on.

Then the fighter broke free and went to work like a butcher at a chopping block. When the German left, he was covered with blood— Jim Mayo's blood. He laughed harshly.

"I'll be back," he said. "I'll be back tomorrow. We're going to put you in a ring to see how you Americans take it."

Ponga Jim backed up and sat down. After he had bathed his face again, he lay down and stared up at the ceiling through his swollen eyes. He had to get out. In time these beatings would kill him. If he had a chance to recover, and could start from scratch, it might be different. Now, there was no chance. Or was there?

For a long time he thought, and out of the thinking came a dim memory of a fight he had seen ten years before, of a fellow who used a Kid McCoy type of stunt. Out of that memory came a plan.

But it was a plan that covered only one phase. It did not cover escape. He had to get away, had to get out and let the authorities know what was being planned here.

It was then he heard the plane. Only a few minutes later, another, then several at once. He sat up abruptly. The transports were coming. That meant the day was soon to come.

IN THE MORNING he was still stiff and sore. He was battered, and he knew his cuts would open easily. A glance into a mirror showed he was hardly to be recognized. But he shadow-boxed a little to loosen up, and rubbed his muscles. He was, he knew, in no shape for such a battle as he would now have. But he was in better shape than Hugo Busch believed.

Valdes was with them when they came to get him. He frowned when he saw Ponga Jim's face.

"Been giving it to you, has he? Well, I don't like it."

Jim said nothing, and he was led to a ring that had been pitched in the open under some trees. Seats had been placed around, and there were at least thirty German officers there. One of them, an elderly man, scowled when he saw Mayo's face. He put a monocle in his eye and studied Jim briefly. Then he removed the monocle and started away. He took three steps but then walked back briskly.

"Good luck," he said briefly. "For myself, I don't care for this sort of thing."

Ponga Jim was stripped to the waist, and they were tying on the gloves when he looked up to see Carisa coming down the lane with Don Pedro and Von Hardt. She involuntarily put a hand to her mouth when she saw Jim's face.

Busch got into the ring, and Jim barely had time to take the piece of tissue paper from under his arm and put it a little higher, so it would not be noticed. The action passed unseen.

Someone struck a bell, and Busch walked out. Jim came to meet him, then lifted his left arm. From the armpit the thin sheet of tissue paper floated toward the floor.

For an instant, Busch stared. Involuntarily, his hands dropped. An instant only, but it was enough. Ponga Jim threw his right high and hard.

There was a sodden smack, then Hugo Busch crumpled to the canvas without so much as a sound.

For a moment, there was dead silence. Then, from the crowd there arose a roar of anger, mingled with a few cries of approbation, and one definite hand clap. It was from the elderly officer with the monocle.

Lifted from the floor, Busch was showered with water. For an instant he stared, wondering. Then with a cry of rage, he shook off his handlers and rushed.

"Enough."

The voice did not seem loud, but suddenly everyone froze. Even Hugo Busch stopped his rush in midstride.

Not a dozen feet away, standing alone at the edge of the crowd, was Armando Fontes.

In his right fist he held his huge pistol. It was aimed at Don Pedro Norden!

CHAPTER IV

Armando Fontes was holding a large sweet potato in his left hand, and was gnawing at it contentedly. He was still wearing his soiled whites. His belt barely retained his bulging stomach.

"If you move," Fontes said, "I will kill Don Pedro. Señor Mayo, get out of the ring and walk to me."

For just a moment there was startled silence.

Ponga Jim, holding his breath, crawled through the ropes. Only then did anyone move. A German officer, at the opposite end of the line from Don Pedro, reached for his gun.

Fontes scarcely seemed to move, but the gun roared, and the German fell facedown, blood spattering the ground.

"Next time, Don Pedro," Fontes said, undisturbed, "it is you. If you no want to die, tell these men to stand still."

"Don't move," Norden said. "The fool really will shoot."

Fontes backed slowly away after Jim Mayo. Around the corner of the stable, the Brazilian wheeled about and darted between two sheds. Almost at once a heavy cart laden with hay moved into the space, and a silent, unspeaking *obrero* began to work over the wheel.

Fontes knew his way. Quickly, and with devious turns, he led Mayo into the rocks along the side of Mount Jua. Behind them, men were scattering out. The cart in the opening between the sheds would delay pursuit. It would save a minute, perhaps two, for the line of stables and sheds was unbroken for some distance in either direction. And every second counted.

Armando, for all his weight, moved with surprising agility. He stopped once to hand Jim his .45 Colt.

"I take it from the guard," he said, "the *carabinero* was angry—but no matter."

Only a few paths led across the face of Mount Jua at this point. Don Pedro had obviously planned to have the mountain protect his rear, and certainly, only one who knew the paths could have traveled where Fontes was going.

Surprisingly, at the foot of the mountain trail the battered Model A was standing in the shade. They got in, and the motor coughed into life. Over a rocky, broken road, Fontes guided the car, seemingly more by instinct than sight.

"You saved me a beating," Ponga Jim Mayo said.

The Brazilian shrugged. "I don't like those men. They make troubles."

PONGA JIM WENT into the side entrance of the hotel and reached his room unnoticed. Armando sat down on the bed and took off his torn fedora, wiping his forehead.

"Is hot," he said. He looked solemn. "I wished to shoot him, that Don Pedro."

There was a light tap on the door, then even as Ponga Jim's gun slid into his hand, the door opened and Juan Peligro stepped in. He glanced quickly at Fontes.

"Who is this?" he demanded.

Mayo introduced them. Quickly, Peligro turned to Jim. "I have located your ship. It is in the Acaraú River. There are twenty men aboard, men other than your crew."

Ponga Jim explained quickly what he had overheard at the Castillo Norden, and what had happened there. When his story ended, Peligro looked at Fontes with respect.

"You could work for me, my friend," he said.

Armando shrugged. "It is no good work for other man," he said. "I work for myself. When I want to rest—I rest—want to work, I work. I like it this way."

Suddenly, a car rolled up to the front of the hotel. They all heard it. They also heard the sharp commands as men unloaded. Ponga Jim rushed for the door just in time to see a file of Norden's thugs come up the steps. He ducked back into the room. It was empty.

He stared about, unbelieving. But Peligro and Fontes were gone. Then he noticed the open window, its curtain blowing in the light breeze. A fist pounded on the door, and there was a sharp command to open.

Ponga Jim went out the window to the ledge, then dropped to the roof of the shed below it, and then into the street. A German rushed at him. They grappled for an instant, then Jim broke free and punched him solidly in the jaw.

Even as the man dropped, Jim jerked open a door and walked into a cantina. He walked through to the next street, went outside, dodged through the light traffic, and stepped into the car in front of his own hotel. It was a large, powerful car from the Castillo Norden.

The man on guard at the door of the hotel wheeled as the motor roared into life. Then as the guard realized what was happening, he raised his gun and took careful aim. Ponga Jim was dead in his sights, and for an instant, Mayo looked death in the face.

From across the street there was a great coughing gunshot. The soldier folded, his rifle going off harmlessly into the air. Even as Ponga Jim let the clutch out, he saw Armando Fontes, his huge pistol dangling in his fingers, leaning against the corner of the building across from the hotel.

The big car swung into a curve, and Jim stepped down on the accelerator and opened her up. Whatever else she had, the car had power. He headed out the road toward Castillo Norden, and when the car hit the highway it was doing ninety.

Norden's road was guarded. That was all right with Mayo. He roared past the first guard station with the motor wide open, and saw two men waving wildly as he went through.

Peligro had told him just where the amphibian was. It was gassed up and kept ready for instant flight. If he could get to it, and away, things would start to look up.

The big car whirled down the private road to the landing field. Dust clouds billowed out behind. Yet even as he swung onto the field, he saw Don Pedro, Von Hardt, Valdes, and Busch starting for the amphibian, whose propeller was turning lazily.

Crouching behind the wheel, Ponga Jim headed straight for them. They took one look and dived for shelter. He let the car shoot past the flying boat, then spun the wheel and turned it on a dime. For a split second he thought the big car would roll over, but it righted itself and he pointed it at the nearest transport in the row.

Jamming down the accelerator then shifting into neutral, Ponga Jim leaped from the running board. He landed hard, and scrambled to his feet, spitting dust. Beyond the amphibian he heard a tremendous crash as the speeding car smashed into the plane. Then there was an explosion, and both were in flames.

Mayo ran to the amphibian and crawled inside. The German pilot looked up. Mayo pulled his .45 and stuck it in the man's face. He herded the German out the hatch. An instant later he had it rolling down the runway. He eased back on the stick and the ship took off. It cleared the low hedge easily and mounted into the sky.

He climbed, cleared his guns with a burst, then swung the ship around. She was specially built, faster and more maneuverable than the basic model. He went back over the field, the four wing guns blazing. He saw men lift their rifles, then tumble into the dust. One man rushed for a .50-caliber machine gun on a hangar roof, but a burst of fire caught him and threw him bodily to the ground below. Ponga Jim drew the stick back and climbed steadily away from the Castillo Norden. One glance back showed the flames still roaring. Then he headed for the Acaraú River, and the *Semiramis*.

HIS HEAD WAS ACHING fearfully. His swollen face still throbbed. In his dive from the car he had injured one leg, not badly, but enough for it to be painful. He flew steadily toward the river, remembering its position on the chart. It was, he remembered now, one of the few rivers along this section of the coast that could be entered by a ship of any size.

What would happen now, he could not guess. Juan Peligro and Armando Fontes were free, so far as he knew. If they could remain free they would be fortunate. What had been done was enough to force Don Pedro to move. The shooting in Fortaleza and the burning of the planes would be sure to excite comment in regions beyond Norden's control. Peligro, too, would be in touch with his government, and possibly with Vargas.

If Don Pedro hoped to win he must act at once. There was no chance for delay, no time for hesitation. His power had been flouted. The people of Fortaleza would know that there was opposition. Such petty officials as Duro would begin to shake in their boots. Such men always followed the winning side, and now there could be doubt.

Below he saw the winding thread of the Acaraú, and he circled the plane above the *Semiramis*. Then he made a shallow dive and waggled his wings. It was his old signal to his crew all was well. If any were on deck, they would be expecting him.

Ponga Jim had lost his own cap, so now he picked up a beautiful

Panama that had been left in the cabin of his plane. From his pocket he took his gun and reloaded it. Then he took another from a locker in the plane, slipping it into his waistband.

Finally, he glided down to a landing, let the amphibian fishtail into the wind, and lay just a few yards from the *Semiramis*'s beam. After anchoring the plane, he stood up and straightened his clothes. A boat was coming toward him. Mayo now planned to try a colossal bluff, counting on the fact that no one aboard would know him but his own men.

As the boat drew alongside, he stepped in. Holding out his arm, hand open, he snapped a greeting.

"Heil Hitler!" he said.

The man in the launch returned the salute clumsily.

"To the *Semiramis*!" Mayo barked. "A message from Don Pedro."

Expecting nothing else, the man turned the launch and ran over to the accommodation ladder. Ponga Jim got up, pulled down the brim of his Panama, and eased his automatic in its shoulder holster. Then he went up the ladder.

Norden's captain, a wide-faced *mestizo,* was at the gangway with another man. Beyond them, working over some running gear, was Big London. The surprised Negro turned abruptly away from Jim, then stepped around the corner of the hatch where he could watch without seeming to notice. But Mayo had no time to waste.

As the captain opened his mouth to speak, Ponga Jim thrust the automatic into his stomach.

"Manos arriba!" he snapped.

The man gulped and lifted his hands, as did the man beside him. Ponga Jim spoke no Portuguese, but Spanish was close enough. Jim drew their guns and tossed them to London.

"Get the crew out," he said.

In a matter of minutes, the crew was on deck ... the ship taken back before the guards realized just what was happening. The surprise was complete.

PONGA JIM GRABBED BROPHY. "Get under way," he said quickly. "I want you to run up to Fortaleza. There are two ships there, the *Nissengate* and the *Chittagong.* Both are loaded with munitions. Sink them."

Slug Brophy jerked a thumb at the armed freighter nearby. "What about him?"

"Leave him to me," Mayo said grimly. "Get four bombs aboard the amphibian. They won't notice because this ship lies between."

Brophy snapped into action, and Jim noticed the guns being cleared for trouble. Within twenty minutes after he landed, he was taking off. He climbed to a thousand feet, swung around, and started back for the armed freighter.

Even as he swung back he could see the *Semiramis* pulling up to her anchor. The captain of the armed freighter was shouting something at the *Semiramis* when Ponga Jim released his first bomb.

Ponga Jim had come in slowly, taking his time, and the crew of the ship were expecting nothing. The bomb hit the starboard bridge, glanced off, and struck the deck. It exploded with a terrific concussion.

Jim swung back over again, ignoring the men trying to man an AA gun, and let go with another. That bomb hit the water within a foot of the ship and the explosion blazed a fountain of water high into the air. The freighter heeled over violently, and Ponga Jim could see flames roaring in the 'tween decks through the gaping hole torn in her deck and hull by the first explosion.

He banked steeply and soared off over the hills, heading to Natal. As he left he saw the *Semiramis* open fire on the crippled freighter with her 5.9-inch guns.

Quartered at Natal there were American troops. Also, there would be, he hoped, some Vargas officials who were loyal. Despite himself, he was worried. Don Pedro Norden was no fool. He was an utterly unscrupulous and ruthless man who knew how and when to act. That Ponga Jim had won this last move was due largely to the daring of his performance and the fact that Don Pedro underrated him.

CHAPTER V

It was dark when he flew back to Fortaleza. Earlier, he had located a small lake in an uninhabited region. It was set among some wooded sand dunes, and as he glided in he could see no signs of life. He paddled ashore in his rubber boat, and concealed it in some thick brush, then he started walking toward the city.

Flying up, he had seen no sign of the *Semiramis,* and he was worried. He had swung wide to get a glimpse of the field at Norden's estate; it was empty. The planes had gone. Even the signs of the fire had been eradicated. All that had him worried, too; it would have been more to his liking for there to have been government officials circulating, asking difficult questions ... forcing Don Pedro to spend time and energy in a cover-up.

The streets of Fortaleza were quiet, too quiet. A few men walked here and there about their business. A few straggled into the theaters. A group of hard-faced men stood on a corner, talking in low voices. As he passed, Ponga Jim saw them turn to look. The Panama was pulled low, and his face showed but little in the vague light.

He walked on. There were other clusters of men. These groups stood in strategic positions, and he saw the city was dominated by them. Several planes flew over the town, headed inland. A woman passed him, her face stiff with fear, and hurried down a side street.

"You must get off the streets, amigo," a low voice whispered. "They mean to kill you on sight."

Mayo turned to find Peligro at his elbow.

"What of you, *chiquito*?" he said grinning. "From what I heard you aren't exactly welcomed around here yourself."

Juan Peligro shrugged. "I fear you are right, señor. They do not appreciate my talents. Don Pedro has practically occupied Fortaleza. The planes are flown inland."

"To Teresina and his mines and plantations, I'll bet. He has bases there for them." Jim looked around. "What will happen now?"

"I don't know," Peligro shrugged. "At midnight the word is to go out. The killings will start, there will be risings all over Brazil. In Colombia, too. There is to be peace with the Axis and war with the Allies."

Ponga Jim looked at him. "From where will they send the message? Here? Or from Castillo Norden?"

"From the Castillo. I heard—only now—that Norden is soon to leave. That is to be the signal. He himself, you see, plans to be unaware of the murdering until it is completed. If it is successful then he will make a speech, and later will give medals and jobs to the murderers."

Up the street there was a crash of glass and a shout of fury. The bunch nearest Jim started for a store, and one man put his shoulder against the door. It burst open, and the thugs from the street corner dragged a shouting shopkeeper into the street. One struck him, another kicked him.

"We might as well start here," Ponga Jim said grimly. He turned on his heel and walked up behind the nearest troublemaker. Mayo grabbed him by the collar and hurled him into the street. From a brown shirt nearby came a shout of rage. The other men whirled about. Ponga Jim's first punch knocked a man rolling. Grabbing a stick from another, he laid about him furiously. Another man tumbled, and then someone fired. Instantly, Jim went for his gun. Standing in the middle of the sidewalk, he fired coolly and steadily. Two men dropped, and another staggered, then ran off.

Suddenly at the corner, a heavy gun boomed. Glancing over, Mayo saw Armando Fontes standing in the street with his big pistol. Juan Peligro had gone into action, too, and cheered by their support, shopkeepers and other Vargas sympathizers rushed into the streets with weapons.

Then something happened that stopped them all, both sides, dead in their tracks.

A dull boom sounded from the east. Next the scream of a shell. As one man, the people stopped fighting and stared toward the harbor. The *Semiramis* steamed in, swung broadside, and then her 5.9s began to fire.

For the first time in the three years he had owned her, and in all the actions she had come through, Ponga Jim Mayo could stand on the sidelines and watch his ship in action. Only a dark shadow on the water now, lighted by constant blasts of gunfire, but he knew every line of her, every spot of rust, every patch of red lead.

Shells screamed overhead, blasting the hangars of the airfield into flaming ruins and turning level runways into pitted, pockmarked uselessness. Then the fire ceased, and when it opened again, the guns were fired on the *Nissengate*.

It was point-blank range. Jim could almost hear Gunner Millan's crisp orders, could see the powerful muscles of Big London and Lyssy, passing shells to the crew.

A shell exploded amidships. Another blasted the stack into a canted, swaying menace, hanging only by its stays. The after wheelhouse vanished in the crimson blare of an explosion, and then a shot pierced the hull and exploded.

All sound was lost in a tremendous blast as though someone had suddenly exploded a balloon that was miles in diameter. The burst of air and the concussion left them deaf and silent amid crashing glass of broken windows in the town. They stared at each other, mouths open, and eyes goggled at the tremendous pillar of flame that shot suddenly skyward.

People began to run. Nordenistas, Falangists, and the supporters of Vargas all in one mass, they ran.

Peligro grabbed Ponga Jim's arm, but Jim was waiting, his eyes bright. The *Semiramis* swung a little, and the 5.9s covered the *Chittagong*. The latter vessel was armed, and her own guns began to roar, but the crews kept overshooting badly.

A shell from the *Semiramis* landed on the poop of the *Chittagong* and exploded. Then more guns began to hammer, and Jim could see, even at that distance, the black figures of men as they dove overboard from the *Chittagong*. Three were fighting desperately to launch a boat. Then the ship caught fire.

Jim wheeled, and with Juan Peligro beside him, started on a run for the edge of town. Only a couple of hundred yards, and then Armando Fontes came alongside in his panting Model A. They scrambled in, and following Jim's directions they started over the sand hills toward the amphibian.

They left the car in the brush and walked down to the water, and Jim got the rubber boat from the brush. They had reached the plane and Mayo was getting in when he saw a flicker of movement.

A boat had appeared at the tail of the ship, and he saw himself staring into three submachine guns. He thought, for one breathless instant, of risking a dive into the lake, then gave up. Even if he succeeded, Fontes and Peligro would be shot down like sheep.

"Get in." It was Hugo Busch. "Get in the plane."

Mayo reluctantly stepped aboard. Von Hardt was sitting there, gun in hand.

When the plane was in the air, Busch came back to where they were sitting. He grinned widely as he sat down nearby.

"You've been putting on a show, Mayo," he said, "and Norden is quite unhappy. What I'd have done to you would be nothing to what you'll get now."

Busch turned his head to stare at Fontes. "Where did you pick this up?" he said. "He looks like somebody you found in a Hollywood comedy."

Fontes said nothing. But he stared at Busch, his eyes sullen. Then coolly, he rolled his quid and spat. The tobacco juice splashed on the German's chin and shirt collar, and Busch went white with fury.

With a lunge, the German grabbed Fontes by the throat, but bound as he was, the Brazilian was powerless to defend himself.

"Hugo!" Von Hardt's voice cracked like a bullwhip. "None of that."

Busch subsided, his face livid. Armando Fontes rolled himself into a sitting position and stared at Busch, still sullen and unperturbed.

TWENTY MINUTES LATER, still bound, the three were taken from the plane to the library of Castillo Norden. Don Pedro and Carisa Montoya sat waiting for them, Don Pedro staring with cruel eyes. Nearby, Carisa sat, more beautiful than ever.

Norden studied the three, then looked up.

"Leave them, Herr Busch," he said sharply. "Tell Enrico to get the radio warmed up. It is almost time."

Don Pedro got up. Despite himself, he was alive with anticipation and could not refrain from showing it. He looked at Mayo.

"So? You thought to interfere? Well, you have courage, even if you have no brains. You have changed my plans, Captain Mayo. But for the better. I have decided not to wait. The zero hour was to have been three days from now. But this interference has decided me. The time is now." Don Pedro Norden shoved his hands down his coat pockets, and his hard eyes gleamed with triumph. "In just fifteen minutes the word goes out. The hour to strike has come."

Fifteen minutes!

Then it was too late! All he had planned, his trip to Natal, everything was in vain. They could do nothing to warn the officials now. Brazil would be caught flat-footed. There was, nowhere, any knowledge of such a power as Norden had welded together. Nowhere but in Berlin and Tokyo.

Shoved down into chairs, Mayo and his two companions were bound hand and foot. Don Pedro seemed to have forgotten them. He pressed a button and several men came in. To each he handed a brief, typewritten sheet. His orders rapped out thick and fast.

Norden had planned well, the plan was set to function, and each man was dropping into his position to await the final order.

Ponga Jim glanced at Peligro. The Colombian was perspiring, his face a deathly pallor. Armando Fontes, his eyes narrow, was staring at Norden.

Carisa Montoya, her face stiff, watched what was happening. At Natal, Major Palmer was ready with his bombers and fighters, but he would be too late, and once the plan was under way his force would be too small.

The plan was simple, concise, beautifully organized. The risings in Cananea, Registro, and other Japanese-inhabited localities would make each a central headquarters for a series of forces striking out into loyal territory. Rio Grande do Sul, with its large German population, would fall into the conspirators' hands like a ripe plum. With submarines to halt naval interferences, rapid moves could in a few hours have much of Brazil in the hands of Don Pedro; the entire South American situation would be changed, forever.

The new government of the Argentine would do nothing. Chile would be uneasy, but would sit quiet. Paraguay was ready, Uruguay might fight, although surrounded by enemies.

With the fall of Brazil, Don Pedro would set up a dictatorship, refuse to allow the passage of bombers to Africa, and the southern supply route to Egypt would be forced into the North Atlantic, where German submarines hunted like packs of wolves. Axis sub and plane bases in Brazil would give them complete control of the Caribbean and passage around the Cape of Good Hope. Tunisia, Egypt, India, Iraq, Iran, and Russia would be denied help except what could reach them through the blockade of the Pacific.

The United States military would be too late. The move within the country, carefully supplemented by just a little outside help, would be successful and the situation of the Allies would suddenly become infinitely more hazardous—even desperate.

Ponga Jim glanced at the clock. Five minutes. Suddenly, he looked at

Carisa. The intensity was gone from her expression. It was suddenly calm and resolute. For an instant, their eyes met, then they flickered away and stopped.

Slowly Mayo's eyes followed. Don Pedro's automatic lay forgotten on his smoking stand beside his desk, not six feet from Carisa's hand. Their eyes met, and almost imperceptibly, he nodded.

Abruptly he spoke.

"You can't get away with this, Norden," he protested. "Take a tip from me and get out from under while you can."

Norden turned a little in his chair, as Jim had hoped he would do. The man was superbly confident.

"Get out from under? Don't be absurd, Captain. I have a foolproof plan. You have seen enough here today to tell how perfectly it will function. I'll admit, however, that your ship has caused me no end of inconvenience.

"Right now, though"— he glanced down at an order at hand—"we know where she is; the *Semiramis* is in a small harbor not far from Natal. We will have her attacked at daybreak by three dive-bombers. She cannot escape.

"News of her action never left this province. That was carefully arranged. By the time that information reaches Rio, I will be in command there."

"You've overlooked something," Jim said. Carisa had edged a trifle closer to the gun. "That I made a trip to Natal while in the amphibian."

Don Pedro's eyes flickered. "To Natal?" He studied Mayo thoughtfully. "What difference could that make?"

"This difference," Jim told him flatly, "that our officer there immediately sent word to the United States. Ships and planes in force will arrive here in a matter of hours. They may even be coming in now."

Even as he spoke, Ponga Jim knew the folly of what he said. Palmer and Wagnalls had done no such thing. Palmer had said his hands were tied, that there was nothing he could do but inform President Vargas of the plot.

CHAPTER VI

But Jim Mayo could see the possibility disturbed Norden. The plan was too perfect to risk making any changes. It all must work, or the parts each became insecure. Ponga Jim's suggestion, simple as it was, left him uncertain. He did not believe the story, yet it could be.

"So?" He studied Jim, and Jim smiled slowly. "I just wanted, Don Pedro, to let you stick your neck way, way out. I wanted you in so deep you couldn't pull back. When you give that order in just one minute, you'll seal your own doom."

"Don't take me for a fool!" Norden snapped. "You're bluffing!"

He started to get up, and in that instant, Carisa reached out and grasped the gun. Even as the butt slipped into her hand, Don Pedro, sensing something wrong, whirled about.

With a snarl of fury, he grabbed Carisa's hand. Instantly, Jim hurled all his weight forward and his chair tipped over under Norden's feet. The big man fell over him with a crash, the gun breaking loose from his hand and flying across the room.

Norden struggled to get up, and Carisa tripped him again. Ponga Jim, remembering an old trick he had used before, rolled atop the fallen man. Fontes and Peligro were struggling madly to escape, and Carisa scrambled to her feet and ran across the room after the gun. In that instant, the door opened, and Von Hardt stepped in.

His mouth opened in a cry for help when Armando Fontes suddenly heaved from his chair and lunged across the room. He hit Von Hardt with what resembled a flying tackle, knocking the man clear out into the spacious hall.

Von Hardt shouted wildly. Fontes leaped up from the fallen man, then wheeled and darted back into the room, kicking shut the door. Carisa had struck Norden over the head and was fighting desperately to get Jim untied. Peligro was still bound.

In a few seconds both men were free. Norden was struggling to get up, and Ponga Jim walked across and slugged him, knocking the financier into a heap. Peligro rescued their guns and tossed Jim's to him.

Shouts were ringing through the house now, and they could hear running feet. Mayo grabbed Carisa.

"Quick," he shouted. "Which way to the radio room?"

Leading the way, Carisa opened a small door in the corner and ran down a hall. Behind them, fists were thundering on the library door.

They found the radio room empty, and Peligro dropped into place at the controls. The typewritten orders lay beside the radio, stacked neatly on the left-hand side of the mike.

Ponga Jim grabbed the microphone as Fontes and Carisa began moving a filing cabinet against the door. "Mayday ... Mayday ... Calling SS *Semiramis* ... calling *Semiramis* ... calling—"

The reply was distinct and clear. "*Semiramis* ready ... what is it? ... *Semiramis* answering Mayday ... *Semiramis*—"

"Mayo speaking. Get out of that harbor now. Bombers to attack at daylight."

A machine gun rattled and the door was riddled with bullets. Ponga Jim turned, watching the door, and talking coolly and calmly. As he continued to broadcast, sending a warning to Rio describing the day's events and the plot, he grabbed up the pile of typewritten orders and shoved them into his pocket.

Fontes had drawn back to one side and had his gun ready. Carisa, her face deathly pale, was holding the small automatic she had taken from Don Pedro. Mayo signed off as the door began to splinter.

Fontes's gun exploded, and there was a shrill scream of pain outside the door. Peligro began methodically smashing the radio.

Seeing a window, Ponga Jim darted across. Four feet below and two feet to one side was the parapet of a lower section of roof. While Fontes kept up occasional blasts at the door, Jim opened the window and lowered Carisa, then Peligro, to the parapet.

"All right," Jim said, "you're next."

Fontes shrugged. "You, señor. I will stay."

"Nuts," Jim said. "Beat it."

Fontes swung to the wall, and Peligro caught his feet and held them until he was balanced. Ponga Jim leaped to the sill and with his gun in hand, dropped one leg outside, then the other.

The door came in with a splintering crash, and Jim's automatic bucked in his hand. The first man plunged over on his face, and then a bullet smashed the wall near Jim, stinging his face with tiny fragments of mortar and stone. He fired back, edging along the parapet. The gun locked open, out of ammunition.

Mayo turned, balancing on the edge of the parapet, then dropped to the roof.

Peligro was waiting for him.

"Quick. The others are below."

Dropping to the ground, the two men darted through the thick shrubbery and headed for the amphibian.

But the search was closing in. Behind them there was shouting, and off to the left they heard the crashing of men in the brush. Everywhere, their enemies were searching. Leading the way now, Ponga Jim took them into a low place on the edge of the airfield.

"Stay here and keep out of sight. I'll get that ship, bring her down here to take off; you come running."

Without waiting for a reply, he pushed his way into the brush. He took his time, working his way carefully, to make no noise. Norden would kill now. He would kill without hesitation.

The amphibian was in plain sight, and the motors were turning slowly.

Beside the ship a mechanic was loafing, and Jim could see the glow of his cigarette. There were three other planes on the ground nearby.

Walking swiftly, Ponga Jim started across the field. He was within a few feet of the mechanic when the man saw him—too late. Jim lunged and swung, knocking the man into a heap under the wing. He had no more than regained his balance when a cold voice cut across his consciousness. "You again, is it?"

Mayo turned, slowly. Hugo Busch was standing there looking at him.

"I knew you'd come here," Busch said, "so I waited. They are hunting you back there in the trees.... We will have a little time together so I could finish what I started."

Ponga Jim's mouth felt dry. The lights from the hangars showed the ground smooth and clear of obstacles. He could see the German's broad, powerful shoulders, and he remembered the driving power of his punches.

They were the same height, but Busch was at least twenty pounds heavier than Jim's own two hundred.

"All right," Jim said quietly, "if that's the way you want it."

The German walked in, smiling, superbly confident. Then his left shot out, but Jim went under the punch with a smashing right to the heart. In a split second the two men were standing toe-to-toe slugging it out. Blood flew, furiously, desperately, each suddenly conscious that the end might mean death, each aware of so much at stake, and each filled with a killing fury.

The German hit Jim with a wicked right hook that knocked his head back on his shoulders, and then slammed a left into his body. That punch turned Jim sick at the stomach. He clinched, and hurled the German to the ground. Busch came back up like a cat. Hugo rushed, and Jim took two driving blows to the body, then his head rocked with a wicked right that had him hanging on while Busch ripped into him with short, driving blows.

The German seemed to have limitless strength. He kept coming, boxing skillfully at times, then dropping his skill to fight like a demon.

Yet Ponga Jim was learning. He was surer of himself now. He began to push the fight more and more. He caught the hardest blows on his shoulders and pushed his way ahead. Years of rugged living, of fresh sea air, hard work, and clean living had left him hard as nails. He drove on in now, slugging in a kind of bloody haze, confident of only one thing, that he was going to win. Busch set himself and feinting, threw a hard right.

This was the chance Jim had been waiting for. He put everything he had in his own right. It landed with a thud like an ax striking a log, and Hugo hit the ground. Drunkenly, Mayo almost collided with the plane.

PONGA JIM STARTED the plane forward in a groggy haze. Guiding it by instinct, he paused at the end of the field. Juan Peligro, Armando Fontes, and Carisa came running. Jim took off, circled, then headed back over the flying field. His mind was clearing, and though his body was hurt, felt better than he had expected. He had taken all the big German had been able to give, and he had won.

The amphibian, he noticed, had been loaded with bombs. It was carrying six. He let one go as he swung in toward the field, another over the sheds, then he swung around, and in a rattle of machine-gun fire, let go two more over Castillo Norden. As the plane circled away, they could look back and see flames leaping high.

Peligro was at the plane's radio, and now his eyes brightened.

"They are coming!" he said excitedly. "Your navy is coming!"

They landed once more on the small lake near Fortaleza and started back toward the city.

PONGA JIM MAYO'S FACE was cut and swollen. Peligro looked tired, and Carisa Montoya walked almost in a dream. Only Armando Fontes looked the same; his round, fat face was sullen, his eyes somber when they passed the light of a window.

The streets were empty. Two bodies lay in the gutter where they had fallen earlier, and the sidewalks were littered with broken glass. A heavy smell of smoke from the explosion and fire tainted the air, and the waters of the bay were littered with wreckage. It was almost day, but the moon was still bright.

In the vague light the streets looked like those of a long-deserted city. Yet as they rounded a corner, a file of soldiers in Brazilian uniforms turned into the street from the opposite direction. They marched past, stepping briskly along, a cool, efficient, soldierly body of men. "That means that Vargas acted," Ponga Jim said. "Everything will be over soon enough."

They reached the steps of the hotel and started in when two men came out. One was Major Wagnalls from Natal. The other was Slug Brophy, Jim's chief mate.

The major smiled and held out a hand. "So you made it! One of our boys just radioed word that Castillo Norden was in flames, the hangars destroyed, and three planes burning on the field.

"A transport landed there a few minutes ago from Rio. Von Hardt has been arrested by Major Palmer, and they found Hugo Busch beaten unconscious. A mechanic said you did it." Wagnalls looked at Jim. "I didn't think anybody could do that."

"Neither did I," Mayo said simply. "I guess I was lucky."

"What about Don Pedro?" Peligro interrupted. "He is the one we want."

Wagnalls's brow creased. "That's the missing item. He escaped. It doesn't matter, for the government will confiscate his holdings here, so his power is broken. But I dislike to see him free.

"Especially," he added, "since Señorita Montoya will soon be known as a government agent ... President Vargas was suspicious, and Miss Montoya knowing Don Pedro, volunteered to investigate."

"What I want to know," Mayo demanded, "is how they captured my ship?"

Brophy grinned sheepishly. "Duro, the port captain, Du Silva, and an army officer came out. They had three girls along, so we didn't expect trouble.

"They came aboard, and Duro said he had to search my cabin for dope. We started for the cabin. No sooner had we left the deck than men came up the ladder and deployed about the deck."

"There's still some fighting going on but all the principal plotters are taken care of but Don Pedro," Wagnalls said. "But we'll have him soon."

"I don't think so."

Ponga Jim Mayo felt himself turn cold. His back was to the speaker, but he needed no more than those few words to tell him who it was. The voice had been low, but heavy with menace. He turned.

Thirty feet away, Don Pedro Norden stood in the street near the mouth of a narrow alleyway. In his hands he held a submachine gun. His brilliantly conceived plot had fallen to pieces, the men he hated had won. Yet he had a gun, and the little group before the hotel were covered, helpless.

Norden's clothing was torn and bloody, his face looked thinner, harder, more brutal. If ever a man was seething with hate, it was this one. Never in his life, Jim knew, had he been so close to death. The man was fairly trembling with triumph and killing fury. The architects of his defeat—Juan Peligro, Major Wagnalls, Brophy, Carisa, and Ponga Jim—were all in range. He could in one burst of fire wipe the slate clean of his enemies.

Norden's teeth bared in a grimace of hate, and when he spoke his voice was choked with emotion. "Perhaps I will be captured, but not yet...."

The submachine gun lifted, and Jim thought that even at that distance he could see the man's finger tighten.

A gun roared, and the submachine gun began to chatter, but the muzzle had fallen, and the bullets merely bit against the stones of the street and ripped the dust into little fountains of fury.

Don Pedro Norden, a great black hole between his eyes, the back of his head blown away, fell slowly on his face.

Turning, they saw Armando Fontes, the big pistol clutched in his right hand, leaning nonchalantly against a corner. With a match in his cupped left hand, he was lighting a cigarette.

For a long moment, they stared, relief soaking through them. Ponga Jim looked at the disreputable little man.

"All right, Armando," he asked. "Tell us. Who are you agent for? What's your part in this?"

Fontes shrugged, his eyes lidded. He drew on his cigarette and took the occasion to slip the big gun back into his waistband.

"I, señor? I am but a little man. A little man who likes his government."

He turned, and with a deprecating wave of his hand, walked down the street, and away.

Pirates of the Sky

Turk Madden came in toward the coast of Erromanga at an elevation of about three thousand feet. The Grumman amphibian handled nicely, and flying in the warm sunshine over the Coral Sea was enough to put anyone in a good mood. Especially when Tony Yorke and Angela waited at the end of the trip in the bungalow by Polenia Bay. A night of good company, especially Angela's, would take his worries away. The war in Asia was expanding. Someday soon America would be involved, and all this—the express freight and passenger business he had worked so hard to build—would be no more.

Curiously, Turk's eyes swung to the interior. The island was only about twenty-five miles long, and perhaps ten wide, yet it was almost unknown except for a few isolated spots along either coast. Several times, he had considered taking time out to fly over the island and down its backbone.

Madden shrugged. Flying freight, even when you were working for yourself, didn't leave much time or gas for exploring. When he saw Traitor's Head looming up before him, he banked slightly, and put the ship into a steep glide that carried it into Polenia Bay. Deftly, he banked again, swinging into the cove, and trimmed the Grumman for a landing. It was then he saw the body.

The ship skimmed the water, slapped slightly, and ran in toward the wharf, but Turk Madden's eyes were narrowed and thoughtful. Violence in the New Hebrides was bad medicine and there, floating on the waters of the cove, almost in the bay now, was the body of a native with his head half blown away.

None of Yorke's boys came running to meet him. Instead, a white man in soiled white trousers and a blue shirt came walking down to the wharf. He was a big man, and he wore a heavy automatic in a shoulder holster.

TURK CUT THE MOTOR, and tossed the man a line, then dropped his anchor. He was thinking rapidly. But when he stepped up on the wharf, his manner was casual.

"Hello," he said. "I don't believe I've met you before. Where's Yorke?"

"Yorke?" The big man's eyes were challenging. He lit a cigarette before he answered, then snapped the match into the water with studied insolence. "He sold out. He sold this place to me. He left two weeks ago."

"Sold out?" Madden was incredulous. "Where'd he go? Sydney?"

"No," the man said slowly. "He bought passage on a trading schooner. He was going to loaf around the islands awhile, then wind up in Suva or Pago Pago."

"That's funny," Madden said, rubbing his jaw. "He ordered some stuff from me. Told me to fly it in for him. Some books, medicine, food supplies, and clothes."

"Yeah," the big man nodded. "My name is Karchel. He told me he had some stuff coming in. My price included that."

"You made a nice buy," Turk said. "Well, maybe I can do some business with you once in a while."

"Yeah," Karchel said. "Maybe you can." His eyes turned to the plane. "Nice ship you got there. Those Grumman amphibs do about two hundred, don't they?"

"Most of them," Madden said shortly. "This was an experimental job. Too expensive, so they didn't make any more. But she's a honey. She'll do two forty at top speed."

"Well," Karchel said, "you might as well come up and have a drink. No use unloading that boat right now. An hour will do. I expect you want to get away before sundown."

He turned and strolled carelessly up the path toward the bungalow, and Turk Madden followed. His face was expressionless, but his mind was teeming. If there was one thing that wouldn't happen, it would be Tony Yorke selling out.

Tony and Angela, he was sure, loved their little home on Polenia Bay. If they had told him that once, they had told him fifty times.

Now this man, Karchel, something about his face was vaguely familiar, but Turk couldn't recall where he had seen it before.

"You don't sound Dutch," Karchel said suddenly. "You're an American, aren't you?"

"Sure," Turk said. "My name is Madden. Turk Madden."

Instantly, he realized he had made a mistake. The man's eyes came up slowly, and involuntarily they glanced quickly at the brush behind Turk. Another guy, behind me, Turk thought. But Karchel smiled.

"I heard that name," he said. "Weren't you the guy who made all that trouble for Johnny Puccini back in Philly?"

Sure, Turk thought. That would be it. How the devil could he ever have forgotten the name of Steve Karchel? Shot his way out of the pen once, stuck up the Tudor Trust Company for $70,000, the right–hand man of Harry Wissler.

"If you want to call it that," Turk said. He stepped up beside Karchel. "Johnny was a tough cookie, but he wanted to organize all the mail pilots. I was working for Uncle Sam, and nobody tells me where to get off."

Karchel dropped his cigarette in the gravel path.

"No?" he said. "Nobody tells you, huh?"

Two men had come out of the brush with Thompson submachine guns. They looked tough. Covered all the time, Turk thought. Those guys had it on me. I must be slipping. Aloud, he said:

"You boys got a nice place here." He looked around. "A right nice place."

"Yeah," Karchel chuckled coldly. "Lucky Yorke was ready to sell." He motioned up the steps. "But come on in. Big Harry will be wanting to see the guy who thumbed his nose at the Puccini mob."

Turk walked up the steps and then the mosquito netting flopped from the door, and a man stepped out. He was a slim, wiry man with a narrow face. His eyes were almost white, his hair lank and blond. He was neatly dressed in a suit of white silk, and there was a gun stuck in his waistband.

"Who's this punk?" he snapped. "Didn't I tell you if you found any more to cool 'em off?"

"This guy's different, Chief," Karchel said. "He's a flyer. Just flew in here with some stuff for Yorke. I told him how we bought the place, and the stuff would come to us."

"Oh?" Big Harry Wissler sneered. "You did, did you?" He stepped up to Madden, his white eyes narrowed. "Well, he lied. We wanted this spot, so we just moved in. Some of these damned niggers got in the way, so we wiped 'em out."

"What about Yorke?" Turk said. "And Angela?"

Wissler's eyes gleamed. "What? What did you say? Who's this Angela?"

Madden could have kicked himself for a fool. Somehow then, Angela Yorke had managed to get away.

"What d'you mean?" Wissler snapped. "Speak up, you damn fool! Was there a woman here? We heard she'd left!"

"She had," Madden said quickly. "I didn't think."

"Oh? You didn't think!" Wissler sneered. Then he wheeled, his eyes blazing. "You idiots get out an' find that woman! Find her if you tear the place apart. The one who finds her gets a grand. If you don't have her by night, somebody gets killed, see?"

The man was raging, his white face flushed crimson, and his small eyes glowed like white-hot bits of steel.

"Take this punk away. Put him somewhere. I'll take care of him later."

Karchel's hand was shaking when he took Turk's gun. The two men with tommy guns covered him so he was powerless. Then, they hurried him from the verandah and down to a big copra shed.

"The chief's got the willies," Karchel said. "We better watch our step."

"Why stick with him?" Turk said. "You'll get it in the neck yourselves, if you aren't careful."

"You shut your trap," Karchel snapped abruptly. "I would've burned if he hadn't helped me out of the pen. You couldn't leave him, anyway. He's got eight or ten million hid away. He'd follow you till the last dime was gone. He'd get you. Nobody ever hated like that guy."

BEHIND THE COPRA shed a steep cliff reared up from the jungle growth, lifting a broken, ugly escarpment of rock at least two hundred feet. Here and there vines covered the side of the precipice, and from the rear of the shed to the foot of the cliff was a dense tangle. Once, three months ago, Turk had helped Yorke find an injured dog back in that tangle.

A sudden thought came to him with that memory.

"Damn! My plane's sinking!" he shouted.

Karchel stopped abruptly, staring. Madden swung, and his big fist caught the gunman on the angle of the jaw, then he leaped around the corner of the copra shed and ran!

Behind him rose a shout of anger, then one of the men who had been with Karchel sprang past the corner and jerked up his submachine gun. Turk hit the ground rolling, heard bullets buzzing around him like angry bees, one kicking mud into his face. Then he was around the corner and into the brush. He dropped to his hands and knees and crawled between the spidery roots of a huge mangrove, wormed his way around the bole of the tree, and then on through another.

He halted, breathing hard, and began to work his way along more carefully. This was the way the dog had come, trying to find a place to die in peace. Almost before he realized it, he found himself at the foot of the cliff.

Again he halted, pulled aside a drapery of vines. He stepped quickly into a crack in the rock and found himself in a chimney of granite, its walls jagged and broken. It led straight up for over two hundred feet. Carefully, taking his time, he began to climb.

It was nearly a half hour later that he came out on top, and without waiting to look back, walked quickly into the jungle and started for the top of Traitor's Head.

He had been climbing for some time when he heard the movement.

Instantly, he dropped flat on his face and rolled over into the grass beside the trail. The movement came to him again, and he edged along in the brush, peered out.

A GIRL WAS COMING down the trail, moving carefully. In one hand she gripped a sharpened stick, a crude weapon, but it could be a dangerous one.

"Angela!" he gasped.

"Turk!" Her eyes brightened and she ran toward him. "I saw you flying in, tried to warn you, but you didn't see me. I was on the summit of the Head."

"Where'd they come from?" he asked. "How long have they been here?"

"They came in about three days ago. They've got a steam yacht hidden, with a lot of gunmen aboard. They've two planes, too. They killed Salo, our foreman. Tony came running down the beach and knocked one of the men down. They grabbed him then, and started beating him. I knew I couldn't help him by going down there, so I hid."

"A good thing you did," he said. "That blond-headed man? He's Harry Wissler, a gangster from the States, and as crazy and dangerous as they come. The big man is Steve Karchel, he's almost as bad."

"I heard them say they were going to hijack some ships," she told him. "They have a fast motorboat and two planes. They want to use this for a base, and loot ships going to and from Australia."

"That's absurd!" he said. "They couldn't get away—" He hesitated. "They might, at that. They wouldn't leave any survivors, and they'd sink the ships. There's a war on now, that might make the difference."

"What are we going to do, Turk?" Angela said. Her gray eyes were wide, serious. "We've got to do something! Tony's down there—they may kill him any time. And then some ship will come along . . . it would be awful!"

"Yeah," he replied, nodding slowly. "Where's their yacht?"

"In Cook Bay. But they won't leave it there long. It is too exposed."

"So's Polenia, as far as that goes. But the cove is okay. That is sheltered enough. Did you hear them mention any particular ship?"

"The *Erradaka*. I remember her very well because I once went from Noumea to Sydney on her. But they expect to get her before she reaches Noumea."

THE *ERRADAKA* was a passenger liner of some fifteen thousand tons, running from San Francisco to Sydney. She passed within a comparatively short distance of the island.

"Our problem now is to hide," he told her. "They've got orders to find us—or else."

"We'll go where I've been." She walked faster, and he was glad to step out and keep moving. "It's in a place they'd never discover in years!"

They reached the round top of Traitor's Head, and she walked straight forward to the very edge of the precipice. Then she stepped carefully over the edge!

He gasped and jumped to catch her arm, but she laughed at him.

"Come on over!" she said. "See! There's a ledge, a few steps, and a cave!"

An instant his eyes strayed out over the edge. It was a long drop to the sea, and yet a more secure hiding place couldn't be found. The cave was invisible from above, and one had to dare that narrow, foot-wide ledge before they could see the black opening. Inside it was dry and cool, and somewhere he heard water running.

"How in the world did you ever find this?" he demanded, incredulous.

"I climbed the Head one day, just to be doing it, and saw a rat go over here. I hurried up to see why a rat should commit suicide and saw him disappear in the rock. I decided to investigate, and found this. Even Tony doesn't know it's here!"

Turk Madden looked around the bare, rock-floored cave. A perfect hideout if ever there was one. Their greatest danger was to be seen from the sea when coming or going. A boat or plane might see them, as it was coming through the entrance to Polenia. Otherwise, with food and water, they could remain indefinitely.

He stepped toward the opening, then stopped dead still. A low murmur of voices came to him, and Turk tiptoed to the cave entrance, motioning to Angela for silence. Above on the cliff edge, two men were talking.

"They aren't up here, wherever they are," one man growled. "The chief's in a sweat about the dame; it's a waste of time, if you ask me."

"There's worse ways of wasting time, Chino," a second man said. "I'd like to find her. A grand is a lot of dough."

"What d'you think about goin' after these ships?" Chino asked. "I don't know a damn thing about ships."

"It's a steal. A war goin' on, lots of ships missin' anyway, an' if we don't leave anybody to sing, what can go wrong? Durin' the last war, a German tramp freighter did it for a couple of years. If they did it, why can't we? It's like Harry says. When everybody is fightin' there's always a chance for a wise guy to pick up a few grand."

"Well," Chino said. "I'm going back down in that jungle. I want to see if I can't find something. Coming?"

"I'll stick around," the man said, slowly. "I'm fed up crawlin' through the brush."

Turk Madden tiptoed back to Angela.

"One of them's leaving," he whispered. "There may be a chance!"

HE PICKED UP the stick Angela had carried. Then he turned and slipped back to the cave entrance. Stopping, he felt on the rocky floor to find a loose fragment of stone. Suddenly, there was a gasp behind him and he looked up.

A burly, flat-faced man was standing in the cave entrance, his eyes gleaming with triumph.

"Hold it, buddy," he said softly. "I don't want to take no dead meat back to the chief. All you got to do is come quiet."

"How'd you find this place?" Turk demanded.

The man chuckled wisely. "I seen your tracks back a ways. I said nothing to Chino, because I want that grand for myself. Me, I done some huntin' as a kid, so I figured the lay. I seen half a heel print from a woman's shoe right on the rim where there was a little dust."

"That's clever, plenty clever." Turk took a firm grip on the stick. Half concealed by the darkness of the cave, he had inched himself forward to striking distance. Suddenly, like a striking adder's head, the sharp stick leaped forward, the point tearing a jagged gash through the gunman's wrist!

Involuntarily, the man's hand jerked up and his fingers opened wide. He dropped the gun and stepped back with a cry of pain. And in that split second, Turk Madden stepped in.

Slugging the man in the belly with a bludgeoning right, he knocked every bit of breath from his body. Then a short, vicious left hook slammed the man on the chin and drove his head against the jagged rock beside the cave entrance. The man staggered and then fell clear. Where the leering gunman had stood an instant before, now the cave entrance was empty and behind the falling man a cry trailed up through the still air.

Quickly, Turk stepped outside and up the narrow ledge. It was the work of an instant to brush out the tracks, then he retreated as swiftly as he had come forth, picking up the heavy automatic as he returned to the cave.

"That was close," he whispered.

For three hours, they waited in the cave, hearing the sounds of the searchers above. The gunman's cry had obviously carried far enough for Chino to hear, yet when they came searching, there was nothing. The men came and went, then darkness began to gather, and finally Chino spoke up.

"To hell with it!" he snarled. "I must've been dreamin'! Buck probably went off huntin' in the brush."

"No tracks left here," Karchel insisted. "Where could he have got to?"

"If you ask me," one of the men said abruptly, "I don't like it. No guy as tough as Buck vanishes into thin air. If he ain't here he went somewhere, didn't he? Well, I don't like it!"

"Afraid of ghosts?" Karchel sneered.

"Maybe I am," the man said doggedly. "Funny things happen in these islands! I been hearin' plenty!"

"Oh, shut up!" Karchel snapped, disgusted.

THEY LEFT. "You know, Angela," Turk said softly, "we've got something there. Those guys may not think they are superstitious, but all of us are a little. And maybe—"

"Maybe what?" Angela asked anxiously.

"I'm going out," he said. "I'm going out to get Tony. And I'm going to throw a scare into those guys they'll never forget!"

It was two hours before he slipped through the brush near the house, and paused on the edge of the jungle, studying the layout thoughtfully. Yorke might be imprisoned in the copra shed, and he might be held in the bungalow itself.

Several windows were lighted, and Turk could see men moving about, apparently getting ready to leave. One of the men came out and stood near the roots of a giant ficus tree. Madden glimpsed his face in the faint glow of a lighted match as the man touched it to a cigarette.

With a quick slice of his pocketknife, Turk cut a strip of liana from a long vine hanging near him. Then, soundlessly, he made a careful way over the damp earth to the giant tree. Like a ghost he slipped into the blackness among the roots. Before him, he saw the man stir a little, saw the faint gleam of light on the metal of a gun. He stepped closer.

He made a crude running noose in the end of the liana, and with a quick motion, dropped it over the man's head, jerking it tight! With a strangled cry, scarcely loud enough to be heard a dozen feet, the man grabbed at his throat. Then, Turk stepped in quickly, and slugged him in the stomach. Without a sound the man tumbled over, facedown in the mud.

Taking his gun and cartridges, Turk slipped off the crude noose and slipped back among the roots. Working swiftly, he had almost completed a semicircle around the house when he heard the man cry out.

Someone ran past him swearing, and Turk saw lights go out suddenly in the house. In the darkness, he could distinguish a stream of shadowy figures, starlight gleaming on their guns, as they poured from the house.

"What the hell's wrong now?" Wissler was demanding.

"It was Gyp Davis," Karchel said, with disgust. "Something jumped on him in the dark, or that's what he says. Some slimy thing got him by the throat, he says, then kicked him in the belly."

Wissler made an ugly sound, half a snarl.

"These yellow-bellied tramps!" he sneered. "Gettin' scared of the dark! You tell Gyp and Brownie to get those ships ready. We're taking off before daybreak. See that there's plenty of shells in those crates. And a half dozen of those bombs the Doc makes. We won't have any time to waste on this job!"

Suddenly, there was a burst of excited voices, and stepping forward in the brush, Turk Madden saw a cluster of figures coming toward the house. One of them was dressed in white, and his heart sank.

"Got her, Chief!" Chino exclaimed, eagerly. "We found the dame. She was in the brush up on Traitor's Head. Do I get the grand?"

Wissler stepped toward the girl, and grabbed her roughly by the arm, pulling her toward him. Then he stepped back again and let the flashlight travel over her from head to foot.

"Yeah," his voice was thick. "You get the grand. You take her up to the house and lock her up. Make sure she's there to stay."

Turk wet his lips. Well, here it was. There was only one answer now. He slipped both guns from his waistband and clicked off the safety catches. Go out there shooting, get Wissler and Karchel, anyway.

He took a step, then stopped dead still, feeling the cold chill of steel against his neck.

"Hold it, buddy!" a harsh voice said. "And don't get funny with that gun."

The man reached out from behind with his left hand to get the right-hand pistol. Then Turk dropped the other gun into the brush, speaking quickly to distract the man's attention so he wouldn't hear the sound of its fall.

"Okay," he said. "You got me. Now what?"

The man prodded him into the open and marched him across the small clearing to where Wissler and Karchel were standing.

"Got the guy, Chief. That Madden fellow."

Wissler stepped toward Turk. "Tough guy, are you?" He slapped Madden across the face with one hand, then with the other. But Turk stood immovable. A wrong move now, and they'd kill him. If they did, then Angela and Tony were done for, to say nothing of the hundreds of innocent people on the *Erradaka*.

Wissler laughed coldly. "All right, tie him up an' lock him up. I'll tend to this guy and that dame when we come back."

SOMEWHERE DOWN THE BEACH, the motor of a plane broke into a coughing roar. It wasn't the Grumman. Probably one of the aircraft they were going to use for the attack on the *Erradaka*.

Three of the men hustled him away to the copra shed. He was hurriedly bound, then thrown on the floor. The three men left, and it was only a few minutes until Madden heard two planes roar away toward the sea. It would be dawn soon, and the *Erradaka* with several hundred passengers would be steaming toward a day of horror and bloodshed.

He rolled over, trying to get to the wall. Reaching it, he forced himself into a sitting position and managed to get to his knees. This done, his fingers could just reach the knot behind his ankles.

It seemed that it took him hours to loosen the knot, although as he realized afterward, it could only have been a few minutes. When the ropes fell loose, he staggered to his feet. It was growing light outside and it was gray in the shed. He moved the length of the building, searching for something he could use to free his hands.

In a corner of the shed, he found an old wood saw. By wedging it into the crack in the end-boards of a worktable, he managed to place the saw teeth in the right position. Then he went to work. Finally, a strand of the rope fell apart and he hastily jerked the loosened ropes from his wrists, rubbed them violently. Now—

"Pretty smart, guy," a voice sneered.

HE TURNED SLOWLY. Chino stood in the door laughing at him, a gun in his hand. Turk Madden's brain went hot with rage. Now, after all this struggle, to be deprived of escape? Chino was coming toward him, chuckling with contempt.

With one sweeping movement of hand and arm, Turk grabbed the saw and hurled it flat at Chino's face. Chino leaped back with an oath, and the gun roared. Turk felt the bullet blast by his face and then he sprang. The gun roared again, but Madden was beyond all fear. Chino's face was bleeding from a ragged scratch of the saw, and he lifted the gun to take aim for a killing shot when Turk dove headlong in a flying tackle. They hit the ground rolling, and Turk came out on top, swinging both hands at Chino's face.

The gun blasted again, and he felt the searing pain of a powder burn, then he knocked the gun from Chino's hand and sprang to his feet. The gunman scrambled up, his face livid with rage. Turk threw a punch, short and hard, to the chin. The gunman went down. Turk swept up his gun and started running for the door.

A man loomed in the doorway, and Turk fired twice. The man staggered back, tumbling to the ground. And another stepped up behind him, taking careful aim with a pistol, but Turk fired from the hip, and the man staggered, his bullet clipping a notch in a beam over Madden's head.

Then Turk fired again, hurled his now empty automatic after the shot, and grabbed another from the man in the doorway.

He made the house in a half dozen jumps, felt something tug at his clothes, then felt the whiff of a bullet by his face, the reports sounding in his ears, flat and ugly. A big man with a scarred face was standing in the door of the bungalow firing at him. Dropping to one knee, Turk fired steadily and methodically, three shots hitting the man, another taking a stocky-built blond fellow who came around the corner.

Then Turk scrambled through the door over the fallen man's body and rushed inside. There was no one in sight, but on the table was a tommy gun, a Luger automatic, and several other weapons. Turk sprang past them, and seeing a closed door, tried it. It was locked. He shot the lock away and stepped inside, gun ready.

Angela Yorke was tied in a chair in the center of the room. Tony Yorke, his face white and battered around the eyes, was lying on his back against the wall. Hurriedly, he cut the girl loose, handing her the gun.

"You two watch your step. I think I made a cleanup, but if any more show up, shoot—and shoot to kill!"

ANGELA CAUGHT HIS ARM, her face white. He brushed something away from his eyes, and was startled to see blood on his hand. He must have been shot.

"What are you going to do?" the girl exclaimed.

"I'm taking the Grumman. She's got guns that came with the ship, and I never bothered to dismantle them. I've got to stop those guys before they get to the *Erradaka*!"

"But you'll be killed!" she protested.

He grinned. "Anything's possible, but I doubt it."

THE GRUMMAN TOOK OFF after a short run, and Turk Madden swung the ship out to sea. The gunmen would land somewhere and wait there for the psychological moment. Their best chance was when the crew and passengers were at breakfast. And the first thing would be to get the radio room. Then sweep the decks with machine-gun fire, board the ship from the yacht, and kill the passengers.

Turk climbed to six thousand feet and opened her up. The Grumman responded perfectly, her twin motors roaring along in perfect time, fairly eating up the miles. The other ships were well ahead of him, he knew, but they would be in no hurry, for the yacht had to come up before they could attack.

Switching to the robot controls, he carefully checked the tommy gun and the other weapons he'd brought along. His ship carried two guns anyway, and with the additional armament he wouldn't lack for fighting equipment. He left Tanna off to the east, then swung the ship a bit and laid a course for Erronan.

Erronan! His eyes narrowed. Why hadn't he thought of that before? It was the perfect base for an attack on the shipping lane. There was a good landing on Tabletop, the flat mountain that was the island's highest point, nearly two thousand feet above the sea. From there it would not be much of a jump to the course of the *Erradaka*. No doubt the attacking ships had settled there to await the proper hour of attack. Well, he grinned wryly, it wouldn't be long now.

He cursed himself again for letting the sending apparatus on his radio get out of whack. He slipped on the earphones and could hear the *Erradaka* talking to another ship near the coast of New Caledonia. He turned his head, watching the blue expanse of sea beneath him and searching for the yacht. Then, suddenly, he picked it up, and a moment later, the *Erradaka*.

The yacht was taking a course that would bring her up with the *Erradaka,* and he heard the passenger liner calling her, but the yacht did not reply. Suddenly, a flicker of motion caught his eyes, and he turned to see two ships closing in on the liner. They were flying fast, one slightly above and behind the other.

Then, even as he watched, the first ship dipped a wing, and glancing down, he saw a tarp suddenly jerked from a gun on the yacht's fo'c'sle-head. The *Erradaka*'s radio began to chatter fiercely, and then the gun roared and the shell crashed into the radio room, exploding with a terrific concussion. Fired rapidly, the second shell exploded at the base of the fo'm'st, dropping it in wreckage across the deck.

THEN THE FIRST SHIP DOVE, and he saw the mass of people who had rushed out on deck suddenly scatter as the plane's machine guns began chattering. He had time to notice the ship was an older Fiat. Not so bad. At best they'd do about two hundred miles per hour, which would give him a little margin. The other ship was a Boeing P-26, somewhat faster than his own ship.

He swung her over hard and put the Grumman into a steep dive. He came down on the tail of the Boeing, both guns firing. The Boeing, seeming to realize he was an enemy for the first time, pulled into a left chandelle.

Madden let it go and swung after the Fiat. For just an instant, he caught the outlaw ship full in his sights and saw a stream of tracers streak into his tail. Then Madden swung up in a tight loop, missing a stream of fire from the Boeing by a split second. He wheeled the Grumman around in a skid, but the Boeing was out of range, and the Fiat was climbing toward him.

He reached for altitude, saw pinkish tracers zip across his port wingtip, and went into a steep dive. Suddenly, he realized the yacht was right below him, her deck scattered with figures and a cluster of them around the gun. He pressed the trips on his guns and saw a man stagger and plunge over on his face.

The others scattered for shelter, and his guns swept the yacht's deck with a flaming blast of machine-gun fire. Three more of the fleeing gunmen fell headlong. One of them threw up his pistol and fired, then his body jerked, fairly lifted from the deck by the burst of bullets. Madden banked steeply and saw the topmasts of the yacht miss him by inches.

His stomach felt tight and hard. He was in a spot, and knew it. Only a few feet above the water and the Boeing above and slightly behind, closing in fast. There was no chance or room to maneuver. He saw a stream of tracers cross his wing, missing by inches, then he glimpsed the looming hull of the *Erradaka* dead ahead. He clamped his jaw and flew straight at the huge liner.

His twin motors roaring, he swept down on the big ship, the Boeing right behind him. Then, just as it seemed he must hit, he jerked the Grumman into a quick, climbing turn, saw the starboard davits of the ship slip away beneath him, and he was climbing like a streak.

He glanced around, but the Boeing pilot had lost his nerve and swung off. Now he was desperately trying to close on the Grumman before Madden could get too much altitude. The Fiat suddenly loomed before Turk's sights and he pressed the trips, and saw a stream of tracers pound into the fuselage of the plane. He saw the Fiat's pilot jerk his head back, saw the man's mouth open as from a mighty shout, and then the Fiat swung around and plunged toward the sea, a stream of orange fire behind it!

TURK MADDEN SWUNG the Grumman around, driving toward the Boeing with all he had. The Boeing held, guns flaming, and steel-jacketed bullets punched holes in the Grumman's wing, cracked the canopy and tore at the rudder. Then the other plane pulled up abruptly. In that split second the Boeing's belly was exposed. Turk fired a burst past the undercarriage and into the body of the ship. Yet still the Boeing seemed unharmed.

Turk did a chandelle, brought himself alongside her even as he saw the pilot jerk off his goggles and hurl them from him. The ship was wavering drunkenly, and the pilot fell over the edge of the seat, arms dangling. With a long whine that cut across the nerves like a tight board shrieking in an electric saw, the Boeing spun and dropped, a huge pearshaped flame stretching out and out as the plane fell into the sea.

Turk Madden swung the Grumman and headed toward the yacht. If only he had a bomb now. He shrugged—no use thinking of that. He saw the yacht's gun was ready for another shot at the liner, and even as he went into a shrieking dive, he saw the flame leap from the muzzle of the gun and saw the gunners grab for another round. Then, he was spraying the deck with bullets, and he saw two men fall. Then something happened to the Grumman, or to him, and he jerked back on the stick and lifted the ship into a steep climb. But he felt sick now, and dizzy.

The ship wobbled badly, and he circled, let the ship glide in for a landing. It hit the waves, bucked a little. He cut the motor and tried to get up. The plane pitched in the sea and he slid to the floor.

He forced himself to his knees, startled to see the deck was red where he had rested. But he held himself there and pulled the tommy gun toward him. Even as he waited, he saw he was a little astern of the two ships, and about halfway between them.

Wissler wouldn't sink him. He would need the plane now. His eyes wavered to the liner, and he saw she had a hole through her forepeak and another on the waterline. He wondered why she wasn't moving, then looked aft and could see the steam steering-engine room was blasted. The splutter of a motor drew his attention and as the hull of the Grumman pitched up in the mild swell he saw a motorboat speeding toward him from the yacht.

He let the door swing open in case he fell and couldn't lift himself to see, and then leaned against the edge. Below him the water was stained with a little red. He didn't know where he was shot, and didn't even believe he was. Yet there was blood.

This was going to be close. If Wissler wasn't in that boat—but he would be. Leave it to Wissler to be there to kill the man who had hit so hard and fast. If he could cook Wissler, and maybe Karchel, there wouldn't be any raiding of peaceful ships, nor any attacking of plantations. The others would scatter without leadership.

THE SPEEDBOAT SWUNG in alongside and cut the motor. Just beyond the plane. They'd ease her in slowly now. Maybe.

Turk Madden grinned. Puccini tried to get tough with him back in the States, and Puccini was a big shot. All right. Now let Wissler see what it meant to cut himself a piece of this cake. He felt sick, but he lifted the machine gun. Then Steve Karchel saw him and yelled, his face dead white and his gun coming up. As the body of the plane slid upward and the boat sank a foot or two into the trough of a wave, Turk grinned.

There was the roar of the gun, and suddenly Steve Karchel's chest blossomed with crimson. The man sagged at the knees and sat down, his chest half shot away. Madden turned the gun and swept the boat. Flame leaped from somewhere, and there was a shocking explosion. Madden felt himself getting sicker, and he clung to the door. When he opened his eyes, the motorboat was drifting just beyond the Grumman's wing, and all aflame.

Then he saw Harry Wissler. He was standing in the stern, and his face was white and horribly red on one side from the scorching of the flames that were so close. The man's lips were bared in a snarl of hatred, and he was lifting his six-gun carefully.

Funny, what a fellow remembered at a time like this. That Wissler always stuck with a revolver. No automatics for him. Well, okay. Possibly he'd like this one.

The tommy gun was gone somewhere. Slipped out the door, maybe. But not the Luger. Turk lifted it. The gun felt terribly heavy.

He heard a report, and something smashed into the doorjamb. Then he began firing. From somewhere another boat was approaching, but he kept shooting until the gun was empty.

Slowly, the hulk of the speedboat tipped, and with it all that was left of Harry Wissler slid into the sea.

WHEN TURK OPENED HIS EYES, he was lying in a clean white bunk and a couple of men were standing over him.

"Live?" one man was saying. "Sure, he'll live. He was shot, but it was mostly loss of blood from these glass cuts in his head." The doctor shook his head admiringly. "He certainly made a grand cleanup on that bunch of would-be pirates."

Turk smiled.

" 'Has-been' pirates, now," he murmured as he passed out again.

Flight to the North

Turk Madden nosed the Grumman down gently and cut his motor, gliding in toward the dark waters of the cove. A dead stick landing on strange water in the middle of the night, and no flares to be chanced—it was asking for trouble.

True he had been assured by the Soviet Intelligence that it could be done, that the cove was wide enough and deep enough, and there were no dangers to navigation.

"If I get away with this," he muttered savagely, "anything can happen! And," he added grimly, "it probably will!"

It was bright moonlight, and he swung in toward the still waters of the cove with no noise save the wind-wash past the plane. The dark water lifted toward him, the amphibian hit lightly, then slid forward to a landing.

He would turn her around before the ship lost momentum. Then if anything happened . . .

The shore was dark; ominously still. If Powell and Arseniev were there they were to signal with a flashlight, but there was no signal. Madden hesitated, fuming inwardly. If he took off and left them, it would mean abandoning them to death. But if something had happened, if the plot had been discovered, then it would mean his own death to delay.

Suddenly he found himself wishing he was back in the East Indies running his airline in person instead of being up here in a lonely inlet on the coast of the Japanese island of Hokkaido waiting to pick up two secret agents.

From a single plane flown by himself, he had built his passenger, express, and freight service to three ships operating among the remote islands of the Indies. Then, wanting a change, he had taken a charter flight to Shanghai. From there he had flown for the British government to Vladivostok, only to be talked into flying down the coast of Japan to pick up Powell and Arseniev.

Arseniev he had known in China. He had been flying for Chiang Kai-shek when the OGPU agent had been working with Borodin and Galen.

He liked the Russian, and they had been through the mill together; so he accepted the offer.

Madden glanced shoreward again, tempted to take off. Then with a grunt of disgust he heaved his two-hundred-pound frame out of the pilot's seat, let go his anchor, and got his rubber boat into the water. "This is asking for it," he growled to himself, "but I can't leave while there's a chance they're still ashore. If the Japanese found them now, a firing squad would be the best they'd get."

The moonlight was deceiving, and the rocky shore was dark. Filled with misgiving, he paddled toward a narrow strip of beach. He made the boat fast to a log, and stepped out on the sand. Again he felt the urge to chuck the whole business, to get out while the getting was good. But he walked up the beach, stepping carefully.

It was too quiet, too still. Where were the men? Had they been captured? Had they merely failed to make it? Or were they here, without a light, unable to signal?

Loosening his gun in its holster, he stepped forward. He was rounding a boulder when he saw a shadow move. Instinctively, he crouched.

"Move," a cool voice said, "and I'll shoot."

Turk knew when to stand still and when to move. Now he stood still. A dozen men materialized from the surrounding shadows and closed in. Swiftly, they took his gun and shoved him up the trail between them.

"Well," he told himself, "this is it." The Japanese had no compunctions about their treatment of foreigners under any circumstances, and spies—well, death would be a break.

Ahead of him was a low shack, barely discernible against a background of rocky cliffs. A voice challenged, and one of the Japanese replied, then a door opened, and they were revealed in a stream of light. Shoved rudely forward by his captors, Turk Madden almost fell through the door.

Two men were lying on the floor, bound hand and foot. One was a slender, broad-shouldered man with the face of a poet. The other was short, powerful, his face brick-red, his eyes frosty blue. The latter grinned.

"Sorry, old man," he said, "we couldn't make it. These blighters had us before we reached the cove."

Madden turned around, squinting his eyes against the glare. There were six Japanese in the room, aside from one with the attitude of an officer who sat at a table studying a chart. There was a coal oil light on the table beside him. None of the men were uniformed, or showed any distinguishing marks. All were armed with automatics and rifles. One carried a light machine gun. Their behavior, however, was definitely military.

The officer looked at Turk, his eyes narrow and heavy-lidded. "An American?" The Japanese smiled. "You sound like one. I am Colonel Kito Matasuro. I once lived in California."

"That makes us pals," Madden assured him, grinning. "I was a deckhand once on a San Pedro tugboat."

"But now I am a soldier and you are a spy," Matasuro murmured. "It is most unfortunate—most sad—but you must be shot."

He indicated Arseniev. "He will mean promotion for me. We have wanted him for some time. But like a shadow, he comes and goes. Now we have him. We catch three—we eliminate three."

Turk was acutely conscious of the flat hard butt of his .380 Colt automatic pressing against his stomach. It was inside his coat and shirt, but in his present predicament it might as well have been on the moon.

Despite the harsh realization that his time was only a matter of minutes at best, Turk found himself puzzling over the situation. Why were these men, obviously military, on this stretch of lonely coast in civilian clothes? Why were they here at all? Only a short time before it had been reported devoid of human life, but now there were signs of activity all about him.

Matasuro turned and rapped out orders. "Sorry," he said, getting to his feet, "I would like to have talked to you of California. But duty calls—elsewhere."

With three of the men, he went out. From somewhere a motor roared into life, then another, and still another. A plane took off, and then the others followed. They sounded like pursuit jobs.

For a few minutes they stood in silence. Then Madden said, without looking around, "Fyodor, I'm taking a chance at the first break."

"Sure," the Russian said. "We're with you."

One of the Japanese soldiers stepped forward, lifting his rifle threateningly. He spoke angrily, in Japanese.

The door opened suddenly, and another Japanese came in. He was slim and wiry, his voice harsh. He merely glanced at the prisoners, then snapped orders at the three guards. Hurriedly, they cut the ropes that bound the ankles of the two Intelligence men, and jerked them to their feet. The officer and two soldiers walked out, and the guard behind shoved the prisoners into line and pointed to the door. Madden glanced quickly at Arseniev as the last of the men stepped out, leaving only the guard. "The table!" he snapped. Then he kicked the door shut with his foot, and lunging forward, struck the upright bar with his head. It fell neatly into the wide brackets.

Instantly, Arseniev kicked the table over and the light crashed and went out. Powell had wheeled and kicked the remaining guard viciously in the stomach. The man gasped, and fell forward, and the Britisher kicked him again, on the chin.

Turk, whose hands had not been tied, spun Arseniev around and stripped off the ropes that bound his wrists, then, as the Russian sprang to get the rifle, he did the same for Powell.

"Come on!" he hissed sharply, "we're going out of here."

Turk jerked the bar out of place and threw the door wide open. Outside, clear in the moonlight, stood the three Japanese, hesitating to shoot for fear of killing their comrade. Arseniev threw the rifle to his shoulder and fired, and they plunged outside. The officer had gone down, drilled through the face by the Russian's shot, but the other two jerked their rifles up, too late. Madden's automatic barked. Once . . . twice . . . One was down, the other fled, firing into the night.

"Get their guns, and let's go," Turk said. "My plane may still be okay."

Running, the three men got to the beach and shoved off in the rubber boat. The amphibian floated idly on the still water where he had left it, and they scrambled aboard.

Turk almost fell into the pilot's seat while Powell got the boat aboard, and the Russian heaved in the anchor.

The twin motors roared into life, and in a minute the ship was in the air. Turk eased back on the stick and began reaching for altitude. Glancing back they could see the flat space of the landing field.

"How many planes took off?" Turk asked. "Did you hear?"

"Twelve," Arseniev said. He looked grave. "Where do they go? That is what I am thinking."

"It has to be Siberia," Turk said, at last. "If to China, why the disguise? If to my country, they would be bombers. Pursuit ships cannot reach Alaska from here."

"If they go to make war," Powell said, "they wouldn't be in mufti. There's more in this than meets the eye."

"Maybe," Turk suggested, "a secret base in Siberia from which they could strike farther west and south?"

Arseniev nodded. "Perhaps. And how many have gone before these? Maybe there are many. In the wilds of the taiga there are many places where hundreds of planes could be based."

"What's the taiga?" Powell asked.

"The forest that extends from the Urals to the Sea of Okhotsk, about twenty-five hundred miles from west to east, about seven or eight hundred north and south. I've been through part of it," Turk said; "looks dark and gloomy, but it's full of life. Miles and miles of virgin timber, lots of deer, bear, elk, and tiger in there."

Turk leveled off at ten thousand feet, and laid a course for Vladivostok. His eyes roved over the instrument board, and he told himself again how lucky he was to have this ship. It was an experimental job, an improvement on the OA-9. No bigger, but much faster, with greater range, and capable of climbing to much greater heights. Also, it was armed like a fighting ship.

THE MEN SITTING behind him were silent. He knew what they were thinking. If Japan had a base far back in the great forest of Asiatic Russia, they could strike some terrible blows at Russia's rear while the Soviet was fighting a desperate battle with the invading Germans. It might well be the turning point of the war, and the three men—American, Russian, and British—had a like desire to see Germany defeated.

"You know Ussuria?" Turk asked Arseniev.

The Russian shrugged. "Who does, except in places? There are still wild lands along the ocean, and in the north. I am from the Ukraine, then Moscow, Leningrad, and Odessa. I have been all over Russia proper, but Siberia?" He shrugged once more.

Turk banked slightly, skirting the edge of a cloud. He was watching for the coastline. "I lived there a year when I was kid."

Powell looked at him in astonishment. "Aren't you a Yank?"

Madden grinned. "Sure, I was born in Nevada. But when I was two my father went to the consul's office in Cairo. Then to Zanzibar, then to Tiflis in Georgia. My mother died in Zanzibar, and when I was eleven the revolution broke out. About the same time the old man died of pneumonia.

"Me, I lived around the towns of southern Russia, sleeping in haystacks and wagons, eating when I could. I lived a few months in the Urals, and then went to Siberia. I took up with an old hunter there, and lived and hunted with him for a year. He got killed, so I went south to Samarkand, and into India.

"I got back to the States when I was sixteen. Stayed two years, then went to sea. I've been back twice since."

Arseniev rubbed his chin thoughtfully. "You know a place? Where planes could land?"

Turk nodded. "I was thinking of it. Koreans used to hunt gold up in there. It might be some Japs came with them. It's a small lake almost due north of Lake Hanka and back up in the Sihoti Alin Mountains."

"Want to try it?" Arseniev suggested. "We could refuel at Khabarovsk."

"Hell," Powell interrupted, "why get him into it? He's a commercial flier. You can't get paid enough for that kind of work, and taking a ship like this where it may get into unsupported action isn't sensible!"

"I agree," Turk said, grinning over his shoulder, "so we'll go. We'll land at Khabarovsk, refuel there, and you'd better tell them at Vladivostok what happened. Then we'll hop up there and look around."

In his mind, Turk went back over those Ussurian hills and forests, trying to locate the lake. He remembered those years well enough, and how he and the old Russian had hunted ginseng, trapped mink, and lived on the berries and game of the forest. They had gone west from the forks of the Nahtohu River, and come on the lonely little lake, scarcely a half-mile broad, and three-quarters of a mile long.

LEAVING THEIR PLANE at the field, the three men divided. Turk drifted down the streets, then found a quiet bar, and seated himself. He was eating a bowl of *kasha* and some cheese and black bread when three men sauntered in. They sat down near him, ordering vodka.

One was a huge man with a black beard, slanted Mongolian eyes, and an ugly scar along his cheekbone. His nose had been broken, and when the man reached for his glass, Turk saw the man's hands were huge, and covered with black hair. The other two were more average looking, one short and fat, the other just a rather husky young man with a surly expression. The bearded man kept glaring at Madden.

He ignored it, and went on with his eating. Knowing his clothing set him off as a foreigner, Turk thought it was merely the usual curiosity. The big man talked loudly, and the three looked at Turk, laughing. Then the big man said something louder, still in Russian. Above the noise in the room Turk was unable to distinguish the words.

It was obvious they did not believe he understood Russian, and it began to be equally obvious that the big man was seeking to provoke a quarrel. The crowd in the bar did not like the big man, he could see, but he himself was a foreigner. Finally, above the rumble of voices, he heard the big man use the words "dumb" and "coward."

Turk looked up suddenly, and something in his glance stopped the voices. He spoke to the man serving drinks. "Vodka," he said, motioning to the gathering, "for those. For these—nothing."

There was momentary silence, and in the silence, Turk jerked a thumb at the big man, and said, contemptuously, *"Gnus!"* using the Russian word for abomination applied in the taiga to the swarms of mosquitoes, flies, and midges that make life a curse.

The crowd roared with laughter. *"Gnus! Gnus!* Ha, that's a good one!"

His face swollen with anger, the big man got to his feet. Instantly, the crowd was still. From the expressions on their faces, Turk could see that most of them were frightened. Continuing to eat, he let his eyes slide over toward the men's table. There was an eager light in the eyes of the other two men, and Madden was sure this was what they had been working up to all evening.

The big man, whom he had heard called Batou, came toward him, and Turk continued to eat. When he was close by, the big man reached out suddenly. Turk's head slipped to one side to avoid the clutching hand, and then he kicked the big Russian viciously on the shin.

With a bellow of pain, Batou bent over, grabbing at his shin. Then Turk grabbed him by the beard with one hand, and jerking him forward, leaped to his feet and smashed a heavy right fist into Batou's midsection. The big fellow gasped and Turk shoved him so hard against the wall that he rebounded and collapsed to the floor.

There were audible gasps in the room, and then Madden quietly sat down and started to finish his cheese and *kasha*. Out of the corner of his eye he watched the two men at the table and Batou with apparent unconcern.

He finished his meal as the Russian got up. Stealthily, he observed the other man's rise. Batou's face was vicious as he strode across the room. "So!" he roared, "you t'ink it iss so easy to—"

Turk came up from the table, his left fist swinging.

The blow missed Batou's chin, slid along his face, and ripped his ear. With a cry of rage, Batou swung with both hands, but Turk went under them, and slammed both fists into the big man's stomach. Then he straightened up and grabbing Batou by the beard jerked his head forward into a driving left, and kicked his feet from under him.

Accustomed to winning fights by sheer size and strength, Batou was lost, helpless. He staggered to his feet, and in that instant, the other two men closed in. Adroitly, Turk sidestepped and kicked a chair in the taller man's path, then he struck the other man with a wicked pivot blow and caught him entirely unprepared and knocked him staggering into the wall. Turk closed in on the big fellow, jabbed a left to his mouth, then three more hard ones in rapid-fire order, hooked a hard right to the fellow's cheek and smashed his lips to pulp with a left hook.

He wheeled at a yell, and the younger man was on his feet, a knife poised to throw. Wide open and off balance, too far away to reach the man, Turk Madden was helpless. He didn't have a chance and he knew it. The man's hand moved back to throw, then there was a swish and a dull thud. Turk stared unbelieving.

The haft of a knife was protruding from the man's throat!

Turk spun about and Arseniev was standing in the door, another knife ready to throw. He smiled, lifting one eyebrow at Turk. "Turnabout is fair play, no? You save me, I save you. What is the trouble?"

Turk turned, just in time to see Batou and the other man slipping out the back door. He shrugged, letting them go. Briefly, he explained.

"I have heard some rumors," Arseniev said gravely, "that there is treachery here. This Batou. He is a bad man, a renegade. He murdered and robbed during the revolution. Then he went away to Korea. Now he is back here, and for no good. I believe this fight was deliberate."

They returned to the plane, and as they approached, Turk noticed three soldiers were on guard around the ship. Arseniev spoke to them briefly, the men saluted, and marched away. Powell was waiting inside the ship.

Turk slipped into the pilot's seat, and took the plane out on the field. There he turned into the wind, and in a few seconds they were aloft. Madden banked steeply, and flew west. Arseniev and Powell were surprised at the direction taken.

"If anyone's watching, that may keep them guessing awhile," he said, "even if not for long."

"If we find these planes, what then?" Powell asked.

Arseniev indicated the two-way radio. "We'll contact Khabarovsk, and they will send out a fleet of bombers. We'll show them a thing or two. Besides," he indicated the lockers, "we have a few messages for them ourselves, if necessary."

After flying a dozen miles due west, Turk swung the Grumman and started north, reaching for altitude. At twelve thousand feet he leveled off and soon left the hamlets and cultivated fields behind. He swung away from the railroad, and headed for the coast.

"I'll follow the coast to the Nahtohu, then follow it west to the forks. After that, finding the lake should not be hard."

He checked his guns. The Grumman mounted four machine guns forward; .30 calibers. Aft, there were three gun ports and two automatic rifles available.

"What have you been doing with this crate?" Powell demanded. "I thought you were flying express in the Indies?"

Turk grinned. "I was, but those East Indies are a long way from tamed yet. Lots of times I was flying gold, pearls, rubies, diamonds. Flying over wild country, over Moro, headhunter and cannibal country, and there's lots of renegades. Sometimes I had trouble."

Below them a cold gray sea was running up on the shore, boiling among worn black rocks, and curling back in angry white foam along the huge cliffs that lined the sea. The forest below them did not seem green, it seemed black, lonely, and forlorn like the woods of a dead planet. Here and there on the heights there was snow, and down below in the occasional clearings they could see it, too.

Turk studied the dead gray of the sky. "Storm making up," he said, "but there's plenty of time. That's the Nahtohu coming up." He swung the Grumman to cut over the woods and intersect the river trail.

"Madden!" Arseniev's voice was sharp. "A Nakajima fighter is coming down toward us!"

"Okay," Turk replied. "Get those automatic rifles and stand by aft. But don't shoot unless I give the word, or he starts. Then pour it into him!"

He flew right straight ahead. His mind was working swiftly. It would have to be quick, it would have to be surprise. The fighter's armament was no better, but his speed and maneuverability were much greater.

He glanced around. The fighter hadn't offered to open fire. It must be that he was uncertain. Turk slowed up suddenly to let the Nakajima overtake him. It did, coming at such a terrific rate that when the Grumman abruptly lost speed the fighting plane drew ahead. Madden suddenly banked steeply toward the Nakajima, and at the same instant, opened fire with his full forward armament.

The savage blast of fire caught the uncertain Japanese unprepared. A shell exploded against his instrument board, riddling his body with fragments. As he sprang up in the cockpit, a hurricane blast of machine-gun fire swept the ship from wing to tail assembly, and the Nakajima rolled over and started for earth, screaming like a dying eagle.

Turk pulled the ship into an Immelmann and wheeled back over the spot where the plane had been. But the pursuit ship was a gone gosling. It was headed for earth with a comet's tail of fire streaming out behind. Paralleling it fell the black body of the pilot, turning over and over in the air.

He'd had no chance to think, let alone to act.

"Nice work," Powell said, coming forward. His eyes were narrow, and he was sweating. "You don't gamble much, do you?"

Madden looked up quickly. "Gamble? With a war at stake?"

Powell laughed, his voice a little harsh. "Some would. You had me worried there for a minute!"

Turk eased back on the stick and began to climb. He glanced at the altimeter. Slowly the needle left ten thousand behind, then twelve ... fifteen ... sixteen....

Powell looked uncomfortable, and loosened his collar. Arseniev, who had rejoined them, was watching Powell curiously.

At twenty thousand Turk leveled off and continued west. "What now?" Powell's breathing was heavy in the thin air. "Better land and look around on foot, hadn't we? If they see us we'll have a flock of pursuit jobs around us faster than we can think, and they'll do what you do, shoot first, then talk!"

"No," Turk said. "If they are down there, we're going to call Khabarovsk, then attack."

"Attacking twelve pursuit ships?" Powell said, his face getting red. "You're no combat pilot! You're mad!"

"Didn't you know that?" Turk grinned. "And that's not true, I flew in Spain."

Powell turned, looking at Madden. "You flew in Spain?"

"That's right," Turk nodded. "And I was a prisoner for a while during the siege of the Alcazar at Toledo. Remember?"

"Remember . . ." Suddenly, Powell's hand flashed for a gun, and Turk shoved the stick forward. The Grumman's nose dropped and Powell, overbalanced, plunged forward, his head smashing against the wall. He slumped in his safety belt, and Turk eased the stick back and brought the ship to an even keel. Arseniev's eyes were bright.

"All the time he was a traitor!" he whispered hoarsely. "All the time!"

"Sure," Madden agreed. "I couldn't place him at first. He's a German, lived in England for several years, but he was with Franco. You'd better tie him up."

Arseniev glanced down as Turk banked the ship. On the shores of a small lake were lined a long row of planes. Half of them were in the process of being camouflaged with branches and reeds. The others still were uncovered. There must have been a hundred.

Arseniev, his face white, bound Powell hand and foot, then he stepped over to the radio. "Calling Khabarovsk . . . calling Khabarovsk . . . enemy airdrome located . . . between the forks of the Nahtohu . . . position 138 degrees east, 47 degrees 2 minutes north. . . . Approximately one hundred planes."

Turk glanced down again. Below them the airdrome was a scene of mad activity.

"Heard us!" he snapped. "Get set, I'm going down! Get on those bombs!"

Turk pulled the Grumman into as steep a dive as she would take and went roaring toward earth. When the ship was built she had been fitted with a bomb rack, and he had taken her just that way. Now it would come in handy.

Roaring toward the ground he saw one of the pursuit ships streaking along the field, and he opened up with the guns. The ship was just clearing the trees at the end of the field when it dipped suddenly, smashed into the timber and burst into flame.

The Grumman dove into the field so close that frightened Japanese scattered in every direction, then Arseniev pulled the bomb release, and Turk brought the ship out of the dive. For an instant he didn't think the wings would stay with her, but they did, and the ship was shooting away over the trees when the thunder of the bursting bombs reached their ears. He did a quick wingover and started back, his forward armament chattering wickedly.

He strafed the field from beginning to end, and a pursuit ship that had started to make the run for a takeoff spilled over into flame. He saw men start across the field.

Behind him, Arseniev was busy dropping incendiary bombs, then the Grumman began to climb, and Turk looked back over his shoulder. Several blazes were burning furiously around the field, two planes had definitely crashed there, and several were on fire.

He turned south. "We're getting out of here, Fyodor. Better inform your boys!"

Madden heard the voice replying behind him, then Arseniev switched off the radio.

"There's a force coming!" he yelled.

Turk tooled the Grumman on south, then swung away from the mountains toward the marshes. Suddenly the motor sputtered, coughed, and Turk worked, his face changing. The motor sputtered again, missed, then died.

"What is it?" Arseniev demanded.

"Gas!" Turk indicated his fuel gauges. "Must have winged us as we were leaving."

He put the Grumman into a slow glide, studying the earth below. It was marshland, with occasional ponds and lakes. But all were small. Suddenly, just ahead, he saw one that was somewhat larger. He pushed the stick forward, leveled off, and landed smoothly on the lake water. With what momentum remained, Turk tooled the ship into a small opening in the marsh. Nearby was a small island of firm ground.

"Better get on that radio and report," Turk said. "I'm going to look around."

He tried a hummock of grass near the plane, and it was solid. A flock of birds flew past, staying low. Turk turned to look at them, scowling. Then he looked up, studying the sky. There were clouds about, and the wind was picking up, but not much yet. Along the horizon there was a low black fog.

Suddenly, complete stillness fell over the marsh. Above, the clouds had ragged edges, and the black fog along the horizon suddenly lifted, and then the sun was covered.

"Arseniev!" Turk shouted. "Quick! We've got to get the ship lashed down. We're going to have a storm!"

In a mounting wind they labored desperately, furiously. There were no birds in sight now, and it was beginning to snow. When the ship was lashed down, Madden turned, wiping the sweat from his brow.

"Come on," he said. "We've got to make some shelter!"

"What about the ship?" Arseniev protested. "That will do, won't it?"

"Might be blown out on the lake. Start cutting reeds, and work like you've never worked before." Turk glanced around hastily. "Don't cut them there, or there. Just over there, and work fast!"

The wind was blowing in gusts now, cold as ice, and the snow was lifting into the air. Turk bent his back and slashed reeds with the bolo he always carried in the ship, sweat broke out on his face despite the cold, but he labored on, swinging with his bolo like a madman. Uncertain, Arseniev followed suit, not sure why they were cutting, but working desperately against time.

Leaping back to the bunches of reeds left uncut, Turk began binding them together with stout cord brought from the plane. Then he wove the long reeds closely together among the clumps, drawing them down low above the ground, and working the gathering snow close around the edges. Running to the plane, he caught up a canvas tarp and raced back, doubling it over on the ground under the covering of the reeds that was partly a hut, partly just a low shelter.

Suddenly there was a shout from Arseniev. Turk looked up, wondering. Powell had somehow broken his bonds, and had leaped from the plane. Turk went for his gun, but his hands, numbed by cold, fumbled, and before he could draw it the man had leaped to a hummock of grass, dodged behind a clump of reeds, and when they next saw him he was running at full tilt over the marsh. Once he fell waist deep in water, then scrambled out, and trotted on.

"Let him go," Turk said. "Maybe it's better than a firing squad, at that."

"What do you mean? You think—" Arseniev began.

Turk shrugged. "He's partly wet, he has no shelter, no weapons. What do you think? He'll die before this night is out. Feel that wind, and imagine yourself wet—in that."

Arseniev shivered. "I can't." He looked around. "What now?"

"Crawl in between the canvas," Turk said. "I'll join you in a minute." He walked back and forth, piling the reeds over the canvas and feathering them against the wind. Then he trampled the snow down, and after a while, lifted the canvas and joined Arseniev.

The instant he was inside it felt warmer; over them they could hear the lonely snarl of the wind, and out on the lake the lashing of the waves, but over their covering of reeds the snow sifted down, gathering over them in a thick, warm blanket.

IT WAS MORNING when he awakened. He turned over slowly, warm and comfortable. No wind was blowing, but he knew that it was cold outside. He touched Arseniev on the shoulder, then crawled out.

The world was white with snow everywhere. The lake was crusted with ice, and even the reeds bent heavily under the weight of the snow. The plane was almost covered with it.

"We've got to make a fire," Turk said, "and then uncover the ship. The way it is, a searching plane couldn't find us."

Sweeping the snow from a place on the ground, Turk went back to the shelter and brought out a handful of dry reeds. Arseniev collected some driftwood from the edge of the lake, and soon a fire was ablaze. Then they went to work, clearing the snow from the ship. It was a job, but it kept them warm.

Arseniev stopped once, looking over the white, empty expanse. "I wonder what his real name was?" he said.

"I don't know," Turk said. "I never heard."

It was an hour later when they heard the mutter of a plane. Soon it was circling above them, and then it leveled off and landed on solid earth not far away from the island where they'd spent the night.

Two men came running to them over the frozen marsh. "Marchenko!" Arseniev yelled. "It is good to see you, believe me!" The other man was Bochkarev, a flyer noted for his Polar exploits. They shook hands all around.

Two hours later, the Grumman was towed to solid earth and repaired. The big Russian ship took off, then the Grumman. Turk headed the ship south, toward Khabarovsk. They were flying low over the snow when Arseniev suddenly caught his arm.

Powell.

They knew him by the green scarf that trailed from his neck, a bright spot of color on a piece of ground swept clear by the driving wind. The man lay where he had fallen, frozen and still.

Turk Madden eased back on the stick and climbed higher. Ahead of them, the sky was blue, and the sun was coming out from the clouds. In the clear cold air the sound of the motors was pleasant, a drumming roar of strength and beauty.

Coast Patrol

Dense fog blanketed the Siberian coast. It was cold, damp, and miserable. Turk Madden banked the Grumman steeply and strained his eyes toward the fogbound earth.

He could not see anything but the gray cottony thickness. Occasionally a jagged peak of the Sihoti Alins loomed through the clouds, black and ugly where the wind had swept the snow away.

It was warm in the cabin of the plane, and glancing over his shoulder, Turk smiled to see Diakov asleep. The Ussuri Cossack gunner possessed an amazing ability to sleep at any time or place. And he never dozed. He was either instantly asleep or wide-awake. Well, a few more miles of patrol and they could return to Khabarovsk, to food and a warm bed.

Turk swung the ship lazily, detecting a rift in the fog. Then, quite suddenly, he saw the freighter.

She was moored fore and aft, just inside the river mouth. A freighter of no less than four thousand tons tied up at a rocky shelf in the mouth of a lonely stream on a coast that rarely saw anything bigger than a fishing smack or occasional whaler. Since the war had begun, even the few Udehe fishermen had gone back up the coast to colder but safer waters.

Glancing back, he saw Diakov was awake. The big Cossack's black eyes were alert. "You see something? What is it?"

"A ship," Madden said. "A big freighter, tied up in the river."

"No Russian ship would be here," Diakov said. "I think not."

"I'm going down and have a look-see," Turk said. He rolled the plane around in a tight circle, heading upstream. His sense of direction had always been his greatest asset. He remembered that river, too. For two weeks he had been flying over it every day, and before that at odd times. Upstream there was a wide bend with a little backwater where he could land ... with luck.

He landed.

Fog was around them like a shroud. Diakov straightened, his face pale under the tan. "Well," he shrugged, "I tell myself it is your life, too, so why should I be afraid? Nevertheless, I am afraid."

He leaped ashore and took a turn around a tree with a line, making the plane fast, then another tree, lashing it bow and stern. Then he got out skis and checked his rifle. "How far you think?" he asked.

"About three miles." Turk grinned at him, the smile making his lean brown face suddenly boyish. "You stay here, Muscovite. If I don't come back, you go over the mountains to Sidatun."

The Cossack lifted an eyebrow. "Even a ghost couldn't cross the Sihoti Alins now," he said. "We fly out, or die."

It would have been simpler to have flown to Khabarovsk to report the ship, but finding a thread of river on that coast in a fog like this would be harder now than finding a Jap in Chungking. This way he could investigate first and have something definite to report.

A snow-covered forest trail followed the river. An expert on skis, Turk made good time and in only a matter of minutes stood on the edge of the forest, not a hundred yards from the ship.

The ladder was down, but the name of the ship was invisible in the fast-falling snow. Vladivostok, the nearest Siberian port, was miles away to the south, almost four hundred miles, in fact. Across the narrow Sea of Japan, however, were the Japanese islands.

Could it be a raiding party from Japan? It didn't seem likely. In any case, it was his job to find out. It was a chance he had to take.

Already, falling snow had covered him with a thin sifting of flakes. Moving carefully, taking every advantage of flurries of wind that veiled his movement, Turk crossed to the ship. He had abandoned his skis in the brush, so when he reached the ladder, he did not hesitate, but mounted swiftly.

There was no challenge, only the whisper of snow. The deck was white and still, unbroken by a footprint. Hesitating, flattened against the bulkhead, he studied the situation. Something here was radically wrong. It was almost an hour since he left the plane, and the snow had begun then, yet there had been no movement on the deck in that time. Every sense in his body was alert, and he hesitated, dreading to move, aware that his steps would be revealed in the snow.

Turk slid his hand inside his leather coat and loosened his Colt. Then he moved swiftly to the passage that led to the saloon and the officers' quarters.

The door opened easily under his hand, and he stepped into the warm passage. The door of the mate's cabin was on his left, but a glance showed it to be empty.

Before him was the door of the saloon. He opened the door, pushed it wide with his left hand as his right gripped the butt of his automatic.

A man lay with his cheek on the table, face toward the door, arms dangling. Between his shoulder blades was the protruding haft of a knife. His cap, bearing a second mate's insignia, lay on the table.

On most freighters the second mate had the twelve-to-four watch. The man had been murdered while eating, so apparently he had been killed just before taking over his watch. It was now nearly four.

Turk stepped back and closed the door gently, then mounted to the bridge. The wheelhouse was empty, except for a man lying sprawled on the deck. Even before he knelt over the body, Turk could see from the way the head lay that the man's neck was broken. There was a large welt on his head, and over him, a broken shelf.

Another cap lay nearby. Turk picked it up and glanced at it. *Third Mate.* He sized up the situation. "Nine bucks to a dime," he muttered thoughtfully, "somebody came in the port door. This guy rushed him, and the guy used judo on him. Threw him into that shelf."

Grimly, Turk stepped out on the bridge and closed the door. Visibility was low. He'd be unable to take off in this. He descended to the captain's deck and tried the starboard door. It was locked. Rounding the deckhouse, he tried the port door and it opened gently under his hand.

THE VERY PRETTY BRUNETTE with the gun in her hand showed no surprise and no fear. "Come in," she said, "and close the door, or I'll kill you."

"Thanks," Turk said, "it's getting cold out there." If she had said she'd shoot him, he wouldn't have been surprised. But she said "kill," and he had a very good idea she meant it. "No need to hold that gun on me," he said pleasantly, "unless you're the one who murdered the mates."

She stiffened. "Who ... murdered?"

"Yeah," he said. "Somebody played rough around here. Somebody who uses jujitsu and a knife. They got the second and third mates."

"Not Richards? Aaron isn't killed?" Her eyes were wide.

Turk frowned. "I don't know your pal Richards. I only know that you've got two less mates than you had, and I want to know why. I also want to know who you are, what this ship is doing here, and where the skipper is."

She stared at him suspiciously, making no move to put the gun down.

"It's all right," he said, exasperated. "I'm an American. I've been flying coast patrol for the Russians because of the war."

She hesitated, then decided to believe him. "This is the *Welleston,* out of Boston. My father, Mace Reardon, was in command. We were bound for Vladivostok with aviation fuel, machine oil, and M-3 tanks when Pearl Harbor was bombed. We had trouble with our radio, and the war had been going on for several days before we heard of it. Dad took the ship north around Sakhalin Island, hoping to slip down the Siberian coast to Vladivostok.

"When we got this far, Aaron—I mean Mr. Richards, the mate— suggested we tie up here and communicate with Vladivostok to get an escort through the most dangerous water."

Madden nodded. "Not a bad idea. Your Mr. Richards was smart. But how were you to communicate with them? Your radio would warn the Japs, and this is an American ship."

"We didn't use the radio. Aaron told Sparks to set out overland for Sidatun."

"For *where?*" Turk's eyes narrowed.

"Sidatun. It's several miles back from the coast. Sparks was good on skis, so he went."

"And Richards sent him?" Turk was beginning to understand ... or suspect. "Where's Richards now?"

"I don't know." The girl was frankly puzzled. "Mutiny broke out, just after Sparks left. My father was ..." She hesitated, and for the first time her poise wavered. "... killed. Then Aaron told me to stay inside and not to let anyone in but him."

A breath of cold air on the back of his neck warned Turk. He turned, letting his gun slide into his hand with that smooth efficiency that only comes from long familiarity and practice. He was just a little too fast for the tall, handsome man who stood in the doorway. "Hold it, buddy," Turk said softly. "I never like to kill people I haven't met socially."

"Aaron!" the girl cried out sharply. "I've been so worried. Where have you been?"

Richards ignored her question, his eyes intent, staring at Turk. He was a bigger man than Turk, which meant that he was well over six feet and weighed more than Madden's compact one eighty.

"Who is this man?" Richards asked coolly.

"The name is Madden," Turk replied, studying the man keenly. "I'm an American. I run a commercial airline in the East Indies. Made a long flight up to Shanghai with a special passenger, and then went on patrol for the Soviet Army of the Far East. Come in and close that door."

Richards complied, moving warily and keeping his hands in sight. He didn't do anything suspicious, but something told Turk he was to be carefully watched.

Richards faced him again. "I'm afraid, Tony," he said to the girl, "that anything this man has told you is a lie. He cannot be on patrol. No plane could possibly land in this weather."

"I land planes in all kinds of weather," Turk said calmly, "and what you think or do not think does not happen to matter in the least. I am an officer of the Soviet government at the moment, and the cargo of this ship is the property of that government. The ship is flying the American flag, and I am a citizen of the United States. I want to know exactly what has happened on this boat."

"There was a mutiny," Richards said coldly, "a very minor one. I handled it. Everything is now under control. We need no help."

The man was listening for something. Turk remembered the door behind him was locked, the ports dogged down. Yet he felt an acute sense of impending danger.

"I wonder if the second and third mates thought it was minor?" Turk demanded. "Who murdered them? Did you?"

Richards stiffened, and his eyes widened just a little, then turned cold and dangerous. "I think we might ask the crew about that, or *you*. You might be a Jap agent."

Turk laughed. "Yeah, I'd bet a lot of dough one of us is, and it isn't me. The second mate wasn't murdered by a stranger or by a crew in mutiny. He was murdered by someone he knew and trusted."

"How do you know that?" Tony asked sharply.

"Because he was stabbed in the back while eating by someone he knew was behind him. The third mate was killed by someone with a knowledge of jujitsu. But he was expecting trouble."

"Well, Mr. Sherlock Holmes," Richards sneered, his eyes hard, "you think you have it all figured out, don't you? Trying to pin it all on me? Well, I think you're a renegade, that you haven't any plane, and have no connection with any government whatsoever."

Tony Reardon was looking at Turk, her eyes cold. "Maybe you'd better put up that gun and leave," she said. "Whatever you came here for won't work. I know Mr. Richards, and now that my father is dead, he is in command. Your efforts to prejudice me against him won't do. I've known him for over a year, and he is not only the captain now, but my fiancé."

Turk grinned. "Which apparently makes him the head man around here. All right, darling, suppose you ask him why he sent Sparks out to die."

"What do you mean?" she demanded.

"You said he sent him to Sidatun to communicate with the Soviet officials. Sidatun, baby, is not several miles away, but several hundred, and across a range of mountains. In this weather even a man who knows the country couldn't make it."

"I don't believe it!" Tony said desperately.

Turk was watching Richards. The mate was half crouched, his eyes malevolent. Madden slipped his hand inside his coat and tossed a roll on the table. "Look at that map, honey."

There was a sudden step on the deck outside, and a sound of footsteps on the ladder. Triumphant light leaped into Richards's eyes at the sound, but Turk sprang for the door. Richards leaped to intercept him, swinging even as he sprang. Turk was lunging right into the path of the blow, and there was no way to avoid it. It struck him a smashing wallop on the chin and knocked him staggering into the wall. Even as he fell back, Richards steadied himself and lifted his gun.

Off balance and helpless, Turk was cold meat, when Tony caught Richards's arm, jerking it aside. The shot smashed a picture an inch over Turk's head.

Before the mate could free his gun hand, Turk sprang close and, grabbing him by the collar, literally jerked him from his feet, dragging him to the door. Throwing it open, Turk dumped Richards out at the feet of three startled Japanese sailors.

Madden drew back swiftly and slammed the door, turning the key in the lock. Tony Reardon's face was deathly pale. "What is it?" she asked. "What's happening? I don't understand!"

A shout of anger came from outside, and then a pounding on the door. It was a steel door, and Turk was unworried.

Her face was strained and Turk could see she was on the verge of hysteria. She had kept her father's death bottled up inside her, and now this.

"Hold it, kid," Turk said kindly. "You sit down and take it easy. We'll get out of this. The way I figure it, this Richards has sold out to someone. Now the Japs have arrived. Richards must have got in touch with them somehow."

He checked his gun. Without doubt they would move the ship at once. Every minute they stayed was dangerous. And that meant that unless he could do something promptly, they would be out on the Sea of Japan headed for a prison camp or death.

Turk crossed the room in a stride and peered out the port. A Jap seaman was opening the valves to get steam into the winch, another had put down his rifle and was clearing a line that had become fouled with some tackle. They would be casting off in a matter of minutes.

Tony came up to him. Her eyes were wide, her face tear-stained, but she was composed again. He looked down at her. "You've got nerve, kid," he said, "and that's what it's going to take."

"What are we to do now?" she asked simply.

"We've got to get out of here and away," he said, "an' there's a good chance we'll get killed trying. They can't release that line up there, an' don't dare cast off aft until they do, else they'll have the ship broadside to the current, an' probably run her aground.

"They will be getting up more steam now. When they do, the chances are someone will slip ashore an' cut the line. Then, like it or not, we'll be headed for Japan."

Turk hesitated. "I'm going to open that door and shoot the guard. It doesn't seem like there's many of them. Then we'll get down that ladder as fast as we can. The snow will help some. They can't see ten feet beyond the bow. It will be the last thing they expect, so we got a chance."

Tony picked up her gun, her chin firm. "Okay, honey," he said, "open the door an' follow me. We're blasting out of here."

Luck was with them. The guard stood by the rail, and even as he turned, Madden slashed him on the temple with the .45. They were halfway to the ladder before they were seen. A Japanese sailor patrolling the bridge let out a shout of alarm and threw up his rifle. Turk spun on his heel and snapped a quick shot at the man. It lifted the cap from the man's head, and he dropped out of sight behind the bulwark.

A shot glanced from the deck right ahead of them, and then Tony was running down the icy ladder. Turk turned coolly at the head of the ladder and laced the deck with a pattern of fire. Then he half ran, half slid, down the ladder. He stopped dead still and slid another clip into his automatic before he moved, then ran close alongside the hull.

Glancing back, he saw a sailor leaning out from the ship to level a rifle, and Turk fired. The man's face blossomed with crimson and he lost his hold, sliding through the rail to fall into the opening between the ship and the ledge.

Then, from the edge of the woods, a barrage of fire opened up, sweeping the ship's rail and bridge with a stream of bullets. Running, gasping for breath, the two plunged through the last of the snow and stumbled into the shelter of the forest.

Diakov met them on the edge of the woods, his face beaming, the CZ light machine gun cradled in his arms. "Skis here," he said. "We better leave quick."

"What about her?" Turk protested. "She—"

"Skis for her, too." The Cossack winked broadly. "I find a Jap out here on skis. I brought them along ... a rifle, too."

Turk glanced quickly at the trail to the plane. Obviously, the Russian had been here some time, for his footprints were covered over with new snow. He turned at right angles to the river and started off through the timber. "Wrong way," Diakov protested.

"We'd get there just a few minutes ahead of their pursuit," Turk said, "and not time enough to warm up the plane and take off. No, we've got to lead them back in the hills."

Diakov's eyes lighted. "In the Sihoti Alins? I hope they all follow us, comrade. We will show them something, no?"

In silence the three struck out through the timber. Behind them they knew pursuit would be organized. The Japanese dared not leave when there was a chance that other planes would catch them before they were far out at sea.

Turk said nothing as he followed Diakov through the timber. The big Cossack was a marvel on skis, and it took only a few minutes for Turk to see that Tony Reardon was able to muddle along.

"What kind of shape are you in?" he asked her.

She smiled for the first time. "I'll get the hang of it. I used to do this when I was a kid in upstate New York. Don't worry about me."

After that it was grim business. There was no chance of eluding their pursuers, but they had a lead that they increased after a few miles. Diakov didn't look for easy going, and as often as possible he led them across bare, icy spots where the skis left no trail.

After a while Turk stopped. "You go ahead," he said to them. "I'm going to give these boys something to worry about."

The two headed away. He and Diakov in a murmured conversation had settled on a lonely peak for a rendezvous, deciding shortly after their start that would be their destination.

Turk took a limb from a tree and brushed the trail. The fast-falling snow would fill in the gaps. Then he walked back over a bare spot, carrying his skis. Down below, a half mile behind, he saw a knot of men, several others scattered out behind.

He rested the captured rifle on a branch and steadied it against his cheek. Allowing for the cold, he took careful aim, trying the rifle from several positions. He watched them come closer, then steadied the rifle and fired.

The group split like magic, and in an instant the trail was emptied of all but one man. He got up and, carrying one ski, hobbled into the brush. Taking his time, Turk fired three times, moving himself. Then slipping on his skis, he started out at a fast clip.

Shooting through an opening in the trees, he drove himself down a long slope in long, swift strides, took a quick turn around the bole of a huge tree, and started up a long slope through the brush, moving at an angle. Far below a shot rang out, and he knew he had been sighted, but he did not stop. Another shot, and then he stopped.

Taking a quick glance back, he threw up his rifle and fired. One of the men sprang aside.

"Stung him!" Turk muttered. "Well, that'll keep 'em worried."

He had gone no more than two miles before he stopped suddenly. Above him, on the steep side hill above the vague trail he was following, a huge boulder was poised. Behind it and on up the mountain were several tree trunks, more rock, and the makings of a small slide. He halted, studying the situation thoughtfully. There was a loose collection of rocks under the boulder, but apparently one stone held the bigger boulder in place. Using a broken limb, he cleared out some of the dirt and loose stuff from underneath and experimentally rocked the boulder back and forth.

Smiling, he continued on. Occasionally he glanced back, but kept to the trail, the boulder in sight. Twice he sighted his rifle over his back trail, and finally he halted.

Seating himself on a rock, he waited. From time to time he stood up and moved around to keep warm. Then he saw them coming. Slowly, the men began to wind along the trail below the boulder. Raising his rifle, he sighted carefully, took a long breath, and let a little out of his lungs. Then holding the rifle loosely, he squeezed the trigger.

He fired not at the men themselves, but at the spot where the rock was holding the slide suspended above the trail. Nothing happened. He shifted his position a little and fired again. Immediately there was a terrific roar, and he saw the slide wipe a black path across the mountainside.

When he moved on again, it was with the knowledge that two fewer men followed him.

It was dark when Turk reached the hollow at the base of the peak. The spot was secluded, and the path he had taken brought him there only a few minutes after Diakov and Tony arrived. The Cossack was cutting dry wood from the underside of a fallen log to build a fire. When it was burning, they sat around talking in low tones. There was small chance of pursuit until daybreak, which was hours away. Traveling even in the day was not easy. At night, with boulders, ice slides, and heavy snow laced with fallen trunks, it would be infinitely more dangerous.

Diakov brewed tea over the fire, and after they had finished a bar of chocolate that Turk shared among them, Turk cleared a wider place in the snow and shifted the fire. Then he spread dry leaves from the bottom of a snow-covered pile over the warm ground where the fire had been. Tony could hardly keep her eyes open, and an instant after she touched the ground, she slept. Diakov and Turk shared watches.

IT WAS JUST turning gray when Turk awakened. Diakov was putting fuel on the fire. "I went back to look," he said softly. "They are three miles back, but a mile and a half east of us. They have lost our trail and talk of returning."

Turk scowled. "That means we must make the plane today. The ship won't leave until these fellows return."

Turk awakened Tony and they hastily slipped on their skis and hit the trail. It was all downhill now. They had reached a high elevation and the trees had thinned out to a few fir, some Siberian larch, and spruce. The lower reaches along the valleys were covered with dense forest with few trails. Giant poplars reached toward the sky, some of them hundreds of years old. Sliding in among the trees, Turk led the way at a rapid pace. There was no time now for delay. Whatever was to be done must be done at once.

There was a chance that, casting about, the Japanese would find their trail, but the risk had to be taken. The air was still and very cold, but the brisk movement kept them warm. Several times Turk stopped to study the back trail, but they moved so rapidly that almost before they realized it, they shot out of the woods beside the river.

The Grumman was lying quietly in the backwater, her wings heavy with snow. Hastily, while Diakov and Tony brushed the snow away, Turk worked over the twin motors. After a few choking tries, they kicked off, roaring into life with a thunder that awakened the still cold of the taiga.

Tony got into the cabin, and then Diakov cast off. Instantly, gambling against the Japanese hearing his signals, Turk began to call the landing field at Khabarovsk. He glanced at his watch. Murzin would be on now. He sent his call out again.

"Madden, Ussuri Coast Patrol, calling Khabarovsk. Coast Patrol calling Khabarovsk."

After a minute he heard Murzin. "Come in, Madden. Where you been, comrade?"

"SS *Welleston,* bound for Vladivostok, tied up in river mouth south of Nahtohu River. Mutiny aboard. Situation serious. Come loaded for bear."

"Stand by, Coast Patrol."

Turk Madden swung the Grumman around and headed for the shore. He was at home now. In the air, flying his specially built amphibian, he was always at home. For what she was, the ship was fast and maneuverable. He saw the gray line of the sea and then he was over it. Glancing down, he saw the freighter. There was no fog now, and he could see the line of men coming wearily through the trees from their fruitless chase.

Instantly, he banked, then pushed the stick forward and sent the ship down in a steep dive, opening up with the machine guns. A blur of snow lifted near the men, and the line melted. He hauled back on the stick and the Grumman climbed steeply, then he swung back over the freighter and cleared her deck with a burst of fire.

Then Diakov was hammering on his back and pointing. He looked up to see a V of planes coming toward him about five hundred feet up. Turk's face turned grim and he climbed even more steeply. The Grumman went up and up and up, reaching for altitude. When he looked again, he could see the planes more closely. Three light bombers all painted with the rising sun. They were probably there in case the Russians had brought up a destroyer, or to sink the ship if it looked like it would get away. After all, it was an American ship.

Madden swung the Grumman around. Stand by, they said. That meant to keep the situation in hand. One of the planes was climbing to meet him, and coming up fast. He had outflown the Japanese before, and could do it again, but in a ship like this, against a war plane, even the best of flying would have to be nine-tenths luck to come out alive. He streaked away from the climbing aircraft and went into a dive over the next lowest bomber.

The fellow swung away, and Turk's first burst of fire missed. Then he did an Immelmann and came in on the bomber's tail. His second burst painted a string of holes along the bomber's fuselage, and he saw the string reach the pilot. The bomber shot up, suddenly fell off, and going into a slow falling turn, burst into a bright rose of flame.

A streak of tracers shot by him, and Turk pulled the Grumman around, diving straight for the trees and the low-hanging fog with the other plane after him. The Japanese was a flier, and with his greater speed was coming up fast. Turk felt an icy blast of air as Diakov swung open the roof hatch behind the wing and deployed his gun mount. The Cossack slammed his machine gun onto the pivot and opened up as Turk banked the ship steeply, his wingtip almost grazing the treetops, and roared into the fog bank. The war plane pulled up slightly, and Madden's Grumman bucked and pitched through the mist with prayer the only force keeping him out of the invisible treetops.

Turk pulled up, into the clear, but the other plane had swung around and was coming at him from the side. The big Grumman was in a spot, and Turk banked around and headed straight for the nearest war plane, his twin motors wide open and all his guns hammering. The Japanese held on grimly, and the two planes shot at each other with terrific force, but in the split second before they would have come together, the Japanese lost his nerve and pulled back on his stick. The plane shot up, and Diakov raked his underside with a wild burst from his gun. Then he shot on by, and only had Diakov's shout of triumph to know that he had scored again.

Strangely, the last aircraft was streaking off over the Sea of Japan and climbing. Turk banked a little and glanced down to find himself coming in toward the freighter. A Jap on the shore was desperately trying to cast off. Turk shoved forward on the stick and opened up immediately with a burst of fire. The man crumpled, seeming to come all apart at the seams, and a second man, rushing for the woods, was caught on the edge of the raking burst and fell, his body tumbling in a complete somersault.

Turk came around and trimmed back for a hot landing on the river just before the freighter. The Cossack sprang ashore with a line, and Turk, leaving him to make the ship fast, grabbed his automatic and dashed for the ship.

Richards. The man was still aboard, and he needed to be apprehended.

Turk reached the top of the ladder just as Richards stepped out of the amidships house. The man's face turned livid and, without regard for Turk's gun, sprang at him. Madden hesitated only a second, then shoved the gun in his pocket and sprang forward, throwing punches with both fists.

Richards was not only big, he was tough and powerful. They grappled and he rolled over and scrambled free. Both men came up at the same time. Turk started to close in, but Richards kicked him away, and when Turk struck out, he caught his arm in a flying mare. Turk relaxed and went on over in an easy roll, landing on his feet. He spun around, slipped a fast left, and smashed a big fist into Richards's stomach. The mate backed up, his face dark with fury and pain. Turk followed, stabbing a left to the face, then crossing a jarring right to the chin. Richards's knees wilted and he almost fell. He lunged forward, and Turk broke his nose with a driving right hook. Richards went down, hitting the deck hard.

Aaron Richards scrambled to his feet. Wheeling, he rushed for the gangway that led to the bank of the river. He bent over and plucked the large pin that allowed the gangway to swivel back and forth out of its hole. As Turk closed on him, Richards turned and swung the heavy piece of metal. It hit Turk a stunning blow on the back of his shoulder and knocked him flat on the deck, his pistol coming loose and rattling into the scuppers.

By the time Turk had picked himself up, Richards was stumbling down the ladder and out onto the muddy ground. When he saw Turk appear at the ship's rail, he turned and, taking hold of the gangway railing, gave a mighty heave. The entire assembly, now disconnected at the top, came loose. Scraping down the side of the hull, it crashed into the gap between the ship and the riverbank. The mate took to his heels.

Diakov was returning from scouting the trees, and Richards straight-armed him like a football player. The big Russian went down, and Richards disappeared into the stand of fir along the water. Turk watched as he picked himself up, but instead of giving chase he limped toward the *Welleston.*

"There are still some left, comrade! They've a boat down the river!"

At that moment a heavy engine roared to life beyond the trees. Turk ran to the other rail in time to see a Japanese torpedo boat arc out into the river. She was going all out, bow high in the water and her stern sunk deep, a cloud of blue-gray exhaust trailing from her pipes. Within minutes Aaron Richards would make the inlet, and from there the open ocean.

Turk backed up, yanked off his low boots and coat and, vaulting the railing, took a running dive into the icy water. The height and the cold took his breath away, but within a dozen powerful strokes he was alongside the Grumman and scrambling onto the hull. His clasp knife made quick work of the mooring rope, and then he was pulling himself into the cockpit and firing the engines.

He flew down the river with the throttles wide open, leaving Diakov on the bank bellowing encouragement. As the plane clawed for altitude, Turk struggled out of his freezing shirt and turned up the mostly ineffective cabin heater.

As the water deepened, the patches of fog thinned, and then ahead of him he could see the torpedo boat. She was shooting across the swells like an arrow, kicking up blasts of spray and leaving a long wake. Turk put the plane into a shallow dive. Fast as the Japanese craft was, the Grumman came down on it at over a hundred fifty miles per hour. Turk triggered his forward guns, the burst cutting the water across the bow.

There were only two men visible on deck—a Japanese sailor at the helm, and Richards, who was struggling to pull the cover from the boat's antiaircraft machine gun. Turk wheeled around and came back, angling in on the fast gray boat carefully. The man at the wheel had begun evasive maneuvers, and Turk could tell it was throwing off Richards's aim; his gun flamed, but it was a moment before he hit the Grumman, and then the bullets found only the wingtip.

Turk held his fire as Richards swung his gun, and then he let go with a long burst just before the traitor could fire. The steel-jacketed slugs tore up the decking, forcing Richards to dive for cover, and continued ripping back and down into the engine compartment. Turk shot past, barely off the water, then pulled back on the stick, heading up toward the clouds.

Outside his left-hand window he saw his port engine stall and die. The drag pulled at the plane, and he leveled out, trying to compensate with his rudder. He turned the nose of the plane back toward land and was glancing at the motor for any signs of bullet damage or fire when the starboard engine died.

"This could be better!" he muttered to himself.

Grimly, Turk put the ship into a long glide and aimed for the calm water just inside the bar at the mouth of the river.

The amphibian set down upon the water smoothly, and when it came to a halt, Turk turned and flipped on the two-way radio switch.

"Calling Khabarovsk ... calling Khabarovsk. Madden, Coast Patrol. Down at sea off Kumuhu River. Please send help. Out of petrol."

"Khabarovsk airdrome answering Madden, Coast Patrol. Stand by."

Another voice spoke through the radio. "Diakov calling from S.S. *Welleston*. I found the crew tied up. We're coming to fish you out. Are you all right, comrade?"

"Okay for now. Go pick up Richards first, no immediate danger ... only I wanted to be shipwrecked with a beautiful dame."

"Well," a cool voice said in his ear, "you're not very complimentary!"

Turk turned and his jaw dropped. "Tony! What are *you* doing here!"

"I was in the plane, and you just jumped in and took off, so here I am!"

Turk must have left his mike switched on. "Comrade Madden ... do you want to countermand that rescue order?"

Diakov waited for a reply, but there was no sound but the lapping of water against the hull. The Cossack had spent three years in the United States and had seen many movies. He sighed deeply.

Wings Over Khabarovsk

The drone of the two radial motors broke the still white silence. As far as the eye could reach the snow-covered ridges of the Sihoti Alin Mountains showed no sign of life. Turk Madden banked the Grumman and studied the broken terrain below. It was remote and lonely, this range along the Siberian coast.

He swung his ship in a slow circle. That was odd. A half-dozen fir trees had no snow on their branches.

He leveled off and looked around, then saw what he wanted, a little park, open and snow-covered, among the trees. It was just the right size, by the look of it. He'd chance the landing. He slid down over the treetops, setting the ship down with just barely enough room. Madden turned the ship before he cut the motor.

Taking down a rifle, he kicked his feet into snowshoes and stepped out into the snow. It was almost spring in Siberia, but the air was crisp and cold. Far to the south, the roads were sodden with melting snow, and the rivers swollen with spring floods. War would be going full blast again soon.

He was an hour getting to the spot. Even before he reached it, his eyes caught the bright gleam of metal. The plane had plunged into the fir trees, burying its nose in the mountainside. In passing, it had knocked the snow from the surrounding trees, and there had been no snow for several days now. That was sheer luck. Ordinarily it would have snowed, and the plane would have been lost beyond discovery in these lonely peaks.

NOT A DOZEN FEET from the tangled wreckage of the ship he could see a dark bundle he knew instinctively was the flyer. Lutvin had been his friend. The boyish young Russian had been a great favorite at Khabarovsk Airport. Suddenly, Turk stopped.

Erratic footprints led from the crashed plane to the fallen body. Lutvin had been alive after the crash!

Madden rushed forward and turned the body over. His wild hope that the boy might still be alive died instantly. The snow under the body was stained with blood. Fyodor Lutvin had been machine-gunned as he ran from his fallen plane.

Machine-gunned! But that meant—

Turk Madden got up slowly, and his face was hard. He turned toward the wreckage of the plane, began a slow, painstaking examination. What he saw convinced him. Fyodor Lutvin had been shot down, after his plane had crashed, had been ruthlessly machine-gunned by his attacker.

But why? And by whom? It was miles from any known front. The closest fighting was around Murmansk, far to the west. Only Japan, lying beyond the narrow strip of sea at Sakhalin and Hokkaido. And Japan and Russia were playing a game of mutual hands off. But Lutvin had been shot down and then killed. His killers had wanted him dead beyond question.

There could be only one reason—because he knew something that must not be told. The fierce loyalty of the young flyer was too well known to be questioned, so he must have been slain by enemies of his country.

Turk Madden began a systematic search, first of the body, then of the wreckage. He found nothing.

Then he saw the camera. Something about it puzzled him. He studied it thoughtfully. It was smashed, yet—

Then he saw. The camera was smashed, but it had been smashed after it had been taken apart—*after the film had been removed*. Where then, was the film?

He found it a dozen feet away from the body, lying in the snow. The film was in a waterproof container. Studying the situation, Turk could picture the scene.

Lutvin had photographed something. He had been pursued, shot down, but had lived through the crash. Scrambling from the wrecked ship with the film, he had run for shelter in the rocks. Then, as he tumbled under the hail of machine-gun fire, he had thrown the film from him.

Turk Madden took the film and, picking up his rifle, started up the steep mountainside toward the park where he had left the Grumman. He was just stepping from a clump of fir when a shot rang out. The bullet smacked a tree trunk beside him and stung his face with bits of bark.

Turk dropped to his hands and knees and slid back into the trees. Ahead of him, and above him, was a bunch of boulders. Even as he looked a puff of smoke showed from the boulders, and another shot rang out. The bullet clipped a twig over his head. Madden fired instantly, coolly pinking every crevice and crack in the boulders. He did not hurry.

His final shot sounded, and instantly he was running through the soft snow. He made it to a huge fir a dozen feet away before the rifle above him spoke. He turned and fired again.

Indian-fashion, he circled the clump of boulders. But when he was within sight of them, there was no one about. For a half hour he waited, then slid down. On the snow in the center of the rocks, he found two old cartridge cases. He studied them.

"Well, I'll be blowed! A Berdianka!" he muttered. "I didn't think there was one outside a museum!"

The man's trail was plain. He wore moccasins made of fur, called *unty*. One of them was wrapped in a bit of rawhide, apparently.

His rifle was ready, Turk fell in behind. But after a few minutes it became obvious that his attacker wanted no more of it. Outgunned, the man was making a quick retreat. After a few miles, Madden gave up and made his way slowly back to his own ship. The chances were the man had been sent to burn the plane, to be sure a clean job had been made of the killing. But that he was wearing *unty* proved him no white man, and no Japanese either, but one of the native Siberian tribes.

IT WAS AFTER SUNDOWN when Turk Madden slid into a long glide for the port of Khabarovsk. In his coat pocket the film was heavy. He was confident that it held the secret of Lutvin's death.

There was a light in Commissar Chevski's office. Turk hesitated, then slipped off his helmet and walked across the field toward the shack. A dark figure rose up from the corner of the hangar, and a tall, stooped man stepped out.

"Shan Bao!" Madden said. "Take care of the ship, will you?"

The Manchu nodded, his dark eyes narrow.

"Yes, comrade." He hesitated. "The commissar asking for you. He seem angry."

"Yeah?" Madden shrugged. "Thanks. I'll see him." He walked on toward the shack without a backward glance. Shan Bao could be trusted with the plane. Where the tall Manchu had learned the trade, Turk could not guess, but the man was a superb plane mechanic. Since Madden's arrival from the East Indies, he had attached himself to Turk and his Grumman, and the ship was always serviced and ready.

Turk tapped lightly on Chevski's door, and at the word walked in.

Commissar Chevski was a man with a reputation for efficiency. He looked up now, his yellow face crisp and cold. The skin was drawn tightly over his cheekbones, his long eyes almost as yellow as his face. He sat behind his table staring at Turk inscrutably. Twice only had Turk talked with him. Around the port the man had a reputation for fierce loyalty and driving ambition. He worked hard and worked everyone else.

"Comrade Madden," he said sharply. "You were flying toward the coast today! Russia is at war with Germany, and planes along the coast invite trouble with Japan. I have given orders that there shall be no flying in that direction!"

"I was ordered to look for Comrade Lutvin," Madden said mildly, "so I flew over the Sihoti Alins."

"There was no need," Chevski's voice was sharp. "Lutvin did not fly in that direction."

"You're mistaken," Turk said quietly, "I found him."

Chevski's eyes narrowed slightly. He leaned forward intently.

"You found Lutvin? Where?"

"On a mountainside in the Sihoti Alins. His plane had crashed. He was dead. His ship had been shot down from behind, and Comrade Lutvin had been machine-gunned as he tried to escape the wreck."

Chevski stood up.

"What is this?" he demanded. "Who would machine-gun a Russian flyer on duty? We have no enemies here."

"What about Japan?" Madden suggested. "But that need make no difference. The facts are as I say. Lutvin was shot down—then killed."

"You *landed*?" Chevski demanded. He walked around from behind his desk. He shook his head impatiently. "I am sorry, comrade. This is serious business, very serious. It means sabotage, possibly war on a new front."

CHEVSKI WALKED BACK behind the table. He looked up suddenly.

"Comrade Madden, I trust you will say nothing of this to anyone until I give the word. This is a task for the OGPU, you understand?"

Madden nodded, reaching toward his pocket. "But, com—"

The Russian lifted a hand.

"Enough. I am busy. You have done a good day's work. Report to me at ten tomorrow. Good night." He sat down abruptly and began writing vigorously.

Turk hesitated. Then, he went out and closed the door.

Hurrying to his own quarters, he gathered his materials and developed the film. Then he sat down and began studying the pictures. For hours, he sat over them, but could find nothing. The pictures were of a stretch of Siberian coast near the mouth of the Nahtohu River. They were that, and no more. Finally, almost at daylight, he gave up and fell into bed.

It was hours later when he awakened. For an instant he lay on his back staring upward, then glanced at his wristwatch. Nine-thirty. He would have barely time to shave and get to Chevski's office. He rolled over and sat up. Instantly, he froze. The pictures, left on the table, were gone!

Turk Madden sat very still. Slowly, he studied the room. Nothing had been taken except the pictures, the film, and the can in which it had been carried. He crossed the room and examined the door and window. The latter was still locked, bore no signs of having been opened. The door was as he had left it the night before. On the floor, just inside the door, was the fading print of a damp foot.

Madden dressed hurriedly and strapped on a gun. Then he went outside. The snow was packed hard, but when he stepped to the corner he saw a footprint. The snow was melting, and already there were three dark lines of earth showing across the track under his window, three lines that might have been made by an *unty* with a rawhide thong around it!

Suddenly, Turk glanced up. A squad of soldiers was coming toward him on the double. They halted before him, and their officer spoke sharply.

"Comrade Madden! You are under arrest!"

"Me?" Turk gasped, incredulous. "What for?"

"Come with us. You will know in good time."

They took him at once to Commissar Chevski's office. Turk was led in and stopped before Chevski's desk. There were five other men in the room. Colonel Granatman sat at the table beside Chevski. In a corner sat Arseniev of the Intelligence. He looked very boyish except for his eyes. They were hard and watchful. The other two men Madden did not know.

"Comrade Madden!" Granatman demanded. "You flew yesterday over the Sihoti Alin Mountains? You did this without orders?"

"Yes, but—"

"The prisoner," Chevski said coldly, "will confine himself to replies to questions."

"You reported that you found there the body of Comrade Fyodor Lutvin, is that right?"

"Yes." Turk was watching the proceedings with astonishment. What was this all about?

"What are the caliber of the guns on your ship?" Granatman asked. "Thirty caliber, are they not?"

"Comrade Olentiev," Granatman said, "tell us what you found when Commissar Chevski sent you to investigate."

OLENTIEV STEPPED FORWARD, clinking his heels. He was a short, powerful man with a thick neck and big hands. He was, Madden knew, an agent of the OGPU, the all-powerful secret police.

"I found Fyodor Lutvin had been shot through the body with fifteen thirty-caliber bullets. His plane had been shot down. The gas tank was riddled, feedline broken, and instrument panel smashed. Most of the controls were shot away.

"I found the tracks of a man and where he had turned the body over, and followed those tracks to where a plane had been landed in the mountains nearby.

"On return I reported to Commissar Chevski, then received the report of my assistant, Blavatski. He ascertained that on the night of Thursday last, Comrade Lutvin won three hundred rubles from Comrade Madden at dice."

"Commissar Chevski," Granatman asked slowly, "who in your belief could have attacked Lutvin in that area?"

"The colonel is well aware," Chevski said quietly, "that Russia is at war only with Germany. If we have a killing here, it is my belief it is murder!"

"Colonel Granatman," Turk protested, "there was evidence of another sort. I found near the body a can containing aerial photographs taken along the coast near the mouth of the Nahtohu River."

"Photographs?" Granatman frowned. "Did you report them to the commissar?"

"No, I—"

"You developed them yourself?" Granatman interrupted. "Where are they?"

"They were stolen from my quarters last night," Madden said.

"Ah!" Chevski said. "You had photographs but they were stolen. You did not report them last night. You flew over a forbidden area, and you, of all those who looked, knew where to find Fyodor Lutvin's body!"

Granatman frowned.

"I would like to believe you innocent, Comrade Madden. You have done good work for us, but there seems no alternative."

Turk Madden stared in consternation. Events had moved so rapidly he could scarcely adjust himself to the sudden and complete change in affairs. The matter of the three hundred rubles had been nothing, and he had promptly forgotten it. A mere sixty dollars or so was nothing. In Shanghai he had often lost that many hundreds, and won as much.

"Say, what is this?" Turk demanded. "I'm sent out to look for a lost plane, I find it, and then you railroad me! Whose toes have I been stepping on around here?"

"You will have a fair trial, comrade," Granatman assured him. "This is just a preliminary hearing. Until then you will be held."

Olentiev and Blavatski stepped up on either side of him, and he was marched off without another word. His face grim, he kept still. There was nothing he could do now. He had to admit there was a case, if a flimsy one. That he had gone right to the body, when it was where it wasn't expected to be—that there was no other known plane in the vicinity but his own—that the gun calibers were identical—that he had landed and examined the body—that money had been won from him by Lutvin—that he had told an unverified story of stolen photographs.

THROUGH IT ALL, Arseniev had said nothing. And Arseniev was supposed to be his friend! The thought was still puzzling him when he became conscious of the drumming of a motor. Looking to the runway, not sixty feet away, he saw a small pursuit ship. The motor was running, it had been running several minutes, and no one was anywhere near.

He glanced around quickly. There was no one in sight. His captors were at least a dozen feet away and appeared to be paying no attention. Their guns were buttoned under their tunics. It was the chance of a lifetime. He took another quick glance around, set himself for a dash to the plane. Then his muscles relaxed under a hammering suspicion.

It was too easy. The scene was too perfect. There wasn't a flaw in this picture anywhere. Deliberately, he stopped, waiting for his guards to catch up. As he half turned, waiting, he saw a rifle muzzle projecting just beyond the corner of a building. Even as he looked, it was withdrawn.

He broke into a cold sweat. He would have been dead before he'd covered a dozen feet! Someone was out to get him. But who? And why?

The attitude of his captors changed suddenly, they dropped their careless manner, and came up alongside.

"Quick!" Olentiev snapped. "You loafer. You murderer. We'll show you. A firing squad you'll get for what you did to Lutvin!"

Turk Madden said nothing. He was taken to the prison and shoved into a cell. The room was of stone, damp and chilly. There was straw on the floor, and a dirty blanket. Above him, on the ground level, was a small, barred window.

He looked around bitterly.

"Looks like you're behind the eight ball, pal!" he told himself. "Framed for a murder, and before they get through, you'll be stuck."

He walked swiftly across the cell, leaped, and seized the bars. They were strong, thicker than they looked. A glance at the way they were set into the concrete told him there was no chance there. He lay down on the straw and tried to think. Closing his eyes, he let his mind wander back over the pictures. Something. There had been something there. If he only knew!

But although the pictures were clear in his mind, he could remember nothing. Thinking of that lonely stretch of coast brought another picture to his mind. Before his trip to pick up Arseniev from the coast of Japan he had consulted charts of both coasts carefully. There was something wrong in his mind. Something about his memory of the chart of the coast and the picture of the coast near the Nahtohu River didn't click.

THE DAY PASSED SLOWLY. The prison sat near the edge of a wash or gully on the outskirts of town. The bank behind the prison, he had noticed, was crumbling. If he could loosen one of the floor-stones—it was only a chance, but that was all he asked.

Shadows lengthened in the cell, then it was dark, although the light through the window was still gray. Pulling back the straw, he found the outline of a stone block.

The prison was an old building, put together many years ago, still with a look of seasoned strength. Yet time and the elements had taken their toll. Water had run in through the ground-level window, and it had drained out through a hole on the low side. But in running off, it had found the line of least resistance along the crack in the floor. Using the broken spoon with which he was to eat, he began to work at the cement. It crumbled easily, but the stone of the floor was thick.

Four hours passed before he gave up. He had cut down over three inches all around, but still the block was firm, and the handle of his spoon would no longer reach far enough. For a long time he lay still, resting and thinking. Outside all was still, yet he felt restless. Someone about the airport wanted him dead. Someone here was communicating with the man who wore the *unty,* who had fired at him with the old Berdianka in the mountains. Whoever that person was would not rest until, he, Turk Madden, was killed.

That person would have access to this prison, and if he were killed, in the confusion of war, not too much attention would be paid. Arseniev had been his only real friend here, and Arseniev had sat quietly and said nothing. Chevski was efficiency personified. He was interested only in the successful functioning of the port.

But it was more than his own life that mattered. Here, at this key port, close to the line that carried supplies from Vladivostok to the western front, an enemy agent could do untold damage. Lutvin had discovered something, had become suspicious. Flying to the coast, he had photographed something the agent did not want known. Well, what?

At least, if he could not escape, he could think. What would there be on the coast that a man could photograph? A ship could be moved, so it must be some permanent construction. An airport? Turk sat up restlessly. Thinking was all right, but action was his line. He sat back against the wall and stared at the block of stone. The crack was wide. Suddenly, he forced both heels into the crack, and, bracing himself against the wall, pushed.

The veins swelled in his forehead, his palms pressed hard against the floor, but he shoved, and shoved hard. Something gave, but it was not the block against which he pushed. It was the wall behind him. He struggled to his feet, and turned. It was much too dark to see, but he could feel.

His fingers found the cracks in the stones, and his heart gave a great leap. The old wall was falling apart, the cheap cement crumbling. What looked so strong was obviously weak. The prison had been thrown together by convict labor eighty years before, or so he had been told. He seized his spoon and went to work.

IN A MOMENT, he had loosened a block. He lifted it out and placed it on the floor beside him. What lay beyond? Another cell? He shrugged. At least he was busy. He took down another block, another, and then a fourth. He crawled through the hole, then carefully, shielding it with his hands, struck a match.

His heart sank. He was in a cell, no different from his own. He rose to his feet and tiptoed across to the door. He took the iron ring in his hand and turned. It moved easily, and the door swung open!

A faint movement in the shadowy hall outside stopped him. Carefully, he moved himself into the doorway, and glanced along the wall.

He caught his breath. A dark figure crouched before his own door and, slowly, carefully, opened it!

Like a shadow, the man straightened, and his hand slipped into his shirt front, coming out with a long knife. Turk's eyes narrowed. In two quick steps he was behind the man. There must have been a sound, for the man turned, catlike. Turk Madden's fist exploded on the corner of the man's jaw like a six-inch shell, and the fellow crumpled. Madden stepped in, hooking viciously to the short ribs. He wet his lips. "That'll hold you, pal," he muttered.

Stooping, he retrieved the knife. Then he frisked the man carefully, grinned when he found a Tokarev automatic and several clips of cartridges. He pocketed them, then turned the man over. He was a stranger. Carefully, noticing signs of returning consciousness, he bound and gagged the man, then closed the cell door on him, and locked it. Returning to the cell from which he had escaped, he put the stones back into place, then put the key out of sight on a stone ledge above the door.

Turning, he walked down the hall. The back door was not locked, and he went out into the night. For an instant, he stood still. He was wondering about his own ship. He knew what there was to do. He had to fly to the coast and see for himself. He thought he knew what was wrong, but on the other hand—

Also, there was the business of Lutvin's killer. He had flown a plane. He might still be there, and if he saw the Grumman—

Turk Madden smiled grimly. He crossed the open spaces toward the hangars, walking swiftly. Subterfuge wouldn't help. If he tried slipping around he would surely be seen. The direct approach was best. A sleepy sentry stared at him, but said nothing. Turk opened the small door and walked in.

Instantly, he faded back into the shadows inside the door. Not ten feet away Commissar Chevski was staring at Shan Bao. The Manchu faced him, standing stiffly.

"This ship's motors are warm!" Chevski said sharply.

"Yes, comrade," Shan Bao said politely. "The Colonel Granatman said to keep it warm, he might wish to use it for a flight."

"A flight?" Chevski said. He looked puzzled. From the shadows, Turk could hear his heart pounding as he sensed what was coming. "What flight?"

"Along the coast," the Manchu said simply. "He said he might want to fly along the coast."

Chevski leaned forward tensely.

"The *coast*? Granatman said that?" He stared at Shan Bao. "If you're lying..." He wheeled and strode from the hangar. As he stepped past Turk, his breath was coming hard, and his eyes were dilated.

THE INSTANT the door closed, Shan Bao's eyes turned to Turk.

"We must work fast, comrade. It was a lie."

Madden stepped out.

"A shrewd lie. He knows something, that one." Turk hesitated, then he looked at the Manchu. "You don't miss much. Have you seen a man with a Berdianka? You know, one of those old model rifles. You know, with a *soshki*? One of those wooden props to hold up the barrel?"

"I know," Shan Bao nodded. "There was one. A man named Batoul, a half-breed, has one. He meets frequently with Comrade Chevski in the woods. He threw it away this day. Now he has a new rifle."

"So," Turk smiled. "The ship is warmed up?"

Shan Bao nodded.

"I have started it every hour since you were taken and have run the motor for fifteen minutes. I thought you might need it. Did you have to kill many men getting away?"

"Not one." Turk smiled. "I'm getting in. When I give the word, start the motor that opens the doors. I'll be going out."

Shan Bao nodded. "You did not kill even one? Leave the door open in the cabin. I shall go with you. I was more fortunate—I killed one."

Turk sprang into the Grumman. The motors roared into life. Killed one? Who? He waved his hand, and the doors started to move, then the Manchu dashed over. He crawled into the plane as it started to move. From outside there was a startled shout, then the plane was running down the icy runway. A shot, but the Grumman was beginning to lift. Another shot. Yells, they were in the air.

He banked the amphibian in a tight circle and headed for the mountains. They'd get him, but first he'd lead them to the coast, he'd let them see for themselves that something was wrong.

In the east, the skies grew gray with dawn. The short night was passing. Below him the first ridges of the mountains slid past, dark furrows in a field of snow.

Shan Bao was at his shoulder. Two planes showed against the sky where he pointed. Turk nodded. Two—one was bad enough when it was a fast pursuit job. One was far ahead of the other.

Madden's eyes picked out the gray of the sea, then he turned the plane north along the coast to the mouth of the Nahtohu. That was the place—and that long reeflike curving finger. That was it.

Ahead of him a dark plane shot up from the forest and climbed in tight spirals, reaching for altitude. Turk's jaws set. That was the plane that got Lutvin. He fired a trial burst from his guns and pulled back on the stick. The two planes rose together. Then the pursuit ship shot at him, guns blazing.

Turk's face was calm, but hard. He banked steeply, swinging the ship around the oncoming plane, opening fire with all his guns.

SUDDENLY THE GRAY LIGHT of dawn was aflame with blasting guns as the two ships spun and spiraled in desperate combat. Teeth clenched, Turk spun the amphibian through a haze of maneuvers, side-slipping, diving, and squirming from position to position, his guns ripping the night apart with streaks of blasting fire. Tracers streamed by his nose, then ugly holes sprang into a wing, then he was out of range, and the streaking black ship was coming around at him again.

In desperation, Turk saw he had no chance. No man in an amphibian had a chance against a pursuit plane unless the breaks were with him. Like an avenging fury, the black ship darted in and around him. Only Turk's great flying skill, his uncanny judgment of distance, and his knowledge of his ship enabled him to stay in the fight.

Suddenly, he saw the other two planes closing in. It was now or never. He spun the ship over in a half-roll, then shoved the stick all the way forward and went screaming for earth with the black ship hot on his tail. Fiery streams of tracer shot by him. His plane shot down faster and faster.

The black, ugly ridges of the mountains swept up at him. Off to one side he saw the black shoulder of a peak he remembered, saw the heavy circle of cloud around it and knew this was his chance. He pulled the Grumman out of the power-dive so quickly he expected her wings to tear loose, but she came out of it and lifted to an even keel.

Then, straight into that curtain of cloud around the mountain he went streaking, the black pursuit ship hot on his tail. He felt the ship wobble, saw his compass splash into splinters of glass as a bullet struck, then the white mist of the cloud was around him, and he pulled back on the stick. The Grumman shot up, and even as it zoomed, Turk saw the black, glistening shoulder of icy black mountain sweep below him. He had missed it by a fraction of an inch.

Below him as he glanced down he saw the streaking pursuit ship break through the cloud, saw the pilot grab frantically at his stick. Then the ship crashed full tilt into the mountain at three hundred miles an hour, blossomed into flame and fell, tangled, burning wreckage into the canyon below.

The Grumman lifted toward the sky, and Turk Madden's eyes swept the horizon. Off to the south, not a half mile away, the two Russian ships were tangled in a desperate dogfight.

OPENING THE GRUMMAN UP, he roared down on them at full tilt. Shan Bao crouched in his seat, the straps tight about his body, his face stiff and cold. In his hands he clutched a Thompson machine gun. The nearer ship he recognized instantly. It was the specially built Havoc flown by Arseniev. The other—

The pilot of the strange ship sighted him, and, making a half roll, started for him. Madden banked the Grumman as though to escape, saw tracer streak by. Then, behind him, he heard an angry chatter. He made an Immelmann turn and swept back. The pursuit ship was falling in a sheet of flame, headed for the small bay at the mouth of the Nahtohu. The other ship swung alongside, and Turk saw Arseniev raise his clasped hands.

Shan Bao was smiling, cradling the Thompson in his arms like a baby.

"He thought he had us," he yelled. "Didn't know you had a behind gunner."

"A rear gunner, Shan," Turk said, grinning.

HOURS LATER, the Grumman landed easily in the mouth of the Nahtohu.

"See?" Turk said, pointing. "A breakwater, and back there a stone pier, a perfect place for landing heavy armaments. It was ideal, a prepared bridgehead for invasion."

Arseniev nodded.

"Lutvin, he was a good man, but I wonder how he guessed?"

"As I did, I think," Turk told him. He sensed a difference in the coastline, a change. The chart showed no reef there, yet the breakwater was made to look like a reef. As it was, it would give the Japanese a secure anchorage, and a place to land tanks, trucks, and heavy artillery, land them securely."

"That Chevski," Arseniev said. "I knew there was something wrong, but I did not suspect him until he ran for a plane when you took off. But Granatman found the photographs in his belongings, and a code book. He was too sure of himself, that one. His mother, we found, was a Japanese."

Turk nodded.

"Lutvin suspected him, I think."

Arseniev shrugged.

"No doubt. But how could Chevski communicate with the flier who flew the guarding pursuit ship? How could he communicate with Japan?"

Shan Bao cleared his throat.

"That, I think I can say," he said softly. "There was a man, named Batoul. A man who wore *unty,* the native moccasins, and one with thong wrappings about the foot. He came and went frequently from the airport."

"Was?" Arseniev looked sharply at the Manchu. "He got away?"

"But no, comrade," Shan Bao protested gently. "He had a queer gun, this man. An old-fashioned gun, a Berdianka with a *soshki.* I, who am a collector of guns, wished this one above all. So you will forgive me, comrades? The man came prowling about this ship in the night. He"—Shan Bao coughed apologetically—"he suffered an accident, comrades. But I shall care well for his gun, an old Berdianka, with a *soshki.* Nowhere else but in Siberia, comrades, would you find such a gun!"

Flight to Enbetu

Colonel Sharpe bent over the map as Turk Madden spoke. "Sure," he said, "I know the spot, I was there once. It's inland from Enbetu, the railroad from Hakodate to Wakkanai forks off here. Years back I was all over Hokkaido."

"Excellent. We bomb Wakkanai at dawn tomorrow. And naturally, before the attack, we want all communication with Hakodate and Japan proper destroyed. You will cut that railroad, also the telephone and telegraph lines that follow it."

"And Ryan takes care of the radio?"

"Right. The radio and power stations will be destroyed. Forty minutes later, which should allow time for any reasonable hitch in his plans, we attack. Everything must go on schedule."

He understood the situation perfectly. Wakkanai was a tough nut to crack but its defenders could also call on scores of Nipponese planes from Hakodate. Should this happen the attack would meet with disaster.

The Kurile Isles had been attacked many times, and Wakkanai was the next step. But there was nothing in the Kuriles even remotely approaching Wakkanai.

The job of the saboteurs was essential. They had a fair chance of getting their mission done, but a very small chance of getting out with a whole skin, or even part of one.

Colonel Sharpe straightened.

"Well, that's the setup, Madden. You move out at two thousand hours, and you should be over your goal by midnight. Within a mile of your destination the Japs have an emergency landing strip. That field is unguarded at present.

"At ten minutes past midnight two lights will be shown to indicate the width of the field. These lights can be shown momentarily only. You will not see the men handling the lights. They are Ainu, natives of the island. They will show their signals and leave. With your mission complete, you will take off and return here."

Madden studied the map thoughtfully. It wasn't as if he didn't know the country, or what he was going into. He did know all of that. But their success depended upon surprise, upon secrecy, and he knew something was wrong.

Two hours before he had opened his strongbox and found that a small, carefully drawn map of the northern tip of Hokkaido had been stolen. It could hardly be coincidence, on the eve of the attack.

The door opened suddenly, and two men came in. Sparrow Ryan was a former stuntman and speed flyer. Like Madden he had been an itinerant soldier in many countries. He had the alert but battered look of a professional.

The other man was tall, good-looking Lieutenant Ken Martin. Martin had been a top-notch collegiate running back not long before. He was dark, sallow, and his eyes had a faint suggestion of the almond. This was one of the reasons he had been chosen.

With the exception of Madden, who knew the country and had made previous secret flights to Japan, all of them would pass for Japanese in dim light, it wasn't much but it was one of the few advantages they had.

"Hi, Turk!" Ryan grinned tightly. "Here we go again!"

"Yeah," Turk agreed, "don't let 'em get you! This has got to be good."

"Listen, honey-chile," Ryan said. "I've studied those charts until I know that country better than the natives. We'll hit them and get away before they know it."

Lieutenant Martin interrupted. "How about this fellow Sauten? I don't like the idea of taking him with us. He's a known criminal and not to be trusted."

Turk looked up from the map.

"Chiv Sauten is a tough baby. I want tough guys. This is no job for milquetoasts."

"But the man's a gangster!" Martin insisted. "We've got to draw the line somewhere. He would sell out to anyone!"

"I don't think so," Turk said shortly. "And I'm not going to marry the guy, I'm going to fight alongside him."

"If they'd known he was a criminal, he'd never have gotten into this unit," Martin persisted. His young, good-looking face was hard. "For one, I don't like going into a tough spot with a man like that."

"He might not have gotten in," Turk agreed, "but he's in now. He volunteered for this job, and for my money, he goes."

Colonel Sharpe frowned a little.

"I didn't know about this man," he said, glancing accusingly at Madden. "Did you cover for him when he joined up?"

"Yes." Madden's voice was positive. "Frankly, sir, I'm a bit fed up on this lily-white stuff. We're fighting a war, not picking men acceptable to somebody's maiden aunt. That guy can handle a tommy gun.

"He's been kicked around and knocked down plenty. He got up. He's been shot at, and hit, and he kept shooting. I don't give a hoot in Hades if the man strangled his grandmother. If he's willing to go on this job, who are we to stop him?"

Sauten came in then. He had a thin, hard face and looked as tough as his reputation.

"Ship's ready. Scofield and Gorman are standing by."

His eyes flickered over the room, resting momentarily on Martin, then moving on.

"Okay. We'll be right out," Madden said briefly. He picked up his 'chute. "See you later, Colonel."

Ryan and Martin had the toughest part of the job. Turk was thinking of that as he climbed into the B-25 and got settled. They would be working in a populated area where discovery was almost a certainty. But the two Cantonese they had with them both looked more Japanese than Chinese, and Sparrow Ryan was small and wiry. Tucker, the navigator, was built along similar lines.

Chiv got in behind Turk.

"It's a good night for it," he said. He checked the magazine on the tommy gun. "Lieutenant Martin was in on that Morley job, wasn't he?"

"Right. The other two were killed. If it hadn't been for him, the whole mission would have been a washout. As it was, he got back with the necessary information, or most of it. He was a lucky stiff to make it out at all."

Turk Madden liked the feel of the ship in the air, despite the fact that it seemed odd not to be at the controls. But Scofield handled the medium bomber like a pursuit plane. Nick Gorman was navigator, and a good man. It would take a good man, for hitting the landing strip in the dark would be worse than finding one of those coral atolls far to the southeast.

The Morley job had been a mess. Vic Morley had gone out with Martin and Welldon. Their plane had been shot down, and Morley and Welldon had been captured. Martin had escaped, then, and only after great trials, got back to their base.

This time was going to be different. It had to be different.

They had been in the air three hours when Gorman touched his arm.

"This is it," he said, "two minutes!"

"Take her down," Madden told Scofield, "and put her on the ground in a hurry."

It was nine minutes past midnight.

Scofield glanced over his shoulder, indicating the altimeter with a finger. It was at a thousand feet. They dare not stay long at that low level. Yet no lights had appeared.

A minute passed, then another. Chiv Sauten shifted his tommy gun, waiting. Gorman glanced at Madden questioningly.

Had their man been captured? Should he play it safe and turn back? Madden set his jaw. To heck with it, he thought. They had come to do a job, and they were going to do it, come what might.

Directly below them was the landing field. Turk's memory for terrain was almost photographic.

He slid forward in the cockpit.

"Give her to me," he said. "I know this field. I might stand a shade better chance at bringing her in blind than you."

Madden leveled off and then nosed down for the field. Ahead, he knew, was a mountain. To the right and to the left were trees. He could see nothing but the loom of one great peak. He could only pray that he was bringing the big Mitchell in right. He let the ship down fast, pulling the nose up a trifle.

Sweat broke out on his brow as he felt the ship sideslip as it dropped away beneath him. It could crash any moment now, any . . .

Two lights flashed suddenly, ahead and to the right. He banked the ship, then flattened her out. A split second later the wheels touched, and the plane rolled forward on the level ground. The lights vanished.

Turk let the B–25 run as far as he dared, then braked her cautiously, his eyes straining against the dark, the big ship swung around, facing downfield.

Madden stepped down, and Chiv Sauten and Monte Jackson closed in beside him.

"Good luck, men," Scofield said softly, and the three of them moved away into the darkness. The last thing Turk saw was Nick Gorman standing by with his tommy gun at the ready.

With every sense alert, Madden led the way. Every moment now was fraught with danger. This was the heart of Japan's own territory. This was the first time American soldiers had set foot on Japan proper since the war began, except as prisoners. If successful, the Kurile Islands would be exposed to attack, along with the whole northern shore of Hokkaido.

He hesitated once, staring about him. There was something wrong about this setup, something very wrong. A subtle sense of danger was flowing through him. He felt as though his back were naked to a bullet-ridden draught.

It was no feeling of the danger ahead. That danger he had faced many times. This was something else . . . the missing map, he'd have to watch his own back on this one. He thought, then, of what Martin had said of Sauten—that the ex-gangster would sell out to anyone.

Yet Sauten was a silent, capable man. Common sense told him Chiv was not to be trusted. His instincts made him less certain. The fellow felt right, whatever his past record had been.

He wasn't kidding himself about his chances on this mission, and he knew the others weren't. They weren't expected to come back alive. He knew that was what they thought at Headquarters. But Turk Madden had his own ideas.

You don't come through a lot of dangers without acquiring confidence. Turk knew just exactly what he faced, just exactly what chances he had. The odds were a thousand to one against them but experience with danger in many odd corners of the world had taught him that positive, determined action by men of quick wits and valor can do some strange things to the ordinary ratio of chances.

He moved forward, beside him, Sauten was like a ghost. Jackson was behind them both.

Madden's feet warned him when he reached the path. He could see nothing, but his soles found its hard smoothness, and his leg muscles felt the downward slope toward the roadbed.

The rail line showed abruptly, two glistening lines of steel. Accustomed to working alone as he always had, Sauten's nearness was disturbing. He kept his companions with him until their eyes were more accustomed to darkness, then at his signal, they vanished. He dropped to his knees and started digging under a tie.

WHEN THEY HAD PLACED their mines, five under each rail, they armed them with detonators and drew back a short distance. Turk wiped his face with his sleeve and felt Jackson near him.

"The culvert's just below us," the man whispered, "the one on the map."

They moved on to the culvert. Sauten was already there, his explosives on the ground. Silently as possible, the three men went to work. This was to be the main, the vital part of the job. If the road were blasted here, it would take weeks to repair. Not only were they preparing the culvert for demolition, but the cliff above as well.

They worked swiftly, silently, with grim determination. There was a vague intimation of light now. Several times Turk looked up. Each time he saw Chiv Sauten peering around.

Finally, Turk Madden straightened up.

"Okay," he said, "now we go back."

"No! Somebody's coming," Sauten said. "And coming very quietly!"

Madden gave a hand signal, and the three of them dropped back into the rocks, on lower ground. From their new position, they could watch the skyline.

Suddenly they saw them—six Japanese soldiers moving slowly, carefully down the track. In the instant before the attack, Madden was grimly aware of one thing—these soldiers were looking for something. They knew!

His hand slid to his knife. It was a commando-style fighting knife, thin and deadly, an eight-inch, double-edged knife with a point so sharp an expert could almost sink it through a man. The last of the Japanese was passing when he moved. Some almost imperceptible sound must have warned the man. He turned his head suddenly.

Turk was close, but not close enough for a blow. He took a chance and let the knife go, throwing it underhand and hard.

He heard it thud as it hit, and he followed it in, slugging the man as he fell. Then he wrenched the knife from below the soldier's heart and went for the next one, hitting him low and hard.

He heard Sauten and Jackson close in. A blow caught him in the mouth, and he tasted blood. He stabbed quickly with the knife, felt it hang on some equipment, then slide off and into the man. He stifled the fellow's cry with a hand.

A soldier swung a rifle butt, and Turk dropped back onto his hands, kicking out viciously with both feet. The Japanese staggered, and Madden threw his body against the man's knees. He went down.

The knife slipped from Turk's hand, but he went in fast, reaching for the man's throat. It was a brutal, ugly bit of fighting. Someone kicked him in the head, and, desperately, he broke away from the man on the ground and rolled free. He came up fast, and a fist slugged him in the mouth, then a boot toe caught him in the stomach.

A sickening wave of pain and nausea went over him, and he was back on the ground. A soldier closed in, kicking at his face. Turk grabbed the man's ankle and hung on.

They both went down. Then he was up, and the Japanese lurched toward him. Turk had grabbed a rifle from the ground as he came to his feet, and before the imperial soldier could start another assault, Turk brought the rifle down, striking with an overhand butt stroke that crumpled the soldier's skull like an eggshell.

He turned then, swaying, gasping for breath. A shadow moved toward him, and he saw a gun leveled at his stomach, and for a moment he thought he was cold meat. It was Chiv Sauten.

"I thought you were a Jap," Chiv said.

"Where's Monte?" Madden demanded.

"Here," Jackson said, coming up the embankment. "I rolled down there with that guy. He nearly got me."

"You hurt?" Turk demanded.

"A scratch," Monte replied shortly. "Let's go!"

They moved off then. Surprise had done it, Turk knew, sheer darned fool luck and surprise.

Madden set a fast pace and as he moved, his mind worked swiftly. The Japanese could have taken the plane. If so, he and the men with him were stranded in Japan.

Turk halted suddenly. Ahead of them was the airfield, less than a dozen yards away.

Turning abruptly, he went off the path and across the brush- and tree-clad hill. Like ghosts, the two men followed him. Sauten remained at Madden's elbow, Monte, his breath coming hard, trailed a little behind.

It was warm and still. Turk eased down over a rock, feeling for the earth. He found it, and lowered himself gently. Then he turned. A bead of sweat trickled down his spine. He moved forward, stepping cautiously and placing each foot solidly before moving the next.

Suddenly, he stopped. A faint, sickening sweet smell. Perspiration dripped from his chin, and a slow drop slid past his ear. He knew that smell, could feel its aftertaste in his own mouth.

Blood!

Cautiously, he put out a foot. At the second step, his toes touched something. He leaned forward. He could see the body. It was a man, short, and very broad. Beside the man was something metallic. Turk reached for it. A flashlight.

He straightened uneasily. This was one of the men who had guided the plane to the field. He recognized the broad, powerful build, typical of the Ainu. And the flashlight confirmed his suspicions.

The Japanese had known. Calmly, quietly, they had stood by and let the plane be guided in. Then they had killed the men who flashed the signals.

The feeling of unseen menace he'd had earlier possessed him again. The soldiers along the track had been no casual patrol. They had been searching for the flyers. They had known, as he had suspected.

If they knew, it could mean but one thing. The American plan of attack had been betrayed.

Sauten moved up beside him. The man's lips moved, and the whisper was ghostly. Turk had never believed a man could speak with so little sound, so little exhalation of breath.

"We're in a spot," the gangster said softly, "there's Japs south of us, and there's Japs across the field. I heard those nearest, saw the gleam on a rifle barrel."

What worried Madden was the plane. Had they taken the plane? He moved forward, touching Sauten.

Keeping the brush behind them, and the blackness of the looming cliff, they worked across the top of the field toward the Mitchell.

There was double danger now. If the plane were not taken, Gorman or Scofield might fire on them.

Crouching low, he saw the silhouette of the plane against the vague sky. Uneasily, he glanced downfield. Something was happening down there. There was no real sound, but a subdued whisper of movement, deadly, mysterious.

What had happened at Wakkanai? Had Ryan managed to wreck the radio? Or had he landed and walked into a trap—a trap that would soon engulf the whole American attack? For, Turk knew, if the enemy had known enough to prepare for this advance movement, they would be ready, multifold, for the attack to come.

Turk moved ahead, halted, then started on again. Suddenly, a figure shot up from the ground ahead of him, and he glimpsed a flicker of movement. Instinctively, he ducked, and just in time to let a rifle butt miss. Lunging, he let go with a wicked left hook for the body.

It landed, a glancing blow, partially blocked.

"Why you dirty—!" The voice was low and hoarse with anger. "I'll—!"

"Nick!" Madden gasped. "It's me! Madden!"

"We thought they'd got you," Nick whispered. "Let's get to the plane!" Lunging to his feet, he made a quick dash for the few remaining yards. Madden followed, then Sauten.

"Where's Monte?" Scofield demanded.

"Here."

Monte's voice was low with effort. He fell against Scofield, and the pilot felt blood on his hand. Jackson's whole side was soaked with it.

Hurriedly, yet gently, they got him into the ship. Scofield stared down the field. It was pitch dark.

"I don't like it," he said grimly, "but here goes!"

They climbed into the ship. Turk hesitated, remembering the subdued sounds. Then he shrugged, and crawled in.

The plane's motors broke into a roar of sound. Surprisingly, no one fired on them. The Japanese, and they must be all around, made no effort to stop them. Turk scowled. Suddenly, on the inspiration of the instant, he picked up the rocket pistol from the lifesaving equipment.

He stepped to the door, and even as the ship started to roll, he fired a shot into the air. There was a brief moment, then the flare burst.

The Mitchell was thundering down the narrow field, her twin motors roaring, and dead ahead, across the field, was a heavy barrier of logs!

Madden's face went white. He started to speak, then saw Scofield. The pilot's eyes were wide, his face grim. Turk saw him push the throttles wide, and at the same instant, he pulled back on the stick.

Turk grabbed his tommy gun. If she crashed, and he lived through it, he was going out fighting.

The Mitchell lifted, sagged, and headed straight at the barrier, her engines a thunder of impossible sound! Desperately, his face cold and stiff, Scofield held back on the wheel. Suddenly, her run seemingly not long enough, the B-25 lifted, a wheel touched the top log, and the ship shot over—they were free!

BELOW, A MACHINE GUN broke into a wicked chatter, bullets slamming into the fuselage, and in the fading light of the flare, they saw Japanese soldiers pour out upon the landing strip, weapons blossoming fire.

Steadily, the big ship climbed. Madden sank back, his face gray, and his mouth dry. He looked at Gorman and thought for a moment that the navigator was going to faint. Only Chiv Sauten showed no emotion, nothing but widened eyes.

"The torpedoes back in Chi thought they were hard guys," he said, just loud enough to be heard. "They thought they were tough! Boy!"

But Turk Madden was already thinking ahead. Their mission was complete. All of it had taken but a few minutes of actual time, a very little while. The bombers would be in the air now, they would be well on their way to Japan. What of Sparrow? Had he succeeded? Or did it matter?

Sauten looked at Turk.

"Well, we're out of that! And I ain't sorry!"

"No," Turk said, "we're not out of it ... we're going on to Wakkanai!"

"What?" Scofield looked at Madden. "Are you nuts? If the Japs knew about us—" He scowled in concentration.

"Nick," he suggested, "if you knew what we know, and you were a Jap, what would you do?"

Gorman shrugged. "Run in a bunch of Zeros and park them out of sight until just before the attack began. Then knock down every Yank in the air."

Madden nodded.

"My guess, too. The ack-ack will be ready, of course, but unquestionably they'll have pursuit ships somewhere out of sight."

He bent over the chart, and pointing, said to Nick Gorman, "It will probably be here, but it might be here or over here. Try the first one."

Sauten made no sound, but his lips thinned to a queer, strained smile. Thoughtfully, he began to check the tommy gun.

Madden said no more. For an instant, he thought of San Francisco and the Top o' the Mark. He'd always liked the view from there, and it reminded him, somehow, of the view from the Peak in Hong Kong.

This was going to be tough. They might find the enemy field, and they might not. In either case, there was a good chance there'd be more trouble.

The whole area they had to cover was not large. Actually a few minutes of flying time would be enough. They could make it, and still have fuel to get safely back to base—if they were still able to fly.

Then he saw the planes. It was a small field, but a dozen ships were lined up to take off. Behind them, more planes were being wheeled from under camouflage nets. The vague lights were enough to show him that, and the Japanese seemed to be working with no thought of discovery.

Scofield had seen them, too. He glanced around.

"How about it?" his lips framed the question, and Madden nodded.

The Mitchell wheeled around and down in a long, slanting dive. The Japanese airmen heard it, and he saw them suddenly scatter. Anti-aircraft guns flashed, but the B-25 was already too low for the shrapnel.

Scofield took the ship in fast, and the men in the Mitchell manned the guns. Madden opened up with the fifty in the nose. He saw a man run for a ship, let go with the gun, and watched the Jap stumble and fall on his face.

The angry teeth of the bullets gnawed the earth, then ripped at the sleeping plane. An explosion burst in the concealed hangars with a terrific concussion, and as the Mitchell lifted away from the field, Turk could see three of the parked ships were in flames.

"Again?" Scofield asked, but Madden shook his head.

He pointed north.

"Wakkanai," he said. He was worried about Ryan. It wasn't only the man, although the flyer was his friend. It was the job. The mission always came first and Ryan had been betrayed—Turk Madden knew he had.

Someone had stolen his map of Hokkaido before they began the flight. Someone had warned the enemy.

Sauten moved a little, and his black, slitted eyes turned toward Madden. He was cold. Turk thought, the man was like ice.

Then he remembered Martin. Lieutenant Ken Martin had been the hero of another flight over Japan. Martin had doubted Sauten. Turk looked again at the man.

True, he had been a gangster. The man had been a criminal. Why should he believe in a man who had done nothing to warrant belief?

WAKKANAI WAS STILL in the quiet night. As the Mitchell came in toward the great Japanese naval base, Turk's brow furrowed. If Sparrow had gone down there, he had done nothing. There were no fires, had been no explosions. Something was wrong, radically, bitterly wrong!

He got up, pulling on his 'chute. Gorman stared. Turk motioned down, then going nearer, gave it to him.

"I'm bailing out! You go on back!" Gorman's protest was lost as he turned. The port opened, and he spilled out into the night.

Over and over he tumbled through the blackness. Then he pulled the string, and after a moment, the 'chute jerked him up, hard.

Studying the dark ground below, he spilled air from the 'chute, trying to guide himself toward a black spot where there were no lights.

It was wildly reckless but Ryan had failed to succeed with his mission. The whole attack depended on their success and the planes would be over the town within the hour. Perhaps the surprise was gone, yet they could take no chances. The attack was going forward regardless.

He landed in soft earth among some bushes. Quickly, he bundled up the 'chute and checked his gun. He cleared the branches just as something dark slipped by him, and then a white cloud descended, enveloping him into its folds!

Desperate, he fought free, lunging to his feet. Another man staggered erect, and he saw the dark glimmer of light on a gun barrel.

"Skipper?" the voice was low, questioning.

Chiv Sauten!

"What the heck?" Madden demanded softly. "I left you in the ship!"

"Yeah," Sauten nodded agreement as he got himself free of the parachute, "but things looked kind of slow up there. I had this typewriter, so I thought I'd come down and see what was cookin'."

"Let's go!" Turk felt relieved. There was no denying the security he felt with Chiv at his elbow. Then, a cold chill went over him.

Why had Sauten joined him? Had the man come to help or to prevent Turk's effort from succeeding?

He could only drive ahead and take a chance on that.

He knew where the radio station was. The plan had been well studied.

They had landed close together in a small park. Chiv, who had followed Madden by seconds only, had observed a tall building to their rear, a dwelling dead ahead of them. He spoke of this now.

Turk nodded.

"We'll skirt the smaller place, then head for the radio. It isn't over a thousand yards away."

Suddenly, the night was broken wide open by the whine of an air raid siren!

Turk broke into a run. Men were dashing about everywhere, and his running did not attract attention. Nearby, covering him, was Sauten.

Dodging past the dwelling, they rushed across a street and down an alleyway. Lights were going out, and in a matter of seconds the town would be in total darkness.

Suddenly, from ahead of them, muffled by the screaming siren, there was a burst of small arms fire!

A soldier darted from a building and started up the street toward the sound. Then, under the scream of the siren he must have heard the running feet and spun around—too late!

Turk was running full tilt, and he jerked up his tommy gun and smashed the butt into the man's face with all the drive of his powerful shoulders. Behind him, as the man fell, he heard another thud, a heavier one. Chiv Sauten was always thorough.

The shooting had broken into a roar now, and it came from a building dead ahead where there still were lights.

There was no time to hesitate. Turk slid to a stop at the door, then turned the corner quickly and flattened against the wall inside the doorway.

Two Japanese policemen were dead on the steps. At the top of the steps was Lin, one of the Cantonese who had flown with Ryan. He was dead. Fairly riddled with bullets.

Turk started forward, working his way up the steps. Inside the shooting had slowed to an occasional shot. He stepped up, then stopped suddenly, his gaze riveted on the body of the Chinese!

Lin had been shot in the back!

Eyes narrow, Turk cleared the top step. Four Japanese soldiers were crouched by the switchboards, their eyes on something across the room.

"All right," Turk said loudly, "this is it!"

As one man, they wheeled, and, turning, they faced a blasting, hell of fire! Through a haze from his tommy gun, Turk saw one Japanese then another toppling to the floor. Beside him Sauten's weapon was hammering.

Across the room, Sparrow Ryan suddenly lunged to his feet and poured a battering chain of .45-caliber slugs into the switchboard.

Sauten jerked a handful of wires, then, punching a hole in the wall near him, he pulled the pin on an incendiary grenade and dropped it in.

A bullet clipped the door over Turk's head, and he wheeled, firing at a soldier in the side door. There was a dull thud and part of the wall blew out as the grenade sent a rush of hot flame toward the ceiling. The three men ran and, as they reached the door, Madden jerked the pin on another grenade, tossing it over the switchboard into the maze of wires. That would take care of the telephone exchange.

They made the street. Madden wheeled to run, and then something smashed across his forehead, and he felt himself falling. He hit the ground on his hands and knees, struggled to get up, and then another blow landed on his skull from behind, and he slid facedown on the sidewalk, his head roaring with a gigantic blackness shot through with the lightning of pain.

IT COULD ONLY have been minutes later when he opened his eyes. His face, which had been lying on the floor, was stiff with blood from his cut scalp. He tried to move, and the attempt made his head throb horribly. He lay still, gathering strength.

"Who is it?"

The voice was scarcely a whisper.

"Are you a Yank?"

Turk's head jerked. "A Yank?" he gasped. "Yes. Who are you?"

"My name's Morley, I—"

"Vic!" Madden heaved himself to a sitting position. "It's Madden! We thought you were dead!"

"They kept me alive for interrogation," Morley replied bitterly. "But if I ever get out of this—" He hesitated, his voice queer and strained. "Turk, we were sold out. It was . . ."

The door opened, and a brilliant light flashed on. Two Japanese officers stepped in. The stockier of the two looked at Madden. His eyes were malignant.

"You are a fool!" he snapped, his words clipped, but in excellent English. "You think you will surprise us? We have been ready for you for days!"

He stared at Madden, then stepped close.

"You tell me—how many planes come in the attacking force?"

Turk smiled. "Go to the devil," he said quietly.

The officer kicked him in the head. Once, twice, three times. Turk let his head roll with the kicks, and held himself inside against the burst of pain.

"You will tell." The man's voice was distinct. He kicked Turk again, breaking ribs.

"Sure," Turk gasped, "I'll tell."

The Jap's eyes gleamed.

"How many come?"

"Ten thousand," Turk said. "It won't end until Dai Nippon is a heap of smoldering ruins."

"Yes? I have seen your country. They are soft! They will tire of the war, then Japan will be left with all she needs!"

He looked down at Turk contemptuously.

"Bah! I know how many ships come! Their size, their bomb loads, their route!"

He turned on his heel and left the room. The guard loitered, his eyes ugly. He glanced over his shoulder at the door, then walked back to Madden. For a moment, he stood looking down, then slowly, he raised the rifle and pointed the bayonet at Turk's chest.

Madden's eyes were cold.

"Go ahead, yellow belly! Some Marine will feed you one of those soon enough!"

The soldier snarled, and the bayonet came down, and suddenly, with all his remaining strength, Turk Madden rolled over, thrusting himself hard into the soldier's legs!

The Japanese had started to shift his weight, and Turk caught him off balance. The guard toppled, and fell, his head striking the corner of the table as he dropped. He rolled over and, groggy, started to get up. Morley, lying almost beside him, fastened his teeth on the man's ear.

At that moment, the sky turned into a roar of sound, and they heard the shrill scream of bombs, punctuated by explosions.

Madden heaved himself closer to the struggling guard and, drawing his knees back to his chest, kicked out hard with the heels of both bound feet. The man's head slammed back into the wall, and then Madden struggled nearer, and kicked again, kicked with all the strength in his powerful legs.

"Quick!" Madden snapped. "Get his rifle and work the bayonet under the ropes on my wrists!"

Outside, the world was an inferno of flame and the thunderous roar of bombs. There was a fight going on overhead, too, and amid the frightful explosions of anti-aircraft fire and the high, protesting yammer of machine guns, Turk could hear the scream of diving planes.

He could feel the blade of the bayonet working against the ropes. It was slow and hard, for Morley was working with bound hands. Suddenly, everything happened at once. A Japanese officer stepped into the doorway, and the ropes on Turk's wrists came free.

There was an instant of paralyzed astonishment, and then the officer reached for his pistol. The holster flap was buttoned and Turk had time to whip the Arisaka rifle to his shoulder and fire.

His hand still fumbling helplessly at the flap, the officer tumbled back through the door. Turk hastily freed his ankles, then turned to Morley.

Stopping only to grab up the officer's pistol, they dashed from the room and then down the steps.

A shadow loomed nearby, and Turk whirled, the rifle poised.

"Hold it, Skipper." Chiv Sauten stepped into view. "It's me."

There was no darkness now. Wakkanai was a roaring mass of flame, and the pound of exploding bombs roared on, unceasing.

"Sparrow got away, too," he said. "We'd better get out of here."

He led them at a fast walk. They carried their guns ready. Rounding a corner, they came face-to-face with a cluster of men fighting a fire. They ran toward the blaze, hoses at the ready, and showed no interest at all in Madden's armed group. Sauten led the way down an alley, picking up the pace. The roar of wind-captured flames was so great as almost to drown the sound of the nightmare overhead. Somewhere a munitions plant let go, and glass cascaded into the street. An arrow of fire shot across in front of them from a burning building, and then a huge wall fell in, and a great blast of flame gulped at the sky.

Moving through the destruction, Turk felt himself turn sick with horror at what was happening to the town. This was fury such as no man had seen short of Hamburg or Berlin.

Soon they were at the edge of town, and they turned into a small field to see Sparrow's B-25 waiting.

And then, Turk Madden saw the officer who had spoken to them.

The Japanese was standing across the field, with him were three soldiers, one behind a heavy-caliber machine gun. Even as Turk glimpsed them, he saw the officer lift a hand as a signal.

Turk's Arisaka went to his hip, and he fired. The shot missed, but knocked the gunner to a kneeling position. Sauten dropped into a crouch and opened up with the tommy gun, but on the third round the gun went dead.

Madden was halfway across the short intervening space before the gun had stopped pounding. The officer was the only man on his feet, and he cried shrilly and sprang from behind the gun, drawing his samurai sword.

Leaping back before the slashing arc of the great sword, Turk hurled the rifle. Its bayonet point was within four feet of the officer's chest, and Madden's throw drove the long knife deep into the man's body! Turning, Turk Madden ran stumbling toward the bomber. . . .

BEHIND HIM, the bullet-riddled body of the Mitchell once again stood on the Air Corps field. As dawn began to light the sky Turk Madden walked quickly toward the Headquarters office. At his side was Sauten, behind him Sparrow Ryan and Morley limped, trying to keep up. Beyond them planes returning from the raid of Wakkanai were beginning to fill the sky and drop toward the landing strip.

Stepping up, Turk stopped in the doorway. For an instant, there was complete silence.

Colonel Sharpe's eyes widened, then narrowed.

"You? Thank God you're back!"

"Yes," Turk said. "And I know who gave us away. I know who the traitor was who blew up the Morley job and who gave us away this time."

The Colonel's eyes were calculating.

"You do?"

Turk turned to face Martin, and his face was quiet. Then Morley stepped through the door, his face thin and pale, his eyes burning.

"Well, Martin, I see you got back again. I suppose you have another story cooked up as good as the one you told after you betrayed us?"

"He landed in a radio-equipped Japanese plane a few minutes ago," Colonel Sharpe said. "When the rest of you were shot up, he got away in a stolen plane."

"Did you come back, Martin," Morley said slowly, "to betray us again? Or were you afraid of what the Japanese might do to you for failing?"

Turk turned to Sharpe. "The burning fighter planes gave away their airfield and the burning signal station ended up being a guide to the bombers."

Sharpe turned to Morley. "Are you claiming he sold us out?"

"He didn't sell anything, Colonel. He's a Japanese!"

"He's a what?"

Martin's lips twisted with contempt.

"You're right, Morley. My mother was, and I'm proud of it! You Americans forced us into this war but we'll . . ."

His hand lurched to the holster at his hip and the gun swung up, but he never made it, for Turk sprang, driving his shoulder hard into Martin's chest.

Martin staggered, tried to remain erect, but Turk stepped back and hooked a left, high and hard. Martin slammed into the wall, and then slid to the floor.

Madden turned.

"That was it," he said, "he sold us out as he did Morley. He even might have succeeded again, except when they threw me in a cell it was with Morley and he'd figured some of it out.

"I should have guessed. Martin was the only one who lived in the building with me, and who might know where I kept the maps he stole from me. But Vic reminded me of something I had forgotten. Before the war there was an up-and-coming football player at USC. He went back to Japan but this kid was the nephew of Commander Ishimaru of the Japanese air force! It was Ken Martin!"

Chiv Sauten looked down at Martin.

"Yeah?" he said slowly. "What was that he was spoutin' about our starting the war? Didn't he ever hear of Pearl Harbor?"

Vic Morley collapsed into a chair. "I heard it a couple of times while I was locked up. You won't find too many in Japan who know the truth. They've all been told that Japan declared war on the U.S. before the attack and that we forced them into it by cutting off their supplies of steel and fuel oil."

"That's ridiculous!" Sharpe barked. "Our boycott was in protest to their invasion of China!"

"It makes it seem they're in the right, Colonel. That's important for motivating troops, especially with a people for whom honor is so important." Turk nudged the unconscious Martin with a toe. "It even works with men who have been around enough to know better."

"Come on, Morley," Sparrow Ryan said, "I think we'd better get to the infirmary."

Turk paused in the doorway of the building with Chiv Sauten at his side. "When I go out again, buddy, I want you along. You'll do to ride the river with!"

"Me?" Sauten grinned. "You should see my brother Pete. He was fifteen years old before he learned you were supposed to take the cans off the beans before you ate 'em!"

The Goose Flies South

Steadily the motors were droning away, in the thin upper air. "If I was a betting man," Panola said grimly, "I'd give ten to one we never get out of this alive!"

"You asked for it." Captain Runnels replied dryly. "This is strictly volunteer stuff."

"Sure," Panola shrugged. "But who wants to duck a job like this? I asked for it, but I'm not dumb!"

Turk Madden eased forward on the stick and felt the Goose let her nose down. In the heavy, cottony mass of cloud you could see less than nothing. Letting her down was taking a real chance, but they were almost at their destination, and they would soon be ready to land.

There were a lot of jagged peaks here, many of them running upwards of two thousand feet. He was already below that level and saw no sign of an opening to the world below.

The Goose dipped out of the clouds suddenly, and with a rush. A huge, craggy, and black mountainside towered above them. Turk whipped the Grumman over in a steep bank and swung hard away from the cliff. He glanced at Winkler as the ship flattened out. The Major's face was a sickly yellow.

"Close, that!" he said grimly.

"It was," Turk grinned. "You don't see 'em much closer."

He glanced over his shoulder. Runnels and Panola looked scared, but Shan Bao, his mechanic and right-hand man, a tall Manchu, seemed undisturbed.

"How much further?" Runnels asked, leaning forward.

"Not far. We just sighted Mount Stokes, so it'll be just a few minutes."

"Let's hope the place is empty," Panola said. "We'd be in a spot if some ship was lying there."

"It's pretty safe." Turk said. "Nothing down here to speak of, and even less back inland. All this section of the Argentine and Chile is wild and lonely. South, it gets even worse."

It was a cold, bleak, and barren country, sullen and dreary under the heavy gray overcast. Great craggy peaks lifted into the low clouds, and below there were occasional inlets, most of them edged with angry foam. Some of the mountains were covered with trees, and in places the forest came down to the water's edge. In other places there were only bleak plains, windblown and rain whipped.

Then suddenly he saw the mountain, a huge, black, domelike peak that shouldered into the clouds.

"That's the Dome of St. Paul," he said, looking over at Winkler. "San Esteban Gulf is right close by."

HE SWUNG THE PLANE INLAND, skirting the long sandy beach on which a furious surf was breaking, sighted San Quentin Bay with its thickly wooded shores, and then swung across toward the mouth of the San Tadeo River.

The land about the river mouth was low and marshy and covered with stumps of dead trees, some of them truly gigantic in size. Inside the mouth of the river it widened to considerable breadth, and something like seven miles up it divided into two rivers. Turk swung the ship up the course of the Black River, flying low. The stream was choked with the trunks of dead trees, and huge roots that thrust themselves out of the water like the legs of gigantic spiders.

A few miles further, and then he swung inland above a barely discernible brook, and then eased forward on the stick and let the amphibian come down on the smooth surface of the small lake. He taxied across toward a cove lined with heavy timber, and then let the ship swing around as he dropped the anchor in compartive shelter.

"Wow!" Panola shook his head and grinned at Turk as the latter peeled off his flying helmet. "How you ever remembered this place is beyond me! How long since you were here?"

"Twelve years," Madden replied. "I was a kid then, just going to sea. Incidentally, from here on we'd better go armed. I'm just giving you a tip, although of course, that's up to Major Winkler."

"We'll go armed," Winkler said. "And all of you know, we can't take any chances on being found. We've got to get this plane under cover and stay there ourselves as much as possible. If we were caught here, there's not a chance we'd get out of this alive."

Turk watched Shan Bao getting out the rubber boat and then turned his gaze toward the mainland. The amphibian lay in a small cove, excellently sheltered on all sides. The entrance to the cove from the small lake was an S-shaped waterway, ending in a pool. The pool was surrounded on all sides by a heavy growth of timber. It was a mixture of fir, pine, and occasional beech trees. The beach was sandy and littered with washed up roots and trunks of old trees.

There was no sign of life of any kind. And that was as it should be. Not over two dozen men on earth knew that here, off the coast of Patagonia, was to be another experiment with an atomic bomb. An experiment kept secret from the world, and of which no American from the North, no Englishman, and no Russian was to know. It was an experiment being made by a few desperate and skillful German scientists and military men, working with power-mad militarists of the Argentine.

Turk Madden, soldier of fortune, adventurer, and late officer in the Military Intelligence, was flying his own plane, a special-built Grumman Goose with a number of improvements and a greater armament and flying range than the ordinary Goose. Major Winkler was in command, and with them were Captain Runnels and Lieutenant Panola, a recently discharged officer.

Runnels and Winkler were both skilled atomic specialists. Panola was the record man whose task it would be to compile and keep the records of the trip and of the secret experiments, if they were able to observe them. Shan Bao, the Manchu, was Madden's own Man Friday, a hard-bitten North China fighter whom Turk had met in Siberia.

Turk, Winkler, and Runnels went ashore first.

"We've got to set up a shelter," Winkler suggested. "And the sooner the better, as it may rain. What would you suggest, Madden? You've had more of this sort of experience than I."

"Back in the woods," he said instantly. "Find four living trees for the corner posts. Clear out under them and build walls of some of these dead logs we see around. If we cut trees, the white blaze of the cut will be visible from the air. You can spot 'em for miles in the right light. But there's enough brush here, and we shouldn't have to cut anything except under the four trees."

The place he selected was four huge trees with wide-spreading branches near a huge, rocky outcropping. There was nothing but brush between the trees, and it was a matter of minutes for the five men to clear it away. Then they began hauling up logs from the beach. Several of them were large enough to split into four timbers. By nightfall they had the walls erected and a peaked roof of interwoven bows with fir limbs covering it. All was safely under the spreading branches of the trees.

TURK PACED THE BEACH restlessly, and his eyes studied the low hanging clouds. The whole thing had been easy, but he was worried. The ship that had brought them south had heaved to on a leaden sea, and the amphibian had been put into the water. Then, with their equipment and supplies aboard, they had taken off. The whole process, planned and carefully rehearsed, had taken them no more than minutes.

On the flight to the mainland they had seen no one, no ship, no boat, nothing remotely human.

It was miles to the nearest port. The country inland was wild and broken, no country for a man to live in. Yet here and there were Patagonian savages, he knew. And there might be others. Knowing the cold-blooded, ruthless tactics of his enemy, and their thoroughness, he could not but doubt.

When the logs had been moved from the beach, he carefully picked up any chips and covered the places where they had laid with as much skill as possible.

A spring flowed from the rock outcropping near the house they had built. They could reach it without going into the open. They had food enough, although he knew there had once been a few deer in the vicinity. Otherwise, there would be nothing except occasional sea birds, and perhaps a hair seal or two.

Runnels, a heavyset, brown-faced man who had been working with atomic scientists for ten years, walked toward him.

"Beastly place, isn't it? Reminds me of the Arctic. I hunted in Dawson once."

Madden nodded. "Seems too good to be true," he said thoughtfully, "I smell trouble!"

"You're pessimistic," Runnels said. His face grew serious. "Well, if it comes we can't do a thing but take it. We're on our own. They told us if we got caught, we couldn't expect any help from home."

"What's the dope on this experiment?" Turk asked.

"They've got two old German warships. They are in bad shape, but good enough for the experiment. They are going to try sinking them with an atomic bomb about two hundred miles offshore. Then, they are going to try an experiment inland, back in the waste of the plains.

"Our job is not to interfere, only to get information on the results so we can try a comparison with our own."

Turk Madden nodded. He had his own orders. He had been told to obey orders from Winkler up to a point, beyond that his own judgment counted most as he was the most experienced at this sort of thing. Also, if it were possible, he was to try to destroy whatever equipment and results they had. But that was his own job and was to be done with utmost skill, and entirely without giving away his presence or that of his party.

A difficult mission, but one that could be done. After all, he had blown bridges right under the noses of the Japanese. This could scarcely be more difficult.

He walked toward the ridge and, keeping under the trees, climbed slowly toward the top. Now was the time to get acquainted with the country. There was one infallible rule for warfare or struggle of any kind— know your terrain—and he intended to know this.

There were no paths, but he found a way toward the top along a broken ledge, a route that he noticed was not visible from below, if the traveler would but move with reasonable care to avoid being seen. There were broken slabs of rock, and much undergrowth.

He was halfway up before the path became difficult, and then he used his hands to pull himself from handhold to handhold. Yet, before he had reached the top, he slipped suddenly and began to slide downward with rapidly increasing momentum.

Below him was a cliff which he had skirted. Wildly, his hand shot out to stay his fall. It closed upon a bush, and—held.

Slowly, carefully, fearful at each instant that the bush would come loose at the roots, he pulled himself up until he had a foothold. Then a spot of blackness arrested his eye. It was a hole.

Moving carefully, to get a better view, he found it was a small hole in the rock, a spot scarcely large enough to admit a man's body. Taking out his flashlight, he thrust his arm inside, and gasped with surprise.

Instead of a small hole, it was a large cavern, a room of rock bigger than the shelter below, and with a black hole leading off into dimness beyond the reach of his light.

Thoughtfully, he withdrew his arm. Turning his head, he looked below. He could see the pool where the plane was, and he could see the lake. But he was not visible from the shelter. Nor, if he remained still, could he be seen from below.

He pulled himself higher and began once more to climb. Why, he did not know, but suddenly he decided he would say nothing of the cave. Later, perhaps. But not now.

WHEN MADDEN REACHED the crest of the hill he did not stand up. He had pulled himself over the rim and was lying face down. Carefully, he inched along the ground until he was behind a large bush. He rose to his knees and carefully brushed off his clothes. Then he looked.

He was gazing over a wide, inland valley. About two miles away was another chain of hills still higher. The valley itself led away inland, a wide sweep with a small stream flowing through it. A stream that was obviously a tributary leading to the Rio Negro.

North along the coast were great, massive headlands, brutal shoulders of rock of a gloomy grandeur but rarely seen elsewhere. The hills where there was soil were covered with evergreens and with antarctic beeches in thick growth.

Under those trees moss grew heavy, so thick and heavy that one could sink knee deep into it, and there was thick undergrowth also. Yet, a knowing man could move swiftly even in that incredible tangle.

Turk started down the ridge upon which he had lain, sure now that nobody was in sight. Indeed, there was scarcely a chance that a man had been in this area in months, if not in years. He walked swiftly, headed for a promontory not far away where he might have a better view up the coast.

He had dropped from a rocky ledge and turned around a huge boulder when he saw something that brought him up short. For an instant, his eyes swept the area before him, a small, flat plain leading to the foot of the bluff toward which he had been going. There was nothing. Nothing now. Yet there upon the turf of the plain were the clear, unmistakable tracks of wheels!

Turk walked swiftly to the tracks, yet careful to step on stones, of which there were plenty, and thus leave no track himself. Then he stopped, staring at the tracks.

A plane. A fighter craft by the distance between the tires, and the weight as indicated by the impression left on the turf. If not a fighter, then a small plane, heavily loaded. More likely, a fighter. The landing here would not be bad.

Yet why here?

Carefully, and with infinite skill, he began to skirt the plain, examining every nook, every corner. Finally, he found a dead fire. He touched his hand to the ashes. There was, he thought, a bare suggestion of warmth.

He looked around at the campsite. Someone had stopped here, picked up wood, and built the fire. They had warmed a lunch, eaten, and then flown away.

Four small logs had been placed side by side, and the fire built upon them, thus the fire was kept off the damp ground. One of the men, and there had been two, had known something. He was a woodsman. At least, he was not unfamiliar with the wilds. That meant even more care must be exercised.

He shifted his carbine to his left hand and studied the scene thoughtfully. Was the visit here an accident? Had there been a mere forced landing? Or was it by intention?

Squatting on his haunches, he studied the ends of the sticks the fire had left unburned. Several of them were fresh, white and newly cut. But several were older, older and yet as he dug into the bark with his thumbnail, he saw they were still green.

It could mean but one thing. Someone had been here more than once. Someone had built a fire here before. Turning, he walked back to the tracks, and working carefully, he moved across the plain. He found two more sets of tracks.

So that was it. A patrol plane. A plane that flew along this bit of coast, stopped here occasionally while the pilot and his companions cooked and ate a warm meal, probably loafed awhile, and then took off again.

It meant more than that. It meant the Americans had slipped in but a short time after the patrol plane had left. That the fact they were alive at all was due to the fact that Turk Madden had touched the coast south of the San Tadeo River. Had he come right in over the coast they would have met the fighter plane! Or have missed it by the narrowest of margins!

Turk turned quickly, but even as he turned, something whipped by his face and hit the tree behind him with a *thud*!

MADDEN HIT THE GROUND all in one piece and rolled into the brush. Instantly, he was on his hands and knees and crawling. He made a dozen yards to the right before he stopped behind the trunk of a huge beech and stared out across the open.

Almost at once there were four more quick shots. Four shots openly spaced and timed, and Turk heard one of them clip through the trees on his left, and the second flipped by him so close that he dropped flat and hugged the ground, his face white and his spine chilled by the close escape.

The other two shots clipped through the woods some distance off.

"Smart guy, eh?" Turk snarled. "Two shots evenly spaced on each side of where I hit the brush! You're not so dumb!"

Straightening up, he stood behind the tree and studied the situation. It was late, and it was cloudy. By the time he had skirted the plain it would be pitch dark, and he could find no tracks, while he was certain to make some noise and the chances of his being shot, if his assailant waited, would be great.

WALKING BACK OVER THE COUNTRY between the campfire and the hidden base, he scowled over the problem. Who could be in the vicinity? Had one of the men with the plane remained behind? But if so, why? That didn't make sense, for even if the enemy were expecting something of the kind, they would never expect it right here. Quite obviously, the entire coast was patrolled, probably as much against their own people, if any, as against foreigners.

If someone had remained behind in that vast and lonely country it could mean but one thing: They had been betrayed.

And if it wasn't a stranger, it could be only one of the men of his own party! Yet, if so, why shoot?

When he stepped through the door into the shelter under the trees, they were all there. Shan Bao was stewing something in a kettle over the fire. He glanced up, but said nothing.

Runnels grinned at him. "Well, we beat you back, but not by very long!"

Turk looked at him for a moment. "You were out, too?"

"Yeah, all of us. We decided it was as good a time as any to have a look around. We just got back. I went south along the river. Nothing down there."

"I didn't find anything either," Panola said. "Not a thing but some marshy, wet country."

"That seems to be the consensus," Winkler agreed. "Nothing around."

"I wouldn't say that," Turk said slowly.

Winkler got up, frowning. "You found something? What?"

"The tracks of a patrol plane—a fighter. Evidently this region is carefully patrolled. The plane lands over in a little plain across the ridge. It has landed there more than once."

"How could you tell that?" Panola demanded.

"By the tracks. Also by the ends of the sticks used to make a fire. A good woodsman," he added, and he knew if there was a guilty man here he would sense added meaning in what he said, "can read a lot of things where the average man can see nothing."

Turk Madden sat down suddenly. He was mad all through. Maybe one of them had taken a shot at him, but if he had, there was no way to prove it. He would just have to wait. He felt the weight of the .45 automatic in his shoulder holster, and liked the feel of it.

Winkler stared thoughtfully into the fire. "So they are patrolling the coast? That means we've got to go very slow."

"Well," Panola suggested, "the test comes off in three days. If the plane comes back, let's knock him off. It would be at least two days before they'd be able to get down to investigate, and by that time, we'd be gone."

"Why two days?" Runnels asked. "They might have a radio on that ship. Probably have, in fact."

"Even so, I doubt if there would be any search organized for a couple of days. You know how bad the storms are down here. It would be all too easy for a plane to get caught in one of those terrific blasts of wind."

"It won't do," Winkler said. "We've got to keep out of sight."

"That's right," Runnels said. "We're to get our information and get out, and if we can do it without suspicion, so much the better."

THAT MADE SENSE. And yet? Suppose Winkler was the one? Suppose it was also a method of keeping them from finding anything more? And what about Panola?

"As though we were at the end of the world here," Runnels remarked. "Everything still as death except for that wind. A man would starve to death if lost on this shore."

"Yeah, and we're not so far as the crow flies from Buenos Aires. And what a town that is!"

"Have you been there?" Turk asked. "I thought I was the only one who knew South America?"

"Been there?" Panola grinned. "Shucks, man, I lived there for three years! Runnels has been here, too! Weren't you here during the war?"

"Uh-huh. I was on duty as military attaché for a couple of months."

Turk ate in silence. So Panola and Runnels had both been to the Argentine? It was easy to be influenced by all that wealth and glitter. The sixteen families or so that dictated the life in the Argentine could entertain very beautifully. Perhaps one, or both, of the two men had been influenced? Persuaded?

MORNING CAME, and he went down to the ship. Shan Bao joined him after a few minutes. He looked thoughtfully at the Manchu, then glanced around to make sure no one heard him.

"You keep your eyes open, Shan," he said softly. "Watch everybody you see. Anybody do anything wrong, you tell me."

He was working over the plane when he saw Runnels and Winkler come out of the shelter. Turk turned and swung ashore. Panola was taking some weather observations, checking his instruments atop the ridge. It was as good an idea as any.

Stepping quickly over the logs, he got to the shack. None of the men had taken their carbines, and he picked up the nearest one, that of Winkler. A quick examination showed it clean. Runnels's checked the same. Then he picked up Panola's carbine. A quick glance into the barrel.

It had been fired.

Panola.

Turk went back outside and returned to the plane, his mind rehashing everything he could remember on Panola. All of them had been checked very thoroughly by the FBI, yet something had been missed.

Panola was of Italian parentage. He had been born in Brooklyn, raised there, had gone to college, and his war record had been excellent. He knew nothing beyond that, that and the fact that Panola had lived in Buenos Aires for three years sometime during this period.

Another thing remained. How had Panola, if he was the marksman, returned to the shelter so quickly the night before? There must be another route than that over the ridge.

"I think," he said musingly, "a little trip around by plane would do more good than anything else!"

Major Winkler was coming down through the trees.

"Major," he said, when the tall, narrow-faced man had come closer, "I think I'll take a cruise around. This country needs some looking over."

"You think it's wise?" Winkler asked thoughtfully. "Well, go ahead, but be careful!"

A HALF HOUR LATER, when Turk taxied the ship out from under the overhanging trees and the camouflaged shelter built for the plane, Shan Bao was ashore. Madden turned the ship down the pool and, after a run, lifted it into the air, banked steeply, and swung away up the coast.

After a few minutes he lifted the plane into the mists under the clouds. As he swung back and forth up the coast, he studied the terrain below. Suddenly, he saw a house!

It was a huge, gray stone building, back of a little cove with a black sand beach. A yacht was anchored in the cove, and a motor launch was at the small wharf. Easing back on the controls, he shot the amphibian into the clouds. Out of sight.

There was a chance he had not been seen, not recognized, as at the moment he had passed over the cove the mists through which he had flown were thick.

He circled the ship higher, puzzling over the situation. That house was no more than five miles from their own base! Also, it was no more than three miles from where he had been fired upon! Could he have been wrong? Perhaps it wasn't one of his own crowd, but one of these people? And perhaps Panola was in the clear!

Turk scowled grimly and hunched his big shoulders. Then he turned the plane inland toward the Dome of St. Paul. Coming up to the mountain, he pulled back on the stick and climbed to get more altitude. He was still climbing when the fighter shot out of the clouds and came toward him with all her guns spouting flame!

Turk pulled away in a climbing turn as the fighter shot beneath him, he fell away and let go with a burst at its tail assembly. Evidently he missed, for the fighter whipped around and came back at him!

Flying like a wild man, Turk put the amphibian through everything he knew, and suddenly made a break and got away into the heavy gray clouds. It was a momentary respite only, for he knew now that he dared not let the plane return to its base.

The other pilot was obviously not used to fighting, for he had missed several good chances that no member of the Luftwaffe would have missed, or a Japanese, either. Turk swung around and dropped back toward the mountain, and then suddenly he sighted the fighter again.

They saw each other at almost the same instant, but even as they sighted each other, Turk whipped over and dived straight for the rounded top of the Dome.

And behind him, the wind screaming in its wings, came the fighter! Desperate, Turk was remembering something from his own experience, a stunt he had tried long before, in the South Pacific. He was remembering, too, that curious gap in the trees atop the Dome. Heading straight for the Dome in a wild, desperate dive, he saw tracers streaming by him, and then he whipped over and cut through that gap in the trees!

A few yards in either direction and he would have crashed into the trees, and as it was, he cleared the top of the Dome by no more than four or five feet! Then, behind him, came a crash!

He took the stick back and reached for altitude, and glanced to the rear and down. A cone of leaping flame was mounting toward the sky, and he could see something he took to be the pilot's lifeless body, lying off to one side.

Thoughtfully, he turned toward home, flying high into the heavy clouds. If they searched, and they probably would, they would find the wreckage. A cursory examination would show only that the plane had crashed, and they might accept it as an accident.

Yet, if they examined closely what wreckage there was left, and one wing, at least, had fallen clear of the flames, they might find bullet holes. Still, the chances were he had missed. For the first time in his life, he found himself hoping he had missed.

He was gliding in for a landing on the pool when he saw the path, a dim trail along the rocky edge of the brook leading from the river. A path that would be a shortcut to the house on the cove!

When Turk Madden put the plane down he was worried. He got up from the pilot's seat and swore softly. Then he slid the Colt from its shoulder holster and checked the magazine. It was ready. "I think," he said softly, "I'm going to need a gun!"

Shan Bao came out in the rubber boat and took him ashore, after which he left Shan the job of snugging the ship down and checking her.

Runnels looked up when Turk walked in, then his eyes sharpened. "What happened?"

"That fighter showed up. I tricked him into a crash on top of the Dome." Turk spoke quietly, but even as he spoke he was trying to see all their expressions at once.

Panola wet his lips slowly. "Then they know we're here. Or they will. That doesn't leave us much chance, does it?"

"Maybe they won't know," Turk suggested.

"What would prevent them?" Winkler demanded. His long, lantern-jawed face had sharpened with worry. "My heavens, man! They aren't that dumb."

"If they actually send somebody to the top of the Dome to check, I doubt if he'll find evidence of anything except a crash. They'll think he collided with the peak in a cloud. I doubt if he has any bullet holes."

"They may check his guns," Winkler suggested. "Had you thought of that?"

"I hadn't," Turk said. "But if they do, guns often fire in flames, and I doubt if there will be much left to examine. There was gasoline over everything."

"I'd say you were lucky, mighty lucky!" Runnels said. "Great stuff, old man!"

Then he told them of the yacht and the house. They watched his face curiously, but it was Winkler who seemed most worried. He paced the room thoughtfully.

"THIS THING SCARES ME," he said. "They might find us!"

It was just daylight when Turk Madden slipped from the cabin. He took his carbine, and went toward the Goose, then turned away among the trees and started for the trail that led along the creek, the trail seen from the plane.

This was it. He could sense the building up of forces around him, could sense an intangible danger. Someone in his own group, he felt sure, was a traitor. It could be Panola, and yet, it might be either of the others. Winkler had been a good leader, and Turk could understand his natural worry. The atomic tests were to be tomorrow, and if it was to be witnessed and checked, everything must move smoothly and easily. The explosion, unless the time was changed, was supposed to be at ten in the morning.

Panola was to remain here. Winkler, Runnels, and himself would fly to the vicinity, taking advantage of the cloud cover. Then, just before ten, the explosion. They would drop through, make their check when the explosion occurred, and get away—if possible.

He knew what was at stake. The Fascists in the Argentine were strong, and they had been increased by refugees from Germany. More than one atomic engineer had escaped to Buenos Aires, and they had been joined by others. There were rumors of money being sent to them from the north to aid the experiments by those interested in the commercial application of atomic power.

The experiments were strictly hush-hush. Even the Argentine Government was supposed to know nothing about them. The presence of a North American here—well, Turk Madden knew the men he was working against.

Baron von Walrath, one of the shrewdest operatives in the former German Military Intelligence; Dr. Walther Rathow, atomic scientist and militarist; Wilhelm Messner, of the Gestapo; and Miguel Farales, of the Argentine Military Intelligence.

Yet they had seen none of these men. Agents had reported nothing. The whole affair had moved so perfectly that he had become suspicious. And the next few hours would tell the story.

Hurrying, he worked along the trail, then rounding a fallen log, he saw there in the soft earth, the mark of a boot! The shape was not distinct in the moss, but the heel print was plain. It could have been made no earlier than the night before.

As he continued along the trail, Turk watched carefully, and found several more footprints, but none was distinct. Yet someone had left their camp, or the vicinity of it, and had come over this trail. Then almost at the plain where he had seen the tracks of the fighter plane, he saw a double footprint. They were apparently of the same foot, and the second one was superimposed on the first, and that second track pointed toward camp! The man had come from the camp, and returned to it!

Following the footprints, he reached the dead campfire. The man he had followed had come this far. He had waited, he had smoked several cigarettes, and then he had returned the way he had come. He had waited here—for the patrol plane!

Leaving the plain, Madden crossed by way of the woods to the range of hills beyond, stepped through the woods carefully toward the cove. He could see the cold seawater lapping on the gravel beach, and he could hear the bump of the launch hull against the small pier.

Then he leaned forward to peer at the gray house. He leaned forward still further and put a foot out to balance himself. A branch under his foot cracked like a pistol shot, and he jerked back.

Then something struck him on the head, and as he toppled forward he heard a pistol shot ringing in his ears!

HE OPENED HIS EYES and saw a hardwood floor, then blood. His own blood. He closed his eyes against the throb of his head and tried to place himself, to remember what had happened.

"Hang it, Stock," a voice was saying in English, "why did you have to shoot the man? Couldn't you get the drop on him and bring him in?"

"That guy's Turk Madden!" another voice said. "I'd know him anywhere. If you ask me, you better kill him. You leave him alive and you're borrowin' trouble. I heard of him in China, and the guy is poison."

"Thanks, pal." Turk told himself mentally, "but I don't feel very much like poison right now."

"We've got to keep him alive!" The first voice was crisp and hard. "At least until we know where they are. Messner was to have communicated with us as soon as they landed. They aren't far from here, we know that, and he has the patrol plane stops. One of them is sure to be close to where they will be."

"Perhaps, Baron," said a third voice, suave and smooth, "we can make Madden talk. Timeo has convincing methods."

"Not a chance!" Madden rolled over and sat up. His fingers touched his scalp gingerly. The bullet had cut a neat furrow along the right side of his head. He looked up. "Unless there's some money in it."

He glanced up at the three men. Stock would be the big man with the flat face. The man seated in the chair with the smoothly shaven face and the monocle could be no one but a German. That would be von Walrath. And the other was Latin. Probably Farales.

"Money?" Farales leaned closer. "Why should we pay you money? You have nothing we want."

"Maybe yes, and again, maybe not." Turk swallowed. "How about a drink? I'm allergic to bullets. They make me thirsty."

At a motion from Farales, Stock poured a drink and handed it to Madden. He tossed it off, shook his head, and then got slowly to his feet. There was an empty chair, and he fell back into it.

"I'm a businessman," he said then. "I'm not in this for my health. If you guys have got a better offer, trot it out."

He was stalling for time, stalling and watching. Somehow, he had to get out of here, somehow he had to block Messner, whoever he was. Certainly, one of the three men at camp was Messner, formerly of the Gestapo. To think that such a man could be in an American unit, on such a mission. But the man was there. Turk was under no illusions about stopping him. There would be only one way now.

"Who sent you here?" von Walrath demanded. "From what office do you work?"

"Office?" Turk shrugged. He took out a cigarette and put it between his lips. "I work for Turk Madden. I'm in this for myself. I'm goin' to get all the dope I can, and sell to the highest bidder."

"The United States?" Farales asked gently. He was studying Turk through narrowed eyes. "Why should they pay? They already know."

"Do they?" Madden shrugged again. "But you may find out something they won't know. Also, they may want to know how much you know."

"And that's why you're here. To find out how much we know. That's why your government sent you here." Farales's voice was silky.

"My government?" Turk raised an eyebrow. "What is my government? I fought for China before I fought for the United States. I fought for them because they paid me well, and because I like the winning side."

Von Walrath's eyes were cold. "Then you did not believe we Germans could win? The greatest military power on earth?"

Madden chuckled. "Why the greatest? Who did you ever lick? Nobody I can remember except a lot of little countries who never had a war. It's like Joe Louis punching a lot of guys who ride a subway. Anybody can lick an average guy if he's got some stuff. Germany was ready for war, the other countries weren't. Germany never whipped a major power who was even half ready for war."

"No?" Von Walrath sat up stiffly. "And why did we lose this one?"

"Mainly because you never had a chance." Turk warmed to his subject. "Any war can be figured on paper before it begins. You didn't have the natural resources. You were cut off from the countries that had them. You didn't have the industry."

"Next time," von Walrath replied coolly, "we won't need it. Atomic bombs change everything."

"That's right. The smallest nation has a chance now."

"Even," Farales suggested, "Argentina."

Von Walrath stood up suddenly. "Where is your plane now?" he demanded.

"Around," Madden rested his elbows on his knees. His .45 was lying on the table not a dozen feet away. "Supposing we make a deal. You slip me a chunk of dough, and I keep my plane out of this? Your man Messner can't keep it out. I can."

"And why can't Messner keep it out?" Farales demanded.

"First place," Turk looked up from under his eyebrows. He had his feet drawn back and was on his toes now, "because he won't try. Why hasn't he communicated with you? I'll tell you why: because he hasn't any intention of it. Because he has another deal pending."

"You lie!" von Walrath hissed furiously. "I will vouch for Messner!"

Turk chuckled. "Listen, you guys. You're not so dumb. Who will pay most to get the atomic secret now? Who wants it worst? I ask you: who wants it? *Soviet Russia!*"

He lighted another cigarette. "What do you think they'd pay? A hundred thousand? Yes, and maybe more. Maybe a million. If a man had the secret, he could ask plenty, and get it! What can a poverty-stricken Germany give Messner? What can even the Argentine give Messner? Would he get a million from them? From you? Not a chance! What can we give your friend Messner?"

Farales's sardonic black eyes lifted to von Walrath. "He speaks wisely, Señor. What can we give your friend Messner?"

"He lies." Von Walrath's eyes were blaring, yet Madden knew he had injected an element of doubt into the Prussian's mind. "Messner is loyal."

"Then why has he not communicated with us? He is days overdue." Farales looked at Madden. "How long have you been here?"

"We landed a week ago," he lied.

"A week, and still no word. How is this, Walrath?" Farales's voice was cold. "Four times in that week has our plane been at the prescribed places. And it cannot be far. This man walked."

"Wait until the plane comes today before you speak. Messner probably has been unable to get away."

Madden could see that the Baron was uncertain. "There will be word today."

"No," Turk said coolly, "there won't."

He had been stalling for time. Stock was across the room now, mixing a drink. No one was near the table where the gun lay.

"What do you mean?" von Walrath demanded. "What makes you so sure?"

"Simply," Turk said, this was going to be close, "because your pilot is dead, and your patrol plane crashed. It's lying up there," he pointed suddenly toward the wide window and the Dome of St. Paul, "burned to a crisp!"

As he pointed, their heads almost automatically turned, and he was out of his chair and had made three steps before Farales swung and saw him. It was too late. Turk hurled himself at the table, grabbed the automatic and swung with his back to the table. Farales's shout brought a crash from Stock as he wheeled, dropping the glass and grabbing for his gun. Turk shot him in the stomach, and then wheeling, he hurled himself, shoulder first, through the window.

It was no more than six feet to the ground. The instant he hit he flattened against the building and ran along it close to the wall until he reached the end of the house.

The shore there was high, lifting in a straight bank at least ten feet above the shelving gravel beach. He jumped off the bank to the gravel, landing on his feet, and fell back into a sitting position.

As he fell backward, he saw a man on the motor launch grab a rifle, and he blasted with the Colt from where he sat. The bullet hit the cabin of the boat and laced a white scar across its polished side. The man fell over, and then the glass crashed as the fellow thrust the rifle through a cabin port. Turk was on his feet then, but he wheeled and put two quick shots through that port, and then he was running.

He had made a dozen steps before a rifle cracked and a shot hit the rocks ahead of him and whined viciously away over the water. He zigged right, and then dodged back, and seeing a cut in the bank, dropped behind it just as several more shots struck nearby.

He paused just an instant, caught a quick breath, and then ran up the cut. Ahead of him it ended near a cliff and the forest came up to the foot of the cliff. Yet there he would have to dodge across twenty feet of open country before he could make the forest.

"That German is a shot, or I miss my guess," Turk told himself. "He'll have his sights set on that open place, and I'm a dead pigeon!"

Yet even as he reached the end of the water cut, he saw there was a deep hollow and another water drain that fell sharply away. The water that had made the deeper hole had fallen off a corner of the cliff around the shoulder. Perhaps he could get across.

A huge root thrust itself out, and sticking his gun in its holster, he jumped. It was a terrific leap, but his hands just grasped the root, and he swung with all the impetus of his leap and hurled himself at the bank opposite.

He hit it, chest first, and grabbed wildly at the edge. Dust and rock cascaded into his face, and suddenly a rifle barked, and a shot smacked into the bank right between his clutching hands!

Frightened, he gave a mighty heave and hurled himself over the edge and rolled into the woods. A bullet clipped a tree over his head, and he scrambled to his feet and floundered away in the knee-deep moss. Then he saw a fallen log and, leaping atop it, he ran its length, swung by a branch to another, and ran along it.

It wasn't going to be enough to get away. He had to lose them. Yet on one side was the plain, and if pushed into the open they would cut him down in an instant. On the other side was the river.

His breath was coming in great grasps, and his lungs cried out with pain at the effort. Yet he kept on, for speed meant everything now.

He had crossed a small clearing and was entering the woods along the river when suddenly another shot rang out, and he plunged headfirst into the soft, yielding moss. The shot had come from in *front* of him!

Turk Madden was mad. Suddenly, something had seemed to burst inside of him. The traitor, whoever he was, was up ahead, trying to kill him.

"All right!" Madden said suddenly, savagely, "if you want it you can have it!"

He slid the Colt into his hand. Four shots left. He felt in his pocket for the extra clip. Well, they hadn't taken that! Flat in the moss, he began to worm his way through the damp green softness, gun in hand, a fierce, leaping rage within him.

He crawled, and he felt the moss thinning. Was the watcher keeping an eye on him? This guy knew a thing or two, as he was the same one who had dusted the brush so thoroughly on that first day. There was a crashing in the brush back the way he came. Wish he'd shoot some of his own men!

Another crash and then he could hear someone breathing hard. The man had stopped to stare around. Slowly, Turk gathered his knees under him, and then he straightened.

The man, a huge fellow with a blackish, greasy face, was not ten feet away!

As Turk arose, the fellow stared stupidly, then gave a gulp and jerked up the rifle. He was much too slow. Turk put a bullet through his heart, then sprang across the ten feet of space, and grabbed the man's rifle. Then, without hesitating, he threw the rifle to his shoulder and dusted the woods, firing ten shots and spacing them neatly across the forest behind him.

THEN HE DROPPED the rifle and plunged down to the gravel shore of the stream. For thirty minutes he twisted and turned in the woods, and then finally straightened out and headed for home. As he walked, he exchanged clips.

As he came up to the shelter, he found Shan Bao, a carbine in his hands, standing by the door.

"Where are the others?" Turk asked.

"They all went out into the brush. Thought we might be attacked." Shan Bao looked at Madden's head, and the blood. "You have had trouble," he said. "I hope you killed the man who did that."

Turk dug out a cigarette and lighted it. Then he looked at the Manchu.

"I don't know, Shan, but he's got one in the stomach he wishes he didn't have!"

Runnels came out of the woods. He looked flurried, and his eyes were narrow. He glanced at Turk's head.

"Looks like you had it tough!"

"Plenty!" Turk snapped. "Better get your gear aboard the plane. We're moving!"

"Moving?" he frowned. "Winkler won't like that. Better wait to see what he says. After all this is his show."

"Up to a point," Turk Madden replied shortly. "That happens to be my plane. Anyway, they came too close just now. They'll be back. We can't stay here."

"And why shouldn't we stay here?" It was Major Winkler. His face was hot and his eyes looked angry. "I heard what you said, Madden, and we're staying, whether you like it or not."

"No," Turk replied shortly, "we're not. At least, I'm not. I'm taking my ship and getting out. I'm going back in the hills until tomorrow, back where we'll all be safe!"

"You'll stay right here." Winkler's carbine lifted, and Turk cursed himself for a fool. "You'll stay here, and like it. Panola, tie him up! This is mutiny. I'm in command here. We're in no danger, and we'll stay right here until tomorrow."

"I don't believe the gun is necessary, Major," Runnels protested. "Madden will stay."

"You bet he'll stay!" Winkler declared sharply. "I'll personally see that he stays. Tie him!"

Runnels looked at Panola, and the Italian shrugged, then he stepped forward and jerked Turk's hands behind him. Yet even as Panola tied his hands, Turk knew the officer was not tying him tight. Was it because he sympathized or because he hoped he would try to escape, and be shot escaping?

Tied on his bed, Turk relaxed and lay quiet. How soon the Baron would find them, he couldn't guess. Obviously, it couldn't be long. The possible areas now were so limited, for they knew he had come from some place within walking distance, which meant no more than ten miles, or perhaps a bit more. It was rough, rugged country, but they would be looking.

Working a little, he loosened his ropes. Major Winkler had been lying down for several minutes now, and Runnels was sitting in the door.

Panola was nowhere in sight. Had he gone to warn von Walrath and finally to make contact? Yet somehow, Turk found himself doubting that Panola was the guilty man. But even that left only Runnels and Winkler, and Winkler was in command. He would be blamed for the success or failure of the effort.

Winkler got up suddenly and walked outside. He said something to Runnels about being nervous.

"Nothing must happen now," he muttered.

Turk lay still. His hands were free. Now where was Shan Bao? He drew his knees up and worked on the ropes on his ankles. Runnels still sat in the doorway. There was no sign of Panola or Major Winkler.

He put one foot down beside the cot, then turned carefully and sat up. Runnels had not moved. His head lay against the door post, and he was apparently asleep. Turk got up and in two quick steps had crossed the room to his carbine.

He picked up a handful of extra clips and thrust them into his pockets. He retrieved his automatic and more ammunition, then he stepped over to the back wall. In a few minutes he had worked his way through the branches and leaves of the shelter and stood outside.

A shot rang out, and he heard a muffled curse, and then he saw men come streaming into camp. He had made it none too soon. He saw Runnels start up and then go crashing down as he was struck by a gun butt. Then they charged inside, and he heard a shout as they failed to find him.

"And they knew where to look," Madden said viciously.

HE MOVED SWIFTLY through the darkness toward the cliff. He knew where he was going now. He needed shelter, and there was the cave above. He climbed swiftly, and found his way to the cave. For a while he had been afraid he would not be able to find it in the dark, but he did. Then he crawled in and lay still.

They were searching down below, and he heard the voice of von Walrath as well as that of Farales. Something had gone wrong, apparently something more than the fact that he was gone. They kept searching, then finally gave up. But they remained below. He was bottled up, unable to do a thing.

Where was Shan Bao? Had Runnels been killed? And what of the others? Unable to sit still, he turned on his flashlight, shielding it with his hand, and went to the back of the cave. It was a steep, winding passage, and he went down, walking swiftly. It took a sharp turn, and suddenly he realized it was going toward the shore of the pool!

There was dampness here, and occasional pools of water. He walked on, then feeling the air moving against his face, he proceeded more cautiously. It was a large opening, almost concealed behind a fallen log. But he was looking over the pool—and there, not a dozen feet away, was the Goose!

How far had he walked? And what was the Goose doing here?

Considering, he realized he must have walked at least twenty minutes inside the cave. He could have come a mile, but probably it was no more than half that far. In his mind he ran his eyes along the edge of the pool. Then he knew. Somehow, some way, the Goose had been slipped away and hidden in this inlet at the extreme end of the pool.

It was only a delay, for with daylight they would find it with ease. And by daylight the Goose should be winging out to sea instead of lying here.

He crawled over the log, then moved ahead slowly, carefully. He was going to be aboard that plane or dead within the next few minutes. Suddenly, right ahead of him, something moved.

Turk froze. Then he saw a tall, lean form rise before him. Instantly, he grinned with relief. Shan Bao!

"Shan!" he whispered hoarsely, and saw the figure stiffen. Then the Manchu turned and beckoned.

"What is it?" Madden whispered as he came up. "How'd the plane get here!"

"Panola," Shan replied softly. "Panola and me."

"Panola?" Madden scowled. Then Panola wasn't the one. Crawling out along a log to the door of the ship, he puzzled over that. Then he slipped in. The Italian moved, and touched his arm.

"Madden? Man, I'm glad you're here! I can't fly this thing good enough. We towed her down here with the rubber boat. Maybe we can take off."

"We can!" Turk shifted his carbine. "Panola, who's the traitor, Runnels or Winkler?"

"I don't know," he shrugged. "You mean one of them isn't on the level?"

"That's right. And I thought it was you! You, because of your rifle. Somebody fired on me that first day, and your rifle was the only one fired that day."

Panola grabbed his arm.

"But Turk!" he said hoarsely. "I didn't have my own gun that day. I got another by mistake. Major Winkler had mine!"

"Major Winkler?" Turk's jaw set. "Then Winkler is Wilhelm Messner, the Gestapo agent!"

He turned sharply. "Panola, you stay with this ship. Stay with it and don't let anybody aboard but Shan or me. I'm going ashore."

"But what can you do?" Panola protested. "Only two of you?"

"Watch!" Turk snapped harshly. "Shan is worth a dozen. Watch, and you'll see how it's done. This isn't cricket, but it's business!"

He walked back to the gun case and took out a submachine gun, and slid in a magazine. He thrust three more in his belt. Then he went ashore. He went through the woods fast with Shan, also armed with a submachine gun, following close behind.

There was no effort at concealment when he stepped up toward the shelter. His very carelessness made the guard relax. Turk stepped out of the brush and saw the guard suddenly stiffen. Then he let out a low cry and grabbed for his gun.

He never made it. Turk opened up with the tommy and cut him half in two with the first blast of fire. Men scrambled to their feet and the two men mowed them down. Leaping into the open, Turk felt a gun blast almost in his face, and then he shoved the gun against the big man who lunged at him and opened up.

The Baron charged from a door, gun spouting, and Turk Madden cut down on him with his Thompson. The man went flat and rolled over, grabbing feebly at the earth, his hands helpless, his gun rattling on the rocks.

Then someone leaped from the shambles and made a dart for the outer darkness. It was Winkler!

Dropping his tommy gun, Turk sprang after him. Plunging wildly through the brush, the man charged at the cliff and began a mad scramble up its surface with Turk close behind him.

They met at the top, and Winkler, his features wolfish with fury, whirled to face him. He aimed a vicious kick at Turk's face as he came over the edge, but Turk ducked and grabbed his foot. His hold slipped, but it was enough to stagger Messner, and before the Gestapo man could get set, Turk Madden was on top.

In the darkness there on the brink of the cliff, they fought. Messner, like a tiger at bay, struck out. His fist smashed Turk in the mouth, and Madden felt his lips smash and tasted blood, and something deep within him awakened and turned him utterly vicious. Toe to toe, the two big men slugged like madmen. There was no back step, no hesitation, no ducking or dodging. It was cruel and bitter and brutal. It was primeval in its fury.

Turk went down, and then he came up swinging, and Messner, triumph shining in his ugly eyes, smashed him down again and leaped in to put the boots to him. Turk rolled over and scrambled up, smashing Messner in the stomach with a wicked butt.

Relentless, ruthless, Turk closed in. He ducked a left and smashed a wicked right to the body. He felt the wind go out of the German, and he stepped in, hooking both hands to the head and then the body. He caught a long swing on his ear that made his head ring, but he was beyond pain, beyond fear, beyond doubt.

It was a fight to the death now, and he fought. He stepped under another swing and battered at the German's body with cruel punches. Then he straightened and whipped up a right uppercut that jerked the German's head back. Then a crushing left hook, and as the German went to his knees he smashed him again in the face.

The man fell back and then rolled over and got up. Turk started for him, and the man turned, gave a despairing cry, and sprang straight out from the cliff!

It was a sheer drop to the jagged rocks and upthrust roots and jagged dead branches below.

Turk stepped back, his chest heaving with effort, his eyes blind with sweat and blood. Then he turned, and slowly he walked back to the path and went down to the shelter.

Runnels met him, a tommy gun in his hands.

"Get him?" he asked.

Turk nodded. "Yeah." He glanced toward the east where the sky was beginning to lighten. "Shan, fix some coffee. Then we'll get the ship warmed up. We've got us a job to do."

"Madden," Panola said slowly, "I did some looking around myself. Rathow, the atomic scientist, and Miguel Farales are back at the house. The bomb that is to be dropped is there. One of them, anyway."

"You saw it?" Turk exclaimed, incredulously.

"I wired it," Panola said, grinning. "I wired the blasted thing." He added, then, "The other comes over the house about nine. It will be in a big bomber and guarded by a fighter plane. There will be another plane, a big passenger job, of scientists."

"Then that's our job!" Turk said. "We've got to get the fighter. If we can knock out the fighter, the others are sitting pigeons." He turned to Panola. "How'd you wire that bomb?"

"The first person who opens the door on the back of the house will blow that whole cove into the mist," Panola replied grimly. "It isn't more than half the size of our Hiroshima bomb, though."

When Madden's amphibian took off, all were aboard. Turk Madden scowled at the sky, and his hard green eyes searched the horizon for the oncoming planes. They should be along soon. He reached for altitude and squeezed the Goose against the low hanging clouds.

Getting a fighter was anything but simple, and he knew there was every chance it would end in failure. Of course, he could go ahead, observe the experiment, and return so they could report their findings.

Yet, if all could be destroyed, the experimenters who remained in Buenos Aires would be unsure of just what had happened and where the mistake had been made. It would certainly slow up experimentation and increase uncertainty and fear.

Shan Bao saw them first. The Manchu leaned over and touched Turk on the shoulder and gestured.

The bomber was flying at about six thousand feet, with the passenger plane and its observers on right and a bit behind. For a moment the fighter eluded him, and then he saw it high against the sky, flying at probably nine thousand, his own level. He eased back on the stick and climbed, hoping with all his heart that the fighter pilot had not sighted him.

IT WOULD BE touch and go now. There would be no such chance as with the other fighter, a few days before. He could not hope for such a thing twice. Even the maneuver was risky, and the chance of the pilot making a mistake was slight. The man in this ship would probably be tough and experienced. He had one chance in a million, and only one, that was to dive out of the clouds and get a burst into the fighter before he realized what had happened.

They were a good eight or ten miles from the house on the cove now. He leveled off at eleven thousand, thankful it wasn't as heavily overcast as usual, and watched the planes below him.

Suddenly, the Goose seemed to jump in the air. Startled, he looked at his instruments, and then a rolling wave of sound hit him and he jerked his head as if struck, and at the same time the ship rolled heavily.

"Look!" Panola screamed, and following his outthrust arm and finger, they saw a gigantic column of debris lifting toward the sky!

"Somebody opened a door!" Runnels said grimly.

Turk was jolted momentarily, and then suddenly, he saw his chance!

"Hold everything!" he yelled, and swung the ship over into a screaming dive.

The fighter had been jolted, too, and the ships ahead were wavering. In the picture that flashed through his mind, Turk could see their doubt, their hesitation.

Something had happened. What? The bomb at the house had gone up, but how? Why? Would there be enough radioactivity at this distance to affect them? Who among them knew? And what had caused the other explosion? Might this one go, too?

The fighter pilot must have sensed something, or his roving eyes must have caught a glimpse of the plane shooting down on his tail. In a sudden, desperate effort, he pulled his fighter into a climbing turn, and it was the wrong thing.

Turk opened up. Saw his tracers stream into the fighter's tail, saw the pursuit ship fall away, and then banking steeply, he sent a stream of tracer, stabbing at the fighter's vitals like a white hot blade!

There was a sudden puff of smoke, a desperate effort as the fighter flopped over once and fired a final, despairing burst that streamed uselessly off into space. Then it rolled upside down and, sheathed in flame, went screaming away down the thousands of feet toward the crags below.

The other ships must have seen the fighter go, for they split apart at once. One flying north, the other south. With a gleam in his eyes, Turk saw it was the bomber that turned south. "We got 'em," he yelled.

He rolled over and went streaking after the passenger ship. His greater speed brought him up fast, and he could see the other plane fighting desperately to get away.

In that passenger plane would be the men whose knowledge of atomic power could give the militarists of the world a terrible weapon, a weapon to bring chaos to the world. It was like shooting a sitting duck, but he had to do it. His face set and his jaw hard, he opened the Goose up and let it have everything it had left.

Swiftly he overhauled the passenger plane, which dived desperately to escape. It came closer to the hills below, and Turk swung closer. He glanced at the gigantic Dome of St. Paul, coming closer now, and then he did a vertical bank, swung around, and went roaring at the plane!

The pilot was game. He made a desperate effort, and then the probing fingers of Turk's tracer stabbed into his tail assembly. The ship swung off her course, lost altitude, and the pilot tried to bank away from the rounded peak of the Dome. He tried too late. With a terrific crash and a gigantic burst of flame, the passenger plane crashed belly first against the mountainside.

For an instant the flaming wreck clung to the steep side, then it sagged, something gave way, and like a flaming arrow it plunged into the deep canyon below.

Turk shook himself, and his face relaxed a little, then he started climbing.

"Two down," he said aloud, "and one to go!"

He went into a climbing turn. Up, up, up. Far off to the south he could see the plane bearing the atomic bomb, a mere speck against the sky now.

It was an old type plane, with a cruising speed of no more than a hundred and fifty miles per hour. With his ship he could beat that by enough. For the fiftieth time he thanked all the gods that he was lucky enough to have picked up this experimental model with its exceptional speed. He leveled off and opened the ship up.

Runnels had moved up into the copilot's seat. He glanced at Turk, but said nothing. His face was white and strained. Behind him, Turk could hear Panola breathing with deep sighs. Only Shan Bao seemed unchanged, phlegmatic.

As the lean Manchu thrust his head lower for better vision, Turk glimpsed his hawklike yellow face and the gleam in his eye. It was such a face as the Mongol raiders of the khans must have had, the face of a hunter, the face of a fighter. There was in that face no recognition of consequences, only the desperate eagerness to close with the enemy, to fight, to win.

Turk's eyes were cold now. He knew what he had to do. That atomic bomb must go. If his own plane and all in it had to go, the cost would be slightly balanced against the great saving to civilization and the world of people. Yet that sacrifice might not be necessary. He had a plan.

He swung his ship inland for several miles, flying a diagonal course that carried him south and west. The bomber was still holding south, intent only on putting distance between them.

Turk knew what that pilot was thinking. He was thinking of the awful force he carried with him, of what would happen if they were machine-gunned or forced to crash-land. That pilot was afraid. He wanted distance, freedom from fear.

Yet Turk was wondering if the pilot could see what was happening. Did that other flyer guess what was in his mind? And Turk was gaining, slowly, steadily gaining, drawing up on the bomber. It was still a long way ahead. But it was over Canal Ladrillero now, and as Turk moved up to the landward, the bomber followed the canal southwest.

Deliberately, Turk cut his speed back to one hundred and fifty. Runnels glanced at him, puzzled, but Turk held his course, and said nothing. At the last minute, the enemy pilot seemed to realize what was happening and made a desperate effort to change course, but Turk moved up, and the bomber straightened out once again.

There was one thing to watch for. One thing that might get the bomber away. He would think of that soon, Turk realized. And that would be the instant of greatest danger.

"Watch!" he said suddenly, "If he drops that bomb, yell! That's his only chance now."

Runnels jumped suddenly as the idea hit him.

"Why! Why, you're herding him out to sea," he shouted. "You're herding him out there where his bomb won't do any damage!"

"Yeah," Madden nodded grimly, "and where he won't have gas enough to get back."

"What about us?" Panola asked.

"Us?" Turk shrugged. "I think we've got more gas than he has. He wasn't expecting this. We had enough to fly us back to our mother ship. If we have to, we can sit down on the water and last awhile. This is a boat, you know. We could probably last long enough in this sea so that the ship could find us. We'll radio as soon as we get this bomber out far enough."

They were over two hundred miles out, and still herding the bomber before Runnels let out a yell. But Turk had seen the bomber jump and had seen the bomb fall away.

He whipped the ship over into a steep climbing turn and went away from there fast. Even so, the concussion struck them with a terrific blow, and the plane staggered, and then he looked back at the huge column of water mounting into the sky, and then the awful roar as thousands upon thousands of tons of water geysered up and tumbled back into the sea.

Turk banked again, searching for the bomber. It was there, still further out to sea, and Turk turned again and started after him.

"All right, Panola," he said. "In code, call our ship. I hope they survived the wave caused by that bomb."

The bomber was farther out now, and they moved after him, and in a moment, Panola leaned over.

"She's all right. About two hundred miles north and west."

Turk turned the amphibian, keeping the bomber in view, but angling away. "He may reach land," he said over his shoulder. "But if he does he'll crash on the coast of Chile. He'll never make it back to the Argentine!"

Runnels leaned back and ran his finger around inside of his collar.

"For awhile you had me worried," he said grimly. "I thought you were going to tangle with that bomb!"

Turk chuckled. "Not me, buddy! I'm saving this lily white body of mine for the one and only girl!"

"Yeah?" Runnels was skeptical. "And you've got a girl in every port?"

"Nope. I haven't been in every port!"

Tailwind to Tibet

The twin motors of the Grumman muttered their way through the cloud, then pulled the plane into the blue sky beyond. Below, the bare, brown backs of the mountains fell away into the canyons like folds of loose hide. The winding thread of the Yellow River which had pointed their way toward the distant hills had fallen behind. Before them lay only the unknown vastness of the Kuen-Lun Mountains and, beyond, Tibet.

Turk Madden eased forward on the stick and slid down a thousand feet toward the black, thumblike peak on which he had laid his course. Then he banked around it and came in over the black lake.

It was there, just as he remembered it. On the far side the age-old ruins, ancient beyond belief, lay bleak and bare in the late rays of the setting sun. Turk put the ship down gently and taxied toward the crumbling structures, keeping a careful eye out for any of the stone piers that might be under the water.

Shan Bao moved up behind him as he neared the stone platform, weathered and black with age. "We'll tie her up," he told the Manchu. "I want to go ashore."

Sparrow Ryan looked over his shoulder. "Looks older than the mountains!" he exclaimed, staring at the buildings. "Who built these?"

Turk shrugged. "That, my friend, is possibly the ultimate mystery. Nobody knows anything about this part of the world. No competent archeologist has ever worked up here. I've seen Roman ruins that look juvenile compared to these."

When the ship was tied to massive iron rings on either side of the slip, they climbed out. Ryan glanced at Turk. "I'll stay put," he said, "just in case."

Madden nodded and helped lovely film actress Raemy Doone to the dock. Travis Bekart climbed out and stood looking around. There was apprehension in his eyes and a certain watchfulness that Turk didn't like. He was glad the tough little government man was staying behind to keep an eye on things.

The stone platform on which they stood was worn by long ages of wind and water, and it fronted what had once been a magnificent building, over half in ruins now. The architecture was not Chinese but something that predated even the massive monasteries of inner Tibet. The city itself, of which almost a third had been built on stone pilings over the lake, stretched halfway up the sandy hills of the valley.

At the far end of the lake the Thumb Peak pointed a finger at the sky. "I'm glad it's thumbs up!" Turk said, chuckling. "This place is gloomy!"

Their footsteps echoed hollowly on stones no white man had ever trod, and when they spoke they dropped their voices to whispers as though fearful of awakening spirits long dead.

There was no other sound. A stillness of something beyond death lay over the valley. Even the wind found no place to wail or mourn among the ruins or the hollow arches of empty windows. The platform ended in a paved street that ran along the shore behind the first row of buildings, then turned up a gloomy avenue that mounted the hill. A great stone tower had fallen into the street, which was scarcely more than an alley, making a pile of dusty rubble over which they must climb.

Shan Bao slid a long, yellow-fingered hand into the pocket of his leather jacket and drew out a pipe. Raemy glanced at him, seeing the curious expression in his eyes. "These were your people?"

"Who knows? I am a Manchu, and my people are very ancient, but this"—he waved a yellow hand—"this is more ancient. This is older than the Great Wall, older than time. It is perhaps older than the mountains."

Turk stepped to a great stone arch that opened into a vast hall, unbelievable in its height and impressive expanse. They walked inside, a tiny knot of humanity lost beneath a dome so huge as to make them stare, unbelieving.

"Who would ever dream there were such places as this!" Raemy exclaimed. "It's so strange, and so beautiful!"

"Beautiful?" Bekart stared about him distastefully. "It's gloomy as a cavern."

They walked out into the darkening street. A bat dipped toward Turk's head, and, involuntarily, he glanced up.

Beyond the rooftops and on the ridge that enclosed the valley was a small group of horsemen. They were at least a half mile away but clearly visible in the last rays of the sun.

Raemy caught Madden's arm. "Who are they?"

"Can't say," Turk murmured, scowling. "They might be Lolos. We'll get back to the ship. Bekart, you go on ahead with Miss Doone. I'll hang back with Shan Bao as they may come up on us."

"I want to see them!" Raemy protested, lifting her chin defiantly.

Turk grinned. "You'd better go, honey chile. You'd be worth fifty camels up here!"

"I'll stay," she said. "I want to see them!"

Turk barely glanced around, his eyes level and hard. "You'll go," he said, "now!"

"Let's not use that tone, Madden!" Bekart said savagely. "I'll not have it!"

Madden's eyes shifted to Bekart. "You go with her," he said coolly, "and get moving!" His eyes went back to the actress. "Take him along," he said.

Their eyes held. Horses' hoofs sounded on stone. She turned abruptly then. "We'd better go, Travis," she said. "He's right, of course!"

A DOZEN HORSEMEN were riding toward them, loping nearer on their ragged, long-haired Mongolian ponies. When they were almost up to them they reined in, and their leader, a tall, fierce-looking man with greasy black hair, shouted speech strange to Madden's ears.

Shan replied. After attempting several dialects he made himself understood. "He wants to know what we do here," Shan said. "I told him we rest awhile."

"Ask him what he knows of the great mountain, Amne Machin."

Shan spoke, and the big man's face became a mask of incredulity. There was excited talk among the horsemen, then the big man spoke excitedly to Shan, shaking his head many times.

Shan looked at Turk. "He says you cannot go there. That is Ngolok country, and they are very bad men with a queen who is a wicked and evil woman. She has many slaves, some of them his own people."

"Tell him we search for a man who crashed in a plane. Ask him if he knows of any white men up this way."

After some excited talk, Shan Bao turned back to Turk. "He says once long ago a big bird landed back in the Ngolok country. He has seen it, but it is not broken. He said there was another bird, not so fat in the belly as ours, that flew near here yesterday."

"Sounds like a fighter," Madden speculated. "Who would have a fighter up here?"

Shan talked some more, and the leader got down from his pony and came forward. Squatting on his haunches he drew a rough map in the sand, pointing out the mountain peaks, then drew a line for a valley. He put his finger on one spot. "The plane is there," Shan Bao interpreted. "That line is a deep valley, and very, very rich. Caravans come from and go there from Sinkiang, Urumchi."

Turk Madden drew a flashlight from his pocket. There were several in the plane. He flashed the light on and off, then handed it to the chief. The man got to his feet to accept the gift, then bowed very low.

"He says any enemy of the Ngoloks is a friend, but he thanks you," Shan advised.

As the horsemen rode away, Turk led the way back to the ship. "We'll stay here tonight," he said. "I think the place he mentioned isn't more than sixty miles away."

Ryan was waiting for them on the dock with Bekart and Raemy.

"Miss Doone," Madden said, turning to the girl, "your trip may not be a wild goose chase. A ship like the one we're looking for came down safely about sixty miles from here."

"Turk!" Raemy's eyes flashed with joy as she caught him by the sleeves of his jacket with both her hands. "Do you mean it? Is it true?"

"Take it easy," Madden advised. "He might have been killed in the landing, anyway. We only know what this native said, and he was never close to the ship. If he's alive and enslaved to the Ngoloks, we'll have a rough time freeing him."

"Oh, if he's only *alive!*"

Turk's eyes lifted from hers to Bekart's and he was shocked. The former Army flyer's face was dead white, the bones seeming to stand out tight and hard against the tautened skin. His eyes were narrowed and ugly.

Gently, Madden stepped away from the girl. Was Bekart so affected because the girl had grabbed him in her excitement? Or was he afraid that Captain Bob Doone might still be alive?

While the others were busy preparing for night, Ryan walked over to Turk. "What do you think of Bekart?" Madden asked him.

Sparrow Ryan kicked a stone. "Haven't got him figured," he said. "Like I told you in Hollywood before we left, the government checked him thoroughly. His war record is good. Before the war he was an advertising man, before that a number of things. He seems to like the company of wealthy women, but who doesn't?"

"Notice his face when I mentioned the plane was intact?"

"Uh-huh, I did. That hit him right where he lives, Turk, and I'm wondering why. He flew the wingman for Doone, and nobody ever knew what happened but him."

Could Bekart secretly be in the pay of the people who wanted the Pharo counter? Certainly, this improvement in the Geiger counter which had been the sole cargo of the missing plane was infinitely valuable to a number of countries.

MADDEN RECALLED Ryan's words of a few days before. "It's a new gadget. Yank flyer in India dreamed it up. He'd been working in a laboratory where they had to keep testing for radiation. The device for that's a Geiger counter. This guy dreams up a new angle on it, a much more sensitive tube, just the sort of thing that would be ideal for locating secret atomic plants. This Pharo counter is much more sensitive and has a directional device so they can pin down the location of the disturbance within a matter of miles.

"This guy in India," Ryan had said, "had access to the materiel and built a model, but then he was murdered. However, they put the gadget in this steel box and started it for the States over the Hump. They were flying it to Chungking, then Japan, then home. But the plane crashed."

Had that been the reason for the crash? Madden doubted it, and so did the authorities in Washington. The crash had been in the wrong place, almost impossible of access. Three times, under cover of other excuses, the Army had tried to find the plane and failed. Then when they discovered that Raemy Doone, the film star, was financing her own expedition to search for her brother, who had piloted the ship, they had slipped their man, Ryan, into the personnel for the flight. Madden's eyes searched the shadowy line of the hills, and beyond them the mighty, ice-capped peaks and shoulders of the mysterious Kuen-Luns and the towering majesty of the world's mightiest mountain, Amne Machin.

Travis Bekart was utterly ruthless. He was the sort of man who got what he wanted, regardless of price. The cold, bleak fury in his eyes a few minutes ago had not been the look of a man in love and engaged to the beauteous Raemy Doone. It had been the expression of a man thwarted who meant to do something about it.

Then Turk Madden stiffened. Sparrow Ryan, who had started toward him, stopped dead still, his mouth open.

For from the distance over the hills came the mutter of a rapidly approaching plane! A drone that mounted and mounted until suddenly, with a gasp of night air, it swept by, low over the hills! It was a single-engine fighter.

"Think he saw us?" Ryan speculated apprehensively.

"No telling. We'd better figure that he did. Get out that B.A.R. If he comes back and asks for it, he can get it."

The plane did not return, and at daylight Turk Madden rolled from his blankets into a crisp, chill dawn. Gathering a few sticks he built a small fire against a stone wall.

The rest of them crawled from the plane, Sparrow with a gun on his hip, and Shan Bao with his ever-present rifle. Standing it nearby he began to prepare breakfast. Turk's gun, as always, was in his shoulder holster.

Bekart's face looked drawn and worried. "Madden!" he burst out suddenly. "I've come this far without complaint! But this is madness! Sheer, unadulterated madness! This place is ghastly, and who knows what horrors we may run into up close to that mountain? I've heard of the awful chamber of horrors in Samyas monastery in Tibet, and compared to these Ngoloks the people of Tibet are civilized! I insist we turn back!"

"How can you talk that way, Travis?" Raemy protested. "Why, would you want me to waste all I've spent? All my hopes and Madden's time? I wouldn't think of turning back!"

"I insist!" Bekart replied stiffly. "I love you and I can't have the woman I love subjected to such risks! This journey was madness in the first place! With what we know now it is worse than madness!"

"You mean," Ryan interrupted suddenly, "because we now know that Doone landed in one piece?"

Bekart's face whitened and his eyes glittered, but he did not reply, only continued his tirade. "What kind of plane was that, that flew over us last night? I know every plane that flies, and I never saw such a ship before! What would a fighter be doing here, of all places? We've been warned about these people, and every step is nearer to awful death or slavery!"

Turk Madden glanced up. "You knew all that when you came," he said coldly. "We all did. As it happens, neither you nor Miss Doone has anything to say about the further progress of this trip.

"It is true," he added, smiling at Raemy's surprised look, "that she financed this trip to find her brother. That's still our purpose, but we have another. Ryan is a government man. We're after a steel box that was Doone's cargo in the lost plane. That box is of enormous importance, so let's hear no more about it. The trip continues.

"As for Bob Doone," Madden added, "if he is alive, we'll find him. If he is dead, we shall find his grave. Also"—he glanced up, his eyes bland— "I wish to examine Doone's ship to see what happened to it."

Travis Bekart's eyes sparkled dangerously. "What are you implying?" he demanded.

"I?" Turk raised astonished brows. "Why, nothing! Only that's the usual course when a crashed plane is found. We must find the cause of accidents to prevent future trouble. What else would I imply?"

Raemy Doone stared searchingly at Bekart, and there was a cold and curious light in her eyes. Raemy, Turk decided, was an astute young woman.

DARK WATER ROLLED back from the ship. Turk gunned the amphibian and it lifted, the water of the black lake dropping away below. He came back slowly on the stick, skimming over the ridge and lifting the ship toward the gray clouds. In the distance, its mighty granite shoulders lost in crowding gray cumulus, was the icy mass of Amne Machin, the mountain that was a god.

Turk glanced at the altimeter. "I'm going up," he said. "We'll just have a look." They adjusted their oxygen masks and climbed. Clouds came and fell away. They skimmed an ugly ridge, soared past a glacier-created peak, and climbed on. The towering peak of Amne Machin still hung over them.

"Going on up?" Ryan gestured with his thumb.

Madden shook his head affirmatively. Later, when they had descended to a lower level again, he glanced over at Ryan. "Want my guess? I'd say that peak wasn't an inch under thirty-one thousand feet, about two thousand higher than Mount Everest! Joe Rock, one of the two white men who ever got within seventy-five miles, estimated it to be over twenty-eight thousand, but he was conservative. Some of the war flyers figured it to be over thirty-three thousand!"

"Gives me chills to look at it!" Ryan said. "Now where's this plane we're lookin' for?"

"On a plateau. We should be there in a few minutes." The Grumman slid down through scattered clouds and skimmed over a dark forest. Far below them something dark moved on the stone-covered field and vanished under the trees with a queer, bobbing run.

"What was *that*?" Raemy demanded, over Madden's shoulder.

He shrugged. "Nothing I ever saw before. There are rumors of queer animals, animals never before seen."

"Not even in Hollywood?" Raemy was grinning.

"We're not speaking of varieties of wolves," Turk said. "But only in the last few months they have been finding new animals in the Congo. A new type of rhino, a wild boar. Who knows what they'll find up here."

She gestured at the country below. "How much of this is unknown country?"

Madden shrugged. "Probably a chunk as big as Arizona. Tibet itself is just a shade less than the combined areas of Arizona, California, and Nevada. The population is estimated to be about the same as California's."

"Look, Turk!" Ryan exclaimed. "There's the plane!"

"*Stop!*" The voice was cold and deadly calm. "Fly back to the lake where we stopped last night, and start right now!"

Rigid, Turk Madden looked up. Travis Bekart, a .45 Colt in his hand, was crouching behind them. "Put this ship down," he said, "and I'll kill you!"

Madden's eyes were quiet, calculating swiftly. His quick glance had assured him that Bekart had slipped into a chute harness. If he shot, he would bail out immediately.

"Why, sure!" Turk said. "If you feel that way!" Then, instantly, he snapped into a vertical bank. Hurled from his position, Bekart's head slammed into the corner of a seat and he collapsed.

Turk glanced at him and watched Shan take the gun from the fellow's hand, then bind them securely. Raemy watched, her eyes wide and strange.

"What got into him?" Sparrow asked, speaking to nobody in particular.

"I think," Turk said as he skimmed back over the plane below, "that he would rather we didn't see this ship! It makes me kind of curious!"

He banked slightly and studied the plateau thoughtfully. "What do you think, Ryan?"

"I think she looks okay. Put her down. After all, Columbus took a chance!"

"Cross your fingers then!" Turk swung around into the wind and came in for a landing. He knew he wasn't going to like it, but here they were.

As they swooped down, Ryan suddenly touched him on the shoulder. "Pick her up," he said, "there's a lake in that hollow!"

Turk shot past the plateau and circled wide over the valley. Sparrow was right. There was another black lake, almost identical with the one seen previously, and here, too, there were ruined buildings, but here they surrounded the lake on three sides. The lake was scarcely more than a mile from the plane on the plateau.

Turk Madden slid down, leveled off, and came in fast, skimming the water lightly. He brushed the low waves, brushed them lightly again, and then the ship took the water smoothly and he taxied in toward another lonely, lost, and ruined town.

"This country," Ryan said, "must have been quite a place at one time!"

Madden nodded. "Hear about that pyramid they found in Shensi? Over fifteen hundred feet high. The biggest one in Egypt is only a third of that height, and about a third of the baseline. Nobody knows anything about it. Hell, they'll find there was civilization in China six thousand years ago before they are through!

"There's been almost no excavation there, and none in Shensi. All we know of Chinese civilization is what we can see and read, and that's old enough. Somebody should do some excavating in Central Asia, and in extreme western China.

"Nobody knows much about Tibet above ground, or Sinkiang, or Turkestan, so how can they figure on the ancient history?"

When the ship was anchored, Turk got out on a pier and took a rifle with him. "I'll take Shan Bao and Miss Doone," he said. "Stick with the ship, Sparrow. Later, we'll leave Shan an' you an' me will have a look-see. Okay?"

Ryan nodded. Bekart was coming out of it. "Lie still, sweetheart," Ryan said, "or that slap you got on the noggin will seem like a love tap." He looked up at Turk. "Think I'll interrogate this guy. Maybe he'll talk."

"Better wait until we see this ship," Madden advised. "I've got an idea."

He paused when they reached the shore. Rows of ancient buildings of time-blackened stones lined the water's edge. Here, too, some of them were built on stone pilings over the water, evidently as a means of defense. But the city had outgrown what was evidently merely a beginning and had gone ashore, and crawled slowly around the lake. Two mountain streams flowed into the lake, which had only a very narrow visible outlet to the south.

The sky was gray and unbroken by any rift in the clouds. The air was damp, and there was a faint, musty smell. Their footsteps echoed hollowly so Turk was glad when they emerged from the age-blackened walls and started up the scarred slope of the hill.

The bomber lay on its belly some fifty yards away, a dark spot on the white snow. No landing gear was down, but wings and props were intact. Turk glanced at Raemy. "I'd better look first," he suggested.

Her eyes flickered, frightened. "Please. Would you?"

His feet crunched on the thin snow. Here and there the wind had revealed the black rock and gravel surface of the plateau. No vegetation could be seen. The ship looked lost and alone, and his heart began to pound as he drew near. He turned as his hand touched the door and glanced back.

Raemy stood on the snow, a silent, lonely figure. She was tall and stood well up to him when they were together, but now she looked forlorn and very small. "Look!" Shan pointed.

Turk's eyes followed the gloved finger. The cowl of the nearest engine was bullet-riddled. He felt his scalp tighten, and his eyes swept the fallen ship. Left motor shot out, tail assembly shot to shreds. The guy had performed a minor miracle to get down in one piece.

He pulled the door open. It came so easily he almost lost his balance. He peered within. It was dark and empty, with the chill of something long lifeless.

It had been looted of everything portable. If the crew had been alive when they landed, they were gone now. Perhaps to death or captivity. The steel box was missing, and there were dark stains on the instrument panel, the altimeter smashed by a bullet.

Raemy was walking toward the ship. Madden shook his head at her. "No sign of anybody, but the ship was shot down."

"*Shot* down?" Her eyes questioned him. "By the Japanese?"

"There were no Japanese in this area. It must have been someone else."

Her face looked old and tired. She kicked her toe into the crusted snow. "Travis?" she asked. "He flew as fighter escort—"

"Who knows? He acted strange, but it could be something else."

"Are ... any of them—"

"No." He took her by the arm. "Want to look? I think the copilot was hurt. There's some blood."

Shan Bao muttered, and Turk turned. Shan was pointing at a crude cairn of stones. Raemy stumbled toward it, and they followed. Turk's face was somber, yet when he saw the name he felt a wave of relief go over him. Scratched crudely on a stone slab atop the cairn were the words:

WILLIAM A. LYTE, LIEUT., A.A.F.
KILLED OCTOBER 9, 19

The date was incomplete. "Interrupted," Turk said, "by somebody, or something. Lyte was the copilot."

"I should be sorry," Raemy said, "but somehow I can only be glad it isn't Bob."

When they returned to the lake Ryan was waiting. "Found a building that's intact," he said, "a good hideout."

"We'll make this our base," Madden said. "From here on we work on the ground all we can. Save gas and attract less attention. Shan can remain with the ship. We'll go, Ryan."

"And I," Raemy told him.

Madden hesitated. Then he shrugged, smiling at her. "All right, but you're inviting the risk and will have to take the consequences. From here on it will be very dangerous."

"I know."

She spoke quietly and seriously, and Turk looked at her again and was convinced. Ryan walked back inside, and Raemy stood there beside Madden, staring out over the lake.

"Madden," she asked suddenly, "how do you suppose he was shot down?"

Turk hesitated. "There's no answer to that. We've seen one or maybe more planes. Bekart said he couldn't identify the one he saw. Well, I couldn't either. They may have shot your brother down."

Raemy looked at him. "If you think anything else, tell me."

"It's only a hunch, and I've no motive to ascribe."

"You mean Travis?" She looked at Turk seriously.

"Well, it does seem strange, I think, that he should do everything to keep us from landing. Almost as if he knew what we would find."

"Yes, I thought of that. But why would he do it?"

That made Turk hesitate. Raemy and her brother were both wealthy. With Bob Doone dead, all the wealth was hers. Then, if she should marry, and if after awhile she died . . .

"I've no idea," Turk replied.

DAWN FOUND THEM, each carrying a rucksack and rifle, heading down the vague and ancient trail that led through the ruined city. Turk walked in the lead, followed by Raemy. Behind her was Sparrow Ryan.

The light was cold and gray, and the path mounted, skirting the side of the mountain, weaving along through canyons and up steep mountainsides. With every mile the way became steeper and the terrain more rugged. Once they heard a plane and hid, waiting until the sound died away. It was below the clouds from the sound, but it did not fly over them.

Ahead of them the canyon ended suddenly in a wide pool enclosed by a grove of willows and poplar. Beyond the grove green grass waved in a wide field!

They halted under the trees. Before them lay a long and very deep canyon at the end of which loomed the massive towers of an ancient monastery, or what appeared to be such. Nearby, several men worked over an irrigation ditch.

The monastery occupied the whole end of the valley, and buildings were constructed halfway up the steep sides at that end. Suddenly a man on horseback rode from the trees on the far side and neared the workers. He shouted angrily at one, and as the man straightened to reply the horseman felled him with a blow from the butt of a whip.

"Rough, isn't he?" Ryan whispered.

"Wait! One of the men is coming this way."

One of the workmen, carrying a crude wooden shovel, walked slowly toward them. Turk's eyes narrowed. "A white man! If that's your brother," he whispered to Raemy, "don't run out there! Everything depends on care now."

The man plodded to a sluice gate and lifted it to let water into a ditch. As he leaned over, Turk spoke. "Don't look up. If you know English, nod your head."

The man jerked as if shot at the sound of Turk's voice. He rested his hands on the gate, then he nodded.

"Are you from the American plane on the plateau?"

"Russky," he said. His voice carried over the few yards of water. "Nine Yanks here. Three from that plane."

Raemy repressed a gasp and Turk's grip shut down hard on her arm. "You are prisoners?"

"Slaves. There are many of us. Most are Chinese. Can you help us?"

"Yes, but be careful! You work here every day?"

"Today and tomorrow. After tomorrow in a valley six miles east. There will be thirty white men."

The horseman had turned and was watching the man at the gate. "Don't take chances. Is the American named Doone with you?"

"Young is here. Doone is at the Domed House. I will see him tonight in prison."

"Tell him we have come for him. Tell him we'll find a way to help. Can we talk to one in command here?"

"No!" he said violently. "That would be fatal! She is a fiend!"

The horseman had started toward them, but was still some way off. "What are the planes?"

"There are five of them, three fighters and two transports. Be careful, I go." The man closed the gate and shouldered his shovel.

Turk drew back and they retreated into the canyon. "You heard," he said briefly. "Your brother's alive. We've no idea what shape he's in. If they've a valley like that, with so many slaves, they must have a considerable force themselves."

"But planes?" Ryan protested. "This is fantastic!"

"Why? Some of them undoubtedly learned to fly with the Chinese. Some of the flyers might be Chinese who joined them."

"How could anyone dream of such a place?" Raemy exclaimed.

"We've known for years," Turk said, "that Tibet had monasteries full of warlike monks. We've known that the Lolo tribesmen kept slaves, and not long ago the Army sent men among them to search for American flyers. But if any were held as slaves you can be sure they were well hidden before the Army men got there! These Ngoloks are infinitely worse than the Lolos!"

Shan Bao met them at the landing. He spoke to Madden in Mandarin.

"You take it easy," Turk said. "Shan wants to show me something."

Shan led the way to a temple built partly over the water. Part of the wall on the lakeward side was missing, and inside almost half the space was water. Evidently from the iron rings, boats had once been kept there. It was a perfect hangar for the amphibian, even to a ramp leading into the water.

When the ship was concealed, Turk turned to Ryan. "Tomorrow you and I hit that valley!" He glanced at Raemy. "This time you stay here. Some of this won't be pretty to watch!"

She started to protest, but when her eyes locked with his she was still. In the morning when the two started off at daybreak, she looked at him. "Be careful won't you?"

"Of Bob? Don't worry, he'll be all right."

"I mean you!" she said, her chin lifting.

Turk looked around at her and she flushed. "Yeah," he said, "I'll be careful!"

FOR AN HOUR they watched the valley. Thirty-two prisoners worked there, guarded by seven men. All were armed, four of them with rifles.

"The first one will be that guard in the green coat," Turk said. "I'll take him."

The guard was a big man, and he looked rugged. He moved toward the edge of the brush, and like a wraith, Turk rose behind him. He struck the guard on the small of the back with his right fist, shooting the midsection of his body forward as his left forearm slid across the guard's throat. Off balance by the blow to the base of the spine, the guard was pulled back sharply. Then Turk's right arm slipped under the guard's right armpit and his hand clasped the back of the guard's head. With his left hand Turk grabbed his own right forearm. Then he jerked back with his left forearm and pushed with his right hand.

The guard struggled, kicked, and tried to claw madly at Turk's iron grip, but the pressure on his windpipe was too great. Turk held the pressure for a full minute while Ryan watched the other guards.

The nearest worker had noticed but continued with his labors. Then he moved toward them. "Good show, Yank!" he said. "We're all primed and ready!" He picked up the fallen man's rifle, and extracted the ugly knife from the guard's waistband.

Quickly, he donned the green coat and coolie hat, then started along the line of workmen, whispering in a low voice. One of the other guards sauntered toward him, and as he neared, the Australian wheeled suddenly and slashed with the knife. The guard fell, blood gushing from his slit throat.

The Aussie gave a low whistle, and like a cloud the prisoners wheeled and closed over the remaining guards. The man on the horse who had been riding toward Turk's waiting place grabbed at his pistol, but Ryan darted from his hiding place and leaped astride of the horse behind him. Together they tumbled from the horse, Ryan on top. He chopped viciously with the barrel of his own pistol, then again.

Ryan got up, wiping sweat from his face. He walked toward the guard Madden had jumped. He glanced at the guard, then up at Madden. "You're thorough!" he said grimly.

The prisoners crowded around. A tall blond man pushed forward. "I'm Young," he said. "I was in the ship with Doone. They've got him up in the Domed House, questioning him about our cargo. Some strange white man came to the Domed House a while back, and ever since then they've been in a dither."

"We'll get out of here fast. Those with the rifles fall behind for a rear guard. Ryan, you lead off."

Young, who had the pistol from the fallen horseman, walked beside Madden. "God, man!" he said. "You can't guess what it meant to us when we heard you were here. Kalinov told us last night." Young glanced at Turk. "That cargo of ours seems to excite a lot of people!"

"Ryan's here for that reason," Turk said. "I've my instructions, too. We've got to get that steel box for our government."

Young shrugged. "Doone's the only one knows where it is."

"Give me the dope," Madden suggested. "What can we expect?"

"There's at least three thousand men in this monastery. Probably around three hundred modern rifles including twenty or thirty Tokarev semi-automatic rifles. It's as good a gun as our Garand. Also, they have some Degtyarov light machine guns, all stolen or smuggled out of Russia by agents of these people. The Domed House, which you can identify by shape, is the heart of the place. I've told you about the planes. The pilots are Ngoloks.

"They have two flying fields and a couple of emergency fields with a fighter plane located at each. They've a leader with brains named Bo Hau. He's been to China and India and has an education of a sort. Tall, big-shouldered fellow."

No part of the situation looked good. Only a few of the escaped men were armed, and there was little food available. They could expect determined pursuit within a few hours. Turk fell in beside Ryan. "You stick by the ship with the man with the pistol, I'll take the four men with rifles."

"Why not take the plane and knock off one of those emergency fields? Then we'd have rifles and ammunition?"

"And run into a fighter? With this ship of mine? A pursuit ship would fly circles around me! Unless we hit 'em before they got off the ground. Strafe the field—but it would be taking an awful chance!"

"The whole thing is a gamble," Ryan said. "Don't worry about Raemy! That gal has nerve!"

Turk turned to a huge red-bearded Scotsman. "You know where the emergency fields are located?"

"Helped build them! One's about nine miles east in the mountains. Concealed, but impossible to use in bad weather."

"How long to get to it on foot?"

"Three or four hours, if we're lucky. It's pretty rough going."

"All right," Madden told them. "I'll keep Young with me. You," he told the Scotsman, "will lead this party. I'll give you four hours. Your job is to keep that fighter on the ground. Don't damage it if you can help it, and shoot anybody who tries to get it off the ground."

Young watched the rescued prisoners as they turned off into a canyon leading to the mountains. "They've got a mighty slim chance!" he said.

Turk nodded. "So have we all. Four men with rifles can make life miserable around any landing field. Knowing the country they have a good chance of getting away with it. The Ngoloks won't expect them to head that way." He turned toward Young. "We have one prisoner, your former escort pilot!"

Young's face went cold. "He shot us down! Never gave us a chance!"

"Why?"

"We never figured that out," Young admitted. "He'd been very friendly to Doone."

"Doone ever mention that Bekart had met his sister?"

"Come to think of it, Bekart was with him on leave once."

"With Bob dead, she'd inherit everything. That may have been it. He could go back, be the sympathetic friend, marry the gal, and then—"

"Ugly mess!" Young stared at the peaks. "Lyte was shot right through the chest. Three-fifties!"

There was no sign of Shan Bao as they drew near the ruined city. Nor any other sign of life and movement. Fear mounting like a tide in his throat, Turk started forward when Shan burst from a building. "He's gone! I go to hunt for wood, and he got away!"

Turk grabbed Shan's arm. "Raemy?"

"She gone, too! Also, her gun!"

Turk rushed to the plane. So far as he could see, nothing was disturbed. "Go over it, Shan! Quick!"

He looked at Sparrow. "We'd better have a look. Maybe we can catch them before they've gone far."

"No use!" Shan Bao protested. "They gone maybe two hours!"

Turk Madden's face was cold and ugly. Despite Shan's protest, he turned and, helped by Young and Ryan, made a careful survey of all the ruined buildings. There was no sign of life, nor could any tracks be found on the pavement or hard ground.

He had failed thus far to free Bob Doone. The steel box was still in the hands of the Ngoloks, or hidden somewhere. And now Raemy had been taken from him.

When they returned from their trek, Madden checked his watch. An hour to go before they took off. Ryan dug into the food and got out some crackers and cheese while Shan made coffee. In silence, the four men ate.

Turk got up finally and walked outside. He looked big and grim in his worn leather jacket, his head bared to the chill wind, his eyes hard as they studied the gray, barren sky. He turned and came back in, checking his .45 grimly.

"Warm her up, Shan, we'll start now!" He looked around again, then glanced at Young. "Better have a look outside. Watch until I call you."

Minutes later he called Young, then followed Ryan into the ship, they taxied out on the lake, and he revved her up and then started her down the dark water. The motors roared beautifully, and he gave her plenty of time for the air was cold and light. As he eased back on the stick she lifted gently, slapped a wave, and lifted toward the rocky crest of one of the hills skirting the lake.

Turk shot straight away from the lake, climbing steadily. At five thousand he swung in a wide curve and headed back. Then he lifted higher, and higher. Far below and off to his left he could see a tip of the green valley. Young waved him further to the right and he banked the ship and headed for a tall, ice-capped spire of black rock almost due west.

Suddenly, he saw the field. It was on a small plateau, and at one end there was a stone hangar and a smaller building nearby. As he pushed forward on the stick and shot down toward the field he saw men burst from the smaller building and one of them rushed toward the hangar, others lifted rifles and although they must have been firing, he heard no sound of the shooting.

The man running toward the hangar suddenly stumbled and fell headlong and lay there, a dark spot on the pavement near his head. Then Turk opened up and the harsh yammer of his own guns blotted out sound and he saw men fold and go down as if blown by a powerful wind.

He dove toward the smaller building and the men with rifles and saw men scatter in every direction, and then he was over the building and zooming up to swing back over the field. Men had scattered into the brush, but he came down fast and let go with another burst at the smaller building.

When he came around for another pass he saw men running out on the plateau waving their arms at him. He skimmed by overhead, then swung around and came in for a landing.

As HE GOT OUT, he saw men pouring into the smaller building and coming out with rifles. Scotty met him, a broad grin on his face. "We got nine of them, all told. One man got away, but several of ours are after him."

"How about weapons?" Turk demanded quickly.

Young had started on a trot for the hangar.

"There's twelve more rifles," Scotty said, "as nearly as we could figure. We'll know in a minute."

Turk walked toward the hangar after Young. In a few minutes they had the news. Of the thirty men they had in all, aside from his own crew, sixteen of them now had rifles and eight more had pistols. The others had found old iron swords and one a pike.

Turk walked into the hangar, and Young was standing there looking at the ship. Young nodded at it. "Ever see anything like *that*?" he demanded.

"Yeah," Turk walked around it thoughtfully. "Looks like an improved version of a Russian ship they had in Spain during the Civil War. Some of the Russians who fought with the Loyalists flew them."

Scotty came in with the escaped prisoner. "What happens now?" Scotty demanded.

"We get out of here," Turk said, "and quick. We've got a lot to do. At least, Ryan and I have. And we're taking this ship!"

Young's brow furrowed. "I fly a little, but I never tackled anything that looked that hot!"

Madden shrugged. "I'll fly it. Shan Bao knows my ship. You can go back to the lake with him. He could take four or five of you."

"We'll march it," Scotty said, "all of us!" He grinned at Turk. "We might run into a bunch of those 'Loks, and the boys are spoilin' for a fight!"

Turk checked the ship himself. There was plenty of gas, and he found a buried tank near the hangar that was almost full. He yelled at Shan, and the Manchu refueled the Grumman.

When they had gone, he walked outside. The ship had been wheeled out before they left, and he had taken a few minutes to look around. He hadn't wanted to tell them, but he knew what he was going to do. He was going hunting for that other pursuit ship. From what he knew of the fighter he had, he knew she was a plenty hot ship. Also, he was going to teach them a lesson or two. They had it coming.

He walked outside and got into the fighter. He warmed her up. She was a two-motored job, bearing a resemblance to the Russian pursuits he had seen in Spain. What did they call them? He scowled, trying to re-member. Masca—Mosca, something like that.

The motors purred evenly and smoothly. Carefully, he opened her up a little, and the ship trembled with the burst of added power. Turk passed his tongue over his lips. "Here goes everything!" he said softly, and, his eyes widened a little, he started the ship down the plateau.

It gathered speed and he opened the throttle wider. The black cliffs faded in a roar of thundering speed. He felt the lift of the ship as it reached for the air and he came back on the stick and felt the earth fall away beneath him. He eased back further, and the little fighter began to climb.

His eyes were bright. "Whoever built this baby," he said, "knew what he was doing."

Roaring with power the ship shot skyward like an angry hawk, and deftly he put her through her paces. She had it—speed, power, maneu-verability. He swung her around, and headed between two gigantic peaks and darted through to see the green valley far, far below him, and even as he glimpsed it, he saw the Grumman far away to the east and north, and sweeping down toward it was the other pursuit ship!

Turk banked his fighter steeply and whipped around to dart after the other ship like a sparrow hawk after a hen! His twin motors roaring, his heart singing with the lust for battle, he cleared his guns with a burst and then swept down on the other fighter.

It was no P-40 or anything like it, but almost a duplicate of his own ship, and some sixth sense must have warned the pilot, for he suddenly pulled up sharply and swung around, wondering at the actions of his companion fighter. Turk cured him of his wonder in a quick burst as the fighter swung past his guns. It was ineffective, to all appearances, except to warn the enemy fighter that he was in for trouble.

The other ship made a flat turn and started for him, but flying fight-ers was an old story to Turk Madden. He had flown almost every kind of ship in the air. Yet the enemy pilot had been trained well, and he handled his ship like it was part of him.

"Okay, bud," Turk said, "you want to play!" He gave the ship everything she had and started for the other fighter, head on. For what seemed minutes they rushed down at each other, yet Turk knew it was only a fleeting instant, then, suddenly, the other pilot broke and hauled back on the stick. The nose of the plane went up, and he went up and over in a wild, desperate effort to escape what seemed fiery and certain death in a head-on collision. And in the fleeting instant when his underside was exposed, Madden poured a darting stream of fire into the other ship!

He banked steeply and swung away, then circled and started back, but the enemy fighter, smoke pouring from it, was headed for the mountains, far below. Even as he watched, the smoke turned to a sudden, crimson burst of flame—and then where the ship had been there was only a puff of smoke and a few disintegrating fragments.

A hand fumbled for his brow and he wiped away the sweat. Then he headed down and south for the lake. He would be able to land beside Doone's wrecked transport. The plateau was long enough, and from what he knew of it from his visit to the wrecked ship, it was good enough for a landing. Getting off again might be quite a problem. If he ever tried.

The Goose was down on the lake when he circled over and dipped his wings, then he darted away, headed into the wind, and eased the fighter to a landing on the plateau, taxiing to a place close beside the transport.

Scotty and Young were there to greet him as he started down the hills. "Get him?" Young demanded eagerly.

"Yeah." Turk mopped his brow and grinned at them. "I hope there's no more of them!"

He glanced from one to the other. "Either of you ever been in that Domed House?"

"I have," Young said. "Don't know much about it, though."

"I'm going in there," Madden said. "I've a hunch that's where Bekart went and where he took Raemy. We've got to get her back, get Doone, and get that steel box. And it's got to be done fast, commando stuff."

"You can count me in," Scotty said.

Madden shook his head. "No. I'll take Shan Bao because he talks this stuff a little. I'll take Ryan because he's small, tough, and it's his job, anyway. And Young here because he knows something about it, about the Domed House, I mean."

When the last straggler had come in and the rescued prisoners were gathered around, eating and drinking coffee, Turk Madden began going through them, one by one. Each man talked, through interpreters when necessary, telling what he knew of the Domed House, the guard system, the valley itself, the discipline and the probable location of Raemy and Bekart, if prisoners.

The guard was relieved every hour at the temple, and a sharp watch was kept for any movement to attack them. It was dusk when Turk gathered his little group around him.

"Understand this much," he said briefly, "these men are our enemies. They have held American flyers as slaves, they have killed some, tortured others. We must rescue Bob Doone and his sister. We needn't worry about Bekart. He should be punished, but we have enough to do without that. Let's go!"

DARK AND COLD LAY THE VALLEY under a high-riding moon when the four men reached the icy rim and looked down. The descent to which Young had led them was at the upper end of the long, deep canyon. Far below them, chill and mysterious in the moonlight, lay the towers and rooftops of the monastery and village. Among them all, at the highest level, was the huge dome of the Domed House.

The air was crisp and still. The rattle of a stone sounded loud in the clear, sharp air. Turk rubbed his fingers against the chill and scanned the town below with a practiced, soldier's eye. Young moved up beside him. "So far as I know, nobody's ever tried it from here. It's desperately steep, but working down there on a wall, once, I noticed what seemed to be a path up here. That's our only chance."

"We've got ropes if the wall runs close enough, or if the path doesn't lead all the way around."

"The guards are nearly giants," Young warned. "Big men, and powerfully muscled."

From below came eerie sounds, the strange music drifted to them, then a chanting voice lifted momentarily, high and shrill, yet barely audible where they stood. Uneasily, Shan Bao shifted his feet. Turk's feet felt for the path.

It was actually merely a ledge, only inches wide, where a lower stratum of rock had thrust out and weathering had still to chafe it away.

Turk edged along the rocky lip, his mouth dry. Were they visible from below? He thought not, yet he seemed naked, exposed, helpless. A foot edged out, felt carefully, then his weight shifted, for an instant his hands gripped until his foot was sure, then he moved along.

Hours seemed to pass. Sweat popped out on his face and dried away. The ledge zigged to a lower ledge, which zagged away into darkness under an overhang. They felt their way through the ominous darkness, and found, finally, a place where a spring trickled water into a deep crevice. It seemed a good route, and they followed it.

Darkness closed around them. Turk felt his way, then suddenly, warned by falling water, he stopped. It was well he did, for when he put his foot out it encountered empty space. With a pencil flash, he studied the drop. It fell away far below the reach of the finger of light. He drew back, studying the rocky walls. Finally, he found a way that seemed possible. Then they were on a level again.

Turk had not begun to consider escape. He knew that a wise man never enters any hole or any place of danger without first considering a way out. Yet now there was no chance. What had to be done must be done, and there was no time for details. He moved along and smiled to himself to know that three men moved behind him.

They might have been ghosts wafted by some breeze from beyond the grave for all the sound they made.

The deep crevasse in which they walked ended so suddenly that Turk stopped and Young ran into him. They made no noise, and it was well, for they stood on the edge of a pool, no more than twenty feet across. It was a pool surrounded by shade trees, and now, kneeling on the far side was a girl. She bent down and dipped up water with a wooden bowl, and drank from it. Her face was a delicate tracery of old ivory in the moonlight, and when she put down the bowl she knelt there on the stone slab, gazing up at the moon.

Turk held himself very still. Behind him he could hear the breathing of the other men. Suddenly, and why he did not know, Turk decided he was going to speak to her. Carefully, he moved out from the others and skirted the pond on light-stepping feet. When he was no more than a few feet away, he spoke to her gently in Mandarin.

It was a wild chance, but she did not look like a Ngolok woman, nor like a Lolo. At the sound of his voice, she stiffened, and her chin came down, but she did not look at him. She did not turn her head, but looked across the garden. "Who speaks from the willows?" she asked.

He spoke very softly, knowing that now he needed her help, her willing help. "A man who seeks the woman he loves, and her brother, who are prisoners here."

"You are not Chinese?"

"American."

Surprisingly then, she turned her head and spoke in clearest English. "Then speak to me so. I was educated in a mission school and have talked with many Americans."

"You know the prisoner—Bob Doone?"

"Yes, I speak with him often, although it is not allowed." She arose and looked up at Turk. "He is the one you seek?"

"Yes, and the American girl who came today? They did get her, didn't they?"

The girl nodded. "She came in with her hands tied and an American with her. He has been talking with Bo Hau, our master."

"You are a prisoner, too?"

"Yes, they keep me as a hostage to keep the aid of my father, who is in Sining. He sends many caravans here, but he does not like the trade. It is done for my protection."

"You know how we can reach Doone? And his sister?" The others had moved around the pool and stood beside him.

"It cannot be done. They are guarded with great care. Bo Hau has wanted something from the American. The man who came today with the woman, I heard him say he could show them how to get it. That he would use the air!"

"By torturing her in front of her brother!" Young said. He swore bitterly. "To think the guy was once on our side! That we ate at the same mess!"

Turk shook his head. "We cannot accept your decision that it cannot be done. It must be done, and tonight, we'll do it."

She nodded as one who understands when a decision is irrevocable. "Then I will take you there," she said, "but what of the guards?"

Turk put his hand on her shoulder. "You take us." He grinned. "We'll cross our guards when we get to them!"

Without further hesitation she turned and led them across the garden. Had they traveled by any other route than down the water course there would have been walls to climb, but here the gardens of the Domed House ran right against the mountain itself.

Her way took them to a door set in a high wall. She opened it and went in, leading them across a paved court where they moved silently. At the far wall she hesitated. "I will speak to the guard," she said, "and then—"

Silently, Shan Bao glided to the fore. "And then I shall act!" he said, low-voiced.

She opened the door and passed within, but when she had taken five steps she paused and turned slightly, then she spoke softly in some strange tongue. The guard stepped toward her, answering with a question. Swiftly, Shan Bao moved in, but some scarcely audible sound must have come to the guard. He wheeled, grasping his huge sword. Yet big as he was and fast as he was, he had no chance. The Manchu was too close, and his deadly knife darted like a serpent's tongue and the big man fell forward. Shan Bao used the knife once more, and then they moved on.

Young breathed into Madden's ear, "You have that guy around all the time?"

Turk nodded. He started to speak, then stopped, for now they were entering a long, dank passageway that trended down in a long, steep ramp. When they had gone a hundred yards they began to pass barred doors.

"Slaves," the girl whispered, "slaves, and most of them Chinese or Lolos. There is another guard ahead, then the men prisoners. The girl is kept above stairs."

Hardly had she finished speaking when a huge man loomed around the corner ahead of them. His eyes widened and his mouth opened for a bellow that would have rocked the monastery, but Turk was moving. Lunging like a fullback, he plowed into the big guard before the man could lift his sword, and, knocked from his hands, it hit the floor with a loud clang.

The huge man grabbed at Madden, but Turk slipped inside of those mighty hands and smashed a right to the guard's heart with every ounce of his two hundred pounds of whipcord and steel muscle behind it. The big man staggered and went back on his hands and knees.

"The prisoners!" Turk snapped crisply at Sparrow Ryan. "Don't bother about me! Go get Doone!"

The guard rushed, and Turk came to his feet, weaved inside the huge hands, and slashed the Ngolok's face with a lancing left hand, and then he began throwing punches with every ounce of power he had. Smashing the guard back with a wicked overhand right, he hooked a left and right to the body. Wildly, the guard swung, but Madden was inside and fighting for his life. He stabbed a right to the body, then lifted his hand and hacked the edge of it across the guard's Adam's apple!

Gagging horribly, the guard fell to his knees and Madden smashed him to the floor. Then he rolled the big man over and, ripping off the rawhide string he used for a belt, lashed the man's hands behind him. Then he bound his feet together and hurriedly gagged him with a corner of the padded cloth ripped from the man's clothing.

Bob Doone—Turk knew him at once from his resemblance to Raemy—lunged from a cell. A half-dozen others followed from other cells. The Chinese girl was hastily motioning them on, so wiping the sweat from his face, Turk started after her. The others fell in behind.

Now she led them up a steep, winding stair into a wide stone hall. Then up another stair. Suddenly, Turk paused. "Ryan," he said, "you'd better take Doone and get out. Get that steel box!"

"And leave you? Don't be crazy!"

"You've got a job to do!" Turk told him. "Besides, I'll have Shan. From now on, it's up to me. Don't tell Bob I'm after Raemy."

Ryan hesitated, then shrugged. With Young he turned back. Turk walked on down the empty passage behind the slim, young Chinese girl. Suddenly, she gestured at him and stepped into a doorway at one side of the passage. Turk and Shan Bao followed, and no sooner were they concealed than four of the guards appeared, and marching between them were Raemy and Bekart!

Watching, they saw the group turn into a wide doorway and vanish into a room. Turk hesitated a moment, his mind working swiftly. From all appearances the prisoners were being taken to a questioning. This would be the one big chance: when they were not locked in cells!

The long passage was dank and gloomy. Certainly, if modern tendencies were alive among the Ngoloks, they had done little to improve their living conditions. A chill pervaded the great Domed House, the damp, empty chill of a building long cold.

THIS WAS NO SECRET and marvelous lost civilization, it was the den of a barbaric people, constructed long ago, and almost untouched since. The flagstone floor was uneven and dirt gathered in the cracks. Here and there dampness had left stains on the wall and ceiling.

"You'd better go back to the garden," Turk whispered to the girl. "We'll come that way and take you with us!"

He stepped out of his hiding place boldly and walked across to the huge plank door. Without a glance over his shoulder he lifted the latch and stepped within. He heard the light slap of Shan Bao's footsteps behind him and heard the door close softly. He did not turn his head, for his eyes were riveted upon the great hall in which he stood.

They were under the vast dome, and suspended from it was a huge bronze bell!

Towering high under the great dome, the bell was enormous, and across the bottom, which was a mere eight feet from the stone floor, it was fully as wide as it was tall! Directly beneath it was a chair, bolted to the floor. Four of the huge Ngolok tribesmen stripped to the waist stood around the bell, each with a huge mallet. The bell had no clapper, but was to be sounded by blows from the Ngoloks.

Several steps below the bell were Raemy Doone and Travis Bekart. Two guards stood beside them, and facing them was a woman, tall, and thin to emaciation, her face a haglike mask of wickedness and cunning. Behind her was a big man who could be none other than Bo Hau.

The entry of Turk and Shan Bao had been unnoticed as there was a screen before the door to prevent the entry of evil spirits, which according to the Ngolok belief must travel in a straight line and so cannot get around a screen.

Madden took in the scene at a glance. He needed no explanation for the chair beneath the bell. There was no form of torture so quickly calculated to ruin a man's self-possession, none that would drive him into insanity and death so quickly as the awful roar of sound and the vibration. Beneath the bell the vibration would be terrific and centered entirely on that chair.

The guard nearest Raemy took her by the arm and started her for the chair, and then Turk stepped around from behind the screen. His heart jumping, he started toward them. He had taken three steps before Bo Hau looked up, and their eyes met.

"Release her!" Turk commanded.

The old queen's eyes lit with an insane humor. "Kill him!" she said, her tone flat and cold.

The guard near Bekart wheeled, lifting his rifle. Turk's hand shot out and grasped the rifle barrel underneath, then his left hand dropped to the stock just back of the breech. He jerked back with his left hand and shoved up hard with his right and ripped the rifle from the astonished guard's hands. The man sprawled on the floor, and Turk stepped back, his rifle on the queen.

One flickering instant, no more. "Release her," he repeated.

The guard holding Raemy took his hands away from her. Bo Hau was staring at Turk, his eyes alive with fanatic hatred.

"Raemy," Turk said, his eyes shifting from Bo Hau to the queen, "walk back to the door!"

"Aren't you taking me?" Bekart demanded.

"Why should we?" Madden replied harshly. "So you can stand trial for murdering your fellow soldiers?"

"Take me with you!" Bekart pleaded. "Don't leave me here! These people are fiends!"

"You escaped us and went to them," Turk's voice was level.

"But, man! You can't—"

"All right!" Turk relented. "Get along, but one wrong move and I'll shoot you myself!"

Bekart jerked free and ran after Raemy. Slowly, Turk began to back up. In all this time, scarcely more than two minutes at most, Bo Hau had said nothing.

Ngoloks gathered around the bell had moved forward slowly, their eyes on Madden. The man on the floor got slowly to his feet. Turk watched them as he moved back, knowing that Shan Bao covered him, yet wary.

The old woman was scarcely sane. A withered hag, eaten by hatred, her mind twisted by power, and probably in a measure dominated by Bo Hau.

The big Ngolok was grinning now, "You go?" he spoke suddenly, pleasantly. His voice was high-pitched. "You leave so soon? We should so like to have you stay for dinner. Is it not the custom among your people to invite guests to stay for dinner?"

Turk did not reply, and suddenly Bo Hau's face was ugly with anger. "Kill him!" he snapped.

The other guard's rifle swung up, and even as it lifted, Turk swung the rifle he held and fired from the hip. The guard's rifle clattered on the floor, he clutched wildly at his stomach, and pitched over on the stone floor.

"Thank you!" Bo Hau said brightly. "Now my people will come . . . thousands of them!"

Somewhere a gong clanged with huge, hammering blows, and the great Domed House was filled with a clamor of voices mingling with the roar of the gong and running feet!

"Run!" Turk roared at Shan Bao. "Back the way we came!"

Darting down the long hall, they rounded the turn to see a guard looming in the way. Turk's rifle bellowed and the guard went down screaming. From behind them there was a shout, then a shot. The bullet ricocheted from the wall. When they reached the garden, still bright and glorious in the glow of the young moon, Turk stopped. "Take them, Shan!" he said. "Make it quick!"

For an instant, the Manchu hesitated, and Raemy's lips started to form a protest, then they were moving.

Madden walked back and picked up a rifle by the wall where the guard was bound, and with it his ammunition belt. Then he retreated to the rocks on the far side of the pool. Kneeling behind the rocks, he waited.

His mouth was dry and his heart was pounding, but he tried to calm himself. The gate burst open suddenly, and men poured through it. Resting the rifle stock against his cheek, Turk began to squeeze off his shots. Once—twice—three times!

Each time a man fell, and the attack broke and split to either side among the shrubbery. Another man showed in the doorway, and Turk fired again. The man crumpled and fell. He shifted his position and studied the shrubbery. A slight movement warned him, but he waited. Suddenly a man lunged from the nearest bush, a huge knife in his hand. With a scream, he hurled himself at Turk's breastwork!

The rifle barked again, and knocked back by the force of the heavy bullet, the Ngolok toppled into the pool. In the breathing space, Turk reloaded the rifle. Then, carefully, he eased back into the shadows.

Shan would be leading them up the steep climb again by now. He moved back, felt a rock wall, and then a low voice, Ryan's, came to him. "Turk?"

"Yeah!"

"That Chinese gal showed us a new way out. Old steps in the cliff, used years ago. I waited to guide you. They comin' after us yet?"

"In a couple of minutes. I got a few of them, scared 'em a little. Let's go!"

Sparrow Ryan led the way, and they hurried up the steep steps as behind them there was a flurry of movement. Far up the stair Turk heard a stone rattle.

Suddenly, torches were burning behind them, and they could hear shouts and yells as the searching party scrambled through the dark crevasse. Ryan rushed on ahead. Turk turned at a small landing and glanced back. He could see the bobbing torches. Coolly and with care he began to fire.

A torch toppled and a scream lifted. Again and again he fired until the rifle was empty, and then he coolly reloaded and emptied it once more. Then he turned away.

A shadow moved, then the huge, greasy body of one of the mallet holders who had stood by the bell loomed from the shadows. How he got there, Turk could only guess. By some secret stair, no doubt, that opened upon this same landing.

The man was a veritable giant, stripped to the waist with his massive muscles gleaming in the light of the moon. Turk's tongue touched his lips, and he circled warily as the man crouched and came toward him. Accustomed too long to fighting with his hands, he forgot his pistol, forgot everything but the huge man who moved toward him, catlike on his huge sandal-clad feet.

Suddenly, the Ngolok lunged. Turk's left fist *splatted* against his lips, and Madden felt the give of the big man's teeth, but then the fellow had his hands on him, and they slipped around his body, wrapping him in a python-like grip!

Turk's head jerked forward and smashed into the Ngolok's face, but then the big man jerked his head aside and began to crush with powerful arms. Turk's left hand was bound to his side by the encircling arms but with his right he hooked short and hard to the ear, then struck down on the kidney with the edge of his hand. The Ngolok grunted, but heaved harder with his powerful arms. Agonizing pain shot through Turk, and he struggled wildly to get loose, then his right lifted and he dug his thumb into the big man's mouth, keeping it between his cheek and the side of his teeth. Digging all four fingers into the flesh behind the giant's ear and jawbone, he jerked back with all his strength!

The Ngolok screamed hoarsely as his cheek ripped under the tearing thumb, and his grip relaxed. As it did, Turk lifted his knee and stomped down on the huge sandal-clad foot with all his strength. With a roar of pain, the big man let go, and Turk sprang back, staggered, and then setting himself, swung a right hand that had the works on it. The punch caught the huge man off balance and he toppled back, hit the crumbling stone parapet, and went over in a shower of falling stones, his screams echoing upward through the vast chimney where they had climbed.

His back stiff with pain, Turk started on up the stair, his lungs gasping for air, his brain wild with fear of what lay behind. Somehow he reached the top and found Ryan crouching there, awaiting him.

The air on the high plateau was crisp and cold, and he gasped great draughts into his tortured lungs. Then he turned and they stumbled away into the darkness together.

SEVERAL MINUTES MORE and they came up with the rest of the party. Young walked a step behind Bekart, his eyes never wavering from the former pursuit pilot's back. Raemy's face was drawn and pale. Turk caught up with her, and she noted his torn shirt and a dark stain of blood on his cheek where the Ngolok's clawing hand had torn the flesh like a claw. "You're hurt!"

"No, and we've got to keep going," he said. "Can you make it?"

"I think so."

Turk's eyes strayed to the Chinese girl. She was walking along, patiently, quietly. He knew the look. He had seen it in the faces of Chinese infantrymen long ago. They would walk until they dropped.

Scotty met them in the hills with a half-dozen armed men. He grinned at Turk, then looked quickly at Doone. "You all right?"

Bob Doone was walking beside his sister. He looked up and grinned. He was very thin, but his eyes were very bright. "Sure!" he said. "Who could be better?"

A silent group met in the big room where the Goose waited, resting easily on the dark water. Young, Scotty, Doone, Ryan, and Kalinov gathered around Turk. He was brief and to the point.

"We've got to move out—now! They'll be down here, and we haven't weapons enough to fight them off. Scotty, I'd say you and Kalinov should move out right away, keep to the low country and get as much distance between you and this bunch as you can. It'll be rough going, but you'll have to do it.

"Travel light. We haven't much in the way of supplies, but we'll rustle some more and bring them to you, supply you by air.

"Don't fight unless you have to, but keep your riflemen to the rear."

Madden watched them go, scowling thoughtfully. He was worried by

Bo Hau's lack of opposition to the escape from the Domed House. The man had the look of a plotter, a conniver as well as a man of action. Turk doubted that they would get away so easily.

The Grumman had brought more supplies than needed, and a few things were carried by the walking party, which made the plane somewhat lighter. There remained Young, Doone, Ryan, Shan, Bekart, and the two girls. It was still a heavy load. Madden had his own plans, intending to fly the fighter. From what he originally learned, there was still another fighter and two transports somewhere around the valley.

The transports, even if armed, did not worry him. The fighter was another thing.

Bob Doone had avoided Bekart, and he avoided him now as he walked over to where Turk Madden, his thumbs tucked behind his belt, was staring bleakly at the grim hills. The gray clouds had lowered themselves over the peaks now, and the massive grandeur of Amne Machin was shut out.

"Ryan tells me you came for my cargo, too?" Bob suggested.

Turk nodded. "And the sooner we get it and get moving, the better."

"All right. When you're ready, I'll take you to it. I hid it myself."

"Sparrow, you come with us. Shan, get the ship warmed up. Young, if you will, warm up the fighter for me. I'm flying it." He glanced at the Manchu. "And keep an eye on Bekart. He's got something on his mind!"

Turk checked his Colt, and then the three turned and walked from the ancient temple. The wind outside was raw and chill. Bob Doone led off and they started up the street, over the tumbled walls and broken stones. When they were halfway up the hill they stopped and looked back. White caps dotted the lake's black water, and the hills were a sullen gray and black, streaked here and there in cracks and crevices with the white of snow.

On the far side of a plateau a path led downward. "Found it by accident," Doone said. "Came down here, couldn't carry the box very far. Before we crashed I'd seen those natives coming, and they didn't look enticing."

The path dipped into a thick growth of pine, then out and into a small open glade at the end of a canyon. Here, set away by itself, was a temple.

A wide stone-flagged terrace lay before it. They walked across, footsteps echoing hollowly, then up three high steps and through the narrow door.

Inside the light was vague, but they could see a bare and empty room except for one place at a far corner where some animal had gathered sticks and grass for a nest. A huge figure of Buddha loomed at the end.

They walked toward it, and Doone gestured. "See? The Buddha is newer than the rest. Probably some other god was there and they put the Buddha in its place. Didn't work very well from what I heard in the valley, for the people deserted the temple and, later, the town."

He circled the pedestal and the huge stone figure. "Careful! It's balanced very badly there. I think someone started to move it, planning to return the original, and then stopped."

It was not of one solid stone, rather of blocks cunningly fitted together.

Behind the pedestal, Doone got down on his knees and dug at a flat block fitted into the floor. Using a knife, he succeeded in getting his fingers under the edge. He heaved on the slab, and his shoulder touched the pedestal. The figure above teetered dangerously. "Look out!" Ryan warned. "If that thing fell off of there it would kill us all!"

Turk stooped and got one edge of the slab and they lifted it out. In the recess below was the black steel box. Carefully, they lifted it out.

Turk and Ryan each took a handle, and they straightened. Turk went suddenly cold inside. His right hand gripped the handle on the steel box, his Colt was in its shoulder holster in his left armpit. And Travis Bekart was standing before them, in his hands a submachine gun. He was smiling, his coldly handsome face was even colder now, and his eyes were like ice. "So," he said, "here's the payoff! Didn't think I'd let you get away with this, did you, Madden? You messed up my plans for me. I'd an idea of marrying Raemy and living on the fat of the land, then getting rid of her and inheriting it all myself. I got Doone out of the way, and then you had to nose in.

"But I'd no intention of going back a prisoner. Oh, no! I intend to go back, all right! I'll go back alone, and very sad that you were lost, but I'll take the black box with me, and they will be very pleased. I may even get a decoration for it. And there will be other women with money."

"What about Young?" Doone said. "He knows!"

"Young is dead," Bekart replied, with triumph. "I've killed him. I pushed Raemy into the lake when no one was looking, then when the Manchu went in after her, I took this gun and came away. Unfortunately Young never knew what hit him. And now you ... you'll all know, and I'll have made a clean sweep. I'll just leave the girls. Those Ngoloks will take care of them. It will serve Raemy right for not marrying me when she had the chance."

"You talk a lot," Turk said. If only he didn't have that damned box! He could make a try for his gun and—

Bob Doone shifted his feet. "You can't get away with it," he said. He shifted his right foot a little, lost his balance, and hurled his weight against the pedestal of the huge Buddha!

As his weight hit the pedestal there was a grinding crash from the stone beneath the figure and the great mass toppled forward!

Travis Bekart threw up his arms with a scream of fear as he saw the huge stone figure looming over him. For one blinding instant the man's face was a tortured white mask, and then with a mighty crash the stone image hit the man's widespread arms and screaming face, burying him under an avalanche of ancient granite.

The sound died, dust lifted, and Turk staggered forward, pulling on his handle of the box. "Let's go!" he said.

THEY FOUND YOUNG down on his face beside the fighter, his head smashed with the heavy slugs.

"Go ahead," Turk told them. "Get this into the amphibian and take off. Get moving."

Tenderly, he carried the man's body to a place beside the other grave. He scraped out a hollow and rolled the body into it, then covered it with brush and stones. There was no time to make a cross.

He turned and hurried back to the fighter. As he did so, he caught a movement on the lakefront below, and saw a column of men circling the lake toward the temple!

Yet even as he looked, he saw the amphibian taxi out on the water. Scrambling into the fighter, he revved the motors. Young had evidently had them warmed fairly well before he was killed. Staring at the lakefront, he saw the monks begin to deploy along the waterfront, scattering out in a crude, skirmishing line.

Twin motors roaring, he started the ship down the plateau. It bumped, then rolled faster and faster. Swiftly, he shot over the packed snow, then hauled back on the stick and lifted the tiny ship. He was airborne. He climbed steadily, then swung around in a steep bank and raced back for the lakefront.

He could see the monks lifting their rifles now, and he swept down upon them and tripped the triggers on his guns. The leading edge of the wing burst into fire, and he saw the scattered line break and lunge for cover. One man leaped off into the icy water, and then Turk came back on the stick and shot away above the lake, lifting higher and higher, reaching for altitude to put him above the amphibian. The plane below him was heading off across the bleak gray hills, and a thousand feet higher he turned after the fleet Grumman.

He turned once, to glance back toward the valley, and his eye caught a flash of movement. He glanced up, and fear struck him like a blow! Another fighter was dropping out of the gray clouds, guns flaming, and coming down in a wild, screaming dive!

Turk whipped the fighter around and dove for the lake, then shot up, just clearing the black edge of the surrounding ridge by a matter of feet. The enemy fighter was on his tail and coming fast. He swung the ship again, darting this way and that in a mad rush to escape. A bullet hole appeared in the instrument panel ahead of him, and something spattered on his face.

He hauled back on the stick and climbed almost straight up toward the gray clouds, then went over backward in a loop, trying to reverse positions, but as he swept by the other ship he saw a fleeting glimpse of a taut yellowish face! *Bo Hau!*

A burst of tracer flamed past him and he whipped the ship around, fighting for his life. The big Ngolok knew his ship and knew every trick of flying. Another burst, and Turk felt a sharp blow on his leg. There was no chance to glance down, but feeling numb and sick, he whipped the ship around again and dove like a streak for the dark, stone-filled streets below!

As he eased out of a screaming dive he shot the ship for the looming black tower and banked around as if rounding a pylon on a racing course. Bo Hau whipped around it, too, but with a sudden loop, at its bottom no more than fifty feet above the black stone roofs, Turk got Bo Hau's fighter in his sights, and he let go a burst that riddled the engine cowling and cockpit. The fighter dipped suddenly and went crashing into the street, one wing ripping off as it hit the edge of a stone roof.

There was a tremendous burst of flame, and an explosion that rocked Turk's fighter, and then he was speeding away, heading after the amphibian.

His motors began to stutter, then spit, and he leveled off and headed for the ground. Ahead was a long, level stretch, rocky and scattered here and there with dark, dry-looking brush. As he came in, he cut his speed, eased back a bit on the stick, felt her wheels touch, then again, and then the ship hit a bush and the tail flopped up and over.

Something smashed him on the head, and he passed out.

AFTER A LONG TIME, he opened his eyes. He was hanging in his safety belt, one shoulder against the edge of the seat. Holding with one hand, he loosened the safety belt and toppled to the ground below. He sat there for a long time, his head buzzing. Then he got to his feet, gathered up the few things that belonged to him, and started on weaving feet down the trail the marching party had taken.

Sometime during the night he fell down by a bush and slept, and then almost at dawn the cold awakened him. Turk staggered to his feet, staring around him. His head throbbed and he was tired, but his mind was clear. Of all that had happened since he began walking he had no idea, nor where he was. He saw the tracks of a considerable party and started on, putting each foot down with care.

AT NOON, somewhere between delirium and sanity, he heard a hum in the sky and looked up, shielding his eyes. Then it stopped and he walked on. He was walking like that when they found him, Sparrow Ryan and Raemy.

He was walking solemnly along the dim trail, his eyes fixed ahead of him, blood all over his head and caked in his hair and on his cheek, limping with one leg, but walking on.

Raemy saw him first, and she started to run. "Oh, Turk! Turk! I thought you were *dead!*"

Her arms went around him and he felt her soft lips on his and through the fog of pain his memory came back and he looked over her red-gold hair at Ryan, who was grinning with relief.

"Go away!" he said. "Can't you see she wants to be alone?"

Pirates With Wings

Turk Madden heard the man in the copilot's seat roar, "Turk! Look out!" There was panic in his voice.

Turk gave one startled glance upward and then yanked back on the stick. The Grumman nosed up sharply, narrowly missing a head-on collision with a speedy ship that had come plunging out of the sun toward them.

Turk gave the amphibian the full rudder as it was about to stall, and the ship swung hard to the left and down in a wingover. Then, opening the throttle wide, he streaked for a towering mass of cumulus, dodging around it in a vertical bank.

Buck Rodd, the man in the copilot's seat, glanced at Turk, his face pale. "Was that guy bats?" he demanded. "Or was he getting smart with somebody?"

Turk kept the throttle open and streaked away for another cloud, swung around it, and then around another. He was doing some wondering himself, for the action had been so swift that he had no more than the merest glance at the fast little ship before it was gone clear out of sight. Nor did he stop ducking. He kept the Grumman headed away from the vicinity and traveled miles before he finally began to swing back on his original course.

"What's the matter?" Buck Rodd inquired. "Are you afraid that mug will find you again? He's probably scared silly right now."

"Could be," Turk Madden agreed dubiously, "but that near smashup could have been deliberate. Leone warned us to expect trouble from Petex, you know."

"You mean a guy would do a thing like that on purpose?" Buck demanded, incredulously. "Not a chance! Why, if you hadn't pulled up so darned fast we would both have crashed!"

"Oh, sure!" Turk agreed. "But maybe he didn't figure our speed quite right. If he did mean it, he was probably trying to throw a bluff into us. He probably just tried to scare us."

"I can't answer for you," Buck Rodd assured him grimly, "but he sure got results with me!"

GRIMLY, TURK MADDEN, fighting, roistering adventurer of the skyways, leaned forward, searching the green carpet of jungle below them for some indication of the landmarks he wanted. He was not kidding himself about his newest assignment. It was a job that gave every indication of being one of the toughest and most dangerous he had ever attempted, and his life had been one long series of tough jobs.

The vast jungle below him, known to explorers as the "green hell," amounted to more than three hundred thousand square miles of unexplored territory, a dense, trackless region of insects as large as birds, of natives who fiercely resented any encroachments on their territory, and of fevers that were as deadly as they were strange.

This was the land he had promised to survey for oil for Joe Leone's Tropical Oil Company, a job that could only be done from the air.

To make the project all the more dangerous, another outfit was in the field or soon to be there. The Petroleum Exploration Company had long been known by reputation to Turk Madden. He was himself a hard-bitten flyer who was ready to tackle anything if the price was high enough. The Petex was also ready, and they had the men to do it. The difference was that Turk possessed a hankering for the right side of the law, whereas the Petex was unhampered by any code of ethics. It promised to be a dog-eat-dog battle.

Joe Leone, the tough, fat little executive of Tropco, had warned him as to what he could expect. Leone had been weaned on a Liberty motor, had pioneered with an air circus, and had been a wing walker. From that he'd gone to an airline, and from there to the more hectic business of prospecting for oil by use of the magnetometer.

Leone and Madden talked the same language, and Joe pulled no punches in explaining.

"The first one to get a good survey of that region can get a concession. If there's oil there, we want it. An' get this, Turk. The government wants it. The Tropco is doin' the job, but Uncle Whiskers is mighty interested.

"Our country needs oil—an' plenty of it. Where does the oil come from? We ain't supplyin' our domestic needs now. An' don't kid yourself that we're goin' to make any big discoveries anymore. This country has been prospected from hell to breakfast!

"Sure! We'll find oil here an' there, but not enough. Not a drop in the bucket. That Brazilian country is liable to be the biggest thing yet, an' the folks I speak for an' the ones Petex works for are out to get that survey finished an' make a bid. So figure on trouble.

"They'll do anything—and I mean *anything*—to wreck your chance of a survey. They'll sabotage your planes. They'll kill if they come to it, don't forget that. I don't know for sure, but some of the guys behind this Petex outfit may represent another country. At any rate, they don't respect Uncle Whiskers, an' we do.

"I'd figured on you. But there was a tip from Washington, too. They said you'd be the man. Seems they liked your work during the war. So you take that ship of yours an' head for the Matto Grosso. We'll have fuel spotted for you at Cuyaba, an' on the Amazon at Obido. We've got two men to send along, both good sharp boys, rough an' tumble guys."

Turk had nodded thoughtfully. "Who are they?"

"Dick London an' Phil Mora. London's your expert on the magnetometer. Knows it like a book, an' a good radioman. He's just a kid—twenty-two years old.

"You ever hear of that Boy's Ranch out near Old Tascosa? It's a setup something like Boy's Town, an' a mighty good one. Well, this Dick London came from there, an' the kids that leave that ranch are tops, take it from me. Dick had some tough breaks as a kid, but he took to the life on that ranch an' left there mighty interested in electrical science. Somebody helped him get a job at Westinghouse, an' he went from that to a job in the survey of the Bahamas.

"Phil Mora's a college man. Finished his post-grad work and went to Arabia on an oilfield job. He was there a couple of years, then back in the States, then the war. After the war he went to Syria for a year or two, and now this job."

BUCK RODD TURNED toward Turk. He was a big man, even heavier than Turk's two hundred pounds, and a former commercial explorer, searching the jungle for gold, diamonds, orchids, and quinine bark, among other things. With Shan Bao, Turk's long, lean Manchu mechanic, Rodd completed the party of five.

"You said something about a base on the Formosa," Buck Rodd said. "That was a new one on me. Did Leone give you the dope?"

Turk chuckled. "No, Buck, I've actually got almost nothing to go on! A few nights ago in Rio I ran into a big bruiser in a cantina, a drunken prospector with a red beard and red hair on his chest. I bought him a drink, and he told me he'd been hunting rubber and gold in Brazil all his life, so I started talking about this neck of the woods. No sooner did I mention it, though, than the bruiser clammed up. He'd been ready to talk until then, but he shut up and I couldn't get a thing out of him. However, I went back there again, and on the third night we met again and had another drink.

"Well, to cut it short, this guy finally comes out with a funny crack. He says, 'You look big enough to take care of yourself, an' tough enough. If you're goin' to work that country, there's a little lake in the jungle just west of the Formosa River. It would be a perfect base. But you be careful.' "

"Huh! That ain't much, is it? He say anything more?"

"Well, yes. He did say something. He squinted at me sort of funny, and said, 'If you get there, an' they take you to Chipan, tell Nato that Red said hello.' "

"Chipan? Where the devil is that? I thought that was all jungle, that no white man except maybe Fawcett, who got lost down there, had ever seen it."

"That's about right. And I never heard of any such place as Chipan," Turk admitted. "But a lake in that country? Say! That would be a base worth having, and one that would save us days of time. So where are we headed for? The Formosa."

THE AMPHIBIAN DRONED along smoothly, its twin motors purring like contented kittens, and Turk ran his fingers through his black, coarse hair. His green eyes swept the sky, alternately searching for the plane they had seen earlier and studying the vast sweep of the jungle below them.

Fascinated, his eyes shifted from point to point over the land below. To him this had long been the most exciting country on earth because here, in one great chunk, was a great stretch of land that offered nothing but legend. Ever since the early Portuguese explorers had told their strange stories of vast ruined cities in the jungles, men, lured by memories of the Maya and Inca cities and the gold-walled temples to the Sun, had searched these jungles in their minds. Few had actually penetrated their depths, and not many of the few had returned.

In 1925, Colonel Fawcett had gone into those jungles and vanished. Rumors had come out of him alive, ruling a native people. And now this story told by a drunken prospector. The mention of a strange name ... Chipan. And he was to say hello to Nato. Who was Nato? Man, woman, or god? Or was it some figment of the native imagination? Some reptile? Some monster?

Long ago, reading of this jungle, Turk had read where some Latin explorer had sighted a huge reptile, not unlike a prehistoric monster, in the Bemi swamp. And if such there were on earth, surely there could be no more likely place to find it than here, in these far green forests beyond the reach of men. No sunlight penetrated those depths below. There was hot, still heat, humidity, and the unceasing buzz of insects. At night that jungle was a hell of sound, of screams and yells and screeches.

Turk's wingtip scored the misty end of a cloud and he moved out into the vast, unclouded blue beyond, and the ship seemed lost in a droning dream between the green below and the blue above.

Then out of the green came the shaggy brown ridge of a mountain chain, and the silver of a stream. It could be the Formosa.

Phil Mora stuck his head over Buck Rodd's shoulder. "Is that it?" he asked.

Turk swung the ship in a wide circle, studying the terrain below. "It's not the Formosa," he said at last. "My guess is that it is one of the streams west of there, closer against the mountains. Nevertheless, we'll scout around for a landing."

"Savanna over there to our northeast," Rodd offered, inclining his head in that direction. "Looks like there might be quite a bit of open country around."

"There is," Mora said. "Lots of this country through here is open. Several small mountain ranges in here, too."

Turk Madden swung the ship in a tighter circle, moving in toward the spot of open water. It looked not unlike the brief description Red had given him in the cantina, but there was no way he could be sure. He dropped lower, then cut the throttle and slid down toward the smooth dark water. Then he leveled off and, with the stick back, took the water easily and started to taxi toward the shore, keeping a sharp eye out for snags.

When they were in a small cove, Shan Bao dropped the anchor and they swung slowly, turning the nose into the wind. Turk stared around curiously.

The shore was flat and low at this point, the gravel beach giving way to tall grass, and beyond, a few scattered trees. A bit farther along, the wall of the jungle closed in, but here at the cove was timber enough for shelter and fuel, and some camouflage. Dick London was getting the boat out and Turk nodded toward shore.

"Look that bottom over as you go in. I'd like to run her up on the beach if we can. I think we might make a takeoff up there. I think we'll start flying from here tomorrow."

When they were gone, he got up and reached for his shoulder holster, buckling it in place. Then he picked up his jacket and slipped it on. Ashore, Buck was getting a fire started, and they all went to work getting their camp set up. Turk stared thoughtfully around.

"It's late, so we'll sit tight. Tomorrow we'd better have a look at things."

Dick motioned toward the spur of the mountain. "Some funny rocks up there. One of them looks almost like a tower."

Madden turned toward it. The outline was dark against the sky. It did look like a tower. He lighted his cigarette, still staring at it, then tossed the match down and ground it into the sand with his toe.

Chipan—what was Chipan? Staring at the strange shape against the sky of this remote jungle, Turk Madden felt a queer, ominous thrill go through him, a feeling that left him uncomfortable, as though eyes were upon him. He glanced around, and something in the manner of Phil Mora told him the geologist was feeling it, too.

"Odd place," Mora said at last. "Gets you, somehow."

"It does that!" Buck glanced up sharply. Against the darkening sky the shape of the tower was all gone. "I wonder if that is a tower? Or is it just a rock?"

Dick London laughed. "There's nothing of that kind in here. This is all wild country."

Mora shrugged. "So was the jungle in Cambodia before they found the lost city of Angkor. You never know what you'll find under this jungle. You couldn't even see a city from the air unless you were hedge-hopping. Not if it is really covered with jungle."

Buck Rodd had taken over the cooking job from Shan Bao for the evening, and Turk seated himself on a rock watching the brawny prospector throw a meal together, and listening half unconsciously to an argument between Mora and London as to the relative merits of Joe Louis and Jack Dempsey.

It was not only his interest in this area of jungle that had prompted Madden to accept so readily the challenge of this new venture. Prospecting with the magnetometer was new, and as always such developments intrigued him. He was aware that the device would not entirely replace the usual surface methods, but it would outline the areas that deserved careful study and eliminate many others and much waste of time.

Both Mora and London had worked with the magnetometer, the latter a good deal. Even in civilized areas, the cost of such a survey on the ground was nearly twenty times more expensive than by air, while the difference in the time required for the survey was enormous. The magnetometer would be towed a hundred feet or so behind the plane in a bomblike housing, with the plane flying from five hundred to a thousand feet in the air, and at speeds around one hundred fifty miles per hour.

In the nose of the flying eye there was contained a small detector element called a fluxgate, kept parallel to the magnetic field of the earth by a gyro mechanism. As the magnetic field varied in intensity with variations in the earth's crust, the changes were picked up by an alternating current imposed upon the detector. These sharp pulses in voltage were picked up, amplified, and recorded. Once recorded, these observations were sent to geophysicists and geologists who interpreted the information, with the result that possible oil structures as well as mineral bodies could be identified with fair accuracy.

Darkness closed in around the tiny camp, and overhead the stars came out, bright and close. The water of the lake lapped lazily at the amphibian's hull, and Turk leaned back against his rock and stared into the fire. Phil had picked up his guitar and was singing a Western ballad when suddenly there came a new sound.

Turk heard it first. He stiffened, then held up a hand for quiet. The lazy sound of the voice and the strings died and the fire crackled, and the water lapped with its hungry tongue. And then the sound came again, the low, throbbing sound of distant drums.

FROZEN IN PLACE, they listened. Buck Rodd sat up and stared over at Turk.

"They know we're here," he said grimly. "The natives know it, anyway."

"They sound pretty far off," London hazarded.

"Maybe." Turk shrugged. "Sometimes it's hard to tell. They often sound loudest at a distance."

The drums throbbed, then died, then boomed louder still, and then the sound ended abruptly and the silence lay thick upon the jungle and savanna. Waiting, listening, they suddenly heard something else—a woman's voice singing in the distance.

A voice with a strange accent sang, *"Home, home on the range!"*

London sat up. "Oh, no!" he said. "Not that! Here in the middle of the jungle some babe starts singing cow ballads! What is this?"

"Next thing somebody will start broadcasting soap operas!" Rodd said sarcastically. "Ain't a man safe anywhere?"

Turk Madden's scowl grew deeper, and his green eyes narrowed. It didn't make sense. Not any way you looked at it.

Not even, he thought, if the Petex outfit had beaten them to it.

"You can be ready for anything," Joe Leone had said, "they've got Vincent Boling running their show, an' you know what he is. An' he's got Frank Mather, Sid Bordie, and Ben Pace working with him."

Turk knew them all. Bordie and he had tangled only a short time before, and Mather was a man who had done a short stretch in the federal pen for flying dope over the line from Mexico. The three were flying muscle men, and in this game they were playing for stakes that were enormous. And what happened back here in the jungle might never be known.

"Tomorrow we start working," Turk said, looking up suddenly. "Every man carries a gun at all times, but no shot will be fired unless you are first fired upon. If possible we must make friends with the natives, or whoever there is out here. First, remember these boys we're playing tag with are tough. Nobody is to go into the jungle alone unless it is Buck or myself, and I don't want either you, Mora, or Dick going into the jungle alone until you know your way around."

"You think we'll have trouble? Shooting trouble?" London asked.

"Look, guns aren't something to be taken lightly, and neither is shooting when you are shooting at other men. We've got a job to do, and that's the first thing. If they want war, let them start it."

DAYLIGHT FOUND DICK LONDON working over his gear with Mora at his side. Turk came out from under the mosquito bar mopping the sweat from his face despite the early hour. It had been a thick, close night.

"We may get a storm," Turk said, "so let's get busy."

They ate a quick breakfast, and Turk went out with Shan to give the ship a thorough check. Buck Rodd came down to the beach and called out to them.

"You can land up here if you want," he said. "I've just been over this savanna. There's no rocks, no dead trees."

Madden came ashore, wiping his hands on a piece of waste. At a jerk of Rodd's head, he followed him to one side.

"Come have a look," Rodd suggested. "I didn't want the others to know about this."

The two big men walked side by side, up the slight rise to the long level of the savanna. A light wind stirred the tall grass, but scarcely ruffled the heavier leaves of the jungle growth beyond. Buck stopped suddenly and pointed. In a patch of bare ground near an anthill there was the track of a human foot—a sandal track.

"Last night," Buck said, "someone probably came down to look us over."

"Yeah," Turk agreed. He hitched up his belt and grinned. "Well, maybe we'll have trouble, but lets hope we duck it." On a sudden thought, he turned and glanced toward the spur of the mountain. If there was any tower there, he could not distinguish it now. He remarked about it.

"I noticed that, too," Buck agreed, "but if the thing is there, and it is old and weathered, we might not see it. At sundown the outline is sharper against the sky. Should I have a look?"

"No, better not. We've unloaded most of our gear here, so why don't you and Shan stick around and keep an eye on things. Sort of fix the camp up, too. Mora, Dick, and I are going upstairs now."

WITH THE AMPHIBIAN TURNED into the wind, Turk warmed the ship up and started down the smooth water of the lake. The speed built up, and the ship climbed on the step as he put the stick forward. Then he brought it back and the ship took off easily, skimming off over the low jungle, building up speed.

In a wide circle, he swung back toward the lake, his eyes scanning the jungle, yet there was nothing, nothing except ... He stared again, and back in the notch of the hills he saw some taller trees. His eyes sharpened. He knew the trees growing among ruins often grew to greater height.

Over the lake, the magnetometer was slowly trailed back into position, and Mora had his camera ready to shoot the continuous strip of 35mm film that would make an unbroken record of the flight path. At five hundred feet, the amphibian swept back over the jungle and settled down to steady flying. Pointing the ship due north toward the far distant Amazon, Turk held the speed at one hundred fifty miles an hour.

Below them the green jungle unrolled, broken by wide savannas and occasionally by the upthrust of ancient mountain ranges. Leaning back in his seat, Turk glanced around, his eyes less on the jungle than the sky, for it was from the sky that trouble was most likely to come. Remembering the sudden dive of the mysterious plane on the preceding day, he thought of Sid Bordie, the Petex muscle man. It would be like Sid to try something like that. He was tough, but he was also a bluffer, and he always believed other men were more easily frightened than himself.

For two hours they flew north and then started back for their base, flying a route a quarter of a mile west of the first course. Turk glanced over his shoulder as they flew in toward the lake.

"Everything okay?"

"Couldn't be better!" Dick yelled in answer.

Landing the ship, Turk taxied to the shore. He saw Buck Rodd come strolling down to the beach.

"Everything quiet here," Buck said. "I didn't look around any. Mostly too busy."

On foot then, Turk walked swiftly up the slight hill through the tall grass, eager to stretch his legs. Surprisingly, the air was cool. Despite the latitude, they were fairly high here, and now, in the late afternoon, the heat was already slipping away.

He struck straight for the edge of the jungle. There was less underbrush than he had expected and, following a route that paralleled the jungle's edge, he headed toward the spur of the mountain where they had believed they had seen the tower.

As he walked, he saw no tracks, no marks of any man or woman. Yet despite the tower, if such it was, his mind was more curious about the girl's voice, singing "Home on the Range." It was absurd, of course. Had he heard the song alone, he would have been convinced he had only imagined it.

The route led up to the mountainside, and soon he was out of the jungle and making his way through sparse brush and scattered boulders. Then he stopped abruptly. Before him in the path there was a track.

He knelt, studying it. The foot was moccasin- or sandal-clad, small and well shaped. The stride was even and firm, as of someone of light weight and not too tall. He had a feeling the track was not many hours, perhaps not even many minutes old.

More slowly, he walked along. Once his hand went to his shoulder holster for the reassuring grip of the gun. A flyer in the East Indies and South America before the war, and in Siberia, China, and Japan during the war, Turk was no stranger to danger, but he knew that actually, it was always new. A man never became accustomed to it.

The tracks proceeded down the path ahead of him, and then he came around a boulder and stood on the edge of the ridge, and before him was the tower. There was no doubt. It was a tower.

TURK MADDEN HALTED, stirred by a strange uneasiness. It was that peculiar feeling known to those who come first to ancient ruins. The feeling of being watched, of walking upon hallowed ground, of intruding.

It was late evening and the sun was down. The mountains had taken on the darkness of night, and the green of the jungle had turned to deep purple and black. Outlines were vague toward the lakeshore, although even from here he could see the single star that marked their campfire.

Turk stood there, waiting, every sense alert, a big man, well over six feet, and his broad, powerful shoulders heavy with muscle under the woolen shirt.

The tower was black with age, worn smooth by wind and rain. It stood on a small plateau of grass among fallen stones, gloomy, ancient, alone. Yet there was a faint path down the slight incline toward its base, skirting the tower.

Turk knew that there was no known civilization here. The Inca ruins were far to the west, in Peru. The Maya ruins were far to the north, in Yucatán and Honduras, and the Mayas had never been a wandering people. There had been rumors, of course. Two Portuguese seamen in 1533 had a story to tell of vast ruined cities. A Phoenician galley had been found embedded in the mud on the banks of the Amazon. And there had been tales of a still existent Guarani civilization, somewhere in the vast interior.

Slowly, Turk moved down the path, feeling uneasy. He turned around the tower, and before him the hillside broke sharply away upon an inner valley, its steep sides scarred by broken walls and blackened stone. Here and there a wall was intact. In one place, another tower. And before him, in the tower by which he stood, was the black rectangle of an open door.

Turk Madden hesitated. There was no sound but the faint whisper of the wind. He licked his lips and turned toward the door. And then he stopped. Faintly, and far away at first, he heard the sound of a nearing plane. Then he saw the ship. It was coming low over the hills, and incredibly fast.

It could have been the same plane that had narrowly missed them on the day they arrived at the lake, or it might be another ship of the same type. Like a dark arrow it vanished over the lake and into the darkening sky beyond.

Had the pilot sighted their fire? Most likely, unless they had covered it soon enough, for such a fire was visible for many miles. Well, then, they were probably discovered now, their whereabouts known.

Yet there was still the tower. He reached into his pocket for the small flashlight he always carried and stepped up to the door.

The light revealed the inside of the tower, and before him a square stone table, polished or worn until it was smooth as glass. In the center of the table was a plantain leaf, and on it a small cup. Curious, he stepped forward. The cup contained a liquid, and when he placed a hand upon it, the cup was warm.

He hesitated. Obviously, this had been placed here for a reason. An offering to a god? But there was no image here, nothing but the smooth wall. He lifted the cup and tasted the liquid.

He recognized the drink at once. It was something similar to the sweetened *pozole* of the Mayas, a drink made from ground maize. He tasted it again, and then carefully replaced the cup on the leaf.

"Red?"

The voice was so low it sent a shiver through him, and so unexpectedly near. He stood perfectly still, goose pimples running up his spine. It was a girl's voice, and she was behind him.

"No," he tried to keep his voice calm, even. "It is not Red. I am Turk."

There was a whisper of movement, and the girl stepped into the light. She was taller than he had expected, for he was looking for someone like the Mayas, whose women were less than five feet tall, and the men only slightly taller.

She was tall, with very large, slightly oblique eyes. She might have been called beautiful. She was certainly striking, and the garb she wore left little to the imagination.

"I am Natochi," she said softly, in the same low voice.

Nato, if you see Nato—the prospector had told him—tell her that Red said hello. Then this was Nato.

"Red told me to say 'hello,'" he said.

Suddenly, at a thought, he turned the light so that she might see his face, too. She looked at him, her eyes large, serious, intent.

"You are friend to Red?"

"Yes. You speak English?"

"Red tell me how. You will be at this place long?"

"Perhaps a week, perhaps a month. You live near here?"

He had to repeat that, and then she nodded. "Not far."

"At Chipan?" he asked, and was immediately startled by her expression. Stark horror came into her face.

"No! No! Not at Chipan! Nobody lives at Chipan, only the— ghost?"

"Is it near here?" he asked curiously. She shook her head, refusing to reply, so he took another angle. "Are your people friendly?"

She hesitated. "They are sometimes friendly, sometimes not. At first they did not like Red, and then they did. They do not like the other one now."

"The other one?" Turk frowned. "Is there another white man here? Has he just come?"

"Oh, no! He came when Red came, but he does not go away. He cannot go away now."

"What do you mean? Why can't he go?" Turk persisted.

"He has no legs. He stays here now."

Turk stared at her. What the devil was this, anyway? A white man, stuck in this country without any legs! Why hadn't Red mentioned that?

"Was he a friend of Red's?"

"Oh, no! They fight very much, at first! Many fight, with hands closed, but always he is stronger than Red. He is ver' strong, this one."

"You mean he had legs then? And not now?"

She hesitated, obviously uncertain and a little frightened. "The Old Ones, they took his legs. They cut off them."

Shocked, Madden drew back. Then he asked warily, "Why? Why did they cut them off?"

"Because he wanted to go to Chipan. Always he wanted to go. They told him he must not, the Old Ones did, but he laughed and went, so they cut off his legs to keep him from going again." She looked at Turk seriously. "It is very bad to go to Chipan. It is evil there."

Turk studied the situation thoughtfully. He wanted very much to talk to this man, to get him away from here, but also he wanted and needed the friendship of these people, for they could render his base useless if they were antagonized. More than anything now he wanted to get back to camp and to think this over.

"We are friends," he said at last. "We live at the lake. We work much. Tell your people we will not go to Chipan. Tell them we will be friends and help them if they wish it. Other men," he added, "may come who are not friends. You must be on your guard, for they may be very bad men. You must come to our camp, and see the others, so you will know them."

She smiled suddenly, and he realized with a start that she was not only striking. She was beautiful.

"I have seen them," she said. "Each one. So have others of my people. We have watched you last night, and today."

They left the tower and parted on the edge of the jungle. He turned and walked swiftly back toward the fire, which was still bright.

BUCK RODD WAS PACING BACK AND FORTH, and when he saw Turk, relief broke over his face.

"Man!" he exclaimed. "We were getting worried! Where have you been?"

Turk accepted the cup that Shan Bao offered him and walked over and seated himself on the ground with his back to the stone.

He took a swallow of coffee, and while Shan was dishing up the food, he explained briefly, amused by their wide-eyed interest.

"Talk about luck!" Dick said with disgust. "You walk out into the jungle and run right into something like that. A beautiful dame, and away out here, too! Why doesn't anything like that ever happen to me?"

"If it did," Phil Mora said, smiling, "you'd probably be so scared you'd still be running."

"What about this fellow with no legs, this white man?" Rodd inquired. "You think that's on the level? It's funny this Red didn't say anything about it."

Turk shrugged. "She said that he and Red fought all the time. Red must have been friendly enough with them, for apparently they let him go. I wonder what's at Chipan that this other fellow wanted so much?"

"That's easy enough!" Rodd said. "Gold, probably. What else would make a man gamble on something like that? You remember what Pizarro found in Peru? The walls of that Temple to the Sun at Cuzco were sheeted in thin plates of gold. From what you say, this Chipan must be a sacred place."

"That wasn't the impression I got," Turk said. "She seemed afraid of it. The place is tabu, that's a cinch. Evil, she said." He glanced over at Mora and London. "Don't you boys get any wild ideas. If you don't want to lose any legs, stay away from that place. And don't ask any questions!"

YET HE WAS less worried about Chipan and the tribesmen, whoever they were, than about the plane he had seen, for it was high time that Bordie or some of the Petex crowd showed up. Certainly any outfit that hired Vin Boling to ramrod such a deal, and men like Pace, Mather, and Bordie to carry it out, was planning on riding roughshod over any opposition. And they had moved in too easily.

Daybreak found Turk and his crew in the air again. This time they flew clear on to Obido to refuel. Surprisingly, Joe Leone was waiting for Turk when he came ashore.

"Came down to handle this gas setup myself, an' just as well I did," he said, his cigar jutting up from his tight-lipped mouth. "Boling's in town. They've got a base back in the jungle."

Turk explained quickly, telling all that had happened except about the native girl and Chipan. For some reason he was reluctant to speak of it.

Previously, he had warned Phil and Dick against any comments along that line.

"Hi, Turk!"

Madden turned at the booming voice and found himself facing Sid Bordie and a man he remembered vaguely as Vin Boling. To Boling's reputation he needed no introduction. The man had ramrodded many legal or semilegal deals in his life and was utterly ruthless, a fighter who would stop at nothing.

"Looks like you fellows were getting started," Boling said, smiling. "But you're late. We'll have this survey completed in no time. Why don't you pull out before you waste more money?"

"We'll finish it!" Leone said grimly. "And don't start anything, Boling. I know how you operate."

The big man chuckled. He was taller than Turk Madden, lithe and hard as nails. In his whites and half-boots he looked rugged enough. Bordie was equally tall, but broader and thicker.

"I want 'em to stay!" Bordie said, his eyes bright with malice. "This Madden is supposed to be good. I want to see how good."

"Want to find out now?" Turk invited. "Nobody's holding you, chum."

Bordie's face flushed dark with anger.

"Why, you—"

He swung from his hip, and it was the wrong thing to do. Turk had been rubbing his palms together, rather absently, holding them chest high. It was an excellent punching position, which was exactly why he held them there. Sid Bordie's punch started, but Turk's rock-hard left fist smashed into his teeth, and then a short right dropped to the angle of Bordie's jaw and the big flyer's knees sagged. But Turk had not stopped punching, the two blows had been thrown quicker than a wink, and the third was a left hook to the solar plexus thrown from the hip. It exploded in Bordie's stomach, and the flyer grunted and hit the dock on his knees.

His feet spread, Turk Madden looked over Bordie's back at Vin Boling. "How's about it, bud? You askin', too? Or just looking?"

Boling's eyes held Madden's with a queer, leaping light. Turk saw the hard gleam of humor there, and something else, a sort of dark warning.

"You're rough, Madden," Boling said sarcastically, "and crude. I'm down here on a job, not swapping punches like any brawler. I'd rather like to take you down a notch, but that can wait."

As Turk turned on his heel and left, Sid Bordie got to his feet, his face pale and sick. His eyes were ugly with hatred, and a thin trickle of blood trickled from his smashed lips.

"I'll kill you for that, Madden!"

Dick London moved up alongside of Turk. "Man alive," he said. "He went down as if you'd hit him with an ax."

Leone rolled his cigar in his jaws. "Son," he said, "I'd sooner be hit with an ax." He shook his head then. "I don't like it, Turk. That's a bad outfit. I'd have felt better if Boling'd blown his top."

Turk nodded. "Yeah, he's a hard case, that one. But whatever he does will be back in the bush where nobody can see, an' if he has his way, there'll be no survivors."

SUNDOWN FOUND THE AMPHIBIAN sliding down to a landing on the lake, and Turk's eyes glinted with appreciation at what he saw. Rodd had constructed, with Shan's help, a small dock, about four feet wide and thirty feet long. Also, he had a boom made of logs tied together and anchored, forming a neat little harbor near the dock.

"We've been busy," Rodd said as they strolled from the dock toward the camp. "An' no sign of your babe in the woods. But say, I've been thinkin' a little about this Red you told me about, an' about the fellow without any legs. I know who he is."

Turk stopped. "What do you mean? Who is he then?"

"Look," Buck began, "I prospected down here before the war. Most of us in that racket knew each other. At first when you talked about this redhead you met, I didn't think much about it, but then it began to tie in. Back in forty-one there were a couple of men took off into the jungle, had some idea of hunting the Lost Gold Mine of the Martyrs. Well, when I came out of the jungle to go back to the States and the Army, it was forty-two, and they were still missing. One of those men was Red Gruber. The other one was Russ Fagin."

"Fagin? I think I know that name," Turk mused. "Wasn't he in that Gran Chaco fuss?"

"That's him. A tough character, out for all he could get and any way he could get it. If this fellow without legs is Russ Fagin, I'll bet he's meaner than ever about now."

"That's a horrible thing," Mora said, "having your legs cut off. I wonder what made them do it?"

"Nobody violates tabu," Madden replied. "He was lucky he got off that easy. Usually, they stake them out on an anthill." He studied the situation. "Shan, you can take the boys out tomorrow. I'm going over to this village wherever it is. Buck, you come with me. We'll talk to this legless gent."

As THOUGH she had been expecting them, Nato met the two men at the edge of the jungle. Her eyes went from Buck to Turk Madden.

"You come now to visit us?" she asked.

Turk nodded assent. "And to see the man without legs," he added.

A shadow crossed her face. "Oh, yes! But please, you must not ask for him at once. My people, they are strange."

Turk looked at her thoughtfully. "You are tall, Nato. What is your tribe? You seem like one of my people."

She was pleased, he saw that at once. "My father," she said softly, "was a Chileno—how you say—Iriss and Spaniss. He was a prisoner here for a long time. He, too, tried to go to Chipan."

"Tell me," Turk asked, "what's at Chipan? Is it a city?"

"A city, yes." She would say no more than that, although after a minute, she looked around at him. "The other man, without legs, he is ver' bad man. He try to kill Red."

"Was Red your friend? Your lover?" Turk asked gently.

She looked at him, startled, then amused. "Oh, no! I was too young! Much too young! Red, he talk with my *padre,* father. He talk much with him. When he go, he say he will come back. You see, we like Red. My people all like him."

"Your mother," Turk hazarded a guess, "she was Guarani?"

For a moment, the girl did not reply, and then she said without looking at him, "You must not speak Guarani. It is tabu. Nor talk of Chipan."

They emerged from the jungle into a cluster of ordered fields. They were *milpa* resembling those of the Maya, yet here agriculture seemed to have progressed beyond the stage of burned jungle, for the fields were scattered with leaf mold gathered from the jungle, and an effort had been made to turn the soil over.

"You plant maize? How many years here?" Turk asked curiously.

She looked at him quickly, pleased by his interest. "Maize two years," she said, "*Jican* two years."

Jican, he decided from her further explanation, was somewhat like the sweet-tasting turnip of Guatemala. There was no time for further questions, for they stood suddenly in the street of the village, a street heavily shaded by towering jungle trees, most of them the *sapodilla.*

Beneath the trees were scattered many huts, some of them facing upon a rough square. Several children were playing in the compound, and they got up and drew back into the black doorways of the palm-thatched huts. They stopped before one of the larger huts, and now a man stepped from it. He was white-haired, and although he seemed old, his body was hard and young-looking.

"Cantal," Nato said, and then indicating Madden and Rodd in turn, she said, "Madden, Rodd."

The chief spoke slowly, looking from one to the other as he spoke, and Madden could gather the gist of what he said from his gestures and expression. Also, there was something faintly familiar about the tongue, and then Turk knew what it was. It was faintly similar to the Guarani language with some words he seemed to remember from the Chamacos.

"What do we do now?" Buck asked softly. "The old boy seems friendly enough. Did you savvy that Chamaco? Seems mixed up, but I could get out a word or two."

Cantal led off, and he took them slowly about the village. It was a sightseeing tour, and Turk was interested despite his impatience to see and talk to Russ Fagin, if that was the name of the legless man. Obviously the maize crop was good, and Turk saw beans, squash, papayas, sapodilla, cacao beans, and after they had walked awhile, they stopped near another hut and were served *yerbe mate* in wooden cups.

Nato spoke suddenly to Cantal, and Turk, beginning to catch the sound of the language now and to sort out the Guarani words, understood she was asking about the man without legs. Cantal seemed to hesitate, and his face became severe. But finally the girl seemed to win him over.

Cantal turned and led them to a large hut that was set off to one side, and around it a low fence. As they passed through, a big man lurched suddenly out of the door on crutches, and as he saw them, his head jerked back as if he'd been struck.

HE WORE A tattered and many times patched shirt and crudely made shorts of some coarse, native cotton material. His arms and shoulders were heavy with muscle, his neck thick, and his face swarthy, unshaven. The eyes that stared from Madden to Rodd and back were hard, cruel eyes.

"Hello, Fagin," Rodd said. "You remember me? We met at Tucava, in the Chaco."

Fagin stared at him. "Yeah"—his voice was harsh—"sure I remember. What are you doin' here?"

"I'm with Madden here, on a little survey job."

"Madden?" Fagin smiled. "What is this, a meeting of the lost souls department? Or a reunion of the veterans of the Chaco?" His eyes held on Madden. "Well, what do you want with me? If you think I want to leave, you're wrong. I won't leave here until I kill every last one of these dirty savages." His voice was low and vicious and shook with repressed hatred. "They bobbed my legs." He chuckled grimly. "An' all because I went to their cursed Chipan!"

He hitched closer on the crutches, his eyes gleaming. "Madden, you're a man with spine. There's gold in that place. Gold, diamonds, everything. It makes Cuzco look like a piggy bank, take it from me. I got there, an' I'd of gotten away, too, if it hadn't been for that Cantal, there. He spotted me, an' when the priests got through, they'd taken my legs so I could never go back.

"Take me back there, man. I'll show you where it is." He hitched closer and the excitement made his veins swell in his head. "Listen, man." His voice boomed loudly, and Turk saw other natives coming nearer, and he suddenly wondered how much of this Natochi could grasp. "There's loot there enough for all of us. Everyone. Gold to buy the world."

"You'd better take it easy," Turk advised softly. "These natives won't like that. They'll understand."

"Understand? Them?" He sneered. "They don't savvy anything, but their pig talk." He leaned forward, thrusting his head out at them. "But you should see Chipan. What a city. It puts the Maya and the Inca to shame. An' old? Why that town's older than Rome. Older than Athens. Probably older than Babylon. You take it from me, this is something.

"You can take me," he hissed, leaning toward Turk. "To the devil with these gugus. Kill the lot of them. You've got guns. Mow 'em down. Let's get their gold an' get out of here."

CANTAL TOUCHED TURK'S ARM, and his face was severe. He spoke quickly. Nato interpreted.

"He says we must go now," she said, her eyes were frightened. "I think he understands, as I do, and it will be bad for you."

"No," Turk said, looking at Fagin, "I won't be involved in any venture that will take me to Chipan. If it is tabu, I shall respect their tabu. If you want to get out of here, to get back to civilization, I'll take you out, some way."

Fagin glared wildly. "Fool!" he screamed. "You blithering fool! There's gold there, I tell you. *Tabu!* What do their fool tabus mean to a white man?"

Madden turned abruptly away and accompanied by the others, walked rapidly off. Behind them, Fagin raved and shouted.

"I'll get there!" he screamed. "I'll get there, an' to the devil with you all. I'll see the whole bunch of you dead. All of them an' all of you!"

Madden stopped when they were well away from Fagin and he glanced at Buck Rodd. The big prospector's face was grim.

"Crazy," Rodd said. "Crazy as a loon." He scowled. "But they seem to be takin' good care of him. I wonder why."

Turk voiced the question to Nato, and she replied quickly, "We do not like the—what do you say?—break of tabu, but we have much feeling for one touched by spirits. The priests took his legs so he could not go back, for there is much danger there, spirits that cause much sickness. But we care for him. We always shall."

"Rodd," Turk said, "there's probably something to this tabu. Lots of white men scoff at them, but usually what a native calls evil spirits is something with a very real foundation. In New Guinea once a guy investigated a tabu and found it originated with an epidemic of smallpox. Tabu was the native method of quarantine. There's probably some good reason for this one."

"Yeah," Rodd agreed, then he looked at Turk. "I wonder if Fagin's nuts or if there is a lot of gold there. Man alive! What a find it would be!"

"Right now I'm thinking of something else," Turk admitted. He shook a cigarette from a pack and handed it to Rodd, then took one himself. "Buck, did you happen to look past him into the doorway? I did, and lying on the table, half covered by a cloth, was the torn end of a package of cigarettes. The same brand as these."

"The devil!" Rodd shoved his thumbs down in his belt and squinted his eyes. "Then he's seen somebody else recently, and if that's true, I guess we both know who."

"Sure, Boling's crowd." Turk shrugged. "This may come to a showdown mighty quick now."

Yet careful questioning of both Natochi and Cantal failed to elicit any information about white men other than Fagin. Wherever Russ Fagin had been, or whomever he had talked to, these two knew nothing about it. Yet Turk could see that his questions aroused curiosity, and before he left the village he had the promise from both Cantal and Nato that if any other white men came around, he would be notified at once.

THE FOLLOWING WEEK passed swiftly and without incident. The amphibian was constantly in the air, shuttling back and forth from the base to Obido, and the film and records piled up swiftly. Yet, as the days went by, Turk found himself growing more and more worried, and the strain was beginning to show on both Mora and London as well. Rodd took it easy. He hunted occasionally, or relieved Mora or London, who instructed him in their work. Often he prospected one of the nearby streams, or roamed the mountains with a sack and a hammer, taking samples. These trips Turk knew were more than prospecting trips, for Buck Rodd was keeping an eye on the country. He was not trusting to the natives.

On the tenth morning, Turk gestured at the stack of film, waiting in its cans to be transported to Obido.

"We'll take that in tomorrow," he suggested, "but today we knock off. I'm taking a flight over the jungle. You come along, Dick, an' the rest of you take it easy around here, but keep your eyes open."

They took off in the bright morning sunlight and headed due north as usual, but when a few miles were behind them, Turk banked the ship steeply and circled low over the jungle.

"Keep your eyes open, Dick," he said, "this is a reconnaissance flight. Boling's outfit has me worried."

With the two Pratt & Whitney motors roaring along pleasantly, Turk moved the ship down to a thousand feet and swung over the green carpet of jungle. Somewhere, not too far away, Boling would have a base camp. Twice his planes had been seen, but if they were actually conducting a survey it was not obvious, or else they were working far to the west.

That Vin Boling or one of the men with him had established secret contact with Russ Fagin seemed obvious, and if they had, they would know about Chipan. Knowing how inflammatory natives can become over violation of a tabu, Turk Madden understood that if the newcomers invaded Chipan it might mean disaster for every white man in the area.

Movement caught his eye, and he turned his head. The small plane they had seen before was just rising over the tops of the trees, and as it lifted, it turned in a wide swing toward them.

Turk yanked back on the stick and began to reach for altitude. What was coming he didn't know, but he wanted to be ready for anything. He went up in a fast climbing turn and it took him over a long savanna, the one from which the small ship had risen.

"Look!" Dick yelled. "There's some planes! Three of them!"

Vin Boling's headquarters lay before him. In air line distance it was no more than twenty miles from his own, with the native village between them. He scowled. It was odd that nothing had been seen of Boling's planes when he had been running a survey with the magnetometer.

He glanced back at the smaller plane and saw it was climbing fast and already a little above him.

"Looks like trouble!" he said, nodding quickly. "If that boy is armed, we may have plenty of it!"

London looked at him, astonished. "You don't mean they'd fight us? Like in war?"

Turk chuckled grimly. "Brother, when you tangle with that crowd it's always war. Petex knew what they were doing when they hired Boling. And Bordie, Mather, and Pace are fit running mates for him."

The small ship was a high-powered job with a terrific rate of climb, and it had passed them in the air. Suddenly, it went into a wingover and came down toward them in a screaming dive.

With one fleeting glance at the small ship, Turk opened the throttle wide and hit the straightaway, streaking off over the jungle. Yet he knew he could not hope to keep away from the smaller ship, which was much faster and more maneuverable than his own.

He saw it pull out of its dive and level off in pursuit, and he deliberately slowed. The heavens were almost cloudless, and there was little chance of escape that way. His only chance lay down below or in a sudden break that would put the ship in his sights. He cleared his guns with a burst of fire and saw Dick's startled glance. Then as the small gray ship came hurtling up on his tail, Turk did a half roll and came out of it only a few hundred feet over the jungle.

Several towering trees loomed before him, and he pointed the nose for them and put the stick forward, screaming in a long, slanting dive. He heard a yell from Dick and saw the bright spark of tracer as it leaped up alongside the cabin then fell away behind. The trees, like a solid wall, seemed rushing to meet them, and when they seemed certain to crash, he yanked back on the stick and the ship zoomed up and over. He put the stick forward and did a vertical bank with a wingtip almost touching the jungle below and turned right back on his trail, hauling back on the stick and grabbing at the space above him.

WITH A QUICK GLANCE around as he turned, he saw the fighter had safely missed the trees, but had overshot on his unexpected turn and was pulling up now in an Immelmann. Kicking the throttle open, Turk streaked away for the rising ship and let go with a burst of fire that streaked by the nose, but as the other ship was pulling out, it staggered suddenly in the air, and Turk banked sharply and swung around.

Although he had not noticed it, one of his bullets must have gone home on the other ship. Coolly, he hung above it and behind, watching the pilot fight the ship. He moved in closer, and, suddenly, the gray ship snapped out of it, pulled up sharply and, banking, swept toward Turk, guns blasting fire.

Cursing himself for a fool, Turk Madden made a flat turn, opening up on the smaller ship. But the burst was a clean miss, and the next thing he knew tracer was streaking by his plane. There was no chance to get away. The issue must be decided here. Pointing the amphibian straight at the gray ship, he opened the throttle wide.

He was hoping the pilot would take it for a suicide attempt, an effort to get him while going down himself. But whatever the pilot of the gray ship thought, he pulled up suddenly, and Turk let go with a burst that riddled his tail assembly.

The small ship fell away sharply, clearing Turk's wingtip by inches, and Madden caught a fleeting glimpse of Bordie's face, white and desperate, as the man fought the falling ship.

Madden pulled out and streaked away. Suddenly he was shaking all over and felt sick and empty inside. He glanced over at London, and Dick's face was as white as his own must have been and his eyes were round and bright. Suddenly, Turk was sweating. He wiped his face and glanced back. A puff of smoke rose suddenly from the jungle, and then a tiny spark of flame. Madden turned his head and started back for camp.

"Do you think he got out of that?" Dick asked hoarsely.

Turk shrugged. "There's no telling. When a ship crashes into the jungle like that, a man's got a chance, anyway. A mighty slim one, but I've known them to walk away. Those trees right there are mighty high, and that jungle's like a web. He didn't have much speed when he hit."

"What now?" London asked.

"Their base," Turk said grimly. "They asked for a fight, an' they can have it."

Yet when he zoomed over the savanna where Boling's planes had been, the craft were gone. However, the tents were still there, and what was obviously a storage tank. Madden turned at the end of the field and came streaking back, his twin motors wide open. He caught a fleeting glimpse of a man ducking from one of the tents, and then he cut loose with his guns and saw the tents go up in a burst of flame.

Turning, he made another pass at the field, this time pointing a finger of tracer at the storage tank, and getting it. There was an explosion and a puff of red rolling flame following a burst of black oily smoke.

At the end of the field, Turk leveled off and headed for the horizon. It had been a hot bit of work, but a good one. He streaked away, then made a wide circle and headed back for his own base. He felt suddenly let down now that it was over, and yet he knew just how lucky he had been. If Bordie had waited him out, or hadn't pulled up when he did, it would have been only a matter of a minute or two until he would have shot down the heavier, less maneuverable amphibian. In the last analysis, in such a scrap, it was how much spine a man had, and the breaks.

Madden mopped the sweat from his face again and swung low over the lake. Then he cut the throttle and came in for a landing. The ship touched the water lightly, then took it and taxied toward the shore.

"Hey!" London leaned forward. "Where is everybody?"

Turk's brows drew together. The shore was empty.

FACING UP THE BANK, they started for the tent, yet even before they reached it, they saw Phil Mora. The geologist and cameraman was struggling to get off the ground, his head bloody.

Turk bent over him. "Phil! What happened? Where's Rodd and Shan?"

Mora's lips struggled to shape the words, and London came running with a pan and some cloths.

"Relax," London said. "Take it easy."

Madden's eyes swept the clearing. A few quick steps in each direction showed him no one in sight. If Rodd and Shan were alive, they were in the jungle. At least, he told himself with sharp relief, they were not lying here. He strode back to Mora.

"Tell me what happened," he pleaded, dropping beside the man.

"Six of them," Mora said. "They came out of the jungle when I was in the tent. Shan had gone to the spring for water. Buck was off looking around in the jungle. They slugged me when I came out."

Dick's head came up sharply. "The film! And the records!"

Turk lunged to the tent, but even before he jerked back the flap he knew what to expect. The cans and the box of records were gone. He stood then, his big hands on his hips, his eyes narrowed in thought. Suddenly all the excitement was gone and his mind was cold and ready.

They must have been close to camp, waiting for him to take off. When he was gone, they had moved in. The fight, then, had been lost. He had shot down their plane, strafed their base camp, but they had slugged Mora and got away with the film and the records. And the records and the film were the whole object of this jungle trip. If they got away with them, Tropco was defeated and Petex had won.

Slipping his Colt from its shoulder holster, Turk checked the load. Then he slipped several extra clips in his pocket. He picked up a submachine gun and packed some ammunition down to the water. After that he helped London move Phil Mora to the tent.

"Dick," he said quietly, "you stick here with Phil. Take good care of him. If those guys come back, which isn't likely, you'll have to fight. You've got a good spot down on the shore behind those rocks. I'd move some ammo down there, and get some guns ready. If Buck or Shan come back, hold them here. We may have to get out in a hurry. I've an idea we're in for trouble from the natives, too."

"The natives?" Dick stared. "Oh, I see. You think that Boling and his crowd will go into Chipan with Fagin after that gold?"

"Knowing them, I do," Turk replied positively. "They won't miss, and that will mean the natives will go hog wild and want to wipe us all out. Better pack all our gear down to the beach and get ready for a quick move."

"What about you?" London demanded.

"Me?" Turk shrugged. "I'm gong after that film and those records."

He took twenty minutes for a smooth, rapid check of the ship, refueled from the small emergency supply they had on hand, and then warmed up the motors. He had only the roughest idea of a plan, but it was an idea that might work.

Not over three miles from Boling's base he had noticed another small lake. Actually, it was a treacherous-looking place, resembling a swamp more than a lake. There was every chance that there were snags, and it was very small, scarcely a patch of water among the mangroves and bamboo. However, with a bit of maneuvering he was sure he could put the ship down, and it would leave him within striking distance of his objective.

Of two objectives, in fact. The tall trees near where he had shot down Bordie's plane formed the apex of a triangle of which the other two corners were the pool for which he was headed and Boling's base camp. Also, he recalled that tall trees were often indicative of ruins and were an evidence often used as such by archeological explorers.

Turk got away into the wind and leveled off low over the jungle. The distance was short, and it was only a matter of minutes until he was circling the pool. He glanced down as he banked the ship, swallowing the sudden lump that came up in his throat.

The pool was there all right, and it was long enough, even longer than he needed, which would be a help in the takeoff.

The catch was that the pool was narrow, and there was a crosswind.

"I'd sooner tackle an irrigation ditch!" he said with disgust.

Then he mentally crossed his fingers and, cutting the speed, came in as slowly as possible. Putting the stick to the right, he gave the ship a little left rudder, careful not to overcontrol, slipping the ship down to the right into the crosswind. Then he flattened the ship out hurriedly and put the amphibian down with sweat beading his forehead. Taxiing as near to the mangroves as he dared, he got a line on one of them and soon had the ship moored.

Settling the .45 firmly in place, he slung the tommy gun over his shoulder and swung into the mangroves.

The earth was soggy with leaves and moss, and the jungle was filled with a strange, greenish light, as though Turk had left the plane to step into some fantastic other world where tree trunks rose into the towering thickness of the jungle roof, their grotesquely swollen bodies wrapped in lianas and swathed in dead leaves and pulpy creepers.

Turk Madden, his dark face streaming with perspiration, pushed and struggled through the dense growth. At times he emerged into an open space where the growth was scattered along the ground, even though the roof overhead was as tightly woven as ever. Only occasionally could he get a fleeting glimpse of the sky, blue and distant.

He halted, and a butterfly with a wingspread of seven inches danced in the air before him. He stopped again as a monkey chattered briefly somewhere off in the green distance. What seemed a mottled branch of a jungle tree stirred slightly, and with the hair bristling along his scalp, Turk slipped the machete he had taken from the plane into his right hand.

It was a boa constrictor, as thick as a man's thigh. Turk stepped gingerly around the tree and moved on, avoiding the many-colored globes of the *curuju* that are filled with a caustic ash. He avoided, too, a column of ants that trailed from a tree into the depths of a green and sickly-looking swamp.

Yet he made time. He found ways through the trees, using the machete but little, keeping his pace steady, and moving as swiftly as he could. When his sense of distance and timing assured him that he was approaching the savanna where Boling had his base, he moved more slowly, and purposively. Still when he finally reached the field, he almost walked into it before he caught himself. Sheathing the machete, then, he unslung the tommy gun.

"Brother," he told himself, "here goes nothing!"

The tents, now in ashes, were not far from him, but the planes had returned. There were two now, so all of the party must be present. Bordie's ship, as well as Bordie himself, was gone. That still left Boling, Frank Mather, and Pace, three tough customers, together with whoever they had to service the planes and maintain the base.

One of the ships was a big transport job, the other a small gray ship like the one Bordie had flown. It was not a fighter, but did mount a couple of machine guns.

Circling warily on the edge of the jungle, Turk searched for the men themselves.

He saw nothing, however, until finally, near a small fire, he saw a man rise and pick up a coffeepot.

"Personally"—the man's voice was strong and clear—"I wish we were out of here. This jungle gives me the creeps."

"Yeah," another voice agreed, "but if they do take that Chipan for a lot of loot, we'll be fixed for life!"

"Will we?" The first man's voice was ironic. "I ain't seen Vin Boling turning loose of anything yet. All we'll get will be what they don't want. I'd rather be out of here."

"I wonder where Sid is?"

"You needn't. When a man takes off in a ship like he had, after a ship Madden's flying, an' doesn't come back in all this time, mister, he ain't comin' back!"

"He could have gone on to Obido or Santarem."

"Sure. He could have done that, but I'll lay five to one he didn't. Sid Bordie washed out on this one. You take it from me."

There was no way to approach closer without being seen, and Turk didn't try for further concealment. He stepped out of the jungle and started walking swiftly through the grass toward the men.

"What about this Madden?" the man with the coffeepot was saying. "I only seen him once, an' that was the day he clipped Sid in Obido."

"Oh, he's tough, all right! Flew in the Chaco an' in China. Ran a hand-me-down airline in the East Indies before the war. He's tough, but he can be had! I wish I had a chance at him. Maybe I ain't no hand with my fists, but with a gun? Say!"

Turk stopped. "All right, chum. Say it!"

The coffeepot dropped with a crash, and the man's head jerked as if he'd been struck. He wheeled toward Turk, his eyes ugly.

He was a short man and stocky, with corn-colored hair in a crewcut. He had a red face and his eyes were pale blue. The other man was in a sitting position, and his face looked as if somebody had washed it in flour.

"Here it is," Turk said quietly. "I don't want you boys, but if you want to buy in, this is your chance. I want those films and the records, and nothing more. What do you say?"

The man on the ground spoke and his voice shook.

"Let him have 'em, Ed. Heck, I want to get out of this. This ain't no place for a man to die. I—"

"Shut up!" Ed snarled viciously. "You may be yella, but I'm not. Madden, you get anything here, you got to take it."

Turk's lips tightened and he felt a strange jumping in his stomach. "Chum, you get one more chance. Drop the rod an' back away with your hands up."

"Like the devil!"

With a whiplike movement of the arm, the short man drew and fired.

It was fast, incredibly fast, and Turk felt the snap of the bullet as it whizzed by his ear, and then he swung up the tommy gun.

Turk Madden shut down on the trigger, and the Thompson jarred in his hands. The short man backed up slowly, his face shocked, his eyes suddenly alive with awful realization. He staggered, then fell.

The other man might have been turned to stone. "Not me!" he gasped hoarsley. "I got a wife an' kids! I—"

"Forget it!" Turk said. "If you've got a wife and kids you're in one rotten racket. Where are those films and records?"

"In the transport," the man said eagerly. He got to his feet. "I'll get them for you."

A sudden movement startled Turk, and he wheeled, dropping into a crouch, the tommy gun ready, and then he could have whooped with joy. Two men were rushing toward him, and they were Buck Rodd and Shan Bao.

"You two! By all that's holy, if I was ever glad to see anybody!"

"We trailed them," Buck said, "we were after the films. You've got them?"

"Yeah. In the transport."

"Hell's breakin' out back there," Rodd said, panting from his run. "Vin Boling's in Chipan with Mather, Pace, and another guy, and they've killed a half-dozen natives. Russ Fagin's with them. We hid in the jungle until they got by us. They've got Nato, too!"

"The girl?" Turk scowled. "That's a help, isn't it. If it was just them and the natives, I'd let them fight it out." He fed shells into the clip of the tommy gun. "Look," he said swiftly, "you two take the film and records and head back for our ship." Quickly, he explained. Then he looked at Shan. "Think you can get her out of there?"

Shan Bao listened to his explanation, then nodded.

"All right, then," Madden said, "get this stuff back to the ship, take off, and get back to our base. Load up and be ready to move out."

"What about you?" Buck protested. "If you're going to tackle that gang, I'm with you!"

"No," Turk said. "This is my deal. You fellows get back. Shan couldn't pack all this stuff in one trip, anyway. I'm going over there in the little ship."

"How will you land?" Rodd protested.

Turk shrugged. "Maybe I won't have to. I want to get that girl away from them, but if I catch that bunch alone, I'm not going to play tag with them. Get going!"

"What about me?" the Boling man protested.

Turk turned on him. "Mister," he said, "unless you can fly that transport, or some of those guys come back, it looks to me like you've got a long walk."

On the run he headed for the small ship. A swift check, and he climbed in. It had been gassed up and was ready to go.

Evidently Boling had the same idea that he did, and after their return they had no idea of staying around.

He warmed the ship up, and then with Rodd and Shan waving good-bye, he took off. The little ship answered to the controls like something alive, and it took only a matter of minutes to let him know that he was flying a really hot job. He skimmed off over the jungle and banked around the tall trees as around a pylon.

Instantly, he saw them. Five men and a girl, one of them moving with a swinging movement as if on crutches, and behind them, some distance off yet moving steadily forward, were the natives. They clutched spears and machetes, and despite the undoubtedly superior armament of the Boling crowd, Turk knew they were in for trouble. Yet the white men had reached the tumbled rocks and ruined, vine-covered walls of Chipan.

Turning, Turk studied the situation below. The ruins of the ancient city covered a wide area, and over most of it the jungle had moved, binding the stones together with vines and creepers. Here and there tall trees grew up from some courtyard or walled enclosure, and except for one comparatively wide space of stone terrace, the city was completely covered. This terrace, bounded by long parapets shaped like the bodies of serpents, led up to a massive pyramid. This pyramid was ascended by a wide row of steps, and, atop it, on a space a hundred square yards, was a temple, and before the temple, an altar. It was toward this place that Russ Fagin was leading Boling.

As Turk zoomed over them Boling waved an arm, evidently thinking him to be Sid Bordie, returned.

Turk skimmed out over the jungle and banked into a turn and started back. The girl was obviously their prisoner. In the hands of such men as these, there could be nothing but ill treatment and death awaiting her. No doubt she was a hostage, but knowing the fanaticism of natives when their tabu has been violated, Turk was sure that she would be of no use to Boling. Which meant she would certainly be killed. If Nato, who had helped them, was to escape, it must be by his hand.

Landing was impossible. The terrace was long enough, but it was littered with fallen stones. He looked at the jungle, swallowed.

"If there's a special god for fools," he said aloud, "I hope he's got his fingers crossed for me."

Turning the ship toward the edge of the jungle behind the pyramid, he came down in a slow glide, then he cut the motor and, with the trees close under him, brought the stick back. He came down in a stall.

There was a tearing crash, and he was hurled violently forward. The safety belt broke and he shot forward as the plane nosed down through the trees and brought up in a tangle of leaves and lianas that broke under him. He fell and then crashed into another tangle of vines. He finally hit the earth under the trees in a mass of dried leaves, reptiles, spiders, and decayed lianas that had hung among the tangle of vines like a great bag full of jungle rot and corruption.

All he could think of was that he was alive and unhurt. His .45 had fallen from its holster but lay only an arm's length away. What had become of the tommy gun, he couldn't guess. He struggled to his feet, badly shaken, and moved away from the debris he had brought down with him.

The plane had hit the ground only a few feet away, but look as he might, he could not find the tommy gun.

He stared at the plane, then at the hole in the jungle.

It was a miracle, no less.

"Brother," he said grimly, "they don't do that twice, an' you've had yours."

He started away, then saw his machete lying not far from the broken wingtip. Recovering it, he started on a limping run, his head still buzzing, for the pyramid.

There was no stair on this side, and he knew that by now Vin Boling would be ascending. He started around the base, then halted, for suddenly through the vines he saw a deep notch in the side of the pyramid. It was a tangle of vines and fallen stone, but might be another entrance. It also looked like a hole fit for a lot of snakes.

Carefully, he approached the opening. Beyond the stones he could see a black opening.

Drawing a deep breath, machete in hand, he went into it.

Once inside he stood in abysmal darkness, the air close and hot, stifling with an odor of dampness and decay. Striking a match, he looked around. On the floor was the track of a jaguar, the tiger of the Amazon. There was mud here and mold. But directly before him was a steep stair. Mounting carefully, for the steps were slippery with damp, he counted twenty steps before he halted, feeling emptiness around him. He struck another match.

Torn and muddy from his fall, he stood in the entrance to a vast hall, his feeble light blazing up, lending its glow to the light that came through from somewhere high up on the pyramid's side. Upon each wall was a row of enormous disks, surfaced in gold or gold leaf, at least a dozen upon a side. Before him was an open space of stone floor and, at the end of the hall, an even more enormous disk.

Stepping forward, Turk glanced up toward the source of the light and saw it was a round opening, and no accident, for he realized at once that the rays of the morning sun would shine through that opening upon certain days, and the golden flood of light would strike upon the great golden disk, and be reflected lightly upon the rows of disks.

Awed by the silence and the vastness of the interior of the great pyramid, he walked forward, his footsteps sounding hollowly upon the stone floor, and then he turned and looked back, and almost jumped out of his skin.

A figure wearing a tall golden headdress sat upon a throne facing the disk. Despite the need for him on the surface, Turk turned and walked toward the tall dais, approached by steps, on which the figure sat. Slowly, he mounted the stair.

It was a colossal figure, much larger than he had first believed, and he could see that it would be bathed in the reflected sunlight from the great disk over the end of the hall. In the lap of the figure was a great dish, and upon it lay several gold rings, and some gems.

Suddenly, Turk heard a shot from above him, and then a yell. The sounds seemed very close, and very loud.

"Here they come!" The voice was that of Pace.

"Let 'em come!" Boling said. "Mather, behind the stone on the right. Pace, stay where you are. Don't waste any shots. Fagin, tell them unless they stop and return to their village we'll kill the girl."

Turk heard Fagin shouting, and he turned, searching for the opening through which the sound must come. And then he saw a bit of light and saw there was a stairway close behind the seated figure. From the light on the top steps, he knew it must lead to the roof.

Taking a quick step back, he picked up a handful of the gems on the dish and stuffed them into his pocket. Then he started for the doorway. But in the door he paused, for before him was a gigantic gong. It must have been ten feet across, and beside it a huge stone hammer.

Stuffing his gun back into his belt, he picked up the hammer, hefted it, and swung.

The sound was deafening. With a great, reverberating boom, the tone rang in the empty hallway. Outside, Turk heard a shout of astonishment, then a yell. Again, once, twice, three times he struck the gong, and then, dropping the stone hammer, he was up the stair in a couple of leaps.

He had hoped the surprise would give him his chance, and it did. He rushed out on a stone platform before the temple to face a group that stood astounded in their tracks, the pyramid still vibrating with the sound of the huge gong.

Nato saw him first. "Quick!" he said. "Over here!"

Boling recovered with a shout. "No you don't, Madden!" he yelled.

He swung up his gun, and Turk snapped a shot at him that missed, and then shoved the girl toward the stair and fired again. The man behind Boling grabbed him and yelled.

"Look out!" His voice rose to a scream. "They are coming!"

The natives had started up with a surge, and Pace fired, then Mather. As their guns began to bark, Turk lunged after the girl, but Boling, more anxious to get her in hopes he could stop the natives with her, rushed after him.

Turk wheeled as Nato dodged onto the stairway, and Boling skidded to a halt.

"Out of my way, Madden! That girl can save us. Without her we're all dead. You, too."

"You fool!" Turk snapped. "They wouldn't stop for her. You've violated tabu. They'd kill her, too."

"You—"

Boling's gun swung up, and Turk lashed out with his left. Boling staggered, but slashed at Turk with the gun, yelling in one breath for Nato to come back, in the other for help. Turk went under the gun and smashed a left and right to the body, and then as Boling wilted, he turned and lunged down the stairway after the fleeing girl.

A gun roared behind him, but the shot only struck the gong, and it clanged loudly, driving the natives to a greater frenzy. Grabbing Nato's hand, Turk raced across the open floor and ducked down the dark and slippery stairway toward the opening where he had come in.

Behind them, the pyramid echoed to shots and yells, and then a high-pitched scream of terror and another shot. At the edge of the jungle, they stopped and looked back. All they could see was a mass of struggling figures, but to that there could be but one end, for if the natives had reached the top of the pyramid there was no hope for Boling's crowd. One, perhaps two might get away, but more likely, none of them.

Turk caught the girl's wrist and plunged into the jungle. Her face was white and her eyes wild.

"We must hurry!" she panted. "They will come for us, too, when finished there. We have violated tabu. No living thing must go to Chipan."

"What about them?" Turk asked grimly, indicating the natives.

"They protect the tabu. That is different," Natochi protested.

Slashing at the wall of jungle with his machete, Turk cleared a space and then moved forward into an opening. He walked swiftly, but as fast as he walked, the girl's terror and her own lithe strength was enough to keep her close behind him.

Twisting and turning, using every available opening, he dodged through the thick undergrowth. They had little time, and then the hue and cry would be raised after them, and the natives would come fast, probably much faster than he could go.

A savanna opened before them. "Can you run?" he asked.

She nodded grimly and swung into a stride even with his own. Together, man and woman, they raced across the tall-grass field and into the jungle beyond. Turk's heart was pounding, and though he strained his ears, he heard no more shooting. Then, after a long time, one shot sounded, far behind them.

"If Boling was smart," he said, "he used that on himself."

WALKING, RUNNING, STUMBLING, and pushing, they made their way through the jungle. Behind them they heard no sound, but they knew the chase was on.

What if Shan had crashed in his takeoff? What if there had been some other trouble? What if they had not found the ship? If they had met with trouble, he thought grimly, if anything had gone wrong, then it would be a last stand on the lakeshore for them. And for Dick London and Phil Mora, too.

His shirt was hanging in rags, partly torn in the plane crash and partly in the jungle. His breath came in hoarse gasps, and he stopped once to brush his black hair from his eyes, staring back. He turned once more at Nato's urging and plunged into the jungle.

How long they were in covering the distance he never knew. The jungle was a nightmare of tangling traps and spidery vines. They fought through it, heedless of snakes or swamps, thinking only of escape, and behind them, somewhere in the green and ghostly silence of the afternoon jungle, came the slim brown natives. Their tabu had been violated, and for this each man and woman must die!

A crash sounded in the jungle behind them, and Turk swung about swiftly, his gun leaping up. A native poised there with a spear, and Turk's gun belched flame. The man screamed and the spear went into the ground. Then, as others rushed forward, Turk emptied the clip into them and turned and burst through the wall of the jungle into the open savanna. Before them was the blue of the lake!

If he had had the strength, he would have whooped for joy. Even as he ran, he jerked out the used-up clip and shoved in another one. The prop on the amphibian started to turn, and with his breath stabbing like a knife, he staggered with the girl down toward the water.

Rodd and London were standing there with rifles, and suddenly they began to shoot. Pushing the girl toward the boat, Turk wheeled on Rodd.

"Get going!" he said. "They've gone crazy! Nothing will stop them!"

They shoved off in the boat, and the plane's door was open to receive them. Once aboard the plane, they pulled in the boat and Shan started the ship moving.

Gasping, Turk stared back toward the horde of natives, all of two hundred of them, gathered upon the site of their camp, stamping and waving their spears.

The twin motors talked strongly to the bright blue sky, and the big ship pulled up, circled once over the lake and leveled off toward the far blue distance where lay the Amazon.

"What about her?" Mora said, nodding toward the girl. She looked from one to the other, her eyes wide.

"She'll do better outside," Turk said quietly. "I'll see that Joe Leone stakes her, and with the job we've done, he'll be glad to. Besides," he added, feeling the hard lump of the gems and gold in his pocket, "I've got enough here, out of their own temple, to take care of her for life."

"Wait until I show her Coney Island," Dick said. "And buy her a couple of hot dogs!"

She laughed. "With mustard?"

"Hey!" Dick gasped. "What is this?"

"Red tell me much about Coney Islands," she said. "He talk always of hamburgers, hot dogs, and of beer."

Turk took over the controls and held the ship steady. He looked down at the unrolling carpet of the jungle. It was better up here. It was cleaner, brighter, freer.

They would be in Obido soon, and tomorrow they would be starting home, down the dark rolling Amazon, the greatest of all jungle rivers. And behind them, in the green solitude of the jungle, the morning sunlight would shine through a round opening and touch with all its radiance upon a great golden disk, and the reflected light would bathe in strange beauty the solitary figure of the mysterious god of Chipan.

Mission to Siberut

S teve Cowan cut the throttle and went into a steep glide. He glanced at his instruments and swore softly. If he made it this time, he would need a rabbit's foot in each pocket. Landing an amphibian on a patch of water he had seen but once several years before, and in complete darkness! But war was like that.

The dark hump beneath him would be Tanjung Sigep, if his calculations were correct. Close southward was Labuan Bajau Bay. The inner bay, visible only from the air, was the place he was heading for. It was almost a mile long, about a thousand yards wide, and deep enough. But picking it out of the black, jungle-clad island of Siberut on a moonless night was largely a matter of instruments, guesswork, and a fool's luck.

Cowan saw the gleam of water. Guessing at four or five feet, he leveled off and drew back gently on the stick. The hull took the water smoothly, and the ship lost speed.

At one place, there was about an acre of water concealed behind a tongue of land overgrown with casuarina trees. Taxiing the amphibian around the tongue of land, Cowan anchored it safely in the open water behind the casuarinas. When he finished, the first streaks of dawn were in the sky.

Mist was rising from the jungle, and on the reef outside Labuan Bajau Bay he could hear the roar and pound of surf. There would be heavy mist along the reef, too, lifting above that pounding sea. Cowan opened a thermos bottle and drank the hot coffee, taking the chill of the night from his bones. . . .

Two days ago in Port Darwin, Major Garnett had sent for him. Curious, he responded at once. Garnett had come to the point immediately.

"You're a civilian, Cowan. But you volunteered for duty, and you've flown over most of the East Indies. Know anything about Siberut?"

"Siberut?" Cowan was puzzled. "A little. I've been on all the Mentawi Islands. Flew over from Emma Haven on the coast of Sumatra."

Garnett nodded.

"No Europeans, are there?" he asked.

COWAN HESITATED.

"Not to speak of. The natives are timid and friendly enough, but they can be mighty bad in a pinch. Villages are mostly back inland. It's heavily jungled, with only a few plantations. There are, I think, a few white men."

"How about that trouble of yours some years back? Weren't they white men?" Garnett asked keenly.

Steve Cowan chuckled.

"You check up on a guy, don't you? But that was no trouble. It was a pleasure. That was Besi John Mataga. He's a renegade."

"I know." Major Garnett nodded. "Furthermore, we understand he is negotiating with the enemy. That's why I've sent for you."

He leaned forward.

"It's like this, Cowan. Intelligence has learned that fifty Messerschmitt 110s were flown from Tripoli to Dakar across the Sahara. They were loaded on a freighter heading for Yokohama. War broke out, and temporarily the freighter was cut off from Japan.

"Just what happened then, we only know from one of the crew, who was supposedly drowned. He got to us and reported that several of the crew, led by the chief mate, murdered the captain and took over the ship.

"The chief mate had some idea of striking a bargain with the Japanese. He'd claim the ship was injured and that he could tell them where it was—for a price."

"And the mate is John Mataga, is that it?" Cowan asked.

"Exactly. Mataga had signed on under an assumed name, but was dealing with the Japanese as himself. Naturally, the freighter had to be hidden until a deal was struck. Our advices are that the deal is about to go through. In the right place at the right time, I needn't tell you what those fifty Messerschmitts would mean to Japan."

"No," Cowan frowned. "Those Messerschmitts would be tough to handle."

"That's it," Garnett agreed. "They must never reach Japanese hands. They must be found and destroyed—and we know exactly where they are?"

"Off Siberut?"

"Yes. Lying in Labuan Bajau Bay. You know it?"

"You bet." Cowan sat up. "What do I do and when do I start?"

"You understand the situation," Garnett said. "We can't spare the pilots for an attack. Indeed, we haven't planes enough. But one ship, flown by a man who knew the locality, might slip through."

Cowan shrugged. "You want that freighter blown up?"

"Yes." Garnett nodded vigorously. "You've had no bombing experience, so we can't trust to that. You must land, and . . ."

But that had been two days ago.

The first night, Steve Cowan had flown the amphibian to a tiny inlet on the south coast of Java, where he remained all day, hidden from hostile scouting planes. Then when darkness fell, he took off again. Time and again he had narrowly missed running into the enemy. Once, south of Bali, he had come out of a cloud facing a lone Japanese plane.

He recognized it instantly. It was a Kawasaki 93, a bomber-reconnaissance plane. In the same instant, he banked steeply and sharply and fired a burst at its tail as it shot by him.

Cowan had the faster ship and could have escaped. But he was conscious of nothing but the realization that if the pilot broke free, it would be only a matter of minutes before speedy pursuit ships would be hunting him down.

His turn had brought him around on the enemy's tail, and he gunned his ship. The Kawasaki tried an Immelmann and let go a burst of fire as it whipped back over in the tight turn. But Cowan was too close behind for the pilot's fire to reach him.

He pulled his ship up so steeply he was afraid it would stall, but then he flattened out. For an instant the Kawasaki was dead in his sights.

Cowan's burst of fire smashed the Japanese tail assembly into a stream of fragments. But their crew was game. They tried to hit Cowan with a burst from the observer's gun.

Cowan saw the stream of tracer go by. Then he banked steeply and swung down in a long dive after the falling ship, pumping a stream of bullets into his target. Suddenly the Kawasaki burst into flame. An instant later, a red, roaring mass, it struck the sea.

The entire fight had lasted less than a minute. Cowan pulled back on his stick and shot upward, climbing until he saw the altimeter at sixteen thousand feet. Then he had leveled off and headed straight for Siberut.

COWAN DRANK the coffee slowly, then ate a bar of chocolate. It would be daylight in a matter of minutes, he knew. Beyond the clump of casuarinas on the shore would be the renegade freighter. Beyond the trees, and probably a mile away.

Carefully Cowan stowed his gear, then checked his guns. He was carrying two of them, a .45 Colt automatic for a belt-gun and a .380. The smaller gun was strapped to his leg inside his trousers. There was a chance he might need an ace in the hole.

The explosive he'd brought along for the job was ready. It had been carefully prepared two days before by one of the best demolition experts in Australia.

Cowan made his way ashore through the mangroves that grew down close to his anchorage. Then he swung down from the trees and walked along the sand under the casuarinas.

Besi John Mataga would not leave the freighter unguarded. There would be some of the crew aboard. And if Steve Cowan knew Besi John, the crew members would be the scum of the African waterfronts where they had been recruited.

How he was to handle that part of it, Cowan didn't know. You could rarely plan a thing like that; so much depended on chance. You knew your objective, and you went there ready to take advantage of any chance you got.

The Japanese would be hunting the ship. They wouldn't pay off to Besi John without having a try for it. But on the other hand, they couldn't afford to delay for long. The planes were needed too badly, with streams of new Curtiss, Bell, and Lockheed pursuit jobs pouring into Australia.

Cowan halted under the heavy branches of a casuarina. The outer harbor was open before him. There, less than a half mile away, was the *Parawan,* a battered freighter of Portuguese registry.

It was at least possible, even if improbable, that Besi John did not know of the inner harbor. In any case, no large ship could possibly negotiate the channel without great risk. The entrance, about two hundred yards wide, was shoal water for the most part and out of sight behind the point of casuarinas.

The *Parawan* lay in about sixteen fathoms, Cowan judged, remembering the soundings of the outer harbor. On the shore close by was a hut, where traders used to barter for rattan and other wood products.

Moving along the point toward the mainland, Steve Cowan studied the freighter from all angles. He would have to get aboard by night; there was no other way. In any event, it wasn't going to be easy.

Keeping under cover of the jungle, Cowan worked his way along the shore. Several times he paused to study the sandy beach. Once he walked back under the roots of a giant ficus tree, searching about in the darkness.

A ripple in the still water nearby sent a shiver along his spine. He watched the ominous snout and drew back further from the water's edge.

"Crocs," he said. "Crocs in the streams and sharks in the bay."

Coming to the bank of a small stream, he hesitated, then walked upstream. Finally he found what he sought. In a clump of thick brush under the giant roots of a mangrove, he found a dugout.

Cowan had known it would be there. The natives would want a boat on this bay, and all the boats would not be upstream at the villages. He was going to need that dugout. The bay, like all the waters around Sumatra, was teeming with sharks.

Walking along the shore under cover of the trees, Cowan stopped abruptly. He had been about to step out into a clearing. There in the open space was the hut where the traders used to meet. Two men stood in front of it.

BESI JOHN MATAGA had his back to him, but Steve Cowan recognized the man at once. No one else had that thick neck and those heavy shoulders. The other man was younger, with a lean, hard face and a Heidelberg scar. Cowan's eyes narrowed.

"They won't find this place!" Mataga said harshly. "It ain't so easy spotted. If they do, they'll never get away. We got our own spies around here."

"You'd better have." The stranger's voice was crisp. "And don't underestimate the Aussies and the Yanks. They might locate this place. It must be known to other people."

"Sure." Besi John shrugged. "Sure it is, Donner. But it ain't the sort of place they'd figure on. White men, they never come here. One did once, but he won't again."

"Who was that?" Donner demanded.

"A guy named Cowan. I had a run-in with him once out there on the beach. I whipped the tar out of him."

"You lie!" Steve Cowan muttered to himself.

He studied Donner. Instinct warned him that here was an even more dangerous opponent than Besi John. Mataga was a thug—this man had brains.

"I'm giving the Japanese just forty-eight hours!" Donner snapped. "They either talk turkey or I'll deal with somebody else. I might start out for myself."

"They'll talk," Mataga chuckled. "Birdie Wenzel knows how to swing a deal. They'll pay off like he wants them to, and plenty. Then we'll tell them where the ship is, and pull out—but fast."

"What about them?" Donner said. He jerked a thumb over his shoulder. "You still think the old man is good for some cash?"

Mataga shrugged.

"I'm goin' to work on him. He knows where the dough is. It's hid aboard that ship, and he knows where. He'll talk before I get through with him!"

The two men turned and walked out to a dinghy where several surly-looking seamen waited. They got in and shoved off.

Cowan studied the hut. Now whom had Donner meant by "them"?

While Cowan mulled it over, a husky seaman came around the corner of the hut, a rifle in the hollow of his arm. He said something through the door of the hut, and then laughed at the reply. He sat down against the wall, rifle across his lap.

Cowan stood half behind the bole of a huge tree and studied the situation anew. As long as that man remained where he was, there was no chance that a dugout could reach the freighter unobserved. The seaman was not only guarding whoever was in the hut but watching the ship as well. Even on the darkest night, it would be difficult to get away from shore without being seen.

Cowan circled around the hut. When he was behind it, he straightened up deliberately and walked toward it. Just as he stopped against the wall, he heard a light step. Wheeling, Cowan found himself facing a slender, hatchet-faced man with a rifle.

The fellow grinned, showing blackened stumps of teeth. Cowan did not hesitate. Dropping his left hand, he grabbed the rifle barrel and wrenched so hard that he jerked it free before the man's finger could squeeze the trigger.

Pulled off balance, the man fell forward into a smashing right uppercut to the wind. As he went down, Cowan struck him with the butt of his own rifle. He fell like a log and lay still.

Cowan wheeled, his breath coming hard. He was just in time. The big fellow he had seen on guard in front came around the side of the hut. Steve Cowan gave no warning, but struck viciously.

HE WAS TOO ANXIOUS, and the punch missed. He caught a glancing blow from the other's rifle and went to his knees. Blinded with pain, he nevertheless lunged forward and grabbed the man by the knees. The fellow struck again. Cowan rolled free, lashing out with a short blow that landed without much force. Both men got up at once.

The big fellow's eyes flashed angrily. He rushed in, swinging wildly. Cowan lashed out himself, but caught one on the side of the head. The guard missed a vicious kick as Steve Cowan fell.

But Cowan was up quickly, and breathing hard. Steadying down, he met the rush with a hard right. The big fellow was fighting savagely, and apparently he had not considered a yell for help. Cowan knew he must get him, must knock the man out or kill him before he could shout.

It was more than a fight to win. It was more than a fight for mere life—although Cowan knew to lose meant death. It was a fight for all the lives that might be lost if those fifty crated pursuit ships out there got into Japanese hands.

The guard charged again, trying to close with him. Cowan struck with a short left to the face, then smashed a hard right to the wind. The guard lunged again. Cowan's left speared his mouth. Then he drove in close, his big shoulders swaying with the rhythm of his punches.

The guard staggered, tried then to shout. But Cowan's rocklike fist smashed his lips again. The man went down, falling into a left hook that knocked him to the sand.

Cowan fell on him instantly and tied his hands behind his back. Then he bound his feet. Panting with the exertion, Cowan started for his first opponent. One glance was enough. The man was dead.

Picking up the guard's rifle, Cowan threw the other man's weapon into the brush. Then he sauntered around the hut, keeping his head down. If observed with glasses from the freighter, he might pass to an unsuspecting watcher for the guard. That individual was heavier, but it was not too noticeable at a distance.

Once around the shack Steve Cowan stepped warily inside, fearing there might still be a third guard. But there were only two people—an elderly man and a girl, both bound to chairs. They stared at him anxiously.

Hastily Cowan knelt and freed them. He glanced then at the man.

"You, I take it, are the captain of that ship out there," he said.

The man nodded, questioning gratitude in his eyes.

"Name of Forbes, Ben Forbes. This is my niece, Ruanne. Had a mutiny off the Cape. Left Dakar for Saigon, French Indochina, the sixth of last December, Mr. Mataga brought us in here after a week's layover at Amsterdam. The island, you know."

Cowan stepped back into the doorway.

"You'll have to stay in here until dark. I think they are watching. They'll believe I'm your guard."

"What happened to him?" Ruanne asked suddenly. It was the first attempt she had made to speak.

"He had a little trouble out back," Cowan said dryly. "He's tied up. There was another man, too."

"That was Ford. The big fellow is Sinker Powell. They were in the black gang," Captain Forbes explained.

"Ford's not going to be in any black gang again," Cowan said quietly. "The Sinker is still around, though."

Forbes couldn't yet contemplate his release.

"Who are you?" he asked. "Turning us loose, maybe I shouldn't ask, but—"

"The name is Steve Cowan. I'm a flyer. Commercial, not Army."

"You'll help me take back my ship?" Forbes pleaded.

"Take it back?" Cowan gave him a sidelong glance. "Cap, there must be twenty men aboard there."

"Are you afraid?" Ruanne looked at him quietly, her eyes inscrutable. "You don't look like a man who would be afraid. But I could be wrong."

Cowan grinned, feeling his face tenderly.

"I only wear this blood on my head when I meet ladies. Anyway"—he looked at Forbes—"I couldn't help you, Captain. I'm a guy who doesn't beat around the bush. I came here for one reason, to blow your ship sky-high, and blown up it will be before I leave this island.

"You can help me, though. If you don't want to, all I ask is that you stay out of my way. I've got a plane, and when this is over I'll fly you out."

Forbes glared at him.

"Blow up my ship? Are you crazy, man! There's cargo aboard that ship for Saigon."

"No," Steve Cowan replied quietly. "There are planes aboard that ship for Japan."

Forbes's eyes narrowed.

"A crank, eh? Young man, if you have an idea you can start injuring Japan by sinking my ship, you're all wrong. You sound like one of these 'Yellow Peril' loudmouths. You talk like a blatherskite! I lived in Japan, and—"

Cowan lit a cigarette. When he dropped the match, he leaned his shoulder back against the wall.

"Cap," he said slowly, "when did you say you left Dakar?"

"On December sixth. Why? What has that to do with—"

"Wait a minute, Uncle Ben." Ruanne's eyes were on Cowan. "He wants to say something."

"You left Dakar on December sixth," Cowan repeated slowly. "On the morning of December seventh, the Japanese raided the Pearl Harbor naval base. Then they invaded the Philippines, attacked Malaya, took Singapore, Balik Papan, Palembang, Menado, Rabaul, and the whole Dutch East Indies. The islands in this part of the world are filled with their ships and planes.

"The United States Fleet struck back at the Marshall Islands. Our planes have begun action from Australia. You are right on the edge of the biggest war in history!"

Captain Ben Forbes stared at him, unbelieving.

"I—I don't believe it!" he gasped finally. "Unless Mataga bribed my radio operator to keep me in the dark. I never trusted him much."

"There's your answer," Steve said slowly. "Cap, your freighter out there has fifty Messerschmitt pursuit ships for the Japanese. Those planes can mean many lives lost, much equipment destroyed. They can, for a time and in a few places, give the Japanese equality or superiority in the air. It might be at the crucial spot."

"I know what a man's ship means to him, Cap," Cowan added. "But this is bigger than any of our jobs. I was sent here to see that that freighter is blown up. I'm going to do it."

"He's right, Uncle Ben," Ruanne said softly. "He's very right."

All through the day they waited, discussing the ship, the crew and the chances there would be. Sinker Powell lay bound and gagged, but he glared furiously and struggled.

Captain Forbes paced the hut.

"I don't like it!" he said finally. "You're going aboard that ship alone. If they jump you—"

"If they do," Cowan said grimly, "it will be up to you, Cap. That cargo must be destroyed."

Forbes hesitated suddenly.

"There's a lot of casing-head gas aboard," he said thoughtfully. "It's stowed amidships in steel drums. There's a tank aft we carried gasoline in, but it's empty now. I was going to have it cleaned when we got to Saigon. But you might dump some of those drums of casing-head. It would make a devil of a fire."

"I'll find a way," Cowan declared. He had not mentioned the explosive he'd brought along. "As soon as it's dark, I'll slip aboard. You and Ruanne had better go out on the point under those casuarinas. I'll meet you there. We'll have to get away fast when we go. The explosion and the flames will be sure to bring the enemy around here thicker than bees around a honeycomb."

HE SAT DOWN outside the hut, as Sinker Powell had been sitting when Cowan first sighted the man. There he stayed, alternately watching and dozing while Forbes watched. It was a long day. At any moment Besi John Mataga might decide to come ashore. That was what Cowan feared most; for going aboard the ship was an anticipated danger.

NIGHT CLOSED IN SUDDENLY as it does in the tropics. Cowan walked back along the shore with Captain Forbes and Ruanne. When he came to the dugout he stopped.

"Go out on the point about halfway," he said, "but stay back in the jungle out of sight. This shouldn't take me long. If I don't get back—" Cowan hesitated, gazing down at Ruanne—"you'd better go back inland to one of the villages.

"The natives are friendly if you treat them right. Then stay there until this war is over or you find a way out. But I'll be back," he declared softly.

They walked on. Cowan loaded the gear he had concealed near the dugout and shoved off.

It was deathly still. No breeze touched the face of the water, no ripple disturbed its surface. Clouds covered the sky. The heat was heavy in the humid, unmoving air. Cautiously Cowan dipped his paddle, and the dugout moved easily through the water.

It seemed a long time before he saw the dark hull of the ship. For an instant he hesitated, fearing a challenge. Then he moved on, with scarcely discernible movements of his paddle. He worked the dugout toward the stern, away from the lighted ports. Except for those two ports, the freighter was blacked out. Even as he watched, their lights flicked out, too.

There was silence, heavy and thick. The dugout bumped gently against the hull. Cowan worked his way alongside with his hands, hoping for a rope line, something by which he could get aboard. There was nothing.

He picked up the coil of line he had brought, adjusted the wrapping on the hook again. Sighting at the dimness where the rail was, he threw the rope. It caught and he hauled it in, testing the line with his weight.

It was now or never. If he fell, there would be no need to shoot him. Sharks would take care of that. As if in answer to his thought, Cowan saw the streak of phosphorescence left by a big fish swimming by. He slipped the band of his carrying sling over his shoulder and went up the line, hand over hand.

He crawled through the rail and crouched there in the stillness. There was no sound, no movement. Treading on cat's feet, as though part of the night itself, he slipped forward.

Amidships—that was the place. It was most dangerous, as there would be more chance of discovery there and less opportunity of escape. But the casing-head gas was stored there. Its burning would insure practically complete destruction. And this had to be a clean job. Not one Messerschmitt was to remain. A clean job—

A sound amidships made Cowan crouch at the base of a winch. He saw a man walk out on deck, barely discernible in the darkness. The fellow stood there, looking toward the shore. Another man walked out.

"Funny Sinker ain't got a fire," one of them said.

"Act your age, Joe," the other replied. "The Old Man wouldn't let him have one. Too dangerous."

"Chiv," Joe said suddenly, low-voiced, "you think Mataga will give us a square cut on this money? After all, look at the chance we're takin'."

"Better forget it," Chiv whispered uneasily. "We got to string with him. I want mine, but I ain't no man to cross Besi John Mataga. You see what he done with the second mate? Cut him to pieces with his own knife. The man's a fiend!"

"Donner's worse," Joe said sullenly. "Me, I'm out for the dough. I'm gettin' mine, see? No wise guy ever crossed Joe Gotto yet. I ain't so wise to the angles in this part of the world. I'd feel better if I was in Chicago, or Memphis, or the Big Town."

STEVEN COWAN SLIPPED along the starboard side of the hatch, crouching low. Amidships, he found, as he had feared, that the hatch was still covered. Working swiftly, he took out the wedges, then slid the steel batten from its place. Lifting the corner of the tarpaulin, he got hold of the end hatch cover and slid it slowly out of place, then eased it to the deck.

Swiftly he eased himself into the hole. Pulling the tarpaulin back over him, he went down the steel ladder in the utter blackness of the hold. It seemed a long time before he reached the bottom. Then he was standing on a tier of cargo.

Momentarily Cowan flashed a light. He was standing on a tier of casinghead drums, piled six high. He put the explosive down and coolly spun the tops from a dozen of the drums. Then, as he stooped to adjust the time on the explosive, his flashlight slipped and fell. The glass broke with a faint tinkle on the dunnage below.

For an instant, Cowan crouched in the darkness, his heart pounding. He dared not strike a match, for by now the air around him was filling with fumes of gasoline. For the life of him he could not recall the time for which the bomb was set!

It might be set to go off in three minutes, or five, or an hour. Possibly even a dozen hours. Steve Cowan had planned to adjust it before leaving. Now he had no idea. All that remained was to throw the switch that put the thing to work.

It might blow him up instantly. It might go off before he was out of the hatch. Or off the ship—

It was a chance he had to take. Cowan turned the button and then straightened to his feet. He moved swiftly and his hands found the rungs of the ladder. He went up, quickly and silently.

Pushing back the tarpaulin, he crawled out on deck. A cold voice froze him in his tracks, with one foot under the canvas.

"So? Snooping, is it?"

The voice was Donner's, and a second later a light flashed in Steve Cowan's eyes.

He heard a startled gasp, saw the muzzle of a gun.

"Who are you?" The voice was cold, deadly. "Tell me, or I'll fire!"

"I'm a refugee," Cowan declared, heart pounding. "I was trying to stow away to get out of here before the Japanese come."

Someone came out of the passage.

"What's goin' on, Donner?" It was Mataga's voice. Then Mataga saw Steve Cowan's face. "Well, for—"

"You know this man?" Donner's voice was deadly. "Get inside off the deck," he snapped.

When they were in the saloon, Besi John sat on the corner of the table. His gross, hard-bitten face was unshaven, and his small eyes were cruel.

"So, Mr. Steve Cowan. After all these years we get together again!"

Mataga's face flamed suddenly and animal fury gleamed redly in his eyes.

"Again! D'you hear? And I'm top dog this time! I'll teach you a thing or two, you dirty—"

"Take it easy." Donner's voice was even. "Who is this man?"

"Him?" Mataga's voice was ugly. "This is Steve Cowan. He's a tramp flyer. The one I told you about who knew this place."

"Flyer, eh?" Donner looked at the Yank. "Where's your ship?"

"Lost it at Palembang," Cowan lied glibly. "Enemy got in too fast and bombed the field before I could get her off. Blew off my tail assembly. I got away into the jungle and came over to the west coast, headed for Padang or Emma Haven.

"The Japanese beat me to it, so I picked up a boat and sailed her here to Siberut. I saw this freighter and decided to stow away and get out."

DONNER STUDIED HIM.

"It's a good story," he said slowly. "Almost too good. But where is the girl?"

"Girl?" Cowan felt an empty sensation in his stomach. "What girl?"

"The one," Donner said coldly, "that left this hair on your shoulder!"

Deftly he picked a long golden hair from Cowan's shirt. Evidently it had been left there when he was making his way through the trees beside Ruanne.

"Blond?" Besi John's eyes were hard. "Why, there ain't a blonde within miles but that Forbes girl!"

"I think," Donner said coolly, "we had better tie this man up until we investigate a little further. I found him trying to crawl into the hatch. A minute later and he would have been out of sight."

He turned.

"Mataga, send a couple of men ashore at once. I don't like the looks of things." He hesitated. "I'll go with you."

STEVE COWAN, tied to the rail on the starboard side, watched the sky grow gray. At first there had been some sounds ashore, but then the island had settled into silence.

Nothing had happened. Down in the hold amidships the time bomb ticked on. Or had it stopped? Was all his work to be futile, after all? Cowan sat against the rail, gazing blindly ahead of him, weary as he had never been. On the deck, a few yards away, Joe Gotto, the ex-gangster was sitting beside Chiv Laran.

Past them, Cowan could see the open manhole in the deck. He stared, then slowly his weariness fell away. He looked at Joe and Chiv thoughtfully.

"Who opened that manhole?" he demanded suddenly.

Joe glanced up lazily, shifting his rifle.

"That?" He shrugged. "Mataga. He said it would have to be cleaned. He's as bad as Forbes was. Always cleaning something."

Cowan eyed the two again.

"You don't look to me like a sucker, Joe," he said. "But your side of this deal doesn't smell so good."

"Shut up," Chiv said harshly. "We ain't turnin' you loose."

"You'd be smart if you did," Steve Cowan declared. "What's your cut on this deal? You ever think of how much you'll get—*if* they split the dough they get for these planes? By the time each of you gets a cut, your end wouldn't buy you a ticket to a safe port. I know that Mataga. He'd doublecross his own mother."

Joe looked at Cowan thoughtfully.

"So what? If he don't collect, we can't."

"No?" Cowan glanced at Chiv, who was listening sullenly. "Why is Mataga keeping Forbes alive? Forbes has a cache of jewels aboard this ship, that's why. Did Mataga tell you that? Or Donner?"

Cowan glanced shoreward, but there was no sign of life.

"Or did they tell you there was a war on? That the Japanese had bombed Pearl Harbor?"

"Is that straight?" Gotto scowled. "Why, I'd like to—"

"What's it to you?" Chiv demanded. "The cops run you out, didn't they?"

"Sure," Joe argued. "But what the devil! If the Japanese and Nazis take the States, my racket is sunk. I can't compete with them guys. When I knock over a bank, I want to know there's some dough in it."

"I know where the jewels are," Steve Cowan said quietly, looking directly at Chiv. "We could get them and get out. Let Mataga have his crummy planes."

"Get out?" Chiv sneered. "You mean swim?"

"No, I mean in my plane. I told Mataga it crashed, but it didn't. It isn't ten miles from here. We could grab those jewels, just the three of us, and take it on the lam."

Joe studied him thoughtfully. Then he glanced sideward at Chiv, whose yellow eyes were narrowed.

"You sound like a right guy," he said. "I like the sound of it. Anyway, if the Japanese are going to use the planes against our gang, why—"

"What the deuce do you care?" Chiv snarled. "Nuts! I don't care who gets the planes. I want some dough! I'm no Yank."

"Those stones are close by," Steve Cowan hinted. "We haven't much time."

"Yeah?" Chiv sneered. "Suppose I let you loose? Then you'd get them! Don't be a sap! Mataga will be back in a little while."

"Sure." Cowan shrugged. "And then you get the dirty end of the deal. You think I'm a sap? Those stones are down in that manhole, Chiv, in a box back in the corner of the tank. That's why Mataga opened it. That's why I wanted to know.

"He's letting it air out a little, that's all. You get that box and we'll get out of here."

Joe said nothing. He glanced at Cowan curiously, shifted his rifle a little.

Chiv got up and looked shoreward. Then he approached the manhole, flashing his light down the rungs of the ladder. It wouldn't reach to the corner.

"You got that plane, sure thing?" he demanded. "Because, if you haven't—"

"You got a rod, Chiv, haven't you?" Joe cut in suddenly. "He's tied up, ain't he? If it ain't there, what do we lose? If it is, we take this guy, still tied, and head for the plane."

"How does he know we won't bump him?" Chiv asked. "We could have it all."

His yellow eyes shifted back to Cowan, and the Yank felt a cold shiver run down his spine.

"I'm the flyer," Cowan said. "I know where the plane is."

"All right." Chiv glanced shoreward again quickly, then he looked at Joe. "Don't let him try anything funny, see? I'll be right back up."

His light thrust in his belt, he started down the ladder.

Joe Gotto sat up a little, watching his prisoner, his eyes very bright. Cowan stared at the manhole. They both heard Chiv slip, heard the hollow thump when he hit the bottom.

Cowan tore his eyes from the manhole.

"Now it's just us, Joe. You're a Yank and so am I. Do the Japs get this load of planes to get our boys with? You're a tough cookie, pal. So'm I. But we aren't either of us rats!"

"What was it?" he asked. "What happened to Chiv?"

"No oxygen. Those tanks are dangerous. I had an idea that in this heavy air, darned little of that gas would escape."

He bent over Cowan and hurriedly unbound him. The Yank straightened up, stretching his cramped muscles.

Cowan grabbed up the shotgun dropped by Chiv Laran and ran with Joe to the gangway. A lifeboat bobbed alongside.

"What happened to Mataga?" Joe demanded. In running forward he had picked up a tommy gun from the petty officer's mess, where it had been left on the table.

"He's hunting Forbes and the girl!"

Steve Cowan sprang ashore when the boat grated on the beach. Then as Joe jumped down beside him, he shoved the lifeboat back into the water.

Turning, he led the way into the jungle, heading for the point. They had gone only a dozen steps when Cowan stopped suddenly, holding up a hand.

"Listen!" he said. Someone was floundering through the brush, panting heavily. Joe lifted his tommy gun, his eyes narrowed.

"Hold it!" Cowan whispered.

It was Captain Forbes. The old sea dog broke through the brush, his face red, his lungs heaving. His clothing was torn by brambles, and his face and hands were scratched.

"They're comin'!" he said. "Right behind!"

"Where's Ruanne?" Steve Cowan demanded.

"At the plane!" Forbes looked bad, the veins in his throat standing out, his lungs heaving. "We found it! I tried to lead them away; they got too close!"

SOMEONE YELLED BACK down the shore. Cowan turned, leading the way toward the mangroves.

"Make it fast!" he whispered. "We've got a chance!"

They were almost to the amphibian before Cowan noticed that Joe had not followed. He wheeled and started back. Ruanne stopped helping her uncle in the cabin door.

"Where are you going?" she cried. "Come on!"

"Can you fly?" Cowan hesitated, the shotgun dangling. "If you can, warm that ship up. We'll be back!"

He turned and plunged back into the jungle. Even as he broke through the first wall of green, he heard the angry chatter of a tommy gun and Joe's raucous yell, then the sound of more guns. Joe cried out suddenly in pain.

Cowan burst into a small clearing just as Donner and Besi John Mataga, followed by a dozen men, came through on the opposite side. A bullet smashed by his head, and Cowan jerked up the shotgun. It roared. Donner grabbed the pit of his stomach and plunged over on his face.

Joe Gotto, down on one knee, was raking the killers with his tommy gun. Steve Cowan fired again, and the line broke and ran.

Lunging across the clearing, Cowan swept Joe Gotto to one shoulder and ran for the mangroves. Beyond, the amphibian's twin motors were roaring music in his ears.

Almost at the same instant, a plane roared by overhead. Cowan glanced up, swearing. It was a Kawasaki. It was circling for a return when Cowan boosted Joe into the cabin and then grabbed the controls.

"Strap him in!" he yelled.

He opened the plane wide and let her roar down the open water, throttle wide. Just short of the trees he pulled back on the stick, and the amphibian went up in a steep climb.

Roaring on over the casuarinas, Cowan gave a startled gasp. A long, slim gray destroyer was alongside the *Parawan,* and a stream of Japanese sailors and marines were running up the gangway!

Then he pulled back on the stick again just as the Kawasaki came screaming back toward him. Opening the ship wide, he fled; for the enemy was on his tail and his only safety at this low altitude lay in speed.

A roaring chatter broke out in Steve Cowan's ears. Turning his head, he saw Joe Gotto, strapped in a seat, firing his tommy gun out the port.

The burst of bullets missed, but the Japanese wavered. In that instant, Cowan skidded around in a flat turn, raking the Kawasaki with a quick burst of fire. But the soldier was no fool. Screaming around in a tight circle, he tried to reach Cowan with his twin guns in the nose, while his observer opened fire from the rear cockpit.

A bullet hole showed in the wing. Then Cowan pulled the amphibian on around and climbed steeply. Rolling over before the enemy could follow, he poured a stream of fire into the Kawasaki's ugly blunt nose.

The engine coughed, sputtered. Then Cowan banked steeply and came back with the son of Nippon dead in his sights. His guns roared. The Kawasaki burst into a roaring flame and went out of sight.

Then for the first time Cowan heard a pounding in his ears. Off to his left a puff of smoke flowered. Glancing down, he realized with a shock that the destroyer's anti-aircraft guns were opening up on him.

He pulled the stick back and shot up into the sky, reaching for all the altitude he could get. He was still climbing in tight spirals when he rolled over a little to obtain a better view.

It was like that, with Steve Cowan watching the scene below, when it happened. He had forgotten the time bomb. He had forgotten everything in the rush of action. How it had been set, he never knew. But suddenly, it turned loose with a tremendous detonation.

A PYRAMID OF FLAME shot skyward until Cowan thought his own wings, hundreds of feet above, must be singed. The puff of explosion struck his ship and sent it staggering down the sky. He got it righted, banked steeply, and circled slowly over the roaring fire below.

The *Parawan* was gone. Where it had been was a mass of flaming wreckage. Beside it settled the Japanese destroyer, ablaze from stem to stern, with the bay around it for many yards a furnace of burning oil.

Steve Cowan leveled off and then pointed his ship south.

"Better have a look at Joe," he said to Ruanne. "He may be hit bad."

"Aw, it's nothin'," Joe protested, blushing. "Take me somewhere where I can join the Army. Boy, what I just seen! And me, I thought Brooklyn's 'Murder Incorporated' was tough!"

Down Paagumene Way

Steve Cowan leaned back against a packing case on the jetty at Paagumene Bay, New Caledonia, lazily watching the shipping. It was growing dark, and would soon be night.

Five ships were anchored in the harbor, all of them with cargoes for American troops. One, her freight discharged, was loading chrome from lighters.

The last rays of sunshine tipped the masts with transient gold. The freighter loading ore would sail tonight. In a few weeks she would be tying up in an American port.

Steve Cowan's eyes strayed to the amphibian, riding lightly on the darkening water. A little refitting and he could fly her home on furlough, his first since being assigned to Army Intelligence. She was a beautiful plane, resembling the Grumman "Widgeon" but built to certain unusual specifications, laid down by Army designers. Because of that she was much faster and more maneuverable than any ship of her type. Moreover, she was armed like a fighter, and had a small bomb bay, so far unused except for freight.

Four years ago he had come out to the Pacific, and they had been four years of unceasing activity. Years that culminated in the Japanese invasion of the East Indies, ending his express and mail-carrying business suddenly and dramatically. Since being commissioned, he had acted as a secret messenger and undercover agent for the Allies.

It would be good to be back in the States again, to walk down the streets, to get away from the heat and humidity, eat a cheeseburger, and have a cold soda or beer.

A boat bumped alongside the jetty and two men clambered out.

"You just get that chrome to the right place at the right time. You get it there, or else."

Abruptly, Steve Cowan stiffened. He knew that voice! Instinctively, he shrank down further behind the packing case.

"You don't understand!" the second man protested. "This job is a cinch. It won't interfere with the chrome deal. We can pick up the classified sailing list from the butler in Isola Mayne's place. With those Jap credentials we got, nobody'd be the wiser. The Japs'll pay heavy to get it back. They got to have it for their subs!"

"Yeah?" the voice sneered. "You pull something like that, *Meyer,*" an odd inflection was put on the name, as if Meyer was being taunted, "Koyama will cut your heart out. Try it and see what happens."

Something in the tone of that ugly, domineering voice rang a bell of memory in Steve Cowan's brain.

Mataga!

Recognition brought a start of dismay. Not twenty feet away, on the edge of the jetty was a man sworn to kill Cowan on sight. And Cowan was unarmed.

Mataga was speaking again. "You do what you're told. All you have to worry about is getting this cargo of chrome to the Japs."

"Besi John" Mataga in New Caledonia! Steve Cowan's eyes narrowed. The renegade from the waters around Singapore was not one to stop at anything. Deadly, brutal, and efficient, he had been working with Jap and Nazi Fifth Columnists for several years. When Singapore fell he went to Saigon. When Java succumbed, he appeared in Batavia. Now he was here, in New Caledonia!

As their footsteps receded down the jetty, Steve Cowan got to his feet. If Besi John was here it meant something big was moving. Something infinitely more important than a shipload of chrome. If he was working with Koyama it meant even more, for the Japanese was a leader of the powerful and notoriously evil Black Dragon Society, which had many underground members in the South Seas. And "Meyer"? Could that be Captain Peter Meyer . . . ?

THE EYES OF M. ESTEVILLE were amused when Cowan met with him the next day. "But, m'sieu," he protested gently, "it cannot be! The vessel you speak of is the *Benton Harbor,* well known to us." He sighed gustily. "As you say, it is true her master is Peter Meyer, a native of Holland, but he is highly respected here. Your story, if you'll forgive me, is utterly preposterous!"

"I know Mataga," Cowan persisted. "And I know what I heard."

Esteville shrugged. "Undoubtedly Mataga is a dangerous criminal. But here? I think not. It would be too dangerous. A fancied resemblance, no more."

"Bah!" Steve Cowan's voice was flat. "I know Mataga. Last night I heard him speaking. As to the other man, he may be your Captain Meyer, or he may not. I know Mataga is here and something's in the wind."

"We will investigate." Esteville stood up, plainly annoyed. "But you are mistaken. Nothing is wrong with that ship. As for your wild tale about the shipping lists, that is fantastic. Even if such information could be obtained, there are no spies in Paagumene."

Cowan's eyes hardened. The man's indifference annoyed him. "I've told you. Now do something, or I will!"

Esteville's eyes blazed. "Remember, m'sieu, that New Caledonia still has a government! We are capable of handling our own affairs. Any interference from you will bring a protest to American officials—a protest too strong to be ignored."

Cowan turned on his heel and walked out. He could scarcely blame Esteville for being doubtful. Cowan's connection with Army Intelligence was secret and, because of strict orders, Cowan did not dare tell him. After all, Captain Meyer, master of the *Benton Harbor,* had an excellent reputation and Esteville might feel justified in rejecting such a wild story without proof.

THOUGHTFULLY COWAN PAUSED under a tree and considered his next step. Summing up, how much did he actually know? That the *Benton Harbor* was the only ship in the roadstead being loaded with chrome, a vital war material, and that she would soon leave for the United States. Also that Besi John, a notorious criminal and Fifth Columnist, was here on shady business.

A shipping list had been mentioned, too, and enemy agents. One of whom was evidently working in conjunction with Japanese submarines, plying along the southern route to Australia. Esteville had said there were no spies and that such a list would be impossible to obtain. Yet Besi John had spoken of both agents and list in a matter-of-course manner. So they *did* exist. How could Cowan find out more about them?

Then he remembered Isola Mayne.

He had never seen her. Pictures, of course. Everyone had seen pictures of Isola Mayne. She was more than a beautiful woman, more than a great actress. She was a legend.

Three years before, she had abruptly retired and, going to Singapore, had settled down, apparently for life. Then came the Japanese invasion, and Isola, in her own plane, had flown to Palembang, and next to Soerabaja. When she arrived in Sydney she moved the war off the front pages. Then she was gone. She vanished into nothingness.

A few days the world wondered, but with the war, they soon forgot.

Yet Steve Cowan knew where she was. He knew, because he had flown supplies to her plantation on New Caledonia. He had not seen her, but knew she was living there in seclusion. And Isola Mayne's brother was

Port Captain! Married to a French woman, he, too, had spent time in Singapore, before that La Rochelle, and then relocated to Paagumene. In these places he had held prominent maritime positions. The spy must be one of the servants of his household, one who had managed in some way to steal a copy of the sailing list.

Unconsciously, Cowan had wandered back to the jetty. He stopped, staring at the dark blobs—freighters on Paagumene Bay. Much more was at stake out at the Oland Point home of Isola Mayne and her brother than appeared on the surface. A sailing list, in the hands of the Japanese submarine commanders, might disrupt the whole military line of supplies with the Far East. Whichever enemy got it—either the Japanese or Besi John Mataga— did not matter much with Cowan. Either way it would be disastrous.

Mataga was on the island, and somewhere nearby was Koyama. Mataga's apparent lack of interest in the list had not fooled Cowan. He knew the man too well. Besi John, *besi* being Malay for "iron," would make his own attempt in his own way, and Mataga would strike with utter ruthlessness.

Cowan took his cigarette from his mouth and snapped it into the bay. He could do nothing here. Oland Point was where the answer would be.

He dropped into the rubber boat and paddled out to the amphibian.

Opening the door of the cabin, he stepped in. A light flashed suddenly in his eyes and a fist smashed out of the darkness and knocked him to his knees. Someone struck him a vicious blow on the head, then another.

Through a fog of pain he struggled to hold himself erect, he heard Mataga's harsh voice.

"Lash the beggar!" Besi John growled. "We got a date at Oland Point."

Cowan struggled, trying to shout. Then something crashed upon his skull and he fell forward into a foam of pain that ate into and through him.

IT WAS ALMOST day when he opened his eyes again. The plane was still in the air. Struggling to master his nausea, he tried to reason things out. Still in the air?

He struggled to rise, but an arrow of torment from his head made him fall back, helpless. But not before he had discovered that he was tied hand and foot.

His brow furrowed, he tried to grope his way back along the trail of semiconsciousness. Something had happened—

Memory of it was veiled in the mists, in the half lights of awareness after he had been struck down. How long, he could not recall, yet something had happened. There was a dim recollection of lapping water, a strange dream of firelight dancing upon a dark hull, a mutter of motors, aircraft engines, and the murmur of voices.

He remembered, vaguely, through darkness and clouds, a round hump, like that on a camel's back.

Somehow, that dark hump stood out in his mind, forcing itself always into the foreground. He had a feeling of having seen it before.

Finally he opened his eyes, and knew that he had passed out again. The plane was resting on the water. He could hear waves lapping against the hull.

He rolled over, and tipping his head back, Cowan looked around the cabin of the plane. Sitting in the hatchway, with his legs dangling toward the water was a huge and heavily tattooed Malay. Seeing that he was, for the moment, unobserved, the pilot tried to move his hands. They were bound beneath him and the tightness of the ropes was cutting into his wrists but more painful than that was a seam in the folded metal of the aircraft . . . a seam that just might have a sharp enough edge to free him!

Moving with the slight swell of the water under the craft, Steve Cowan shifted until the ropes lay across the seam, and then, very slowly, he began to saw up and down. How long he worked he did not know but the progress was horribly slow. He felt strands of the rope part, but when he twisted his wrists they seemed just as tightly held. Dispirited, he glanced up and noticed the native in the door watching him with a know-ing sneer on his face . . . and the Malay watchman was a man he knew!

Yosha was a tough from the oil fields in Balikpapan, a man noted for his viciousness and dishonesty. With a war on, it was not surprising that he and Besi John had washed up on the same shore.

"So, y'get away, eh?" Yosha stood and started aft, his blocky body fill-ing the fuselage of the plane almost completely. "We see about tha'." He drew a parang from its bamboo sheath and took a step toward Cowan. In that instant, a woman screamed. Wildly, desperately, a cry of mortal an-guish came from somewhere on shore!

Yosha stiffened, glancing back toward the aircraft hatchway, startled.

Steve Cowan lunged. He hit the Malay with his shoulder, toppling him over backward. Yosha swung but the plane was too small a space to effectively wield the machete-like parang and the blade scraped sparks along the aluminum skin of the craft. The tip hit a rib in the metalwork and the weapon jumped from his grip.

Yosha's big hand grabbed for the handle of the weapon, as his other clutched at Cowan's shirtfront.

Cowan jerked back, tearing the thin garment from the grasping hand. Both men lunged to their feet. Steve Cowan, quicker in reaction, smashed his head forward into Yosha's face in a frantic "Liverpool kiss." Yosha stum-bled back and Steve jerked at his bindings, growling in frustration and fear.

A cord parted as the Malay stood up. Cowan jerked and twisted, one hand coming loose just as Yosha rushed. Cowan lashed out with a right, his wrist still wrapped in hemp, and the blow set his adversary back, but it was weak, the wrist and hand still numb from being bound. Fighting for his life Cowan swung a wicked blow to the brute's middle. Then he lunged into the Malay, his fists slamming the big muscle-corded body.

Yosha flinched away, staggering across the cabin. Yet now he held the thick-bladed knife ready, his teeth bared in a grimace of ferocious hate. Then, his feet wide apart, he started creeping along the narrow cabin toward Cowan. Cornered, desperate, Cowan feinted a blow as the islander lunged. Risking everything, the American hurled himself against Yosha's shoulder, and thrown off balance, both men toppled through the open hatch and struck the water.

Down, down, down! Then, somehow, Cowan discovered he was free and began desperately to swim for shore with powerful strokes.

As Cowan's head broke the surface, he glanced back. The plane rode gracefully on the blue water, not far away. But with the woman's scream still ringing in his ears, Cowan made no move to find out what had become of Yosha. He continued to swim swiftly toward shore. In a short while Cowan reached the shallows and splashed to land. He crossed the beach at a run. When the jungle had closed around him he felt safe.

Moving swiftly and silently, he worked his way toward the rambling plantation house, stripping the remains of the rope from his wrists. He was unarmed, and none knew better than himself the foe he was facing.

Ahead of Cowan was the wall of the Port Captain's house, and in it an open French window. He crossed the garden swiftly, moving from one clump of shrubbery to the next. Flattened against the wall, he peered in.

Isola Mayne was standing by a table. Her dress was torn. Masses of red-gold hair had fallen about her shoulders. Yet despite these things, never before had Cowan seen a woman look so regal, so beautiful, so commanding.

"You tell me!" Besi John Mataga's voice carried a soft but deadly threat. "If you don't, we kill the maid. Your butler was a fool. He gave us no time to explain." He gestured at the body of a man which Cowan noticed, for the first time, lying in the shadows. "I'll kill you or this woman if I have to. Now, where's your brother's safe? We know he has one. Tell us, and we'll let you go."

"So that's what this is about." Isola Mayne's voice was low, and it made Steve Cowan's nerves tingle. "You want the shipping list? And my butler was a traitor, too? Well, you'll never find the list because it isn't here."

Mataga's face flushed and his eyes glinted with anger. But he merely turned away.

"Go ahead!" he told his men. "We'll see if she's as brave as she pretends."

Isola Mayne's face paled. "You wouldn't dare," she said, but Steve Cowan detected the resolution draining from her voice, and he saw how her eyes widened with horror. The men with Besi John were savage beasts.

Leaning further, he could see the two men holding the maid, a native girl. They had bent her arms cruelly behind her back. The girl's face was white, but her eyes were fearless.

"Don't tell them!" she cried. "They'll kill us anyway."

"Shut up!" Mataga whirled and struck the girl viciously across the mouth.

Instantly, the room burst into a turmoil of action. Isola Mayne, seizing a paper knife, was around the table with a movement that took the renegade by surprise. Only a quick leap got him away from the knife. Then he caught the wrist of the actress and with a brutal wrench, twisted her to her knees.

In the same instant that Isola moved, Steve Cowan had plunged through the door. He hit the room running. The nearest of the men holding the maid dropped her arm and wheeled to face him, grabbing for his gun, but he was too slow.

Cowan went at him with a roundhouse swing that started at the door. It knocked the fellow sprawling into a corner. Springing across the fallen chair, Cowan leaped to close quarters with the other man. A shot blazed in his face, then the American's fist drove deep into the softness of the man's body, and he saw the fellow's face turn sick.

Someone jumped on him from behind. Dropping to one knee he hurled the man over his shoulder, then lunged to his feet just as Besi John Mataga whipped out a gun.

For a second Steve looked straight into the gun barrel. Lifting his eyes he could see death in Mataga's cruel face.

Then Isola Mayne twisted suddenly on the floor and kicked out with all her strength. At the same moment Mataga's pistol roared but the bullet went wild. Cowan moved. He hit Mataga in a sudden lunge and Mataga fell, cursing viciously.

Catching Isola's wrist, Cowan lifted her from the floor, and seizing the automatic from the table where it had fallen, charged for the door and the maid came stumbling after them.

How THEY REACHED the jungle, Steve Cowan never knew. He was aware of moving swiftly, of Isola beside him. When the maid stumbled and fell, he picked her up, almost collapsing after going the last few feet into the jungle. There had been shooting. He distinctly remembered the ugly bark of guns and the white lash of a bullet scar across a tree trunk ahead of him.

"Put me down." The voice brought him back to awareness. It was the maid speaking. He put her down carefully. Her face was white and set, but she seemed uninjured.

Isola was beside her in an instant. "Are you all right, Clara? If anything happens to you here, I'd never forgive myself."

"I'm all right."

Steve Cowan liked the blaze in her eyes. She wasn't afraid, only angry. His eyes went to Isola.

"I'm Steve Cowan," he said. Briefly, he explained. "What we'll do now," he added, "is anybody's guess. We'll have to keep moving until we find a place to hole up. Mataga won't quit. Especially," he added grimly, "now that I'm free."

"You knew him before?" Isola said. Her eyes flashed. "He's a spy."

"Two years ago we had difficulties on Siberut, an island near Sumatra."

They walked on in silence. Despite the maid's injured ankle and knee, he kept them moving along. There was no time for hesitation, Besi John would work swiftly and shrewdly.

Cowan studied the situation. It could hardly be worse. Esteville would not help him. Nominally the French were in charge, and no American Army officials could interfere without disclosing Cowan's true status. Whatever was done he must do himself. He checked the magazine of the automatic. Five shots remaining.

"We've got to recapture my plane," said Cowan. "Then I can fly you to Paagumene Bay." He looked at Isola. "Your butler was a traitor? He was selling you out to the Japs?"

"I guess so," answered the girl. "He'd been with us for years and we trusted him. Oh, it's so horrible!"

They reached the edge of the jungle near where the plane was moored. A boat was alongside of the amphibian, and two Malays were seated in it with rifles across their knees. Another one of Besi John's men was standing in the cabin doorway.

"Well," Isola said, "it was a good idea."

Grimly Cowan sized up the situation. Three men with rifles. That chance was eliminated. They found a hollow beneath the roots of a giant ficus tree. It was dark, almost a cave. Cowan handed the automatic to Isola. "You may need this," he said. "What I have to do, it's best to do quietly."

She did not warn him, she did not suggest that he guard himself, but something in her eyes carried a tender message. For an instant her hand was on his arm as she smiled.

"Don't worry about us," she said.

STEVE COWAN MOVED swiftly. He knew the jungle too well to be fearful. Even less than Besi John's imported Malays did he fear the abysmal darkness under the mighty trees. He was familiar with darkness; they superstitiously distrusted it.

There was, he recalled, a radio at the plantation. Since M. Esteville would not help him, he would help himself.

Night had fallen. Yet moving through the blackness under the trees, Steve Cowan knew it would be a help rather than otherwise. He left the jungle, and slipped swiftly from tree to tree across the lawn near the mansion.

The radio room was on the second story. He heard the murmur of voices inside. Then a guard walked along the porch near the railing. Behind the guard was the lattice he intended to use to get to the second floor. He could have waited, but impatience and hot, goading temper drove him on.

The guard, warned by some sixth sense, turned, and Cowan struck like a panther. His left smashed into the man's windpipe, knocking him gasping against the rail. Then the American chopped him across the eyes with the edge of his hand.

The man fell facedown on the porch, and did not move. His gun had fallen over the rail, but he wore a knife. With the blade in his teeth, Steve Cowan went up the lattice. A man sat at the radio, reading a magazine. Being here, he could only be a Mataga man.

Cowan slid a forearm under the man's chin, and crushed it against his windpipe. Then with a quick jerk, he wrenched the fellow back over his chair. Dragging him to the floor, Cowan spoke softly.

"Lie still and live," he said. "Move and you die."

He reached for a rope, and the native acted. He hurled himself at Cowan, his lips twisted in a snarl. Cowan's knife blade, held low and flat side down, slashed suddenly. Blood cascaded down the man's shirtfront, and he slumped to the floor.

Cowan sat down at the radio. For an instant he held the key, then he began to send.

BENTON HARBOR ... SS BENTON HARBOR ... NEW PLAN ... COME AT ONCE.

KOYAMA.

A door swung open and another man appeared. Evidently he was another guard for he uttered a loud shout when he caught sight of Cowan. Then without hesitation he whipped out a gun and fired at the American. The sound of the shot rocked the building, and before the Malay could pull the trigger again, the American threw the knife—low and hard!

It struck! Horrified, the Malay stared at the haft protruding from his stomach. The muzzle of his own weapon sagged as he reached for the knife and tugged it out. Blood gushed, and he fell.

Cowan caught up the gun and sprang into the hall. Two men were charging up the stairs and he sent slugs whizzing at them. Somehow he missed, so he dodged across the hall into another room, slamming the door after him. Then, crouching, he wheeled as bodies smashed against the door. He fired again, once, twice, until the gun clicked empty, and he dropped the useless weapon.

A noise behind him made Cowan turn quickly. A man had come into the window by means of the vines, and Cowan recognized him at once. It was Yosha, the bloodthirsty Malay who had tried to kill him on the amphibian.

Yosha looked bigger than ever. With bared teeth, he leaped at the American. Cowan's jab missed and he was seized by powerful arms, swept from his feet, and hurled across the room. He hit the wall with a crash but came back fighting, although half stunned.

The Malay met the American with a straight arm and flung him against the wall once more. When Cowan tried a flying tackle, Yosha met it with a smashing knee that knocked him rolling to the floor. A kick to the forehead sent darts of pain lancing through his brain. The Malay was adept in this kind of fighting.

Drunk with agony, Cowan staggered to his feet. He had realized that this battle must be to the death. So he cut loose a terrific left hook which caught Yosha on the chin and rocked him to the heels. But the Malay only snarled, shook his head, and replied with a bludgeoning blow which slashed Cowan across the cheek. Dazed, the American could not avoid the instant attack which followed.

Coolly, but with diabolical fury, the Malay tried to beat him into submission. Yosha had a knife in his belt and evidently meant to use it when he had punished the American to his satisfaction. But Cowan kept his head. He weathered the storm and continued to watch for his opportunity.

At last it came. As the knife flashed out Cowan tried another judo trick. Stepping in, he avoided the thrust, and flipped the blade inward. At the same moment he tripped Yosha. The Malay fell to the floor on top of the knife and rolled over. The knife was sticking out of his chest.

At this instant shots rang out in the direction of the beach. Cowan sprang for the window. He could see stabs of flame as more shots ripped the air. Still dizzy from the pounding he had received, the American cleared the sill and went down the vines outside.

Just what was happening he had no idea, but whatever the diversion, he must make it work to his advantage. Running swiftly, he headed for the woods.

THE RATTLE OF rifle fire down along the beach was growing. He swung away from that direction, cutting deeper into the jungle. Then he reached the ficus. Isola Mayne and the maid were gone!

Shocked, Steve Cowan froze, trying to understand. Isola would not have moved willingly, he knew that. The knowledge was no help. He started for the beach, moving fast.

The sound of firing had ceased. He slipped noiselessly through the jungle, and stared out. All was blackness beyond the edge of the trees and he could see nothing. He moved out, creeping slowly. Then he tripped and almost fell. He put his hand down. A dead man.

Feeling around in the dark he found a pistol, which he tucked into his belt, and moved on. His eyes grew accustomed to the darkness, and he saw more bodies. There were corpses of white men among them, white men garbed as sailors.

Whatever the cause of the fight, it had been desperate. Out across the water he caught the outline of a Samson post against the sky. Then he knew.

The only ship in the Paagumene Bay with Samson posts had been the *Benton Harbor*. That meant Cowan's ruse to make Meyer betray himself had been successful. Peter Meyer had received his message.

Meyer, obviously, had been close by. That told Cowan that he had surmised the double cross Besi John Mataga had planned. Meyer's arrival had precipitated a battle.

One of Mataga's sentries must have fired on the ship, and Meyer, fearing a trap, had responded.

Steve Cowan stopped. What now? True, Meyer and Mataga were fighting, but that still didn't help him. The shipload of chrome would be moving out, and the Japanese master spy, Koyama, was still loose. Also Isola Mayne was gone.

Nothing was settled, nothing was improved. He was free, but apparently helpless. Then he recalled the vague, misty dream of his flight to Oland Point, when he had been a prisoner aboard the plane. How long had they been in the air? He had no way of knowing, but he recalled the camel's hump, and the dark sky.

The dark hump . . . *Neangambo!*

He knew then. A Japanese submarine had surfaced in Nehue Bay. Neangambo was an island in the bay, and the dark hump of the hill and trees could be nowhere else near here. It must be the ship that had brought Koyama.

He worked his way along the shore to the edge of a village and as he had hoped, he found a catamaran. He shoved off and after a moment was alone, and slipping across the dark waters.

IT WAS ALMOST daylight when Steve Cowan, drunk with fatigue and his head throbbing with pain from the beating he had taken earlier, reached the shore opposite Neangambo.

The ship he had seen leaving Oland Point, the *Benton Harbor,* was there, and not far away, moored to a piling, was his own plane!

Steve Cowan wet his parched lips. All right, this was it. It was the work of minutes to bring the catamaran alongside the *Benton Harbor.* He paddled around to the bow, moored the boat to the anchor chain, and went up, hand over hand, at the risk of crushed fingers.

The deck was dark and still. He moved aft, slowly. Voices came from the saloon port. He slipped closer, then glanced in.

Peter Meyer, his face sour, sat at one end of the table. Nearby, her hands tied, was Isola Mayne. Behind her was the maid. Koyama sat with his back to the port, and across from him was Besi John Mataga, his face dark with fury.

"So?" Koyama's voice was sibilant. "You thought to betray us. Explain this, if you will."

Besi John laughed harshly. "Don't blame me for that. It was Cowan's work." He looked at the stout shipmaster. "Steuben, I think Cowan knew about what happened. You may resemble Meyer enough to fool some, Herman, but you didn't fool everyone!"

The thin Japanese officer, Koyama, made a gesture of impatience.

"All this is beside the point," he hissed. "Why did you kill our agent, the butler? The Burma man was valuable."

"I tell you I didn't know about it," shouted Besi John, angrily.

The Japanese master spy's anger increased. "You are a fool!" he snapped. "For that you will die." He waved his hand toward the women. "They must die, too. No one who knows our plans must remain alive."

Another voice, suave and smooth, broke in. "You must not do this, Commander Koyama. Miss Mayne is a famous actress, internationally known. She cannot disappear without causing complications. Better turn her over to my authority. I think I can make her see reason."

Esteville! The Frenchman was in this with them. All of which explained why the substitution of Steuben for Peter Meyer had been successful. Without hesitation Steve Cowan turned and walked into the cabin.

Mataga saw Cowan first. Trapped and in danger of losing his life, the renegade had been waiting for a chance to escape from the ship. Like a flash he leaped from his chair, darted through another door, and disappeared. A loud splash revealed he had gone over the side.

Steve Cowan was too busy to follow. As Koyama lunged to his feet and whipped out a gun, Cowan raised his automatic and fired twice.

The Japanese officer's face turned sick, and he fell face forward across the table, dead.

It had happened so suddenly that it was like a slow-motion picture, but almost at once the saloon blazed with shots. Steuben grabbed for his gun, and lunged to his feet, firing desperately. Esteville crouched down, out of sight.

In a haze of powder smoke, Cowan saw Isola and the maid slip out of the door through which Besi John Mataga had disappeared. Steuben was down beside Koyama, now, the smoking pistol clutched in his lifeless fingers. Esteville was hiding behind a table. He had taken no part in the fight and there was no use remaining here any longer. Outside the crew had begun to shout and feet were approaching. So Cowan leaped through the doorway after the two girls, joining them at the railing.

A sailor, in plain sight, opened up with a rifle and Cowan knocked him spinning with one shot. Then with bullets from other members of the crew pattering around him, he swung over the rail and dropped Isola and the maid into the water near the catamaran.

More shots rang out and bullets snipped the water near the slim craft. Luckily the light, just before daylight, was not good, or they would have been slain. He continued to paddle furiously. Soon the freighter was out of sight and the firing stopped.

The plane was ahead, and Steve Cowan swung in close, then crawled aboard. He helped the girls into the cabin and slid into place behind the controls. After several attempts, he got the motors started and warmed them up.

When the ship was in the air, he took stock. The freighter below was moving now. They would get out, and get away fast. Soon Cowan noted two other freighters moving. A convoy, ostensibly bound for America, but, in reality, bound for Japan. The traitorous Pierre Esteville had made this possible.

But even well-laid plans can fail. Cowan swung his ship, and went down in a ringing, whistling dive. Then he opened up with the machine guns. His heavy projectiles blasted the bridge and ripped away the pilot-house windows. The freighter swung suddenly, and turned broadside to the channel.

Banking the Widgeon, Cowan swooped again. From stem to stern he plastered the freighters with gunfire. Then Isola screamed.

Cowan turned in his seat, startled. Besi John Mataga was standing in the middle of the amphibian's cabin, the small hatch to the bomb bay swinging on its hinges. As Cowan slid out of the seat and faced him, he sprang.

There was no choice but to fight, so Cowan met the renegade's rush. He got in one well-placed punch before Mataga closed with him, and the plane dipped dangerously.

Then they were locked in a furious, bitter fight. The plane was forgotten, there was no time to think, to reason, only to act. Slugging like a madman, he broke away from those powerful, clutching fingers. He smashed a left to Besi John's face, then a right to the windpipe. Mataga gasped, and sat down, then lunged and tackled Cowan and they both fell.

Through a haze of blood, Steve Cowan saw Isola had taken the controls. Then the renegade lunged for him, knife in hand. Slapping the wrist aside with his left, Cowan grasped it in his right hand, then thrust his left leg across in front of Mataga's and his left arm over and under Mataga's right. He pressed down, and the half-caste screamed as his arm broke at the elbow, and his body lifted and arched, flying over the American's hip.

The right door had been knocked open, and the maid had been trying, vainly, to get it closed. Besi John's body caught in the doorway and then slipped through. He grabbed at the sill, desperately, and his fingers held for one breathtaking moment.

With a kind of dull horror, Steve Cowan saw Mataga tumbling down, down, down toward the waters of the bay. When he hit, a fleck of white showed, and he was gone.

Cowan turned, drunk with fatigue and punishment. Isola, her hair free in the wind from the open door, was flying the plane. She looked up at him suddenly, and smiled.

He looked down. A long, slim destroyer was sliding past Neangambo Island. Another was off Tonnerre Point in the distance. Evidently the situation was under control.

He collapsed, suddenly, upon the floor.

When he opened his eyes, the ship was resting easily on the water. He looked up. An officer in the blue and gold of the Navy was standing over him.

"All right, old man?" the officer asked, grinning. "You had a rough time of it. We had been checking Esteville, and were suspicious of Meyer. We have him—all of them—in custody."

Steve Cowan looked up. Isola. He had been wondering whose shoulder his head was lying on.

"Then," he said, still looking at her, "I guess everything is under control."

The naval officer straightened. He smiled. The Navy knows something of women.

"Yes," he said thoughtfully, "I'd say it was."

Night Over the Solomons

He was lying facedown under the mangroves about forty feet back from the sea on the southwest side of Kolombangara Island in the Solomons.

For two hours he had been lying without moving a muscle while two dozen Japanese soldiers worked nearby, preparing a machine-gun position.

Where he lay there were shadows, and scattered driftwood. He was concealed only by his lack of movement, although the outline of his body was blurred by broken timber and some odds and ends of rubbish, drifted ashore.

Now, the soldiers worked farther away. He believed they would soon move on. Then, and then only, would he dare to move. To be found, he knew, meant instant death.

He was dressed only in a ragged shirt, and the faded serge pants hastily donned in his escape from the sinking ship. The supply ship had been bombed and sunk in Blackett Strait, en route to Guadalcanal. If there were other survivors, he had seen none of them.

That he had lived while others died was due to one thing, and one thing only—he was, first and last, a fighting man, with the fighting man's instinct for timed, decisive action.

He was not, he reflected, much of a soldier. He was too strongly an individualist for that. He liked doing things his own way, and his experience in China and elsewhere had proved it a good way.

He lay perfectly still. The sun was hot on his back, and beneath him the sand was hot. The shadow that had offered partial concealment had moved now, the sun shone directly down upon him. From his memory of the mangrove's arch he believed he would lack the shadow no more than fifteen minutes. It might be too long.

Yet he dare not move. He was not in uniform, and could be killed as a spy. But the Japanese were not given to hairsplitting on International Law. He was ashore on an island supposedly deserted, but an island where the Japanese were apparently building a strong position.

Overhead, a plane suddenly moaned in a dive, then came out, and from the corner of his eye he saw it skim the ragged edge of the crater and vanish.

That Japanese was a flier. Say what one would about them, they could fly.

In his mind he studied the situation. Soon, he could move. When he moved he must know exactly where he was going and what he intended to do. There must be no hesitation.

Behind him lay the sea. It promised nothing. Before him, the jungle. He had no need to study the island, for he knew it like the back of his hand. He hadn't visited Kolombangara for several years, but his memory was excellent.

Two rounded ridges lifted toward a square-topped crater. The crater itself was the end of an imposing ridge of volcanic rock, not far from Shoulder Hill. Both ridge and hill extended downward from one side of what had once been an enormous crater that had at some distant time been ripped asunder, exposing the entrails of the mountain.

Now, jungle growth had healed the surface of the wound, leaving the riven crater divided into two magnificent gullies whose walls lifted five thousand feet above the sea. Their lofty pinnacles lost themselves in the clouds, towering above a scene majestic in its savage splendor.

Those rugged slopes offered concealment. They might offer food. It was characteristic of Mike Thorne not to think of a weapon. He had his hands. When the time came he would take his weapon from the Japanese.

They would be concentrated near Bambari Harbor. Not large, but perfectly sheltered, it offered excellent concealment from all but close aerial reconnaissance. What supplies the Japanese would need must be landed there. That they were ready for trouble was obvious from their careful preparation of machine-gun and mortar positions at this spot. Here, if necessary, a landing could be effected.

Something big was in the wind. From here a mighty blow could be unleashed at the American forces on Guadalcanal and other Solomon positions. Somewhere on the island the Japanese had a secret landing field.

Suddenly, he tensed. Directly before him there was a stealthy movement in the jungle. A second later, ghostlike, he saw a Japanese soldier slide through the jungle. Even at the bare thirty feet that separated them, the man was all but invisible.

Fascinated by something he was stalking, the Japanese was crouched, staring ahead. He moved again, and vanished.

Mike scowled. What was this?

Something in the manner of the man told Thorne the soldier was closing in for a kill. His intended victim, being an enemy of the Japanese, must be a friend of Thorne.

The American hesitated. To lie still was to remain safe. To interfere was to risk his own freedom or even his life.

Thorne moved. He left the ground in a swift, deadly rush that brought him to the edge of the jungle. Sliding into the dense cover, every sense alert, Mike's big hands opened, then closed. They were all he had, his only weapon.

Stealthily, he advanced. The Japanese had paused and was lifting his rifle. Then, surprisingly, the fellow lowered his gun and Mike, closing in, saw his teeth bare in an ugly grimace. Wetting his lips the Japanese moved forward.

In that instant, Mike saw the girl. She was not twenty feet from the Japanese, facing the opposite direction. She had paused, listening.

Mike lunged.

Catlike, the Japanese whirled, stabbing at Mike's throat with the bayonet.

Instantly, Thorne slapped the blade aside with an open hand and moving in, dropped the other over his opponent, at the same time hooking a heel to trip him. With a quick push, he spilled him and snatched the rifle away.

A shot rang out, and Mike wheeled to see two Japanese coming toward him on the jump. Dropping to one knee, Thorne fired, once, twice. Both men spilled to the ground.

SPRINGING UP, Mike was just in time to meet the barehanded rush of the soldier he had disarmed. But as he jerked the bayonet up, it hung on a liana, and before he could free it, the Japanese had leaped upon him. Thorne staggered back, losing his grip on the rifle, and clawing desperately to get the man's hands free from his throat.

Fighting like madmen, they hit the ground hard. His opponent tried to knee him, but Mike rolled away, driving a powerful right to the man's midsection. The Japanese tried to squirm out, but Thorne was fighting savagely. He leaped up and rushed his enemy, smashing him against the bole of a huge tree with stunning impact.

The man's grip broke, and he fell away. Mike struck out viciously and the soldier crumpled.

"Quick! This way!" Glancing up, Thorne saw the girl beckoning, and out of the tail of his eye he glimpsed a rush of movement across the space where lately he had waited his chance.

Wheeling, he ran after the girl. Vaulting a fallen tree, he plunged into the brush. The girl ran swiftly, picking her ground with the skill of long familiarity.

Suddenly, she stopped. Holding up her hand for stillness, she began to worm swiftly through the jungle. Mike followed. This way, with their momentary start, they might elude the Japanese. The girl was working her way along the ridge, when Mike recalled the cavern.

"This way!" he whispered hoarsely. "Up!"

The girl hesitated, then followed. Mike Thorne took a path that led steadily upward, at times almost closing in around them. Behind, the sounds of pursuit increased, then suddenly died away. The Japanese were cautious now, but they were coming on.

Ruthless and determined, they would be relentless in pursuit. It had ceased to be a matter of hiding away until he could escape. By interfering he had sacrificed all possibility of that. Now it was a matter of a fight to the death.

Once, halting beneath a towering crag, he glanced at the girl. For the first time he realized how lovely she was. Despite the jungle, the desperation of their climb and the heat, she was beautiful.

He was suddenly conscious of his own appearance, the torn uniform and scuffed boots—his open shirt stained with perspiration and his hair, naturally curly now a black tangle over his dark, sun-browned face.

"What will we do now?" she asked. "I know Ishimaru. He'll never stop until we are both killed."

Thorne shrugged. "We can't run for long," he said. "We've got to fight."

"But we can't," the girl protested. "There are only two of us, and we are unarmed!"

Mike Thorne smiled grimly. "No matter how small one's force there is always a place where attack can be effective.

"Hit hard and keep moving. It does the job every time. That's what we'll do. We've got to keep them so busy protecting themselves they can't take time to look for us properly.

"They are getting set for an attack on Guadalcanal. An attack now, from here, could do a terrific amount of damage. So they don't dare let anything happen here. We'll see that plenty happens."

Turning, he led the way up a steep mountain path. They were leaving the heavier jungle behind and worming a precarious way through a maze of gigantic boulders, enormous volcanic crags, and beds of lava. It was a strange, unbelievable world, a world of rocks that looked like frozen flame.

Suddenly they were in a gray fog layer, and Mike stopped, glancing back. They were in the low clouds now, over four thousand feet above the sea.

The girl came up to him. He glanced at her curiously.

"What in the world are you doing in these islands?" he demanded. "At a time like this?"

She smoothed her hair and looked at him.

"My father was here. He persisted in staying on, regardless of everything. But he told me that if the Japanese did come to the Solomons, he would leave Tulagi and come here. There was a place we both knew where he could hide. And he didn't believe they would bother with Kolombangara."

"That's just the trouble," Mike said grimly. "Nobody thinks they will. That still doesn't tell me how you got here."

"I flew. I've had my own plane for several years. I learned to fly in California, and after I returned here, it was easy for me to fly back and forth, to cruise among the islands. I was in Perth when the Japanese came, and they wouldn't let me come back after Daddy.

"Then, three days ago, I finally succeeded. I took off and landed here at Bambari Harbor, and when I went ashore, the Japanese were waiting for me. I got away, but they have the plane."

They moved on, working their way among the crags, still heading onward and upward. They left no trail on the lava, and the jumble of broken rock and blasted trees concealed them.

Once, on the very crest of the ancient crater, where the lip hung over the dizzy spaces below, they came upon a tangle of huge trees, dead and dried by sun and wind, great skeleton-like fingers of trees, the bones and wreckage of a forest. They were worn out and panting heavily when they reached the other side.

Then Mike Thorne saw what he was looking for, a curious white streak on the face of a great, leaning boulder. He walked toward it, skirted the boulder, and, without a word, squeezed into a narrow crack behind it. Following him, the girl saw him turn sharply to the left, in the passage, then to the right, then suddenly they stood in a small open place, green with soft grass. Beyond, the black entrance to a cave opened, and, from a crevice in the rock near the cave mouth, a trickle of water fell into a basin about as big as a washtub.

"You knew this was here?" she asked, staring about wonderingly. "But the water, where does it come from?"

"Seepage. It seeps down from a sort of natural reservoir on top of that peak. Rain collects there in a rock basin and seeps down here. There is always water."

"They would never find us here." She looked at him. "But what now? What will we do?"

"Sleep. We'll need rest. Tonight, I'm going back down the mountain."

"It would take hours!" she protested, glancing at the lowering sun.

"Not the way I'm going!" His voice was grim. "I'm going down the inside of the crater."

Memory of her one glimpse of that yawning chasm gripped her. The idea of anyone suspended over that awful space was a horror.

"But you can't! There's no way—"

"Yes, there is." He smiled at her. "I saw it once. I've often wondered if it could be done. Tonight, by moonlight, I'll find out." He smiled, and his teeth flashed white. "Say, what is your name, anyway? Mine's Mike Thorne."

She laughed. "I'm Jerry Brandon."

HOURS LATER, she awakened suddenly. There was a stealthy movement in the cave, and then she saw Mike Thorne standing in the entrance. He bent over and drank at the spring, then straightened, tightening his belt. She moved swiftly beside him.

"Be careful," she whispered.

"Don't worry," he replied softly. He pressed her hand gently. "So long."

He moved off. One moment he was there beside her, then he was gone. Remembering that almost bottomless chasm, she shuddered.

Mike Thorne moved swiftly. He had no plan. He knew too little about the enemy dispositions to plan. He must make his reconnaissance and attack at one time.

When he reached the lip of the crater, he hesitated, drawing a deep breath. He knew the place. In the past, he had speculated on whether or not a strong, agile man could make it down to five thousand feet from that point.

Taking firm grasp on a rock, he lowered himself over the rim. For an instant his feet dangled in space. Carefully, he felt for the ledge he remembered. He found it, tested it briefly with his weight, then relaxed his grip and felt for a new handhold on the edge itself.

Slowly, painstakingly, he worked his way down the six-inch ledge of rock, feeling with feet and hands for each new hold.

On the way up the mountain he had thought much. Areas for possible landing fields were few. Kolombangara was rough, and the best spot, if not the only spot, was on the floor of the crater itself. There was a chance that when he reached bottom he'd find himself at the edge of their field.

Suddenly, he was in complete blackness. Twisting his head, Mike saw the moon was under a cloud. From his memory of the cliff, he knew he had reached the most difficult point. Carefully, he felt over a toehold, found it, and reached out in the darkness. His hand felt along the bare rock, searching, searching.

A protruding corner of rock met his fingers. He gripped it, shifted his weight. The rock came loose.

For one awful, breathtaking instant, he grabbed wildly, then he felt himself falling.

He slid, grabbed out, felt a rock tear loose from his hand, and fell clear. He must have turned over at least three times before he struck with such force that it knocked the wind from him, then slid, and started to fall again. His hand, grasping wildly, caught a shrub. It pulled, then held.

Breathless, frightened, he hung over the void.

Around him was absolute silence. Slowly, majestically, the moon slid from behind the cloud. To his horror he saw the bush to which he clung had pulled out by the roots, and seemed suspended only by a few stronger roots that might give way at any moment.

Turning his head carefully, he glanced below. Nothing but blackness. The shrub gave a sickening sag, then held.

Moving cautiously, he felt with his toe. He found a toehold, not more than an inch of rock. Then another inch, and he let go with one hand. A heavy root thrust out from the face, and he took hold with a sigh of relief.

ALMOST A HALF HOUR later, he let himself down on the slope, then stepped into the brush. He had worked along silently through the jungle only a little way when he heard a clink of metal against metal. He froze. A sentry stood not twenty feet away, and beyond him bulked the dark body of a plane.

Mike Thorne flattened against the earth. The grass beneath him was damp. He crept softly nearer the sentry. The man turned, rifle on guard, staring out into the dark toward him. Mike lay still. Then the sentry shouldered his rifle and walked away.

Listening, Thorne could hear the man's feet recede, then stop, then start back. Mike moved forward and lay still.

The sentry drew near, paused, and turned away. Swiftly, Mike lunged. His left arm slid around the sentry's throat, crushing the bony part of the wristbone against the man's Adam's apple. His left hand grasped his own right wrist, and Mike gave a quick, hard jerk. The man's body threshed, then relaxed slowly. Grimly, Mike Thorne lowered the body to the ground.

When he straightened again, he carried a heavy-bladed knife. It was a smatchet, evidently taken from some British commando, or picked from the ground after a battle. The rifle he put aside.

Moving forward, he sniffed air heavy with the fumes of gasoline. He hesitated, then felt around. Several tins of gas stood about the plane. It was a Zero pursuit.

Deliberately, he opened the cans and poured one of them over the plane itself. His time was short. He knew the chances of discovery were increased immeasurably by every instant, yet he worked on.

A movement froze him to stillness. A Japanese sentry had stopped not fifty feet away and was staring toward him. The man stepped forward and spoke softly, inquiringly. Mike Thorne crouched, his lips a thin line along his teeth.

This was it. He could see it coming. Suddenly the Japanese jerked up his rifle. There was no hesitation. The man fired as the rifle came up, and the bullet smashed into the pile of cases beside Thorne. Instantly, Thorne lunged. The rifle cracked again, and a bullet whiffed by his cheek. The soldier lunged with the bayonet, and Mike felt the point tear through his sleeve, then he struck viciously with the smatchet.

Blood gushed from the side of the Japanese's neck, but the man scarcely staggered. He wheeled, dropping his rifle, and grabbed at Thorne's throat. Mike tried to pull away, slashing viciously at the sentry with the heavy knife.

The camp was in an uproar. Running men were coming from every direction. With a tremendous burst of strength, Mike hurled the sentry from him, struck a match, and dropped it into the gasoline.

The tower of flame leaped high into the sky behind him, but he had plunged into the brush. He was running wildly, desperately. Running so fast that he never saw the wire until it was too late. He plunged into it, tried to leap, but his foot hung and he fell forward. Desperately, he hurled himself to one side, trying to avoid the barbs. He fell flat, and his head struck one of the anchor pins. He felt the blow, but nothing more.

HIS EYES OPENED on a different world. Weird flames lit the sky, although they were dying down now. They wouldn't, he decided, be enough to attract help. It was too deep within the sheltering bulwarks of the crater.

He was bound to a tree, his right leg around the bole, the toe hooked under the left knee. The left leg was bent back under him. His arms were tied around the tree itself.

Mike's eyes were narrow with apprehension. He knew what this meant. In such a position, in a short time his legs would be paralyzed and helpless. If he were to escape, it must be now, at once. From the tail of his eye he could see enough to know that two planes had been burned, and a fair quantity of supplies.

Suddenly, a shadow loomed between the fire and himself. He tilted his head, and a stunning blow knocked it down again.

"So?" The voice was a hiss. "You?"

He looked up, brow wrinkled with anguish. Commander Ishimaru stared down at him. He remembered the man from an event on the coast of China. He forced a grin. "Sure, it's me, Mike Thorne. How's tricks?"

Ishimaru studied him.

"No change, I see," he said softly. "I am glad. You will break harder, my friend." He bowed, and his eyes glittered like obsidian in the firelight.

The Japanese officer studied him. "Where did you come from?" he went on. "How many are there? Why did you come here?"

"Side issue," Mike replied. "Doolittle and his boys are taking another sock at Tokyo. They sent me down here to keep you boys busy while the big show comes off."

Ishimaru struck him viciously across the face. Once, twice. Then again.

"You tell me how many, and where they are." Ishimaru's voice was level. "Otherwise, you burn."

"Go to the devil," Mike replied.

"You have ten minutes to decide." Ishimaru's voice was sharp. He spun on his heel and walked away.

Mike Thorne's lips tightened. His legs were already feeling their cramped position. The position alone would soon be torture enough, but the Japanese would not let it rest there. He had seen men after Japanese torture, and it had turned him sick. And Mike Thorne wasn't a man to be bothered easily.

If he was to escape, it must be now, at once. From the activity around the landing field he could see that the hour of attack was approaching. The wreckage of the two burned pursuit ships had been hurriedly cleared away. The other planes were being fueled and readied for the takeoff. From his position his view was limited, but there were at least fifty Zeros on the landing field.

More, the Japanese were wheeling attack bombers from concealed positions. In the confusion he was almost forgotten.

DESPERATELY, HE TRIED to pull himself erect. It was impossible. The cramped position of his legs was slowly turning them numb. He strained against the ropes that bound him, but without success.

His arms were not only bound around the tree, but were higher than his head, and tied there. By pressing the inside of his arms against the tree trunk he succeeded in lifting himself a bare inch. It did no good and only caused the muscles in his legs to cramp.

Trying to get the ropes that bound his wrists against the tree bark did him no good. He sawed but only succeeded in chafing his wrists.

A movement in the shadow of some packing cases startled him. Suddenly, to his astonishment, Jerry Brandon emerged from behind the cases. She walked across to him, unhurriedly, then bent over his wrists.

"Get out of here!" he snapped, and was astonished by the fierceness of his voice. "They'll get you! These devils—!"

"Be still!" Jerry sawed at the ropes, and suddenly his wrists were free, then his feet. Slowly, carefully, she helped him up.

"Beat it," he said tersely. "You've done enough. If they catch you, death will be too easy for you. I can't run now. I doubt if I can even walk."

Her arm about him, he tottered a few steps and almost fell. The pain in his legs was excruciating. Suddenly he saw the smatchet he'd had lying on a case beside some rifles. He staggered to the case and picked it up. They each took a rifle.

A Japanese dropped a sack to the ground at the nearest plane and started to turn. He saw them, hesitated, then started forward.

"This is it," Mike said. "Get out of here. I'll get away now. Anyway, no use both of us being caught."

The soldier halted, stared, then turned to shout. Mike Thorne lifted the rifle and fired. His first bullet struck the man in the head and he pitched over. The second smashed into the plane.

Jerry Brandon was beside him, and she fired also. Slowly, they began to back away, taking advantage of every bit of cover, firing as they retreated. A bullet smashed into a tree trunk beside Mike, and he stepped back, loading the rifle again.

They were almost to the brush, and turning, he started for it in a tottering run. Jerry fired another shot, then ran up alongside him. Together they fled into the brush.

Behind them the field was in a turmoil. The escape had come without warning, the sudden firing within the camp had added to the confusion, and it had been a matter of minutes before anyone was aware of just what had happened.

But now a line of soldiers fanned out and started into the jungle.

Mike Thorne stopped, wetting his bruised lips. This was going to be tough. The Japanese would cut them off from his trail up the mountain. They knew where they had lost him before and this time would take care to prevent that. Furthermore, they were closer to the path up the mountain than he.

Worse, the ascent of the precipice down which he had come might be impossible for him in his present condition. And it was a cinch Jerry would never be able to make it.

His own problem was serious, but there was another, greater than that. Death for himself, even for Jerry Brandon, was a small thing compared to the fearful destruction of a sudden, successful attack on grounded planes and ships at anchor. The loss of life would be terrific. But what to do? What could two people do in such a case, far from means of communication....

But were they? The idea came suddenly.

Instantly, he knew it would work. It was the only way, the only possible way. He smiled wryly into the darkness. Was it possible? It meant climbing the cliff in the darkness, climbing along the sheer face, feeling for handholds, risking death at every second. It meant doing what only a moment before he had thought was impossible.

They slid swiftly through the jungle, but now, taking the girl's hand, he chose a new path. He was going to the cliff.

Suddenly, the girl's grip tightened.

"Mike, you're not going to . . . ?"

"Yes, I am," he said quietly. "Something big's coming off. I'm not going to sit by and see the enemy close in on those boys on Guadalcanal."

"But what can you do?" Jerry protested. "Getting up that cliff won't help. And I can't climb it, even in daytime."

"You aren't going to," he told her. "I know a cave in the rocks down below. You can stay there. I'm going up, somehow, some way. If I should fall, you'll have to try. Up on that peak there is heaped-up forest, forest dead and parched by sun and wind, rotting in places, but mostly just dry. We've got to set fire to it."

"Could they see it from there, Mike? It's so far!"

He shrugged. "You can see a candle twelve miles from a plane on a dark night. I'm hoping some scout will sight this flame. It should be visible for miles and miles."

"But won't the Japanese put it out?" Jerry protested.

"They'll try." He laughed softly.

WHEN HE REACHED THE FOOT OF THE CLIFF he stopped dead still. Suddenly, despite the oppressive heat, he felt cold. Above him, looming in the darkness, the gigantic precipice towered toward the stars. Somehow, along the face of that awful cliff, he had climbed down, feeling his way. Now he must go back.

A slip meant an awful death on the jagged rocks below. Yet not to climb meant that many men would die, brave men who would perish in a world of rending steel and blasting, searing flame.

HIS HANDS FOUND a crevice, and he started. Inch by inch, he felt his way along, the awful void growing below him as he mounted upward. Rocks crumbled under his fingers, roots gave way, he clung, flattened against the rock as though glued to it, living for the moment only. His flesh damp with cold sweat, his skin alive, the nerves sensing every roughness in the rock.

Time and again he slipped, only to catch hold, then mount higher. A long time later, his clothing soaked, his fingers torn and bleeding, he crawled over the ridge and lay facedown on the rock. His pounding heart seemed to batter the solid surface beneath him, his lungs gasped for air, his muscles felt limp.

"So . . . I was correct."

The voice was sibilant, cold. Mike Thorne's eyes opened wide, suddenly alert. Ishimaru's voice broke into the feeling of failure, of utter depression that swept over him. "I knew you would try it, American. So foolish to try to outwit Ishimaru."

Mike knew he was covered, knew a move meant death. Yet he moved suddenly and with violence. He had drawn his hands back to his sides unconsciously, and with a sudden push up he hurled himself forward against the soldier's legs.

A gun roared in his ears, and he felt the man go down before him. He lunged to his feet, and Ishimaru, wild with fury, fired from the ground. A searing flame scorched the side of Thorne's face, and then he dove headfirst onto him.

Like a cat, the Japanese officer rolled away. He came up quickly and, as Mike lunged in, grabbed at his wrist. But Mike was too wise in the ways of judo, swung away, and whipped a driving right to the chin. The officer went down, hard.

Feet rushed, and Mike saw a man swinging at him with a rifle butt. He dropped in a ball at the man's feet, and the fellow tripped and fell headlong, rolling over the edge of the cliff. The Japanese made one wild, futile grab with his fingers, then vanished, his scream ringing into the heavens.

Mike's rifle had fallen from his shoulders where it had been slung. Now he grabbed it up and fired two quick shots, then dove into the brush. He staggered through the jungle toward the place he had chosen to start the fire. Heedless of danger, he dropped to his knees, scraped together some sticks, and with paper from his pocket, lit the fire.

A shot smacked dully into the log near him, and he rolled over. The flame took hold, then a volley of shots riddled the brush around him. By a miracle he was unhurt. A Japanese came leaping into the growing fire-light, and Mike's rifle cracked. The soldier fell headlong. Another, and another shot.

The flame caught in a heap of dead branches, flared, and leaped high. In a roaring holocaust, it swirled higher and higher, mounting a fast cre-scendo of unbelievable fury toward the dark skies. The scene around was lit by a weird light, and into it came the Japanese.

Desperately, yet methodically, making every shot count, Mike Thorne began to fire. He sprang to his feet, rushed, changed position, opened fire again. A bullet stung him along the arm, something struck his leg a solid blow. He raised to one knee, blood trickling from a cut on his scalp, and fired again.

Then, suddenly, another rifle opened fire across the clearing. Taken on the flank, the advancing enemy hesitated, then broke for the jungle.

Suddenly, over the roar of the fire, Mike heard the roar of motors. Their planes, taking off!

He saw them mount, swing around, then a bomb dropped. He heard it one instant before it exploded and hurled himself flat. The earth heaved under him, and the fire lifted and scattered in all directions, but roared on.

THEN OUT OF THE NIGHT he heard the high-pitched whine of a diving plane, and the night was lit with the insane lightning of tracer gone wild, while over his head the sky burst into a roaring, chattering madness of sound.

Battle! Planes had come, and there was fighting up there in the dark-ness. He rolled over, swearing in a sullen voice, swearing in sheer relief that his warning had been successful. He fired at a Japanese soldier, saw the flames catch hold anew, and then as his rifle clicked on an empty chamber, he lunged erect, hauling out the smatchet.

Suddenly, something white loomed in the sky, and then a man hit the ground beside him. It was a paratrooper! An American! Then the night was filled with them, and Mike staggered toward the man.

A forward observer grabbed Mike's arm. "What is it? Where the devil are they coming from?"

Mike roared the information into his ear, and the officer began a crisp recital of the information into the radio.

A plane roared over, then explosions came from the chasm below, the night changed from the bright rattle of machine-gun fire to the solemn, unceasing thunder of big bombs as the bombers shuttled back and forth, releasing their eggs over the enemy field.

Mike staggered back, feeling his numbed leg. It wasn't bleeding.

Evidently a stick knocked against his leg by a bullet, or a stone. He turned, dazed.

Jerry Brandon came running toward him. "Mike! Are you all right?"

"Sure," he said. "Where . . . ?"

"I came up the trail. I thought maybe I could make it, and when the fighting started up there, I got through all right."

The Army officer walked back through the smoke and stopped beside Mike. "This is a good night's work, friend," he said. "Who are you?"

Briefly, Mike told him. The officer looked curiously at Jerry. Mike explained, and the officer nodded. "Yes," he said dryly, "we heard about you. Incidentally, your father's safe. He got into Henderson Field last night."

They turned away. Mike looked at Jerry, smiling wearily. "Lady," he said, "tired as I am, I can still wonder at finding a girl like you in the Solomons. If there wasn't a war on . . ." He looked at her again. "After all," he said thoughtfully, "what's a war between friends?"

Jerry laughed. "I think you could handle the war, too," she said.

Afterword

Of all these volumes of the Collected Short Stories series this one is my favorite. Tales that for years have cried out to be presented together have now found a home in the same binding. An era in the life of Louis L'Amour is finally available in a manner where the work almost becomes an autobiography in fiction.

The first several stories in this collection are some of the most recently written, stories that Louis wrote from the early 1950s to the early 1960s; they show the end of an arc that also included "The Moon of the Trees Broken by Snow," a story published in *The Collected Short Stories, Volume One.* The rest of this collection, however, flashes back to Louis's very beginnings as a writer and, in fact, includes the first story he ever published: one recently unearthed and offered here for the first time.

"Death, Westbound" was actually mentioned by Louis in his memoir, *Education of a Wandering Man,* although he didn't mention the title. "I placed my first story for publication," he wrote. "It was a hobo story, submitted to a magazine that had published many famous names when they were starting out. The magazine paid on publication, but that never happened. The magazine folded after accepting my story and that was the end of it."

Interesting, but not exactly true. . . .

Fifty-five years *earlier* Louis had written to a girlfriend of his saying, "I have . . . managed to have one short story accepted by a small magazine one finds on the newsstands. It pays rather well but is somewhat sensational. The magazine . . . is generally illustrated by several pictures of partially undressed ladies, and they are usually rather heavily constructed ladies also. It is called *10 Story Book.* My story was a realistic tale of some hoboes called "Death, Westbound."

Now, I knew for a fact that Dad was trying to impress this gal like all get out. But it *seemed* like he was talking about the same story that he mentioned many years later. A check of his list of story submissions for the nineteen thirties revealed that he had continued to submit work to *10 Story Book* for the next several years.... Not what you'd expect if they had "folded." Much later in life, had Louis felt compelled to mention this early moment of triumph but at the same time deny his connection to the magazine's somewhat sleazy content?

A number of searches showed that very few copies of *10 Story Book* existed in libraries or public archives. So I began to put the word out to magazine aficionados, pulp collectors, and the fairly offbeat subculture of antique pornography collectors. About five years passed with little result other than occasionally calling or e-mailing various people and reminding them that I was still interested. But one day my in-box divulged a scan of "Death, Westbound" by Louis D. Amour. One of my contacts had finally come through. I don't know if the name, D. Amour, was a mistake or an early attempt at a pseudonym, but this was Louis L'Amour's first recorded sale.

Sensational photos (for the 1930s) aside, Dad seems to have been in good company; Jack Woodford is listed in the table of contents of the edition and I assume that this is the novelist, screenwriter, and short-story master of *Jack Woodford on Writing* fame. Other famous writers of the early twentieth century are also reputed to have been published here, too; *10 Story Book* following a model later used by *Playboy,* where the promise of unclothed women draws in readers who otherwise would never have bothered with literature at all; and the literature gave the magazine some class and protection from the opinions of moralists and pro-censorship types.

In this collection, "Death, Westbound" begins a cycle that will carry the reader through stories that relate to many actual events in Louis's early life. It should not be assumed that these stories are always literally true but they are a snapshot of the times—the 1920s and 1930s—and how Louis L'Amour experienced those times. Greatly influenced by Jack London, Eugene O'Neal, and later John Steinbeck, Louis began his career by trying to document the era that he lived in. Whether "Death, Westbound" is a "true story" or not, Louis did ride the side-door Pullman's of the Southern Pacific on many occasions; from Arizona to Texas and back again, and from Arizona to California even more often.

The stories "Old Doc Yak," "It's Your Move," and "And Proudly Die," soon followed, and were drawn from actual people that Louis knew in the time he spent waiting for a ship or "on the beach," as the sailors called unemployment, in San Pedro, California. Louis wrote of that time in an introduction from *Yondering:* "Rough painting or bucking rivets in the shipyards, swamping on a truck, or working 'standby' on a ship were all a man could find. It wasn't enough. We missed meals and slept wherever we could. The town was filled with drifting, homeless men, mostly seamen from all the countries in the world. Sometimes I slept in empty boxcars, in abandoned buildings, or in the lumber piles on the old E. K. Wood lumber dock."

The piled lumber Louis mentions often left gaps or overhangs, some well off the ground, which were shelter of a sort. But if you had a few cents, the vastly preferred place to spend the night was the Seaman's Church Institute, sort of a YMCA for seamen. "Survival," another story of that time, was based on a story that Louis had heard in his time around the Seaman's Institute, but many gaps in the narrative have been filled with his own material, and it is populated with mostly fictional characters.

Louis left San Pedro on a voyage that would eventually take him around the world and "Thicker Than Blood" and "The Admiral" are drawn from that experience. I don't know if the events in these stories are true in whole or in part, but buried in among Louis's papers I found the following photographs...

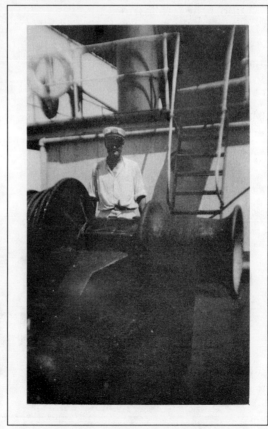

To the right is Leonard Duks, first mate of the SS *Steel Worker* and Louis's nemesis on a voyage that took them from San Pedro west to Japan, China, the Dutch East Indies, the Federated Malay States, Aden Arabia, the Suez Canal, and on into Brooklyn, New York. I don't know if Duks truly lived up to his fictional reputation in "Thicker Than Blood," but Louis didn't like the man and appointed himself as a spokesman for the crew's complaints about the unbelievably bad food and other various working conditions.

The ship did not call in

Shanghai twice, so much of "The Admiral" may be fictional. However, the note on the back of the next photograph suggests otherwise. It reads, "Tony and Joe taken on the beach at Balikpapan (Borneo). Tony is the one in 'The Admiral.'"

Additional photographs from Balikpapan include one of the *Steel Worker* at anchor with much of what looks like their cargo of pipe in the foreground...

And the following, which reads, "Luflander, Malay barber, myself at eighteen, Balikpapan, Borneo."

"The Admiral" was originally published by *Story,* a magazine which was very prestigious at the time, and Louis's being included raised some favorable comment. Dad, more than anything, wanted to continue in this vein. He imagined a cycle of stories about San Pedro and another cycle that took place in Shanghai, both utilizing loosely interconnected sets of colorful characters; hoboes and seamen, soldiers of fortune and gangsters, historical characters and working stiffs just trying to get by.

However, he also needed to get paid. The literary magazines paid on publication and while that was bad enough when the stories were scheduled months ahead of time, often they were not scheduled at all: the story was accepted but the editor had no idea when he would run it and thus no idea when he would pay. The pulp magazines, which published a far less literary fare, paid better and, more important, they paid faster, sending out a check the moment they accepted a story. Ultimately, Louis found this combination hard to beat. At times, though, he did wonder rather wistfully about what kind of career he would have had if he'd been able to keep writing in this more "personal adventure, personal experience" style.

"The Dancing Kate" seems to mix some of the more realistic elements of those "personal experience" stories with those of a pulp adventure while "Glorious! Glorious!" returns to the more anti-heroic style. Louis could not have participated in the Riffian War where the forces of Abd-el-Krim fought both the Spanish and the French Foreign Legions but the *Steel Worker did* sail the Moroccan coast during its final days. "Off the Mangrove Coast" has a plot similar to a story that Louis told about his own life, a story where he and several others unsuccessfully attempted to salvage a riverboat that was supposedly full of the treasure that a rajah from the Federated Malay States took with him when some form of uprising forced him from power. "The Cross and the Candle" is also based on an actual experience, though I do not believe that Louis was there for the climax of the story or that he played a part in solving the murder of the man's ill-fated sweetheart.

"A Friend of the General" is interesting because there is no indication of when it was written. I suspect that Louis wrote it quite late in his career, possibly in 1979 or '80, in order to include it in the collection *Yondering*. Louis's unit, a Quartermaster's Truck Company, *was* based out of Château de Spoir, home of the Count and Countess Dulong du Rosney. The count and countess had indeed moved into a gardener's cottage across the road from the château itself. The "cottage" (more appropriately, the home of the estate manager) was of a style and size that would have attracted notice even in Beverly Hills, so they were nicely housed even though first the German and then the American army had taken over the main residence. The Countess Dulong du Rosney has no memory of Lt. Louis L'Amour, Parisian black-market cafés, or the mysterious "General," but she still may have been the model for the countess in the story. When I spoke to her a few years ago it was obvious that she had that same sense of unflappable self-assurance. The story of the ill-fated arms merchant Milton is one that Louis told many times as if it were true, suggesting that he was teaching boxing at a fencing and martial arts academy in Frenchtown (a section of old Shanghai) at the time.

With "East of Gorontalo" we bid adieu to the group of stories based closely on Louis's life experience, and launch into three different series he created between 1938 and 1948 for Leo Margulies at *Standard Magazines,* a company that owned *Thrilling Adventures* and many others. Although there are few of Louis's personal experiences in the stories of tramp freighter captain Jim Mayo and the "pilots of fortune" Turk Madden and Steve Cowan, many of the locations were places that he had visited during what Louis called his "knocking around" period. In fact, in his collection *Night Over the Solomons,* Louis claimed that in the case of Kolombangara Island in 1943, a story of his had closely echoed reality:

> Shortly after my story ["Night Over the Solomons"] was published the Navy discovered this Japanese base of which I had written. I am sure my story had nothing to do with its discovery and doubt if the magazine in which it was published had reached the South Pacific at the time.
>
> My decision to locate a Japanese base on Kolombangara was not based on any inside information but simple logic. We had troops

fighting on Guadalcanal. If the Japanese wished to harass our supply lines, where would they locate their base?

From my time at sea I had a few charts and I dug out the one on the Solomons. Kolombangara was the obvious solution. There was a place where an airfield could be built, a deep harbor where ships could bring supplies and lie unnoticed unless a plane flew directly over the harbor, which was well hidden. No doubt the Japanese had used the same logic in locating their base and the Navy in discovering it.

He went on to note that while his hero reached the island from a torpedoed ship, both an American pilot and John F. Kennedy had been stranded in the vicinity of Kolombangara under circumstances that would have fit his fictional story to perfection.

Louis's knowledge of the operation and layout of Mayo's ship, the *Semiramis,* came from the time that he had spent as an able-bodied seaman on similar ships and his years of working as a longshoreman and then a Cargo Control Officer at San Francisco's Port of Embarkation during the early days of World War II. The interest in aircraft and the appreciation of the freedom of a tramp flier was gleaned from his good friend Bob Roberts who had lived that life, though never in the Far East.

As Louis moved on through the next two stages of his career, writing crime stories and then westerns, many of the elements found in these early adventure stories continued to appear. His fictional Far East was crowded with types modeled on American gangsters, similar to the crooked sports promoters and gamblers in his stories of the boxing ring, and the *Semiramis* and its crew could almost stand in for a more racially diverse version of one of the beleaguered cattle outfits that his western characters later rode for. In a way his transition from one genre to another was more of a blurring of the lines or a recombining of elements.

For a more in-depth look at all of these stories and more information on this collection visit us at louislamourgreatadventure.com.

Over the next three years we will continue this program with the publication of *The Frontier Stories, Volume Five* in 2007. The following year we will bring out a collection of crime and boxing stories and then, finally, one last collection of westerns, *The Frontier Stories, Volume Seven.* I certainly hope you enjoyed this collection and that you find these next few equally pleasurable.

Beau L'Amour
Los Angeles, California
2006

About Louis L'Amour

*"I think of myself in the oral tradition—
as a troubadour, a village taleteller, the man
in the shadows of the campfire. That's the way
I'd like to be remembered—as a storyteller.
A good storyteller."*

It is doubtful that any author could be as at home in the world re-created in his novels as Louis Dearborn L'Amour. Not only could he physically fill the boots of the rugged characters he wrote about, but he literally "walked the land my characters walk." His personal experiences as well as his lifelong devotion to historical research combined to give Mr. L'Amour the unique knowledge and understanding of people, events, and the challenge of the American frontier that became the hallmarks of his popularity.

Of French-Irish descent, Mr. L'Amour could trace his own family in North America back to the early 1600s and follow their steady progression westward, "always on the frontier." As a boy growing up in Jamestown, North Dakota, he absorbed all he could about his family's frontier heritage, including the story of his great-grandfather who was scalped by Sioux warriors.

Spurred by an eager curiosity and desire to broaden his horizons, Mr. L'Amour left home at the age of fifteen and enjoyed a wide variety of jobs, including seaman, lumberjack, elephant handler, skinner of dead cattle, miner, and an officer in the transportation corps during World War II. During his "yondering" days he also circled the world on a freighter, sailed a dhow on the Red Sea, was shipwrecked in the West Indies, and stranded in the Mojave Desert. He won fifty-one of fifty-nine fights as a professional boxer and worked as a journalist and lecturer. He was a voracious reader and collector of rare books. His personal library contained 17,000 volumes.

Mr. L'Amour "wanted to write almost from the time I could talk." After developing a widespread following for his many frontier and adventure stories written for fiction magazines, Mr. L'Amour published his first full-length novel, *Hondo,* in the United States in 1953. Every one of his more than 120 books is in print; there are more than 300 million copies of his books in print worldwide, making him one of the bestselling authors in modern literary history. His books have been translated into twenty languages, and more than forty-five of his novels and stories have been made into feature films and television movies.

His hardcover bestsellers include *The Lonesome Gods, The Walking Drum* (his twelfth-century historical novel), *Jubal Sackett, Last of the Breed,* and *The Haunted Mesa.* His memoir, *Education of a Wandering Man,* was a leading bestseller in 1989. Audio dramatizations and adaptations of many L'Amour stories are available on cassettes and CDs from Random House Audio publishing.

The recipient of many great honors and awards, in 1983 Mr. L'Amour became the first novelist ever to be awarded the Congressional Gold Medal by the United States Congress in honor of his life's work. In 1984 he was also awarded the Medal of Freedom by President Reagan.

Louis L'Amour died on June 10, 1988. His wife, Kathy, and their two children, Beau and Angelique, carry the L'Amour publishing tradition forward with new books written by the author during his lifetime to be published by Bantam.